DAMIAN A. WASSEL – PUBLISHER

ADRIAN F. WASSEL – EDITOR-IN-CHIEF

DER-SHING HELMER – MANAGING EDITOR

NATHAN C. GOODEN – SENIOR ARTIST

TIM DANIEL – EVP, BRANDING & DESIGN

IAN BALDESSARI – PRODUCTION MANAGER

SONJA SYNAK – SENIOR DESIGNER

DAVID DISSANAYAKE – VP, SALES & MARKETING

SYNDEE BARWICK – BOOK TRADE, SALES & MARKETING,

DANIEL CRARY – COMMERCE & COMMUNICATION

ALEX SCOLA – SOCIAL MEDIA COORDINATOR

CREATED & STORY BY
BRANDON SANDERSON

WRITTEN BY
JACKSON LANZING & COLLIN KELLY

DRAWN BY
NATHAN GOODEN

COLORED BY
KURT MICHAEL RUSSELL

LETTERED BY
ANDWORLD DESIGN

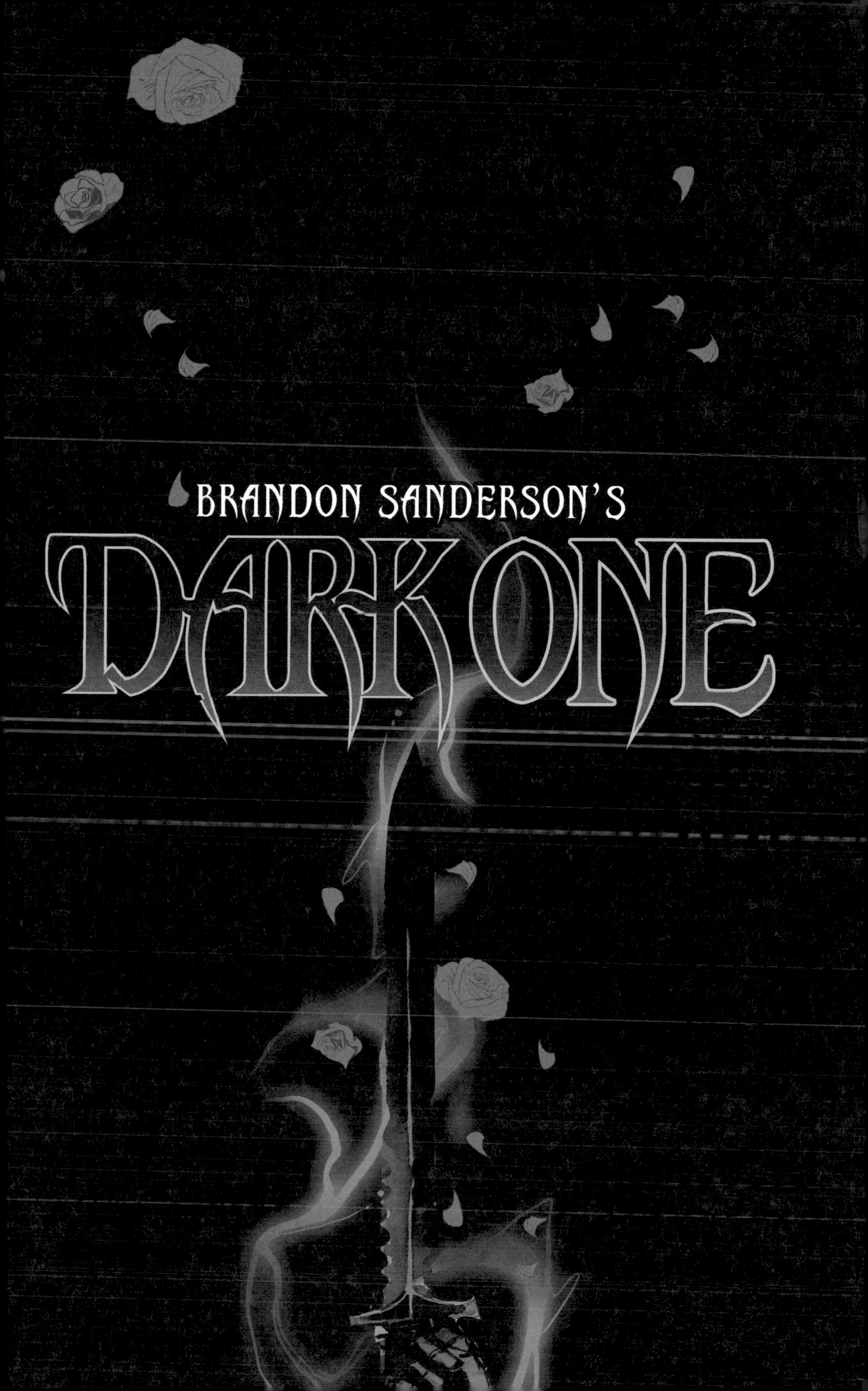
BRANDON SANDERSON'S
DARK ONE

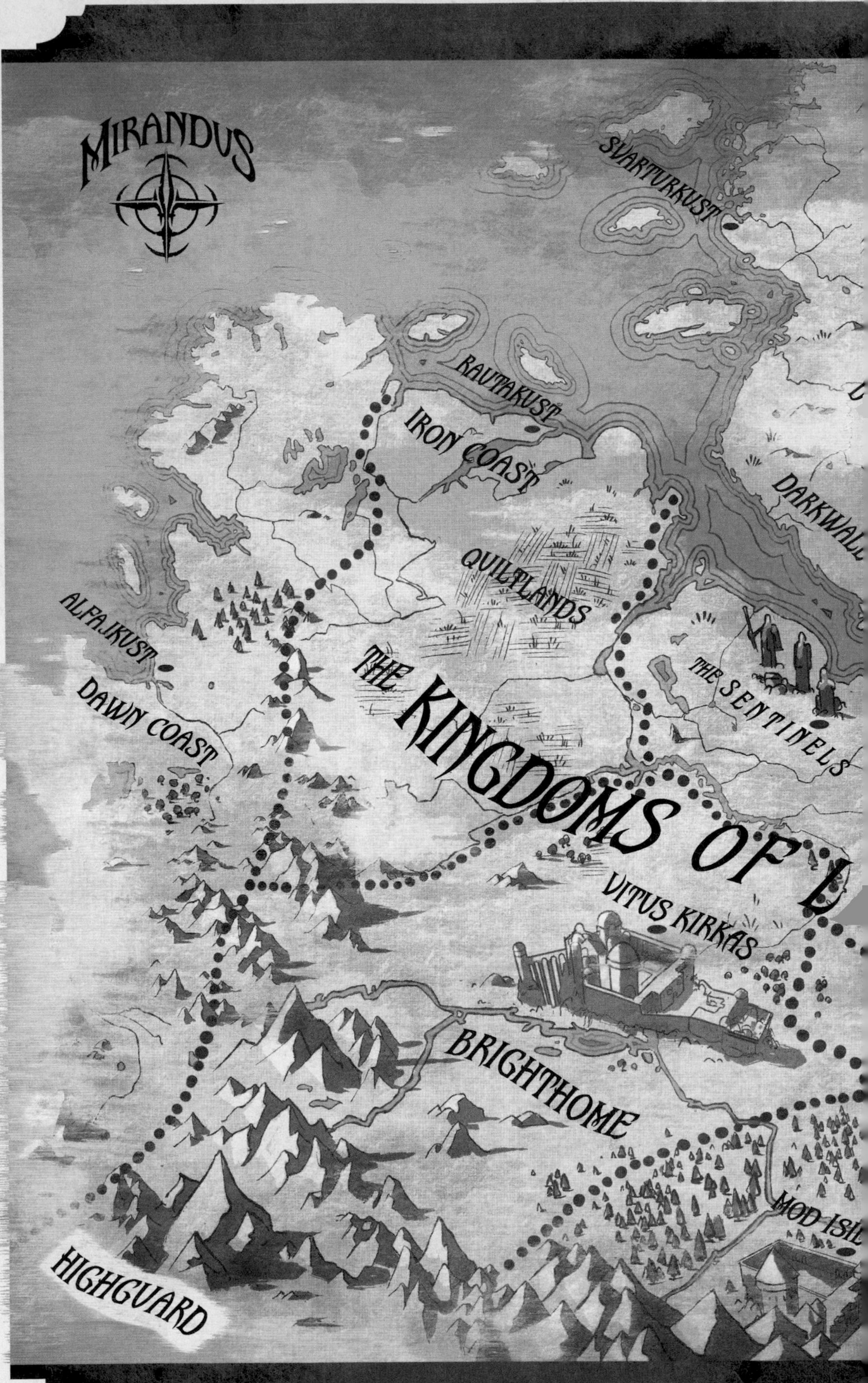

MIRANDUS
SVARTURKUST
RAUTAKUST
IRON COAST
DARKWAL
QUILTLANDS
ALFAJKUST
THE KINGDOMS OF L
DAWN COAST
THE SENTINELS
VITUS KIRKAS
BRIGHTHOME
MOD ISIL
HIGHGUARD

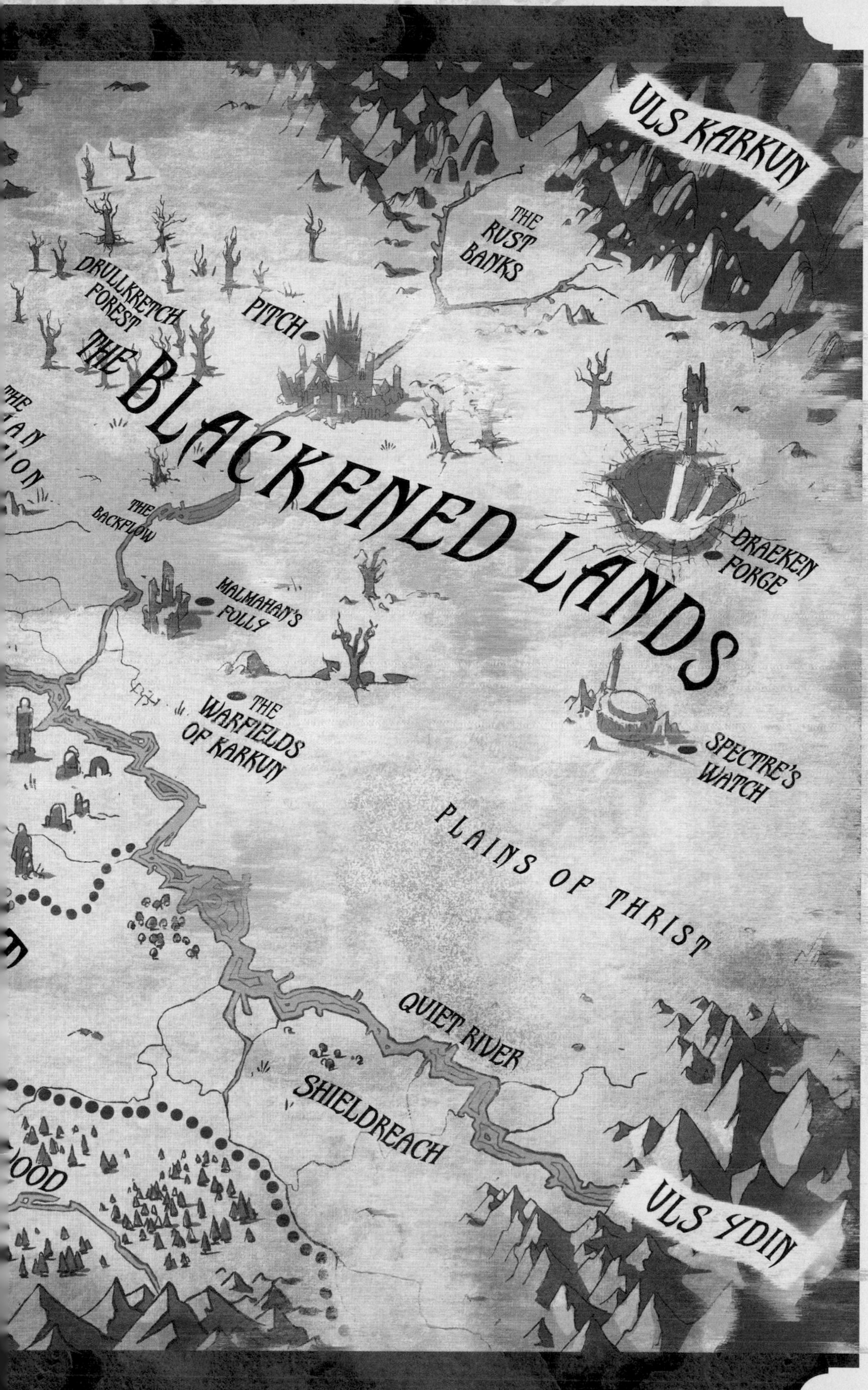

ULS KARKUN
THE RUST BANKS
DRULLKRETCH FOREST
PITCH
THE BLACKENED LANDS
DRAEKEN FORGE
THE BACKFLOW
MALMAHAN'S FOLLY
THE WARFIELDS OF KARKUN
SPECTRE'S WATCH
PLAINS OF THRIST
QUIET RIVER
SHIELDREACH
ULS YDIN

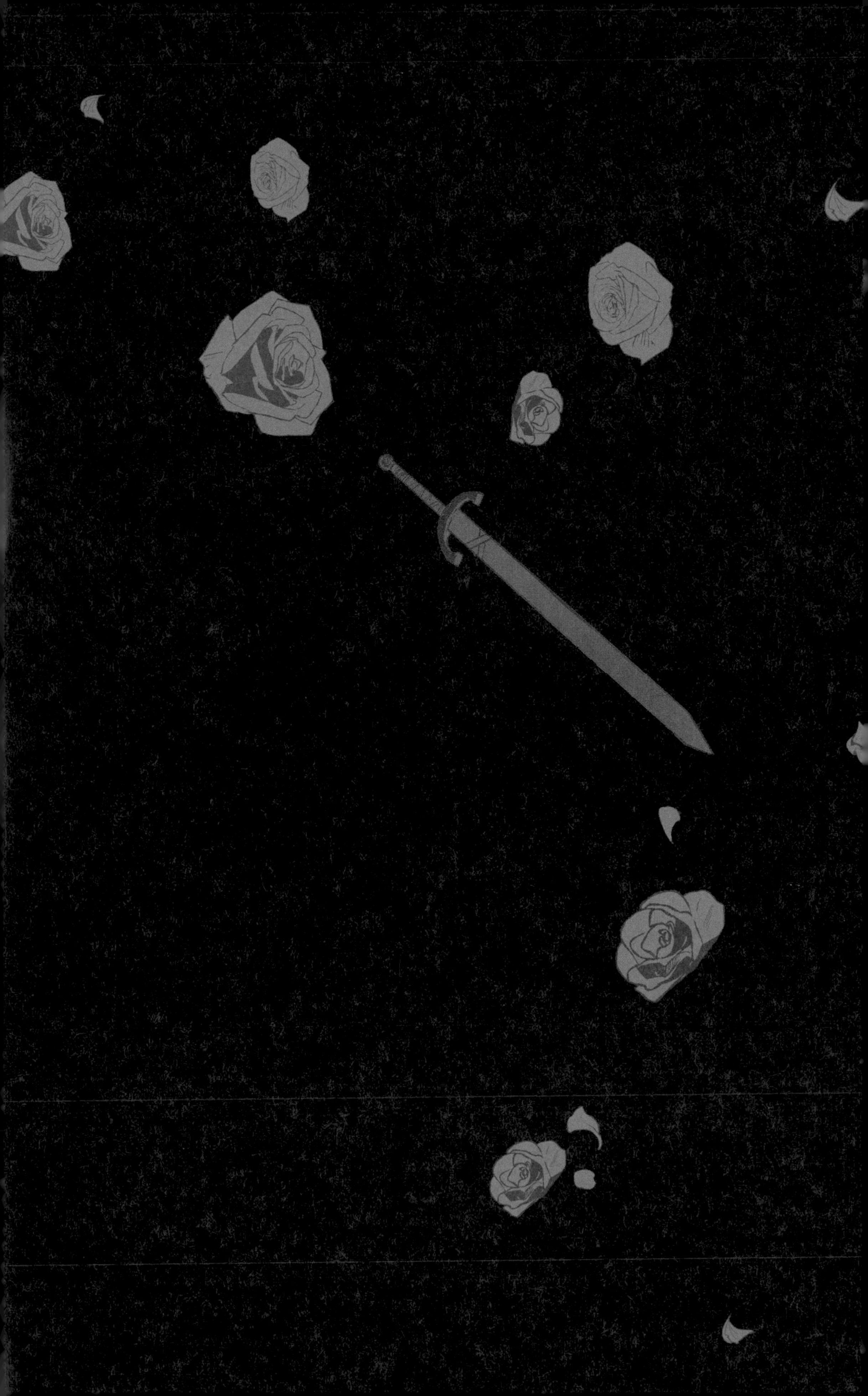

PROLOGUE

THE HEART OF THE CITY

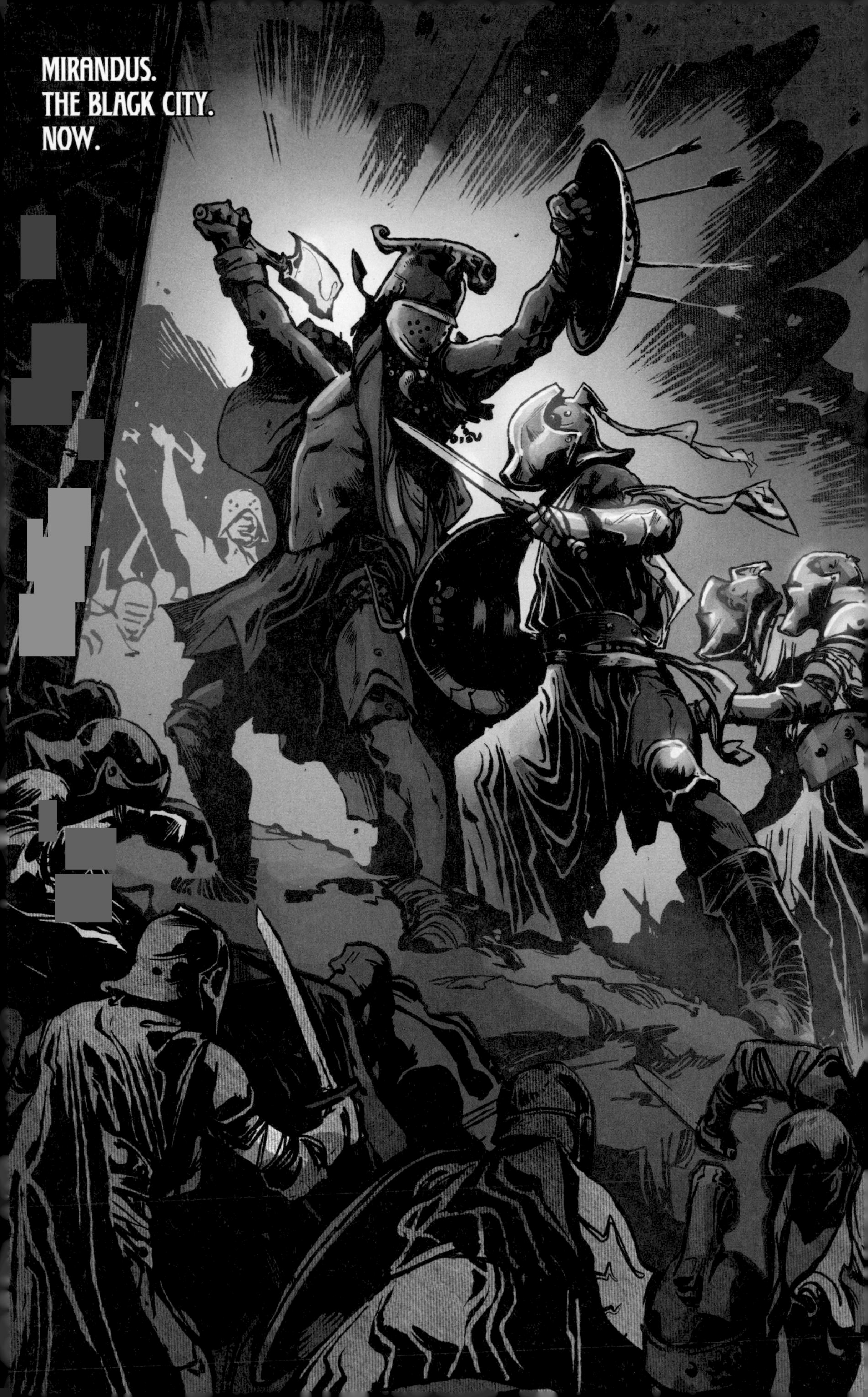
MIRANDUS.
THE BLACK CITY.
NOW.

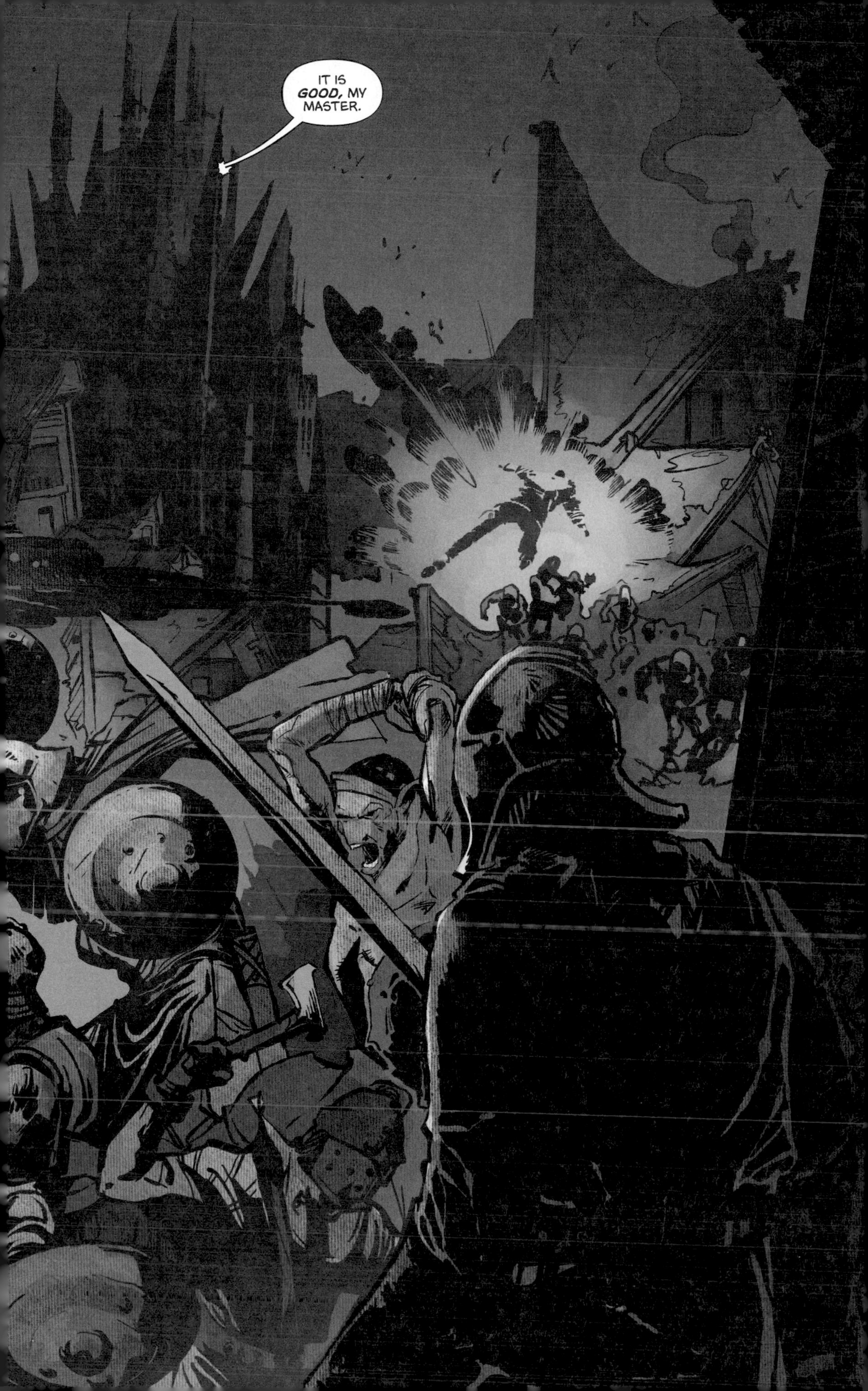
IT IS GOOD, MY MASTER.

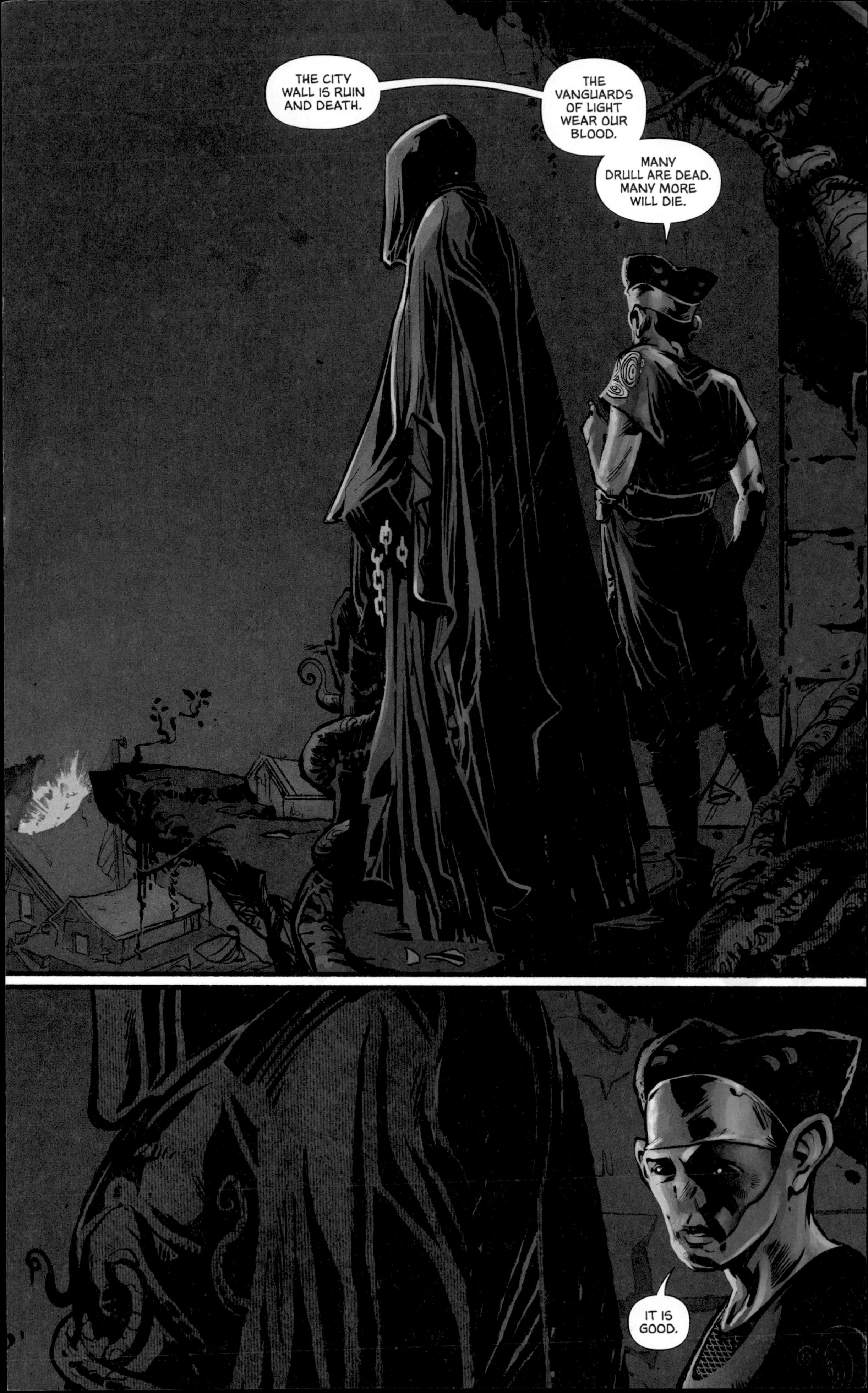
THE CITY WALL IS RUIN AND DEATH.
THE VANGUARDS OF LIGHT WEAR OUR BLOOD.
MANY DRULL ARE DEAD. MANY MORE WILL DIE.
IT IS GOOD.

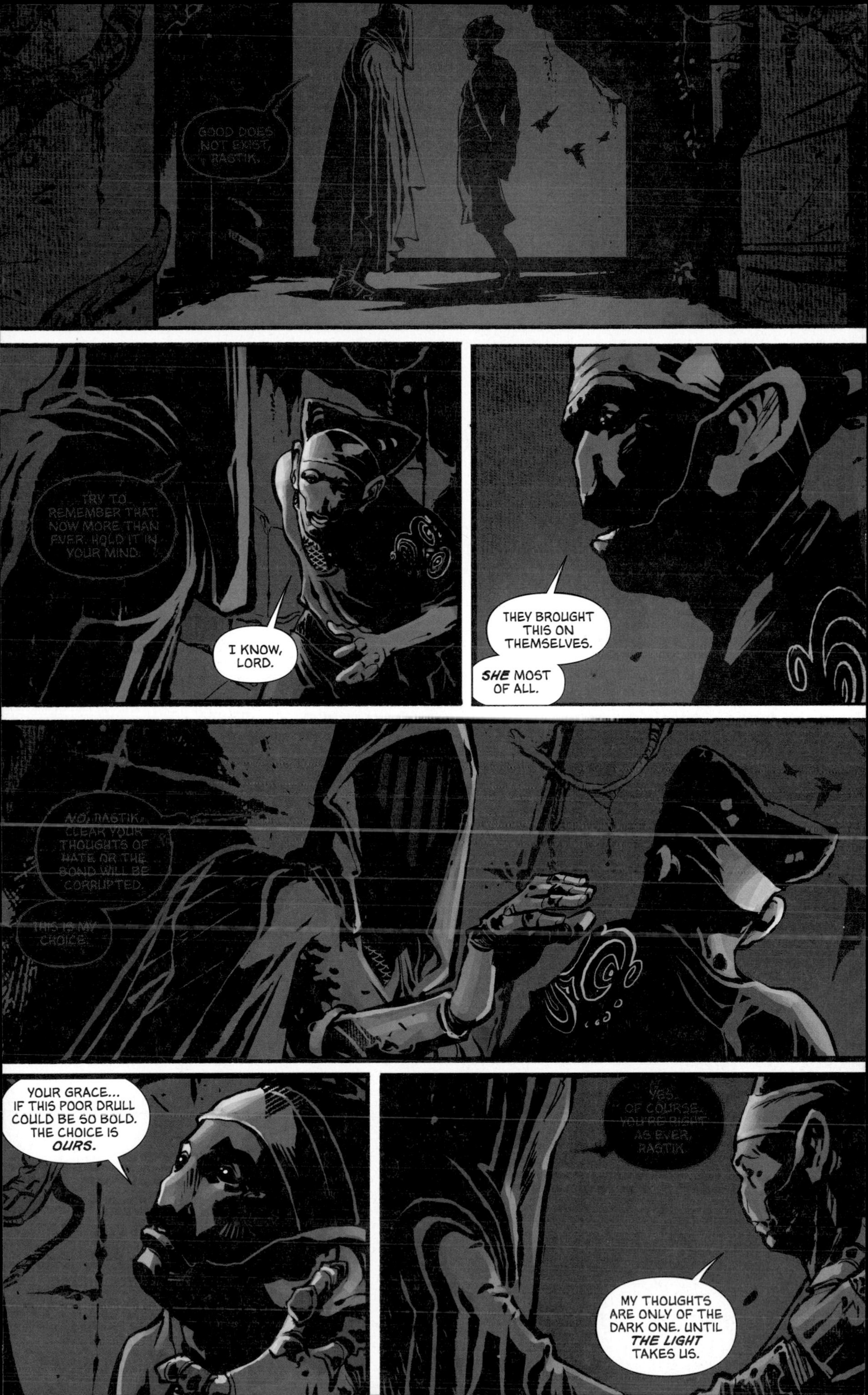
GOOD DOES NOT EXIST, RASTIK.
TRY TO REMEMBER THAT. NOW MORE THAN EVER. HOLD IT IN YOUR MIND.
I KNOW, LORD.
THEY BROUGHT THIS ON THEMSELVES.
SHE MOST OF ALL.
NO, RASTIK. CLEAR YOUR THOUGHTS OF HATE OR THE BOND WILL BE CORRUPTED.
THIS IS MY CHOICE.
YOUR GRACE... IF THIS POOR DRULL COULD BE SO BOLD. THE CHOICE IS *OURS.*
YES. OF COURSE. YOU'RE RIGHT AS EVER, RASTIK.
MY THOUGHTS ARE ONLY OF THE DARK ONE. UNTIL *THE LIGHT* TAKES US.

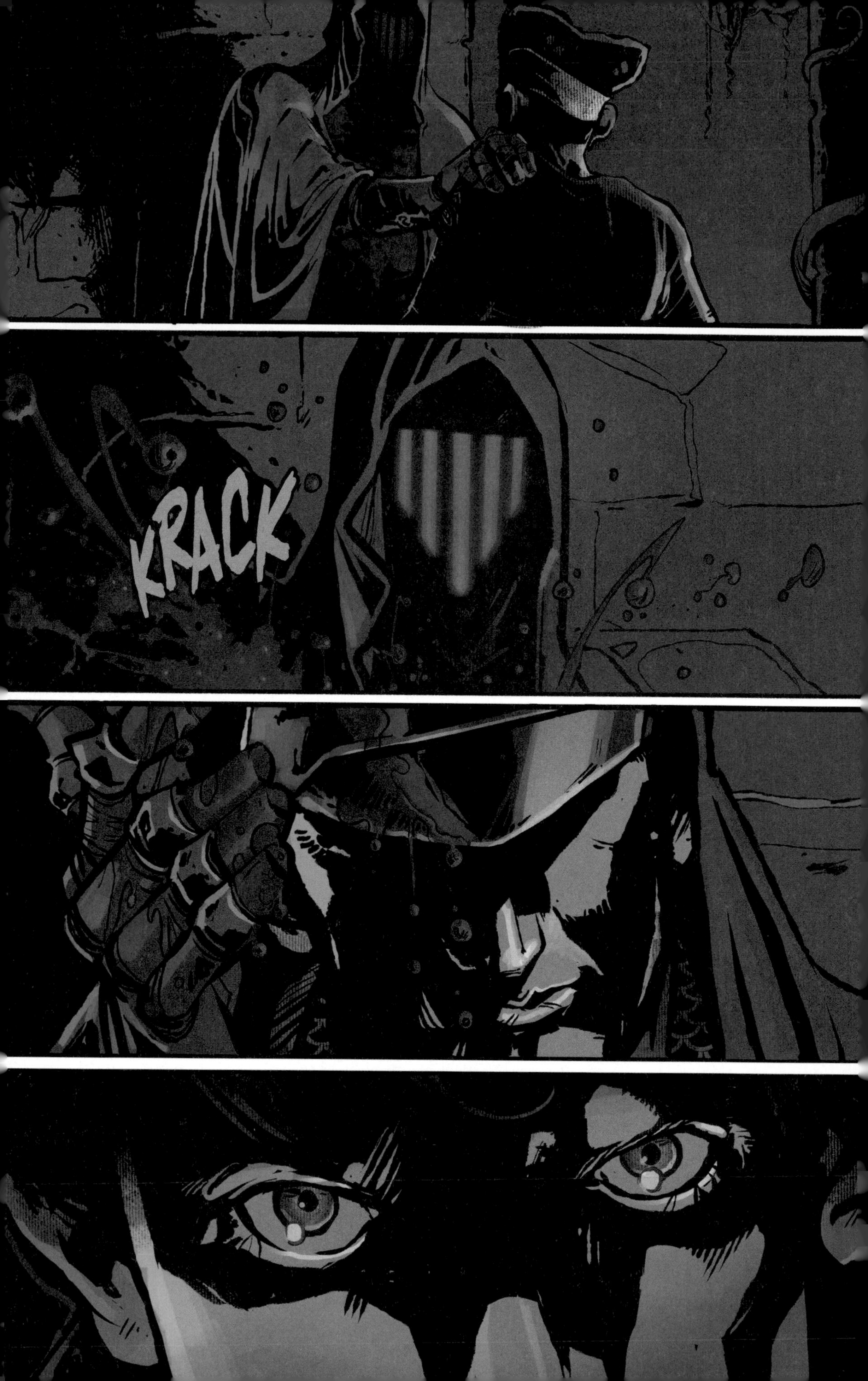
KRACK

THE UNSAFE BOY

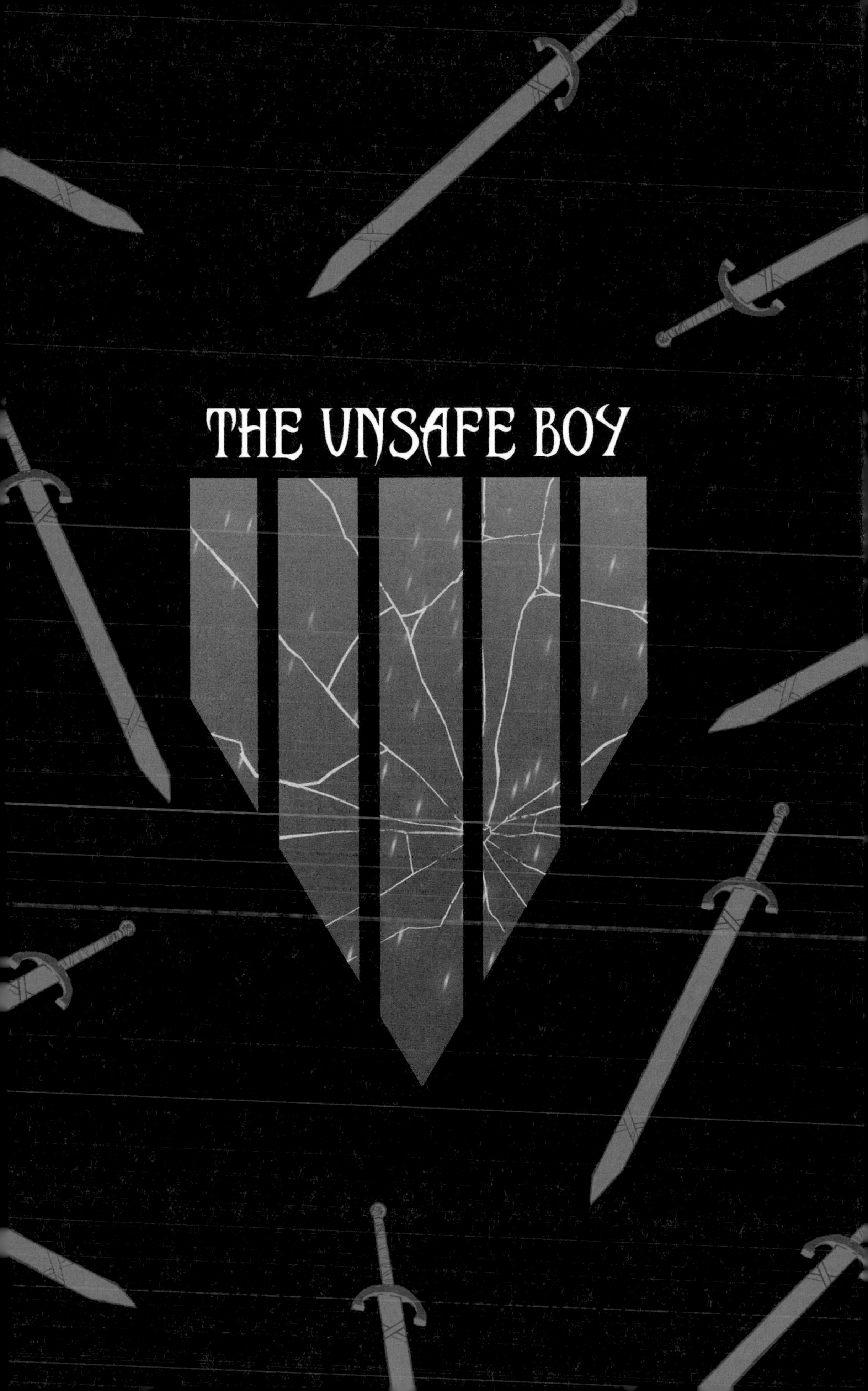

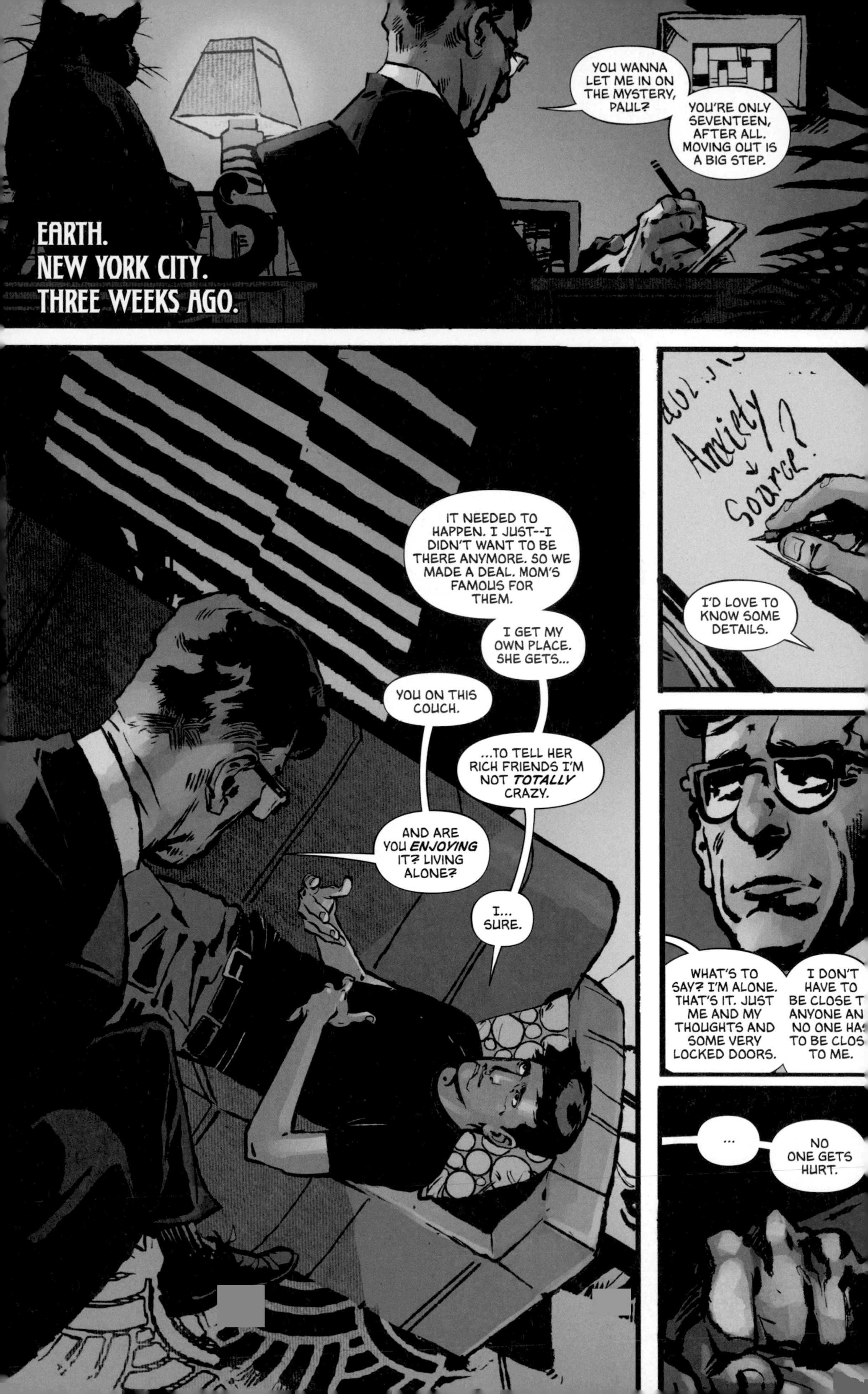
EARTH.
NEW YORK CITY.
THREE WEEKS AGO.
YOU WANNA LET ME IN ON THE MYSTERY, PAUL?
YOU'RE ONLY SEVENTEEN, AFTER ALL. MOVING OUT IS A BIG STEP.
IT NEEDED TO HAPPEN. I JUST--I DIDN'T WANT TO BE THERE ANYMORE. SO WE MADE A DEAL. MOM'S FAMOUS FOR THEM.
I GET MY OWN PLACE. SHE GETS...
YOU ON THIS COUCH.
...TO TELL HER RICH FRIENDS I'M NOT *TOTALLY* CRAZY.
AND ARE YOU *ENJOYING* IT? LIVING ALONE?
I... SURE.
Anxiety
Source?
I'D LOVE TO KNOW SOME DETAILS.
WHAT'S TO SAY? I'M ALONE. THAT'S IT. JUST ME AND MY THOUGHTS AND SOME VERY LOCKED DOORS.
I DON'T HAVE TO BE CLOSE T ANYONE AN NO ONE HA TO BE CLOS TO ME.
...
NO ONE GETS HURT.

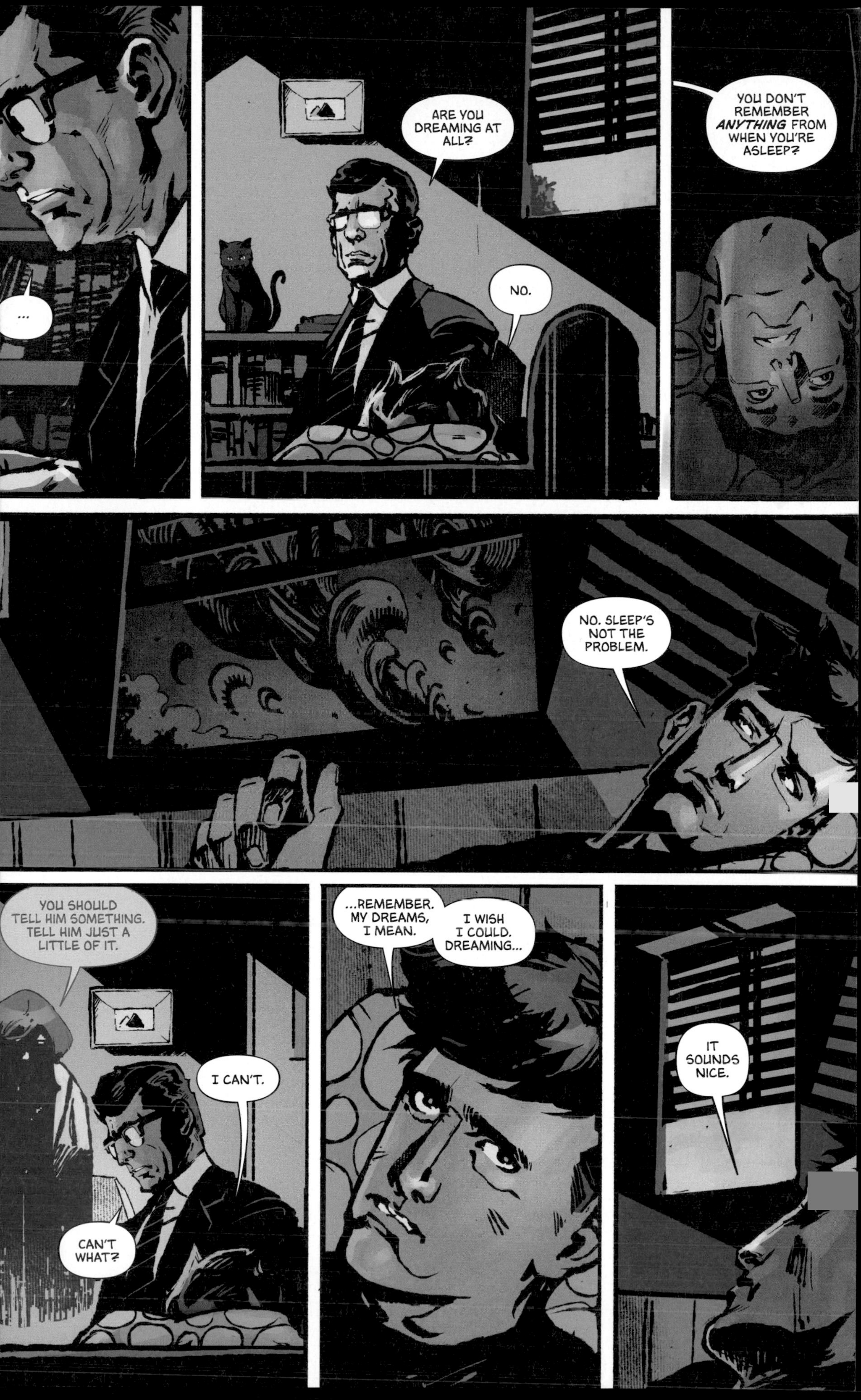
...
ARE YOU DREAMING AT ALL?
NO.
YOU DON'T REMEMBER *ANYTHING* FROM WHEN YOU'RE ASLEEP?
NO. SLEEP'S NOT THE PROBLEM.
YOU SHOULD TELL HIM SOMETHING. TELL HIM JUST A LITTLE OF IT.
I CAN'T.
CAN'T WHAT?
...REMEMBER. MY DREAMS, I MEAN.
I WISH I COULD. DREAMING...
IT SOUNDS NICE.

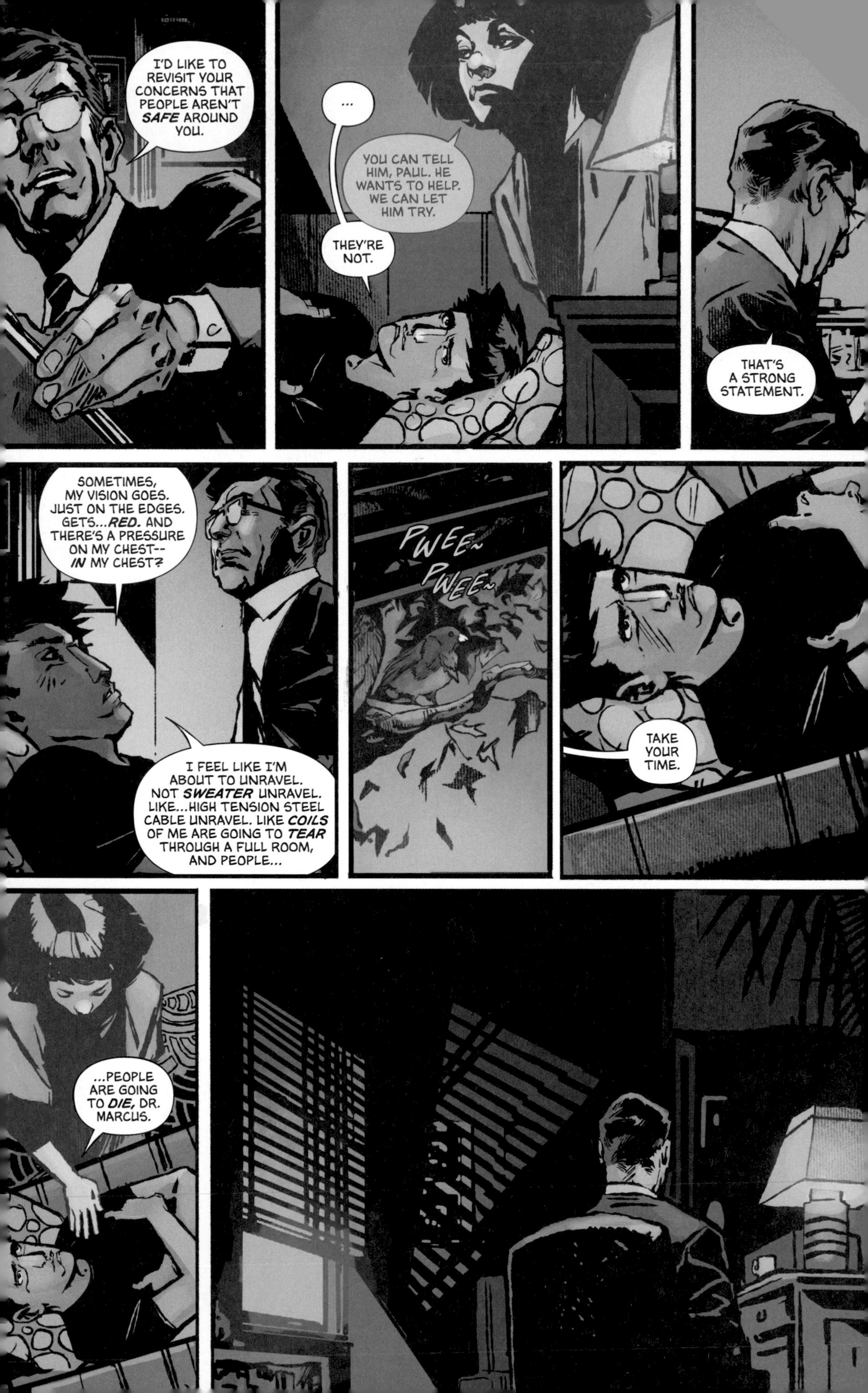
I'D LIKE TO REVISIT YOUR CONCERNS THAT PEOPLE AREN'T *SAFE* AROUND YOU.
...
YOU CAN TELL HIM, PAUL. HE WANTS TO HELP. WE CAN LET HIM TRY.
THEY'RE NOT.
THAT'S A STRONG STATEMENT.
SOMETIMES, MY VISION GOES. JUST ON THE EDGES. GETS...*RED.* AND THERE'S A PRESSURE ON MY CHEST-- *IN* MY CHEST?
I FEEL LIKE I'M ABOUT TO UNRAVEL. NOT *SWEATER* UNRAVEL. LIKE...HIGH TENSION STEEL CABLE UNRAVEL. LIKE *COILS* OF ME ARE GOING TO *TEAR* THROUGH A FULL ROOM, AND PEOPLE...
PWEE~ PWEE~
TAKE YOUR TIME.
...PEOPLE ARE GOING TO *DIE,* DR. MARCUS.

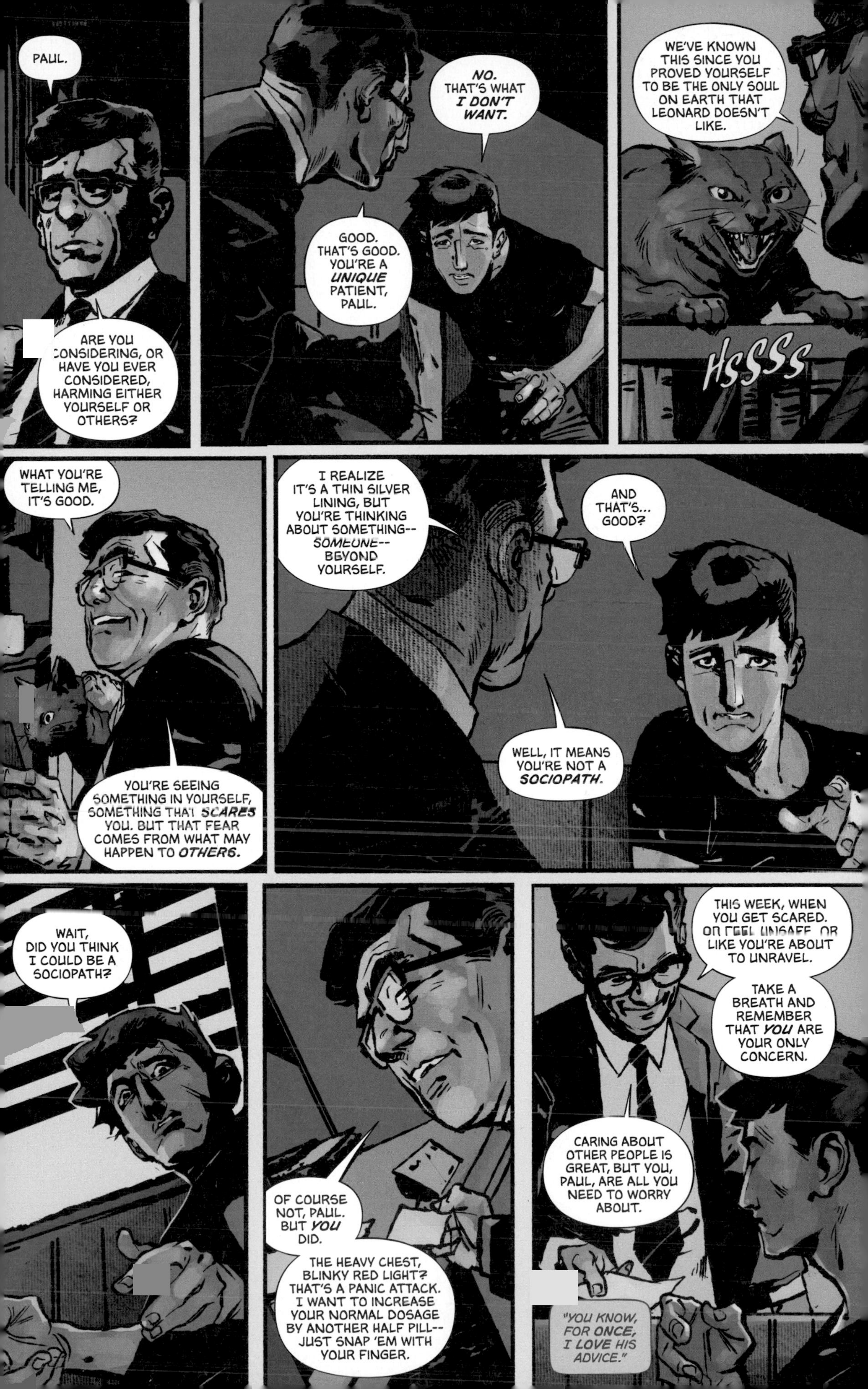
PAUL.
ARE YOU CONSIDERING, OR HAVE YOU EVER CONSIDERED, HARMING EITHER YOURSELF OR OTHERS?
NO. THAT'S WHAT I DON'T WANT.
GOOD. THAT'S GOOD. YOU'RE A UNIQUE PATIENT, PAUL.
WE'VE KNOWN THIS SINCE YOU PROVED YOURSELF TO BE THE ONLY SOUL ON EARTH THAT LEONARD DOESN'T LIKE.
HSSSS
WHAT YOU'RE TELLING ME, IT'S GOOD.
YOU'RE SEEING SOMETHING IN YOURSELF, SOMETHING THAT SCARES YOU. BUT THAT FEAR COMES FROM WHAT MAY HAPPEN TO OTHERS.
I REALIZE IT'S A THIN SILVER LINING, BUT YOU'RE THINKING ABOUT SOMETHING-- SOMEONE-- BEYOND YOURSELF.
AND THAT'S... GOOD?
WELL, IT MEANS YOU'RE NOT A SOCIOPATH.
WAIT, DID YOU THINK I COULD BE A SOCIOPATH?
OF COURSE NOT, PAUL. BUT YOU DID.
THE HEAVY CHEST, BLINKY RED LIGHT? THAT'S A PANIC ATTACK. I WANT TO INCREASE YOUR NORMAL DOSAGE BY ANOTHER HALF PILL-- JUST SNAP 'EM WITH YOUR FINGER.
THIS WEEK, WHEN YOU GET SCARED. OR FEEL UNSAFE. OR LIKE YOU'RE ABOUT TO UNRAVEL.
TAKE A BREATH AND REMEMBER THAT YOU ARE YOUR ONLY CONCERN.
CARING ABOUT OTHER PEOPLE IS GREAT, BUT YOU, PAUL, ARE ALL YOU NEED TO WORRY ABOUT.
"YOU KNOW, FOR ONCE, I LOVE HIS ADVICE."

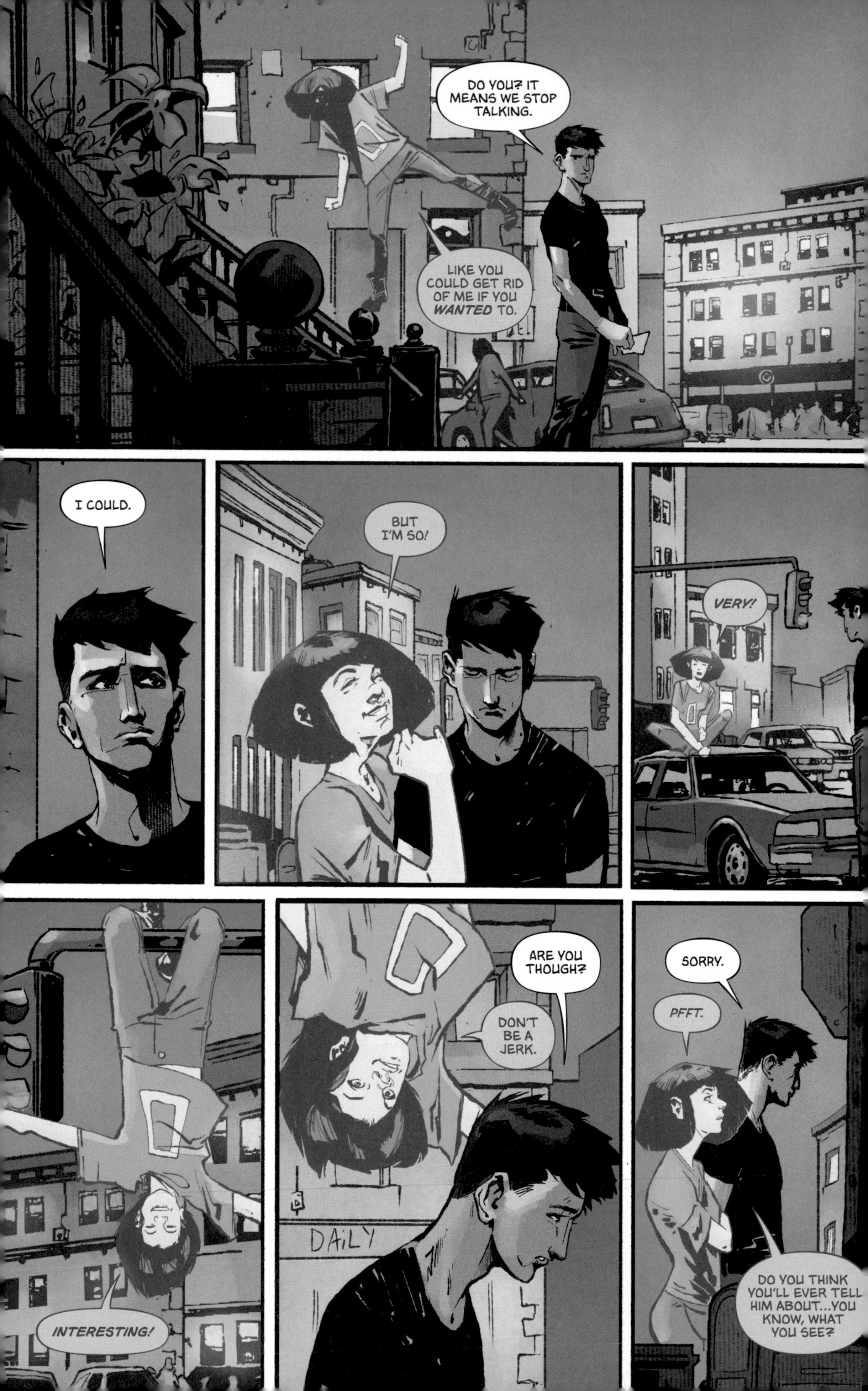
DO YOU? IT MEANS WE STOP TALKING.
LIKE YOU COULD GET RID OF ME IF YOU *WANTED* TO.
I COULD.
BUT I'M SO!
VERY!
INTERESTING!
ARE YOU THOUGH?
DON'T BE A JERK.
SORRY.
PFFT.
DO YOU THINK YOU'LL EVER TELL HIM ABOUT...YOU KNOW, WHAT YOU SEE?
DAILY

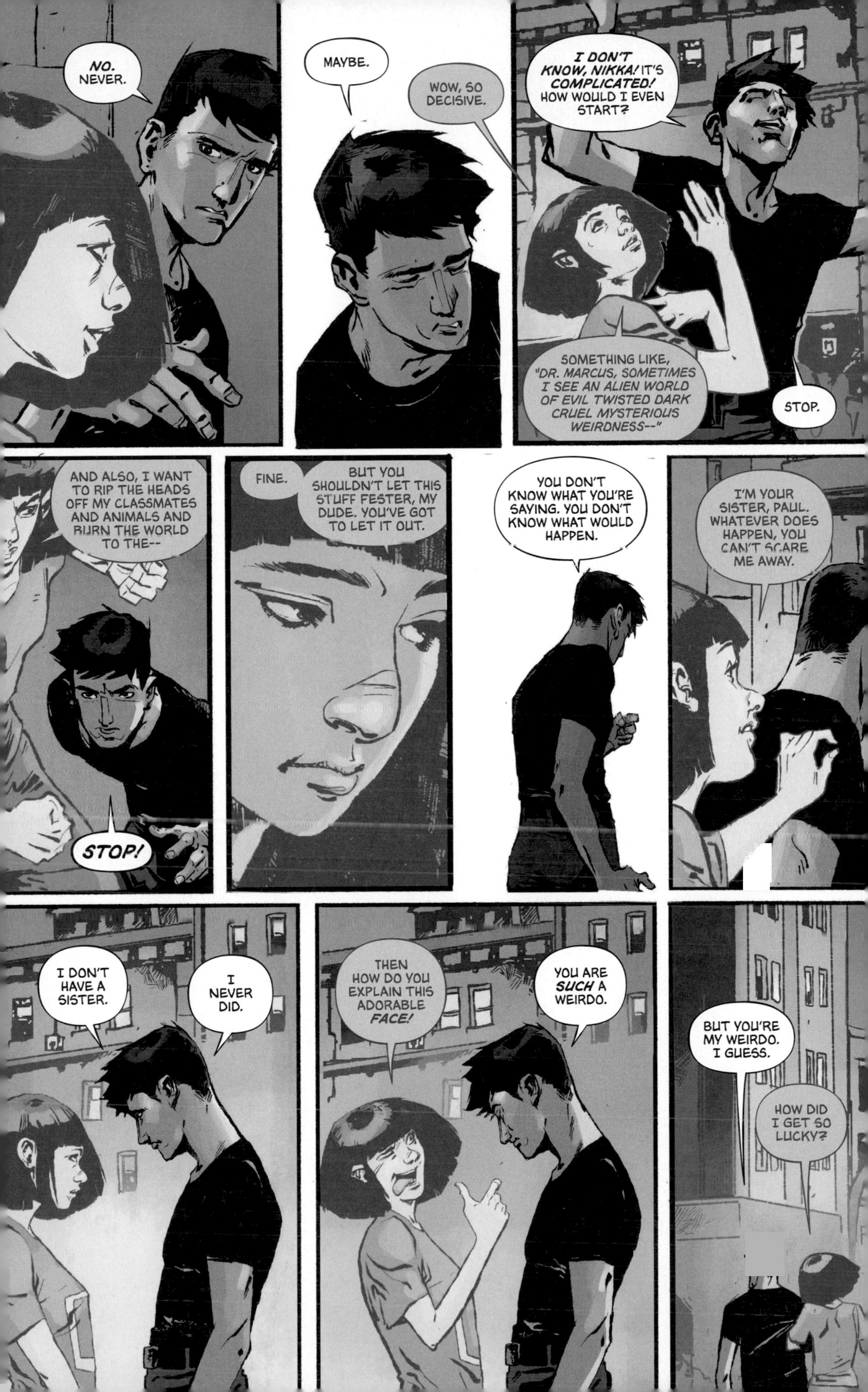
NO. NEVER.
MAYBE.
WOW, SO DECISIVE.
I DON'T KNOW, NIKKA! IT'S COMPLICATED! HOW WOULD I EVEN START?
SOMETHING LIKE, "DR. MARCUS, SOMETIMES I SEE AN ALIEN WORLD OF EVIL TWISTED DARK CRUEL MYSTERIOUS WEIRDNESS--"
STOP.
AND ALSO, I WANT TO RIP THE HEADS OFF MY CLASSMATES AND ANIMALS AND BURN THE WORLD TO THE--
STOP!
FINE.
BUT YOU SHOULDN'T LET THIS STUFF FESTER, MY DUDE. YOU'VE GOT TO LET IT OUT.
YOU DON'T KNOW WHAT YOU'RE SAYING. YOU DON'T KNOW WHAT WOULD HAPPEN.
I'M YOUR SISTER, PAUL. WHATEVER DOES HAPPEN, YOU CAN'T SCARE ME AWAY.
I DON'T HAVE A SISTER.
I NEVER DID.
THEN HOW DO YOU EXPLAIN THIS ADORABLE FACE!
YOU ARE SUCH A WEIRDO.
BUT YOU'RE MY WEIRDO. I GUESS.
HOW DID I GET SO LUCKY?

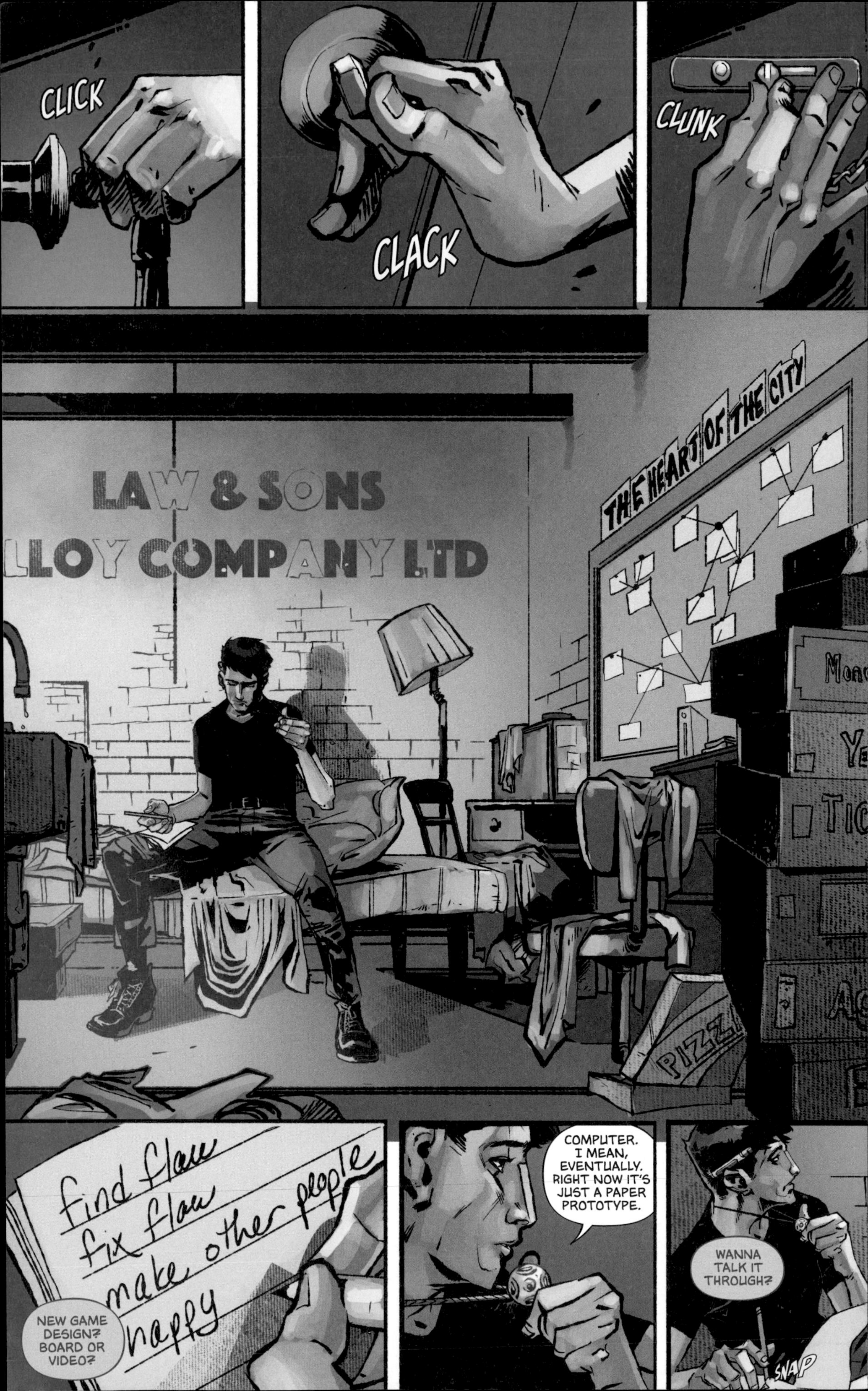

CLICK
CLACK
CLUNK
LAW & SONS
LLOY COMPANY LTD
THE HEART OF THE CITY
PIZZA
find flaw
fix flaw
make other people
happy
NEW GAME DESIGN? BOARD OR VIDEO?
COMPUTER. I MEAN, EVENTUALLY. RIGHT NOW IT'S JUST A PAPER PROTOTYPE.
WANNA TALK IT THROUGH?
SNAP

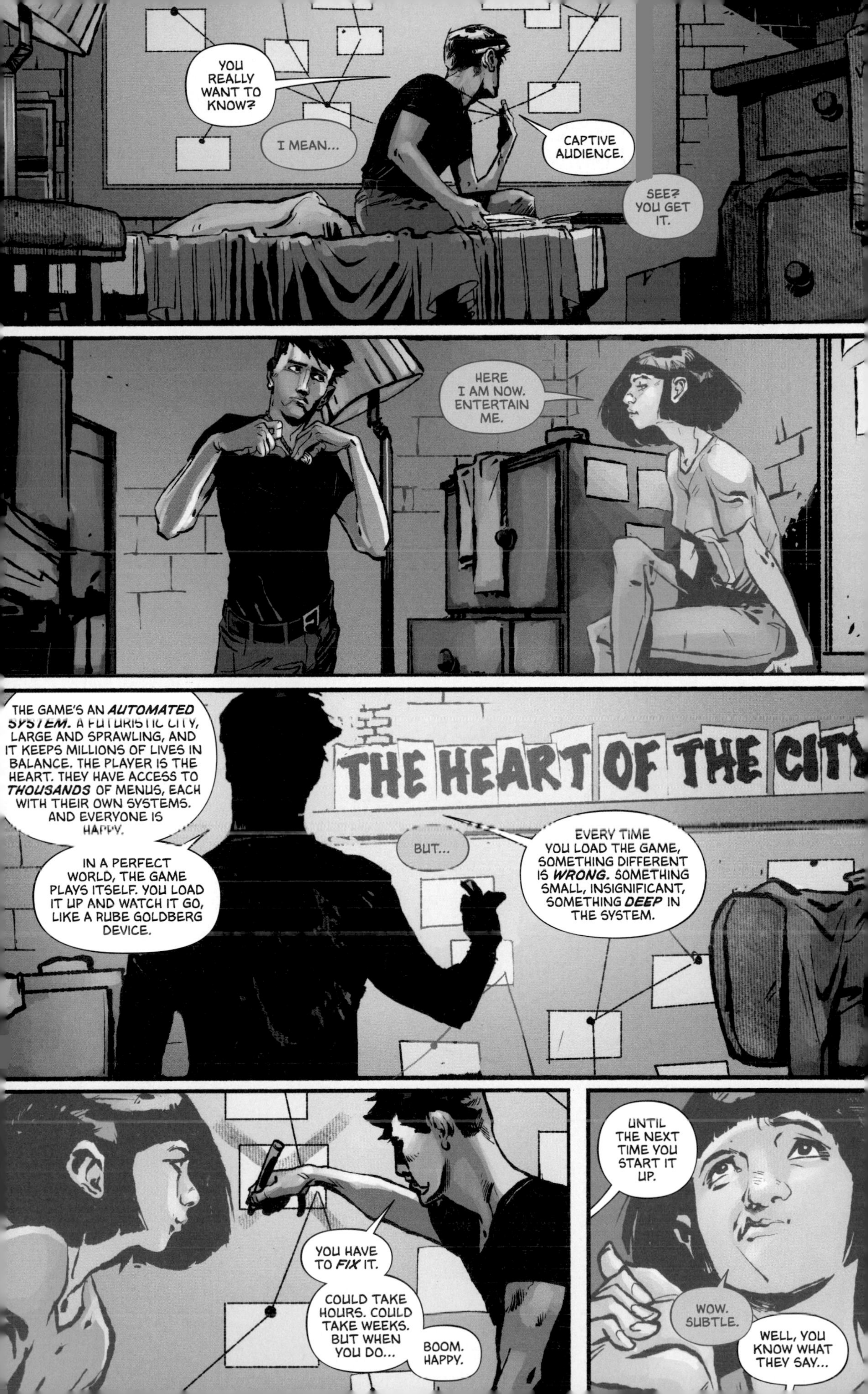

YOU REALLY WANT TO KNOW?
I MEAN...
CAPTIVE AUDIENCE.
SEE? YOU GET IT.
HERE I AM NOW. ENTERTAIN ME.
THE GAME'S AN *AUTOMATED SYSTEM.* A FUTURISTIC CITY, LARGE AND SPRAWLING, AND IT KEEPS MILLIONS OF LIVES IN BALANCE. THE PLAYER IS THE HEART. THEY HAVE ACCESS TO *THOUSANDS* OF MENUS, EACH WITH THEIR OWN SYSTEMS. AND EVERYONE IS HAPPY.
THE HEART OF THE CITY
IN A PERFECT WORLD, THE GAME PLAYS ITSELF. YOU LOAD IT UP AND WATCH IT GO, LIKE A RUBE GOLDBERG DEVICE.
BUT...
EVERY TIME YOU LOAD THE GAME, SOMETHING DIFFERENT IS ***WRONG.*** SOMETHING SMALL, INSIGNIFICANT, SOMETHING *DEEP* IN THE SYSTEM.
YOU HAVE TO *FIX* IT.
COULD TAKE HOURS. COULD TAKE WEEKS. BUT WHEN YOU DO...
BOOM. HAPPY.
UNTIL THE NEXT TIME YOU START IT UP.
WOW. SUBTLE.
WELL, YOU KNOW WHAT THEY SAY...

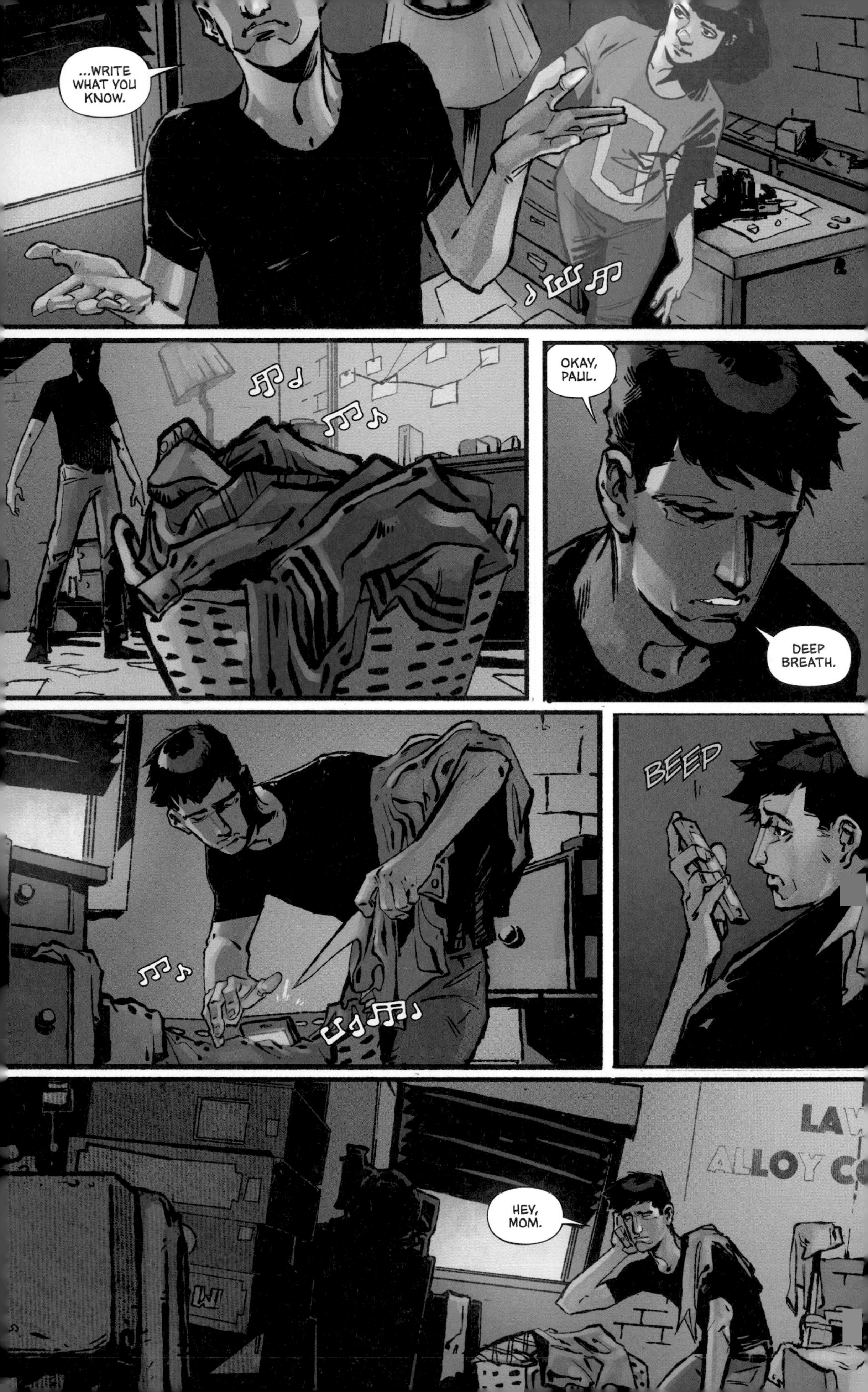
...WRITE WHAT YOU KNOW.
OKAY, PAUL.
DEEP BREATH.
BEEP
LAW
ALLOY CO
HEY, MOM.

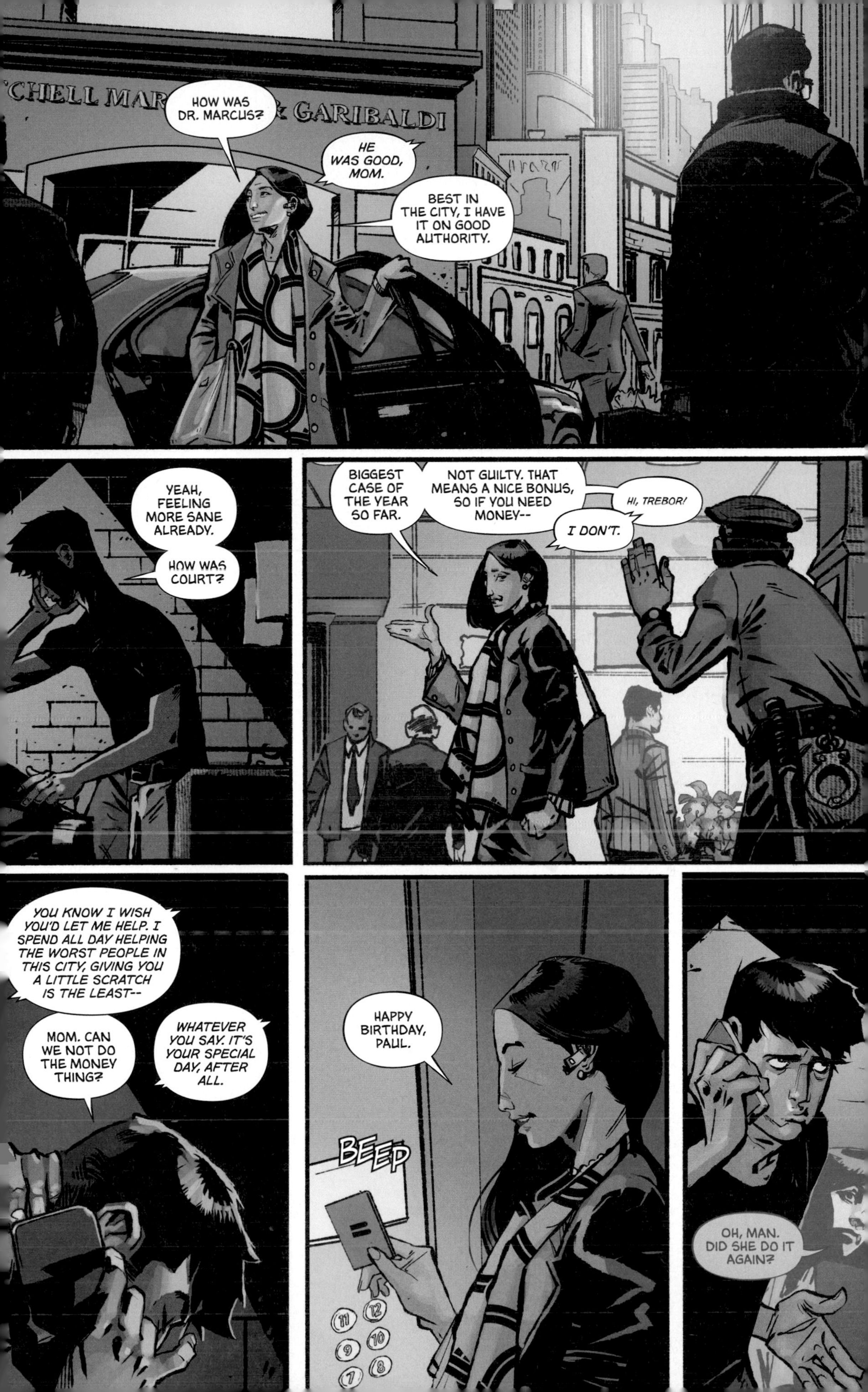
CHELL MAR & GARIBALDI
HOW WAS DR. MARCUS?
HE WAS GOOD, MOM.
BEST IN THE CITY, I HAVE IT ON GOOD AUTHORITY.
YEAH, FEELING MORE SANE ALREADY.
HOW WAS COURT?
BIGGEST CASE OF THE YEAR SO FAR.
NOT GUILTY. THAT MEANS A NICE BONUS, SO IF YOU NEED MONEY--
HI, TREBOR!
I DON'T.
YOU KNOW I WISH YOU'D LET ME HELP. I SPEND ALL DAY HELPING THE WORST PEOPLE IN THIS CITY, GIVING YOU A LITTLE SCRATCH IS THE LEAST--
MOM. CAN WE NOT DO THE MONEY THING?
WHATEVER YOU SAY. IT'S YOUR SPECIAL DAY, AFTER ALL.
HAPPY BIRTHDAY, PAUL.
BEEP
OH, MAN. DID SHE DO IT AGAIN?

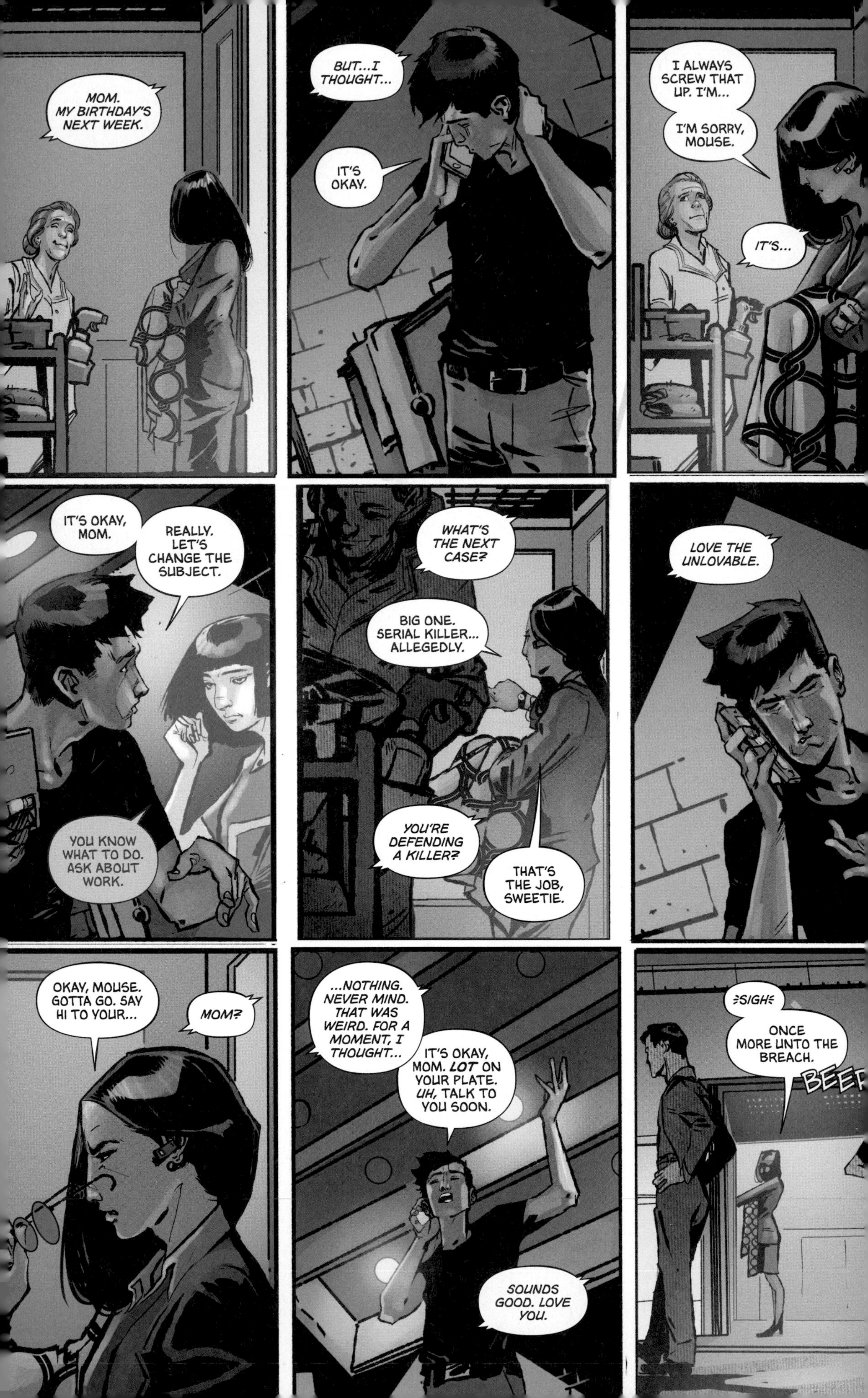
MOM. MY BIRTHDAY'S NEXT WEEK.
BUT...I THOUGHT...
IT'S OKAY.
I ALWAYS SCREW THAT UP. I'M...
I'M SORRY, MOUSE.
IT'S...
IT'S OKAY, MOM.
REALLY. LET'S CHANGE THE SUBJECT.
YOU KNOW WHAT TO DO. ASK ABOUT WORK.
WHAT'S THE NEXT CASE?
BIG ONE. SERIAL KILLER... ALLEGEDLY.
YOU'RE DEFENDING A KILLER?
THAT'S THE JOB, SWEETIE.
LOVE THE UNLOVABLE.
OKAY, MOUSE. GOTTA GO. SAY HI TO YOUR...
MOM?
...NOTHING. NEVER MIND. THAT WAS WEIRD. FOR A MOMENT, I THOUGHT...
IT'S OKAY, MOM. LOT ON YOUR PLATE. UH, TALK TO YOU SOON.
SOUNDS GOOD. LOVE YOU.
SIGH
ONCE MORE UNTO THE BREACH.
BEEP

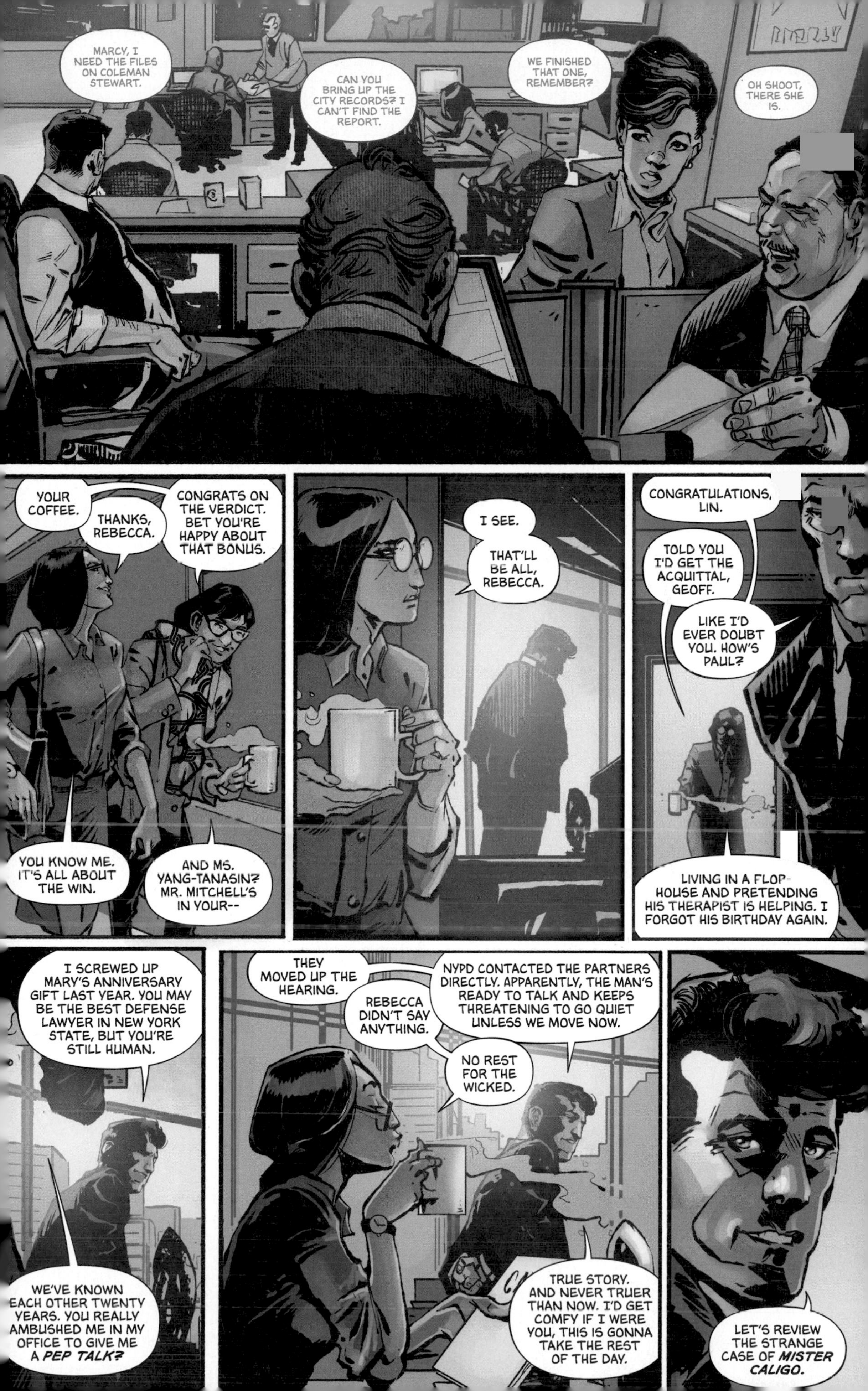

MARCY, I NEED THE FILES ON COLEMAN STEWART.
CAN YOU BRING UP THE CITY RECORDS? I CAN'T FIND THE REPORT.
WE FINISHED THAT ONE, REMEMBER?
OH SHOOT, THERE SHE IS.
YOUR COFFEE.
THANKS, REBECCA.
CONGRATS ON THE VERDICT. BET YOU'RE HAPPY ABOUT THAT BONUS.
YOU KNOW ME. IT'S ALL ABOUT THE WIN.
AND MS. YANG-TANASIN? MR. MITCHELL'S IN YOUR--
I SEE.
THAT'LL BE ALL, REBECCA.
CONGRATULATIONS, LIN.
TOLD YOU I'D GET THE ACQUITTAL, GEOFF.
LIKE I'D EVER DOUBT YOU. HOW'S PAUL?
LIVING IN A FLOPHOUSE AND PRETENDING HIS THERAPIST IS HELPING. I FORGOT HIS BIRTHDAY AGAIN.
I SCREWED UP MARY'S ANNIVERSARY GIFT LAST YEAR. YOU MAY BE THE BEST DEFENSE LAWYER IN NEW YORK STATE, BUT YOU'RE STILL HUMAN.
WE'VE KNOWN EACH OTHER TWENTY YEARS. YOU REALLY AMBUSHED ME IN MY OFFICE TO GIVE ME A *PEP TALK?*
THEY MOVED UP THE HEARING.
REBECCA DIDN'T SAY ANYTHING.
NYPD CONTACTED THE PARTNERS DIRECTLY. APPARENTLY, THE MAN'S READY TO TALK AND KEEPS THREATENING TO GO QUIET UNLESS WE MOVE NOW.
NO REST FOR THE WICKED.
TRUE STORY. AND NEVER TRUER THAN NOW. I'D GET COMFY IF I WERE YOU, THIS IS GONNA TAKE THE REST OF THE DAY.
LET'S REVIEW THE STRANGE CASE OF *MISTER CALIGO.*

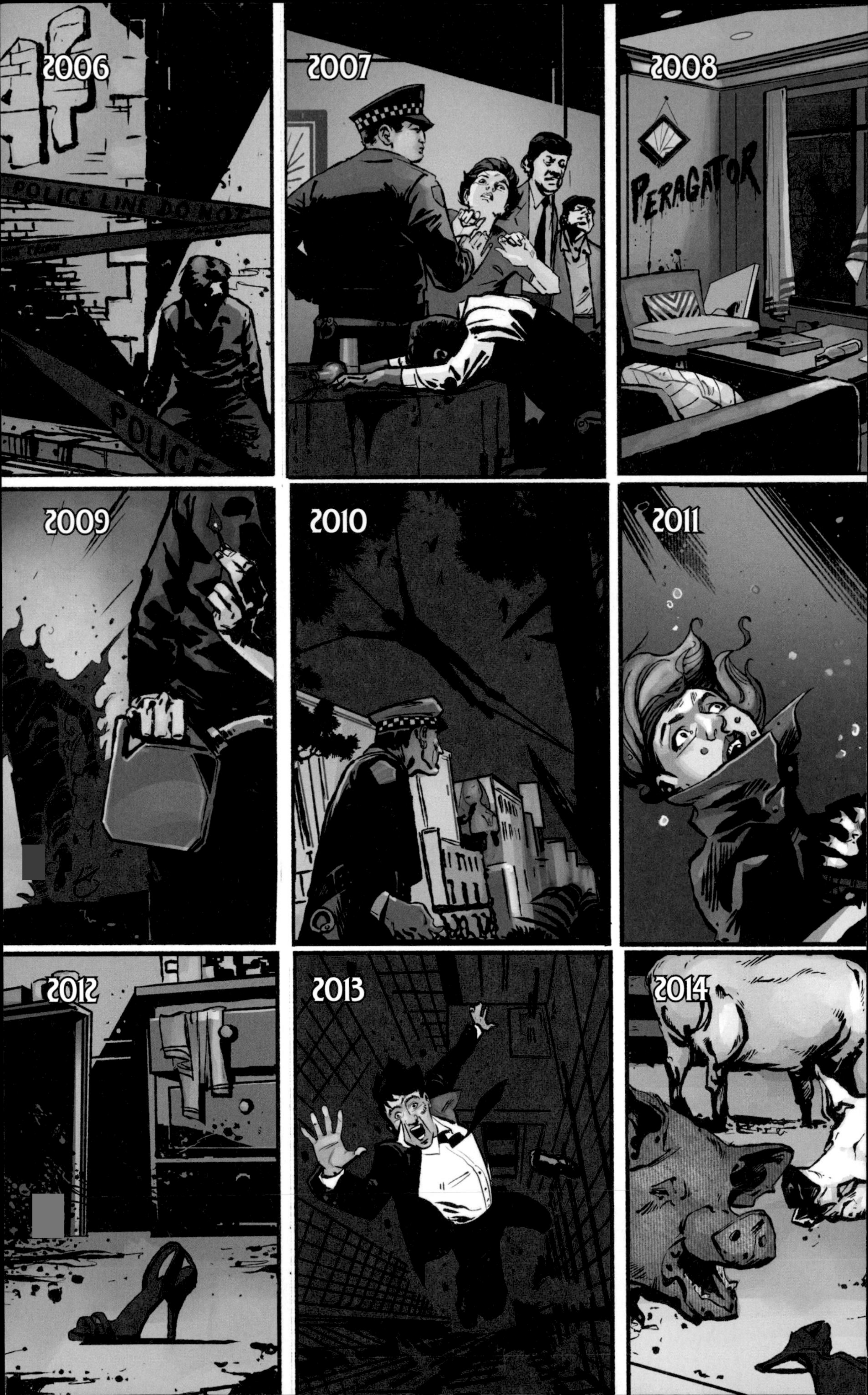
2006
POLICE LINE DO NOT
POLICE
2007
2008
PERAGATOR
2009
2010
2011
2012
2013
2014

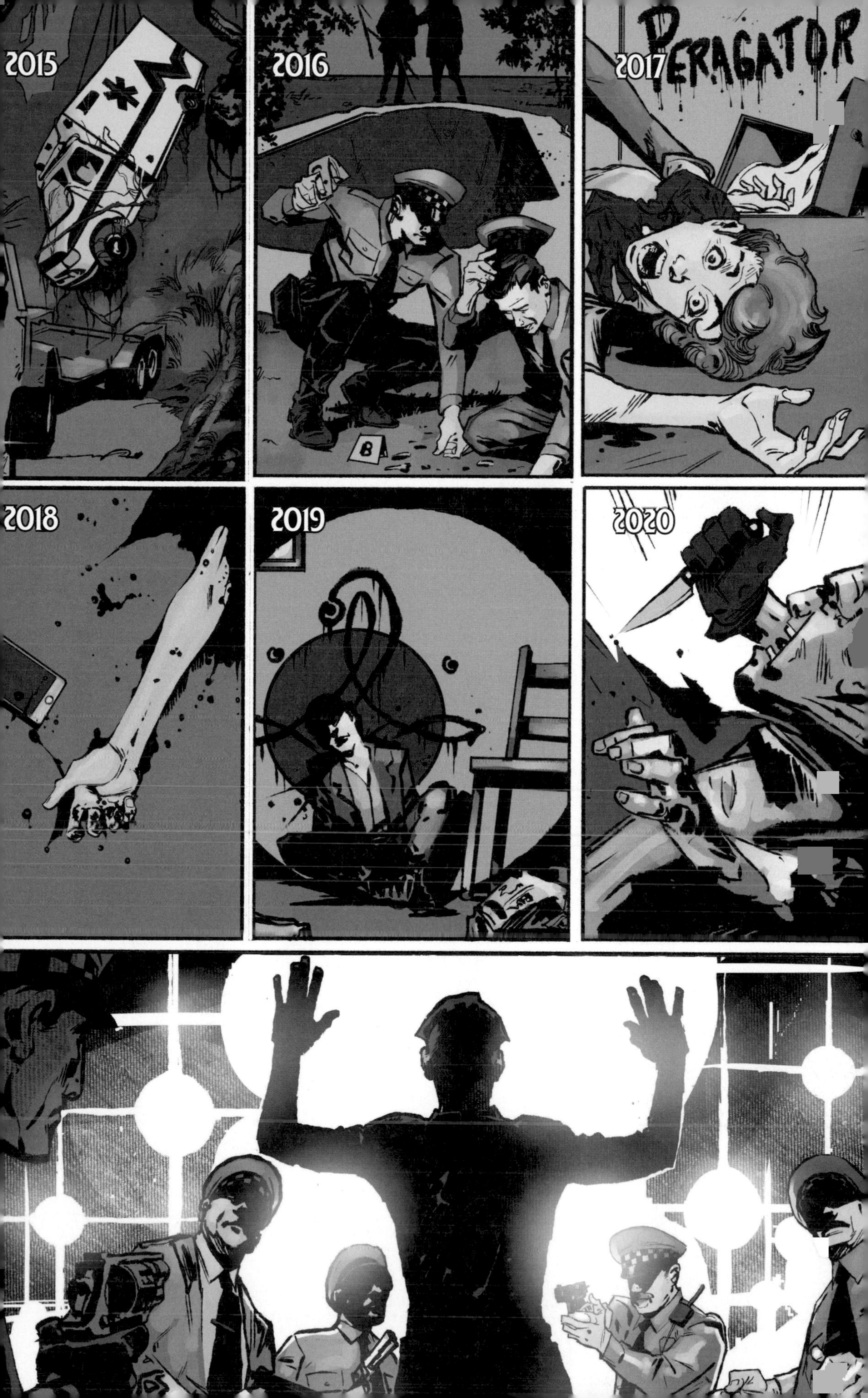
2015
2016
2017
PERAGATOR
2018
2019
2020

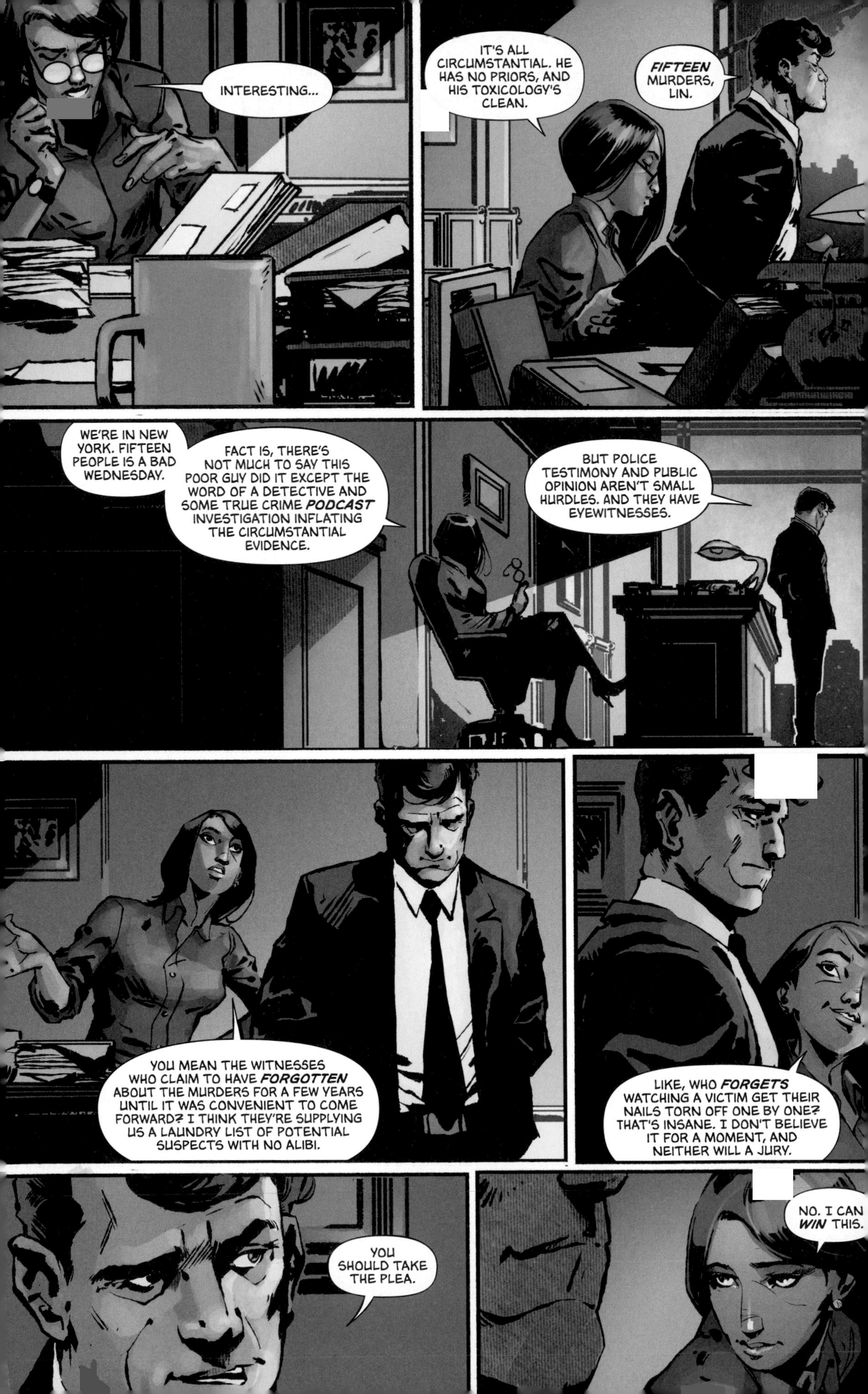
INTERESTING...
IT'S ALL CIRCUMSTANTIAL. HE HAS NO PRIORS, AND HIS TOXICOLOGY'S CLEAN.
FIFTEEN MURDERS, LIN.
WE'RE IN NEW YORK. FIFTEEN PEOPLE IS A BAD WEDNESDAY.
FACT IS, THERE'S NOT MUCH TO SAY THIS POOR GUY DID IT EXCEPT THE WORD OF A DETECTIVE AND SOME TRUE CRIME PODCAST INVESTIGATION INFLATING THE CIRCUMSTANTIAL EVIDENCE.
BUT POLICE TESTIMONY AND PUBLIC OPINION AREN'T SMALL HURDLES. AND THEY HAVE EYEWITNESSES.
YOU MEAN THE WITNESSES WHO CLAIM TO HAVE FORGOTTEN ABOUT THE MURDERS FOR A FEW YEARS UNTIL IT WAS CONVENIENT TO COME FORWARD? I THINK THEY'RE SUPPLYING US A LAUNDRY LIST OF POTENTIAL SUSPECTS WITH NO ALIBI.
LIKE, WHO FORGETS WATCHING A VICTIM GET THEIR NAILS TORN OFF ONE BY ONE? THAT'S INSANE. I DON'T BELIEVE IT FOR A MOMENT, AND NEITHER WILL A JURY.
YOU SHOULD TAKE THE PLEA.
NO. I CAN WIN THIS.

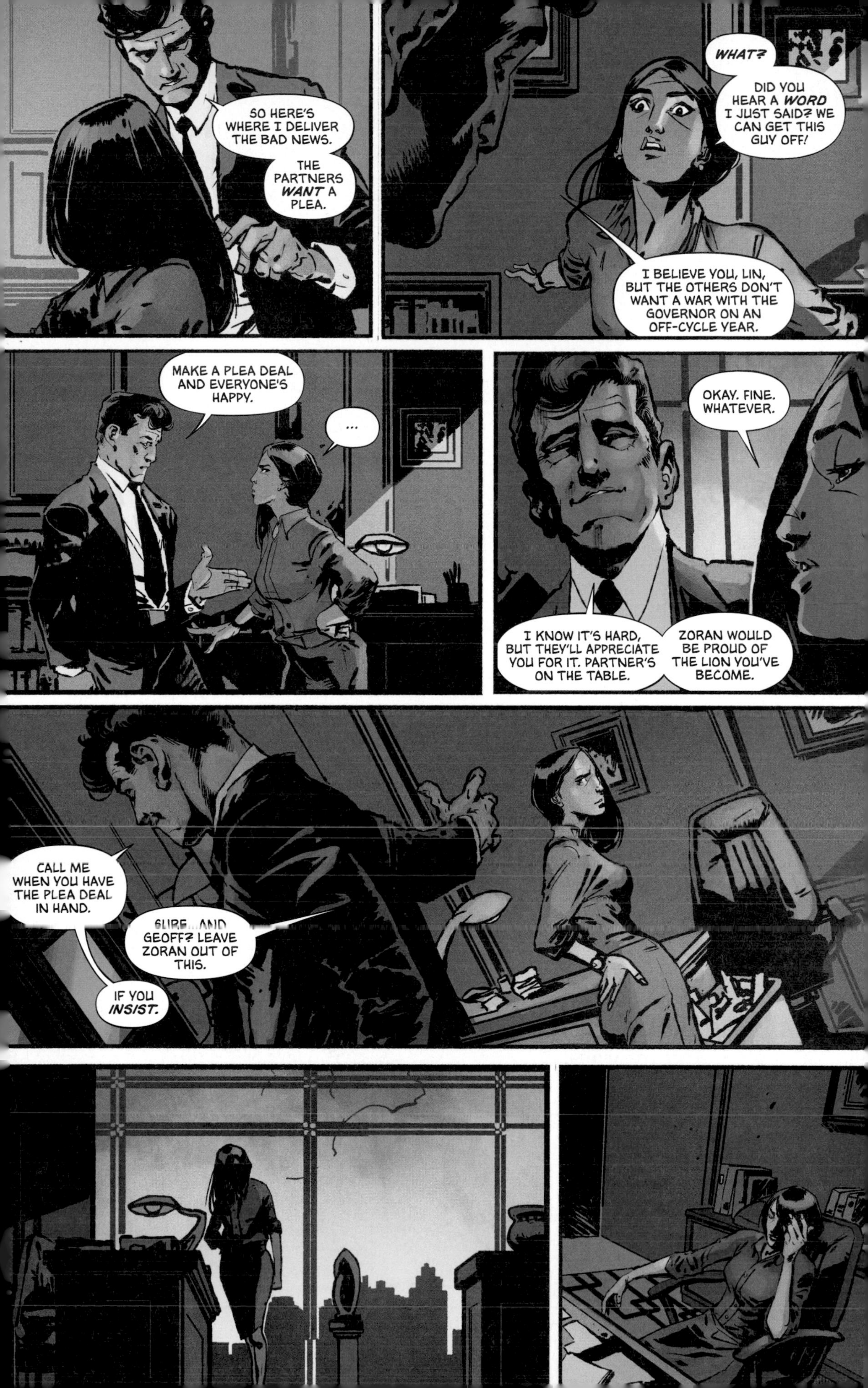
SO HERE'S WHERE I DELIVER THE BAD NEWS.
THE PARTNERS *WANT* A PLEA.
WHAT?
DID YOU HEAR A *WORD* I JUST SAID? WE CAN GET THIS GUY OFF!
I BELIEVE YOU, LIN, BUT THE OTHERS DON'T WANT A WAR WITH THE GOVERNOR ON AN OFF-CYCLE YEAR.
MAKE A PLEA DEAL AND EVERYONE'S HAPPY.
...
OKAY. FINE. WHATEVER.
I KNOW IT'S HARD, BUT THEY'LL APPRECIATE YOU FOR IT. PARTNER'S ON THE TABLE.
ZORAN WOULD BE PROUD OF THE LION YOU'VE BECOME.
CALL ME WHEN YOU HAVE THE PLEA DEAL IN HAND.
SURE...AND GEOFF? LEAVE ZORAN OUT OF THIS.
IF YOU *INSIST.*

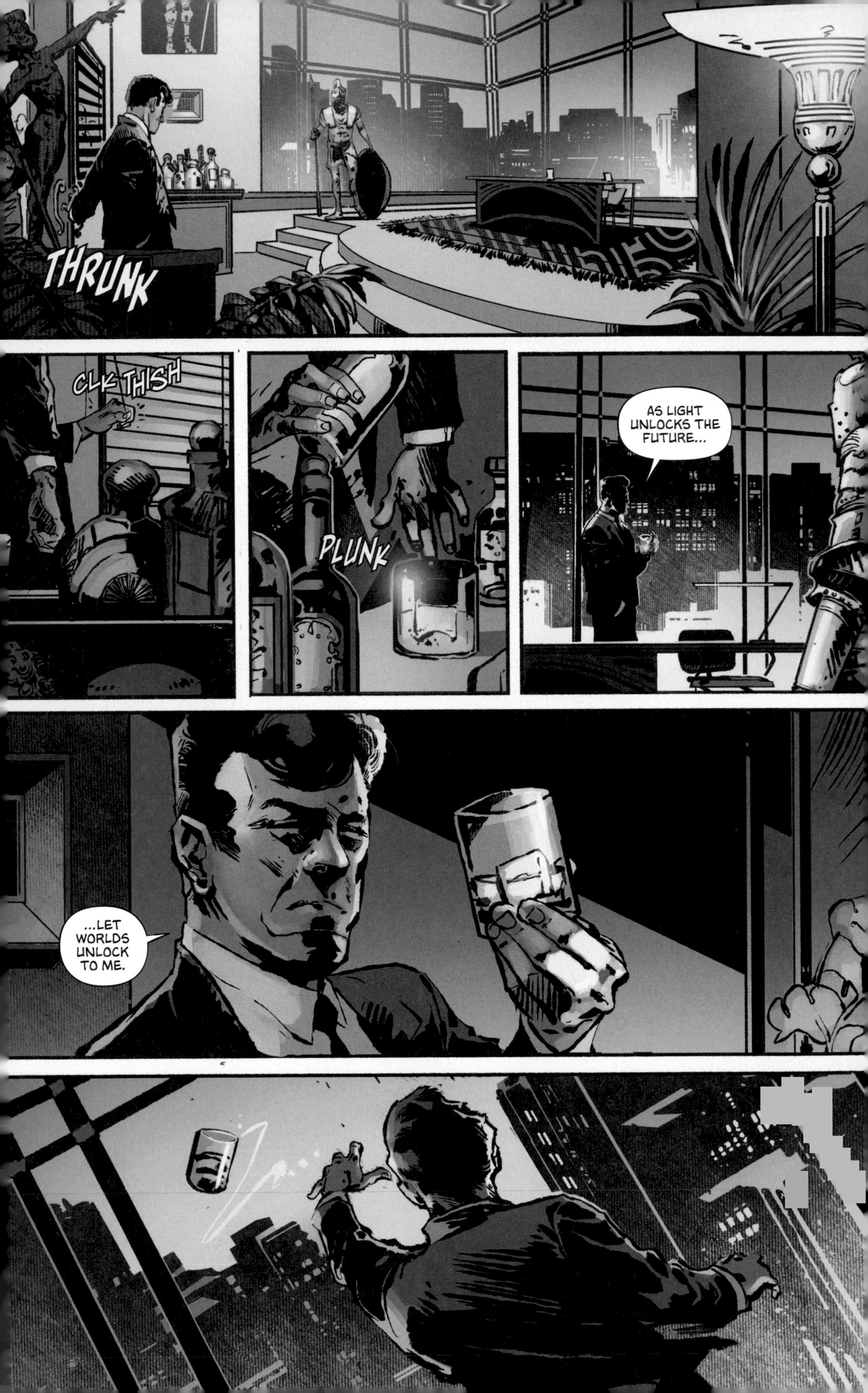
THRUNK
CLK THISH
PLUNK
AS LIGHT UNLOCKS THE FUTURE...
...LET WORLDS UNLOCK TO ME.

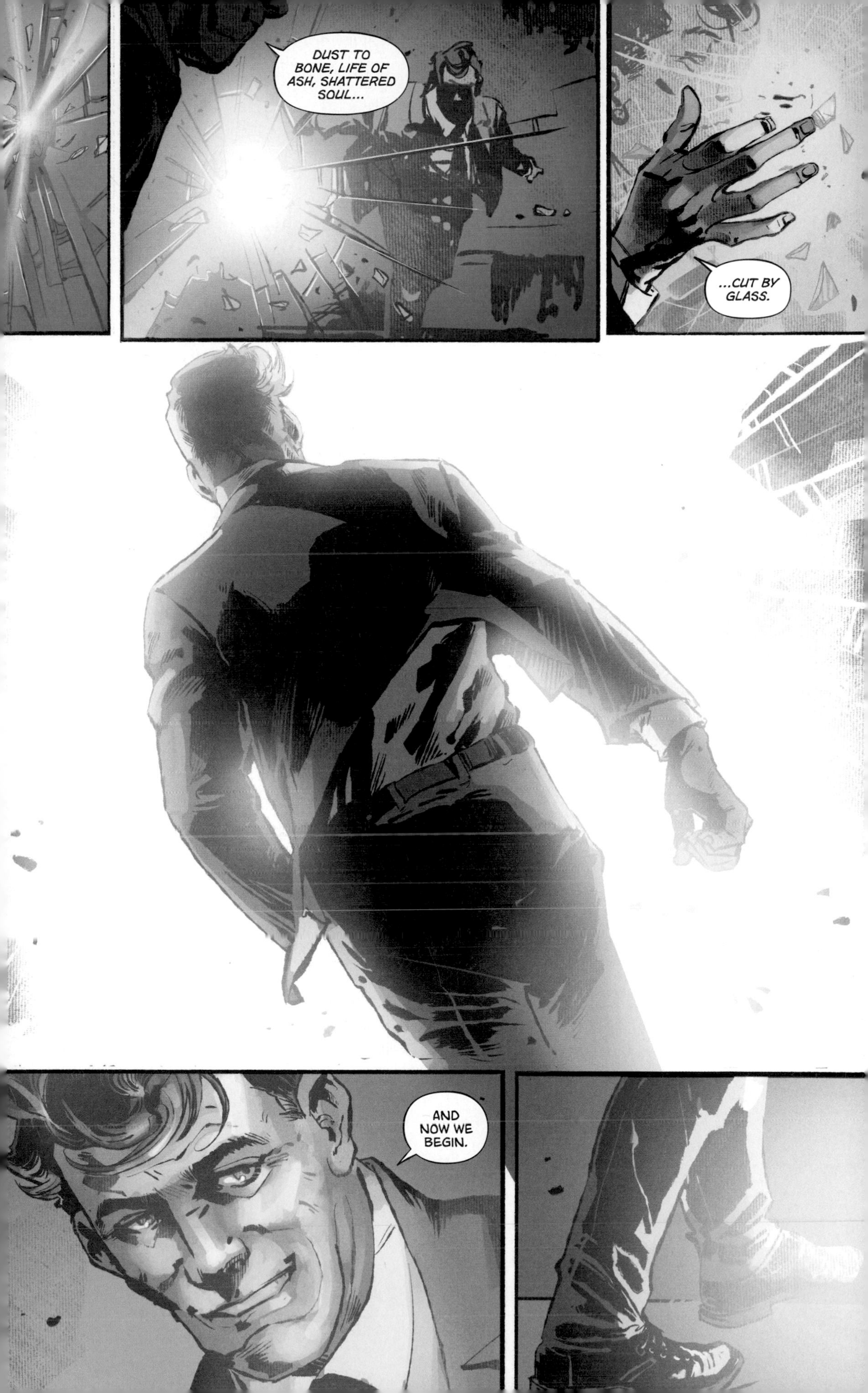
DUST TO BONE, LIFE OF ASH, SHATTERED SOUL...
...CUT BY GLASS.
AND NOW WE BEGIN.

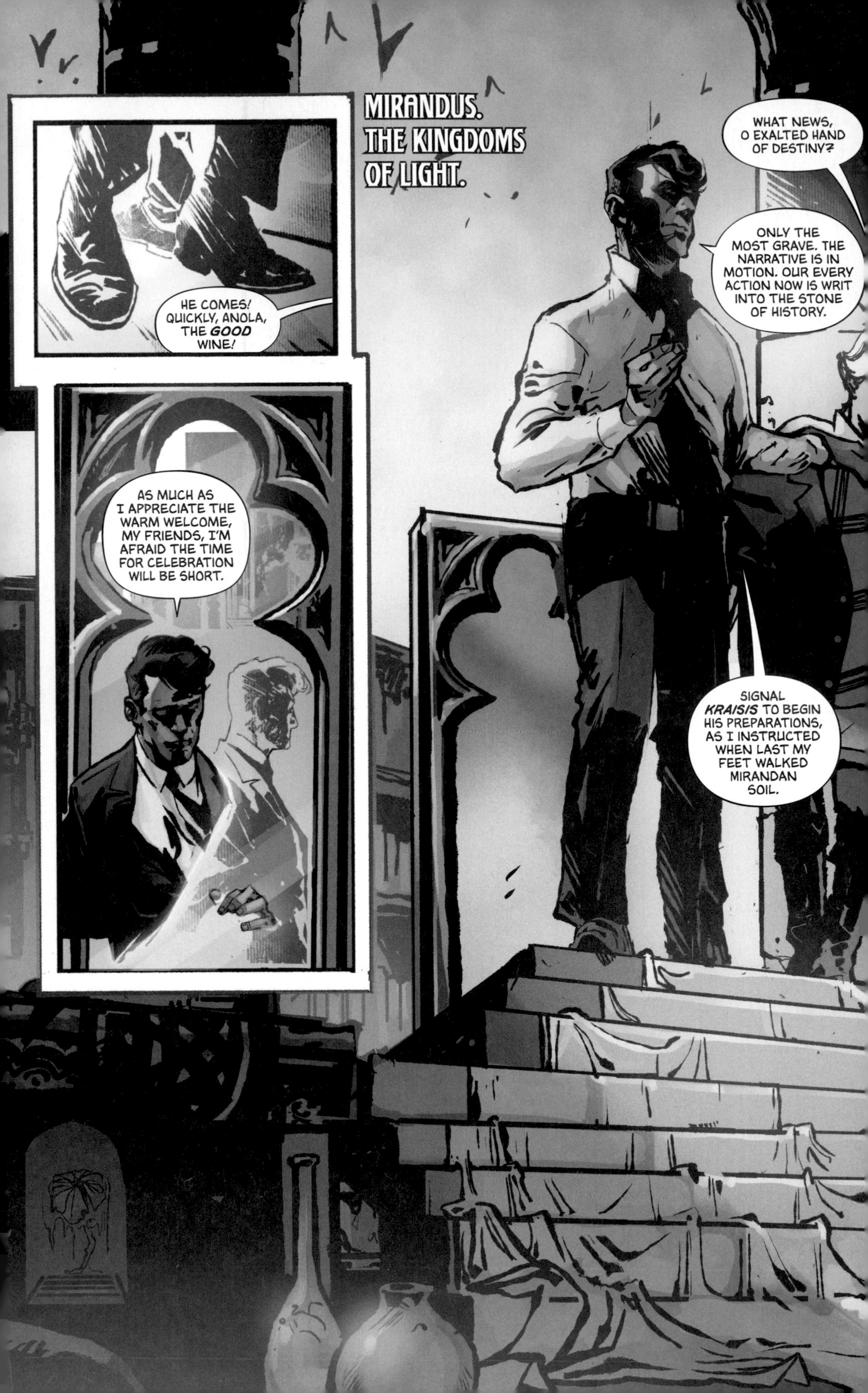

MIRANDUS. THE KINGDOMS OF LIGHT.
HE COMES! QUICKLY, ANOLA, THE *GOOD* WINE!
AS MUCH AS I APPRECIATE THE WARM WELCOME, MY FRIENDS, I'M AFRAID THE TIME FOR CELEBRATION WILL BE SHORT.
WHAT NEWS, O EXALTED HAND OF DESTINY?
ONLY THE MOST GRAVE. THE NARRATIVE IS IN MOTION. OUR EVERY ACTION NOW IS WRIT INTO THE STONE OF HISTORY.
SIGNAL *KRAISIS* TO BEGIN HIS PREPARATIONS, AS I INSTRUCTED WHEN LAST MY FEET WALKED MIRANDAN SOIL.

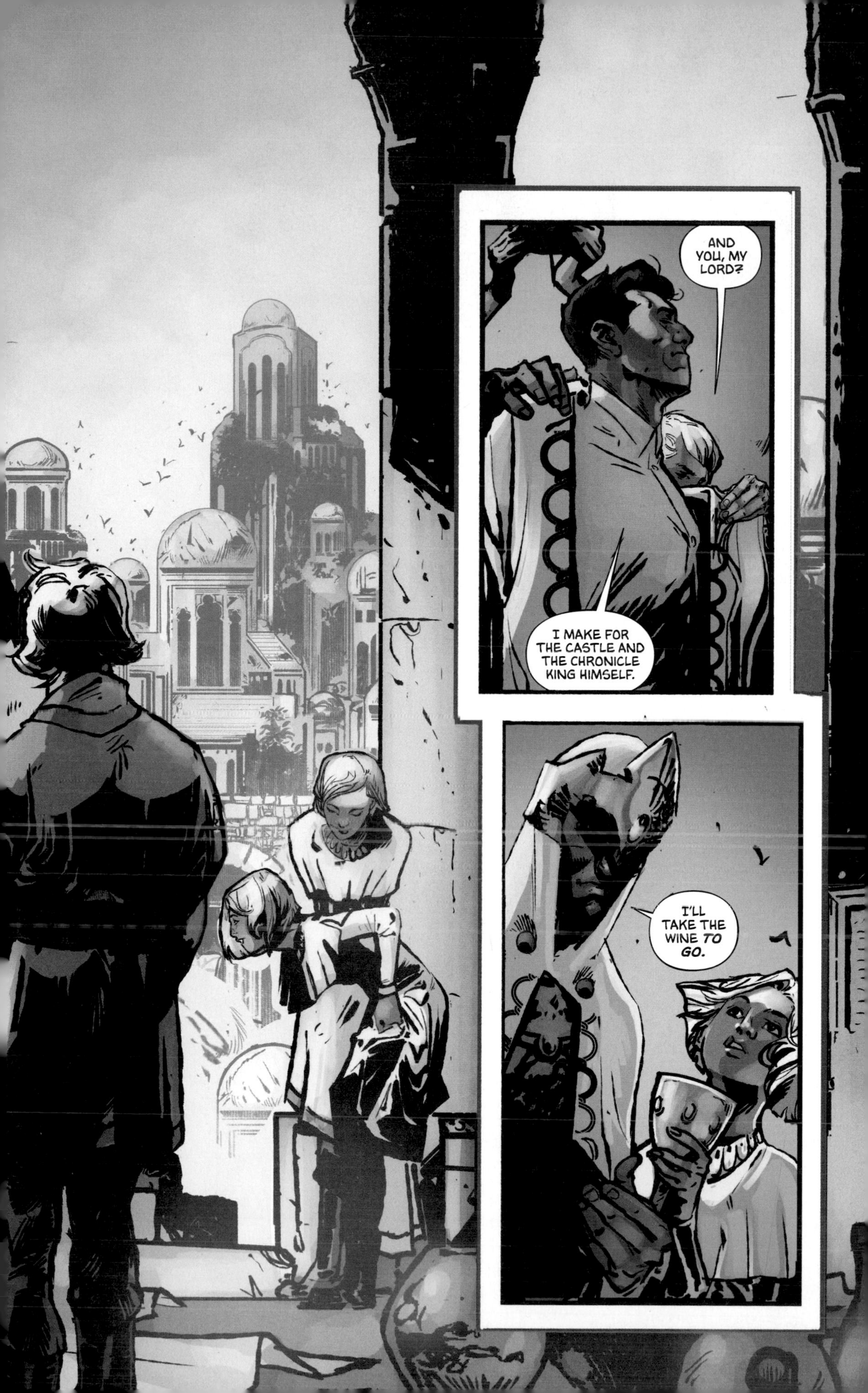
AND YOU, MY LORD?
I MAKE FOR THE CASTLE AND THE CHRONICLE KING HIMSELF.
I'LL TAKE THE WINE *TO GO.*

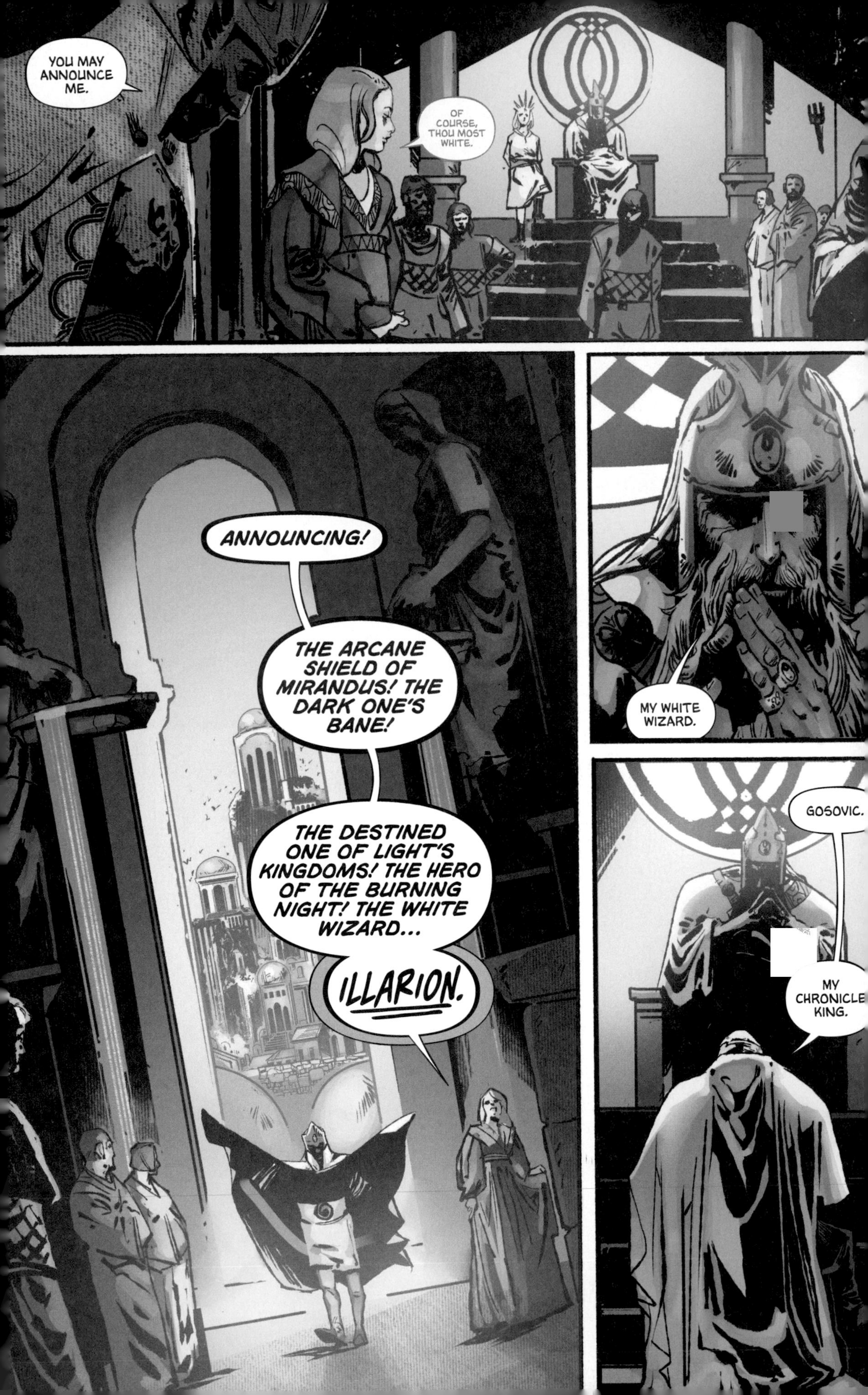
YOU MAY ANNOUNCE ME.
OF COURSE, THOU MOST WHITE.
ANNOUNCING!
THE ARCANE SHIELD OF MIRANDUS! THE DARK ONE'S BANE!
THE DESTINED ONE OF LIGHT'S KINGDOMS! THE HERO OF THE BURNING NIGHT! THE WHITE WIZARD...
ILLARION.
MY WHITE WIZARD.
GOSOVIC.
MY CHRONICLE KING.

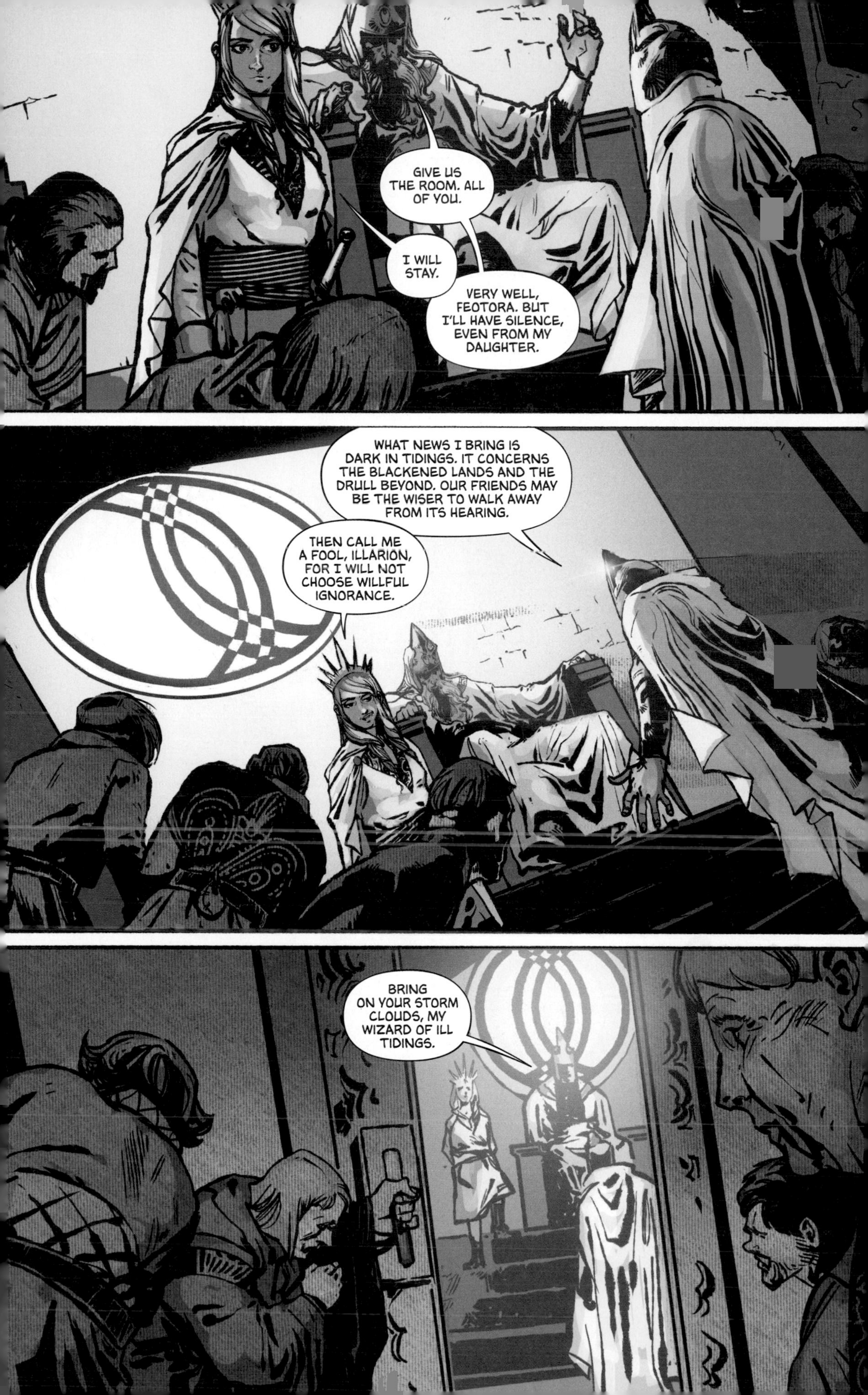
GIVE US THE ROOM. ALL OF YOU.
I WILL STAY.
VERY WELL, FEOTORA. BUT I'LL HAVE SILENCE, EVEN FROM MY DAUGHTER.
WHAT NEWS I BRING IS DARK IN TIDINGS. IT CONCERNS THE BLACKENED LANDS AND THE DRULL BEYOND. OUR FRIENDS MAY BE THE WISER TO WALK AWAY FROM ITS HEARING.
THEN CALL ME A FOOL, ILLARION, FOR I WILL NOT CHOOSE WILLFUL IGNORANCE.
BRING ON YOUR STORM CLOUDS, MY WIZARD OF ILL TIDINGS.

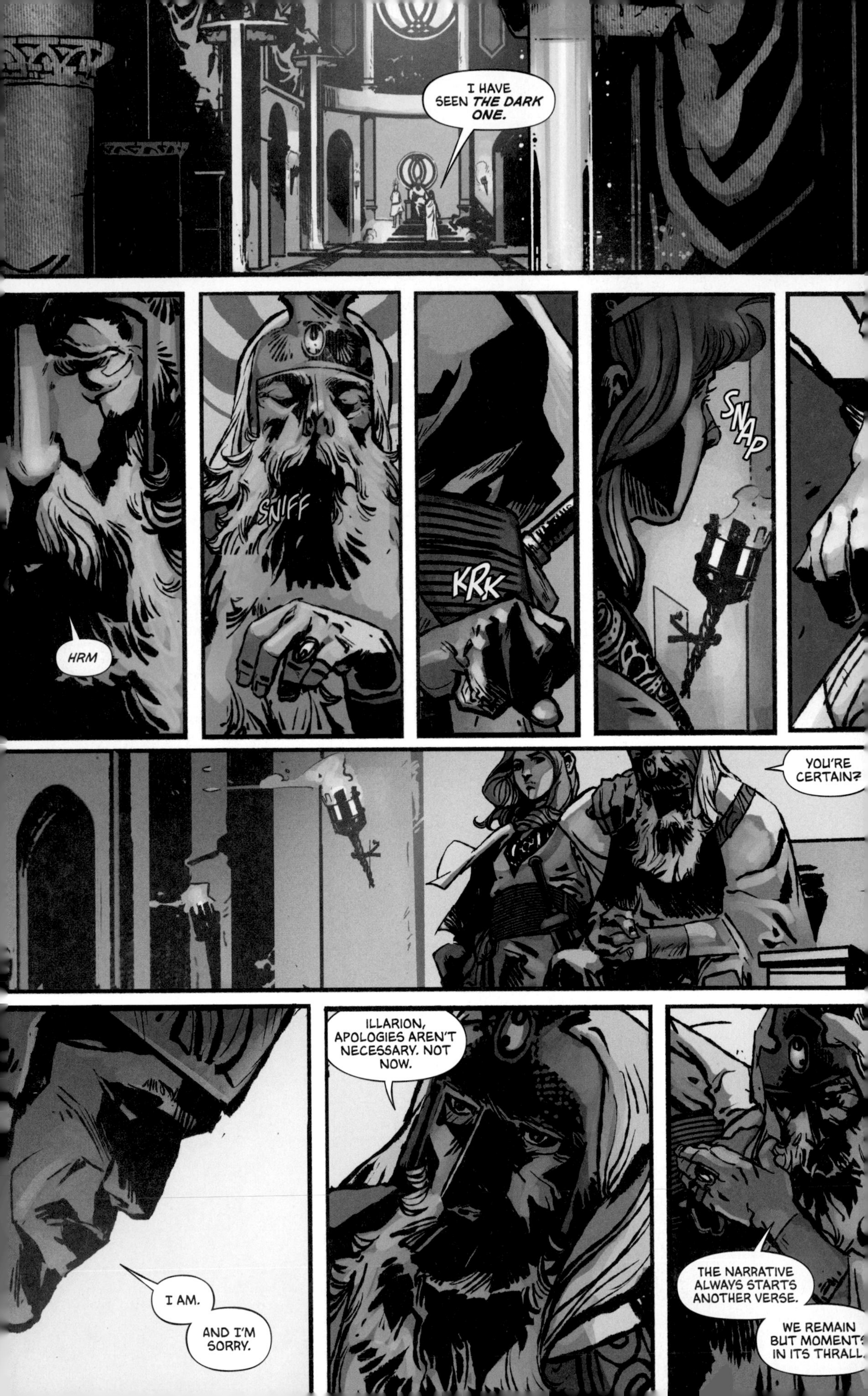
I HAVE SEEN THE DARK ONE.
HRM
SNIFF
KRK
SNAP
YOU'RE CERTAIN?
I AM.
AND I'M SORRY.
ILLARION, APOLOGIES AREN'T NECESSARY. NOT NOW.
THE NARRATIVE ALWAYS STARTS ANOTHER VERSE.
WE REMAIN BUT MOMENTS IN ITS THRALL.

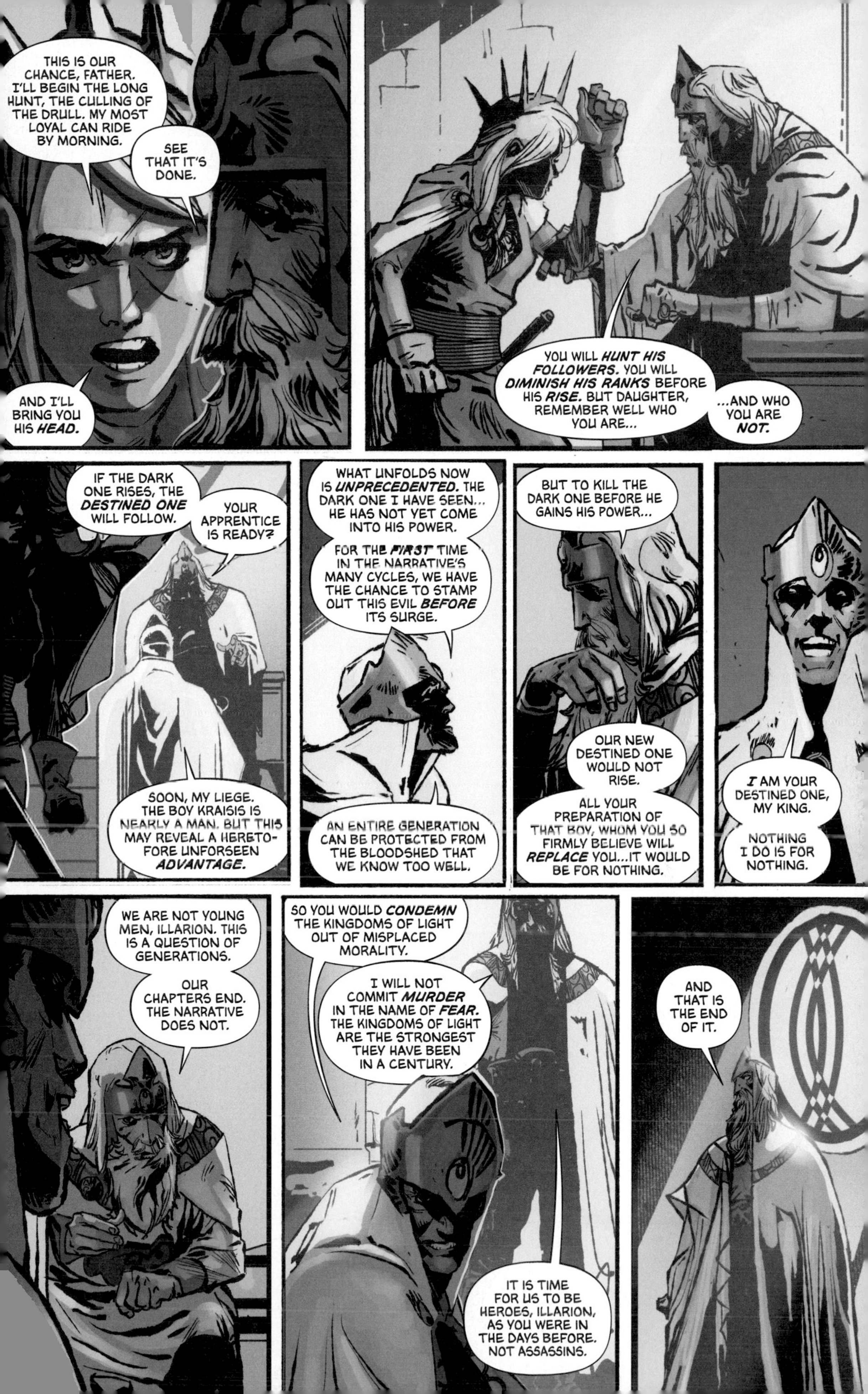
THIS IS OUR CHANCE, FATHER. I'LL BEGIN THE LONG HUNT, THE CULLING OF THE DRULL. MY MOST LOYAL CAN RIDE BY MORNING.
SEE THAT IT'S DONE.
AND I'LL BRING YOU HIS HEAD.
YOU WILL HUNT HIS FOLLOWERS. YOU WILL DIMINISH HIS RANKS BEFORE HIS RISE. BUT DAUGHTER, REMEMBER WELL WHO YOU ARE...
...AND WHO YOU ARE NOT.
IF THE DARK ONE RISES, THE DESTINED ONE WILL FOLLOW.
YOUR APPRENTICE IS READY?
SOON, MY LIEGE. THE BOY KRAISIS IS NEARLY A MAN. BUT THIS MAY REVEAL A HERETOFORE UNFORSEEN ADVANTAGE.
WHAT UNFOLDS NOW IS UNPRECEDENTED. THE DARK ONE I HAVE SEEN... HE HAS NOT YET COME INTO HIS POWER.
FOR THE FIRST TIME IN THE NARRATIVE'S MANY CYCLES, WE HAVE THE CHANCE TO STAMP OUT THIS EVIL BEFORE ITS SURGE.
AN ENTIRE GENERATION CAN BE PROTECTED FROM THE BLOODSHED THAT WE KNOW TOO WELL.
BUT TO KILL THE DARK ONE BEFORE HE GAINS HIS POWER...
OUR NEW DESTINED ONE WOULD NOT RISE.
ALL YOUR PREPARATION OF THAT BOY, WHOM YOU SO FIRMLY BELIEVE WILL REPLACE YOU...IT WOULD BE FOR NOTHING.
I AM YOUR DESTINED ONE, MY KING.
NOTHING I DO IS FOR NOTHING.
WE ARE NOT YOUNG MEN, ILLARION. THIS IS A QUESTION OF GENERATIONS.
OUR CHAPTERS END. THE NARRATIVE DOES NOT.
SO YOU WOULD CONDEMN THE KINGDOMS OF LIGHT OUT OF MISPLACED MORALITY.
I WILL NOT COMMIT MURDER IN THE NAME OF FEAR. THE KINGDOMS OF LIGHT ARE THE STRONGEST THEY HAVE BEEN IN A CENTURY.
IT IS TIME FOR US TO BE HEROES, ILLARION, AS YOU WERE IN THE DAYS BEFORE. NOT ASSASSINS.
AND THAT IS THE END OF IT.

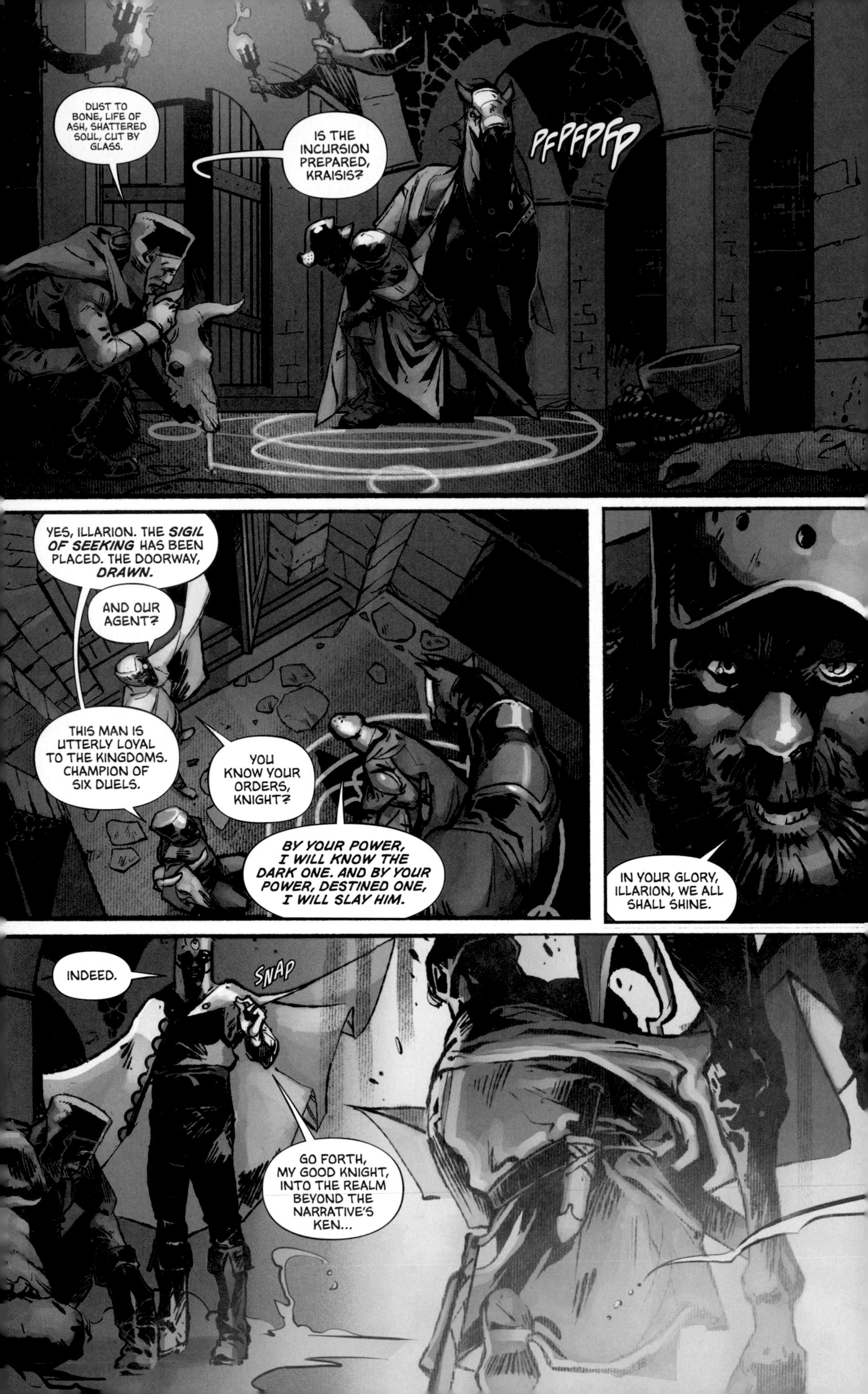
DUST TO BONE, LIFE OF ASH, SHATTERED SOUL, CUT BY GLASS.
IS THE INCURSION PREPARED, KRAISIS?
PFPFPFP
YES, ILLARION. THE *SIGIL OF SEEKING* HAS BEEN PLACED. THE DOORWAY, *DRAWN.*
AND OUR AGENT?
THIS MAN IS UTTERLY LOYAL TO THE KINGDOMS. CHAMPION OF SIX DUELS.
YOU KNOW YOUR ORDERS, KNIGHT?
BY YOUR POWER, I WILL KNOW THE DARK ONE. AND BY YOUR POWER, DESTINED ONE, I WILL SLAY HIM.
IN YOUR GLORY, ILLARION, WE ALL SHALL SHINE.
INDEED.
SNAP
GO FORTH, MY GOOD KNIGHT, INTO THE REALM BEYOND THE NARRATIVE'S KEN...

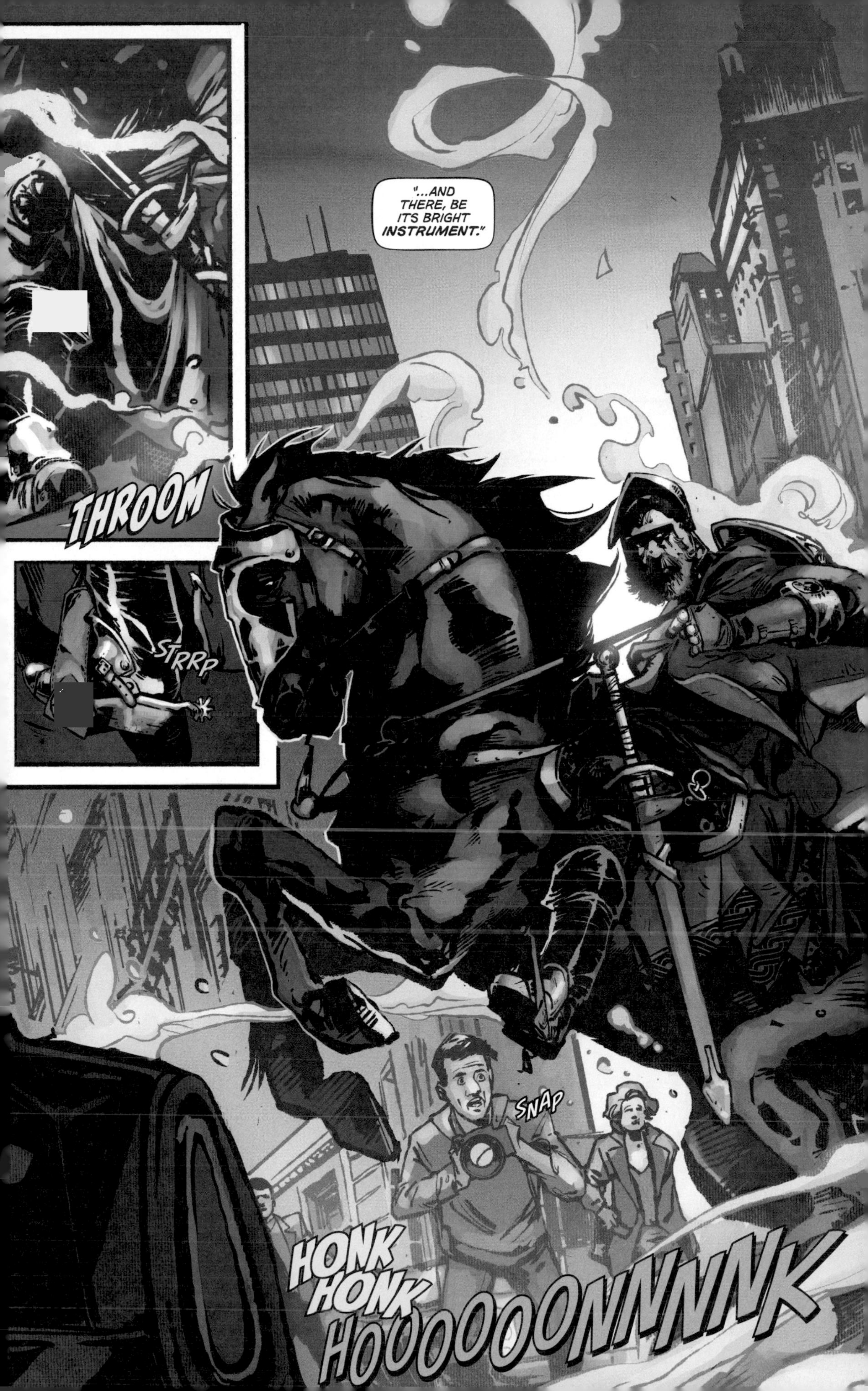
THROOM
STRRP
"...AND THERE, BE ITS BRIGHT INSTRUMENT."
SNAP
HONK HONK HOOOOOONNNNK

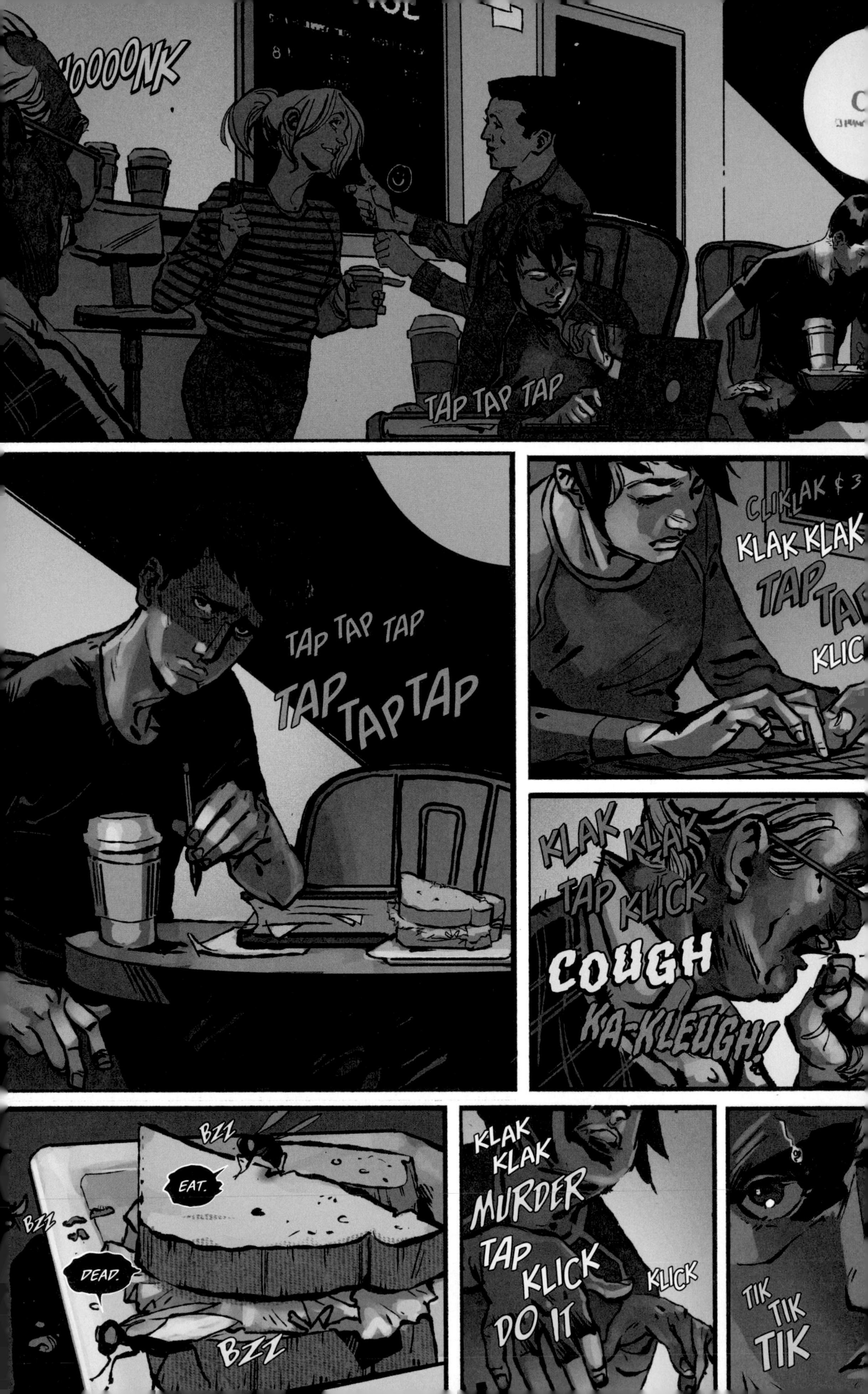
HOOOONK
TAP TAP TAP
TAP TAP TAP
TAP TAP TAP
CLIKLAK
KLAK KLAK
TAP
KLAK KLAK
TAP KLICK
COUGH
KA-KLEUGH!
BZZ
EAT.
BZZ
DEAD.
BZZ
KLAK
KLAK
MURDER
TAP
KLICK
DO IT
KLICK
TIK
TIK
TIK

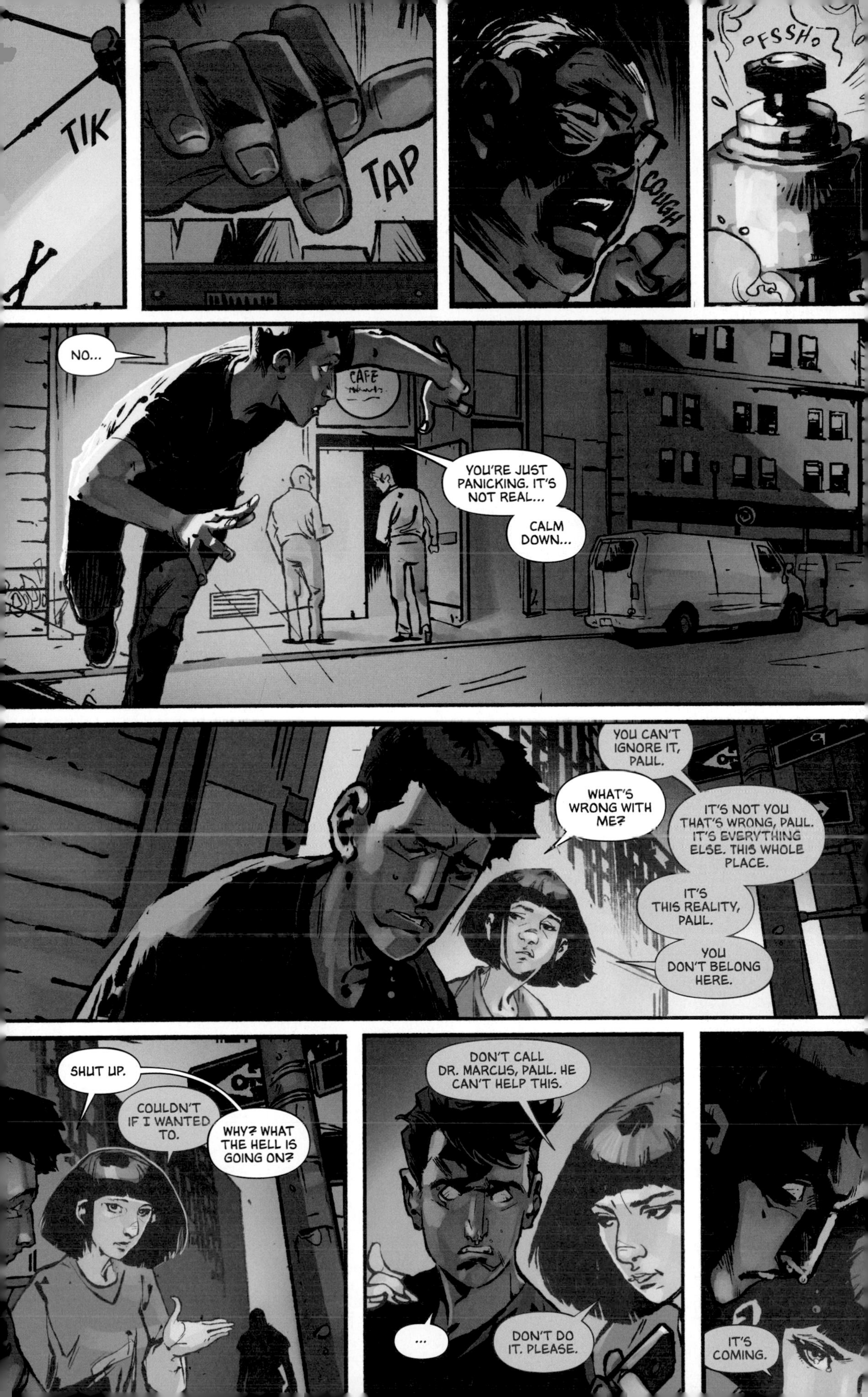
TIK
TAP
COUGH
PFSSHO
NO...
YOU'RE JUST PANICKING. IT'S NOT REAL...
CALM DOWN...
CAFE
YOU CAN'T IGNORE IT, PAUL.
WHAT'S WRONG WITH ME?
IT'S NOT YOU THAT'S WRONG, PAUL. IT'S EVERYTHING ELSE. THIS WHOLE PLACE.
IT'S THIS REALITY, PAUL.
YOU DON'T BELONG HERE.
SHUT UP.
COULDN'T IF I WANTED TO.
WHY? WHAT THE HELL IS GOING ON?
DON'T CALL DR. MARCUS, PAUL. HE CAN'T HELP THIS.
...
DON'T DO IT. PLEASE.
IT'S COMING.

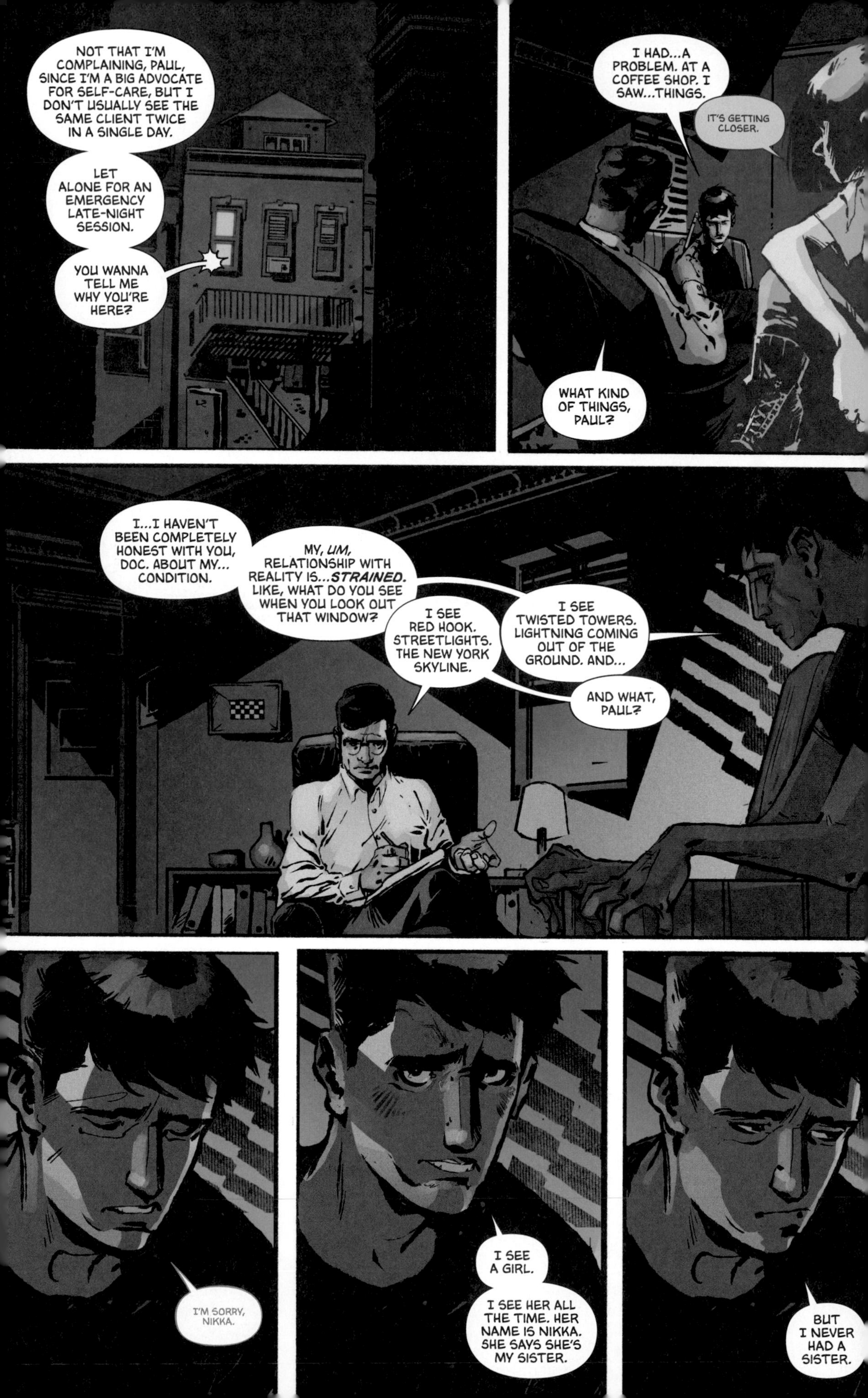
NOT THAT I'M COMPLAINING, PAUL, SINCE I'M A BIG ADVOCATE FOR SELF-CARE, BUT I DON'T USUALLY SEE THE SAME CLIENT TWICE IN A SINGLE DAY.
LET ALONE FOR AN EMERGENCY LATE-NIGHT SESSION.
YOU WANNA TELL ME WHY YOU'RE HERE?
I HAD...A PROBLEM. AT A COFFEE SHOP. I SAW...THINGS.
IT'S GETTING CLOSER.
WHAT KIND OF THINGS, PAUL?
I...I HAVEN'T BEEN COMPLETELY HONEST WITH YOU, DOC. ABOUT MY... CONDITION.
MY, *UM,* RELATIONSHIP WITH REALITY IS...***STRAINED.*** LIKE, WHAT DO YOU SEE WHEN YOU LOOK OUT THAT WINDOW?
I SEE RED HOOK. STREETLIGHTS. THE NEW YORK SKYLINE.
I SEE TWISTED TOWERS. LIGHTNING COMING OUT OF THE GROUND. AND...
AND WHAT, PAUL?
I'M SORRY, NIKKA.
I SEE A GIRL.
I SEE HER ALL THE TIME. HER NAME IS NIKKA. SHE SAYS SHE'S MY SISTER.
BUT I NEVER HAD A SISTER.

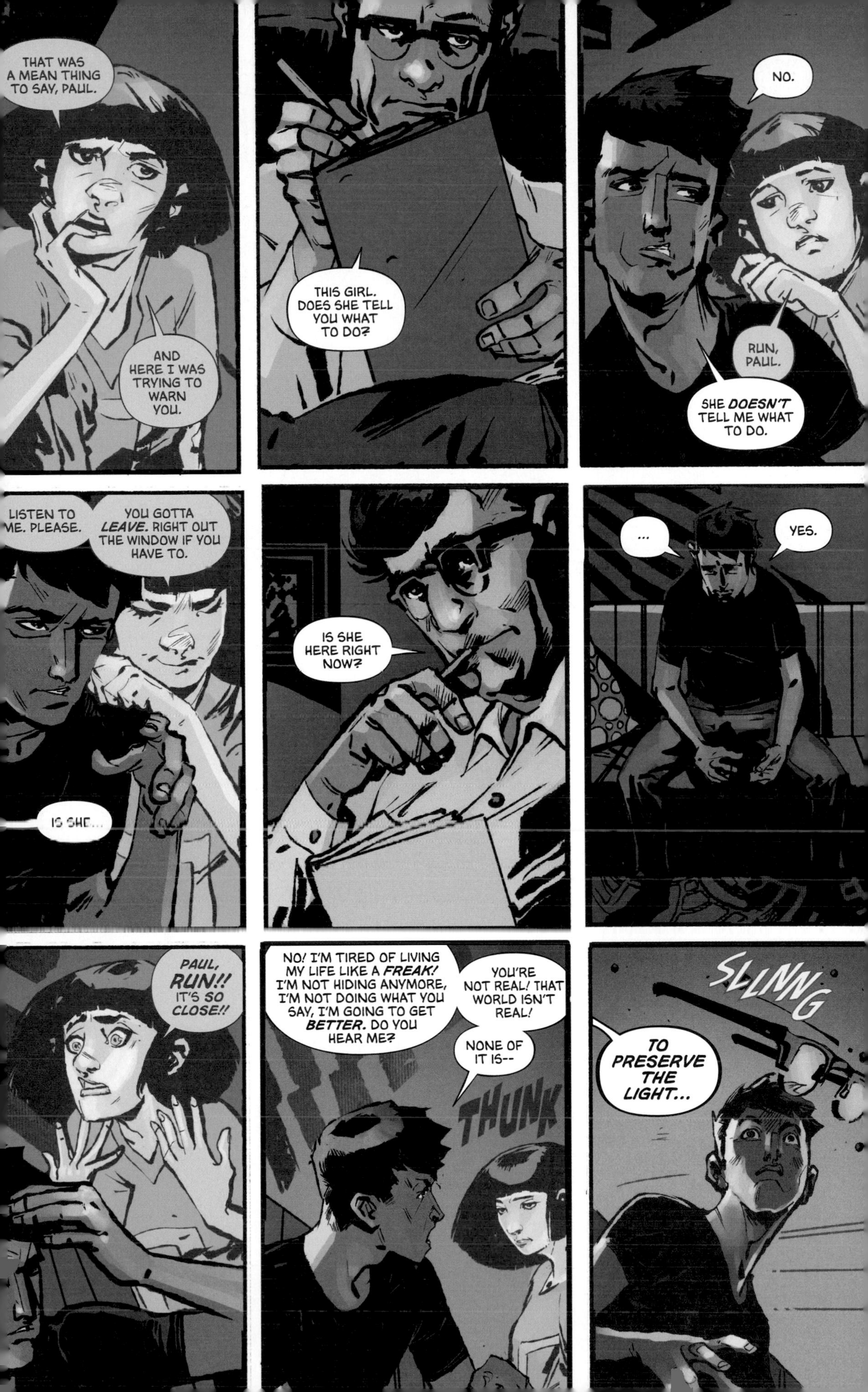
THAT WAS A MEAN THING TO SAY, PAUL.
AND HERE I WAS TRYING TO WARN YOU.
THIS GIRL. DOES SHE TELL YOU WHAT TO DO?
NO.
RUN, PAUL.
SHE *DOESN'T* TELL ME WHAT TO DO.
LISTEN TO ME. PLEASE.
YOU GOTTA *LEAVE.* RIGHT OUT THE WINDOW IF YOU HAVE TO.
IS SHE...
IS SHE HERE RIGHT NOW?
...
YES.
PAUL, *RUN!!* IT'S SO *CLOSE!!*
NO! I'M TIRED OF LIVING MY LIFE LIKE A *FREAK!* I'M NOT HIDING ANYMORE, I'M NOT DOING WHAT YOU SAY, I'M GOING TO GET *BETTER.* DO YOU HEAR ME?
YOU'RE NOT REAL! THAT WORLD ISN'T REAL!
NONE OF IT IS--
THUNK
SLLNNG
TO PRESERVE THE LIGHT...

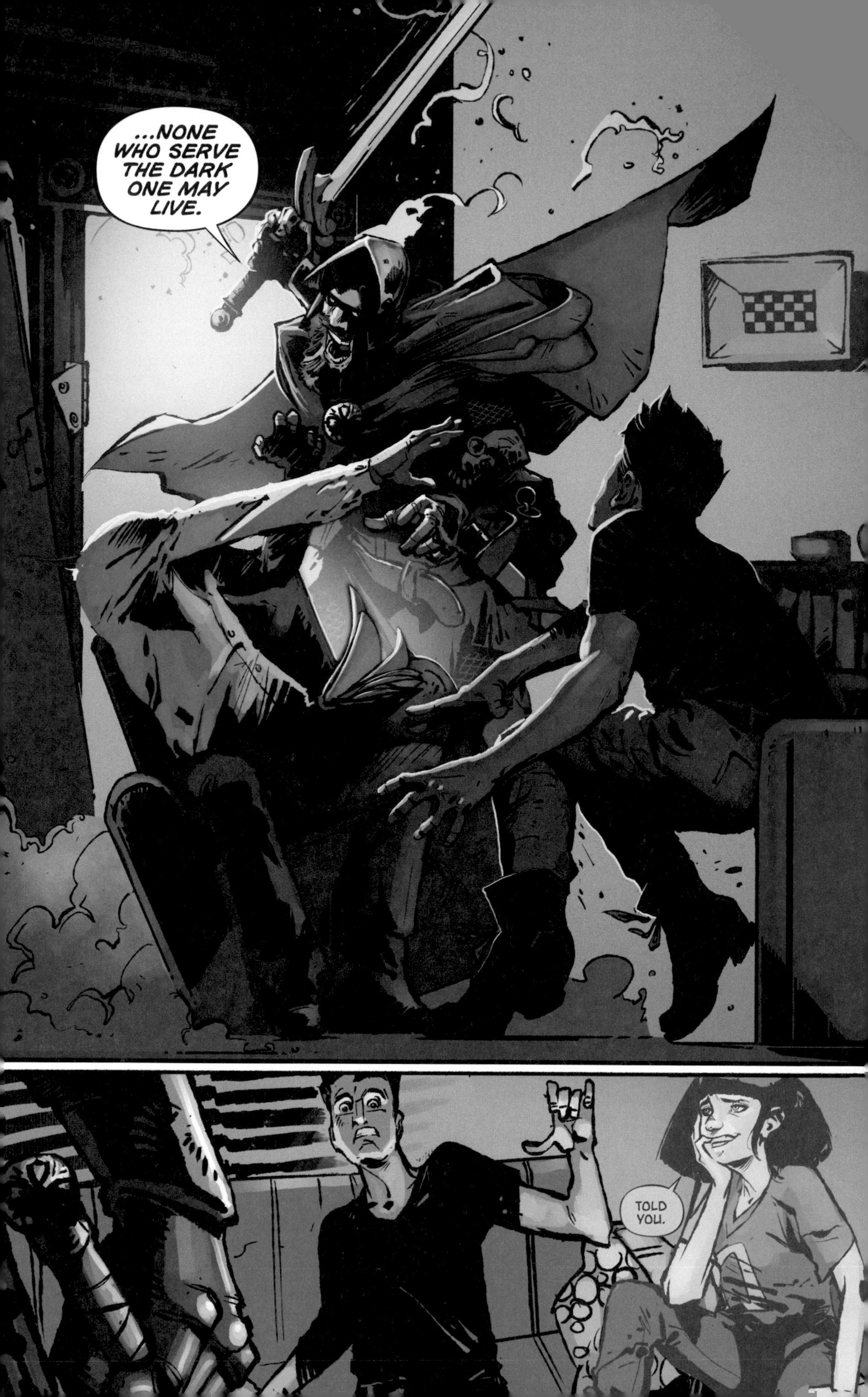
...NONE WHO SERVE THE DARK ONE MAY LIVE.
TOLD YOU.

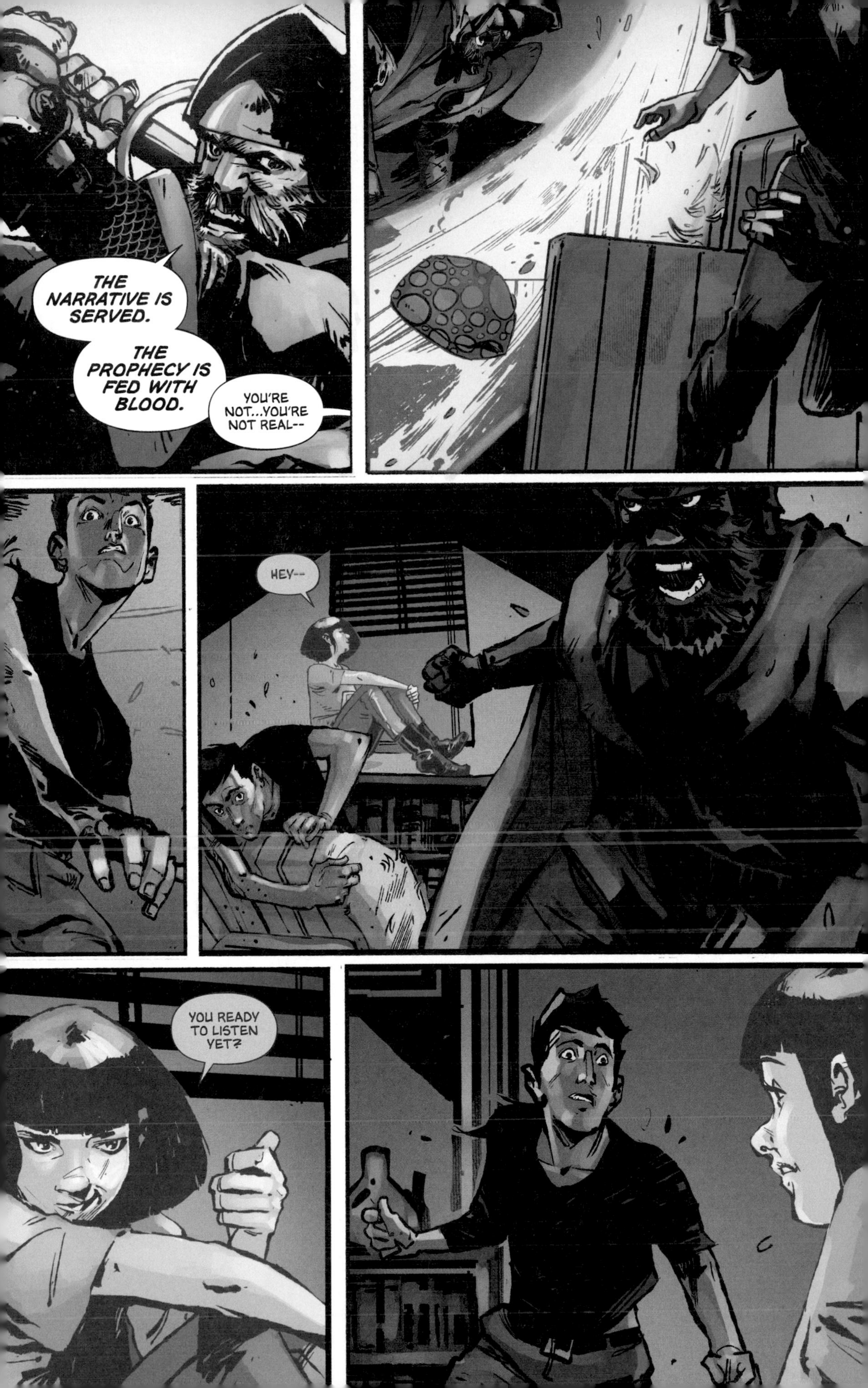
THE NARRATIVE IS SERVED.
THE PROPHECY IS FED WITH BLOOD.
YOU'RE NOT...YOU'RE NOT REAL--
HEY--
YOU READY TO LISTEN YET?

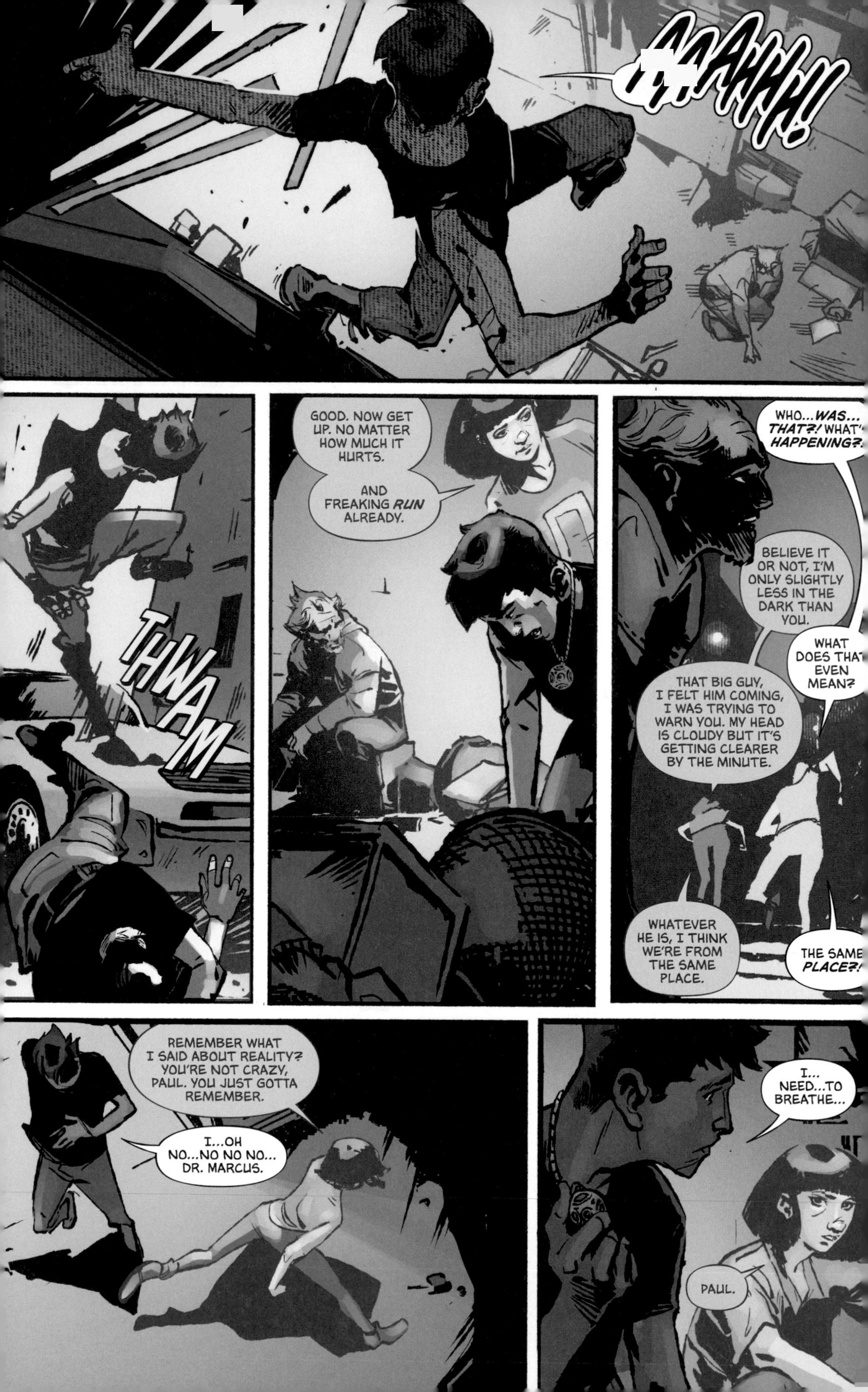

THWAM
GOOD. NOW GET UP. NO MATTER HOW MUCH IT HURTS.
AND FREAKING *RUN* ALREADY.
WHO...*WAS... THAT?!* WHAT'S *HAPPENING?!*
BELIEVE IT OR NOT, I'M ONLY SLIGHTLY LESS IN THE DARK THAN YOU.
WHAT DOES THAT EVEN MEAN?
THAT BIG GUY, I FELT HIM COMING, I WAS TRYING TO WARN YOU. MY HEAD IS CLOUDY BUT IT'S GETTING CLEARER BY THE MINUTE.
WHATEVER HE IS, I THINK WE'RE FROM THE SAME PLACE.
THE SAME *PLACE?!*
REMEMBER WHAT I SAID ABOUT REALITY? YOU'RE NOT CRAZY, PAUL. YOU JUST GOTTA REMEMBER.
I...OH NO...NO NO NO... DR. MARCUS.
I... NEED...TO BREATHE...
PAUL.

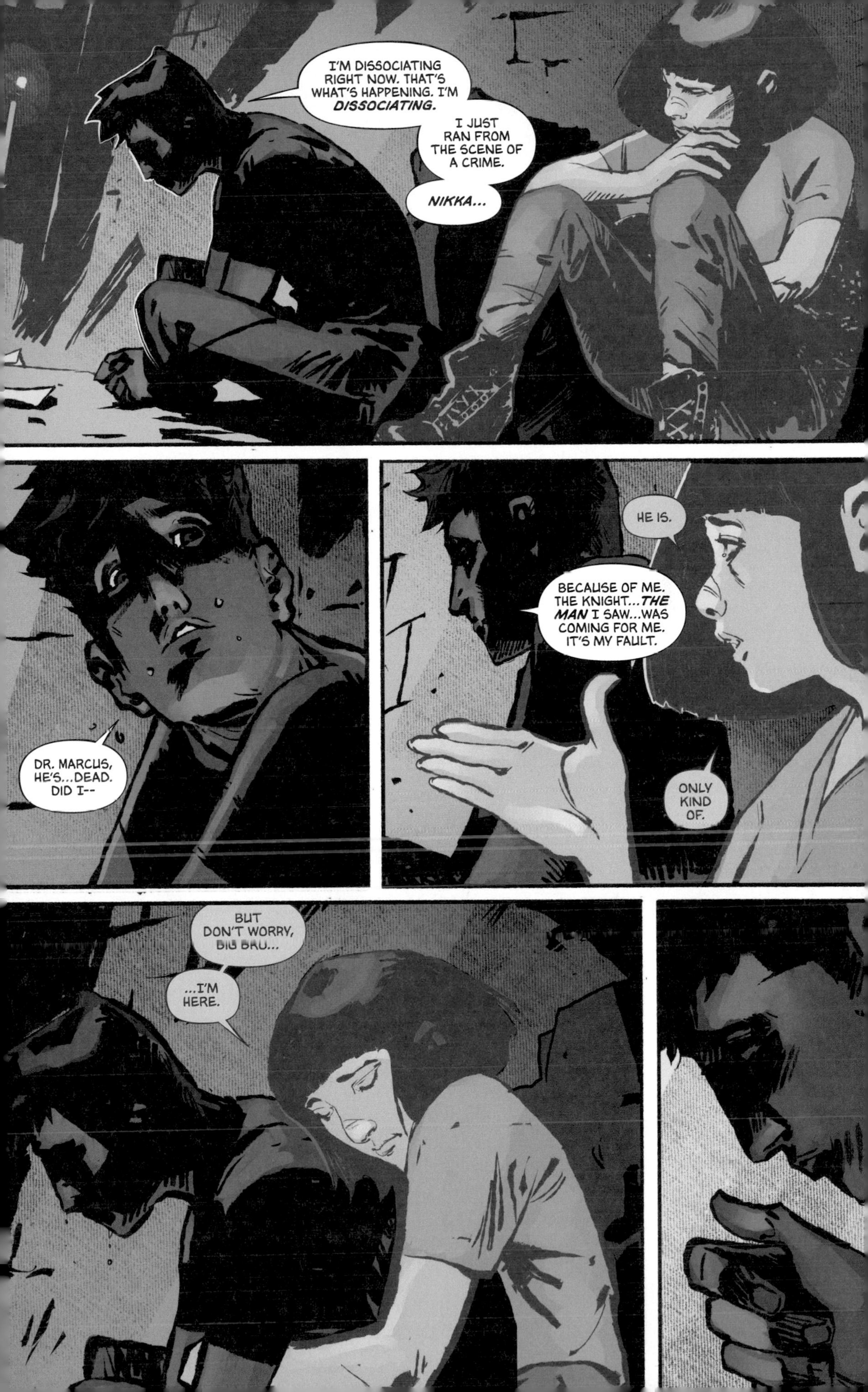
I'M DISSOCIATING RIGHT NOW. THAT'S WHAT'S HAPPENING. I'M *DISSOCIATING.*
I JUST RAN FROM THE SCENE OF A CRIME.
NIKKA...
DR. MARCUS, HE'S...DEAD. DID I--
HE IS.
BECAUSE OF ME. THE KNIGHT...*THE MAN* I SAW...WAS COMING FOR ME. IT'S MY FAULT.
ONLY KIND OF.
BUT DON'T WORRY, BIG BRO...
...I'M HERE.

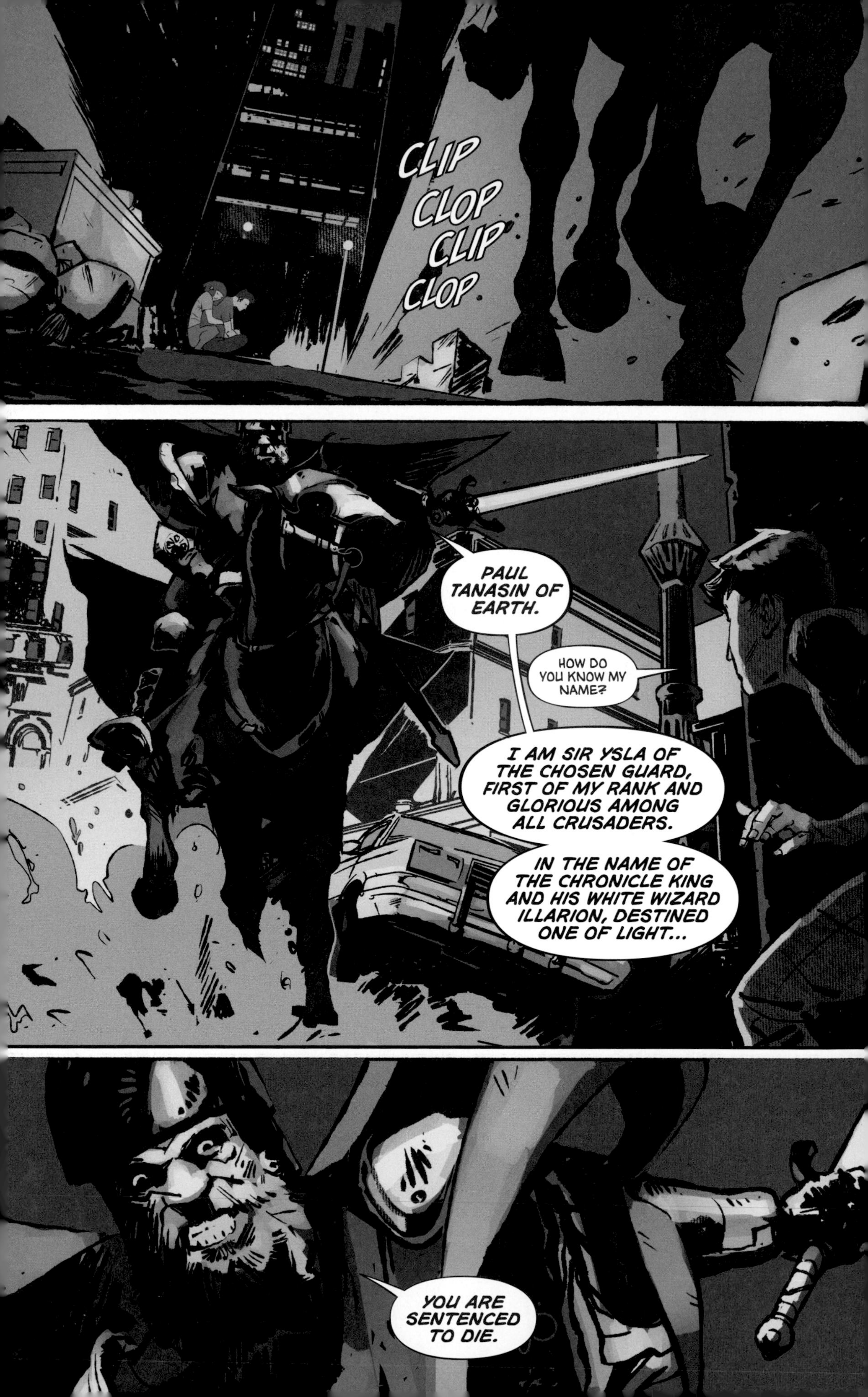
CLIP CLOP CLIP CLOP
PAUL TANASIN OF EARTH.
HOW DO YOU KNOW MY NAME?
I AM SIR YSLA OF THE CHOSEN GUARD, FIRST OF MY RANK AND GLORIOUS AMONG ALL CRUSADERS.
IN THE NAME OF THE CHRONICLE KING AND HIS WHITE WIZARD ILLARION, DESTINED ONE OF LIGHT...
YOU ARE SENTENCED TO DIE.

PLEASE! I DON'T UNDERSTAND, PLEASE *STOP*--

SHREEEE

STOP! CAN'T YOU HEAR ME?

I HAVEN'T *DONE* ANYTHING!

YOU *WOULD* HAVE...

...BUT FOR THE WHITE WIZARD.

TINK

PAUL, YOU HAVE TO STOP HIM! IT HURTS!

PAUL?

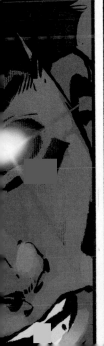

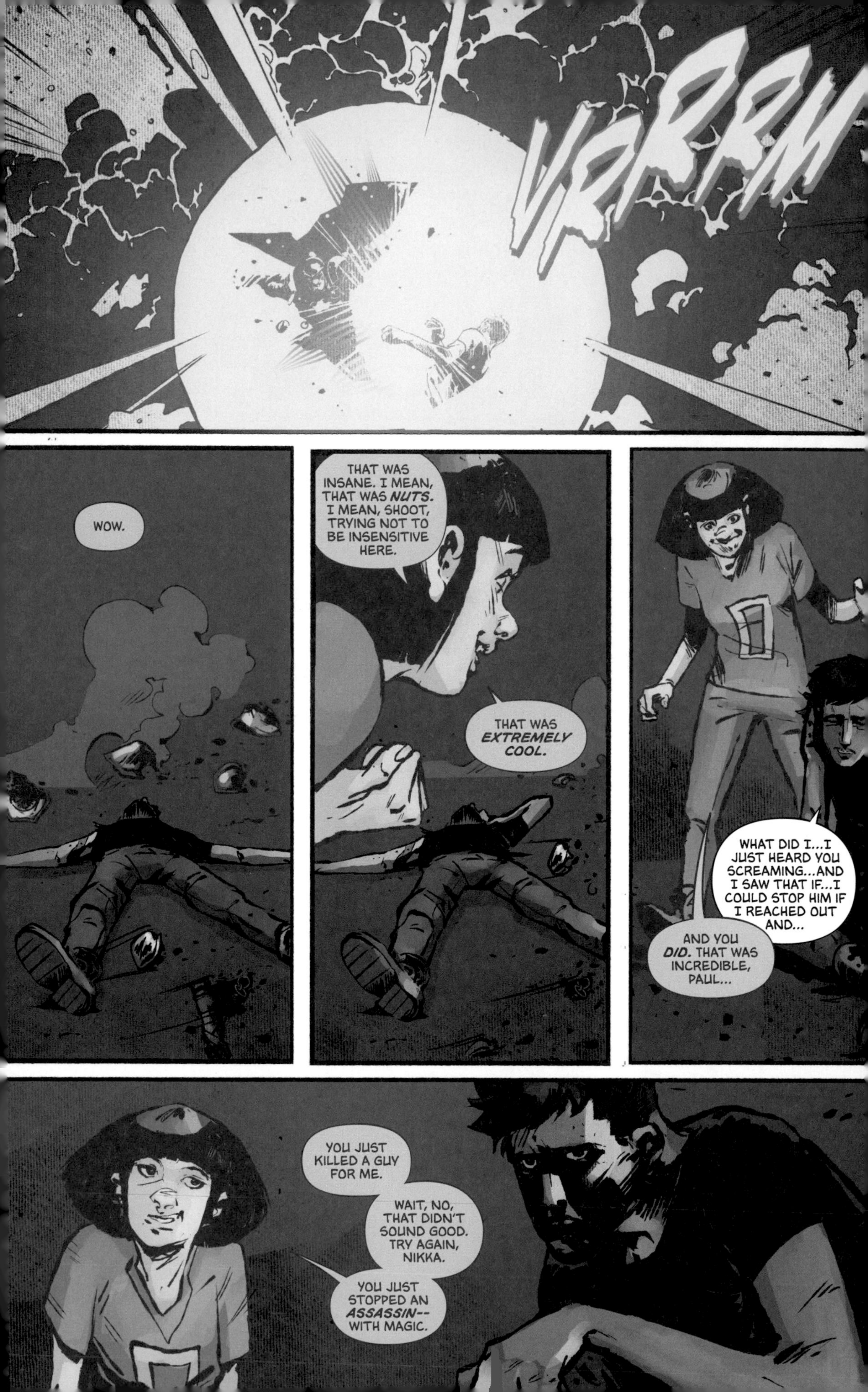
VRRRM
WOW.
THAT WAS INSANE. I MEAN, THAT WAS NUTS. I MEAN, SHOOT, TRYING NOT TO BE INSENSITIVE HERE.
THAT WAS EXTREMELY COOL.
WHAT DID I...I JUST HEARD YOU SCREAMING...AND I SAW THAT IF...I COULD STOP HIM IF I REACHED OUT AND...
AND YOU DID. THAT WAS INCREDIBLE, PAUL...
YOU JUST KILLED A GUY FOR ME.
WAIT, NO, THAT DIDN'T SOUND GOOD. TRY AGAIN, NIKKA.
YOU JUST STOPPED AN ASSASSIN-- WITH MAGIC.

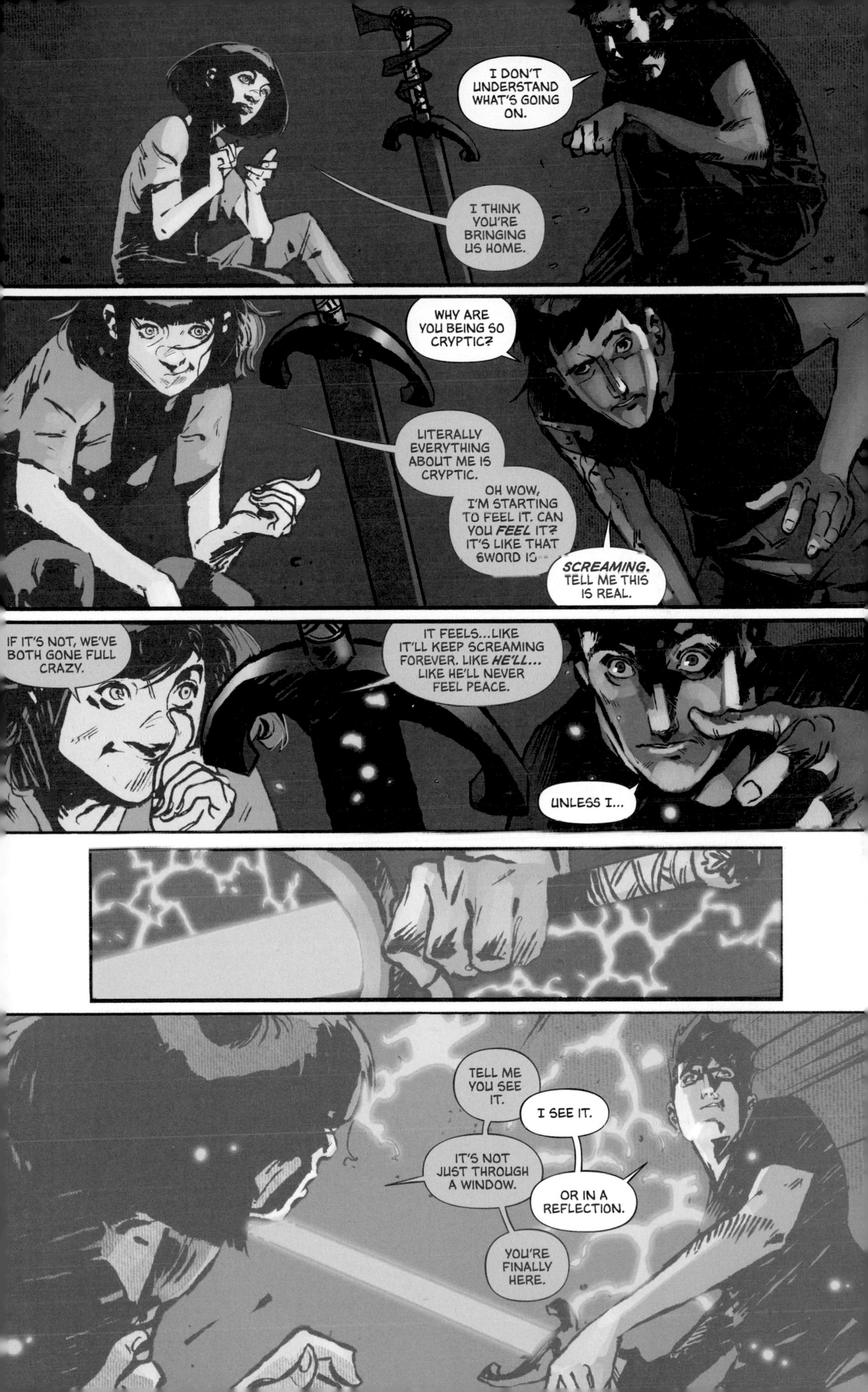
I DON'T UNDERSTAND WHAT'S GOING ON.
I THINK YOU'RE BRINGING US HOME.
WHY ARE YOU BEING SO CRYPTIC?
LITERALLY EVERYTHING ABOUT ME IS CRYPTIC.
OH WOW, I'M STARTING TO FEEL IT. CAN YOU *FEEL* IT? IT'S LIKE THAT SWORD IS--
SCREAMING. TELL ME THIS IS REAL.
IF IT'S NOT, WE'VE BOTH GONE FULL CRAZY.
IT FEELS...LIKE IT'LL KEEP SCREAMING FOREVER. LIKE *HE'LL...* LIKE HE'LL NEVER FEEL PEACE.
UNLESS I...
TELL ME YOU SEE IT.
I SEE IT.
IT'S NOT JUST THROUGH A WINDOW.
OR IN A REFLECTION.
YOU'RE FINALLY HERE.

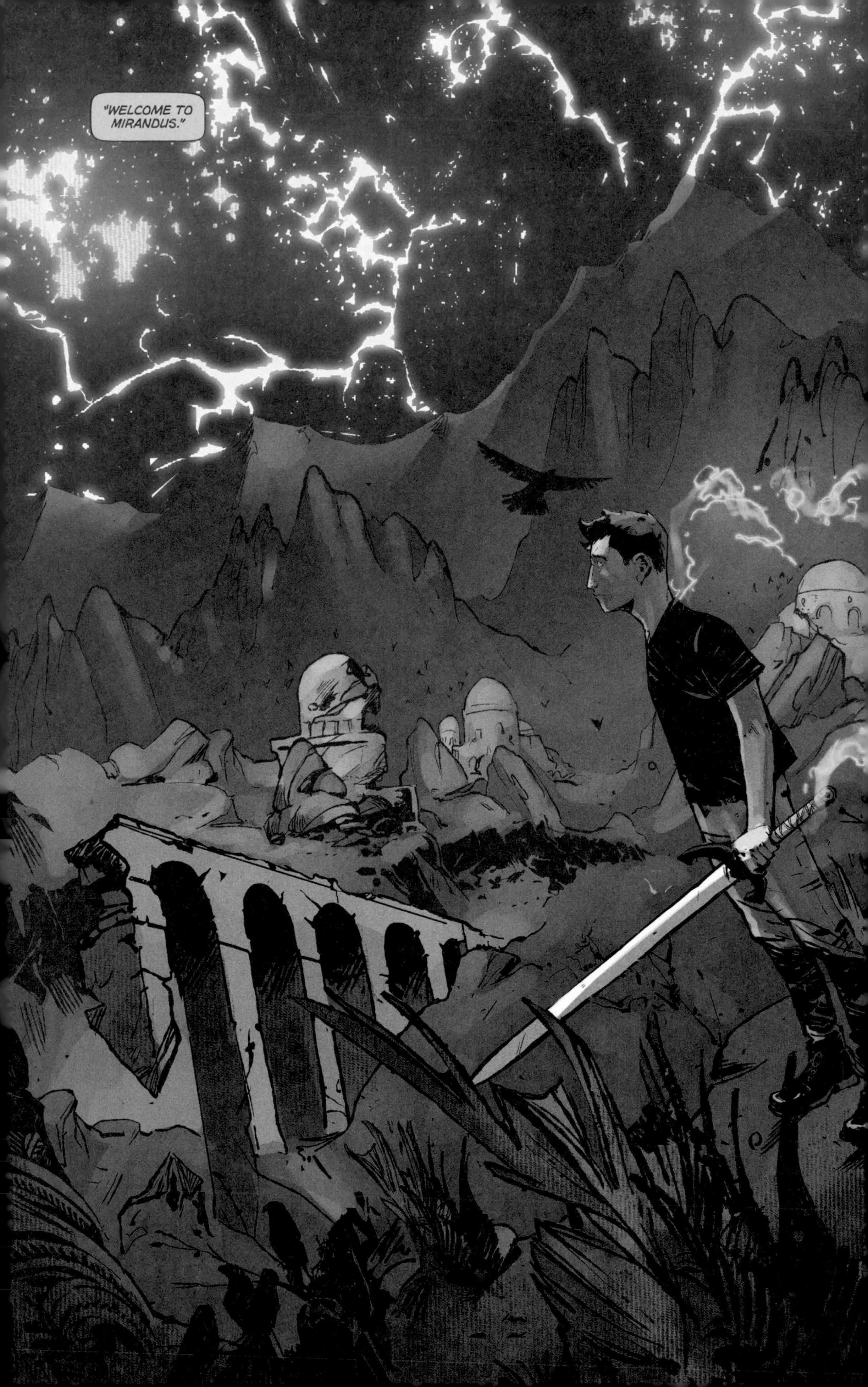
"WELCOME TO MIRANDUS."

INTERMISSION

THE FIRST STORY TOLD

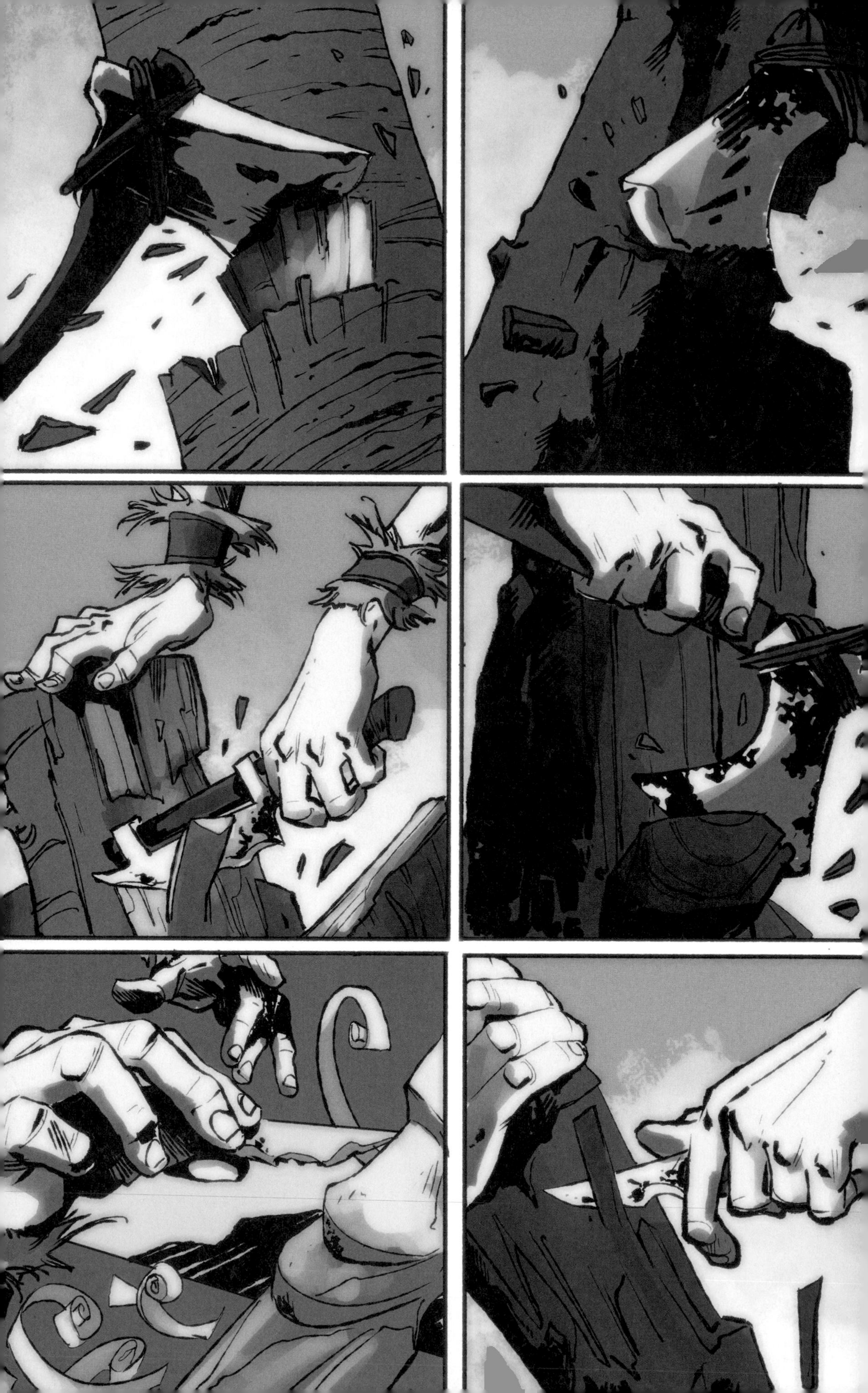

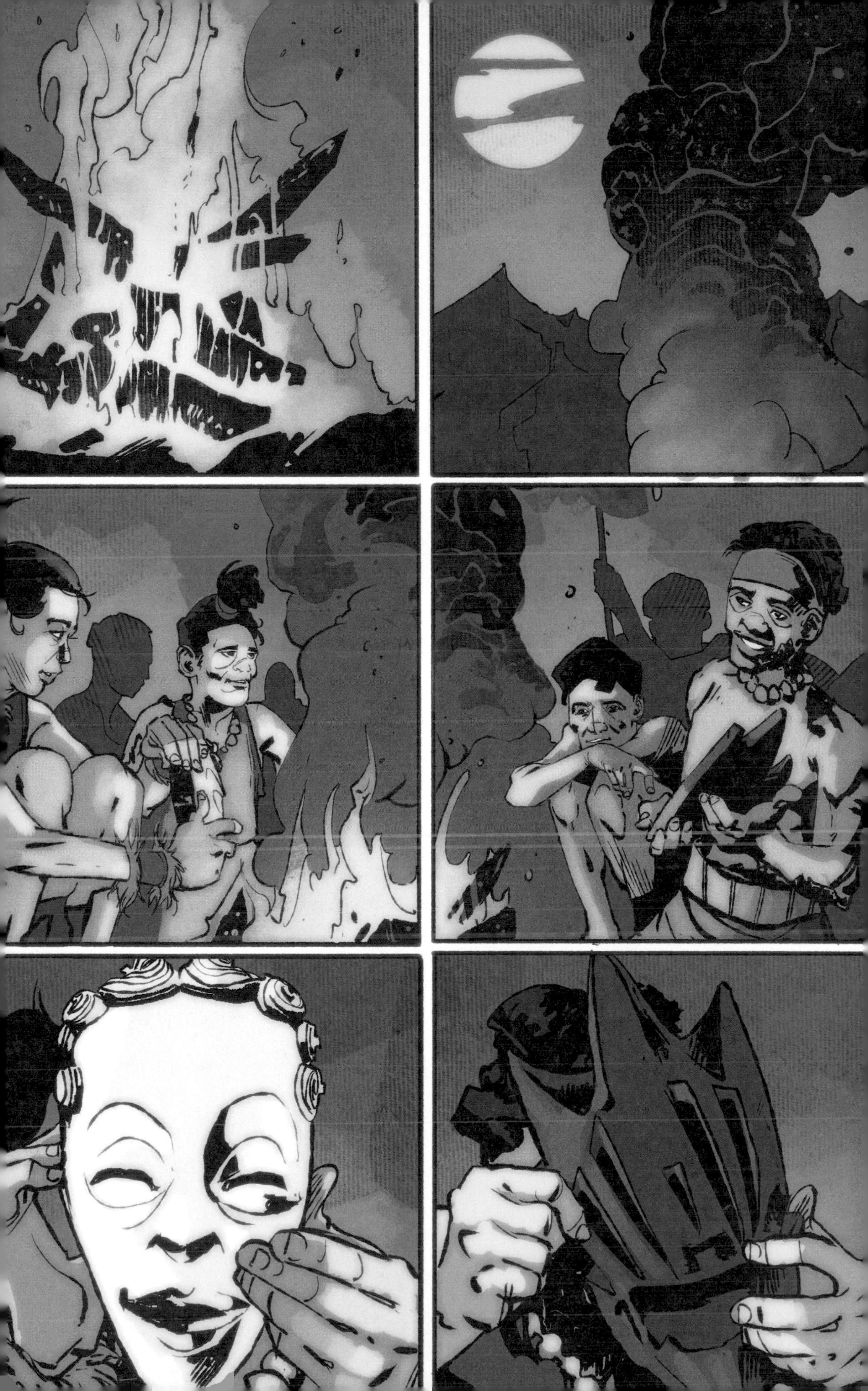

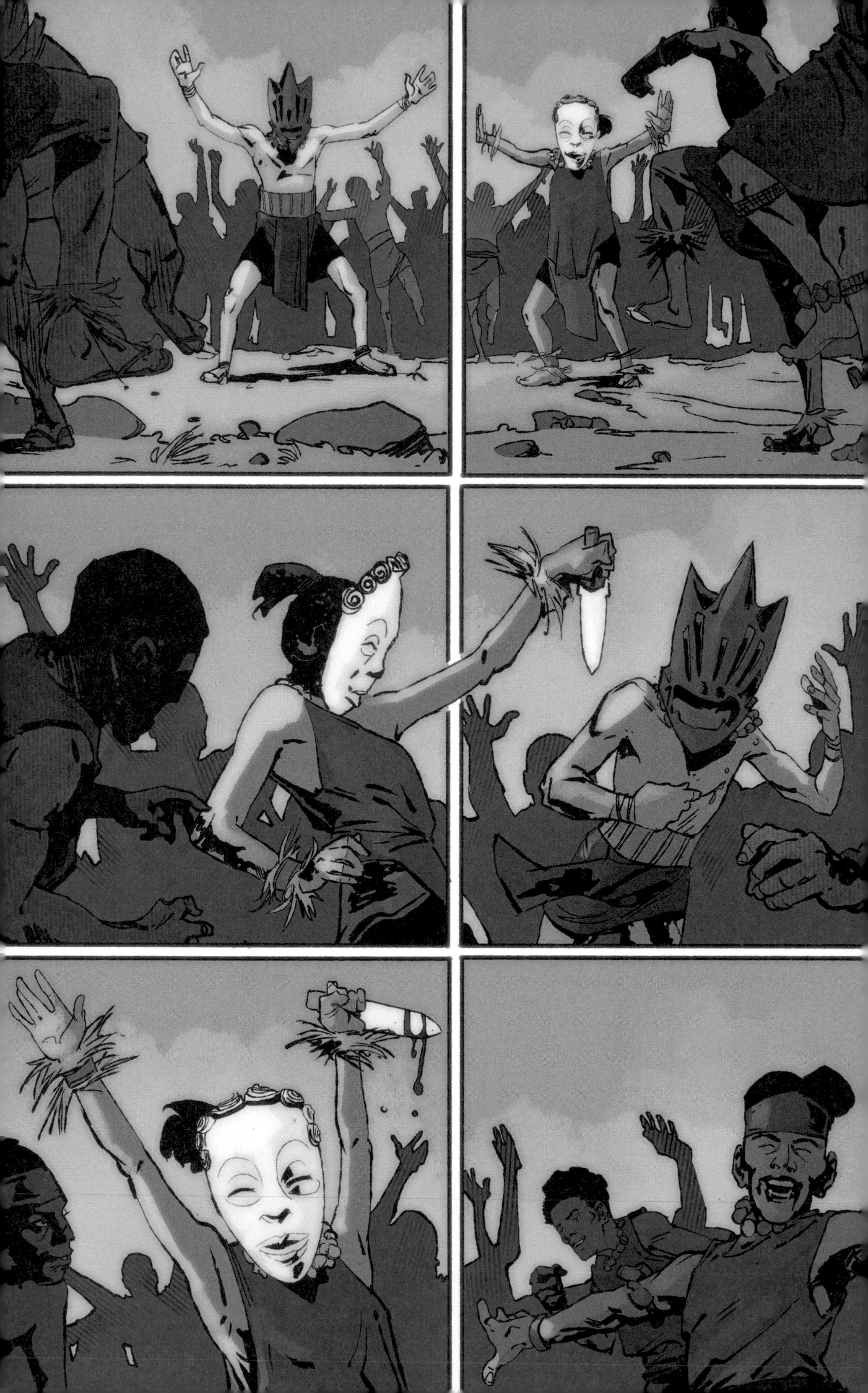

INTO THE SHADOW OF THE WORLD

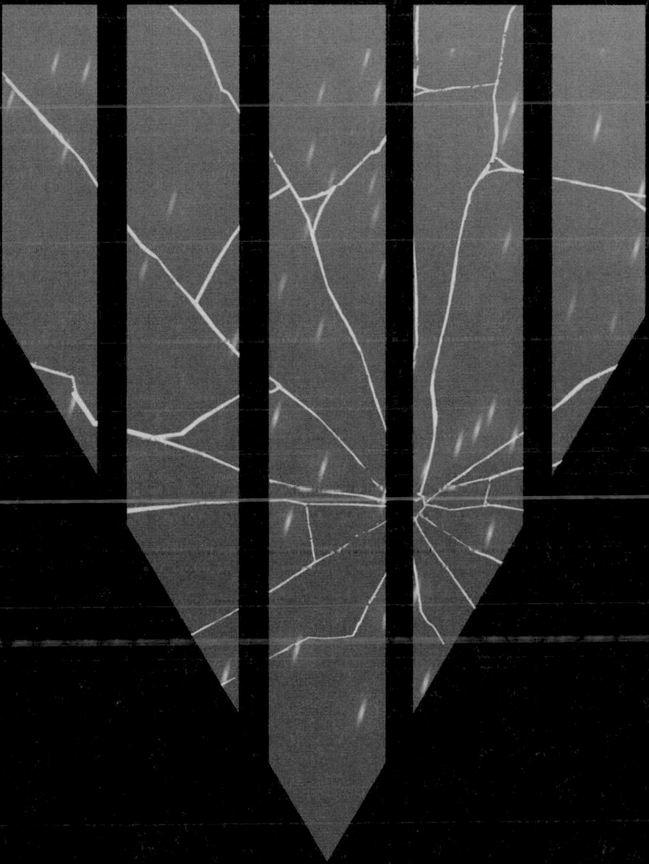

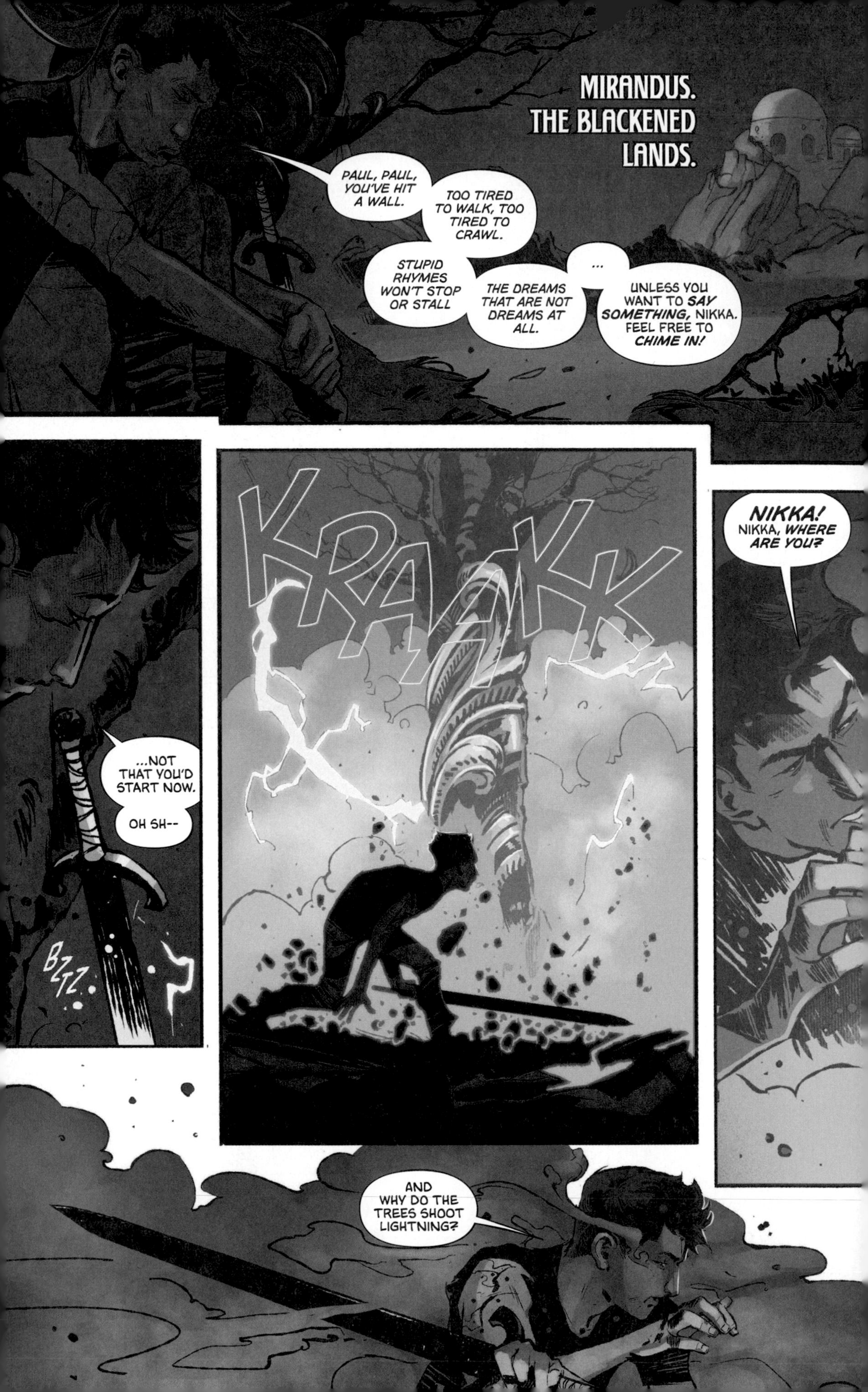
MIRANDUS. THE BLACKENED LANDS.
PAUL, PAUL, YOU'VE HIT A WALL.
TOO TIRED TO WALK, TOO TIRED TO CRAWL.
STUPID RHYMES WON'T STOP OR STALL
THE DREAMS THAT ARE NOT DREAMS AT ALL.
...
UNLESS YOU WANT TO SAY SOMETHING, NIKKA. FEEL FREE TO CHIME IN!
...NOT THAT YOU'D START NOW.
OH SH--
BZTZ
KRAKKK
NIKKA! NIKKA, WHERE ARE YOU?
AND WHY DO THE TREES SHOOT LIGHTNING?

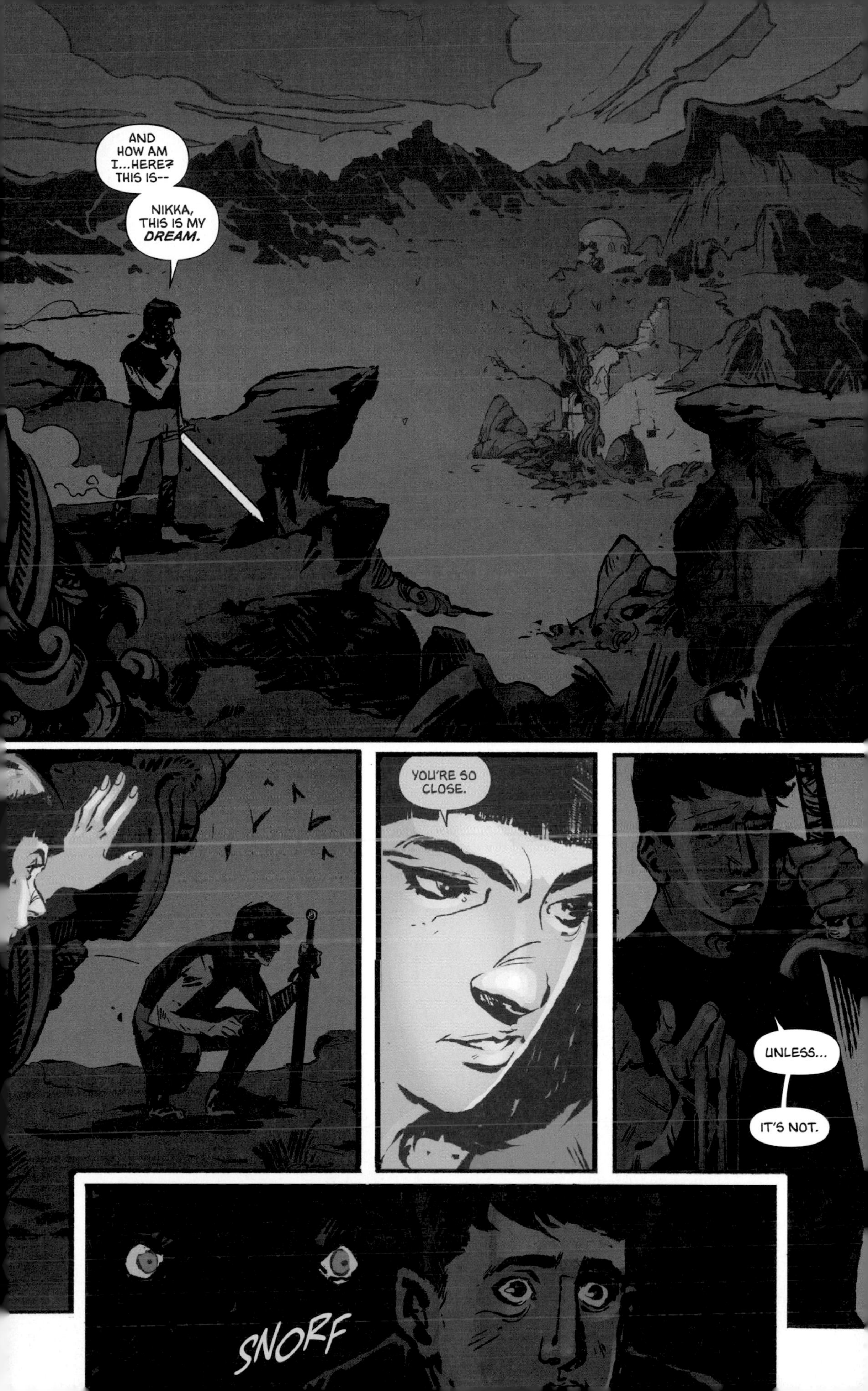
AND HOW AM I...HERE? THIS IS--
NIKKA, THIS IS MY *DREAM.*
YOU'RE SO CLOSE.
UNLESS...
IT'S NOT.
SNORF

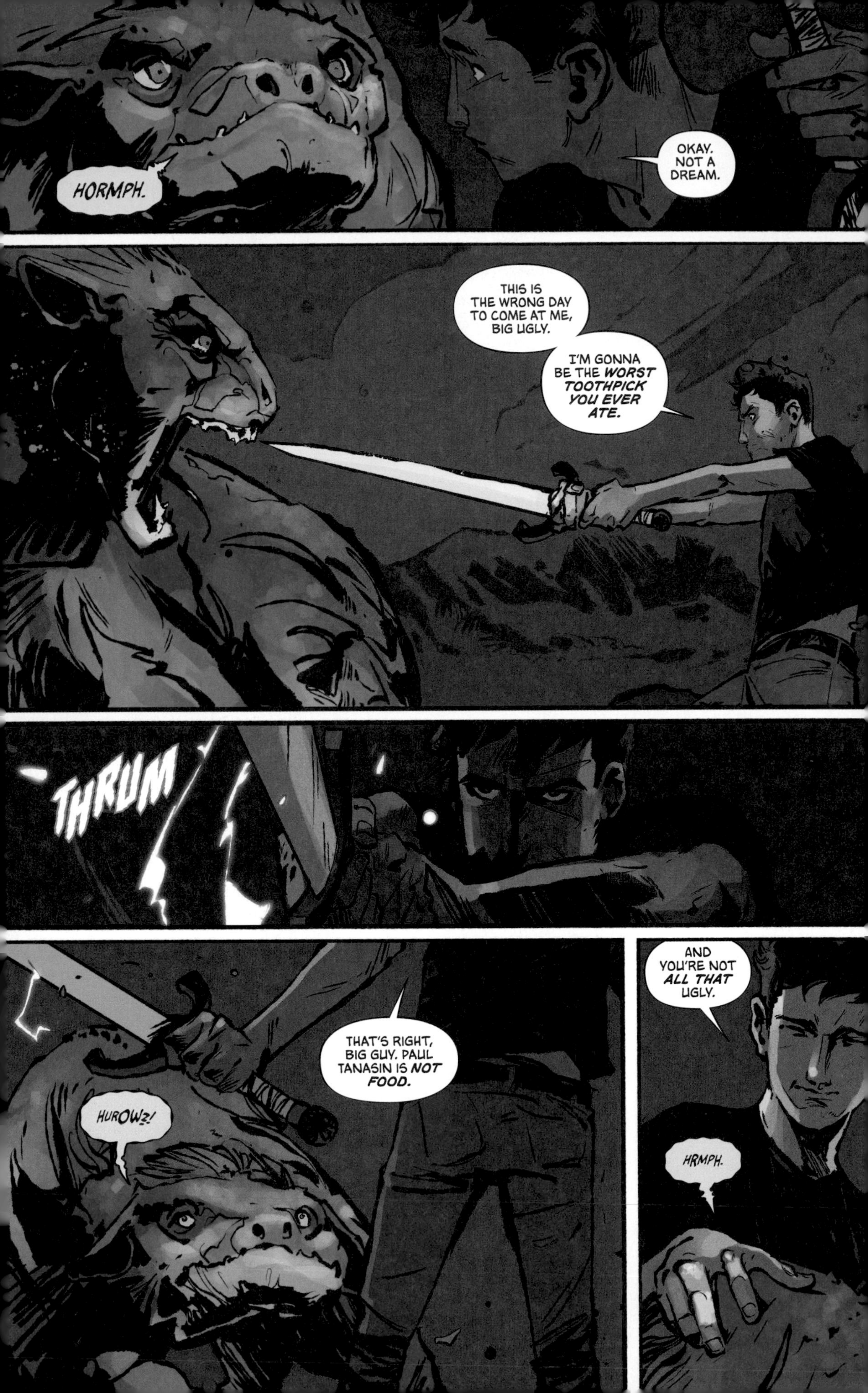
HORMPH.
OKAY. NOT A DREAM.
THIS IS THE WRONG DAY TO COME AT ME, BIG UGLY.
I'M GONNA BE THE *WORST TOOTHPICK YOU EVER ATE.*
THRUM
THAT'S RIGHT, BIG GUY. PAUL TANASIN IS *NOT FOOD.*
HUROWZ!
AND YOU'RE NOT *ALL THAT* UGLY.
HRMPH.

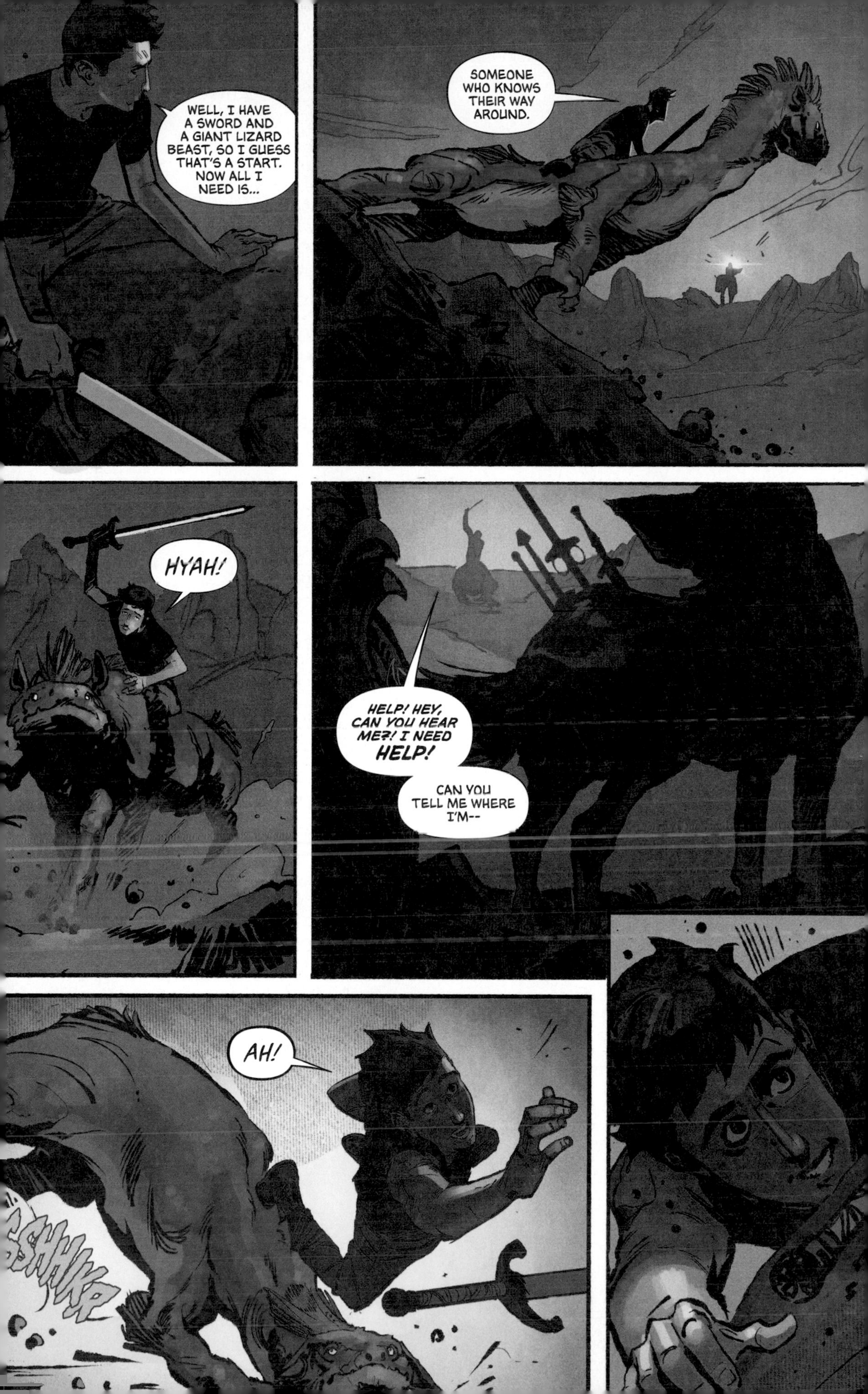
WELL, I HAVE A SWORD AND A GIANT LIZARD BEAST, SO I GUESS THAT'S A START. NOW ALL I NEED IS...
SOMEONE WHO KNOWS THEIR WAY AROUND.
HYAH!
HELP! HEY, CAN YOU HEAR ME?! I NEED HELP!
CAN YOU TELL ME WHERE I'M--
AH!
SHHKP

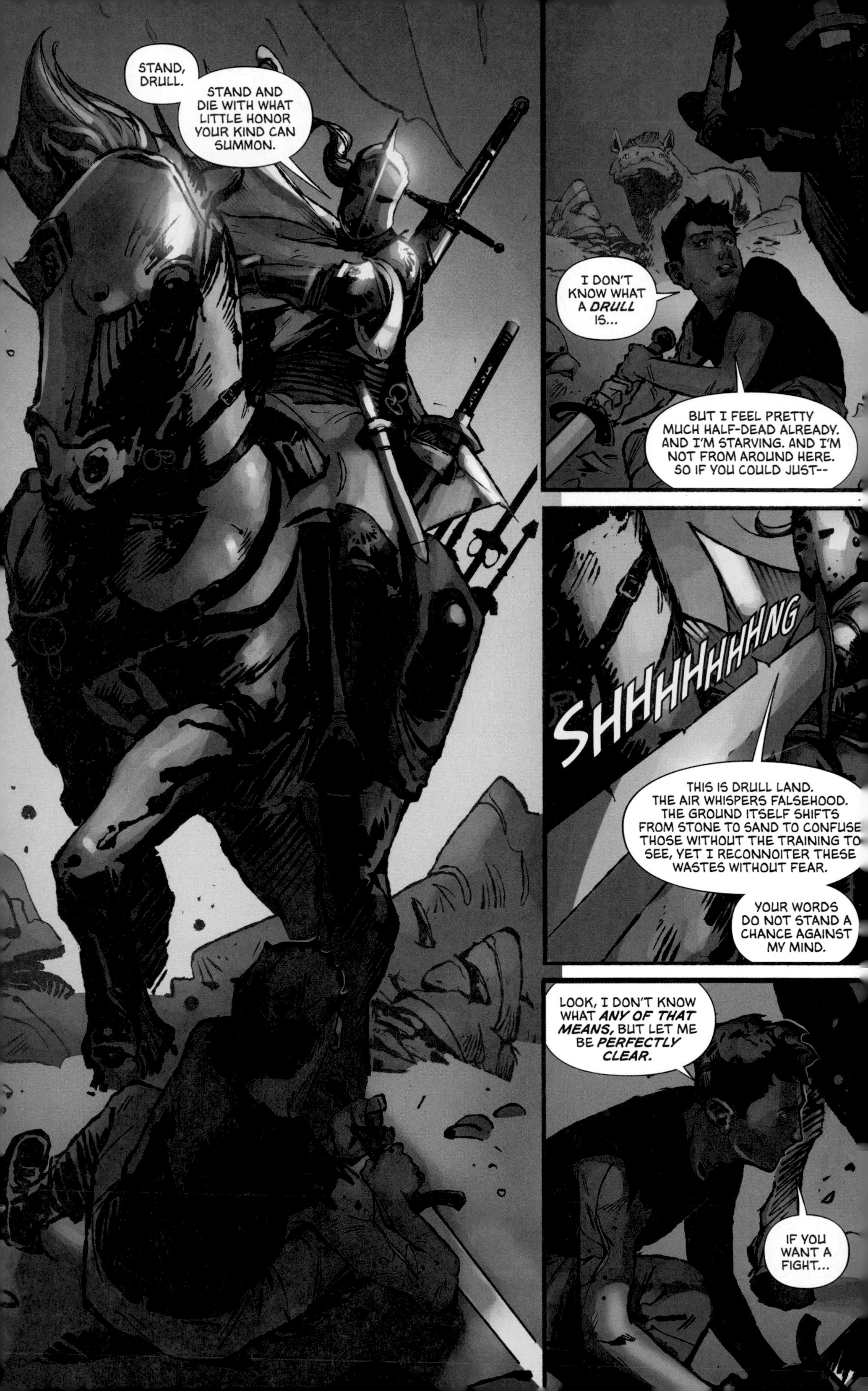
STAND, DRULL.
STAND AND DIE WITH WHAT LITTLE HONOR YOUR KIND CAN SUMMON.
I DON'T KNOW WHAT A *DRULL* IS...
BUT I FEEL PRETTY MUCH HALF-DEAD ALREADY. AND I'M STARVING. AND I'M NOT FROM AROUND HERE. SO IF YOU COULD JUST--
SHHHHHHHNG
THIS IS DRULL LAND. THE AIR WHISPERS FALSEHOOD. THE GROUND ITSELF SHIFTS FROM STONE TO SAND TO CONFUSE THOSE WITHOUT THE TRAINING TO SEE, YET I RECONNOITER THESE WASTES WITHOUT FEAR.
YOUR WORDS DO NOT STAND A CHANCE AGAINST MY MIND.
LOOK, I DON'T KNOW WHAT ***ANY OF THAT MEANS,*** BUT LET ME BE ***PERFECTLY CLEAR.***
IF YOU WANT A FIGHT...

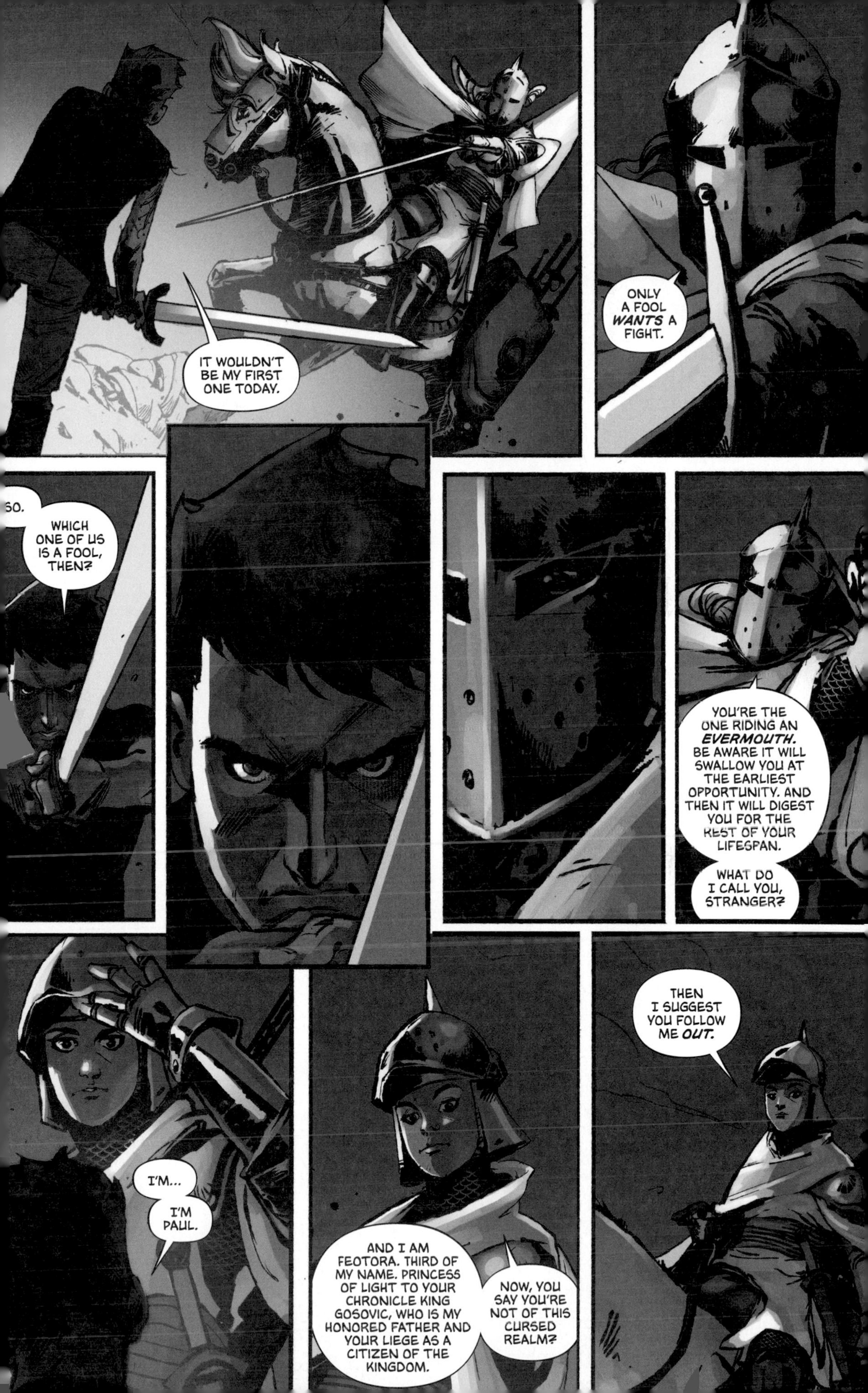
IT WOULDN'T BE MY FIRST ONE TODAY.
ONLY A FOOL *WANTS* A FIGHT.
SO.
WHICH ONE OF US IS A FOOL, THEN?
YOU'RE THE ONE RIDING AN *EVERMOUTH.* BE AWARE IT WILL SWALLOW YOU AT THE EARLIEST OPPORTUNITY. AND THEN IT WILL DIGEST YOU FOR THE REST OF YOUR LIFESPAN.
WHAT DO I CALL YOU, STRANGER?
I'M...
I'M PAUL.
AND I AM FEOTORA. THIRD OF MY NAME. PRINCESS OF LIGHT TO YOUR CHRONICLE KING GOSOVIC, WHO IS MY HONORED FATHER AND YOUR LIEGE AS A CITIZEN OF THE KINGDOM.
NOW, YOU SAY YOU'RE NOT OF THIS CURSED REALM?
THEN I SUGGEST YOU FOLLOW ME *OUT.*

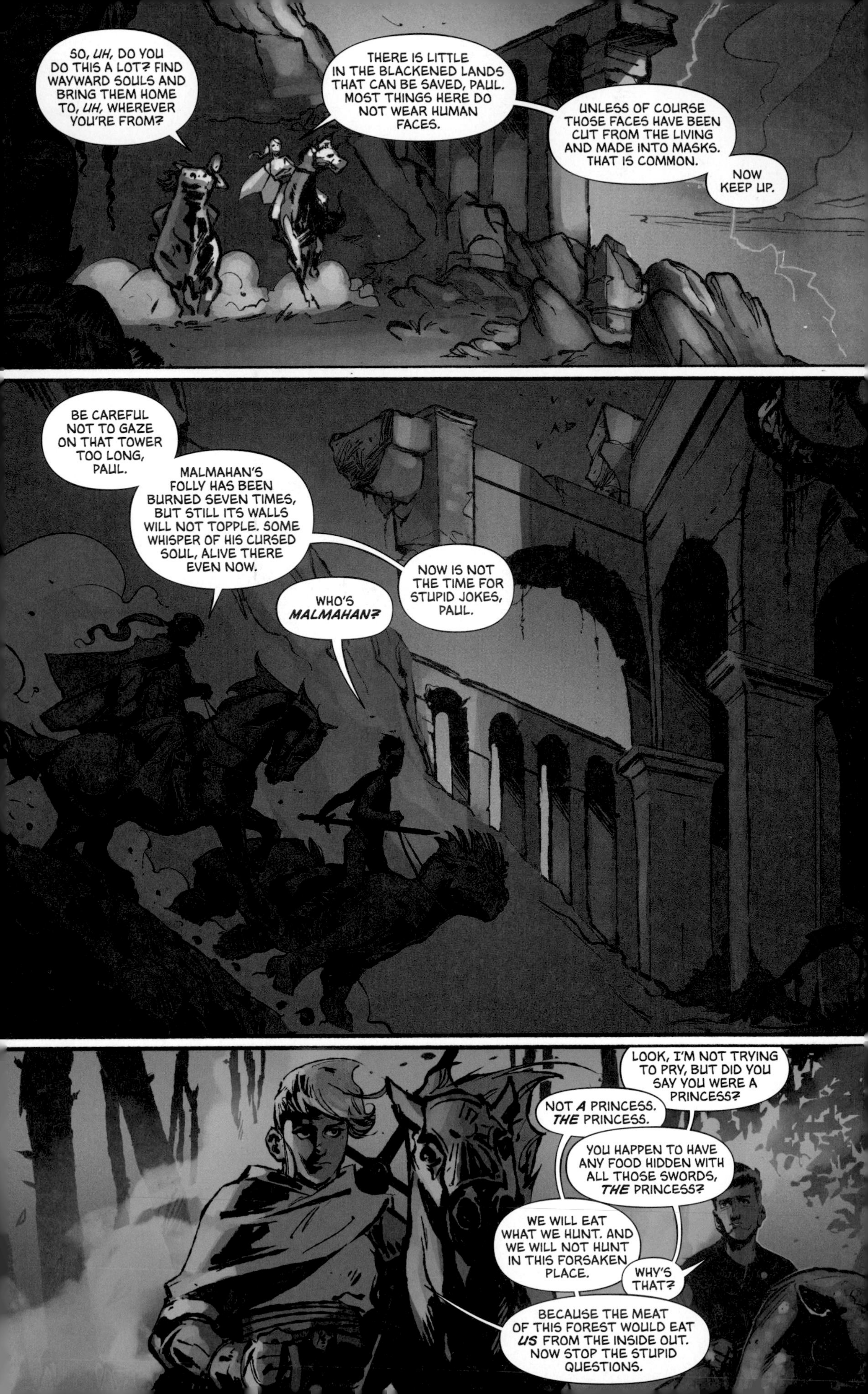
SO, UH, DO YOU DO THIS A LOT? FIND WAYWARD SOULS AND BRING THEM HOME TO, UH, WHEREVER YOU'RE FROM?
THERE IS LITTLE IN THE BLACKENED LANDS THAT CAN BE SAVED, PAUL. MOST THINGS HERE DO NOT WEAR HUMAN FACES.
UNLESS OF COURSE THOSE FACES HAVE BEEN CUT FROM THE LIVING AND MADE INTO MASKS. THAT IS COMMON.
NOW KEEP UP.
BE CAREFUL NOT TO GAZE ON THAT TOWER TOO LONG, PAUL.
MALMAHAN'S FOLLY HAS BEEN BURNED SEVEN TIMES, BUT STILL ITS WALLS WILL NOT TOPPLE. SOME WHISPER OF HIS CURSED SOUL, ALIVE THERE EVEN NOW.
WHO'S *MALMAHAN?*
NOW IS NOT THE TIME FOR STUPID JOKES, PAUL.
LOOK, I'M NOT TRYING TO PRY, BUT DID YOU SAY YOU WERE A PRINCESS?
NOT *A* PRINCESS. *THE* PRINCESS.
YOU HAPPEN TO HAVE ANY FOOD HIDDEN WITH ALL THOSE SWORDS, *THE* PRINCESS?
WE WILL EAT WHAT WE HUNT. AND WE WILL NOT HUNT IN THIS FORSAKEN PLACE.
WHY'S THAT?
BECAUSE THE MEAT OF THIS FOREST WOULD EAT *US* FROM THE INSIDE OUT. NOW STOP THE STUPID QUESTIONS.

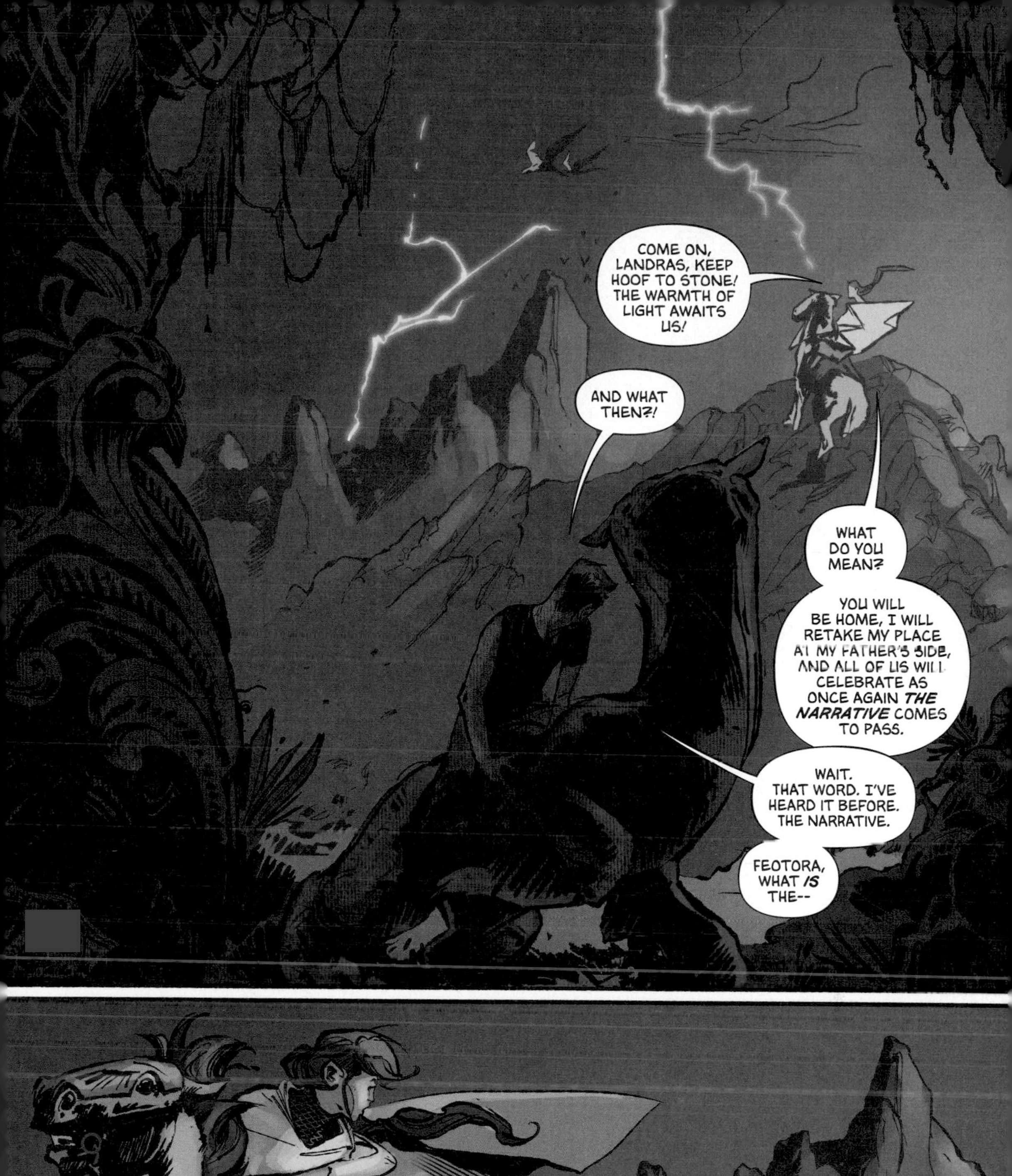
COME ON, LANDRAS, KEEP HOOF TO STONE! THE WARMTH OF LIGHT AWAITS US!
AND WHAT THEN?!
WHAT DO YOU MEAN?
YOU WILL BE HOME, I WILL RETAKE MY PLACE AT MY FATHER'S SIDE, AND ALL OF US WILL CELEBRATE AS ONCE AGAIN *THE NARRATIVE* COMES TO PASS.
WAIT. THAT WORD. I'VE HEARD IT BEFORE. THE NARRATIVE.
FEOTORA, WHAT *IS* THE--

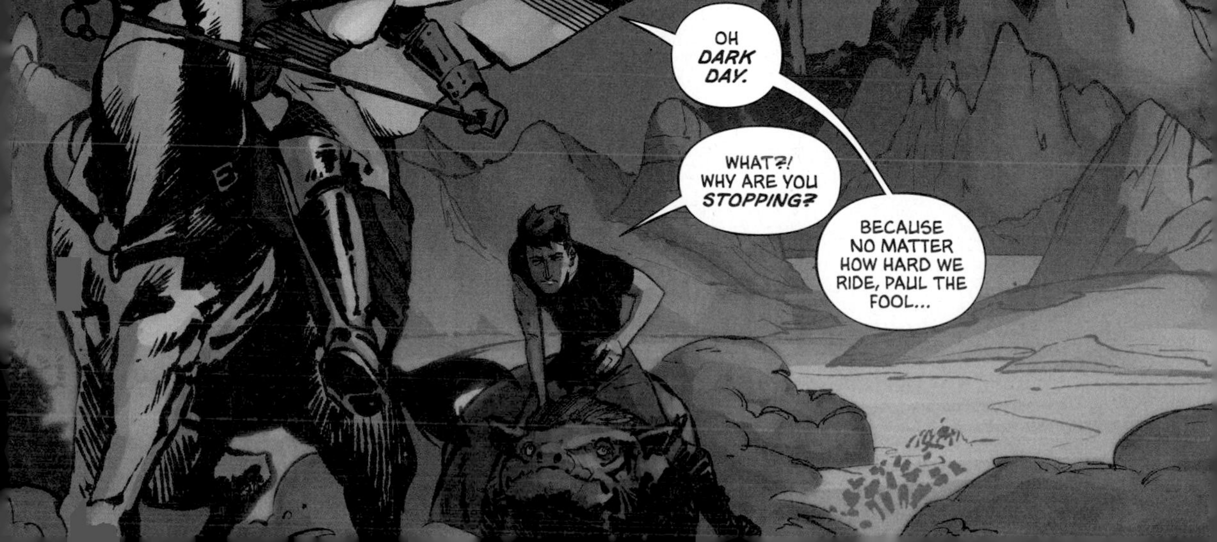
OH *DARK DAY.*
WHAT?! WHY ARE YOU *STOPPING?*
BECAUSE NO MATTER HOW HARD WE RIDE, PAUL THE FOOL...

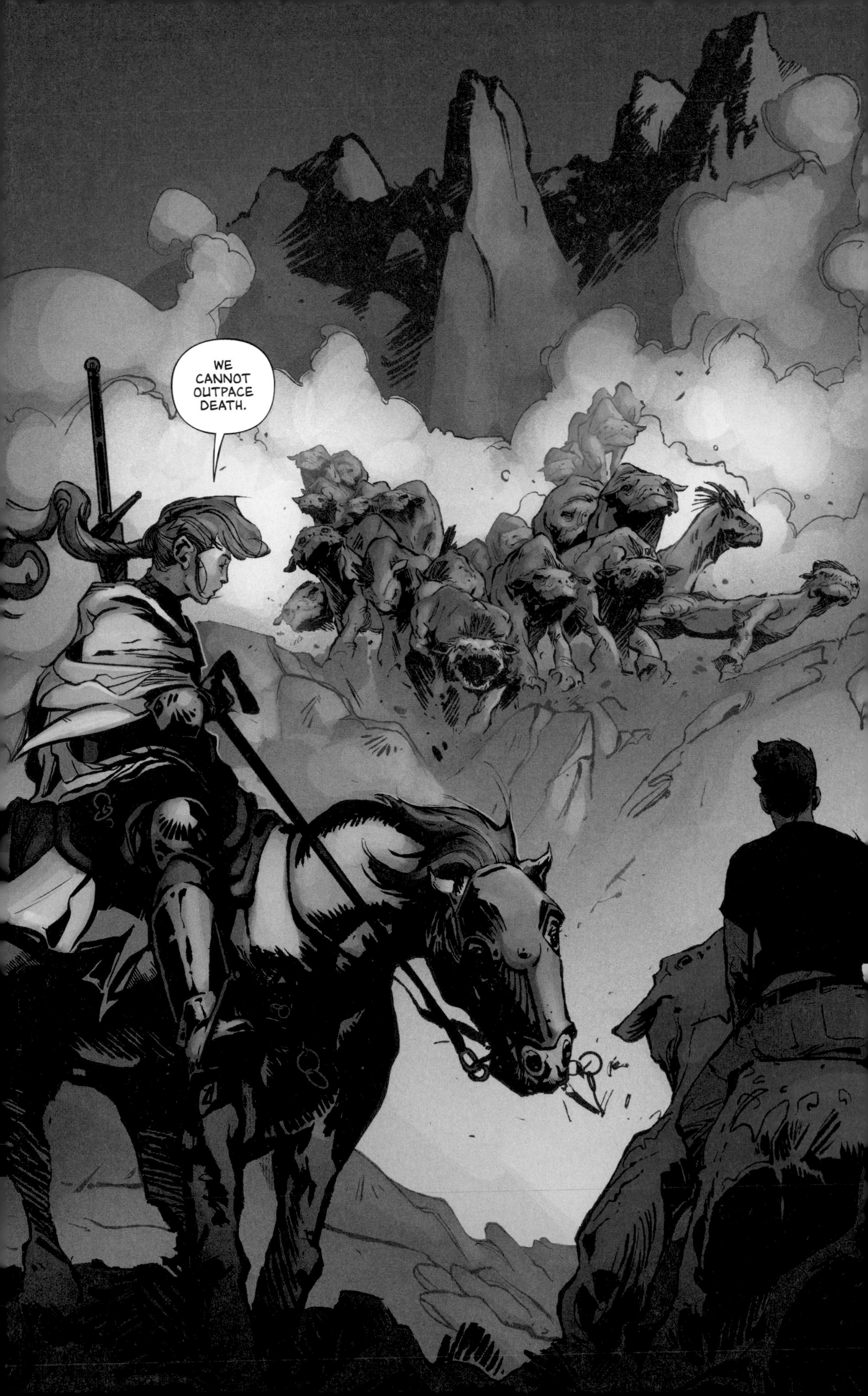
WE CANNOT OUTPACE DEATH.

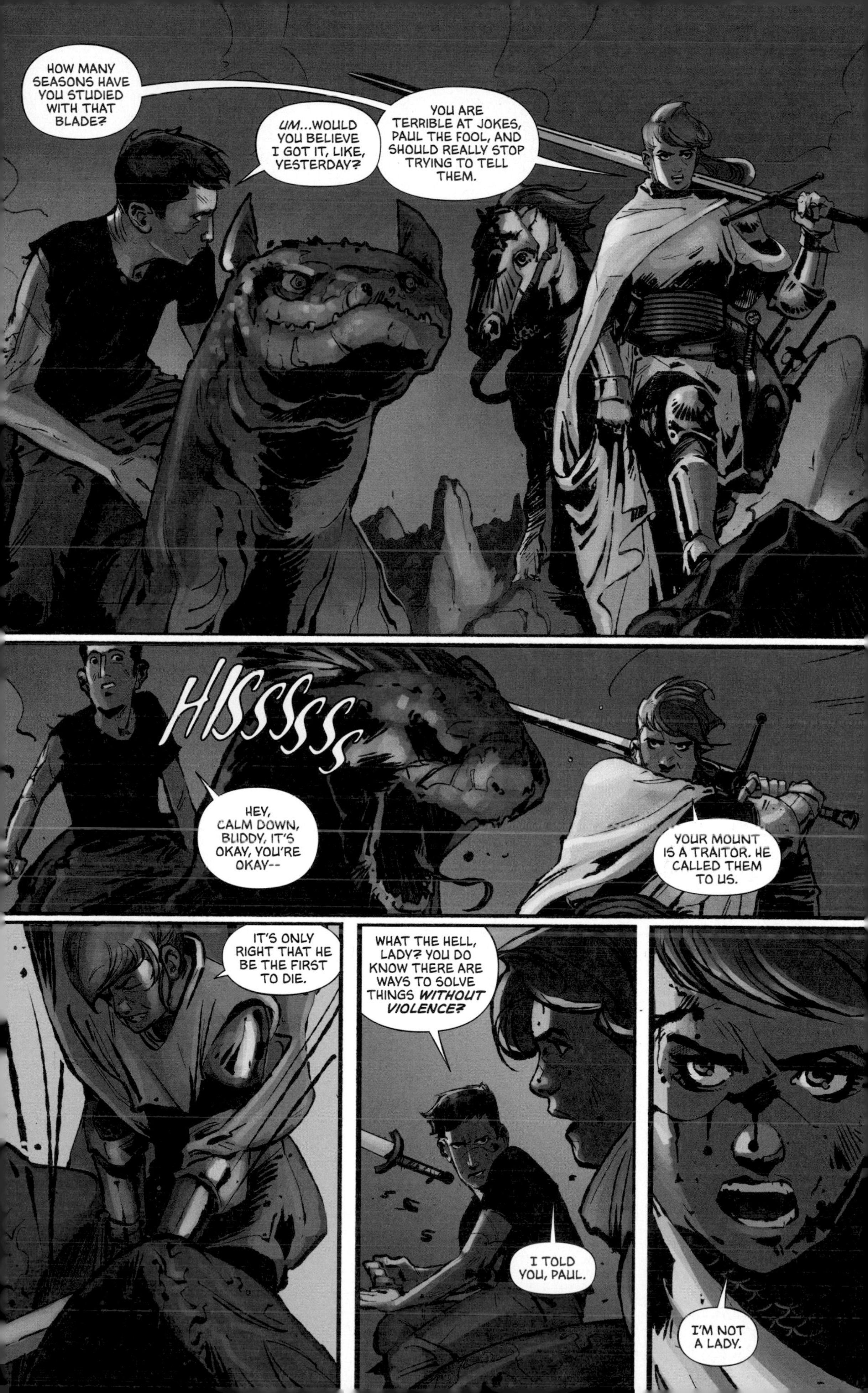
HOW MANY SEASONS HAVE YOU STUDIED WITH THAT BLADE?
UM...WOULD YOU BELIEVE I GOT IT, LIKE, YESTERDAY?
YOU ARE TERRIBLE AT JOKES, PAUL THE FOOL, AND SHOULD REALLY STOP TRYING TO TELL THEM.
HISSSSS
HEY, CALM DOWN, BUDDY, IT'S OKAY, YOU'RE OKAY--
YOUR MOUNT IS A TRAITOR. HE CALLED THEM TO US.
IT'S ONLY RIGHT THAT HE BE THE FIRST TO DIE.
WHAT THE HELL, LADY? YOU DO KNOW THERE ARE WAYS TO SOLVE THINGS *WITHOUT VIOLENCE?*
I TOLD YOU, PAUL.
I'M NOT A LADY.

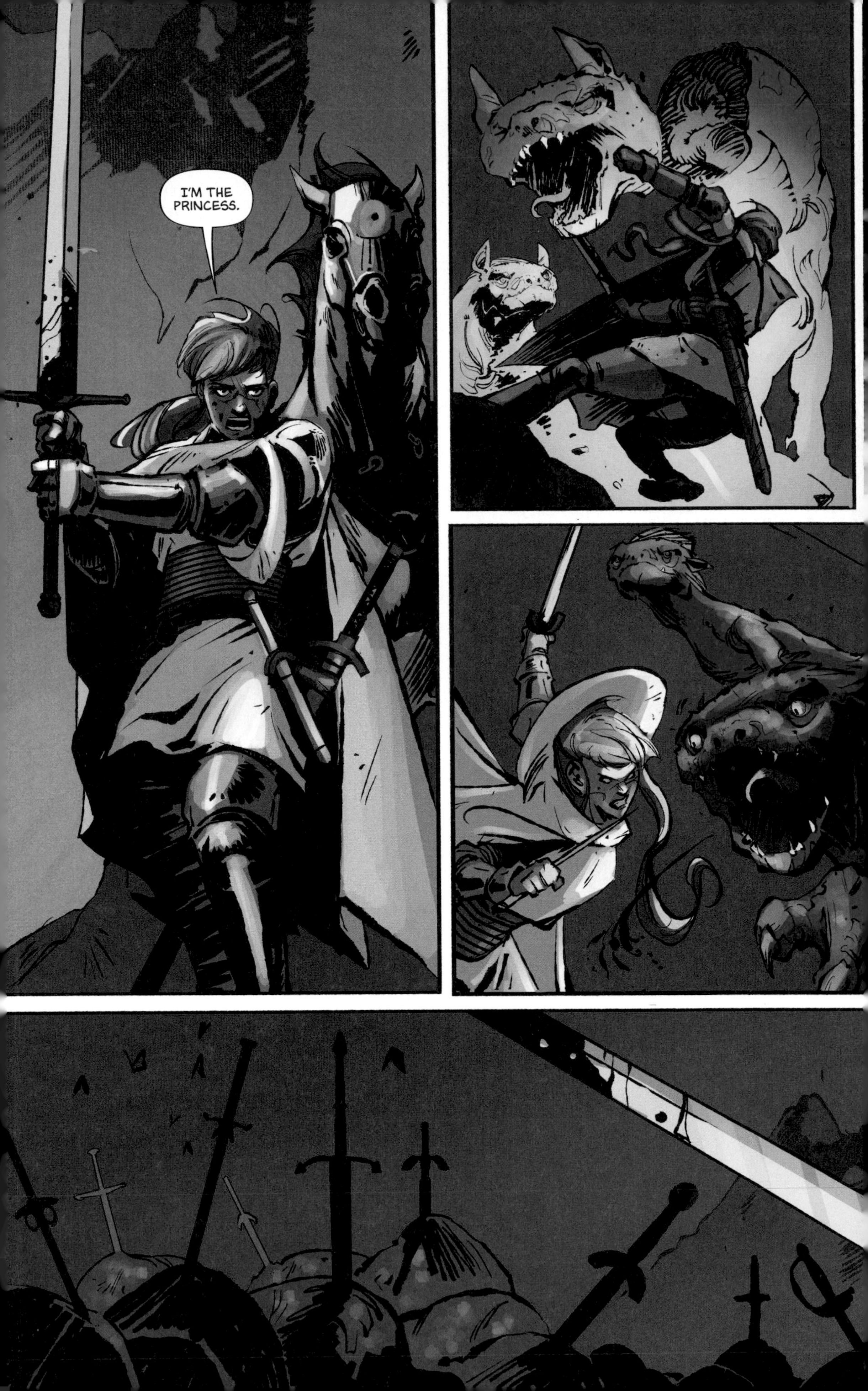
I'M THE PRINCESS.

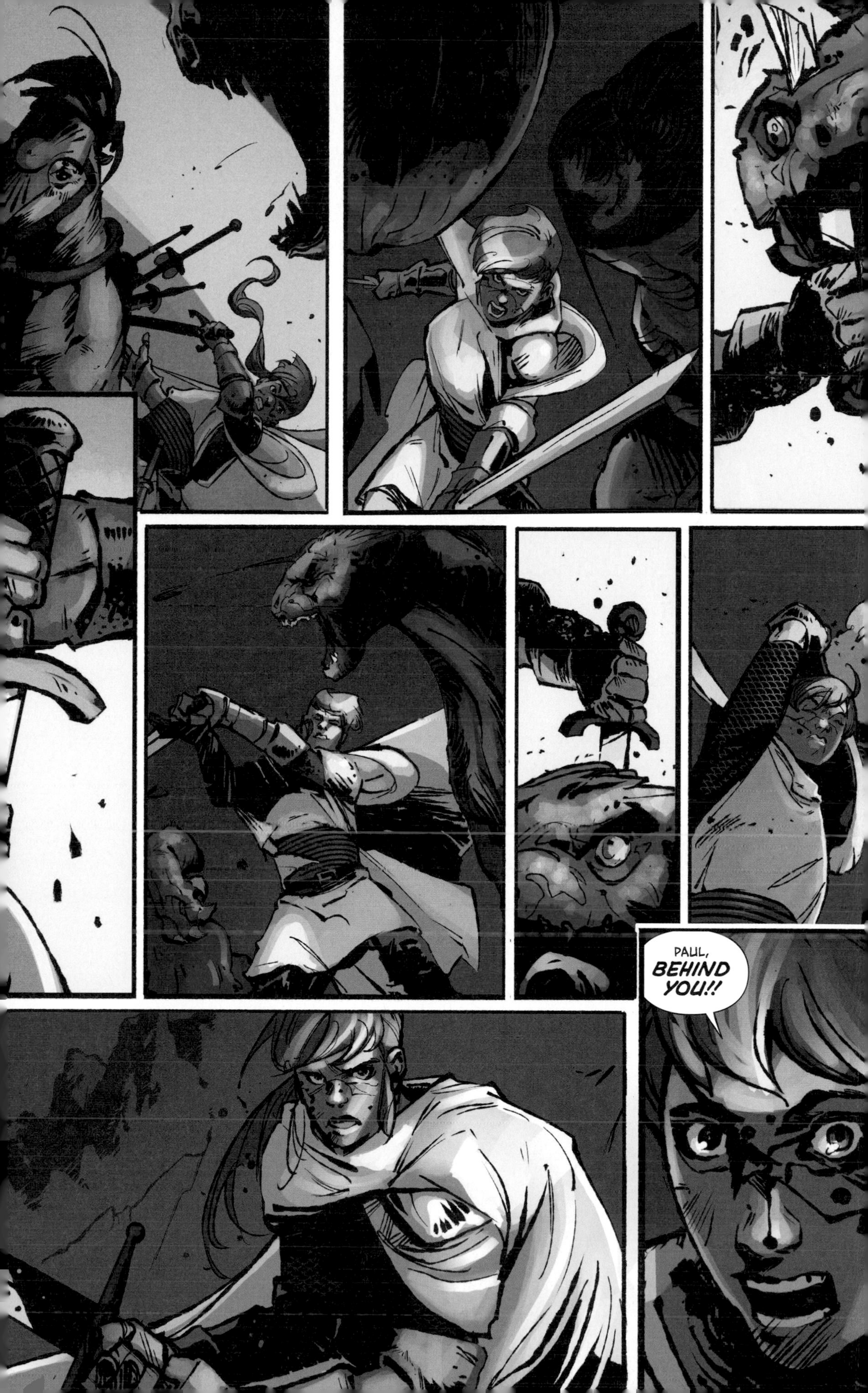
PAUL, BEHIND YOU!!

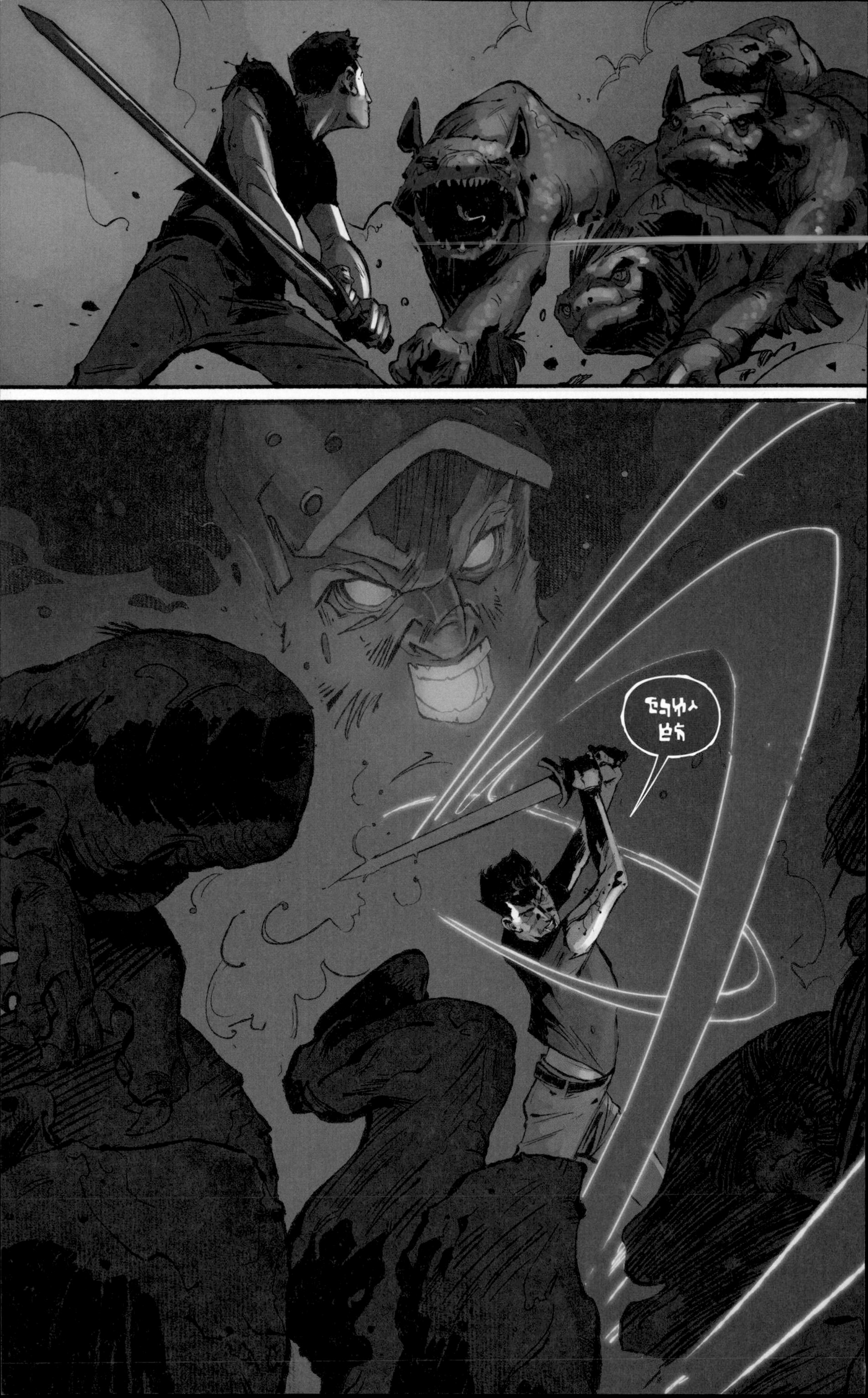

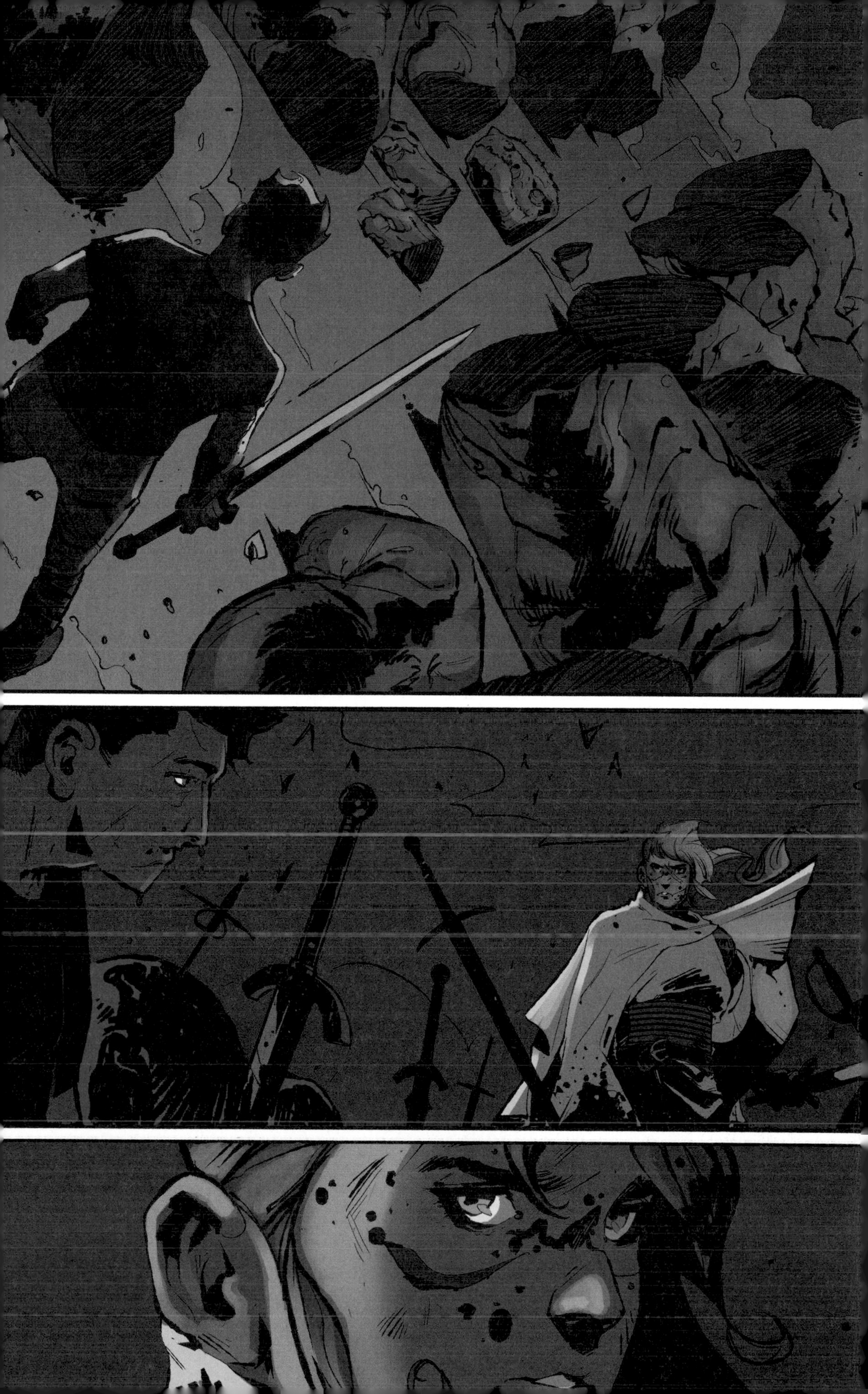

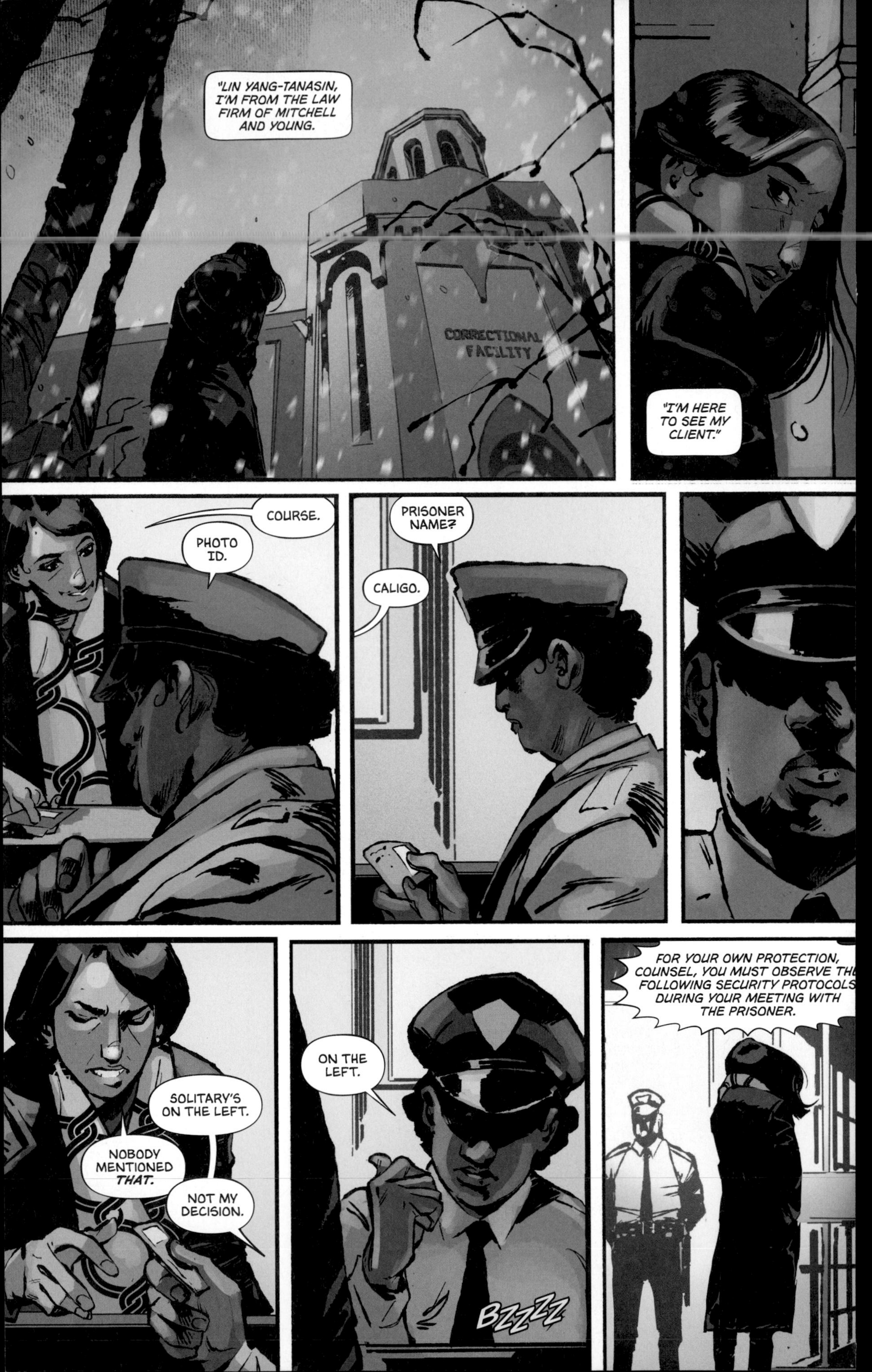
"LIN YANG-TANASIN, I'M FROM THE LAW FIRM OF MITCHELL AND YOUNG.
CORRECTIONAL FACILITY
"I'M HERE TO SEE MY CLIENT."
PHOTO ID.
COURSE.
PRISONER NAME?
CALIGO.
SOLITARY'S ON THE LEFT.
NOBODY MENTIONED *THAT.*
NOT MY DECISION.
ON THE LEFT.
BZZZZ
FOR YOUR OWN PROTECTION, COUNSEL, YOU MUST OBSERVE THE FOLLOWING SECURITY PROTOCOLS DURING YOUR MEETING WITH THE PRISONER.

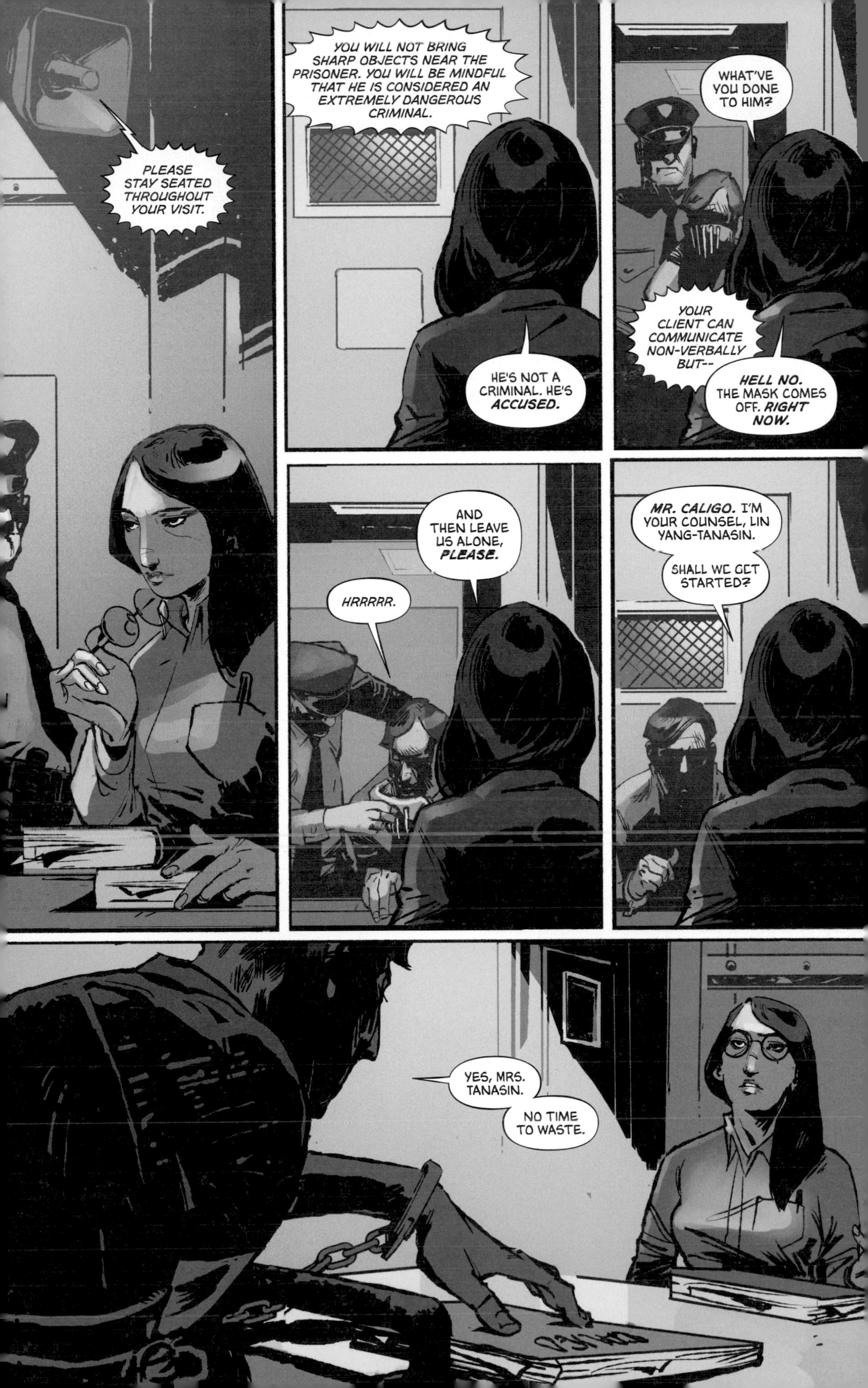
PLEASE STAY SEATED THROUGHOUT YOUR VISIT.
YOU WILL NOT BRING SHARP OBJECTS NEAR THE PRISONER. YOU WILL BE MINDFUL THAT HE IS CONSIDERED AN EXTREMELY DANGEROUS CRIMINAL.
HE'S NOT A CRIMINAL. HE'S ACCUSED.
WHAT'VE YOU DONE TO HIM?
YOUR CLIENT CAN COMMUNICATE NON-VERBALLY BUT--
HELL NO. THE MASK COMES OFF. RIGHT NOW.
AND THEN LEAVE US ALONE, PLEASE.
HRRRRR.
MR. CALIGO. I'M YOUR COUNSEL, LIN YANG-TANASIN.
SHALL WE GET STARTED?
YES, MRS. TANASIN.
NO TIME TO WASTE.

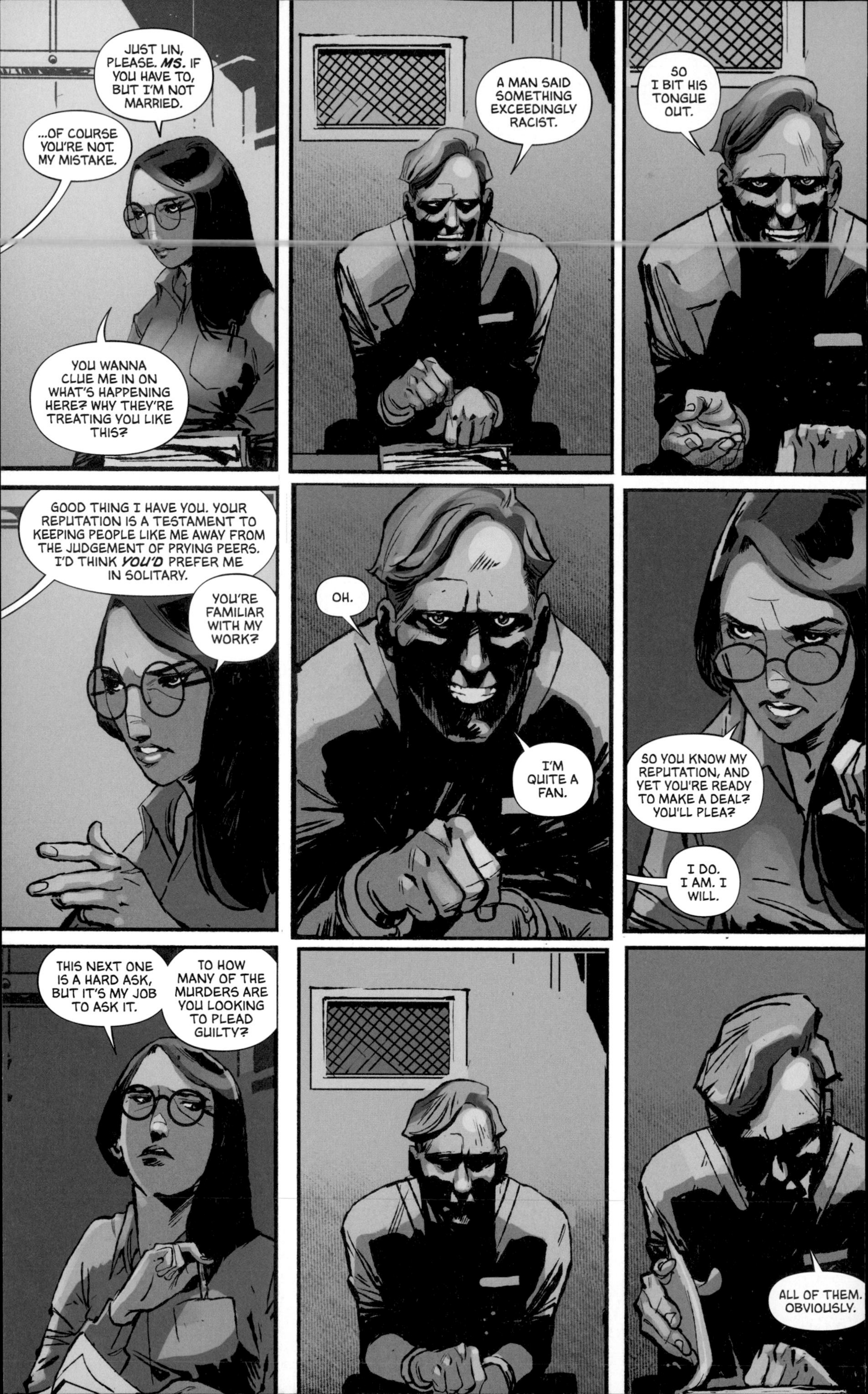

JUST LIN, PLEASE. MS. IF YOU HAVE TO, BUT I'M NOT MARRIED.
...OF COURSE YOU'RE NOT. MY MISTAKE.
YOU WANNA CLUE ME IN ON WHAT'S HAPPENING HERE? WHY THEY'RE TREATING YOU LIKE THIS?
A MAN SAID SOMETHING EXCEEDINGLY RACIST.
SO I BIT HIS TONGUE OUT.
GOOD THING I HAVE YOU. YOUR REPUTATION IS A TESTAMENT TO KEEPING PEOPLE LIKE ME AWAY FROM THE JUDGEMENT OF PRYING PEERS. I'D THINK YOU'D PREFER ME IN SOLITARY.
YOU'RE FAMILIAR WITH MY WORK?
OH.
I'M QUITE A FAN.
SO YOU KNOW MY REPUTATION, AND YET YOU'RE READY TO MAKE A DEAL? YOU'LL PLEA?
I DO. I AM. I WILL.
THIS NEXT ONE IS A HARD ASK, BUT IT'S MY JOB TO ASK IT.
TO HOW MANY OF THE MURDERS ARE YOU LOOKING TO PLEAD GUILTY?
ALL OF THEM. OBVIOUSLY.

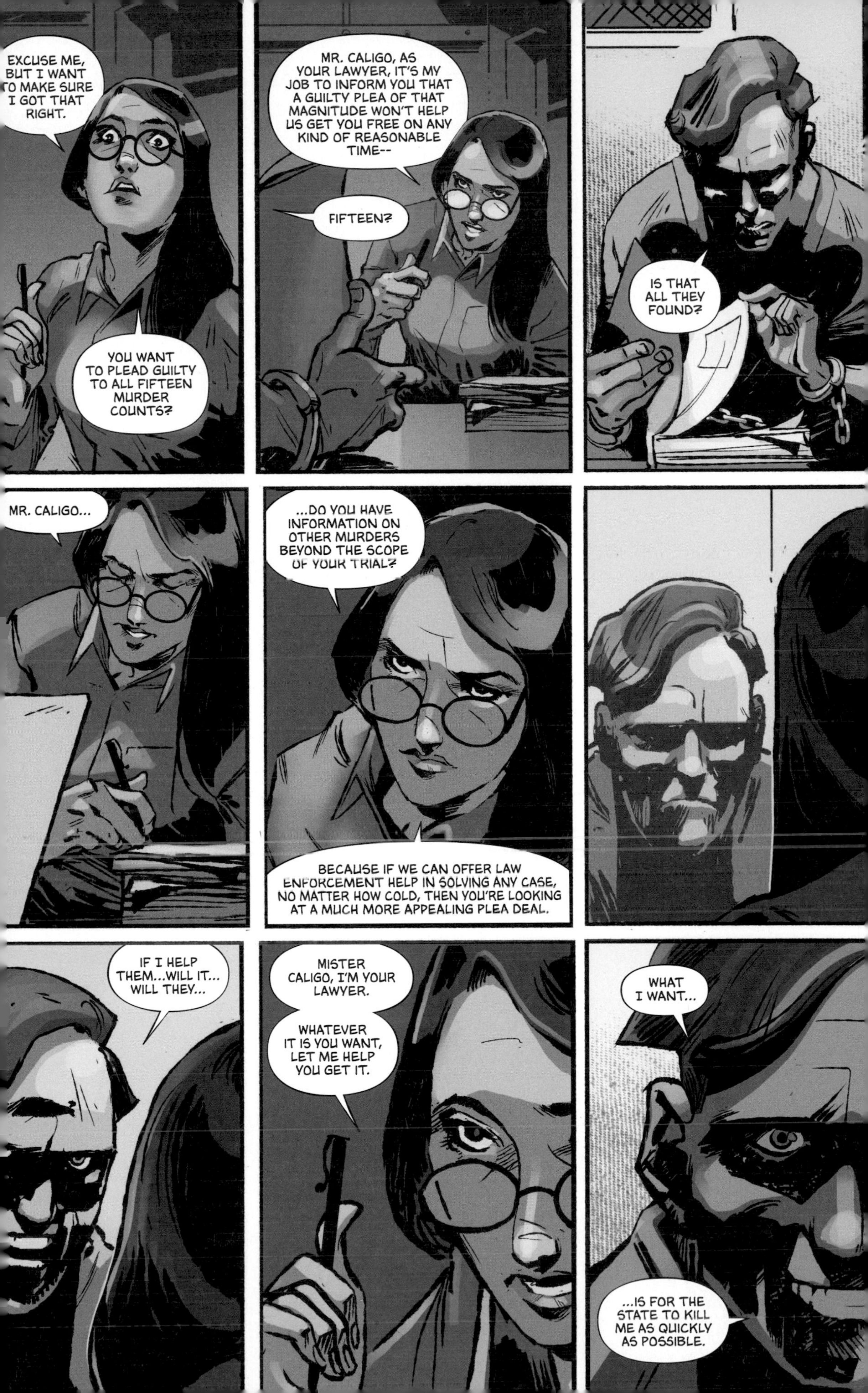
EXCUSE ME, BUT I WANT TO MAKE SURE I GOT THAT RIGHT.
YOU WANT TO PLEAD GUILTY TO ALL FIFTEEN MURDER COUNTS?
MR. CALIGO, AS YOUR LAWYER, IT'S MY JOB TO INFORM YOU THAT A GUILTY PLEA OF THAT MAGNITUDE WON'T HELP US GET YOU FREE ON ANY KIND OF REASONABLE TIME--
FIFTEEN?
IS THAT ALL THEY FOUND?
MR. CALIGO...
...DO YOU HAVE INFORMATION ON OTHER MURDERS BEYOND THE SCOPE OF YOUR TRIAL?
BECAUSE IF WE CAN OFFER LAW ENFORCEMENT HELP IN SOLVING ANY CASE, NO MATTER HOW COLD, THEN YOU'RE LOOKING AT A MUCH MORE APPEALING PLEA DEAL.
IF I HELP THEM...WILL IT... WILL THEY...
MISTER CALIGO, I'M YOUR LAWYER.
WHATEVER IT IS YOU WANT, LET ME HELP YOU GET IT.
WHAT I WANT...
...IS FOR THE STATE TO KILL ME AS QUICKLY AS POSSIBLE.

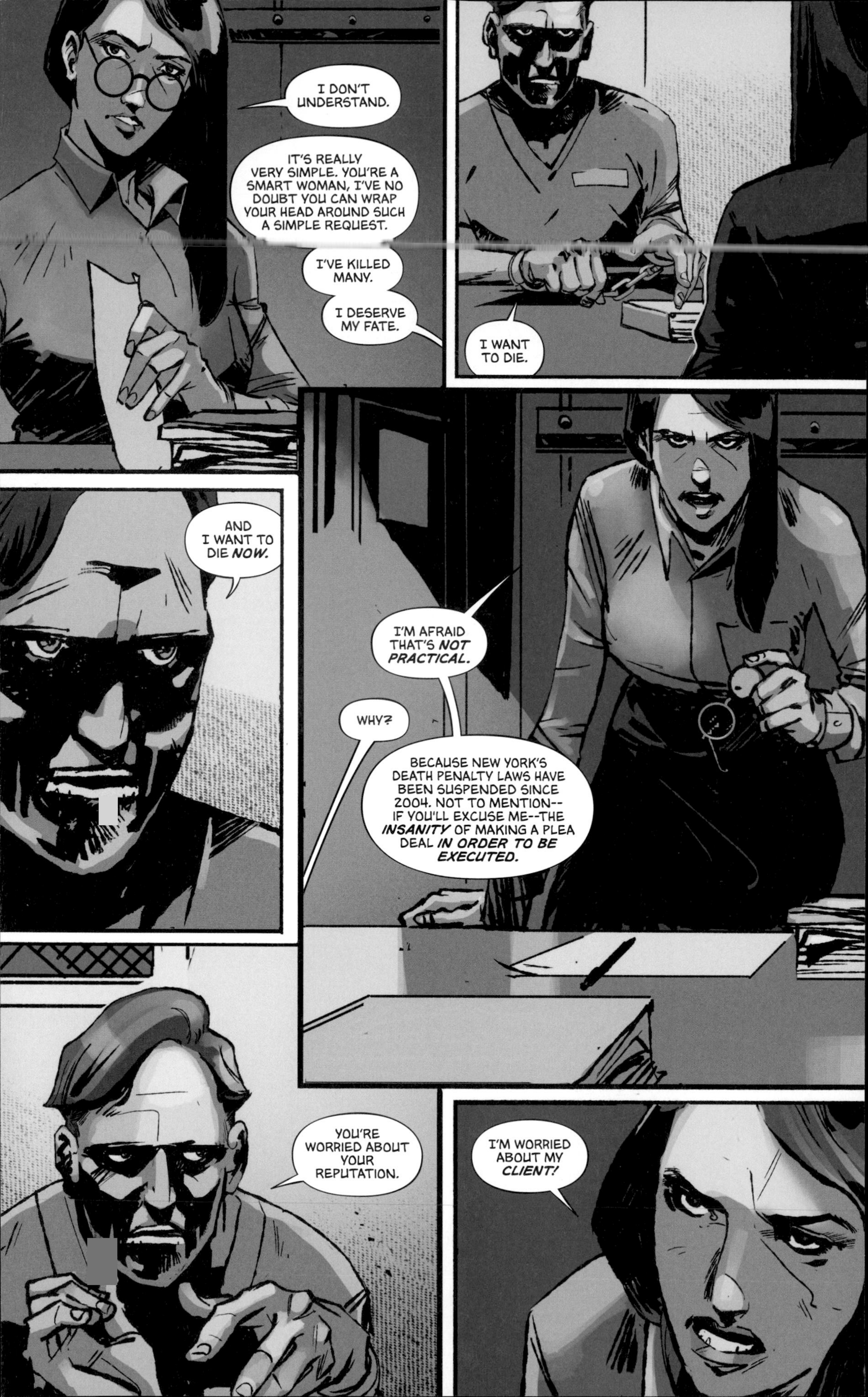
I DON'T UNDERSTAND.
IT'S REALLY VERY SIMPLE. YOU'RE A SMART WOMAN, I'VE NO DOUBT YOU CAN WRAP YOUR HEAD AROUND SUCH A SIMPLE REQUEST.
I'VE KILLED MANY.
I DESERVE MY FATE.
I WANT TO DIE.
AND I WANT TO DIE *NOW.*
I'M AFRAID THAT'S *NOT PRACTICAL.*
WHY?
BECAUSE NEW YORK'S DEATH PENALTY LAWS HAVE BEEN SUSPENDED SINCE 2004. NOT TO MENTION--IF YOU'LL EXCUSE ME--THE *INSANITY* OF MAKING A PLEA DEAL *IN ORDER TO BE EXECUTED.*
YOU'RE WORRIED ABOUT YOUR REPUTATION.
I'M WORRIED ABOUT MY *CLIENT!*

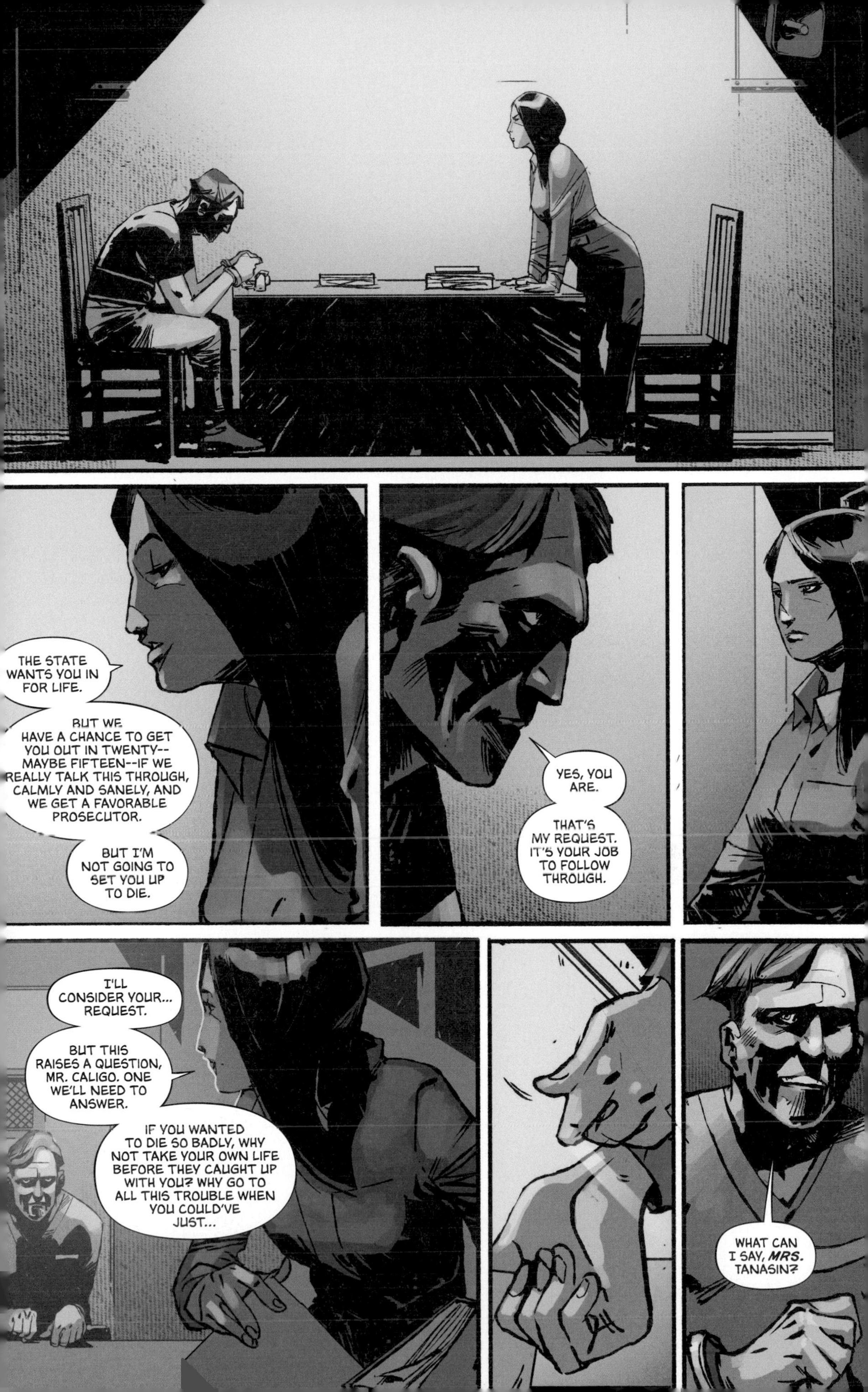
THE STATE WANTS YOU IN FOR LIFE.
BUT WE HAVE A CHANCE TO GET YOU OUT IN TWENTY-- MAYBE FIFTEEN--IF WE REALLY TALK THIS THROUGH, CALMLY AND SANELY, AND WE GET A FAVORABLE PROSECUTOR.
BUT I'M NOT GOING TO SET YOU UP TO DIE.
YES, YOU ARE.
THAT'S MY REQUEST. IT'S YOUR JOB TO FOLLOW THROUGH.
I'LL CONSIDER YOUR... REQUEST.
BUT THIS RAISES A QUESTION, MR. CALIGO. ONE WE'LL NEED TO ANSWER.
IF YOU WANTED TO DIE SO BADLY, WHY NOT TAKE YOUR OWN LIFE BEFORE THEY CAUGHT UP WITH YOU? WHY GO TO ALL THIS TROUBLE WHEN YOU COULD'VE JUST...
WHAT CAN I SAY, *MRS.* TANASIN?

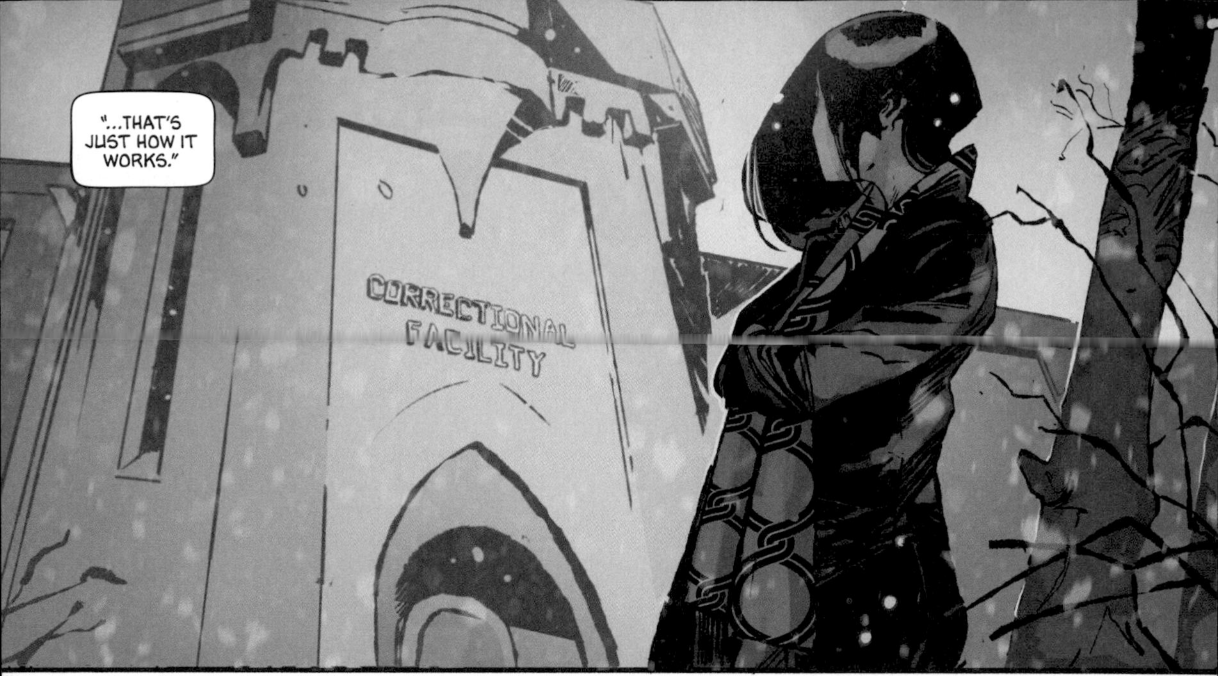
"...THAT'S JUST HOW IT WORKS."
CORRECTIONAL FACILITY
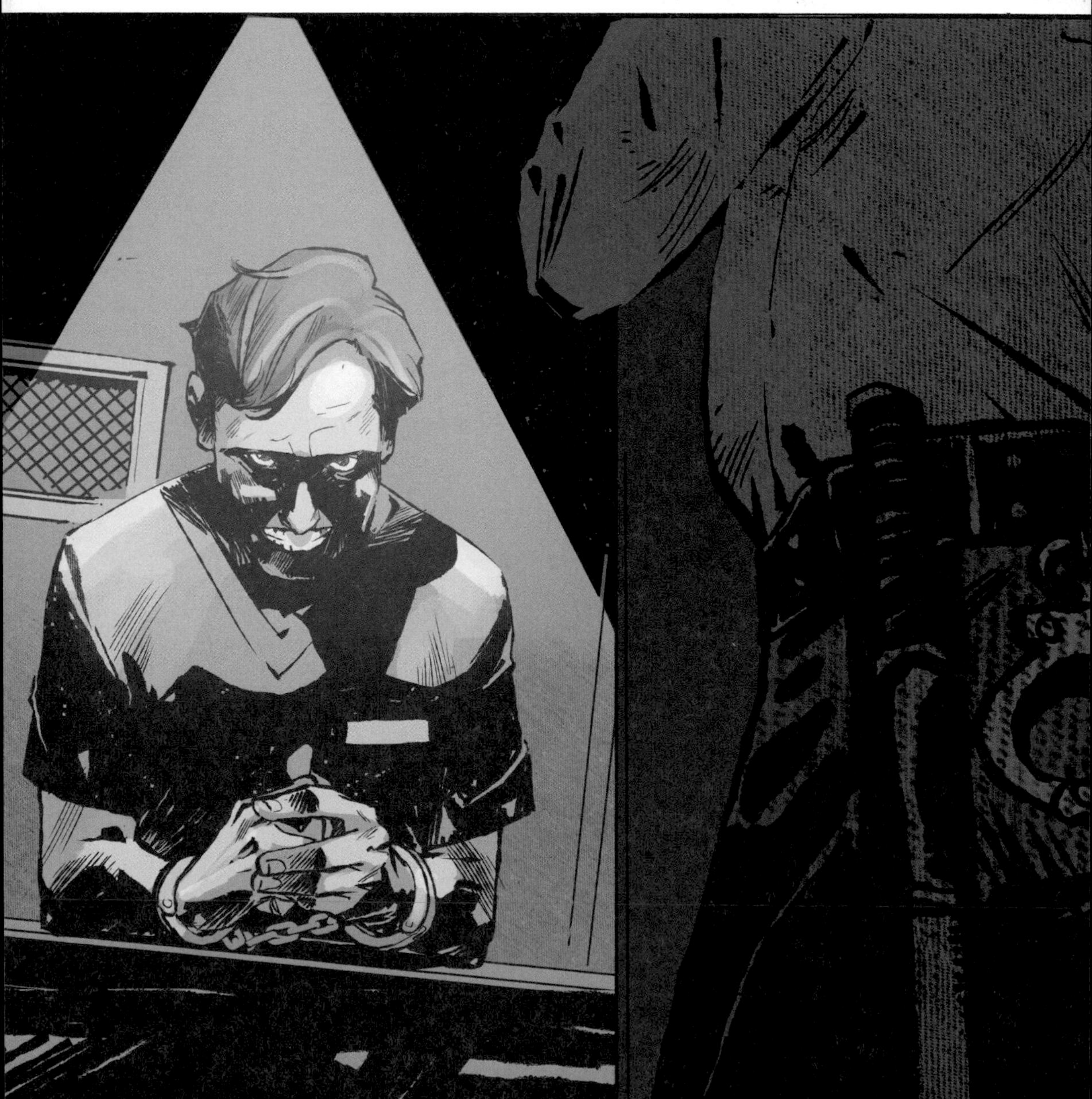

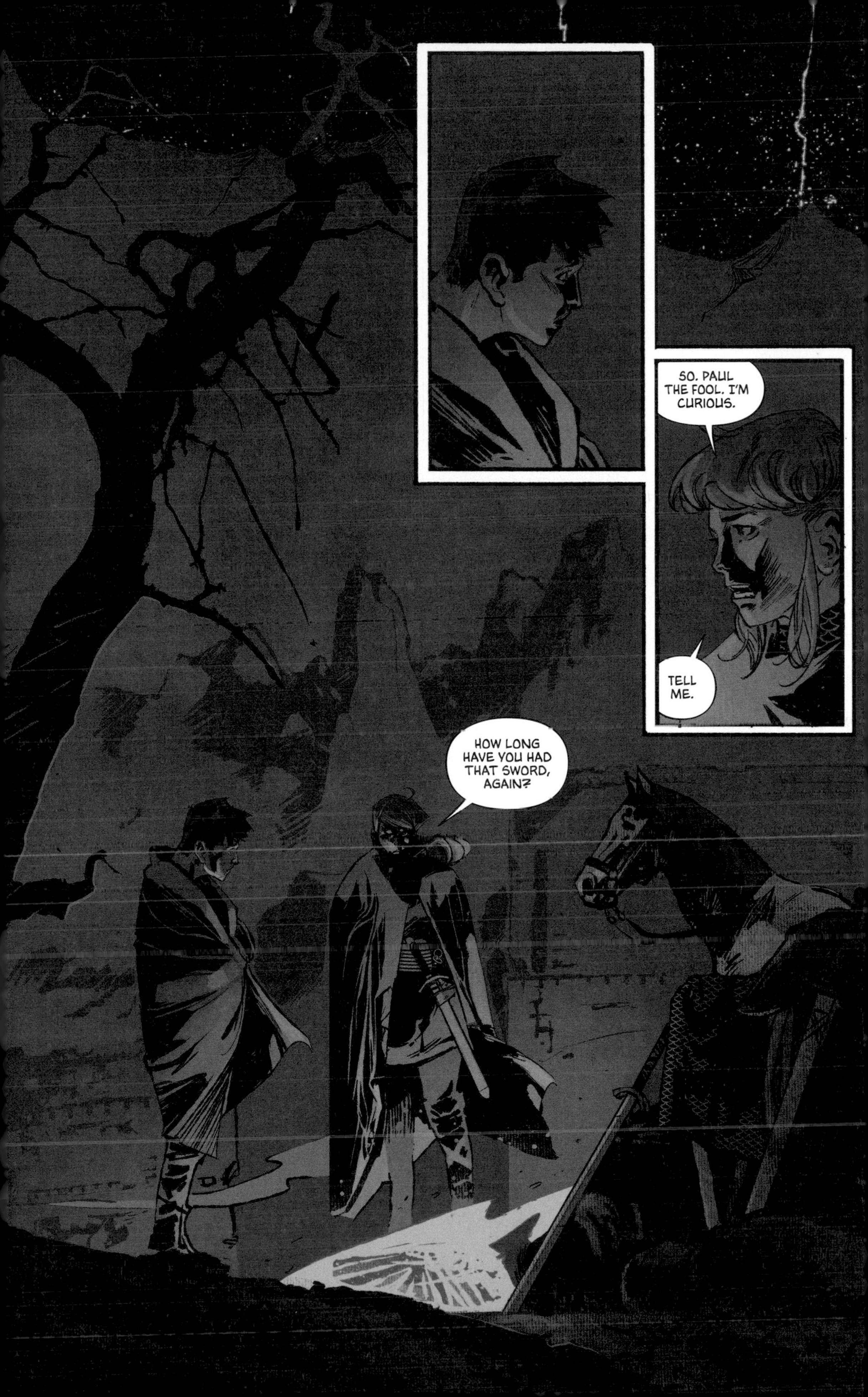
SO. PAUL THE FOOL. I'M CURIOUS.
TELL ME.
HOW LONG HAVE YOU HAD THAT SWORD, AGAIN?

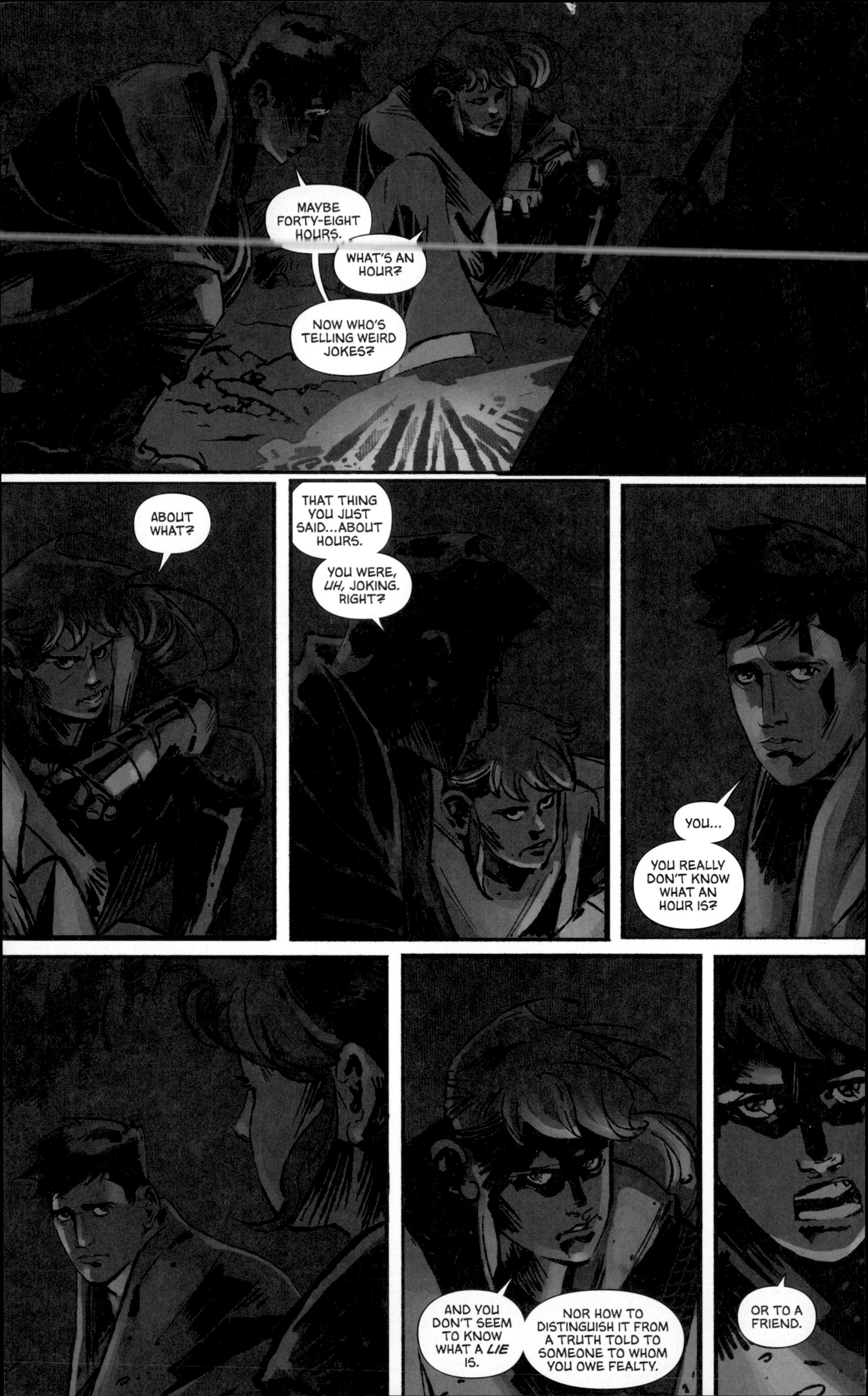
MAYBE FORTY-EIGHT HOURS.
WHAT'S AN HOUR?
NOW WHO'S TELLING WEIRD JOKES?
ABOUT WHAT?
THAT THING YOU JUST SAID...ABOUT HOURS.
YOU WERE, *UH,* JOKING. RIGHT?
YOU...
YOU REALLY DON'T KNOW WHAT AN HOUR IS?
AND YOU DON'T SEEM TO KNOW WHAT A *LIE* IS.
NOR HOW TO DISTINGUISH IT FROM A TRUTH TOLD TO SOMEONE TO WHOM YOU OWE FEALTY.
OR TO A FRIEND.

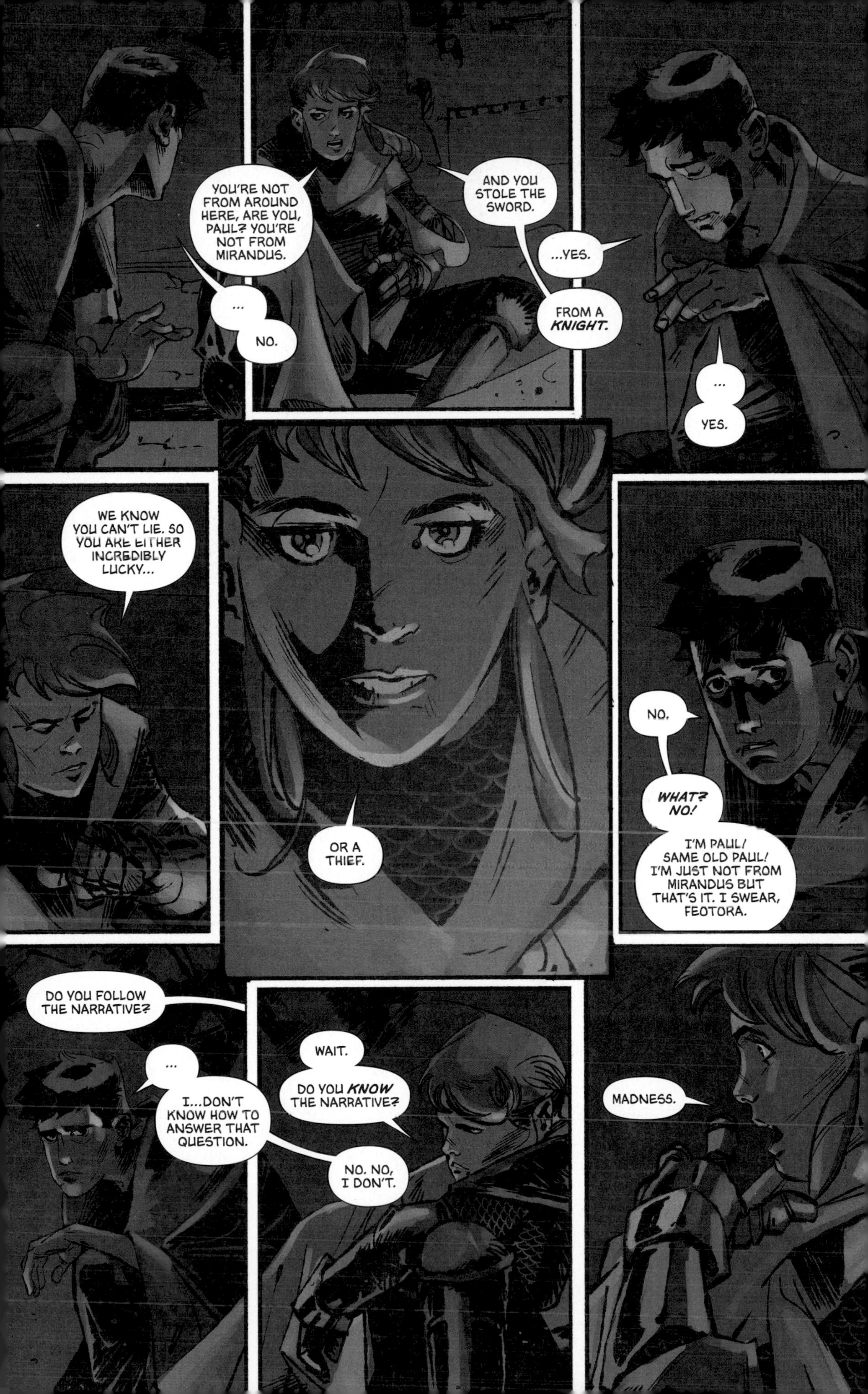
YOU'RE NOT FROM AROUND HERE, ARE YOU, PAUL? YOU'RE NOT FROM MIRANDUS.
...
NO.
AND YOU STOLE THE SWORD.
...YES.
FROM A *KNIGHT.*
...
YES.
WE KNOW YOU CAN'T LIE. SO YOU ARE EITHER INCREDIBLY LUCKY...
OR A THIEF.
NO.
WHAT? NO!
I'M PAUL! SAME OLD PAUL! I'M JUST NOT FROM MIRANDUS BUT THAT'S IT. I SWEAR, FEOTORA.
DO YOU FOLLOW THE NARRATIVE?
...
I...DON'T KNOW HOW TO ANSWER THAT QUESTION.
WAIT.
DO YOU *KNOW* THE NARRATIVE?
NO. NO, I DON'T.
MADNESS.

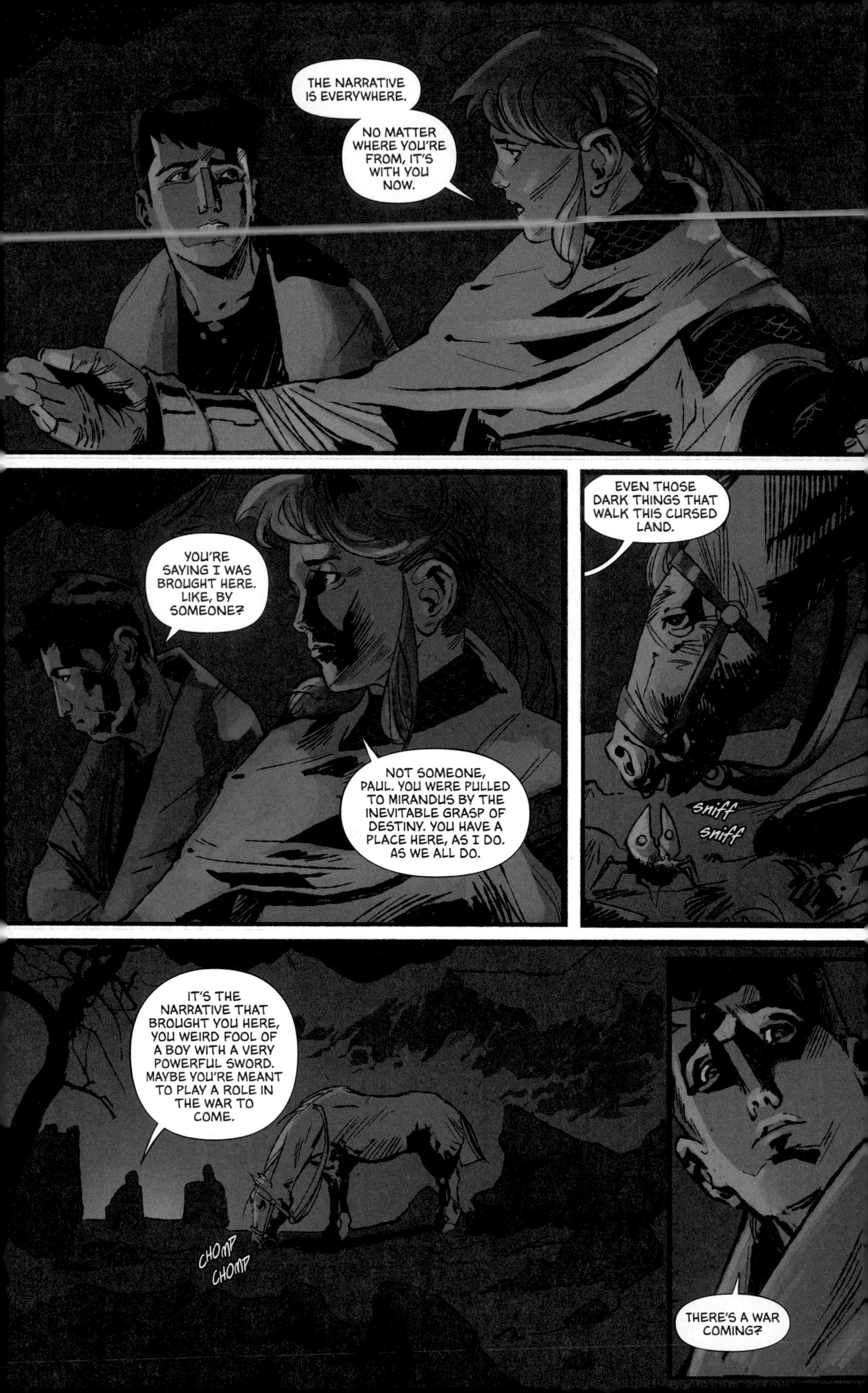
THE NARRATIVE IS EVERYWHERE.
NO MATTER WHERE YOU'RE FROM, IT'S WITH YOU NOW.
YOU'RE SAYING I WAS BROUGHT HERE. LIKE, BY SOMEONE?
NOT SOMEONE, PAUL. YOU WERE PULLED TO MIRANDUS BY THE INEVITABLE GRASP OF DESTINY. YOU HAVE A PLACE HERE, AS I DO. AS WE ALL DO.
EVEN THOSE DARK THINGS THAT WALK THIS CURSED LAND.
SNIFF SNIFF
IT'S THE NARRATIVE THAT BROUGHT YOU HERE, YOU WEIRD FOOL OF A BOY WITH A VERY POWERFUL SWORD. MAYBE YOU'RE MEANT TO PLAY A ROLE IN THE WAR TO COME.
CHOMP CHOMP
THERE'S A WAR COMING?

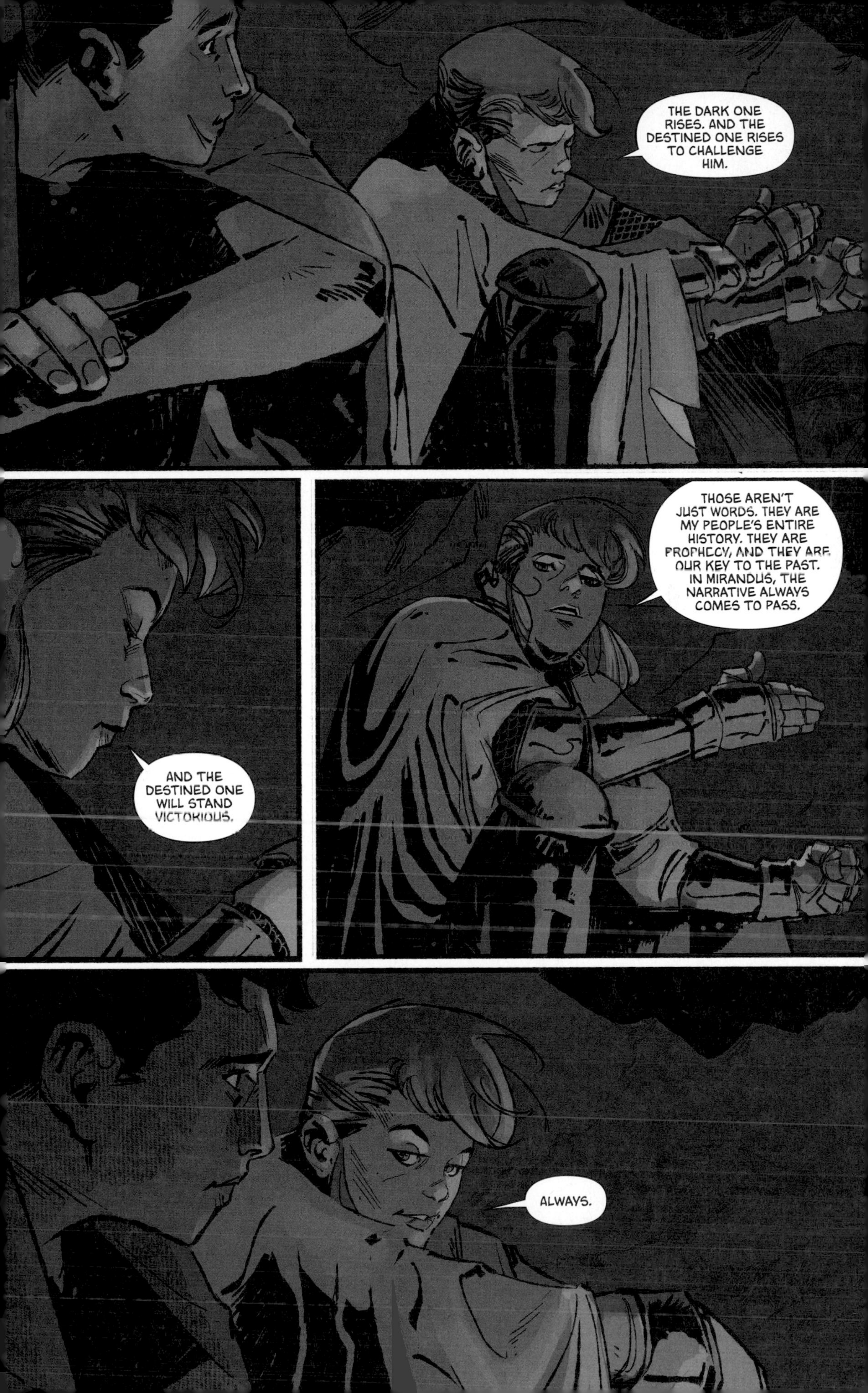

THE DARK ONE RISES. AND THE DESTINED ONE RISES TO CHALLENGE HIM.
AND THE DESTINED ONE WILL STAND VICTORIOUS.
THOSE AREN'T JUST WORDS. THEY ARE MY PEOPLE'S ENTIRE HISTORY. THEY ARE PROPHECY, AND THEY ARE OUR KEY TO THE PAST. IN MIRANDUS, THE NARRATIVE ALWAYS COMES TO PASS.
ALWAYS.

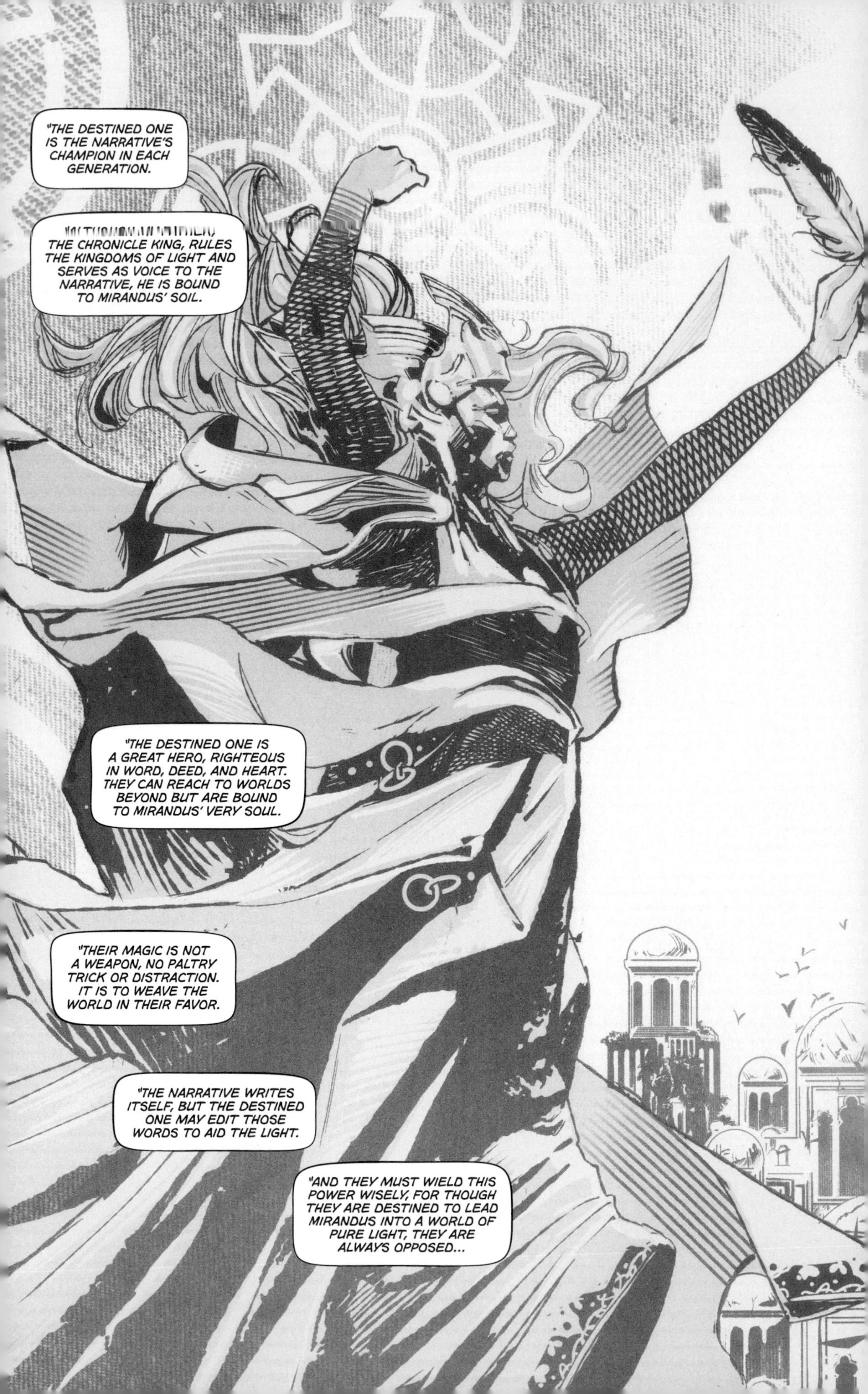
"THE DESTINED ONE IS THE NARRATIVE'S CHAMPION IN EACH GENERATION.
THE CHRONICLE KING, RULES THE KINGDOMS OF LIGHT AND SERVES AS VOICE TO THE NARRATIVE, HE IS BOUND TO MIRANDUS' SOIL.
"THE DESTINED ONE IS A GREAT HERO, RIGHTEOUS IN WORD, DEED, AND HEART. THEY CAN REACH TO WORLDS BEYOND BUT ARE BOUND TO MIRANDUS' VERY SOUL.
"THEIR MAGIC IS NOT A WEAPON, NO PALTRY TRICK OR DISTRACTION. IT IS TO WEAVE THE WORLD IN THEIR FAVOR.
"THE NARRATIVE WRITES ITSELF, BUT THE DESTINED ONE MAY EDIT THOSE WORDS TO AID THE LIGHT.
"AND THEY MUST WIELD THIS POWER WISELY, FOR THOUGH THEY ARE DESTINED TO LEAD MIRANDUS INTO A WORLD OF PURE LIGHT, THEY ARE ALWAYS OPPOSED...

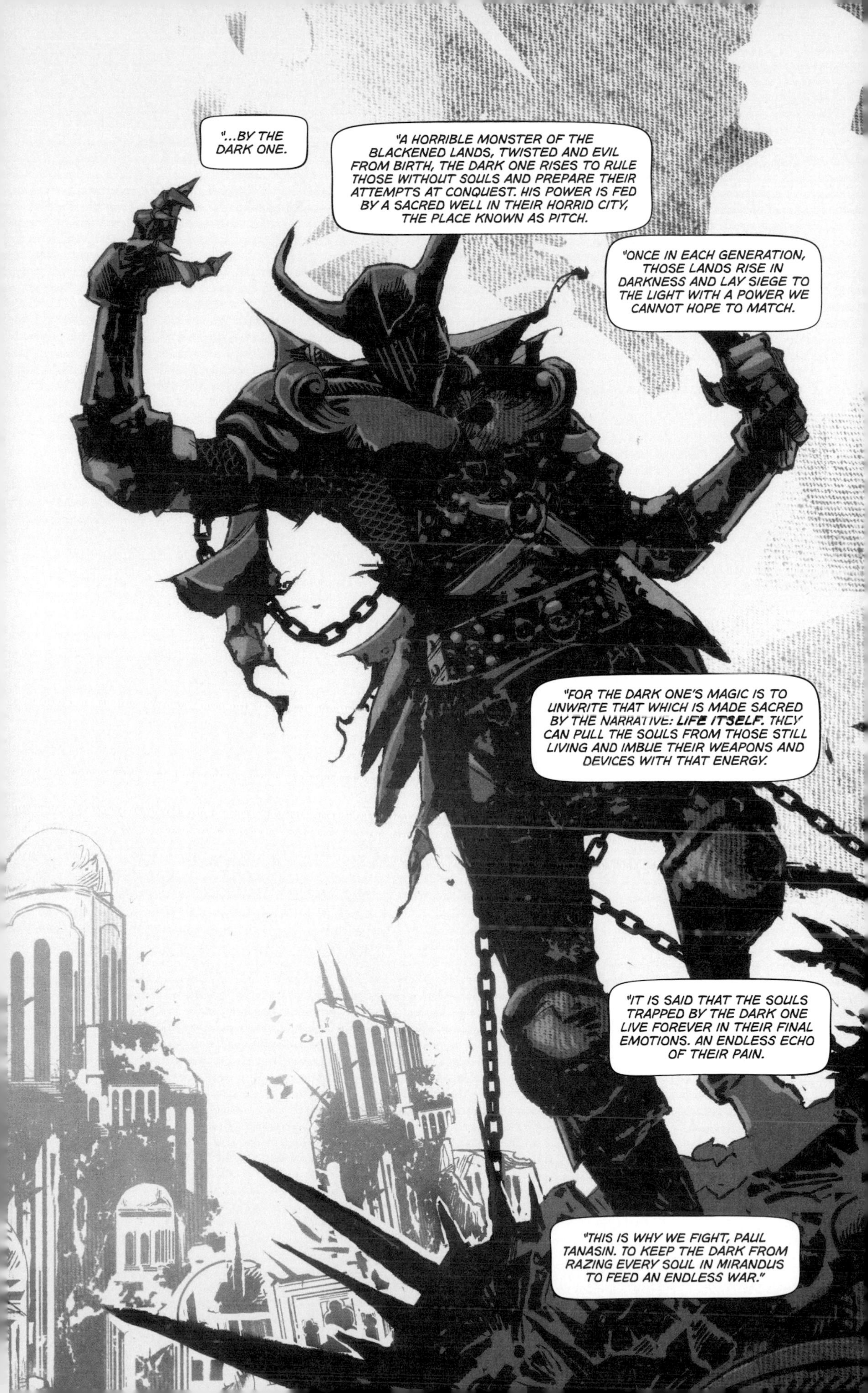
"...BY THE DARK ONE.
"A HORRIBLE MONSTER OF THE BLACKENED LANDS, TWISTED AND EVIL FROM BIRTH, THE DARK ONE RISES TO RULE THOSE WITHOUT SOULS AND PREPARE THEIR ATTEMPTS AT CONQUEST. HIS POWER IS FED BY A SACRED WELL IN THEIR HORRID CITY, THE PLACE KNOWN AS PITCH.
"ONCE IN EACH GENERATION, THOSE LANDS RISE IN DARKNESS AND LAY SIEGE TO THE LIGHT WITH A POWER WE CANNOT HOPE TO MATCH.
"FOR THE DARK ONE'S MAGIC IS TO UNWRITE THAT WHICH IS MADE SACRED BY THE NARRATIVE: **LIFE ITSELF.** THEY CAN PULL THE SOULS FROM THOSE STILL LIVING AND IMBUE THEIR WEAPONS AND DEVICES WITH THAT ENERGY.
"IT IS SAID THAT THE SOULS TRAPPED BY THE DARK ONE LIVE FOREVER IN THEIR FINAL EMOTIONS. AN ENDLESS ECHO OF THEIR PAIN.
"THIS IS WHY WE FIGHT, PAUL TANASIN. TO KEEP THE DARK FROM RAZING EVERY SOUL IN MIRANDUS TO FEED AN ENDLESS WAR."

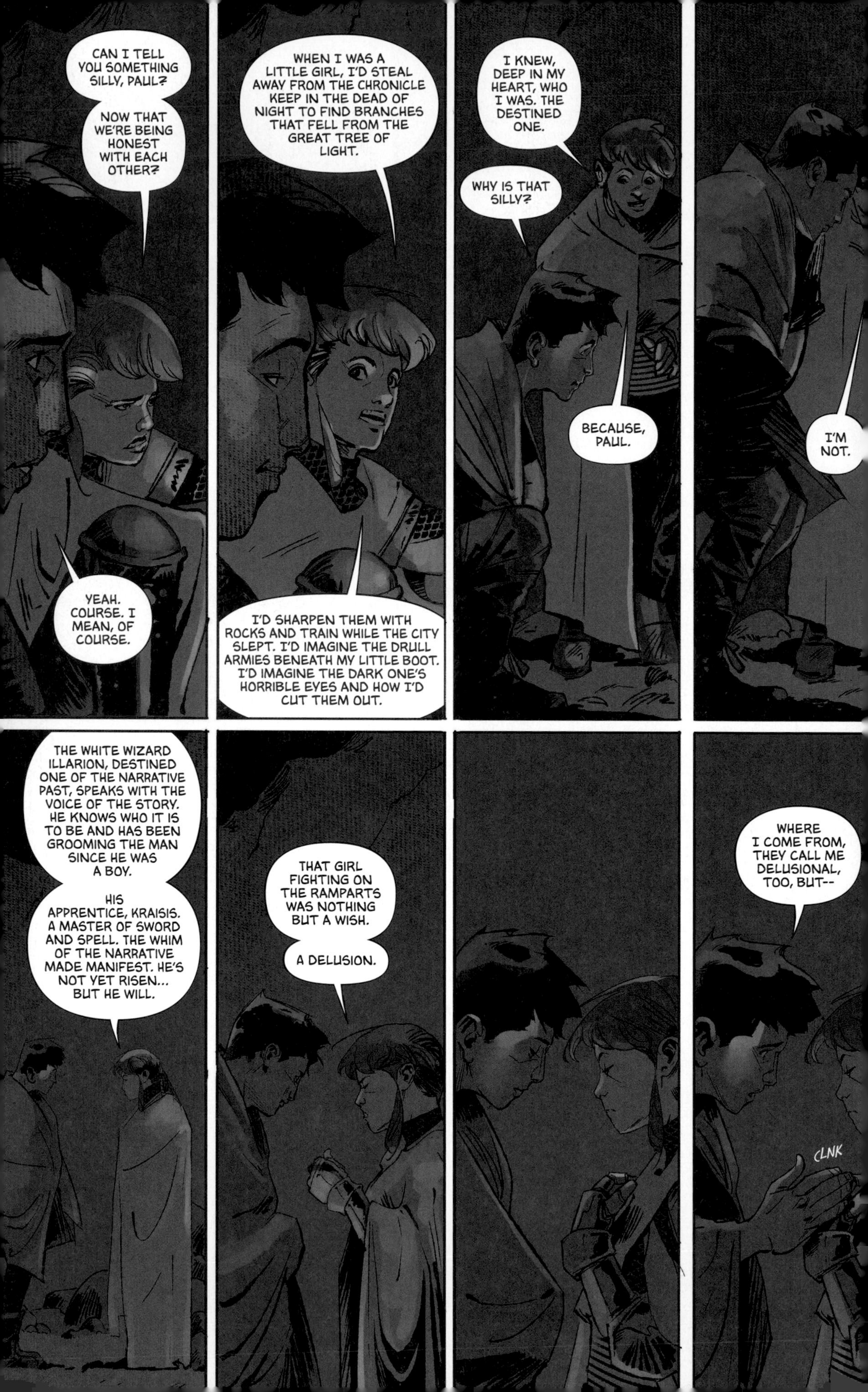
CAN I TELL YOU SOMETHING SILLY, PAUL?
NOW THAT WE'RE BEING HONEST WITH EACH OTHER?
YEAH. COURSE. I MEAN, OF COURSE.
WHEN I WAS A LITTLE GIRL, I'D STEAL AWAY FROM THE CHRONICLE KEEP IN THE DEAD OF NIGHT TO FIND BRANCHES THAT FELL FROM THE GREAT TREE OF LIGHT.
I'D SHARPEN THEM WITH ROCKS AND TRAIN WHILE THE CITY SLEPT. I'D IMAGINE THE DRULL ARMIES BENEATH MY LITTLE BOOT. I'D IMAGINE THE DARK ONE'S HORRIBLE EYES AND HOW I'D CUT THEM OUT.
I KNEW, DEEP IN MY HEART, WHO I WAS. THE DESTINED ONE.
WHY IS THAT SILLY?
BECAUSE, PAUL.
I'M NOT.
THE WHITE WIZARD ILLARION, DESTINED ONE OF THE NARRATIVE PAST, SPEAKS WITH THE VOICE OF THE STORY. HE KNOWS WHO IT IS TO BE AND HAS BEEN GROOMING THE MAN SINCE HE WAS A BOY.
HIS APPRENTICE, KRAISIS. A MASTER OF SWORD AND SPELL. THE WHIM OF THE NARRATIVE MADE MANIFEST. HE'S NOT YET RISEN... BUT HE WILL.
THAT GIRL FIGHTING ON THE RAMPARTS WAS NOTHING BUT A WISH.
A DELUSION.
WHERE I COME FROM, THEY CALL ME DELUSIONAL, TOO, BUT--
CLNK

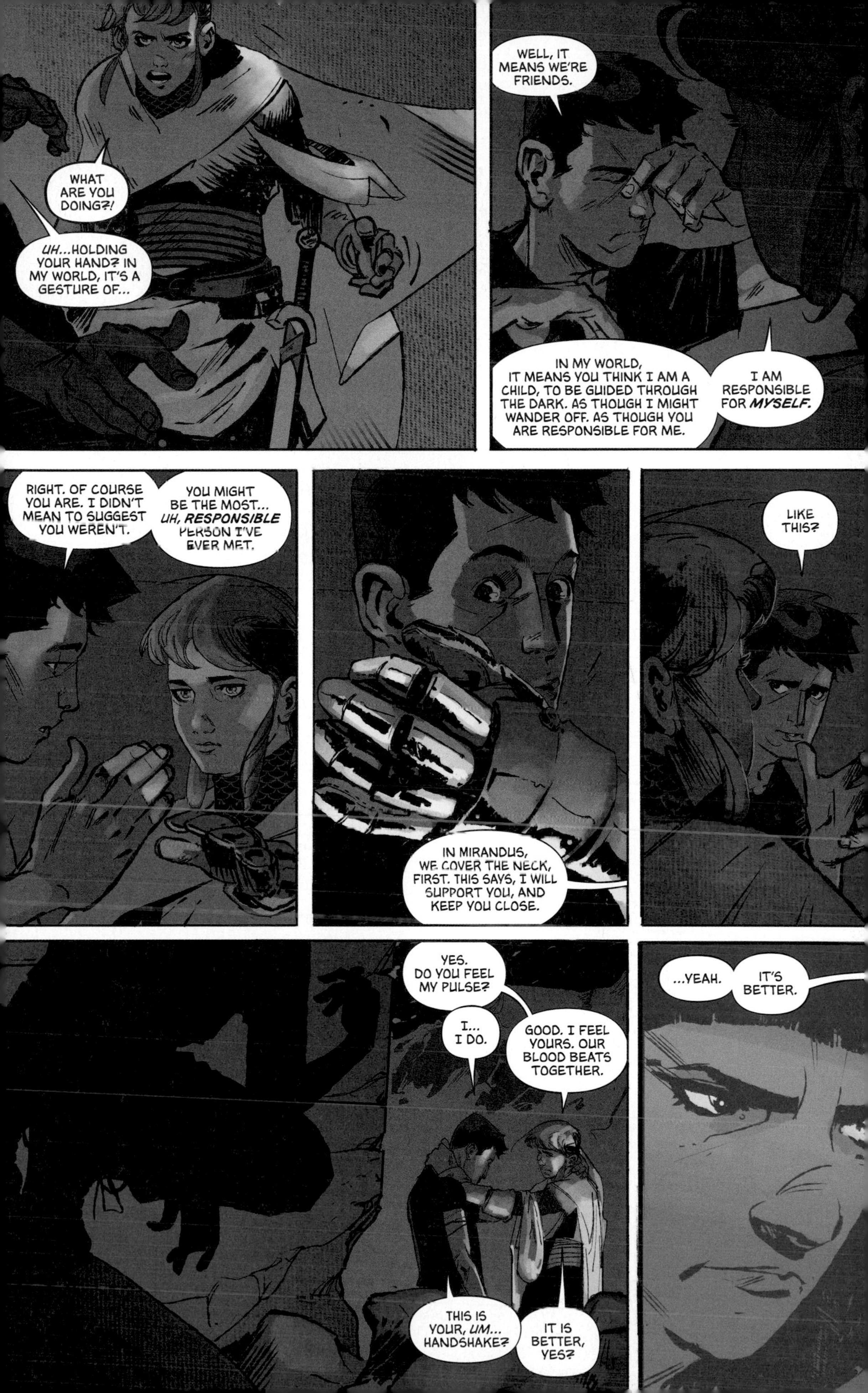
WHAT ARE YOU DOING?!
UH...HOLDING YOUR HAND? IN MY WORLD, IT'S A GESTURE OF...
WELL, IT MEANS WE'RE FRIENDS.
IN MY WORLD, IT MEANS YOU THINK I AM A CHILD, TO BE GUIDED THROUGH THE DARK. AS THOUGH I MIGHT WANDER OFF. AS THOUGH YOU ARE RESPONSIBLE FOR ME.
I AM RESPONSIBLE FOR MYSELF.
RIGHT. OF COURSE YOU ARE. I DIDN'T MEAN TO SUGGEST YOU WEREN'T.
YOU MIGHT BE THE MOST... UH, RESPONSIBLE PERSON I'VE EVER MET.
IN MIRANDUS, WE COVER THE NECK, FIRST. THIS SAYS, I WILL SUPPORT YOU, AND KEEP YOU CLOSE.
LIKE THIS?
YES. DO YOU FEEL MY PULSE?
I... I DO.
GOOD. I FEEL YOURS. OUR BLOOD BEATS TOGETHER.
THIS IS YOUR, UM... HANDSHAKE?
IT IS BETTER, YES?
...YEAH.
IT'S BETTER.

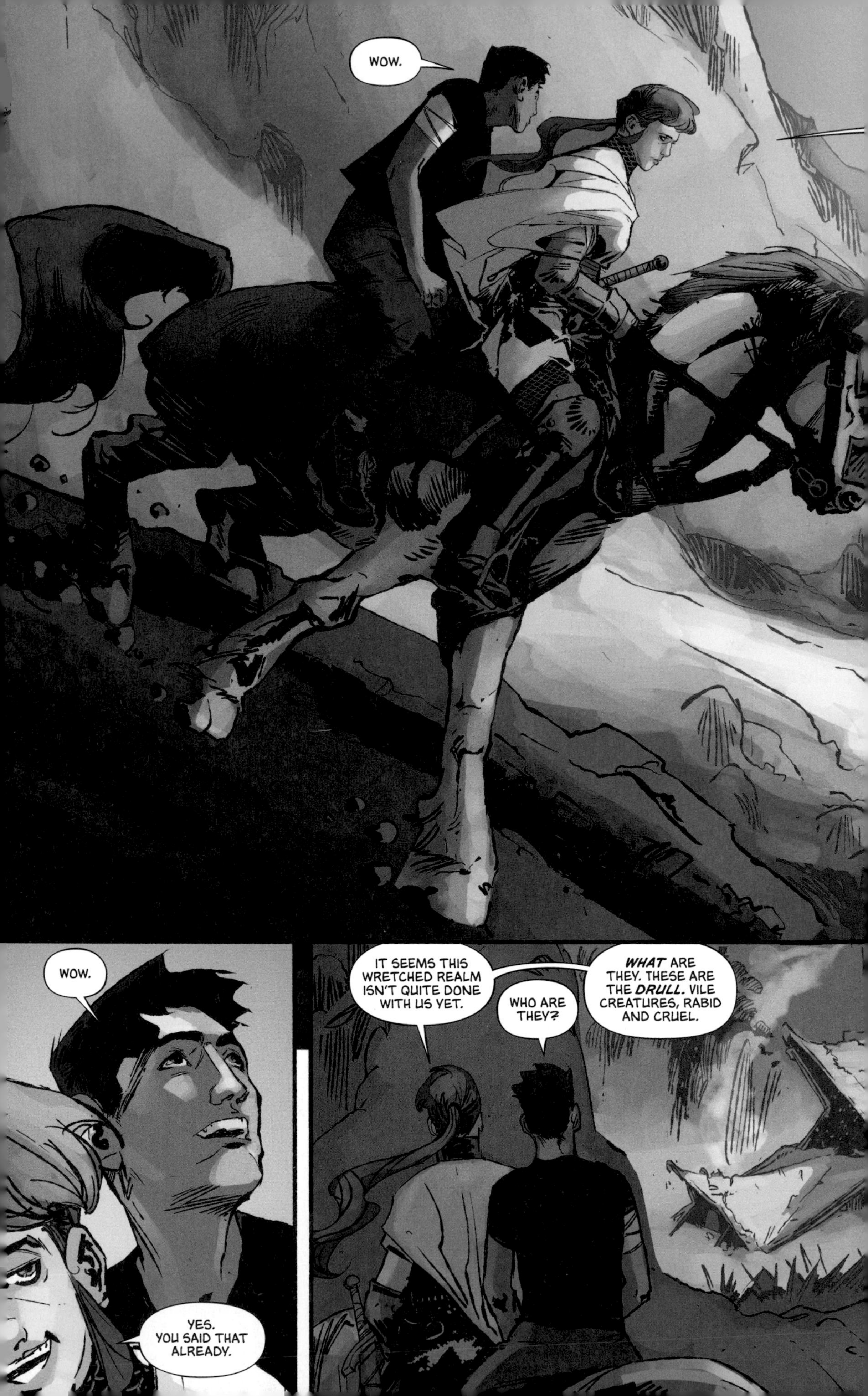
WOW.
WOW.
YES. YOU SAID THAT ALREADY.
IT SEEMS THIS WRETCHED REALM ISN'T QUITE DONE WITH US YET.
WHO ARE THEY?
WHAT ARE THEY. THESE ARE THE *DRULL.* VILE CREATURES, RABID AND CRUEL.

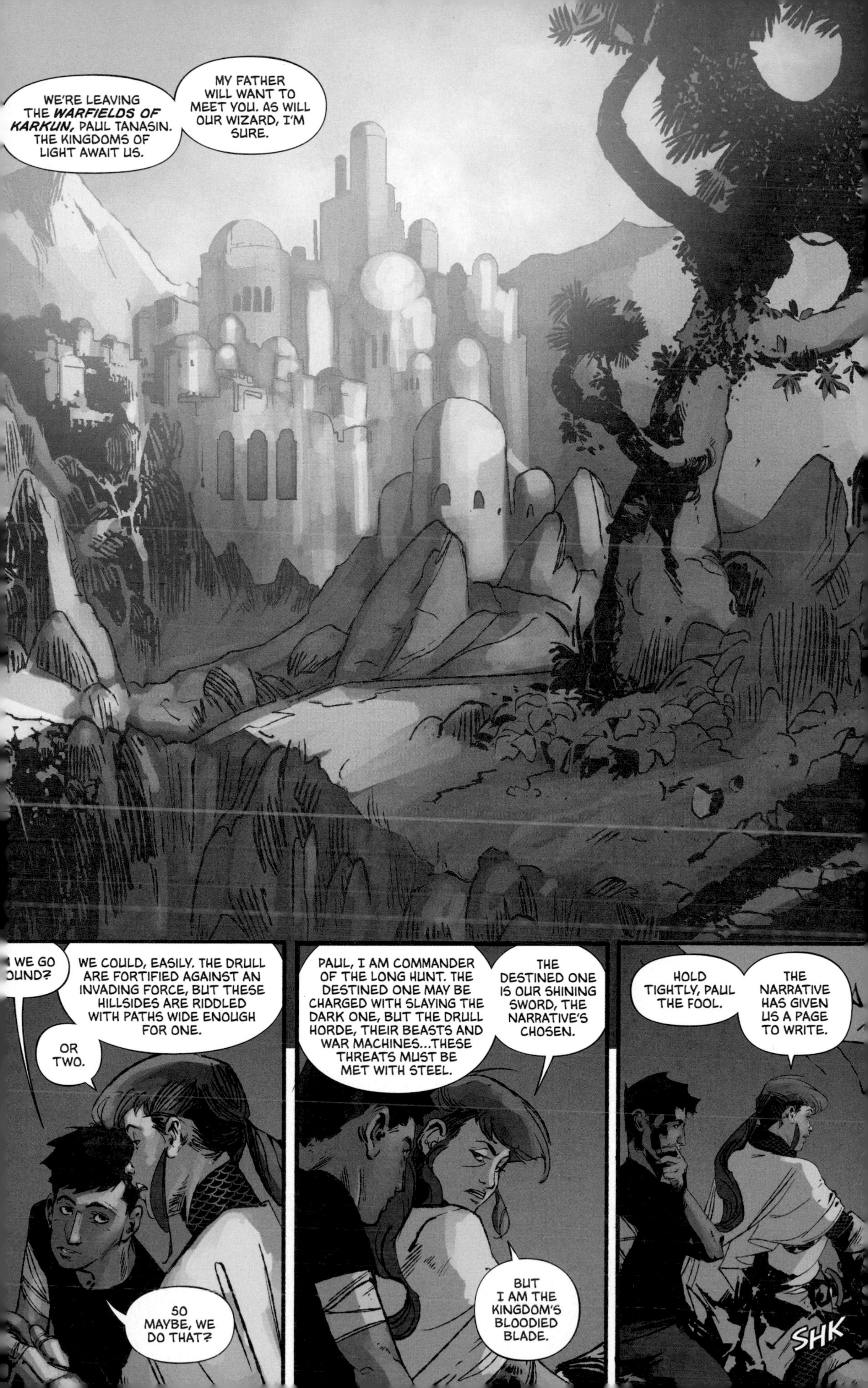
WE'RE LEAVING THE ***WARFIELDS OF KARKUN,*** PAUL TANASIN. THE KINGDOMS OF LIGHT AWAIT US.
MY FATHER WILL WANT TO MEET YOU. AS WILL OUR WIZARD, I'M SURE.
WE GO
WE COULD, EASILY. THE DRULL ARE FORTIFIED AGAINST AN INVADING FORCE, BUT THESE HILLSIDES ARE RIDDLED WITH PATHS WIDE ENOUGH FOR ONE.
OR TWO.
SO MAYBE, WE DO THAT?
PAUL, I AM COMMANDER OF THE LONG HUNT. THE DESTINED ONE MAY BE CHARGED WITH SLAYING THE DARK ONE, BUT THE DRULL HORDE, THEIR BEASTS AND WAR MACHINES...THESE THREATS MUST BE MET WITH STEEL.
THE DESTINED ONE IS OUR SHINING SWORD, THE NARRATIVE'S CHOSEN.
BUT I AM THE KINGDOM'S BLOODIED BLADE.
HOLD TIGHTLY, PAUL THE FOOL.
THE NARRATIVE HAS GIVEN US A PAGE TO WRITE.
SHK

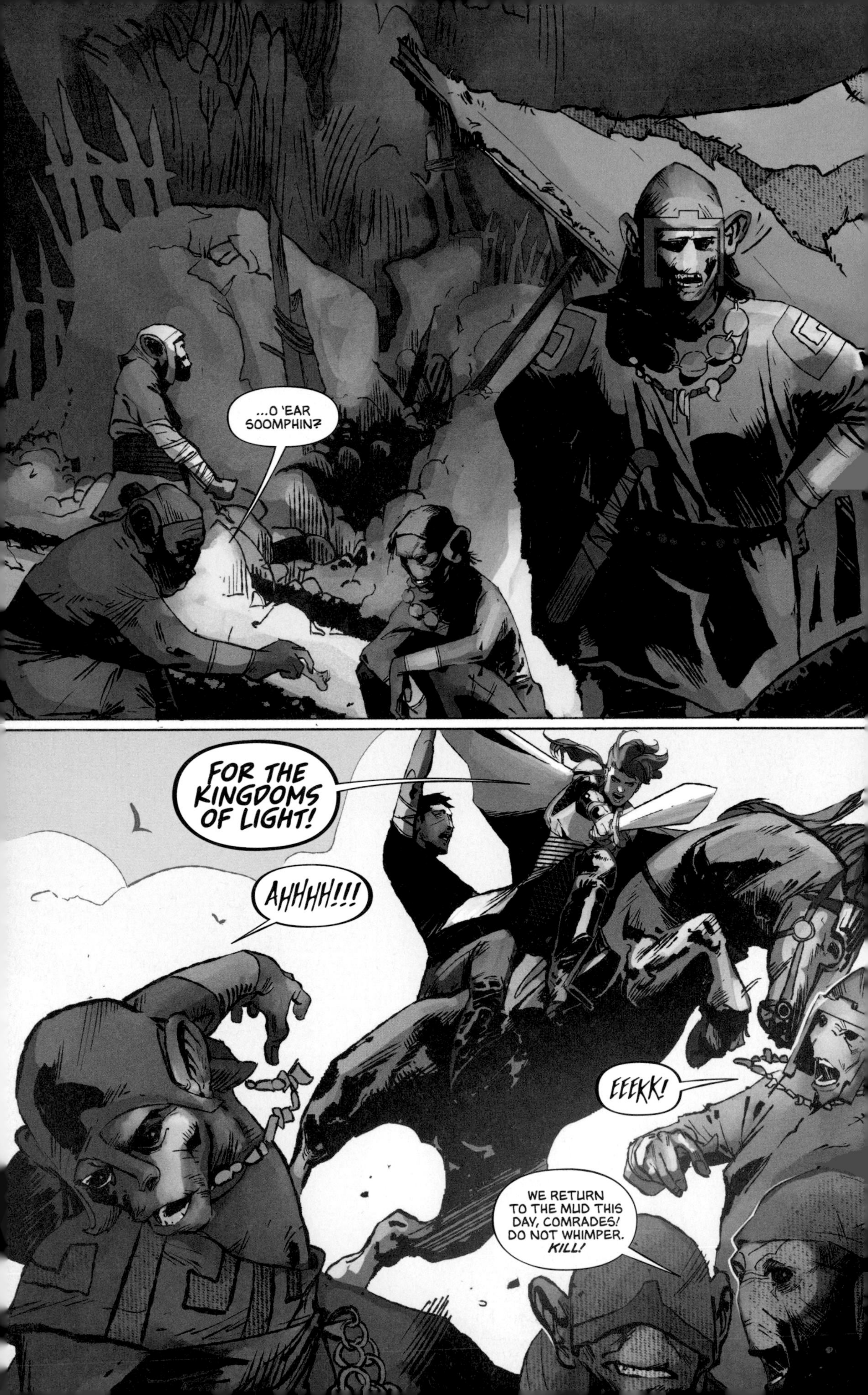
...O 'EAR SOOMPHIN?
FOR THE KINGDOMS OF LIGHT!
AHHHH!!!
EEEKK!
WE RETURN TO THE MUD THIS DAY, COMRADES! DO NOT WHIMPER. *KILL!*

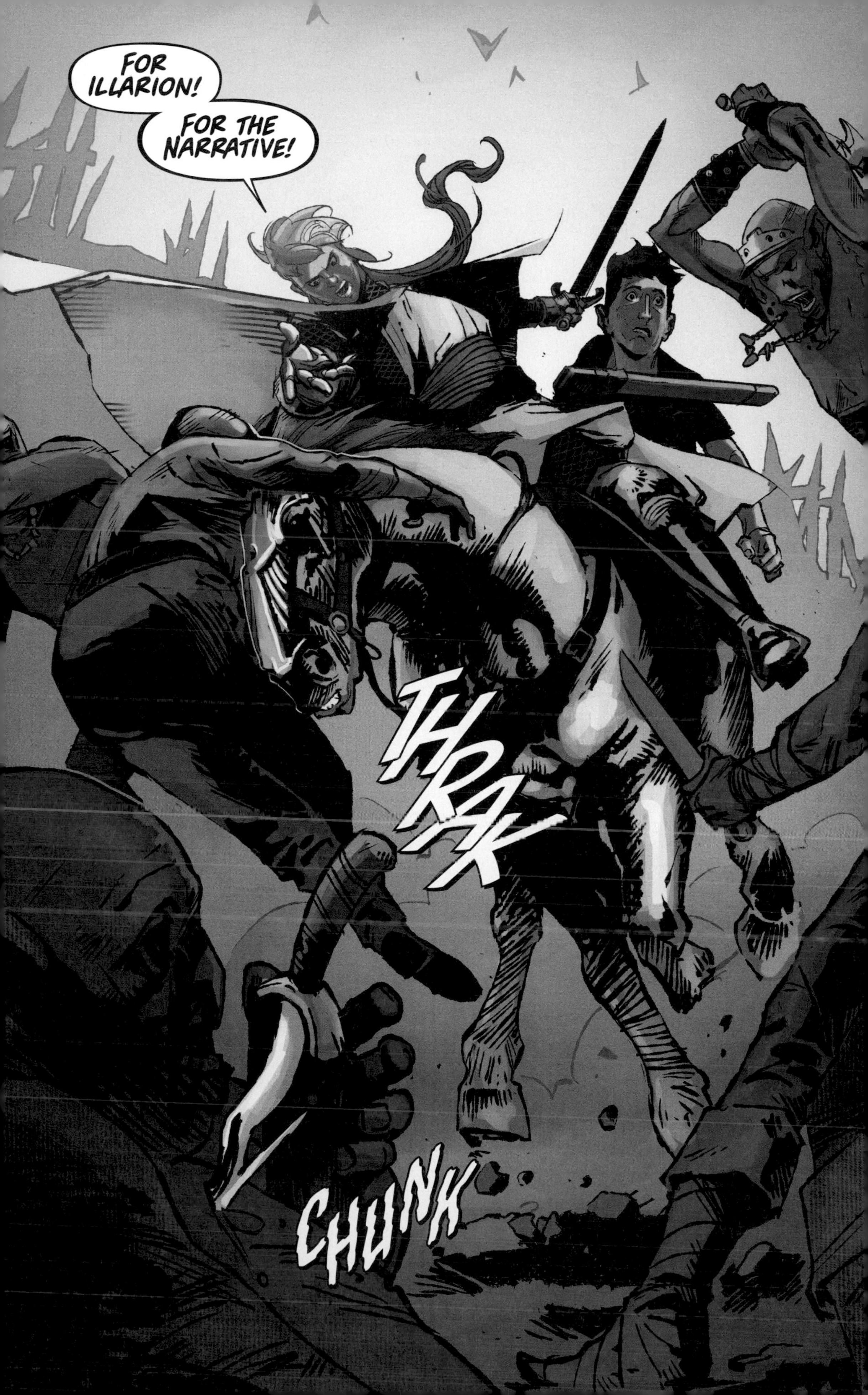
FOR ILLARION!
FOR THE NARRATIVE!
THRAK
CHUNK

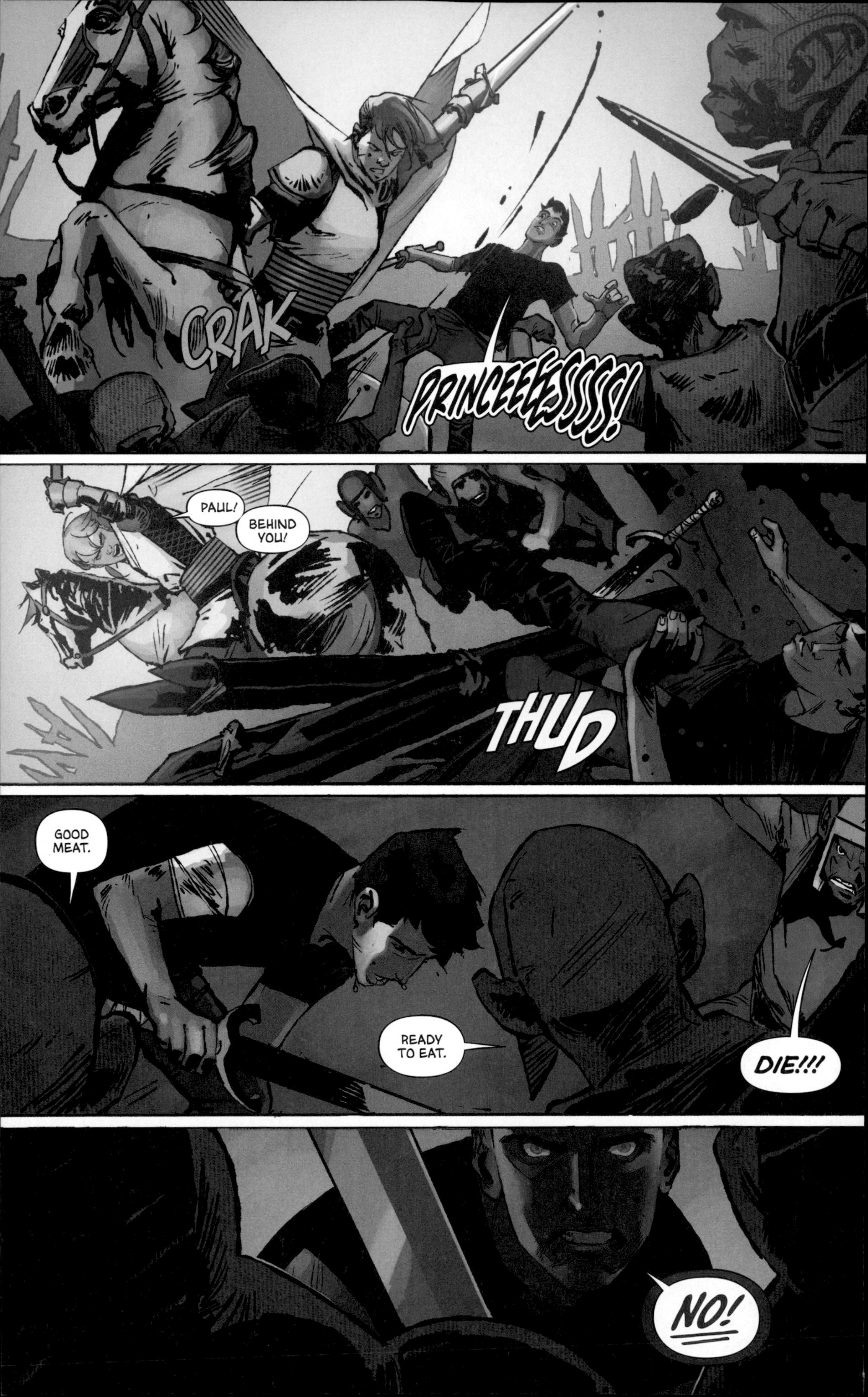
CRAK
PRINCEEESSSSS!
PAUL!
BEHIND YOU!
THUD
GOOD MEAT.
READY TO EAT.
DIE!!!
NO!

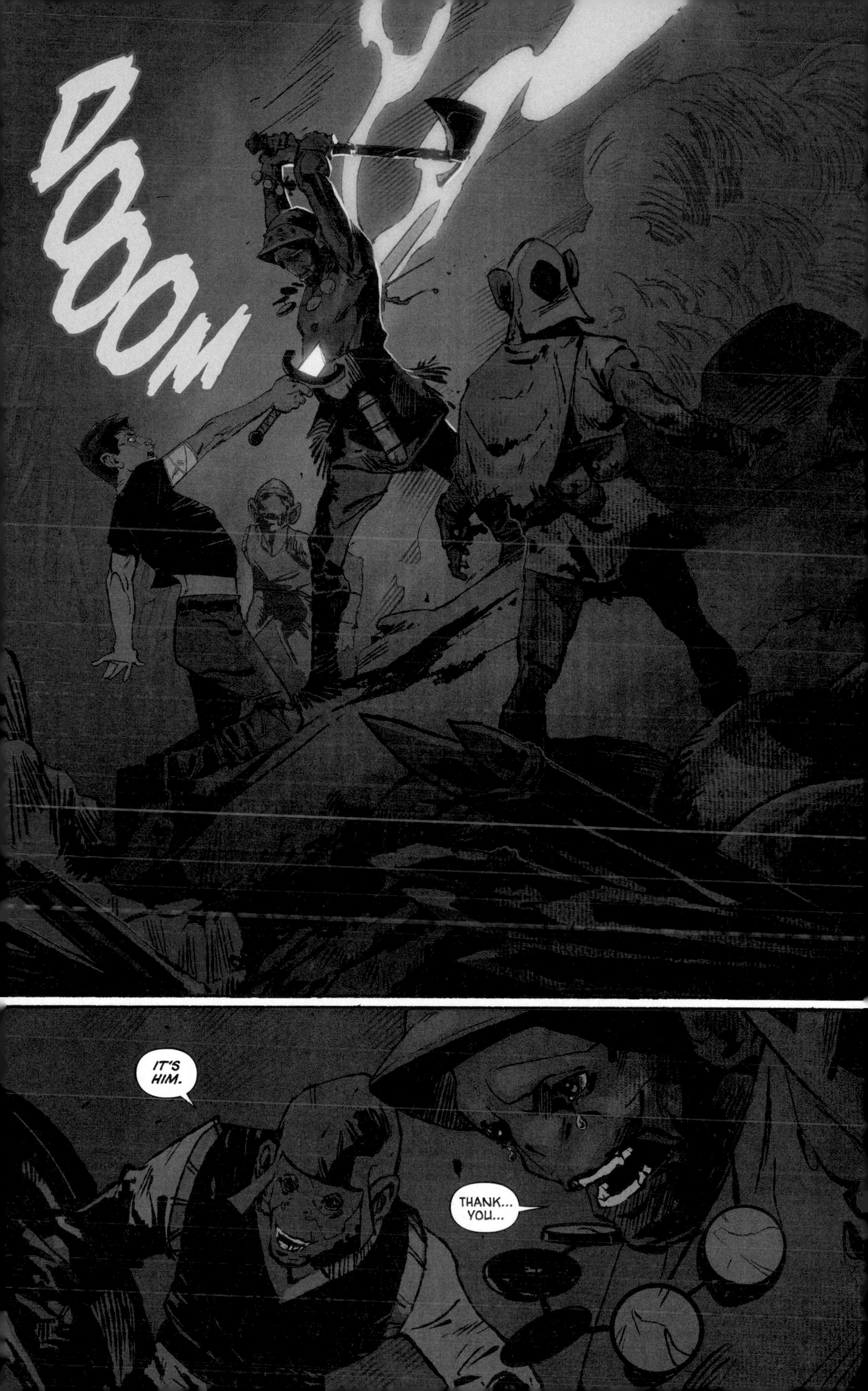
DOOOM
IT'S HIM.
THANK... YOU...

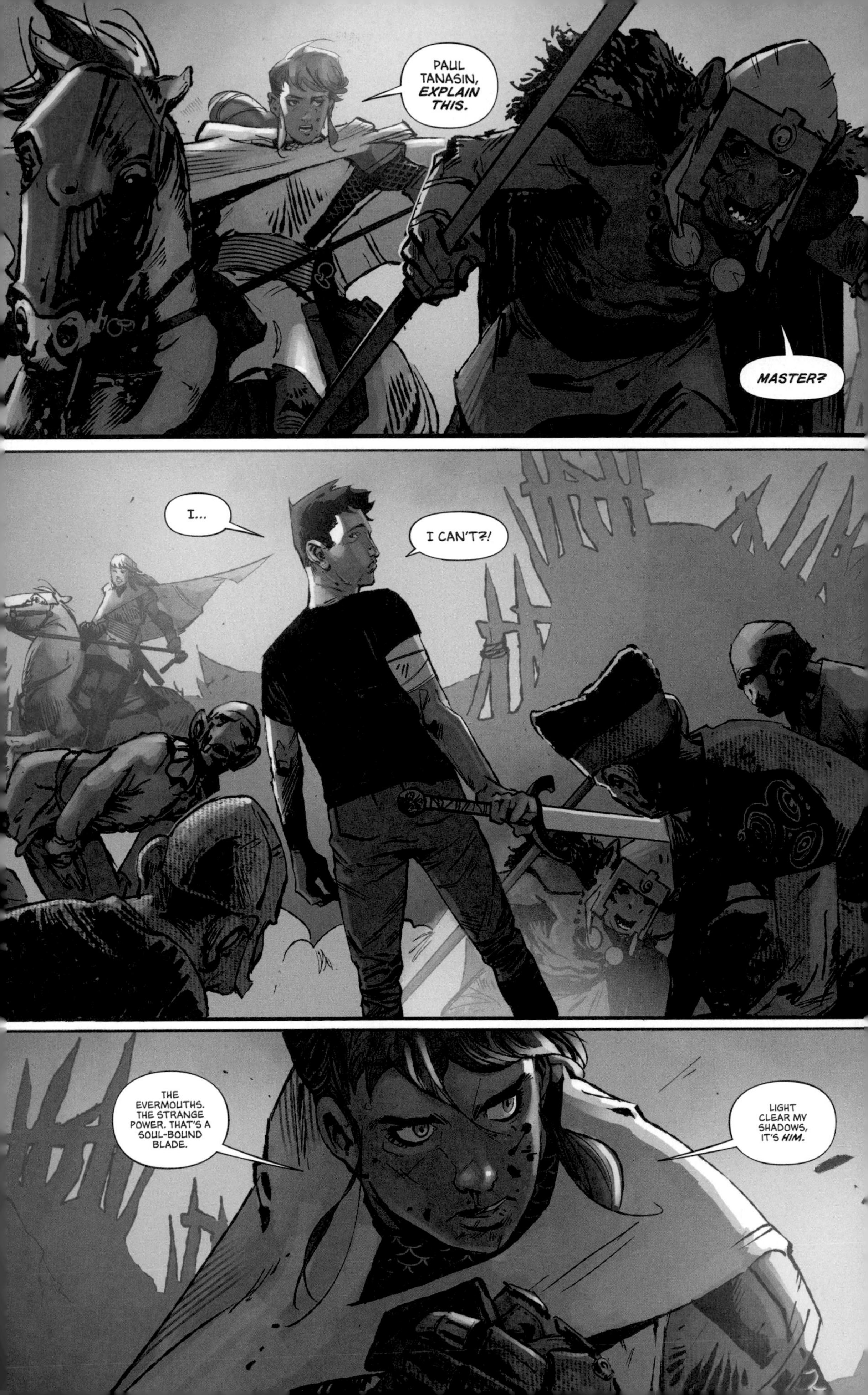
PAUL TANASIN, EXPLAIN THIS.
MASTER?
I...
I CAN'T?!
THE EVERMOUTHS. THE STRANGE POWER. THAT'S A SOUL-BOUND BLADE.
LIGHT CLEAR MY SHADOWS, IT'S HIM.

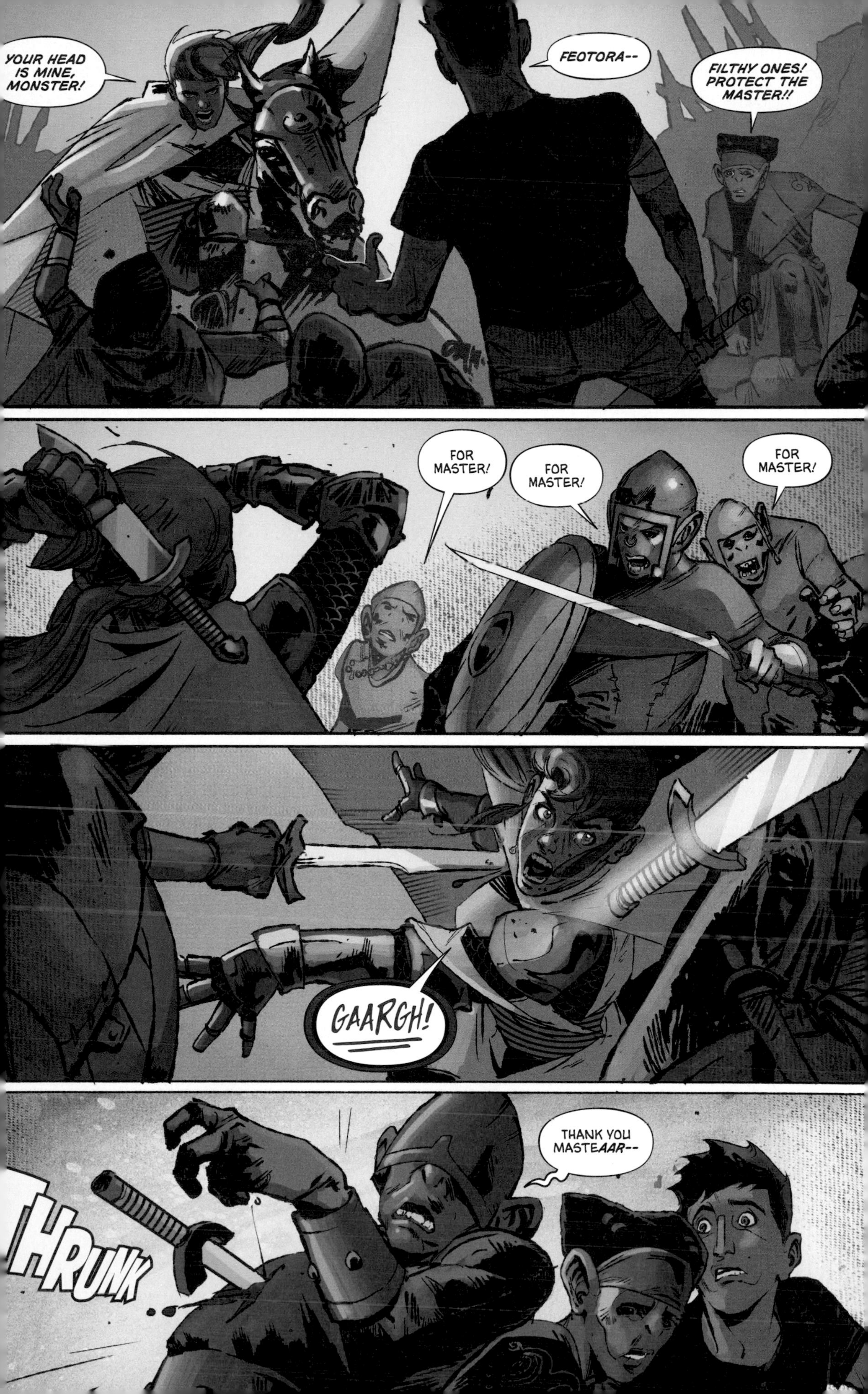
YOUR HEAD IS MINE, MONSTER!
FEOTORA--
FILTHY ONES! PROTECT THE MASTER!!
FOR MASTER!
FOR MASTER!
FOR MASTER!
GAARGH!
THRUNK
THANK YOU MASTEAAR--

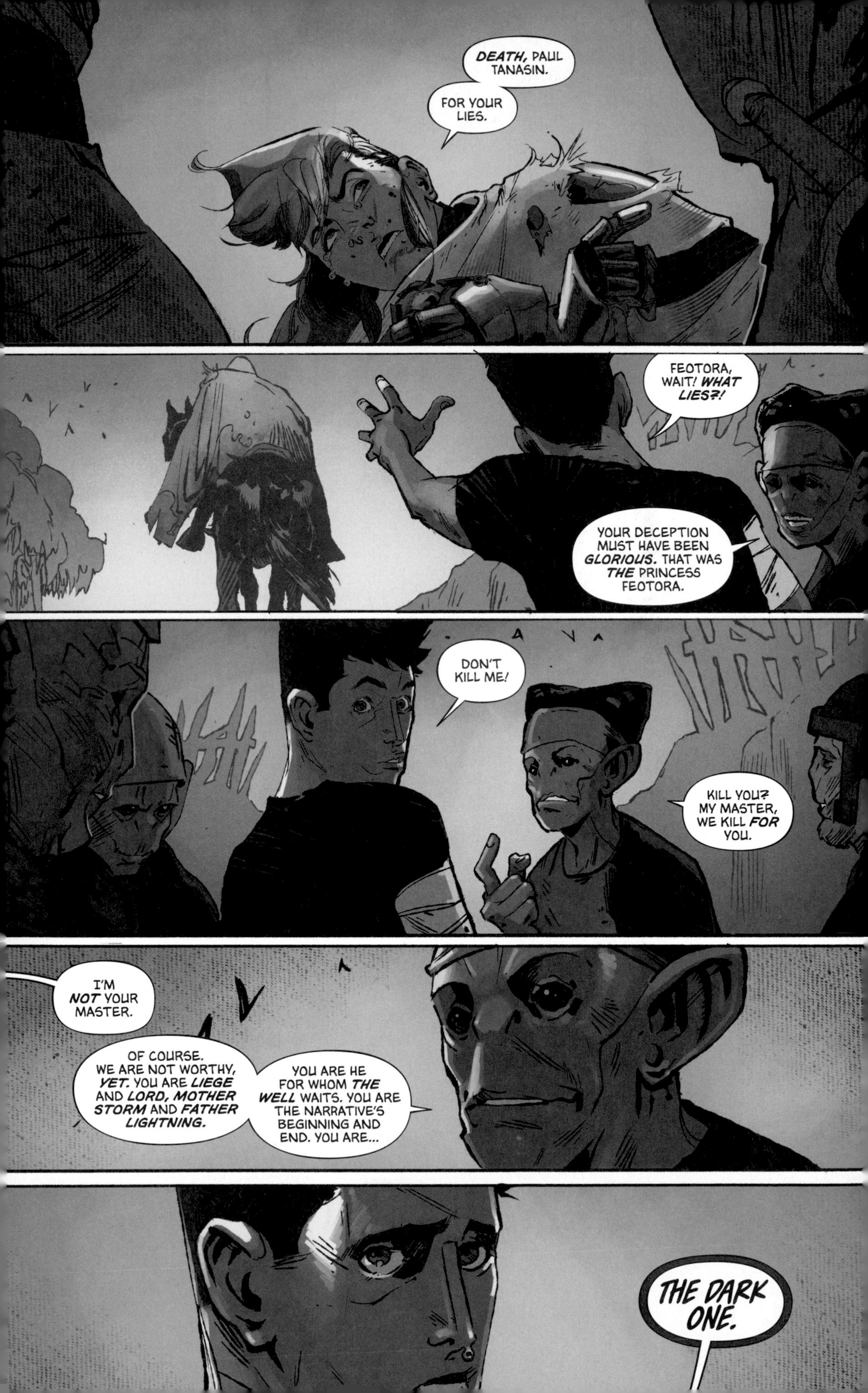
DEATH, PAUL TANASIN.
FOR YOUR LIES.
FEOTORA, WAIT! WHAT LIES?!
YOUR DECEPTION MUST HAVE BEEN GLORIOUS. THAT WAS THE PRINCESS FEOTORA.
DON'T KILL ME!
KILL YOU? MY MASTER, WE KILL FOR YOU.
I'M NOT YOUR MASTER.
OF COURSE. WE ARE NOT WORTHY, YET. YOU ARE LIEGE AND LORD, MOTHER STORM AND FATHER LIGHTNING.
YOU ARE HE FOR WHOM THE WELL WAITS. YOU ARE THE NARRATIVE'S BEGINNING AND END. YOU ARE...
THE DARK ONE.

INTERMISSION

THE GARDEN OF STONE

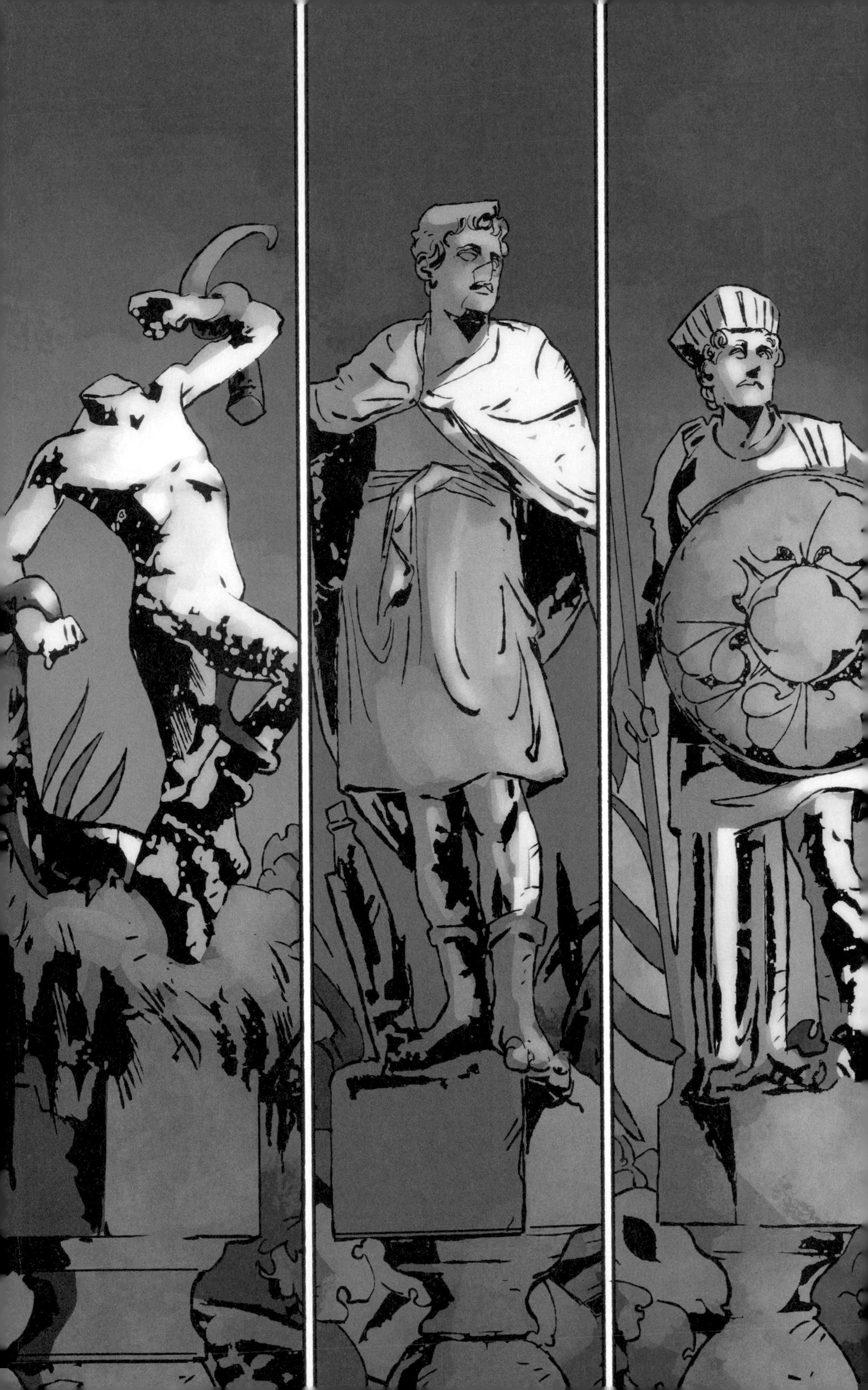

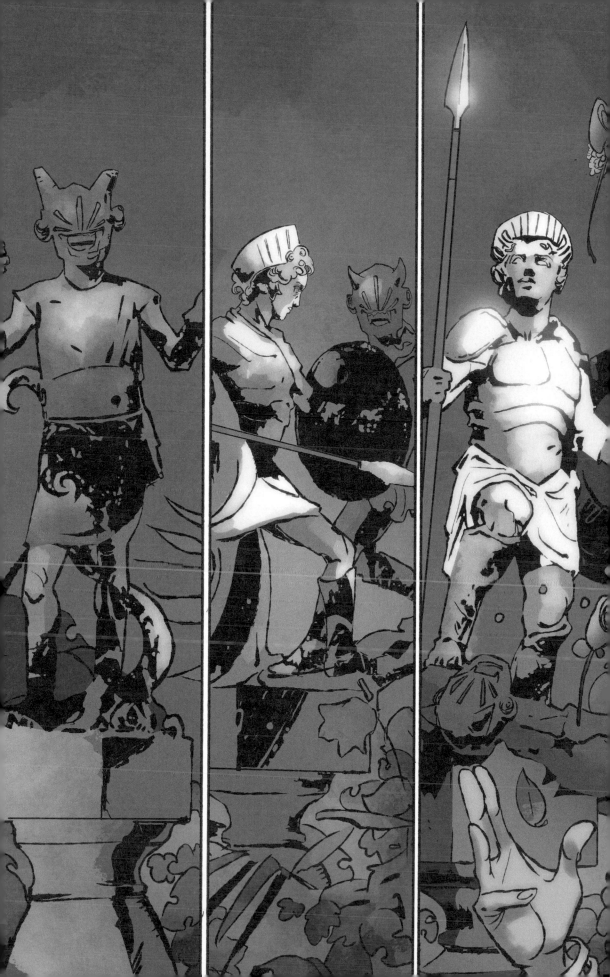

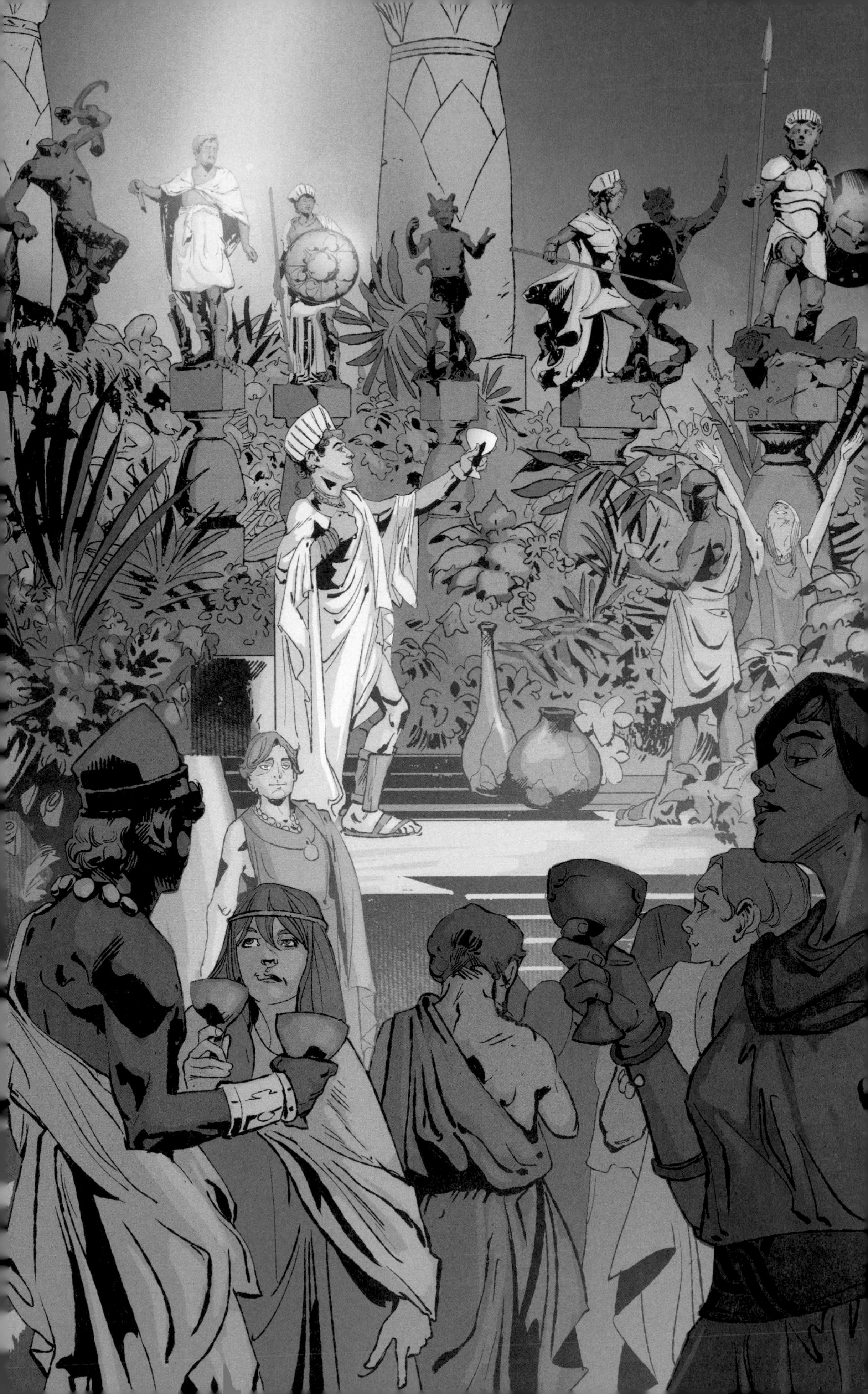

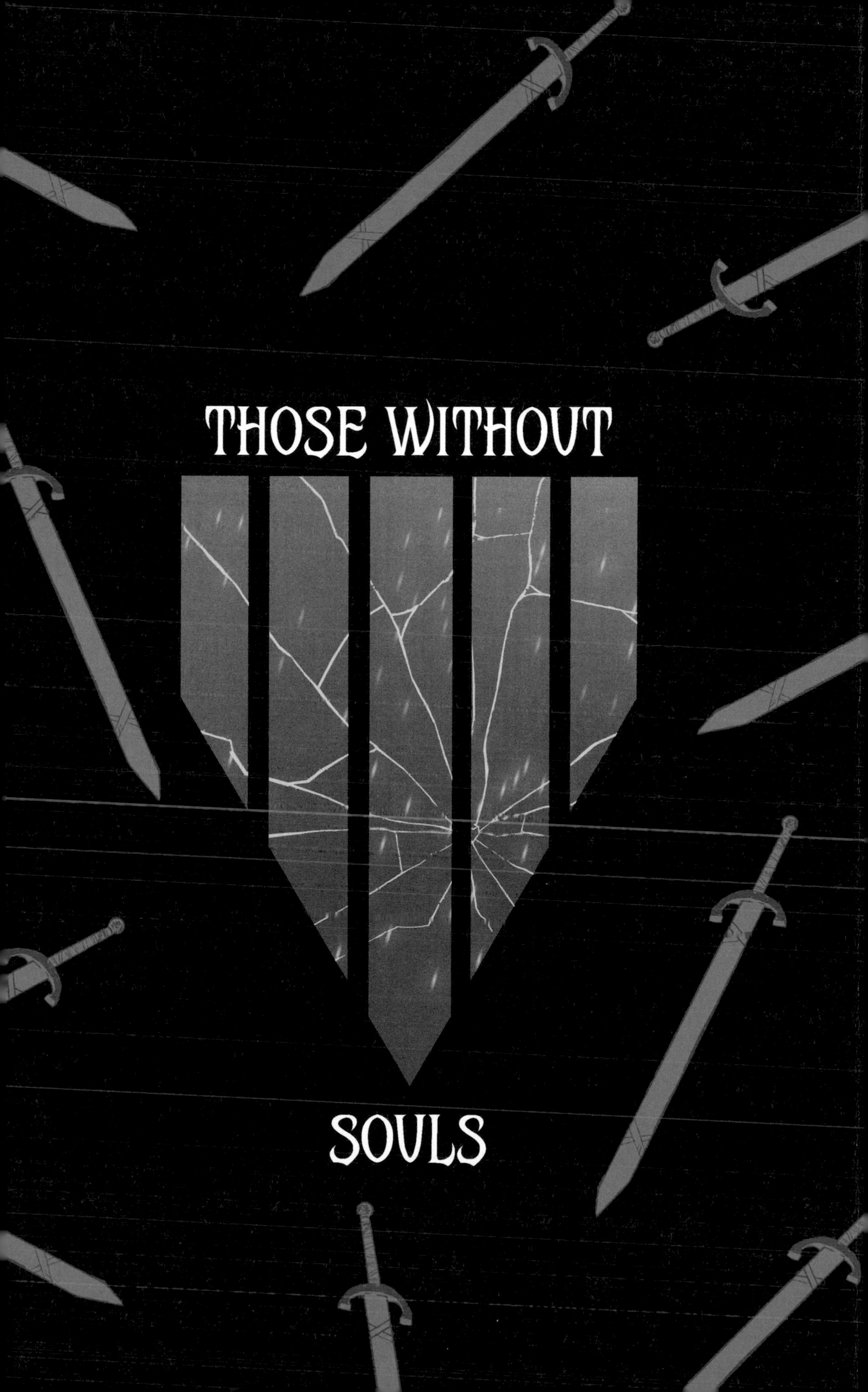
THOSE WITHOUT
SOULS

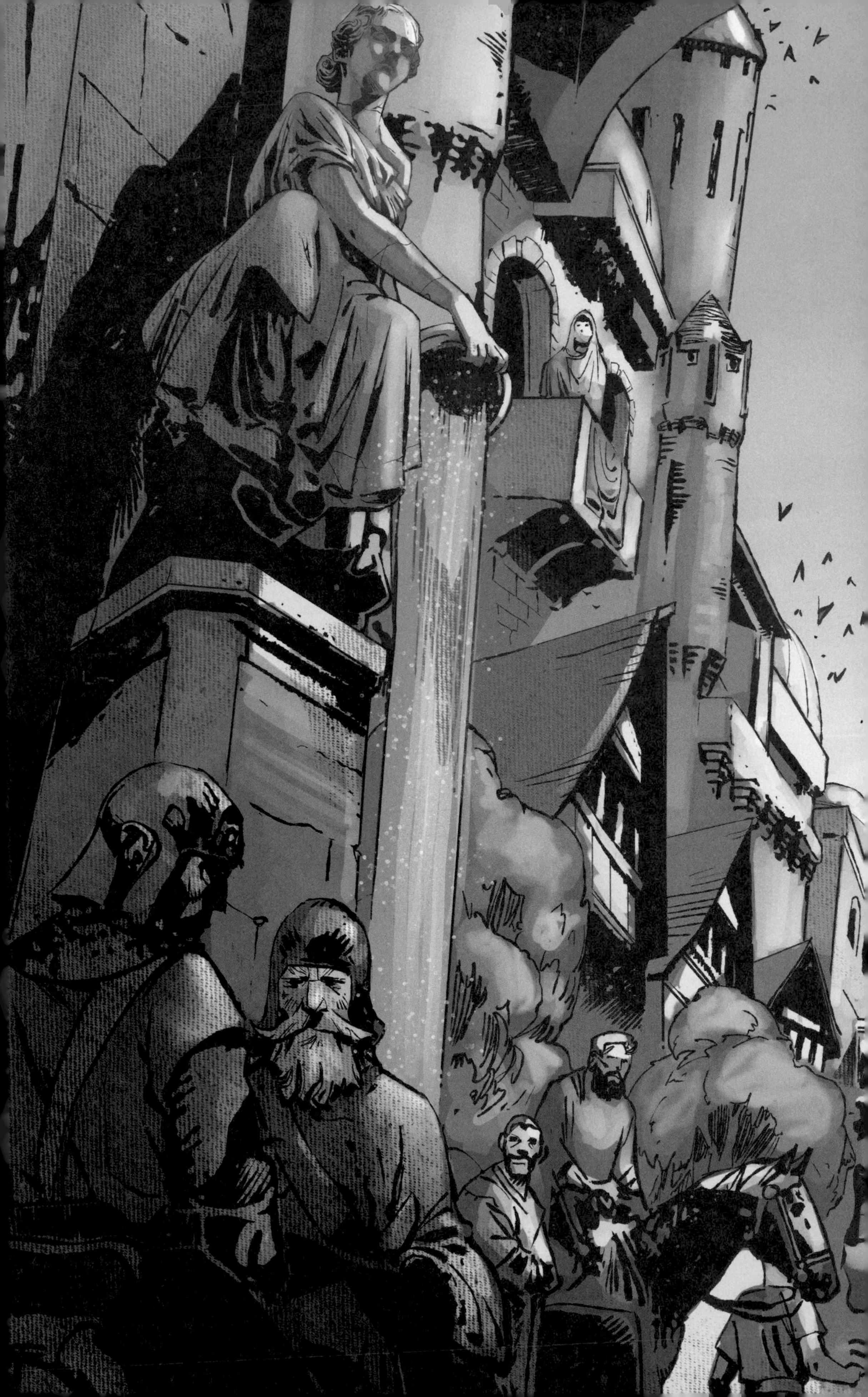

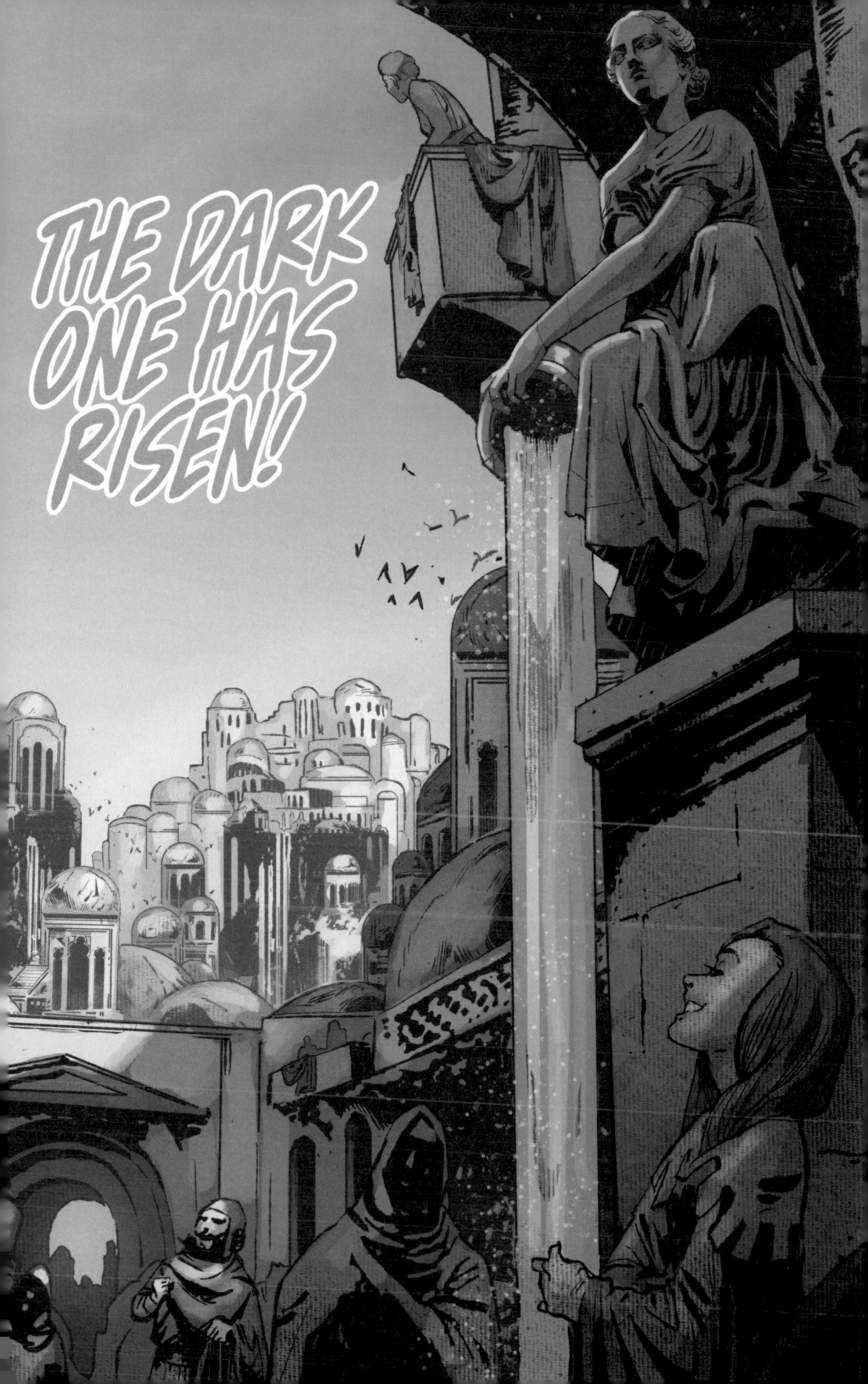
THE DARK ONE HAS RISEN!

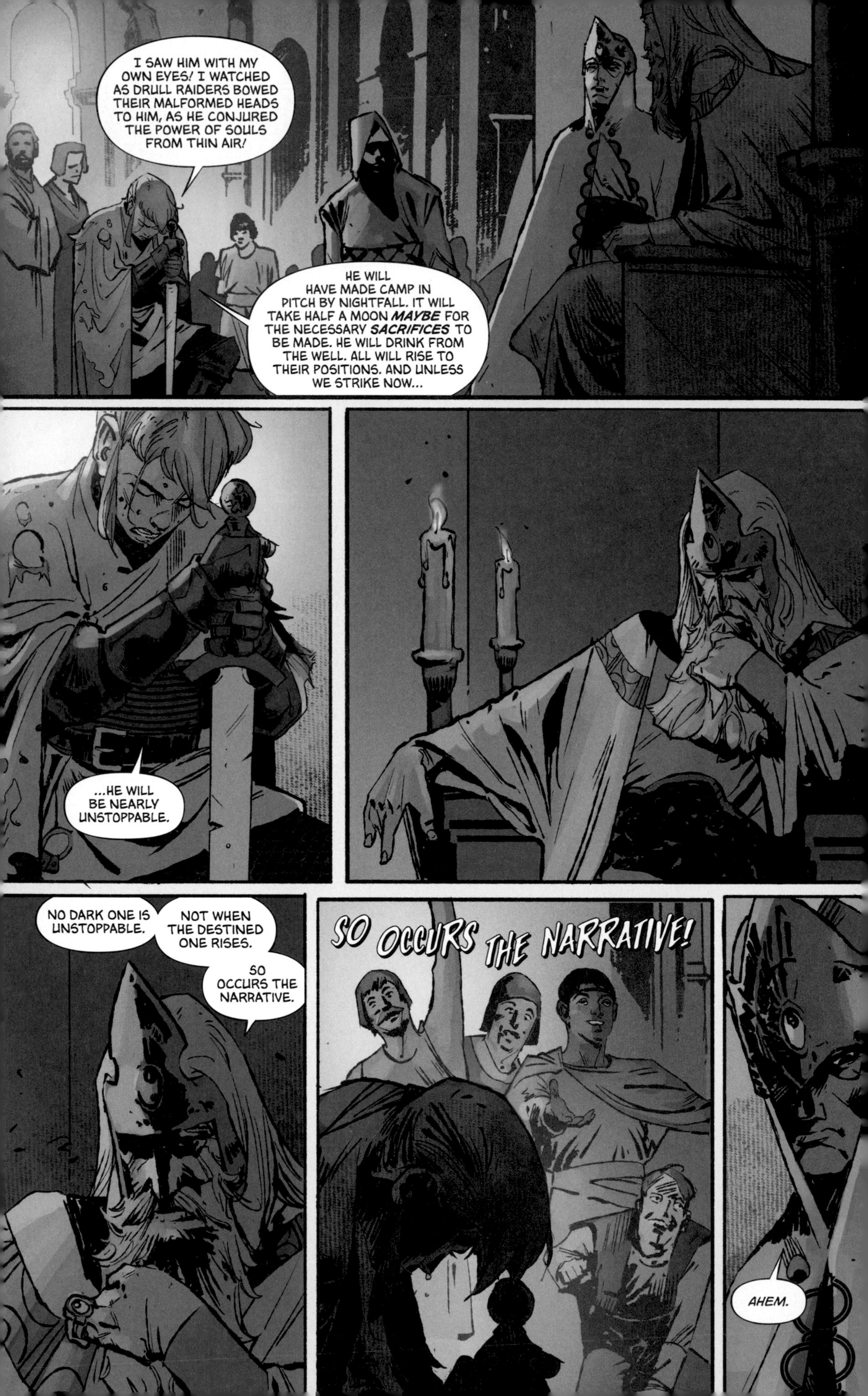
I SAW HIM WITH MY OWN EYES! I WATCHED AS DRULL RAIDERS BOWED THEIR MALFORMED HEADS TO HIM, AS HE CONJURED THE POWER OF SOULS FROM THIN AIR!
HE WILL HAVE MADE CAMP IN PITCH BY NIGHTFALL. IT WILL TAKE HALF A MOON *MAYBE* FOR THE NECESSARY *SACRIFICES* TO BE MADE. HE WILL DRINK FROM THE WELL. ALL WILL RISE TO THEIR POSITIONS. AND UNLESS WE STRIKE NOW...
...HE WILL BE NEARLY UNSTOPPABLE.
NO DARK ONE IS UNSTOPPABLE.
NOT WHEN THE DESTINED ONE RISES.
SO OCCURS THE NARRATIVE.
SO OCCURS THE NARRATIVE!
AHEM.

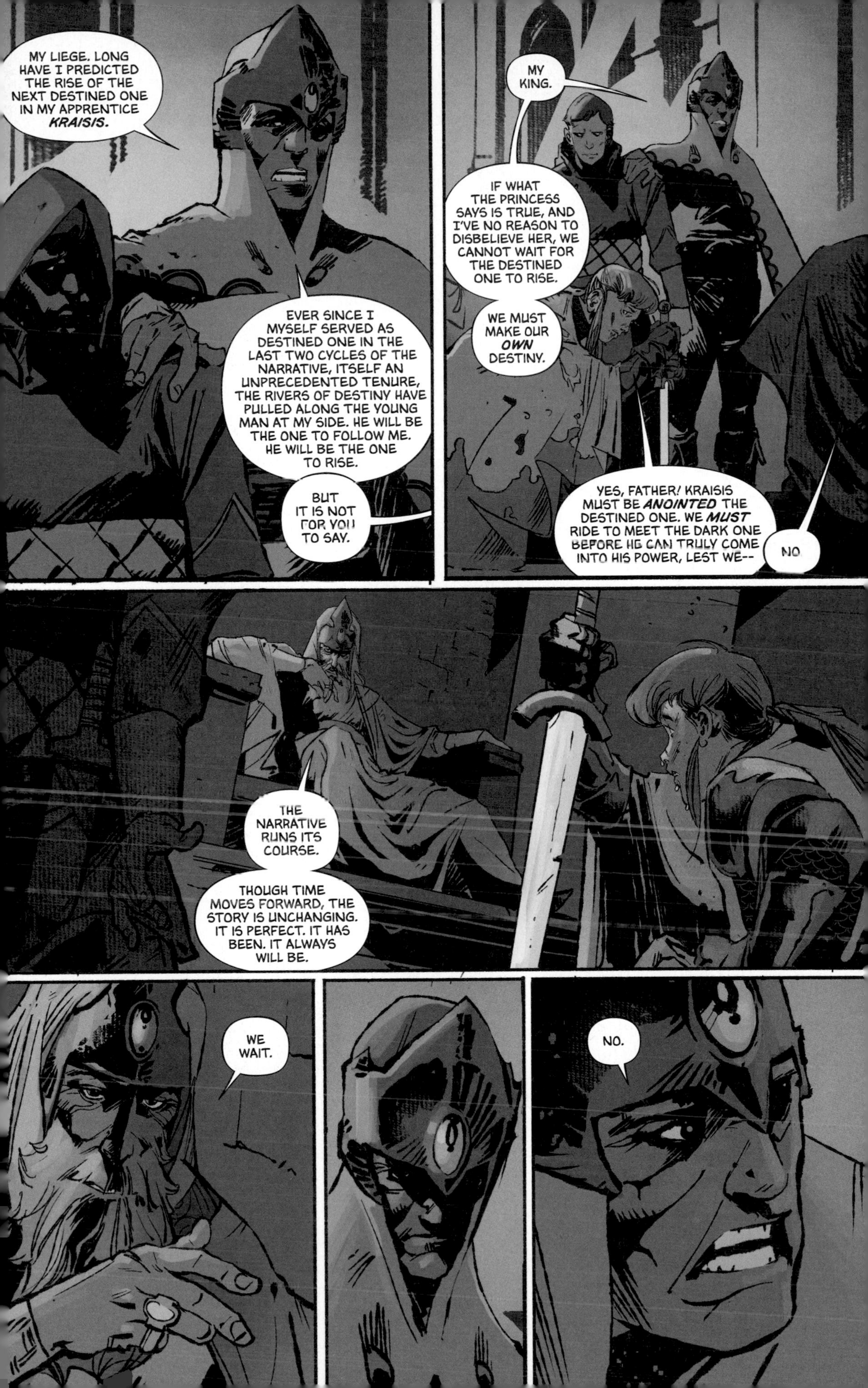
MY LIEGE. LONG HAVE I PREDICTED THE RISE OF THE NEXT DESTINED ONE IN MY APPRENTICE KRAISIS.
EVER SINCE I MYSELF SERVED AS DESTINED ONE IN THE LAST TWO CYCLES OF THE NARRATIVE, ITSELF AN UNPRECEDENTED TENURE, THE RIVERS OF DESTINY HAVE PULLED ALONG THE YOUNG MAN AT MY SIDE. HE WILL BE THE ONE TO FOLLOW ME. HE WILL BE THE ONE TO RISE.
BUT IT IS NOT FOR YOU TO SAY.
MY KING.
IF WHAT THE PRINCESS SAYS IS TRUE, AND I'VE NO REASON TO DISBELIEVE HER, WE CANNOT WAIT FOR THE DESTINED ONE TO RISE.
WE MUST MAKE OUR OWN DESTINY.
YES, FATHER! KRAISIS MUST BE ANOINTED THE DESTINED ONE. WE MUST RIDE TO MEET THE DARK ONE BEFORE HE CAN TRULY COME INTO HIS POWER, LEST WE--
NO.
THE NARRATIVE RUNS ITS COURSE.
THOUGH TIME MOVES FORWARD, THE STORY IS UNCHANGING. IT IS PERFECT. IT HAS BEEN. IT ALWAYS WILL BE.
WE WAIT.
NO.

THE NARRATIVE LIVES, IT IS TRUE...

...BUT IT DOES NOT OPERATE ON OUR TIMELINE OR BY OUR WHIMS. AND THAT WHICH *BREAKS* IT CAN UNDO EVERYTHING WE HOLD DEAR.

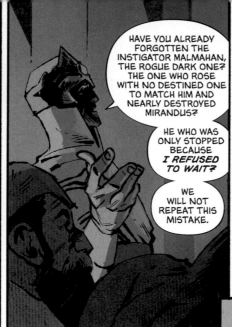

HAVE YOU ALREADY FORGOTTEN THE INSTIGATOR MALMAHAN, THE ROGUE DARK ONE? THE ONE WHO ROSE WITH NO DESTINED ONE TO MATCH HIM AND NEARLY DESTROYED MIRANDUS?

HE WHO WAS ONLY STOPPED BECAUSE *I REFUSED TO WAIT?*

WE WILL NOT REPEAT THIS MISTAKE.

SAYS *YOU.*

SAYS THE *NARRATIVE.* AND, BECAUSE I AM ITS MOST *TRUSTED* SERVANT, THE ONLY DESTINED ONE IN HISTORY TO DEFEAT *TWO* DARK ONES...

YES, GOSOVIC.

SAYS *ME.*

NO.

THE DARK ONE RISES. AND THE DESTINED ONE RISES TO CHALLENGE HIM.

FATHER!

YOU ARE DISMISSED...

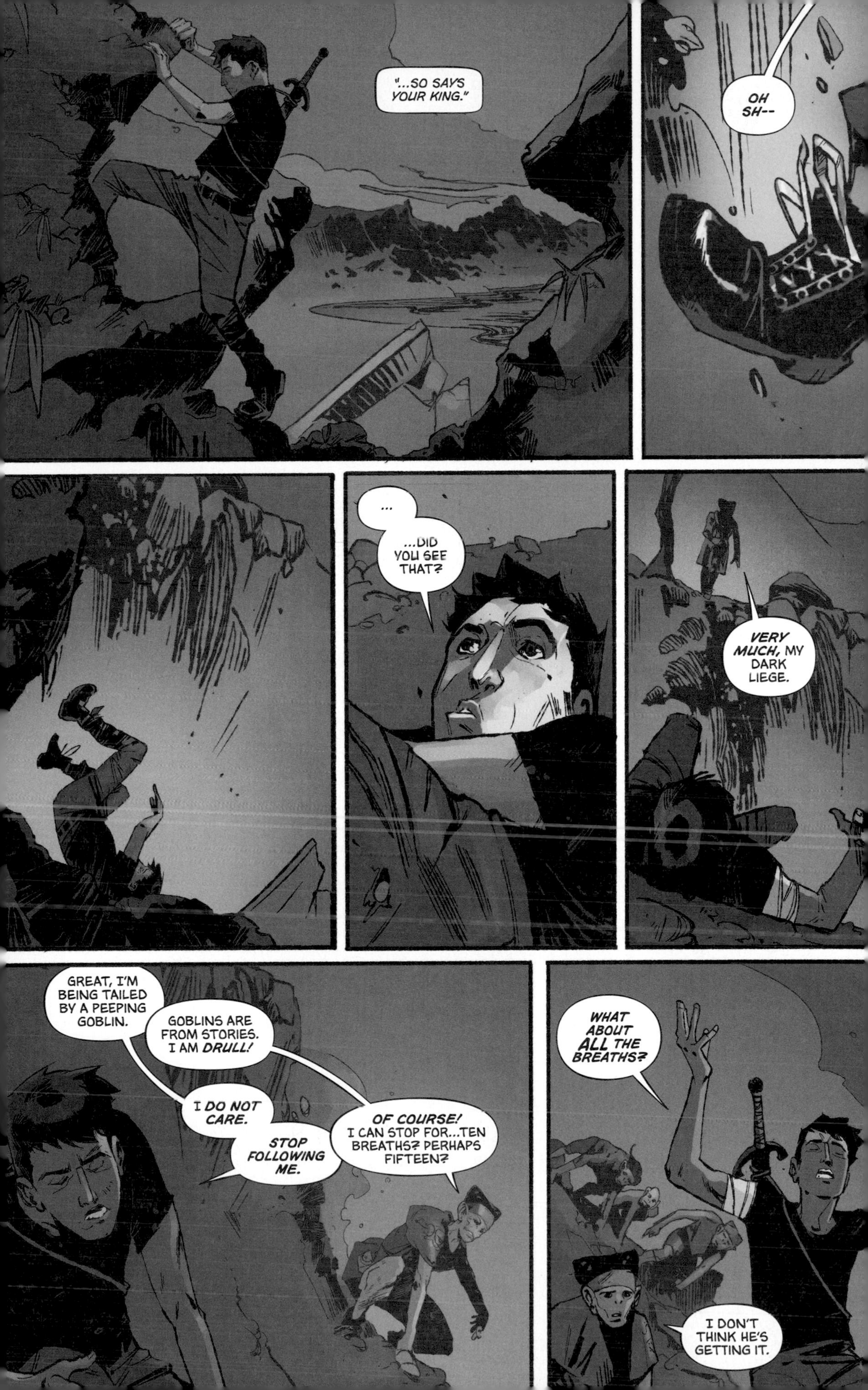

"...SO SAYS YOUR KING."
OH SH--
...
...DID YOU SEE THAT?
VERY MUCH, MY DARK LIEGE.
GREAT, I'M BEING TAILED BY A PEEPING GOBLIN.
GOBLINS ARE FROM STORIES. I AM DRULL!
I DO NOT CARE.
STOP FOLLOWING ME.
OF COURSE! I CAN STOP FOR...TEN BREATHS? PERHAPS FIFTEEN?
WHAT ABOUT ALL THE BREATHS?
I DON'T THINK HE'S GETTING IT.

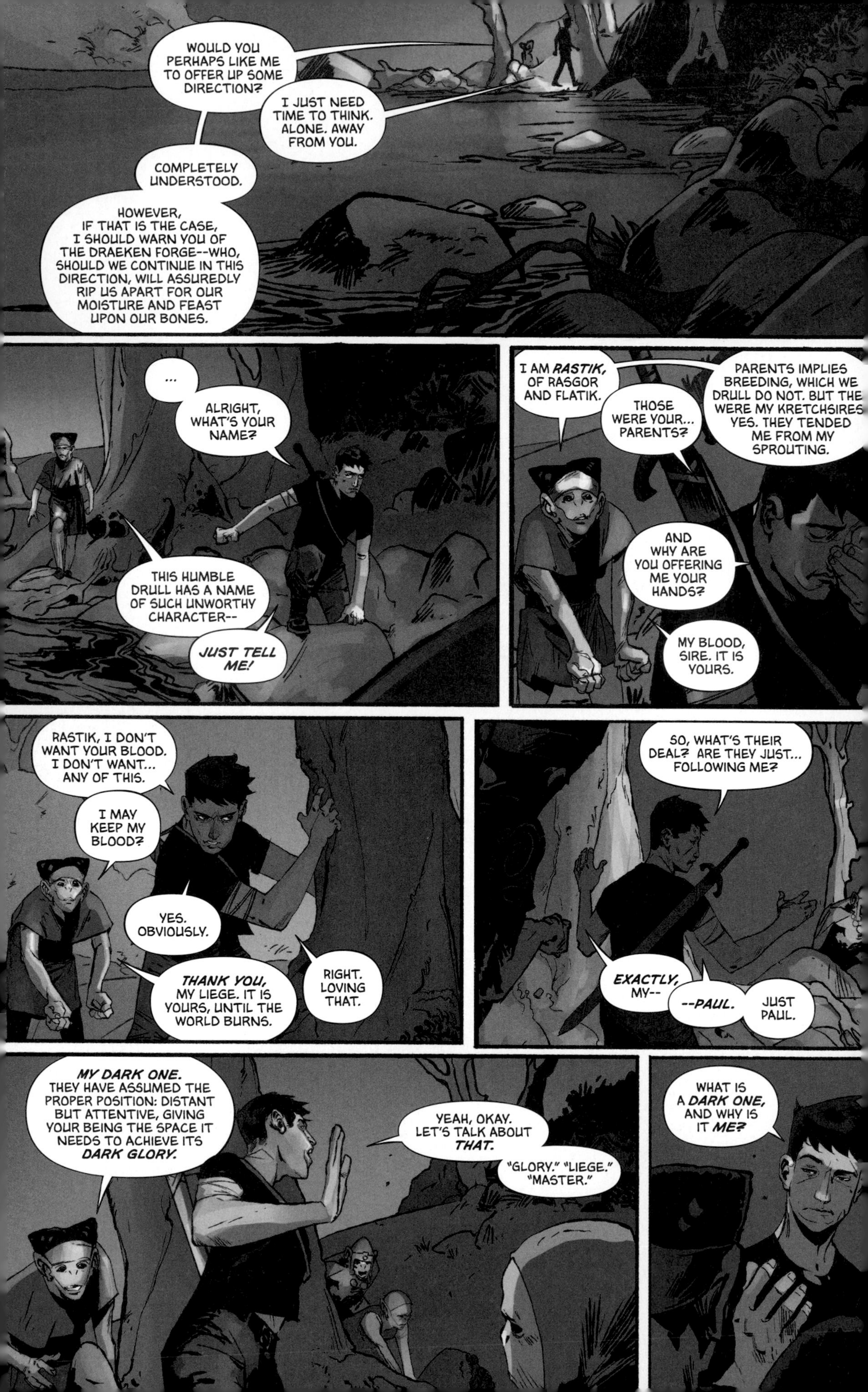
WOULD YOU PERHAPS LIKE ME TO OFFER UP SOME DIRECTION?
I JUST NEED TIME TO THINK. ALONE. AWAY FROM YOU.
COMPLETELY UNDERSTOOD.
HOWEVER, IF THAT IS THE CASE, I SHOULD WARN YOU OF THE DRAEKEN FORGE--WHO, SHOULD WE CONTINUE IN THIS DIRECTION, WILL ASSUREDLY RIP US APART FOR OUR MOISTURE AND FEAST UPON OUR BONES.
...
ALRIGHT, WHAT'S YOUR NAME?
THIS HUMBLE DRULL HAS A NAME OF SUCH UNWORTHY CHARACTER--
JUST TELL ME!
I AM RASTIK, OF RASGOR AND FLATIK.
THOSE WERE YOUR... PARENTS?
PARENTS IMPLIES BREEDING, WHICH WE DRULL DO NOT. BUT THE WERE MY KRETCHSIRES YES. THEY TENDED ME FROM MY SPROUTING.
AND WHY ARE YOU OFFERING ME YOUR HANDS?
MY BLOOD, SIRE. IT IS YOURS.
RASTIK, I DON'T WANT YOUR BLOOD. I DON'T WANT... ANY OF THIS.
I MAY KEEP MY BLOOD?
YES. OBVIOUSLY.
THANK YOU, MY LIEGE. IT IS YOURS, UNTIL THE WORLD BURNS.
RIGHT. LOVING THAT.
SO, WHAT'S THEIR DEAL? ARE THEY JUST... FOLLOWING ME?
EXACTLY, MY--
--PAUL.
JUST PAUL.
MY DARK ONE. THEY HAVE ASSUMED THE PROPER POSITION: DISTANT BUT ATTENTIVE, GIVING YOUR BEING THE SPACE IT NEEDS TO ACHIEVE ITS DARK GLORY.
YEAH, OKAY. LET'S TALK ABOUT THAT.
"GLORY." "LIEGE." "MASTER."
WHAT IS A DARK ONE, AND WHY IS IT ME?

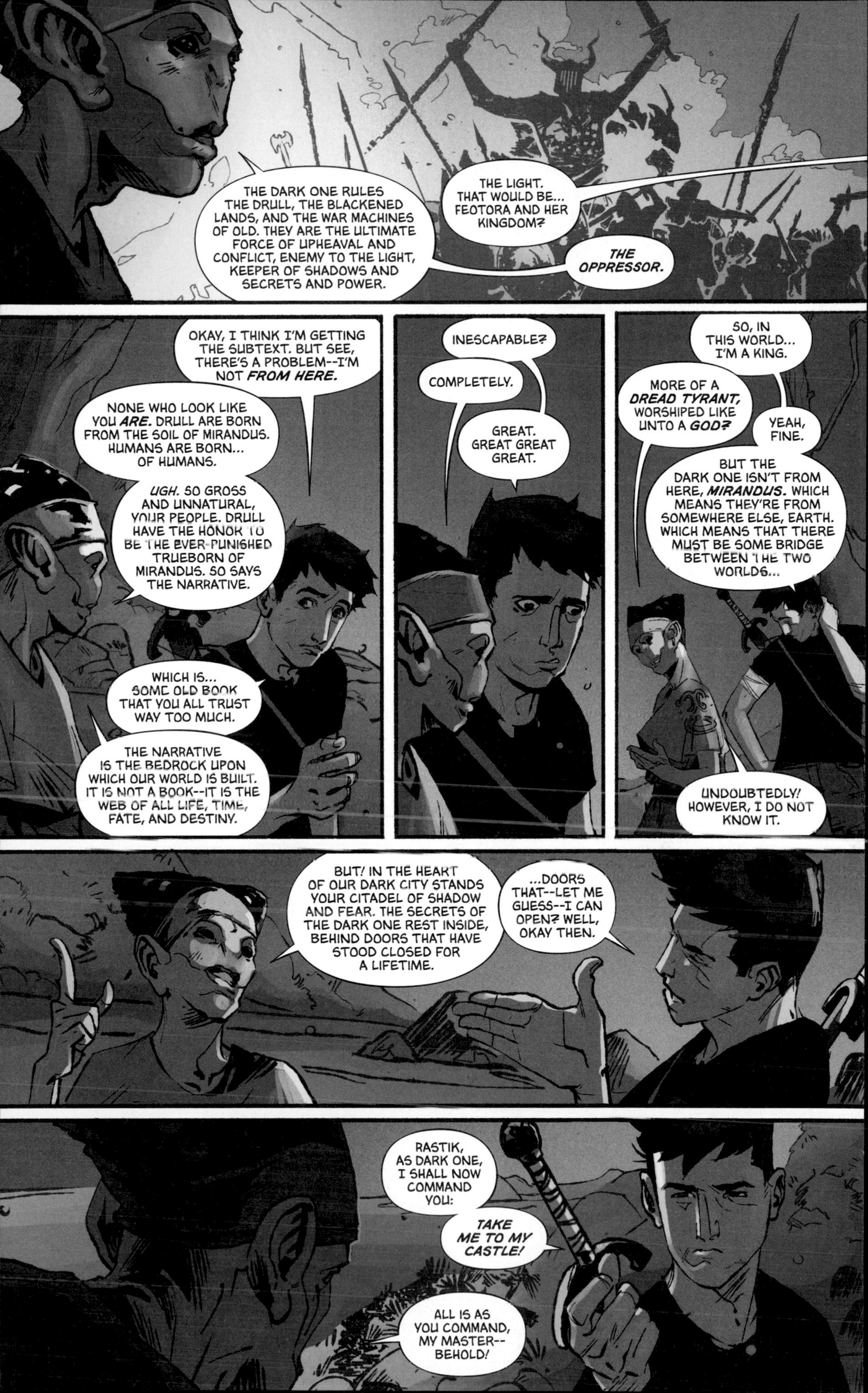
THE DARK ONE RULES THE DRULL, THE BLACKENED LANDS, AND THE WAR MACHINES OF OLD. THEY ARE THE ULTIMATE FORCE OF UPHEAVAL AND CONFLICT, ENEMY TO THE LIGHT, KEEPER OF SHADOWS AND SECRETS AND POWER.
THE LIGHT. THAT WOULD BE... FEOTORA AND HER KINGDOM?
THE OPPRESSOR.
OKAY, I THINK I'M GETTING THE SUBTEXT. BUT SEE, THERE'S A PROBLEM--I'M NOT FROM HERE.
NONE WHO LOOK LIKE YOU ARE. DRULL ARE BORN FROM THE SOIL OF MIRANDUS. HUMANS ARE BORN... OF HUMANS.
UGH. SO GROSS AND UNNATURAL, YOUR PEOPLE. DRULL HAVE THE HONOR TO BE THE EVER-PUNISHED TRUEBORN OF MIRANDUS. SO SAYS THE NARRATIVE.
WHICH IS... SOME OLD BOOK THAT YOU ALL TRUST WAY TOO MUCH.
THE NARRATIVE IS THE BEDROCK UPON WHICH OUR WORLD IS BUILT. IT IS NOT A BOOK--IT IS THE WEB OF ALL LIFE, TIME, FATE, AND DESTINY.
INESCAPABLE?
COMPLETELY.
GREAT. GREAT GREAT GREAT.
SO, IN THIS WORLD... I'M A KING.
MORE OF A DREAD TYRANT, WORSHIPED LIKE UNTO A GOD?
YEAH, FINE.
BUT THE DARK ONE ISN'T FROM HERE, MIRANDUS. WHICH MEANS THEY'RE FROM SOMEWHERE ELSE, EARTH. WHICH MEANS THAT THERE MUST BE SOME BRIDGE BETWEEN THE TWO WORLDS...
UNDOUBTEDLY! HOWEVER, I DO NOT KNOW IT.
BUT! IN THE HEART OF OUR DARK CITY STANDS YOUR CITADEL OF SHADOW AND FEAR. THE SECRETS OF THE DARK ONE REST INSIDE, BEHIND DOORS THAT HAVE STOOD CLOSED FOR A LIFETIME.
...DOORS THAT--LET ME GUESS--I CAN OPEN? WELL, OKAY THEN.
RASTIK, AS DARK ONE, I SHALL NOW COMMAND YOU:
TAKE ME TO MY CASTLE!
ALL IS AS YOU COMMAND, MY MASTER-- BEHOLD!

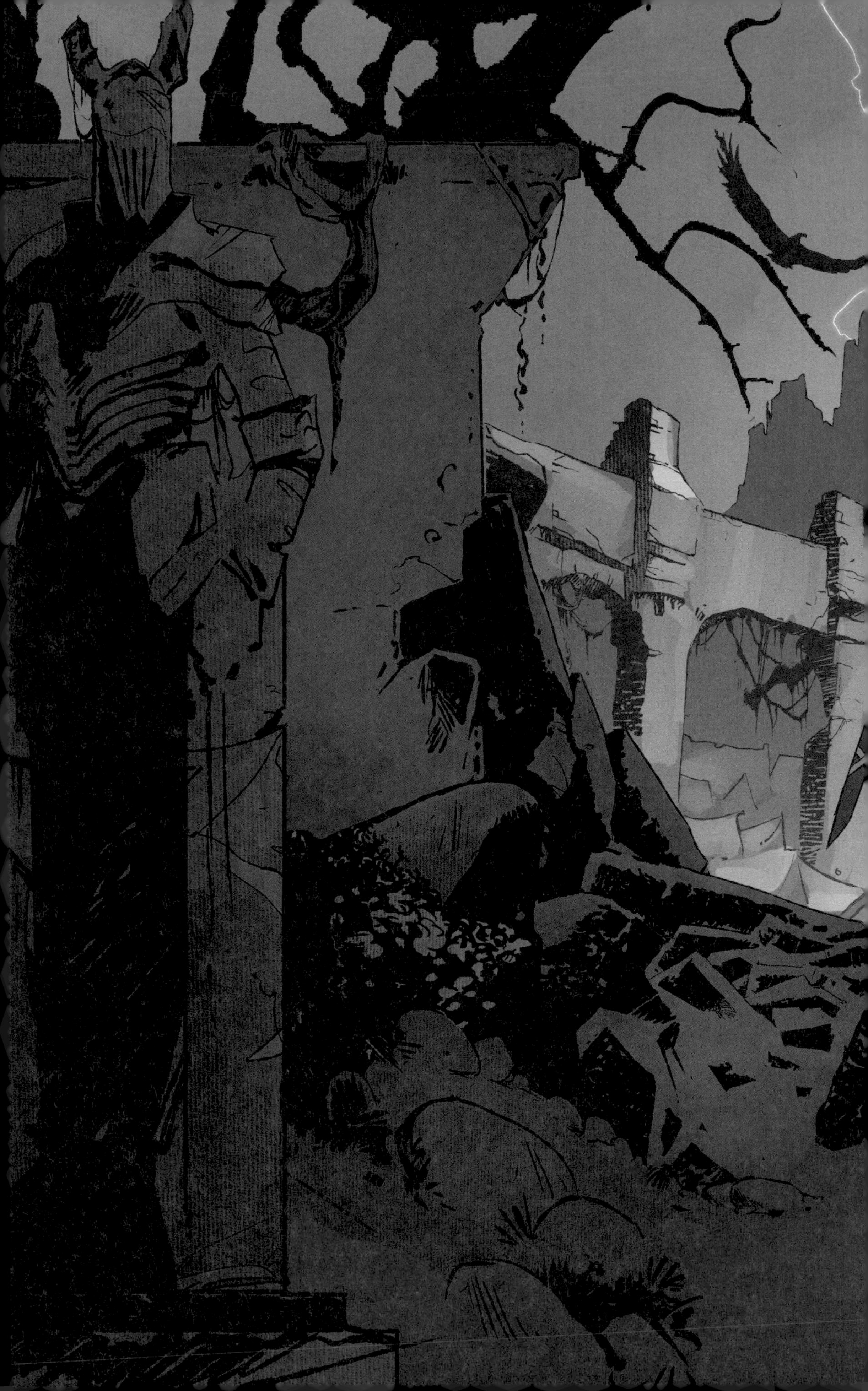

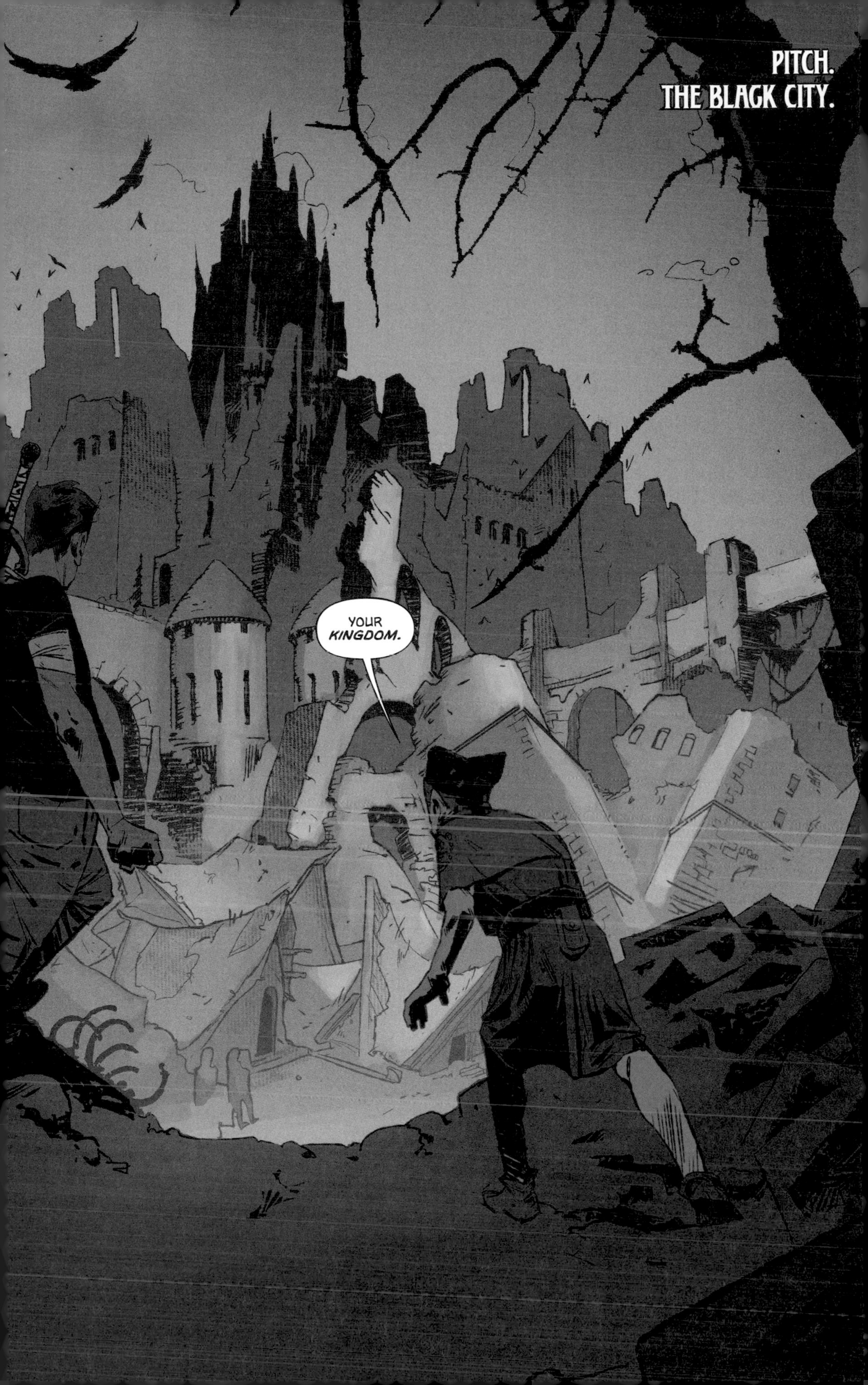
PITCH.
THE BLACK CITY.
YOUR *KINGDOM.*

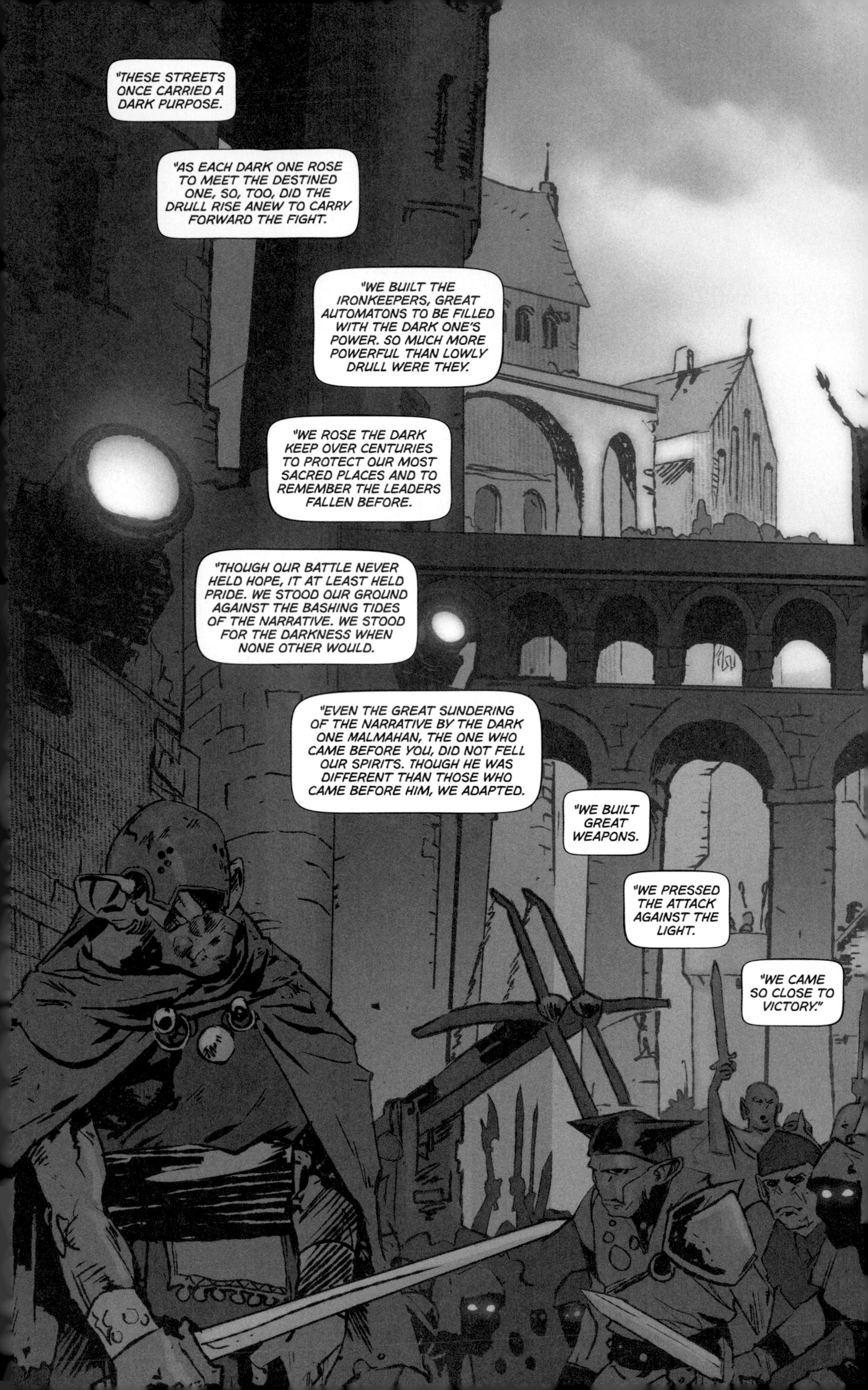
"THESE STREETS ONCE CARRIED A DARK PURPOSE.
"AS EACH DARK ONE ROSE TO MEET THE DESTINED ONE, SO, TOO, DID THE DRULL RISE ANEW TO CARRY FORWARD THE FIGHT.
"WE BUILT THE IRONKEEPERS, GREAT AUTOMATONS TO BE FILLED WITH THE DARK ONE'S POWER. SO MUCH MORE POWERFUL THAN LOWLY DRULL WERE THEY.
"WE ROSE THE DARK KEEP OVER CENTURIES TO PROTECT OUR MOST SACRED PLACES AND TO REMEMBER THE LEADERS FALLEN BEFORE.
"THOUGH OUR BATTLE NEVER HELD HOPE, IT AT LEAST HELD PRIDE. WE STOOD OUR GROUND AGAINST THE BASHING TIDES OF THE NARRATIVE. WE STOOD FOR THE DARKNESS WHEN NONE OTHER WOULD.
"EVEN THE GREAT SUNDERING OF THE NARRATIVE BY THE DARK ONE MALMAHAN, THE ONE WHO CAME BEFORE YOU, DID NOT FELL OUR SPIRITS. THOUGH HE WAS DIFFERENT THAN THOSE WHO CAME BEFORE HIM, WE ADAPTED.
"WE BUILT GREAT WEAPONS.
"WE PRESSED THE ATTACK AGAINST THE LIGHT.
"WE CAME SO CLOSE TO VICTORY."

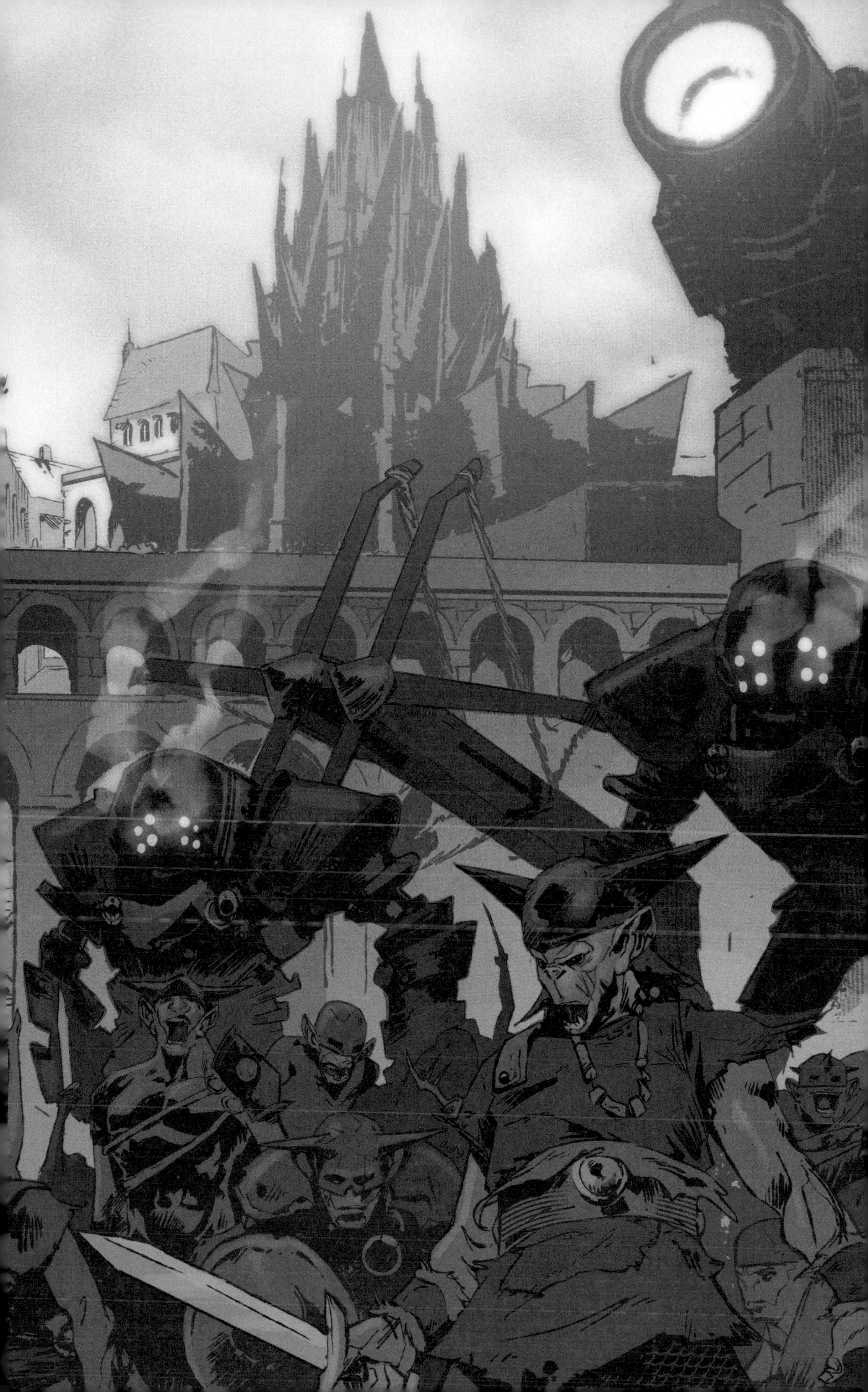

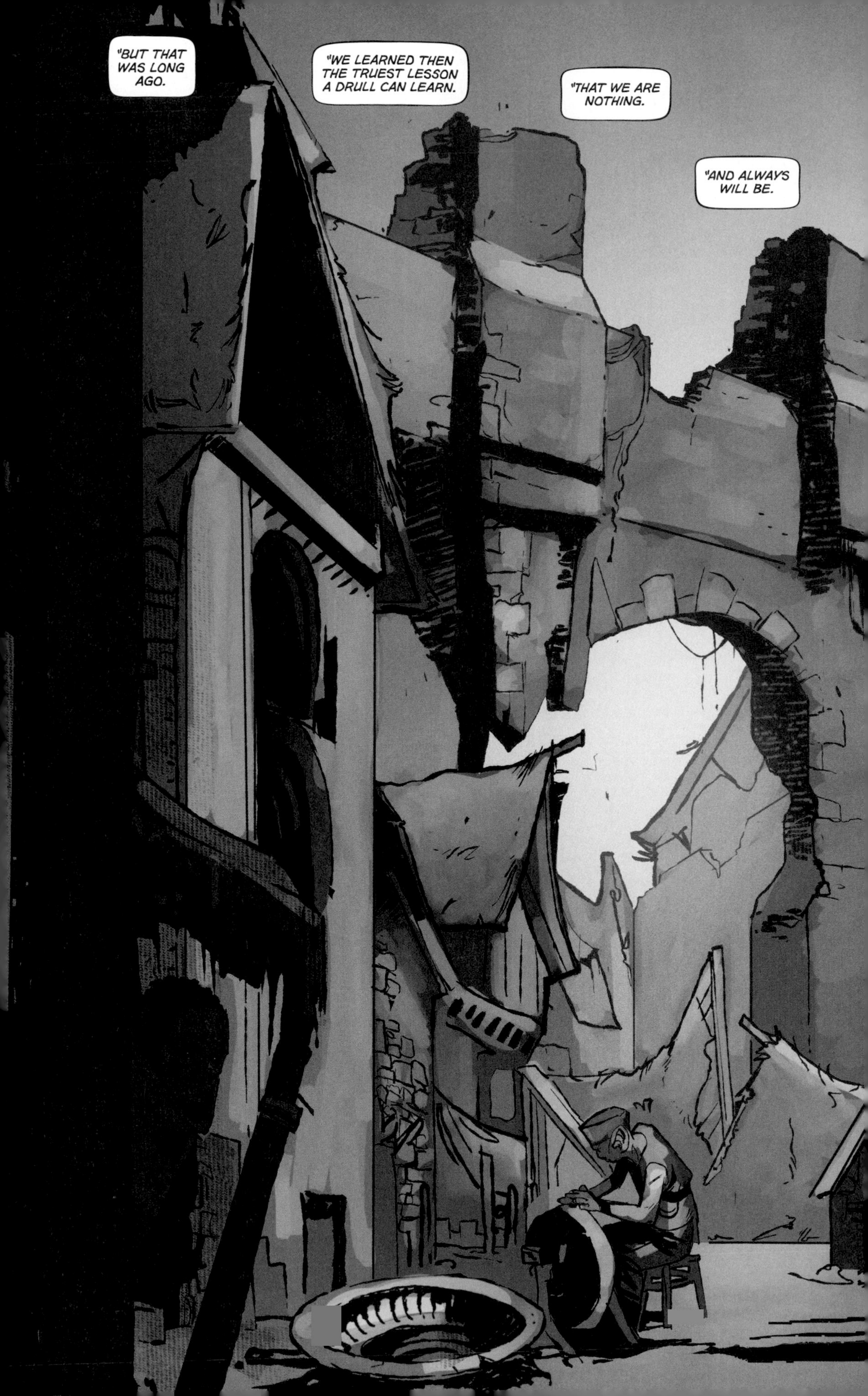
"BUT THAT WAS LONG AGO.
"WE LEARNED THEN THE TRUEST LESSON A DRULL CAN LEARN.
"THAT WE ARE NOTHING.
"AND ALWAYS WILL BE.

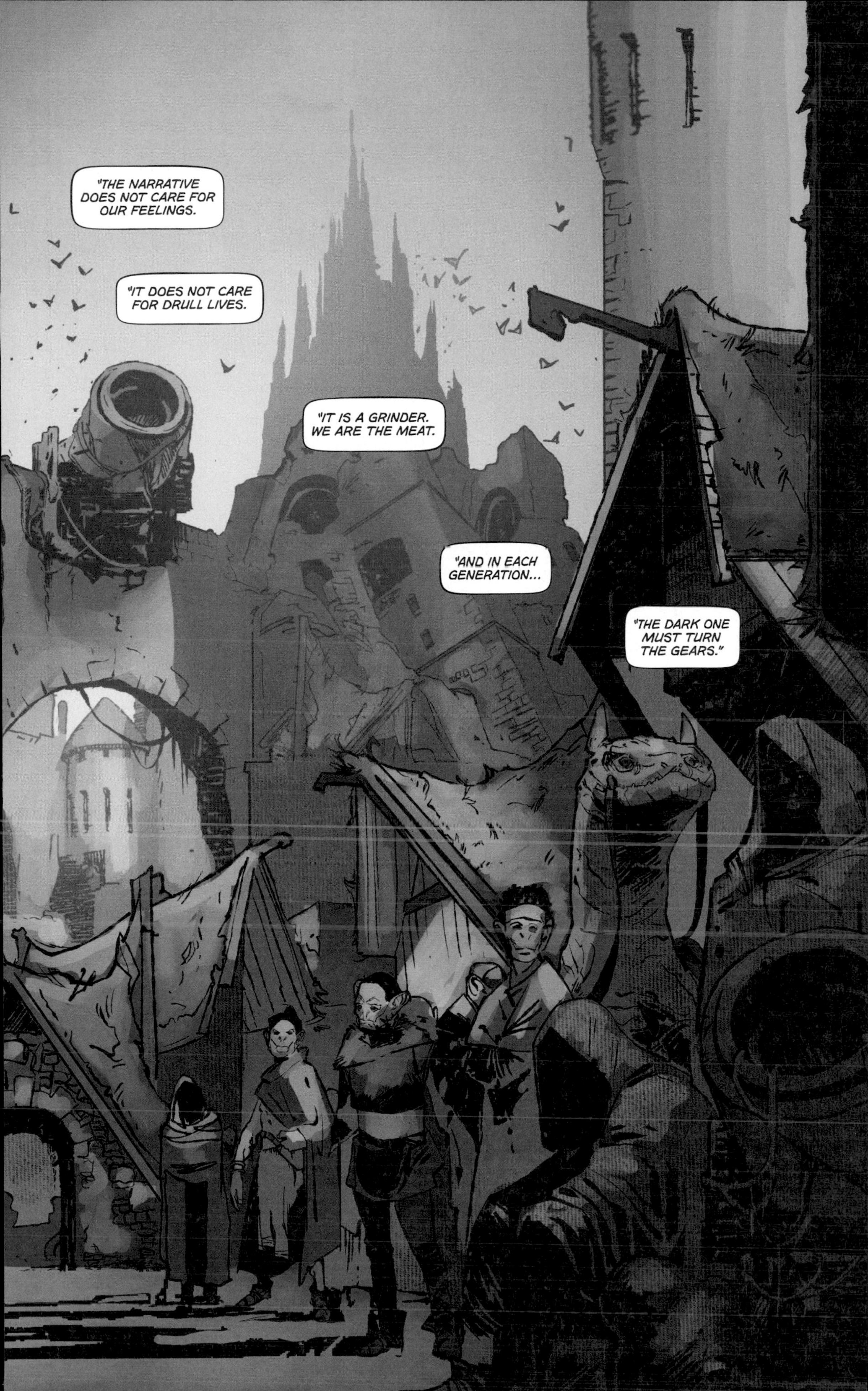
"THE NARRATIVE DOES NOT CARE FOR OUR FEELINGS.
"IT DOES NOT CARE FOR DRULL LIVES.
"IT IS A GRINDER. WE ARE THE MEAT.
"AND IN EACH GENERATION...
"THE DARK ONE MUST TURN THE GEARS."

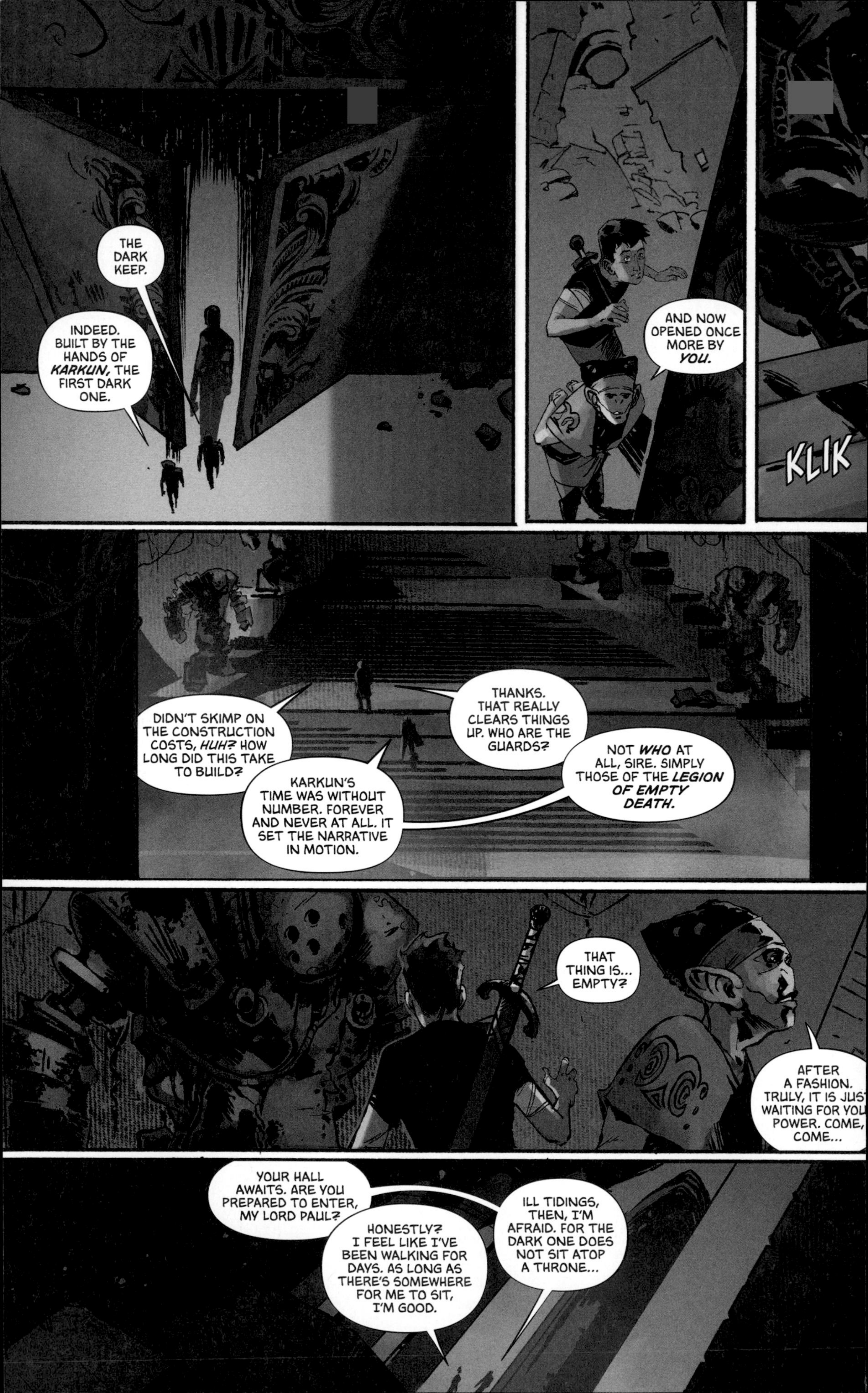
THE DARK KEEP.
INDEED. BUILT BY THE HANDS OF *KARKUN,* THE FIRST DARK ONE.
AND NOW OPENED ONCE MORE BY *YOU.*
KLIK
DIDN'T SKIMP ON THE CONSTRUCTION COSTS, *HUH?* HOW LONG DID THIS TAKE TO BUILD?
KARKUN'S TIME WAS WITHOUT NUMBER. FOREVER AND NEVER AT ALL. IT SET THE NARRATIVE IN MOTION.
THANKS. THAT REALLY CLEARS THINGS UP. WHO ARE THE GUARDS?
NOT *WHO* AT ALL, SIRE. SIMPLY THOSE OF THE *LEGION OF EMPTY DEATH.*
THAT THING IS... EMPTY?
AFTER A FASHION. TRULY, IT IS JUS WAITING FOR YOU POWER. COME, COME...
YOUR HALL AWAITS. ARE YOU PREPARED TO ENTER, MY LORD PAUL?
HONESTLY? I FEEL LIKE I'VE BEEN WALKING FOR DAYS. AS LONG AS THERE'S SOMEWHERE FOR ME TO SIT, I'M GOOD.
ILL TIDINGS, THEN, I'M AFRAID. FOR THE DARK ONE DOES NOT SIT ATOP A THRONE...

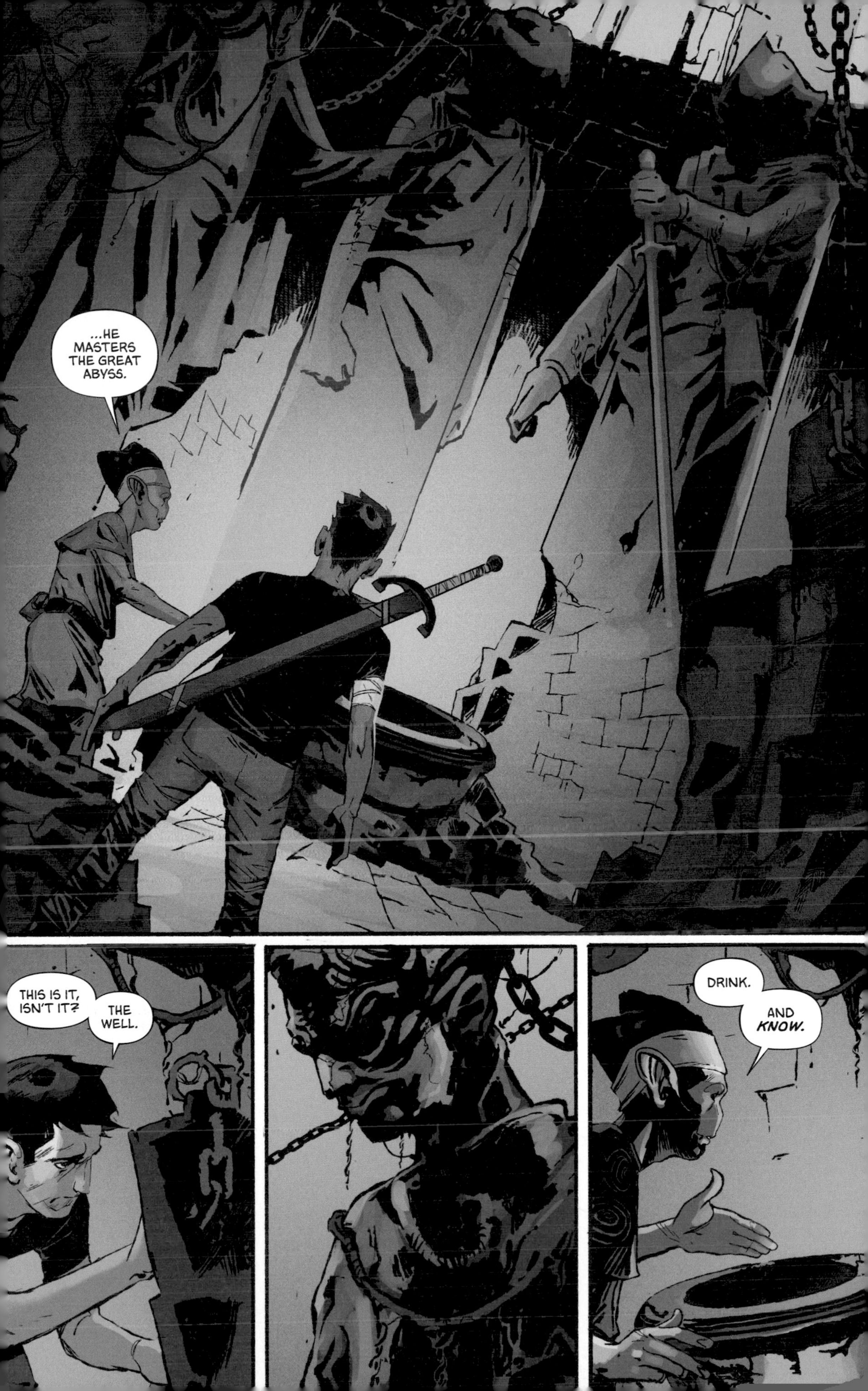
...HE MASTERS THE GREAT ABYSS.
THIS IS IT, ISN'T IT?
THE WELL.
DRINK.
AND *KNOW.*

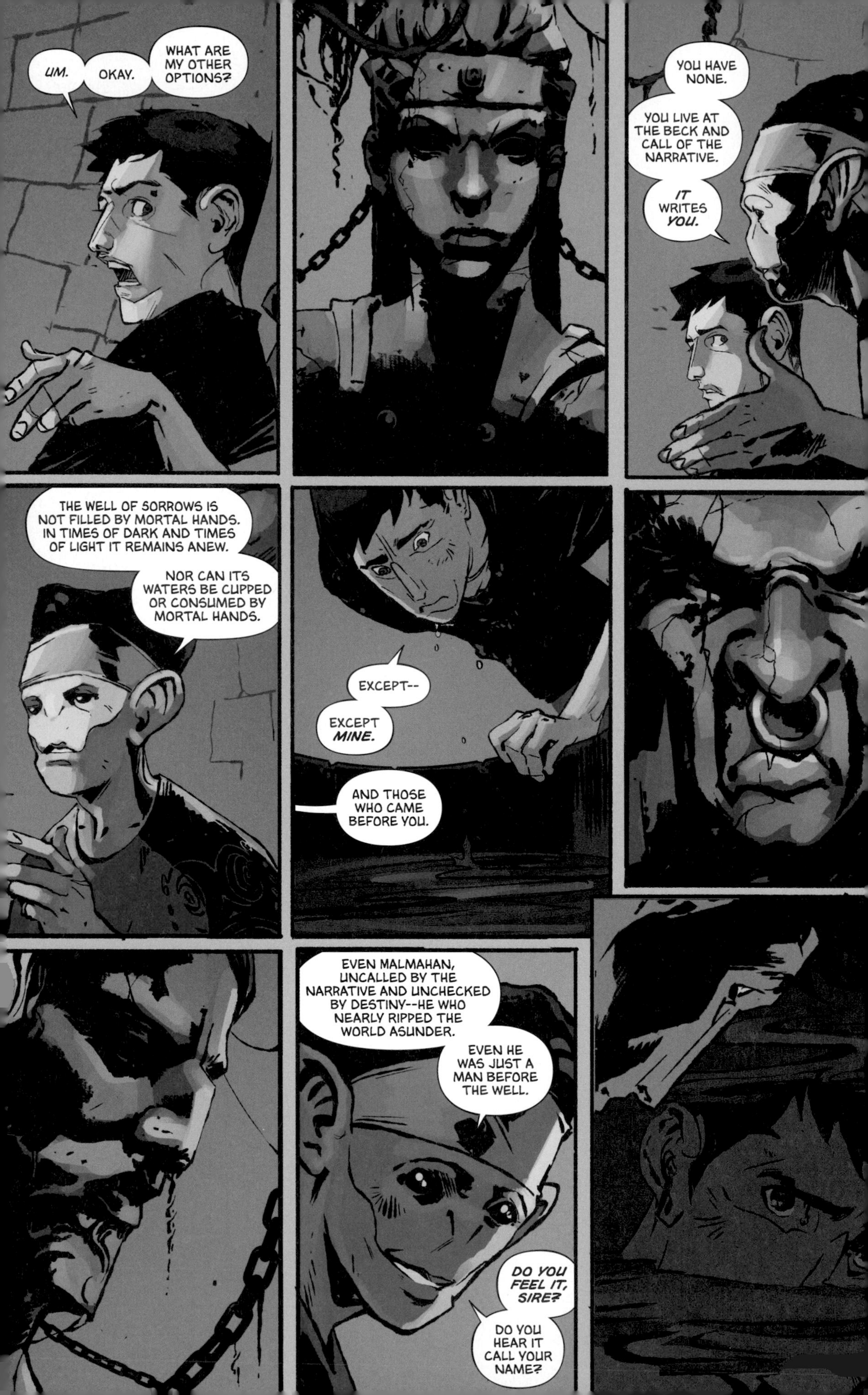
UM.
OKAY.
WHAT ARE MY OTHER OPTIONS?
YOU HAVE NONE.
YOU LIVE AT THE BECK AND CALL OF THE NARRATIVE.
IT WRITES YOU.
THE WELL OF SORROWS IS NOT FILLED BY MORTAL HANDS. IN TIMES OF DARK AND TIMES OF LIGHT IT REMAINS ANEW.
NOR CAN ITS WATERS BE CUPPED OR CONSUMED BY MORTAL HANDS.
EXCEPT--
EXCEPT MINE.
AND THOSE WHO CAME BEFORE YOU.
EVEN MALMAHAN, UNCALLED BY THE NARRATIVE AND UNCHECKED BY DESTINY--HE WHO NEARLY RIPPED THE WORLD ASUNDER.
EVEN HE WAS JUST A MAN BEFORE THE WELL.
DO YOU FEEL IT, SIRE?
DO YOU HEAR IT CALL YOUR NAME?

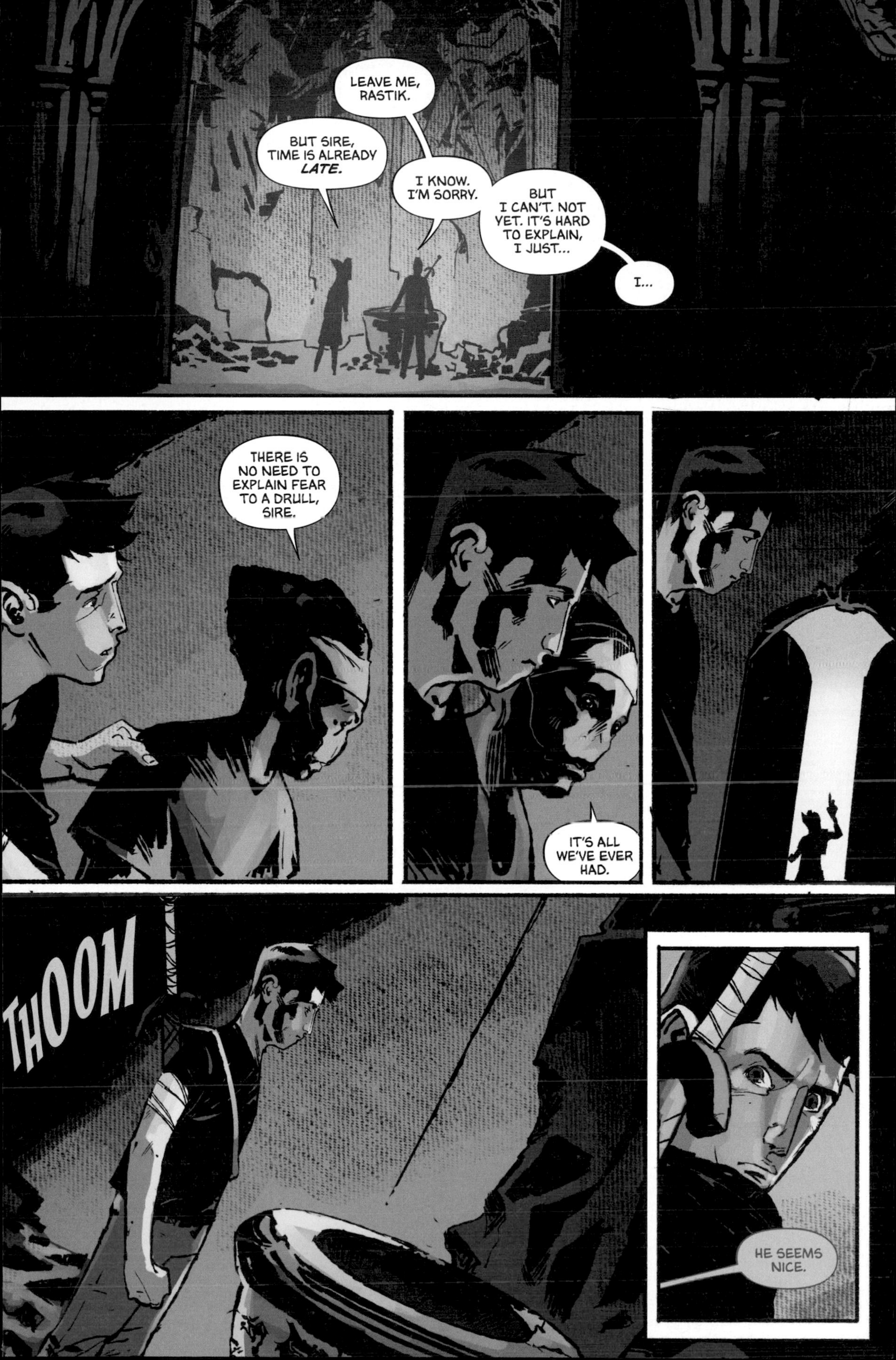
LEAVE ME, RASTIK.
BUT SIRE, TIME IS ALREADY *LATE.*
I KNOW. I'M SORRY.
BUT I CAN'T. NOT YET. IT'S HARD TO EXPLAIN, I JUST...
I...
THERE IS NO NEED TO EXPLAIN FEAR TO A DRULL, SIRE.
IT'S ALL WE'VE EVER HAD.
THOOM
HE SEEMS NICE.

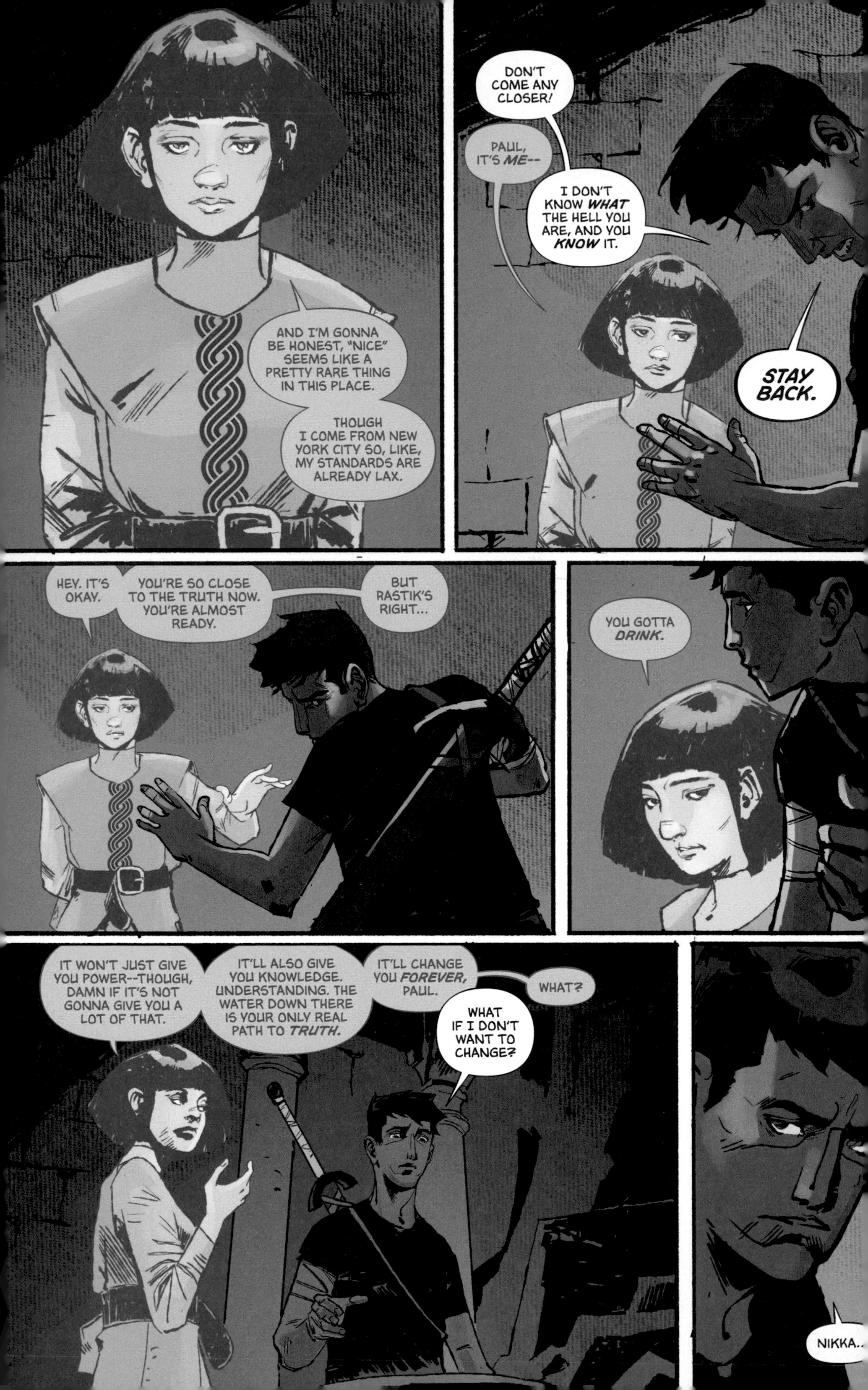
AND I'M GONNA BE HONEST, "NICE" SEEMS LIKE A PRETTY RARE THING IN THIS PLACE.
THOUGH I COME FROM NEW YORK CITY SO, LIKE, MY STANDARDS ARE ALREADY LAX.
DON'T COME ANY CLOSER!
PAUL, IT'S ME--
I DON'T KNOW WHAT THE HELL YOU ARE, AND YOU KNOW IT.
STAY BACK.
HEY. IT'S OKAY.
YOU'RE SO CLOSE TO THE TRUTH NOW. YOU'RE ALMOST READY.
BUT RASTIK'S RIGHT...
YOU GOTTA DRINK.
IT WON'T JUST GIVE YOU POWER--THOUGH, DAMN IF IT'S NOT GONNA GIVE YOU A LOT OF THAT.
IT'LL ALSO GIVE YOU KNOWLEDGE. UNDERSTANDING. THE WATER DOWN THERE IS YOUR ONLY REAL PATH TO TRUTH.
IT'LL CHANGE YOU FOREVER, PAUL.
WHAT?
WHAT IF I DON'T WANT TO CHANGE?
NIKKA...

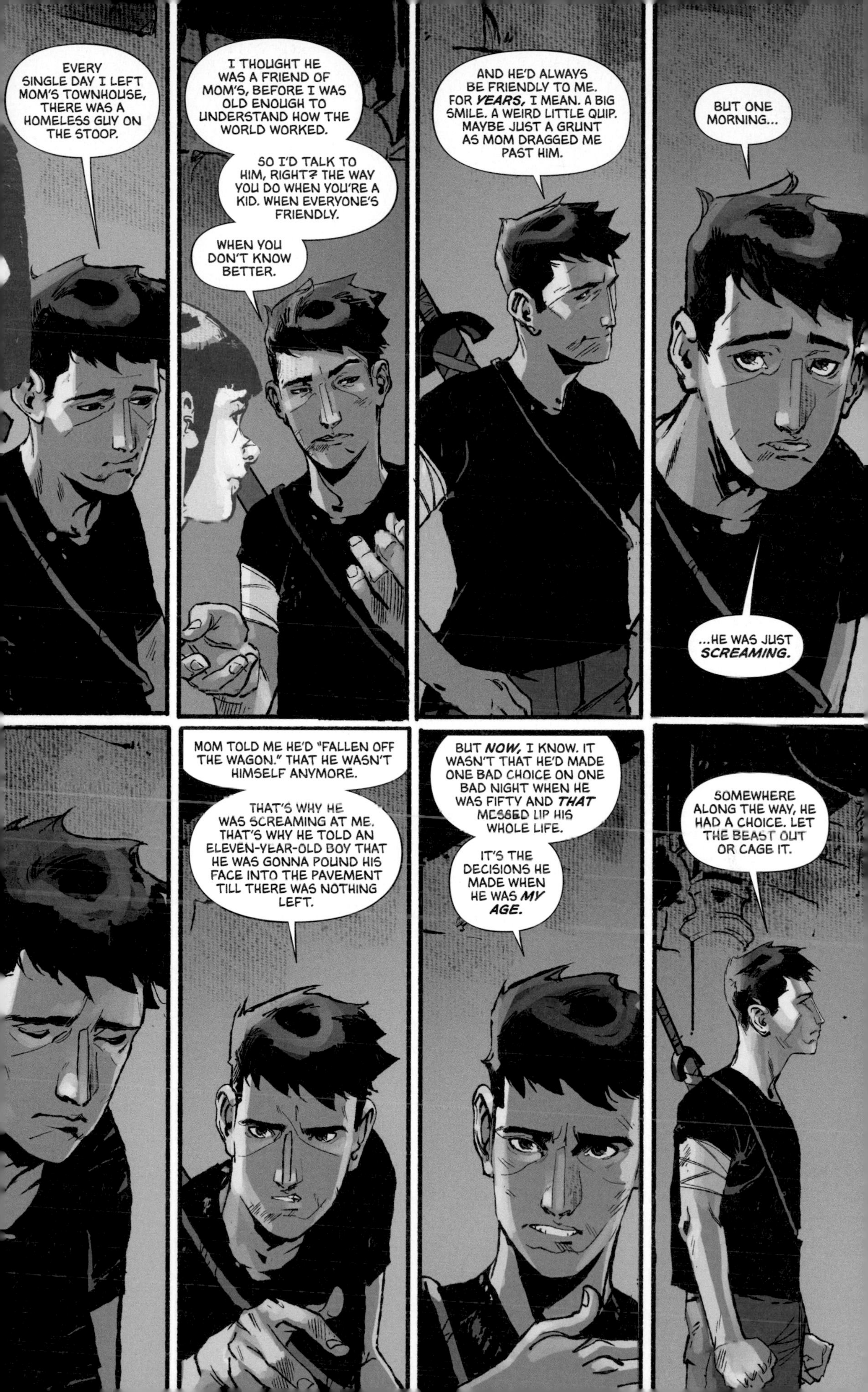
EVERY SINGLE DAY I LEFT MOM'S TOWNHOUSE, THERE WAS A HOMELESS GUY ON THE STOOP.
I THOUGHT HE WAS A FRIEND OF MOM'S, BEFORE I WAS OLD ENOUGH TO UNDERSTAND HOW THE WORLD WORKED.
SO I'D TALK TO HIM, RIGHT? THE WAY YOU DO WHEN YOU'RE A KID. WHEN EVERYONE'S FRIENDLY.
WHEN YOU DON'T KNOW BETTER.
AND HE'D ALWAYS BE FRIENDLY TO ME. FOR YEARS, I MEAN. A BIG SMILE. A WEIRD LITTLE QUIP. MAYBE JUST A GRUNT AS MOM DRAGGED ME PAST HIM.
BUT ONE MORNING...
...HE WAS JUST SCREAMING.
MOM TOLD ME HE'D "FALLEN OFF THE WAGON." THAT HE WASN'T HIMSELF ANYMORE.
THAT'S WHY HE WAS SCREAMING AT ME. THAT'S WHY HE TOLD AN ELEVEN-YEAR-OLD BOY THAT HE WAS GONNA POUND HIS FACE INTO THE PAVEMENT TILL THERE WAS NOTHING LEFT.
BUT NOW, I KNOW. IT WASN'T THAT HE'D MADE ONE BAD CHOICE ON ONE BAD NIGHT WHEN HE WAS FIFTY AND THAT MESSED UP HIS WHOLE LIFE.
IT'S THE DECISIONS HE MADE WHEN HE WAS MY AGE.
SOMEWHERE ALONG THE WAY, HE HAD A CHOICE. LET THE BEAST OUT OR CAGE IT.

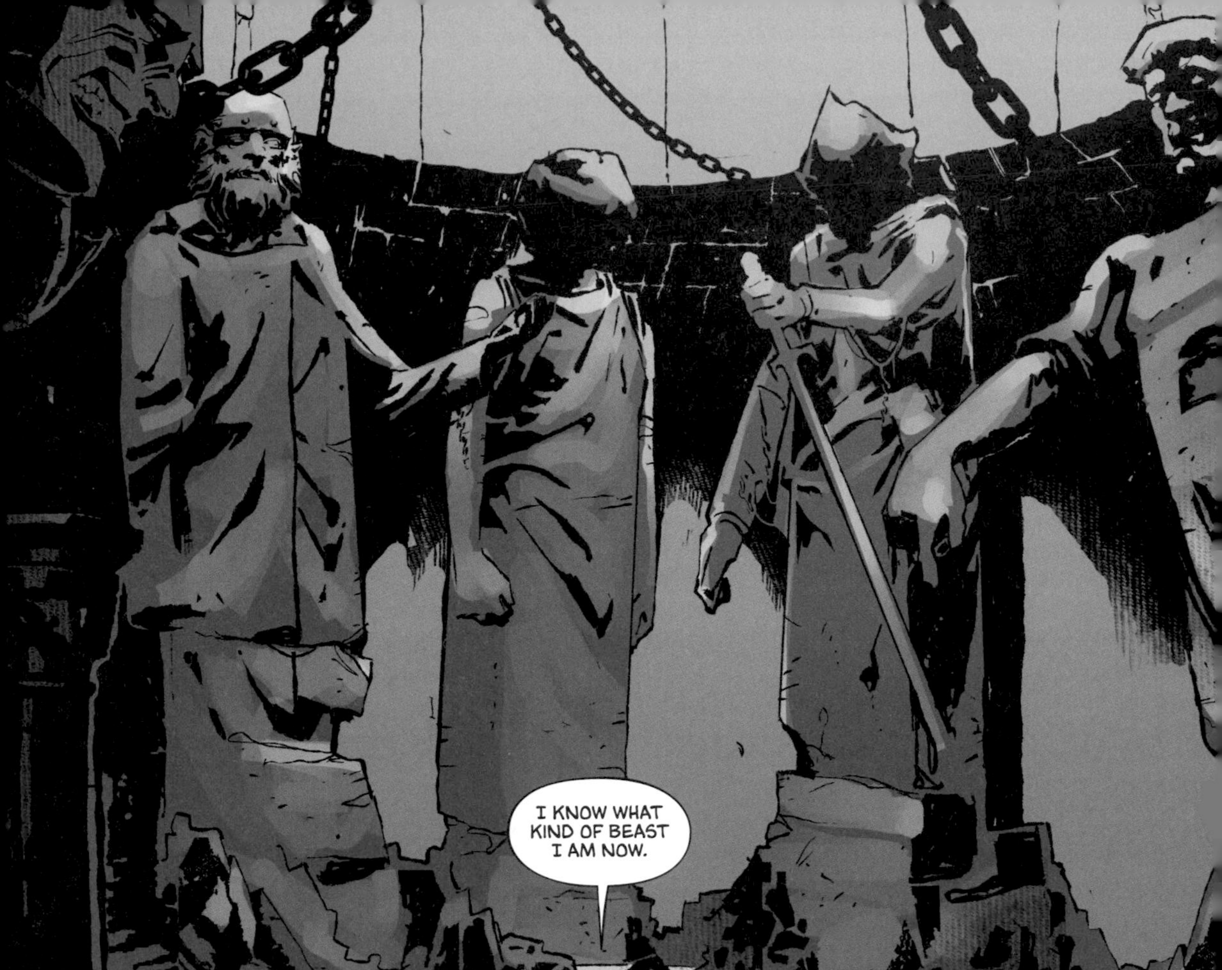
I KNOW WHAT KIND OF BEAST I AM NOW.

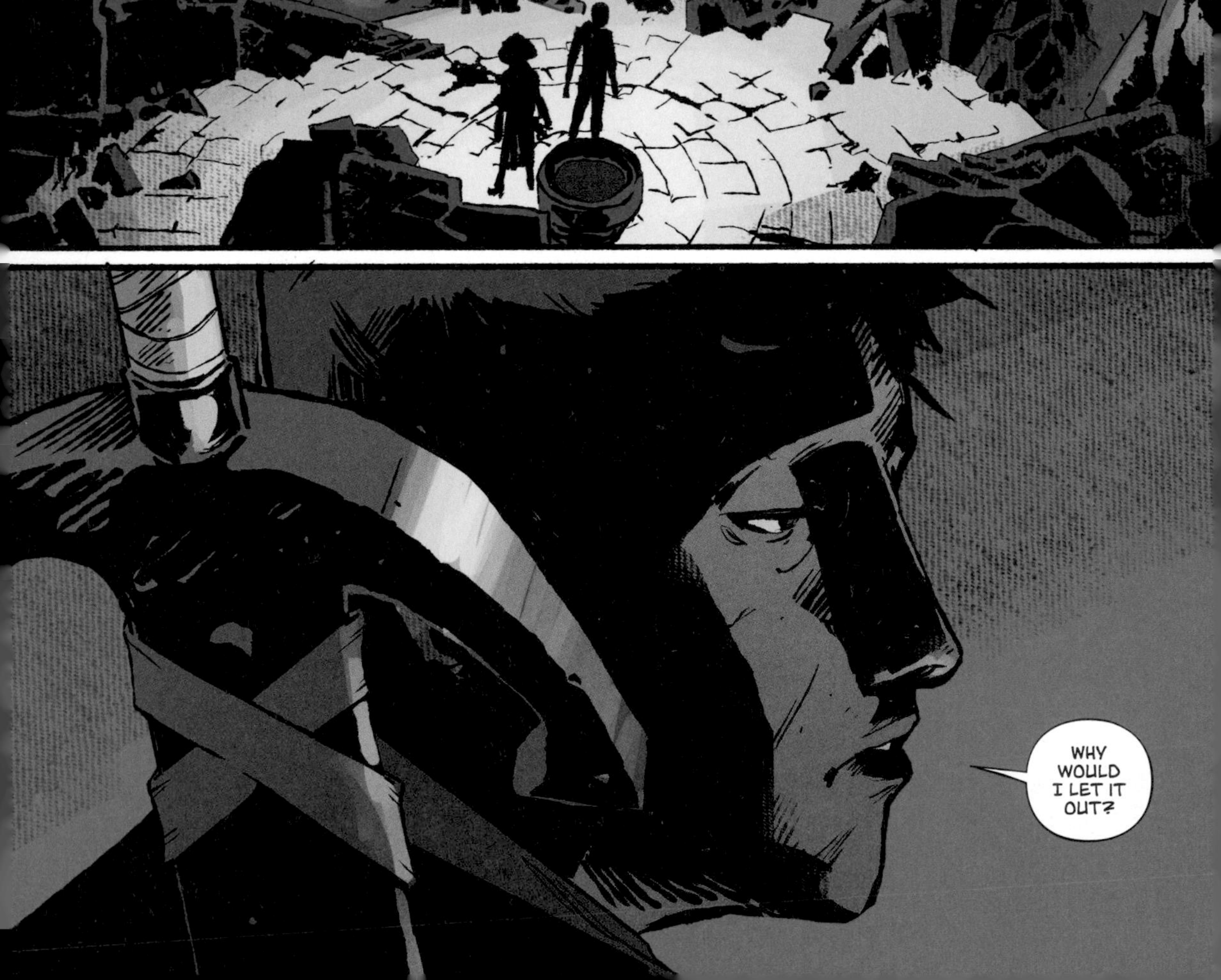
WHY WOULD I LET IT OUT?

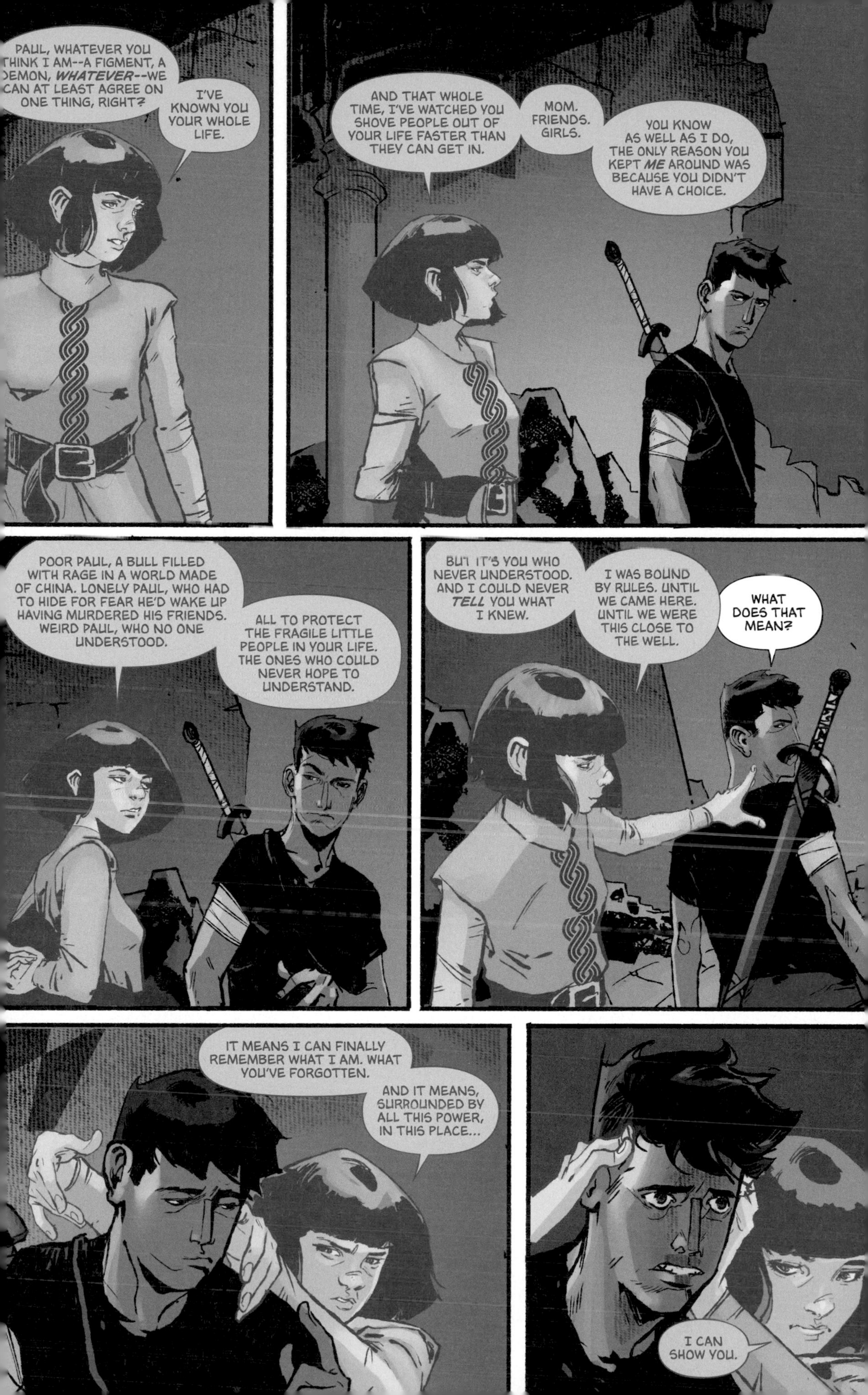
PAUL, WHATEVER YOU THINK I AM--A FIGMENT, A DEMON, *WHATEVER*--WE CAN AT LEAST AGREE ON ONE THING, RIGHT?
I'VE KNOWN YOU YOUR WHOLE LIFE.
AND THAT WHOLE TIME, I'VE WATCHED YOU SHOVE PEOPLE OUT OF YOUR LIFE FASTER THAN THEY CAN GET IN.
MOM. FRIENDS. GIRLS.
YOU KNOW AS WELL AS I DO, THE ONLY REASON YOU KEPT *ME* AROUND WAS BECAUSE YOU DIDN'T HAVE A CHOICE.
POOR PAUL, A BULL FILLED WITH RAGE IN A WORLD MADE OF CHINA. LONELY PAUL, WHO HAD TO HIDE FOR FEAR HE'D WAKE UP HAVING MURDERED HIS FRIENDS. WEIRD PAUL, WHO NO ONE UNDERSTOOD.
ALL TO PROTECT THE FRAGILE LITTLE PEOPLE IN YOUR LIFE. THE ONES WHO COULD NEVER HOPE TO UNDERSTAND.
BUT IT'S YOU WHO NEVER UNDERSTOOD. AND I COULD NEVER *TELL* YOU WHAT I KNEW.
I WAS BOUND BY RULES. UNTIL WE CAME HERE. UNTIL WE WERE THIS CLOSE TO THE WELL.
WHAT DOES THAT MEAN?
IT MEANS I CAN FINALLY REMEMBER WHAT I AM. WHAT YOU'VE FORGOTTEN.
AND IT MEANS, SURROUNDED BY ALL THIS POWER, IN THIS PLACE...
I CAN SHOW YOU.

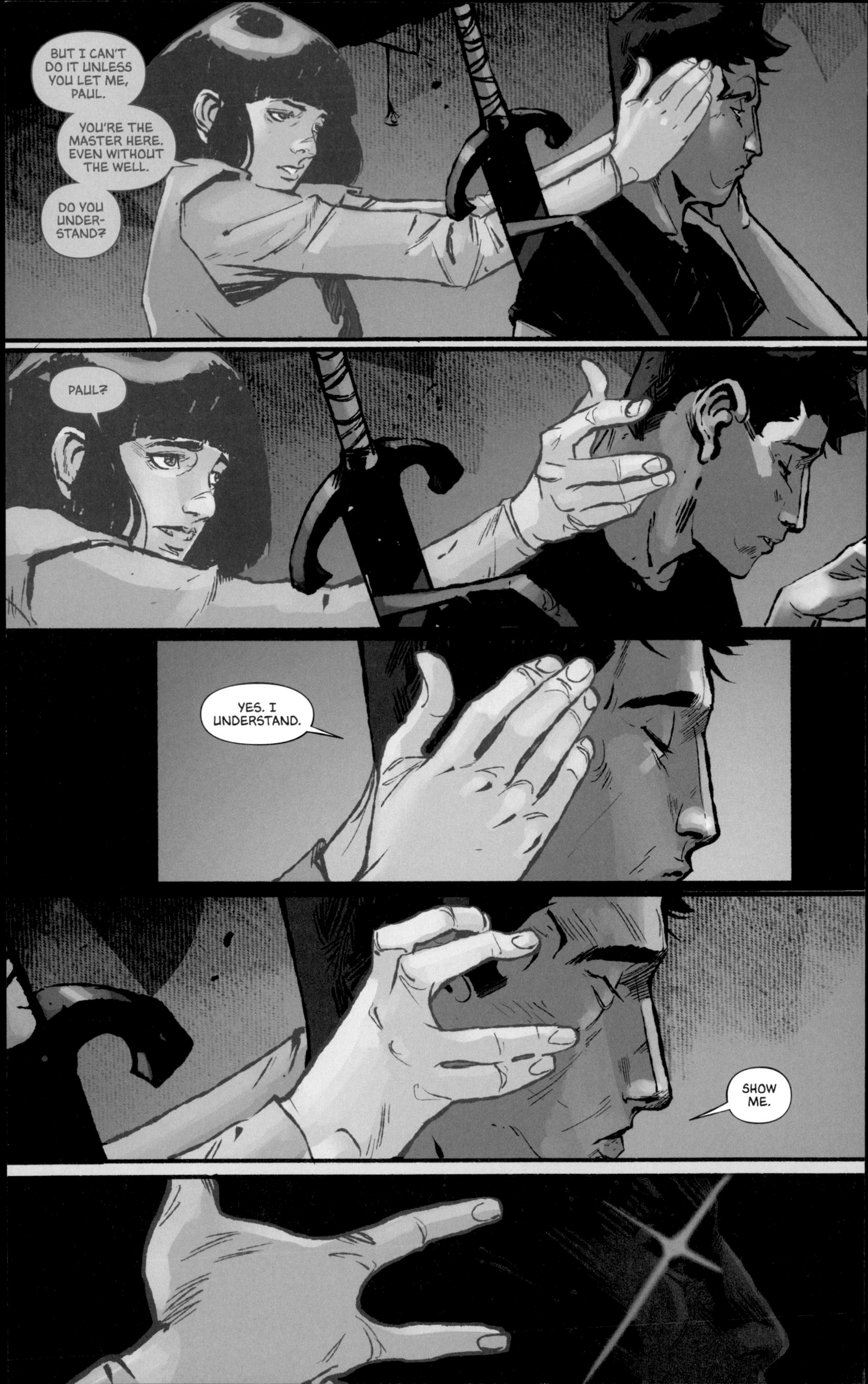
BUT I CAN'T DO IT UNLESS YOU LET ME, PAUL.
YOU'RE THE MASTER HERE. EVEN WITHOUT THE WELL.
DO YOU UNDER-STAND?
PAUL?
YES. I UNDERSTAND.
SHOW ME.

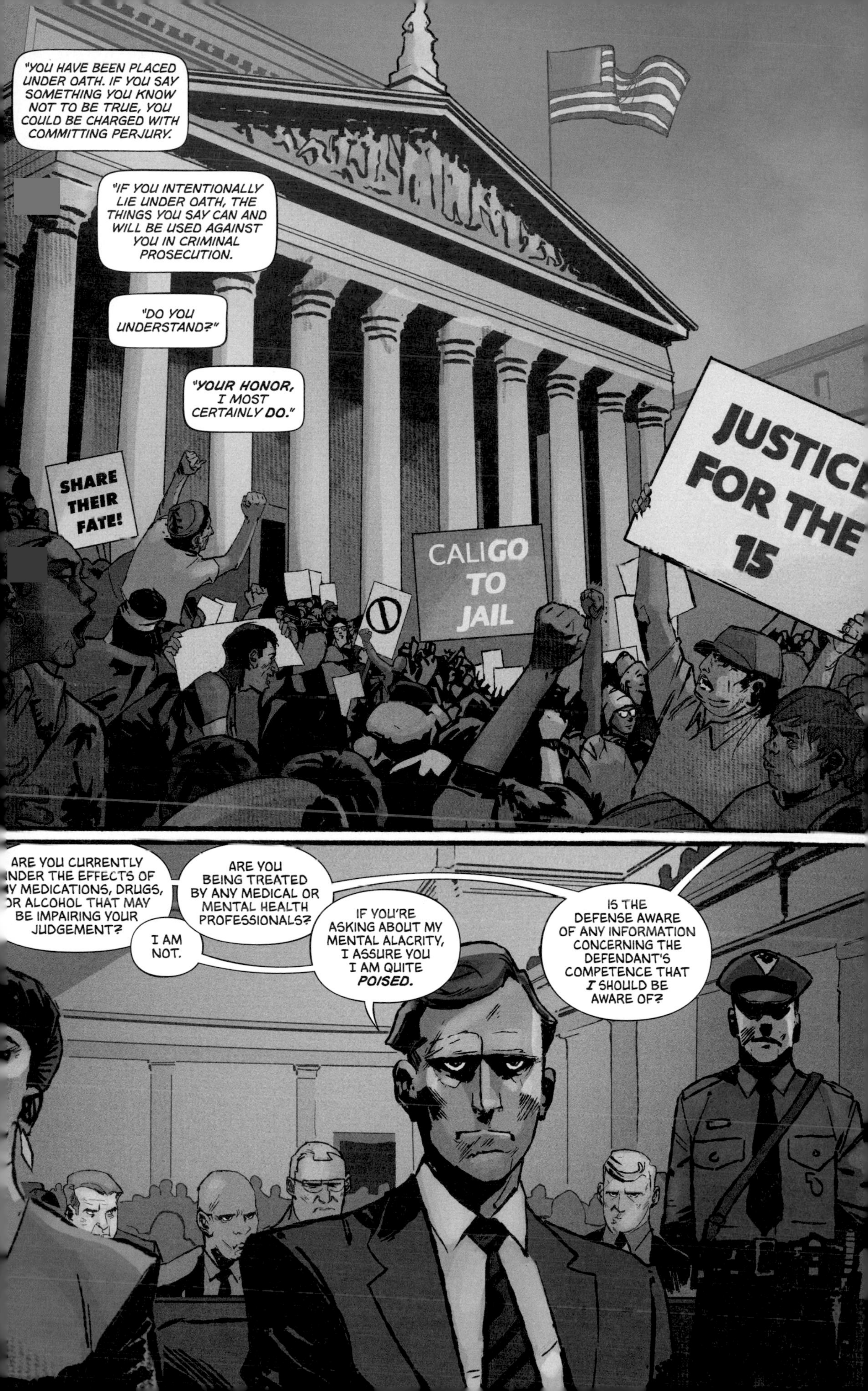
"YOU HAVE BEEN PLACED UNDER OATH. IF YOU SAY SOMETHING YOU KNOW NOT TO BE TRUE, YOU COULD BE CHARGED WITH COMMITTING PERJURY.
"IF YOU INTENTIONALLY LIE UNDER OATH, THE THINGS YOU SAY CAN AND WILL BE USED AGAINST YOU IN CRIMINAL PROSECUTION.
"DO YOU UNDERSTAND?"
"YOUR HONOR, I MOST CERTAINLY DO."
SHARE THEIR FATE!
CALIGO TO JAIL
JUSTICE FOR THE 15
ARE YOU CURRENTLY NDER THE EFFECTS OF Y MEDICATIONS, DRUGS, R ALCOHOL THAT MAY BE IMPAIRING YOUR JUDGEMENT?
I AM NOT.
ARE YOU BEING TREATED BY ANY MEDICAL OR MENTAL HEALTH PROFESSIONALS?
IF YOU'RE ASKING ABOUT MY MENTAL ALACRITY, I ASSURE YOU I AM QUITE POISED.
IS THE DEFENSE AWARE OF ANY INFORMATION CONCERNING THE DEFENDANT'S COMPETENCE THAT I SHOULD BE AWARE OF?

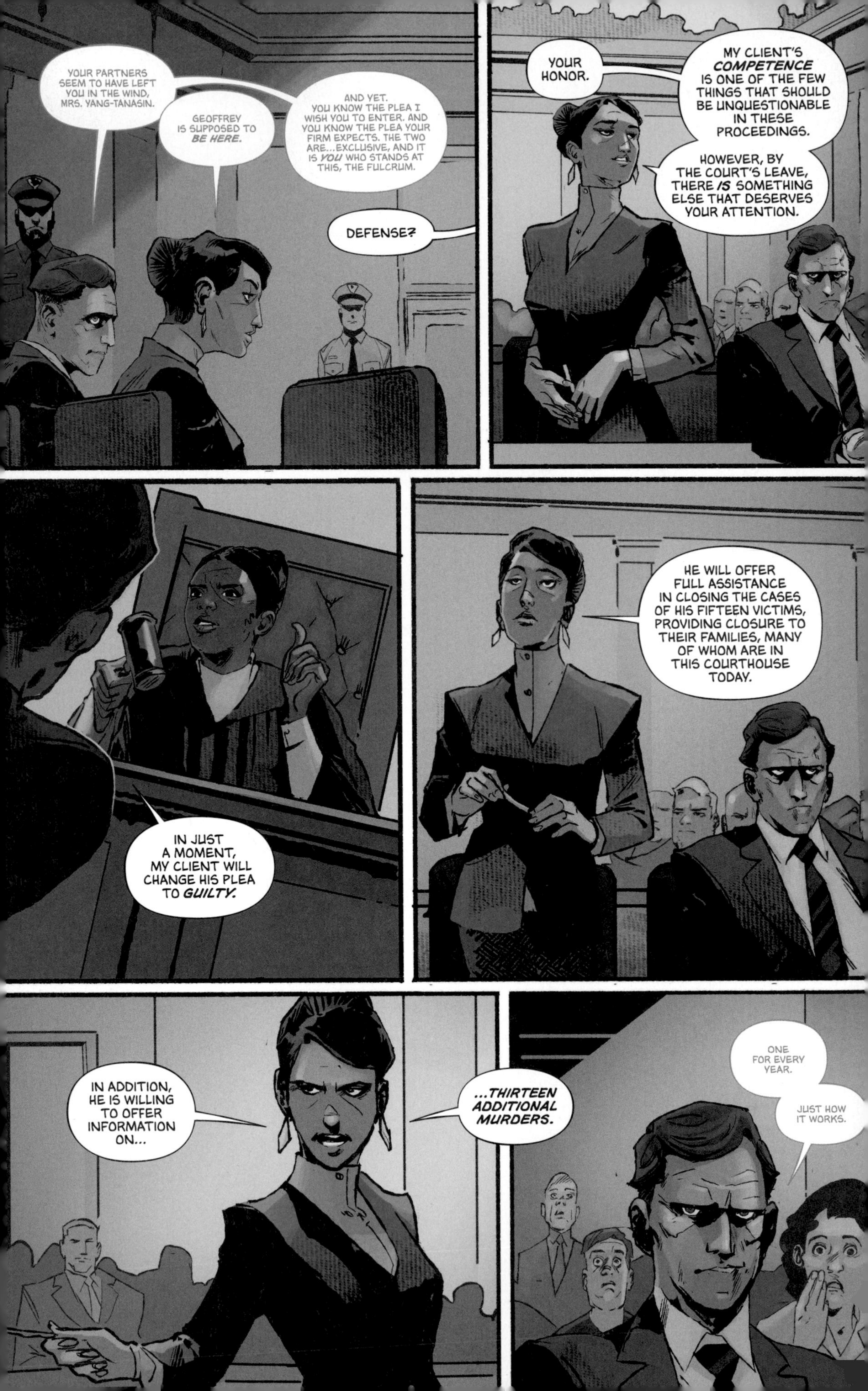
YOUR PARTNERS SEEM TO HAVE LEFT YOU IN THE WIND, MRS. YANG-TANASIN.
GEOFFREY IS SUPPOSED TO *BE HERE.*
AND YET. YOU KNOW THE PLEA I WISH YOU TO ENTER. AND YOU KNOW THE PLEA YOUR FIRM EXPECTS. THE TWO ARE...EXCLUSIVE, AND IT IS *YOU* WHO STANDS AT THIS, THE FULCRUM.
DEFENSE?
YOUR HONOR.
MY CLIENT'S *COMPETENCE* IS ONE OF THE FEW THINGS THAT SHOULD BE UNQUESTIONABLE IN THESE PROCEEDINGS.
HOWEVER, BY THE COURT'S LEAVE, THERE *IS* SOMETHING ELSE THAT DESERVES YOUR ATTENTION.
IN JUST A MOMENT, MY CLIENT WILL CHANGE HIS PLEA TO *GUILTY.*
HE WILL OFFER FULL ASSISTANCE IN CLOSING THE CASES OF HIS FIFTEEN VICTIMS, PROVIDING CLOSURE TO THEIR FAMILIES, MANY OF WHOM ARE IN THIS COURTHOUSE TODAY.
IN ADDITION, HE IS WILLING TO OFFER INFORMATION ON...
...THIRTEEN ADDITIONAL MURDERS.
ONE FOR EVERY YEAR.
JUST HOW IT WORKS.

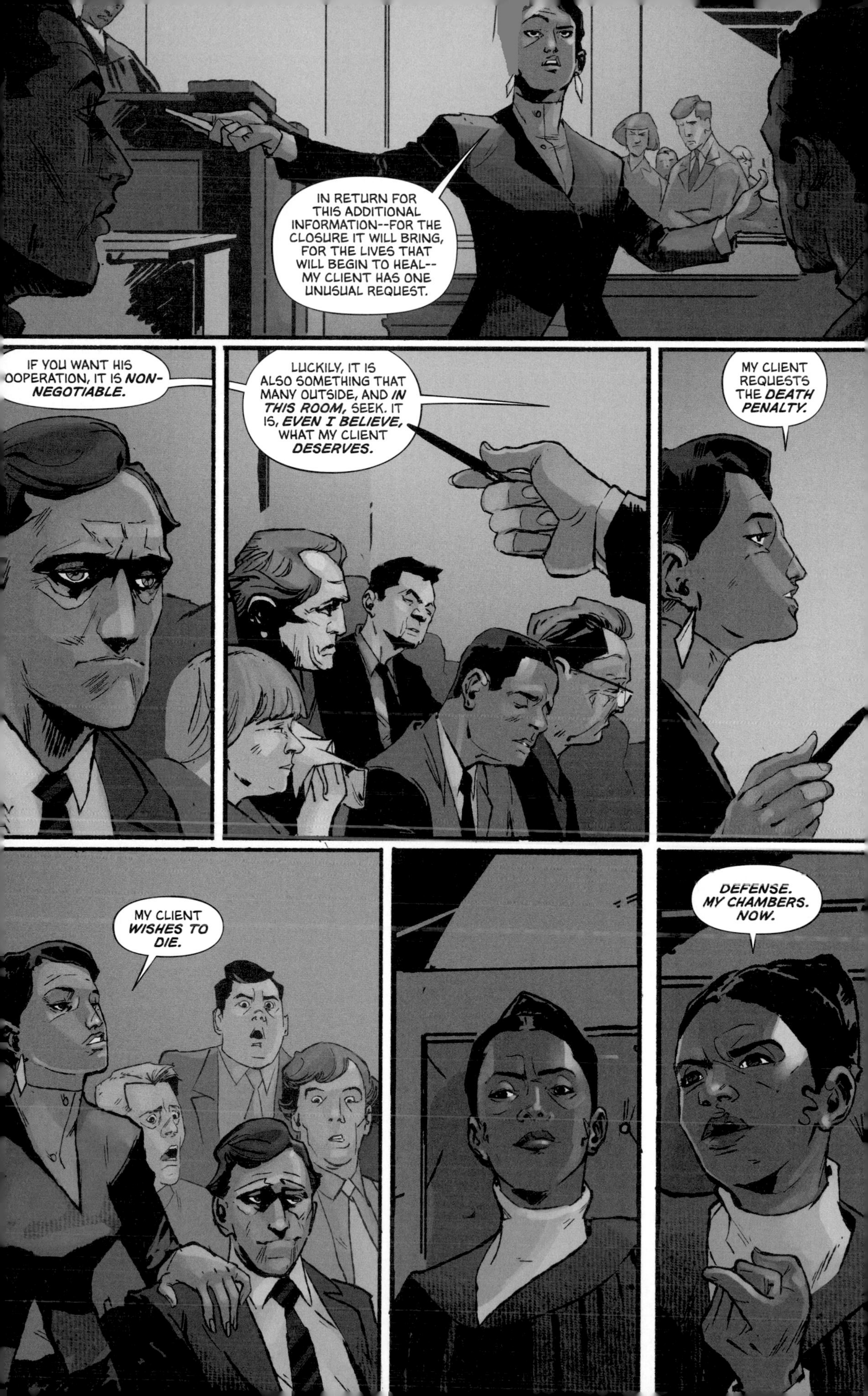
IN RETURN FOR THIS ADDITIONAL INFORMATION--FOR THE CLOSURE IT WILL BRING, FOR THE LIVES THAT WILL BEGIN TO HEAL--MY CLIENT HAS ONE UNUSUAL REQUEST.
IF YOU WANT HIS OOPERATION, IT IS NON-NEGOTIABLE.
LUCKILY, IT IS ALSO SOMETHING THAT MANY OUTSIDE, AND IN THIS ROOM, SEEK. IT IS, EVEN I BELIEVE, WHAT MY CLIENT DESERVES.
MY CLIENT REQUESTS THE DEATH PENALTY.
MY CLIENT WISHES TO DIE.
DEFENSE. MY CHAMBERS. NOW.

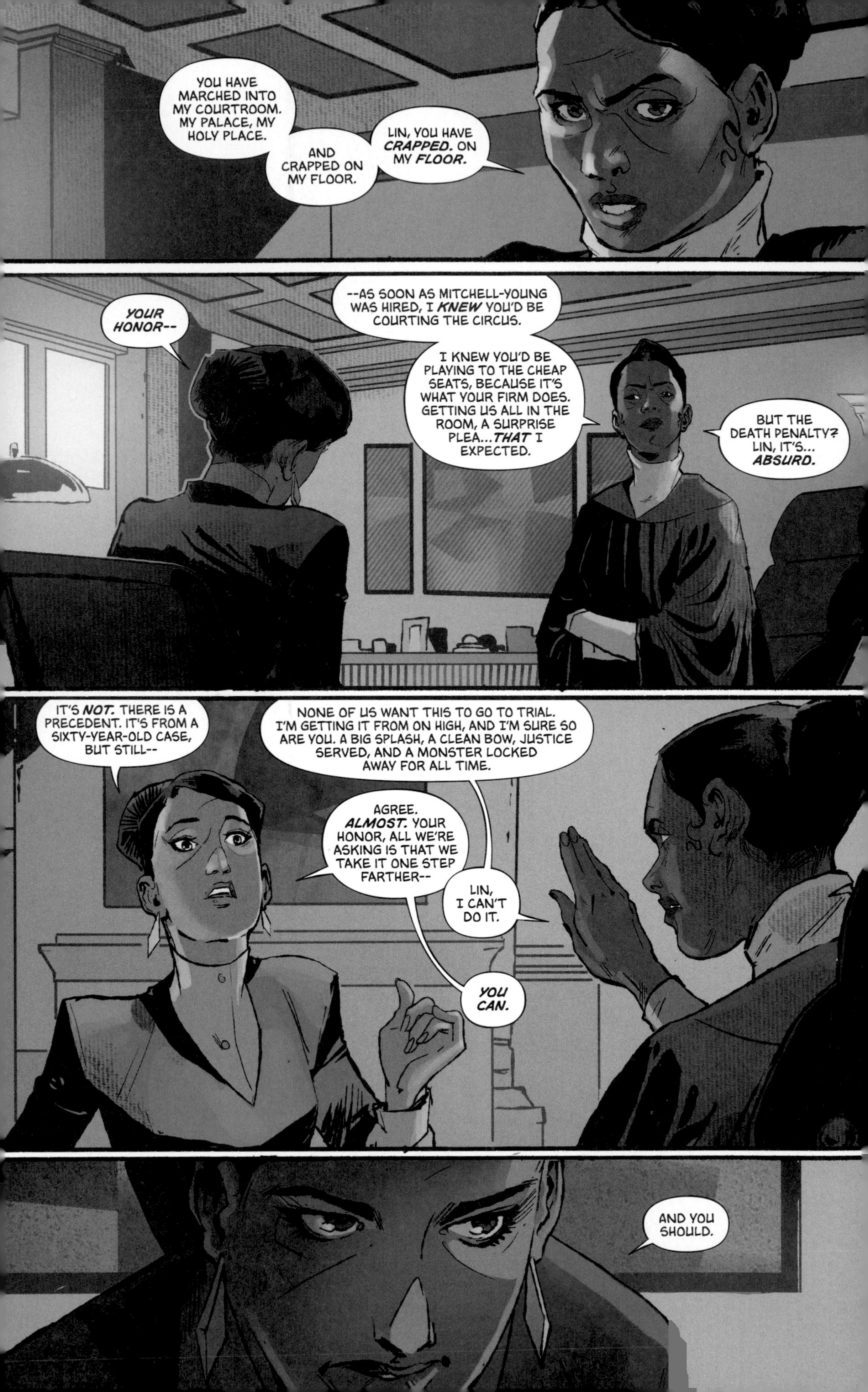
YOU HAVE MARCHED INTO MY COURTROOM. MY PALACE, MY HOLY PLACE.
AND CRAPPED ON MY FLOOR.
LIN, YOU HAVE *CRAPPED.* ON MY *FLOOR.*
YOUR HONOR--
--AS SOON AS MITCHELL-YOUNG WAS HIRED, I *KNEW* YOU'D BE COURTING THE CIRCUS.
I KNEW YOU'D BE PLAYING TO THE CHEAP SEATS, BECAUSE IT'S WHAT YOUR FIRM DOES. GETTING US ALL IN THE ROOM, A SURPRISE PLEA...*THAT* I EXPECTED.
BUT THE DEATH PENALTY? LIN, IT'S... *ABSURD.*
IT'S *NOT.* THERE IS A PRECEDENT. IT'S FROM A SIXTY-YEAR-OLD CASE, BUT STILL--
NONE OF US WANT THIS TO GO TO TRIAL. I'M GETTING IT FROM ON HIGH, AND I'M SURE SO ARE YOU. A BIG SPLASH, A CLEAN BOW, JUSTICE SERVED, AND A MONSTER LOCKED AWAY FOR ALL TIME.
AGREE. *ALMOST.* YOUR HONOR, ALL WE'RE ASKING IS THAT WE TAKE IT ONE STEP FARTHER--
LIN, I CAN'T DO IT.
YOU CAN.
AND YOU SHOULD.

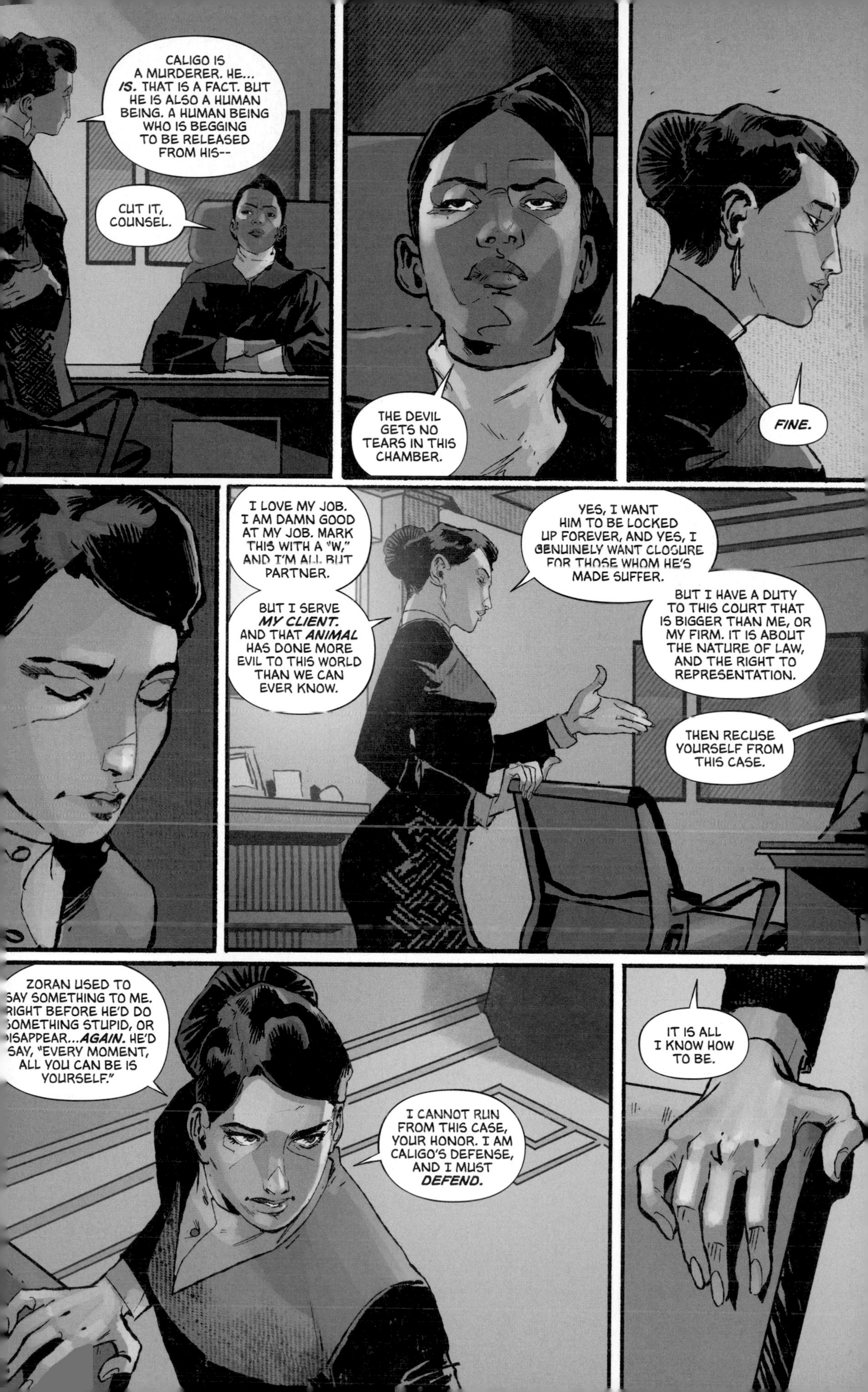
CALIGO IS A MURDERER. HE... *IS.* THAT IS A FACT. BUT HE IS ALSO A HUMAN BEING. A HUMAN BEING WHO IS BEGGING TO BE RELEASED FROM HIS--
CUT IT, COUNSEL.
THE DEVIL GETS NO TEARS IN THIS CHAMBER.
FINE.
I LOVE MY JOB. I AM DAMN GOOD AT MY JOB. MARK THIS WITH A "W," AND I'M ALL BUT PARTNER.
BUT I SERVE *MY CLIENT.* AND THAT *ANIMAL* HAS DONE MORE EVIL TO THIS WORLD THAN WE CAN EVER KNOW.
YES, I WANT HIM TO BE LOCKED UP FOREVER, AND YES, I GENUINELY WANT CLOSURE FOR THOSE WHOM HE'S MADE SUFFER.
BUT I HAVE A DUTY TO THIS COURT THAT IS BIGGER THAN ME, OR MY FIRM. IT IS ABOUT THE NATURE OF LAW, AND THE RIGHT TO REPRESENTATION.
THEN RECUSE YOURSELF FROM THIS CASE.
ZORAN USED TO SAY SOMETHING TO ME. RIGHT BEFORE HE'D DO SOMETHING STUPID, OR DISAPPEAR...*AGAIN.* HE'D SAY, "EVERY MOMENT, ALL YOU CAN BE IS YOURSELF."
I CANNOT RUN FROM THIS CASE, YOUR HONOR. I AM CALIGO'S DEFENSE, AND I MUST *DEFEND.*
IT IS ALL I KNOW HOW TO BE.

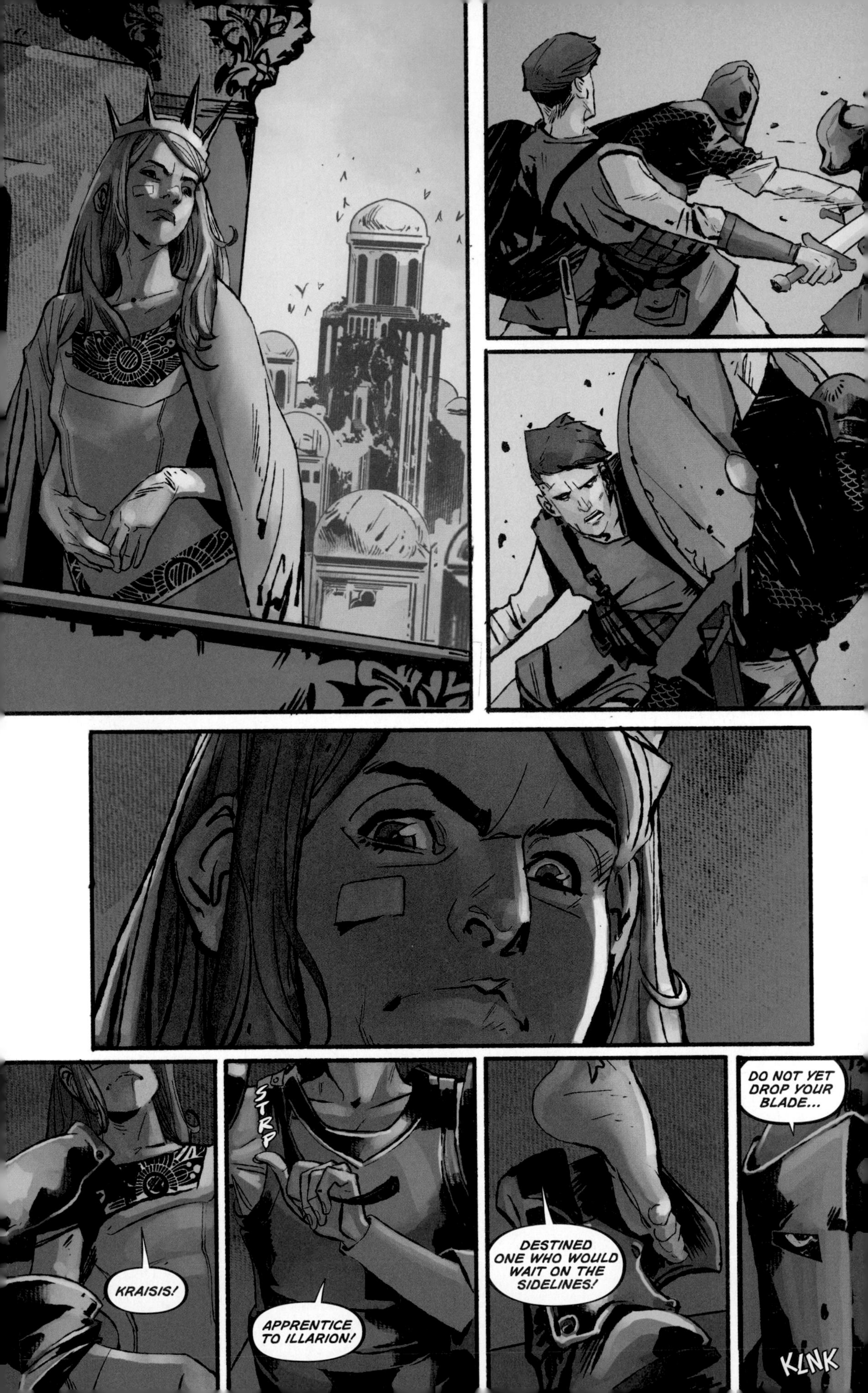
KRAISIS!
STRP
APPRENTICE TO ILLARION!
DESTINED ONE WHO WOULD WAIT ON THE SIDELINES!
DO NOT YET DROP YOUR BLADE...
KLNK

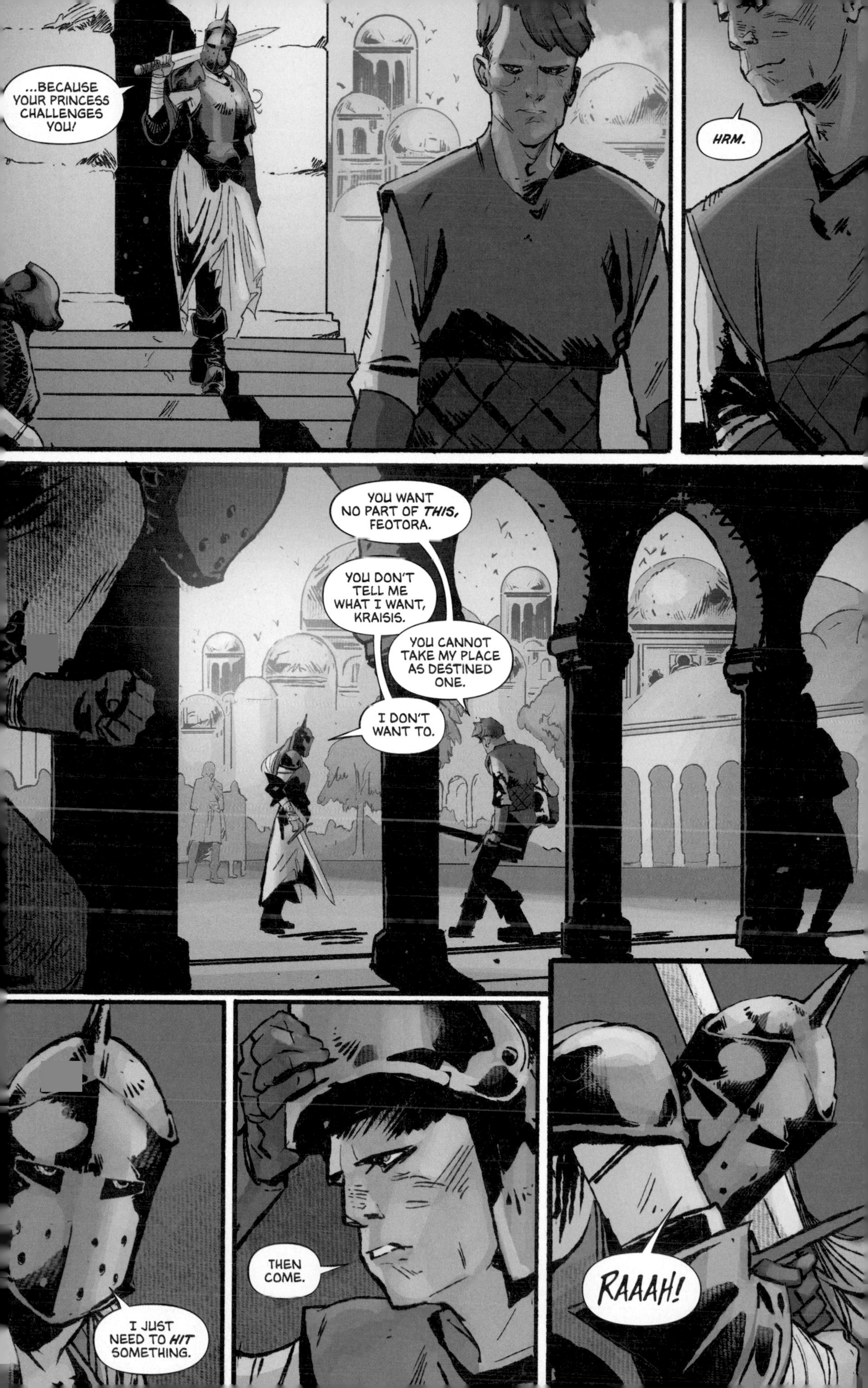
...BECAUSE YOUR PRINCESS CHALLENGES YOU!
HRM.
YOU WANT NO PART OF *THIS,* FEOTORA.
YOU DON'T TELL ME WHAT I WANT, KRAISIS.
YOU CANNOT TAKE MY PLACE AS DESTINED ONE.
I DON'T WANT TO.
I JUST NEED TO *HIT* SOMETHING.
THEN COME.
RAAAH!

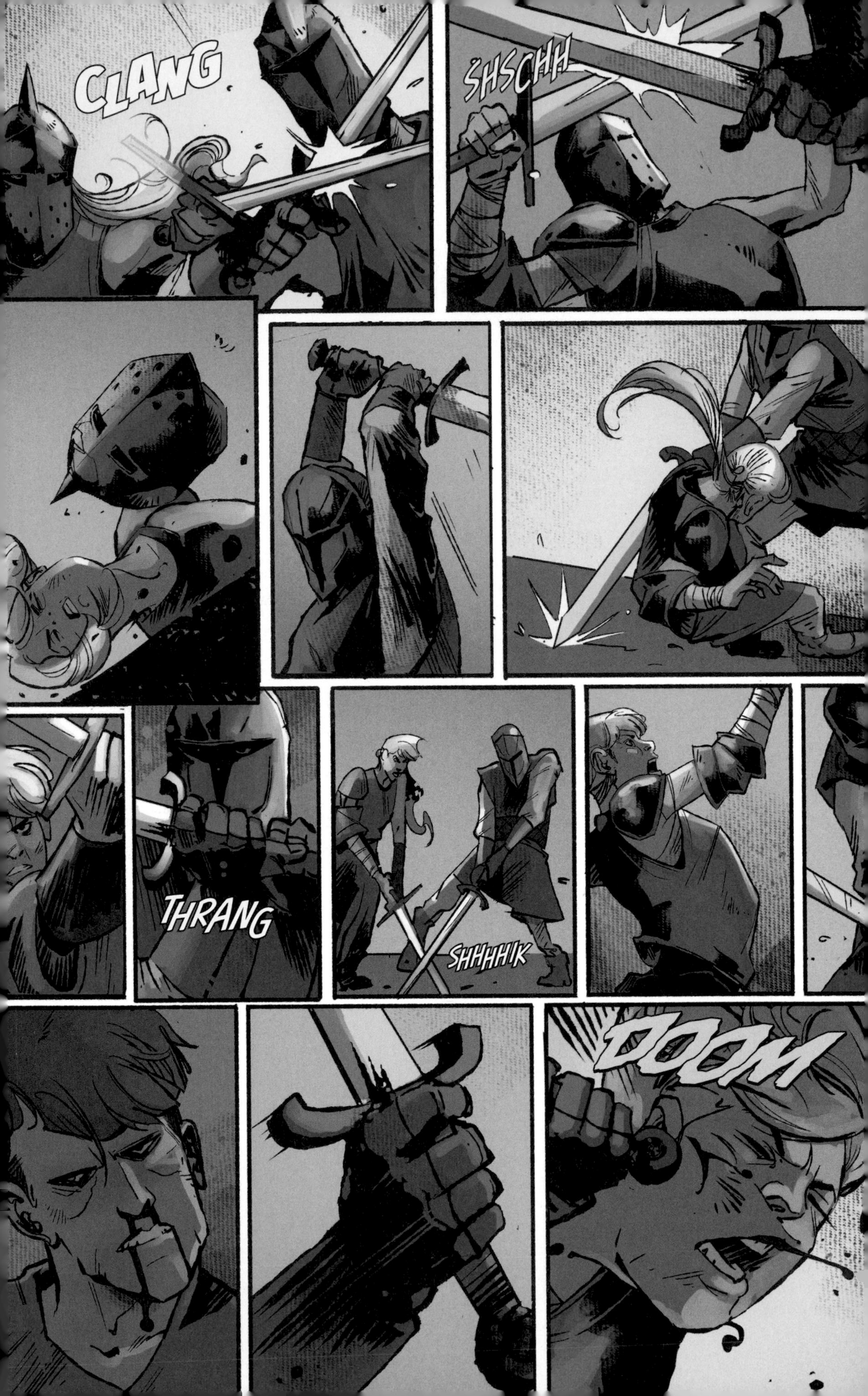
CLANG
SHSCHH
THRANG
SHHHHIK
DOOM

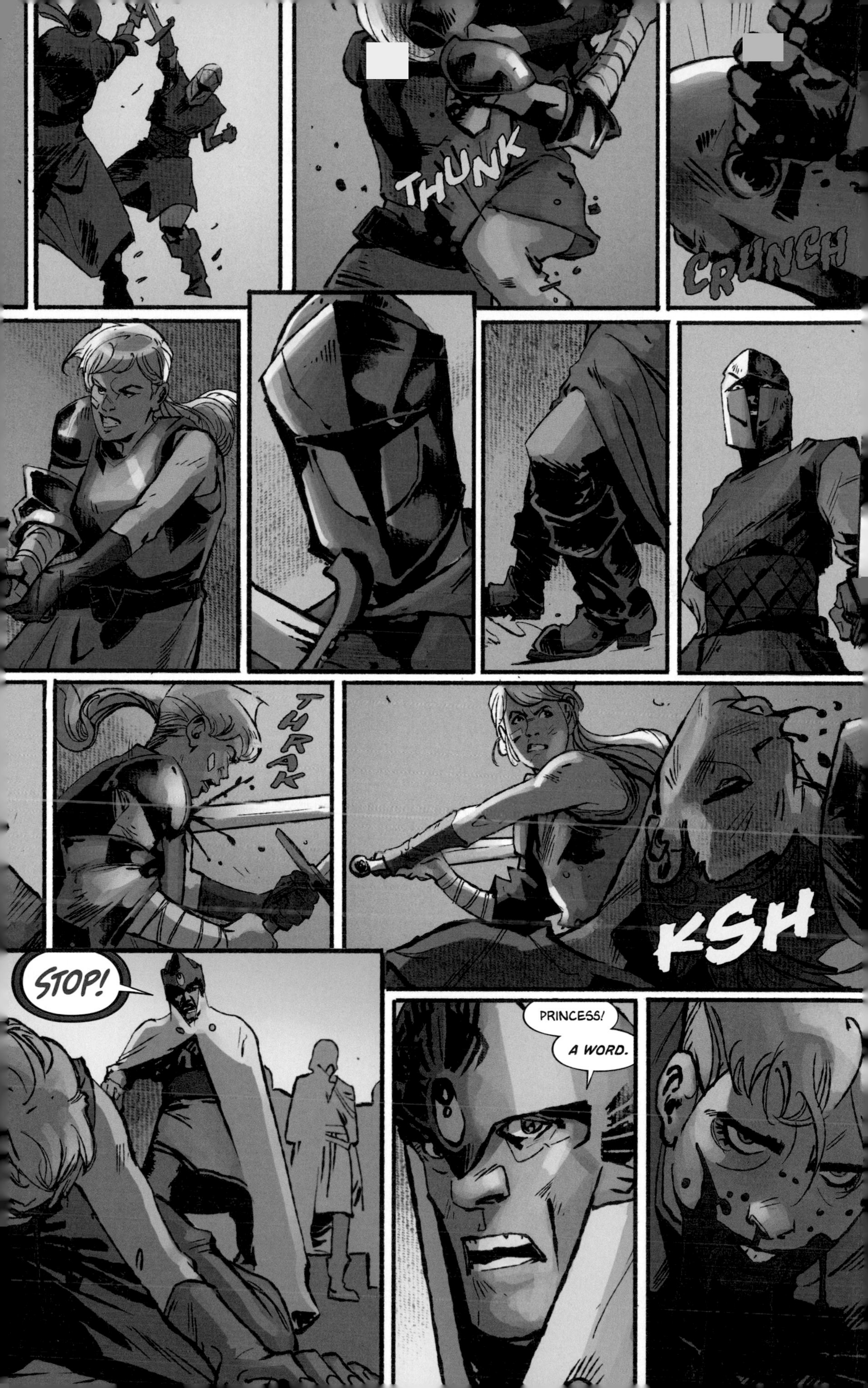
THUNK
CRUNCH
THRAK
KSH
STOP!
PRINCESS!
A WORD.

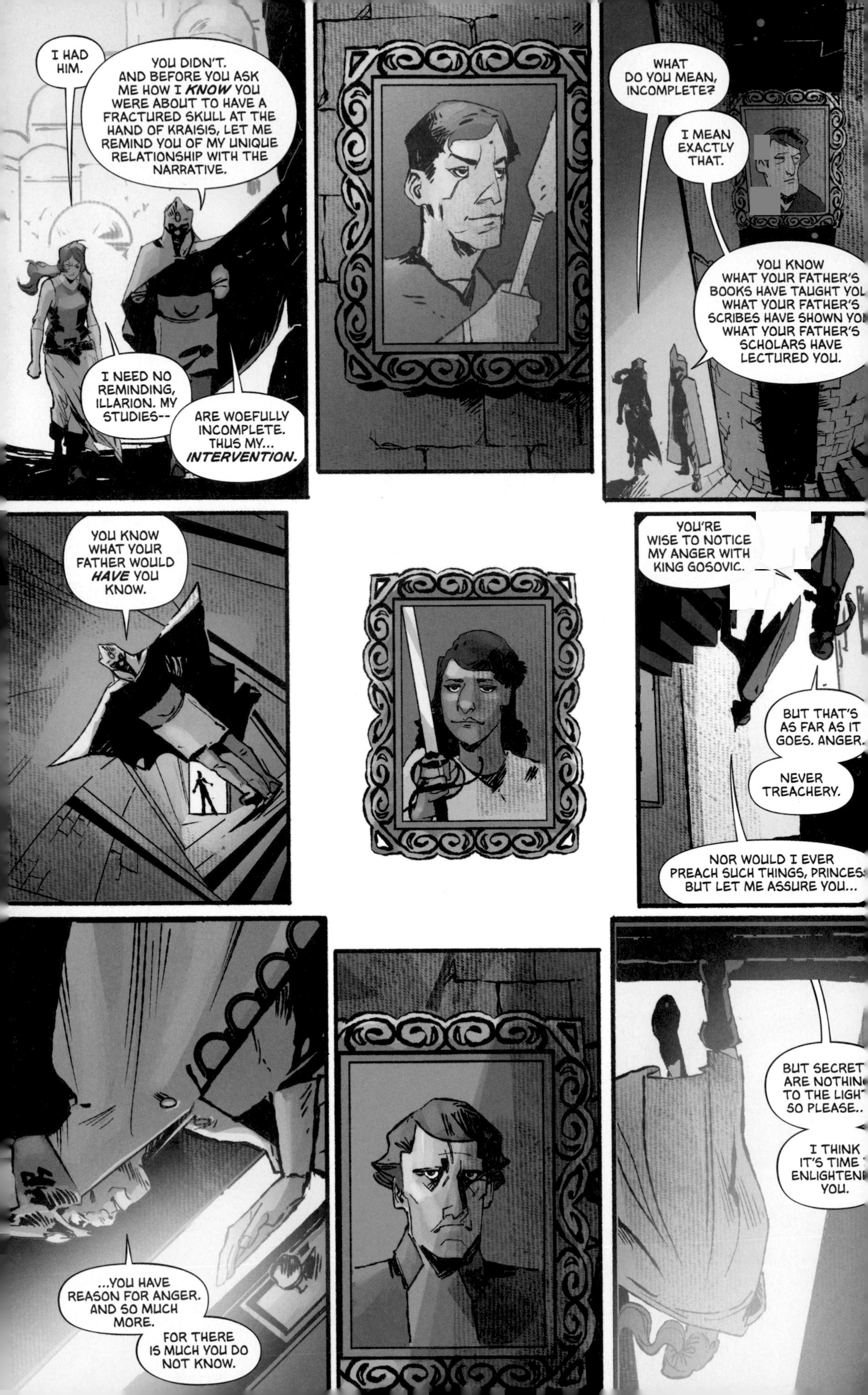
I HAD HIM.
YOU DIDN'T. AND BEFORE YOU ASK ME HOW I *KNOW* YOU WERE ABOUT TO HAVE A FRACTURED SKULL AT THE HAND OF KRAISIS, LET ME REMIND YOU OF MY UNIQUE RELATIONSHIP WITH THE NARRATIVE.
I NEED NO REMINDING, ILLARION. MY STUDIES--
ARE WOEFULLY INCOMPLETE. THUS MY... *INTERVENTION.*
WHAT DO YOU MEAN, INCOMPLETE?
I MEAN EXACTLY THAT.
YOU KNOW WHAT YOUR FATHER'S BOOKS HAVE TAUGHT YOU WHAT YOUR FATHER'S SCRIBES HAVE SHOWN YOU WHAT YOUR FATHER'S SCHOLARS HAVE LECTURED YOU.
YOU KNOW WHAT YOUR FATHER WOULD *HAVE* YOU KNOW.
YOU'RE WISE TO NOTICE MY ANGER WITH KING GOSOVIC.
BUT THAT'S AS FAR AS IT GOES. ANGER.
NEVER TREACHERY.
NOR WOULD I EVER PREACH SUCH THINGS, PRINCESS BUT LET ME ASSURE YOU...
...YOU HAVE REASON FOR ANGER. AND SO MUCH MORE.
FOR THERE IS MUCH YOU DO NOT KNOW.
BUT SECRETS ARE NOTHING TO THE LIGHT SO PLEASE..
I THINK IT'S TIME TO ENLIGHTEN YOU.

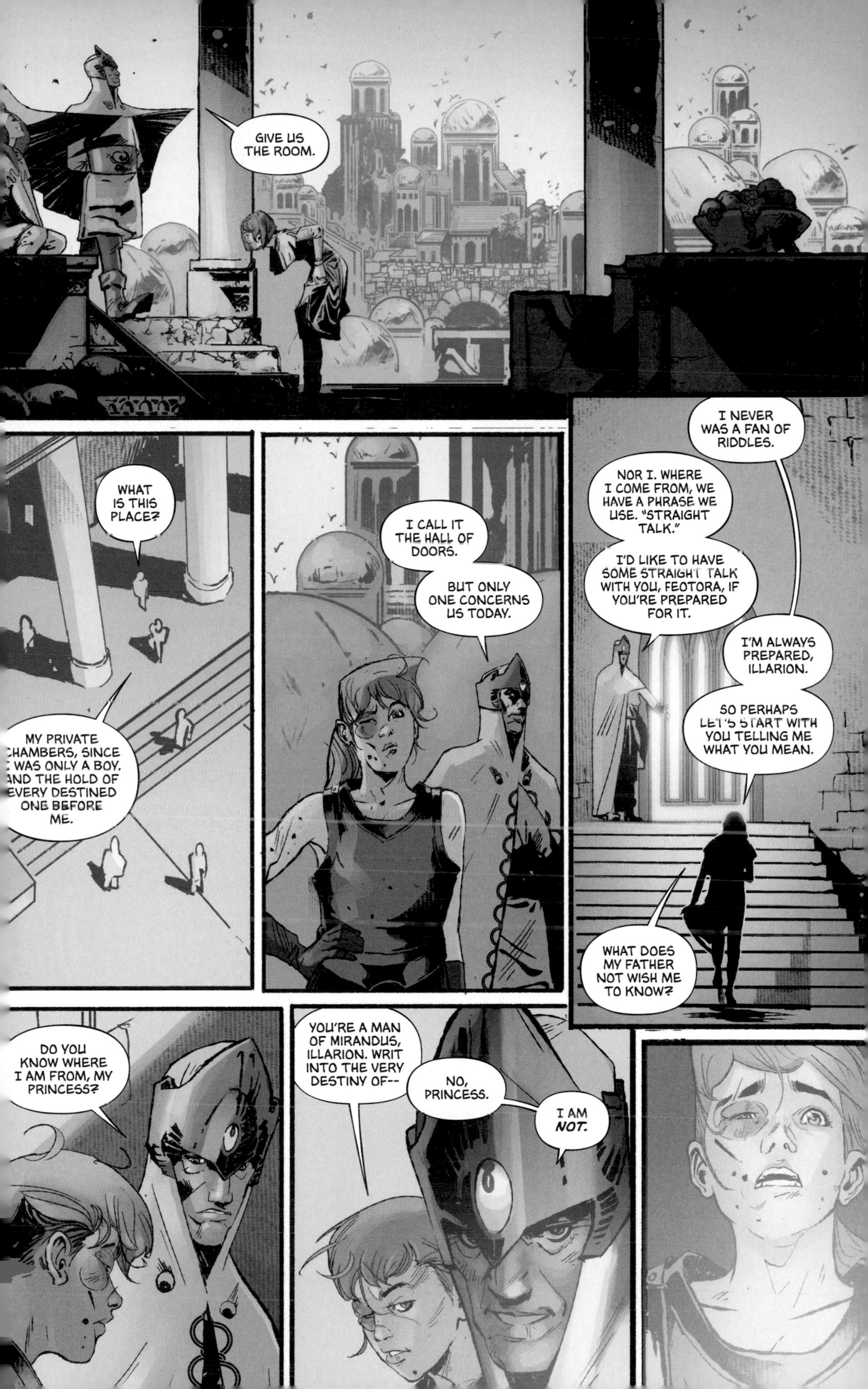
GIVE US THE ROOM.
WHAT IS THIS PLACE?
MY PRIVATE CHAMBERS, SINCE I WAS ONLY A BOY. AND THE HOLD OF EVERY DESTINED ONE BEFORE ME.
I CALL IT THE HALL OF DOORS.
BUT ONLY ONE CONCERNS US TODAY.
I NEVER WAS A FAN OF RIDDLES.
NOR I. WHERE I COME FROM, WE HAVE A PHRASE WE USE. "STRAIGHT TALK."
I'D LIKE TO HAVE SOME STRAIGHT TALK WITH YOU, FEOTORA, IF YOU'RE PREPARED FOR IT.
I'M ALWAYS PREPARED, ILLARION.
SO PERHAPS LET'S START WITH YOU TELLING ME WHAT YOU MEAN.
WHAT DOES MY FATHER NOT WISH ME TO KNOW?
DO YOU KNOW WHERE I AM FROM, MY PRINCESS?
YOU'RE A MAN OF MIRANDUS, ILLARION. WRIT INTO THE VERY DESTINY OF--
NO, PRINCESS.
I AM *NOT.*

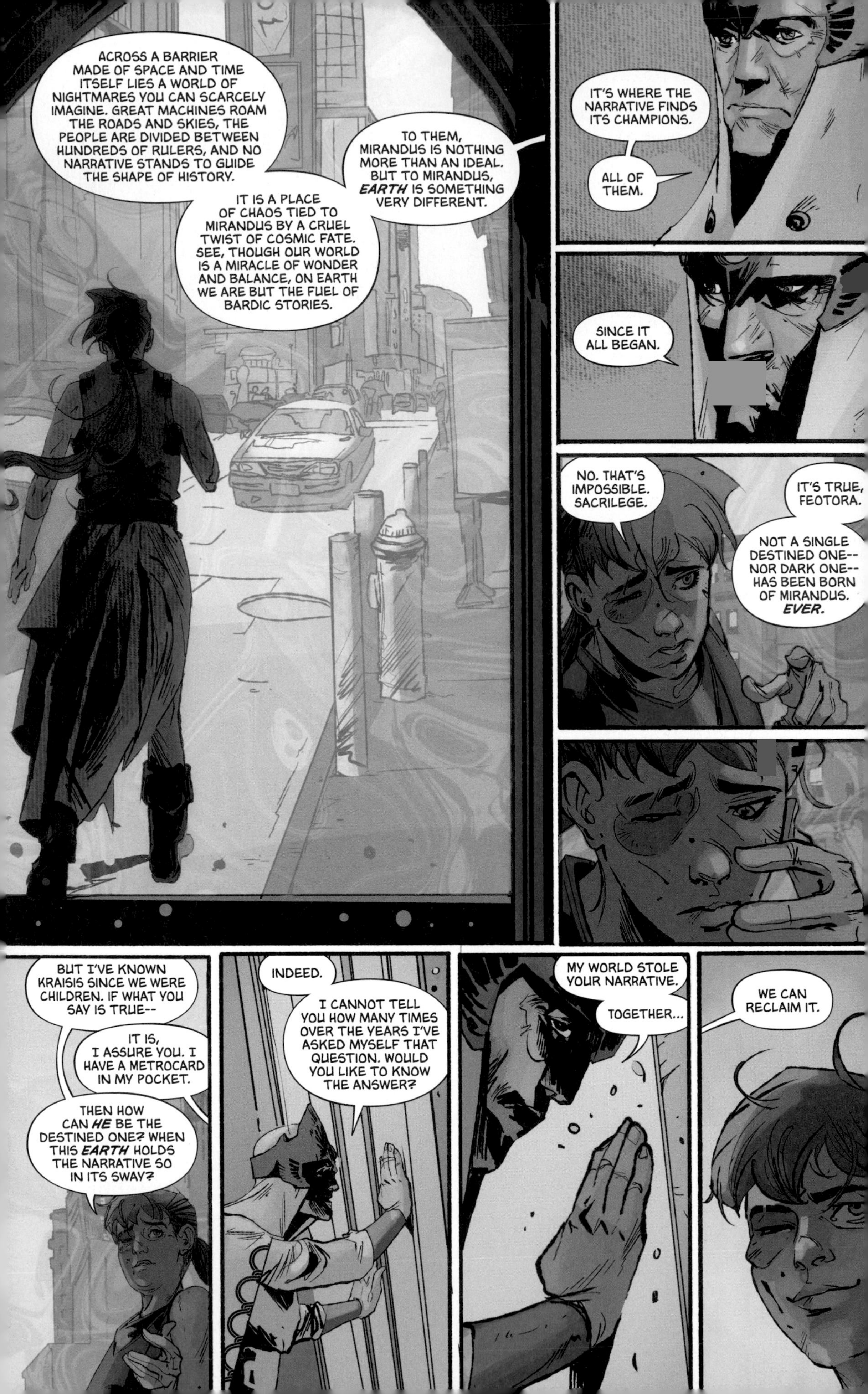
ACROSS A BARRIER MADE OF SPACE AND TIME ITSELF LIES A WORLD OF NIGHTMARES YOU CAN SCARCELY IMAGINE. GREAT MACHINES ROAM THE ROADS AND SKIES, THE PEOPLE ARE DIVIDED BETWEEN HUNDREDS OF RULERS, AND NO NARRATIVE STANDS TO GUIDE THE SHAPE OF HISTORY.
IT IS A PLACE OF CHAOS TIED TO MIRANDUS BY A CRUEL TWIST OF COSMIC FATE. SEE, THOUGH OUR WORLD IS A MIRACLE OF WONDER AND BALANCE, ON EARTH WE ARE BUT THE FUEL OF BARDIC STORIES.
TO THEM, MIRANDUS IS NOTHING MORE THAN AN IDEAL. BUT TO MIRANDUS, *EARTH* IS SOMETHING VERY DIFFERENT.
IT'S WHERE THE NARRATIVE FINDS ITS CHAMPIONS.
ALL OF THEM.
SINCE IT ALL BEGAN.
NO. THAT'S IMPOSSIBLE. SACRILEGE.
IT'S TRUE, FEOTORA.
NOT A SINGLE DESTINED ONE-- NOR DARK ONE-- HAS BEEN BORN OF MIRANDUS. *EVER.*
BUT I'VE KNOWN KRAISIS SINCE WE WERE CHILDREN. IF WHAT YOU SAY IS TRUE--
IT IS, I ASSURE YOU. I HAVE A METROCARD IN MY POCKET.
THEN HOW CAN *HE* BE THE DESTINED ONE? WHEN THIS *EARTH* HOLDS THE NARRATIVE SO IN ITS SWAY?
INDEED.
I CANNOT TELL YOU HOW MANY TIMES OVER THE YEARS I'VE ASKED MYSELF THAT QUESTION. WOULD YOU LIKE TO KNOW THE ANSWER?
MY WORLD STOLE YOUR NARRATIVE.
TOGETHER...
WE CAN RECLAIM IT.

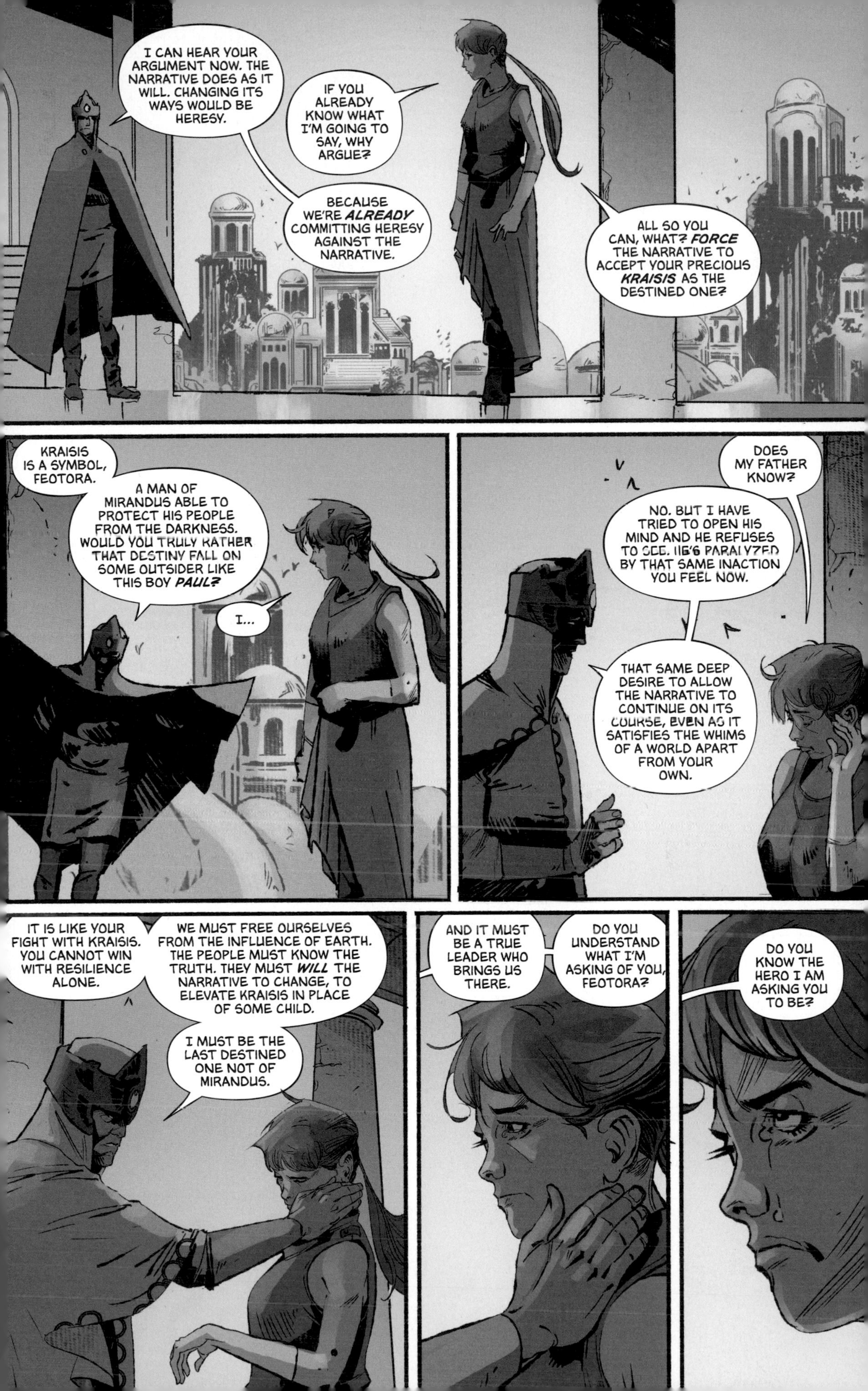
I CAN HEAR YOUR ARGUMENT NOW. THE NARRATIVE DOES AS IT WILL. CHANGING ITS WAYS WOULD BE HERESY.
IF YOU ALREADY KNOW WHAT I'M GOING TO SAY, WHY ARGUE?
BECAUSE WE'RE *ALREADY* COMMITTING HERESY AGAINST THE NARRATIVE.
ALL SO YOU CAN, WHAT? *FORCE* THE NARRATIVE TO ACCEPT YOUR PRECIOUS *KRAISIS* AS THE DESTINED ONE?
KRAISIS IS A SYMBOL, FEOTORA.
A MAN OF MIRANDUS ABLE TO PROTECT HIS PEOPLE FROM THE DARKNESS. WOULD YOU TRULY RATHER THAT DESTINY FALL ON SOME OUTSIDER LIKE THIS BOY *PAUL?*
I...
DOES MY FATHER KNOW?
NO. BUT I HAVE TRIED TO OPEN HIS MIND AND HE REFUSES TO SEE. HE'S PARALYZED BY THAT SAME INACTION YOU FEEL NOW.
THAT SAME DEEP DESIRE TO ALLOW THE NARRATIVE TO CONTINUE ON ITS COURSE, EVEN AS IT SATISFIES THE WHIMS OF A WORLD APART FROM YOUR OWN.
IT IS LIKE YOUR FIGHT WITH KRAISIS. YOU CANNOT WIN WITH RESILIENCE ALONE.
WE MUST FREE OURSELVES FROM THE INFLUENCE OF EARTH. THE PEOPLE MUST KNOW THE TRUTH. THEY MUST *WILL* THE NARRATIVE TO CHANGE, TO ELEVATE KRAISIS IN PLACE OF SOME CHILD.
I MUST BE THE LAST DESTINED ONE NOT OF MIRANDUS.
AND IT MUST BE A TRUE LEADER WHO BRINGS US THERE.
DO YOU UNDERSTAND WHAT I'M ASKING OF YOU, FEOTORA?
DO YOU KNOW THE HERO I AM ASKING YOU TO BE?

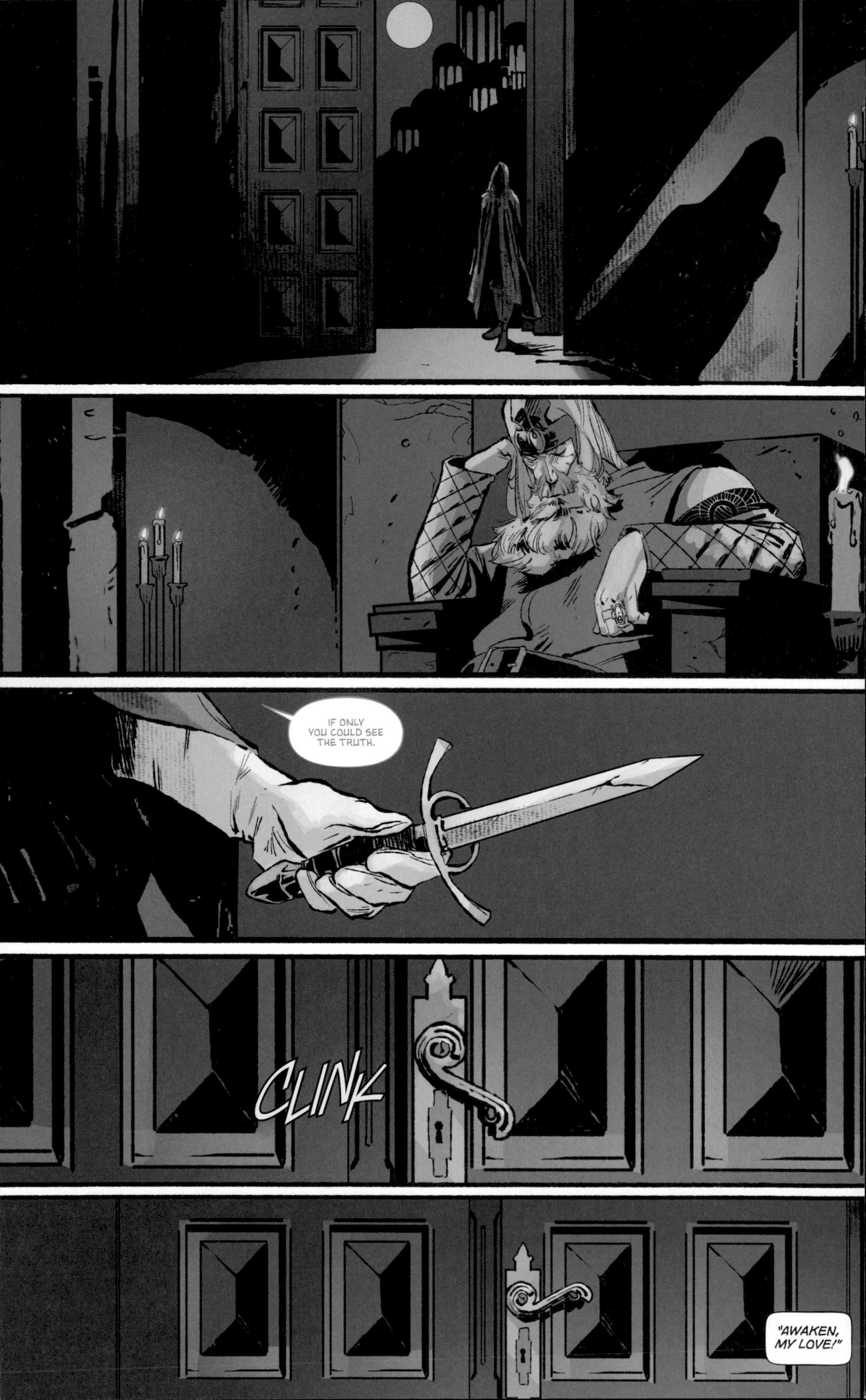
IF ONLY YOU COULD SEE THE TRUTH.
CLINK
"AWAKEN, MY LOVE!"

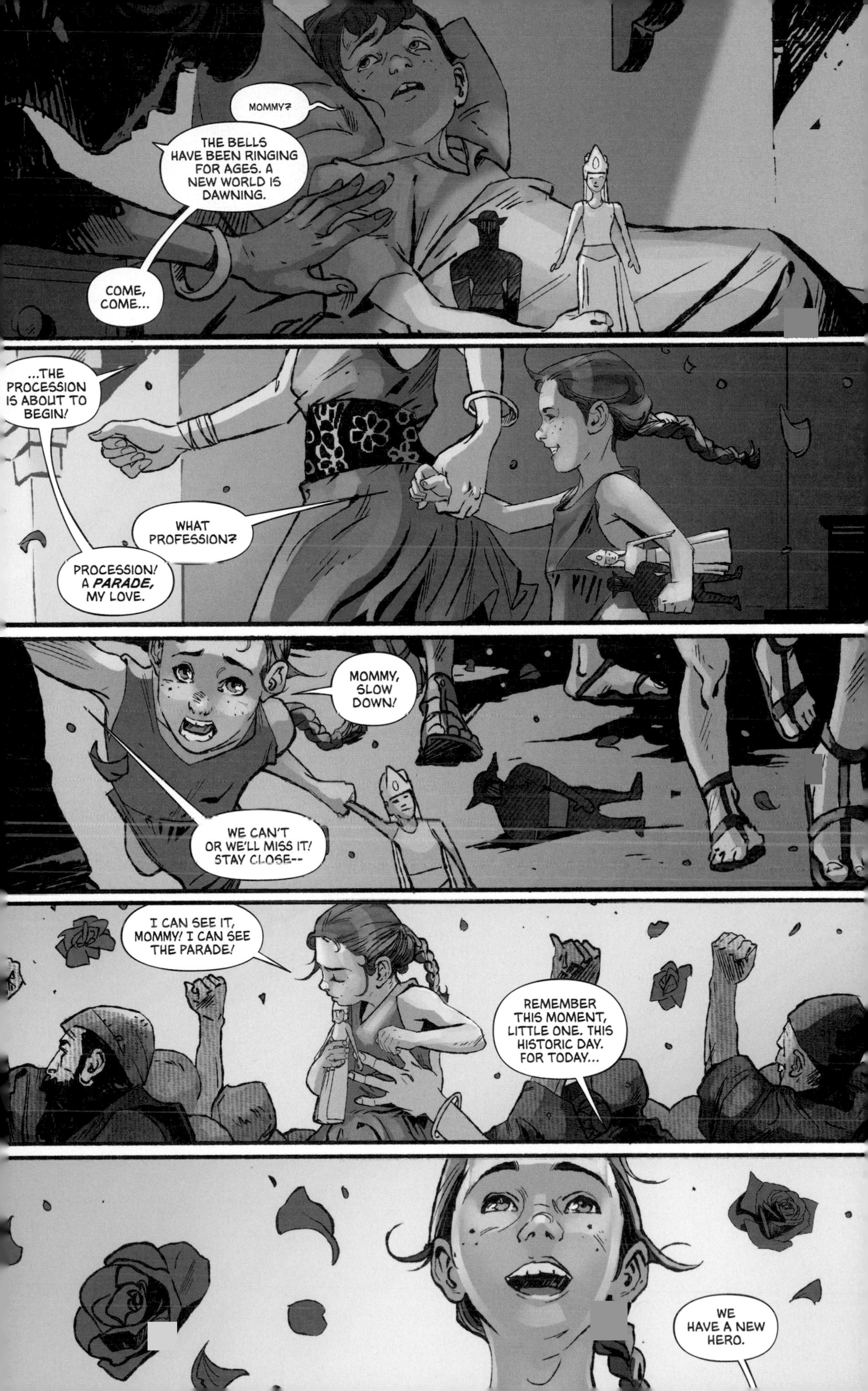
MOMMY?
THE BELLS HAVE BEEN RINGING FOR AGES. A NEW WORLD IS DAWNING.
COME, COME...
...THE PROCESSION IS ABOUT TO BEGIN!
WHAT PROFESSION?
PROCESSION! A *PARADE,* MY LOVE.
MOMMY, SLOW DOWN!
WE CAN'T OR WE'LL MISS IT! STAY CLOSE--
I CAN SEE IT, MOMMY! I CAN SEE THE PARADE!
REMEMBER THIS MOMENT, LITTLE ONE. THIS HISTORIC DAY. FOR TODAY...
WE HAVE A NEW HERO.

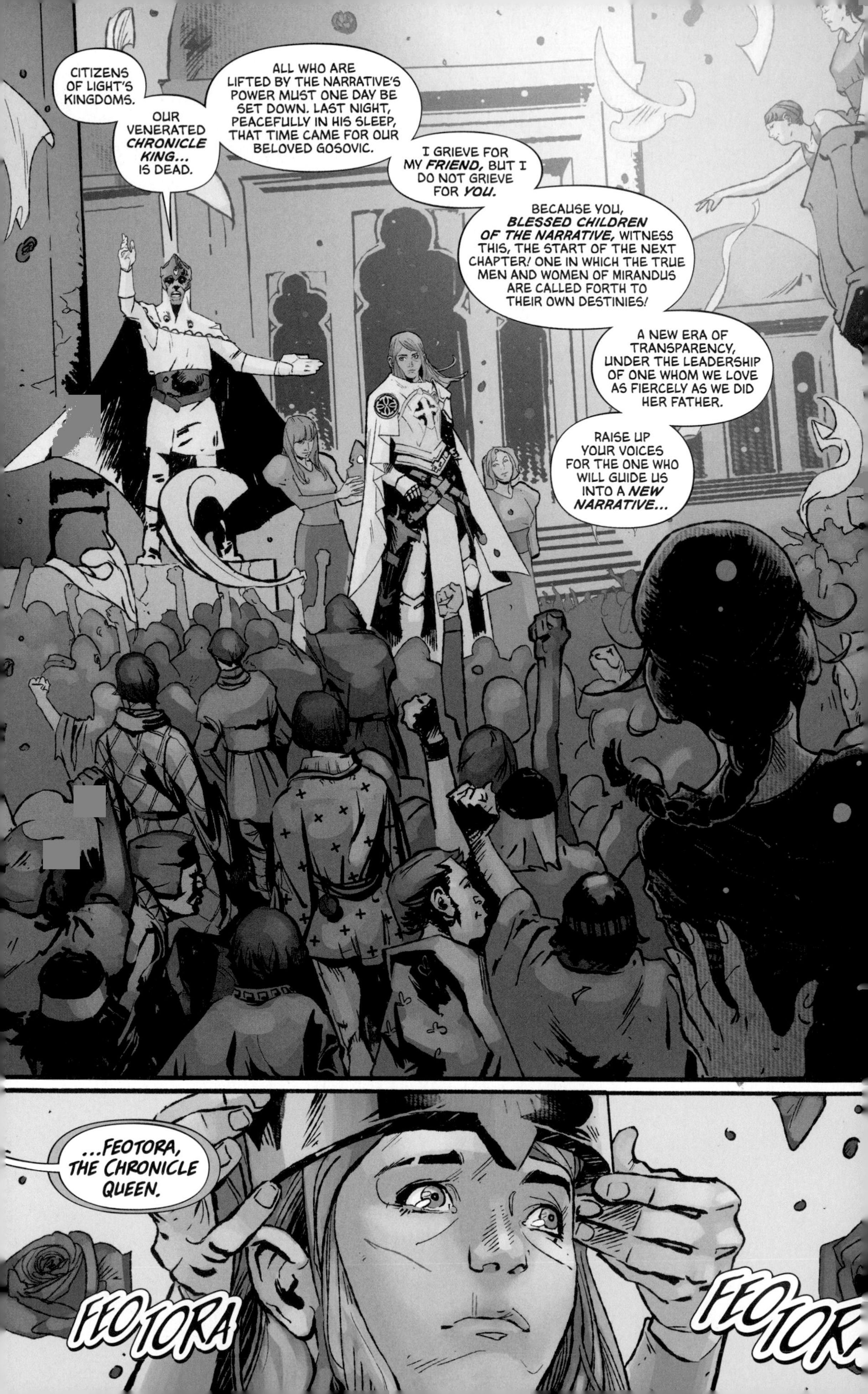
CITIZENS OF LIGHT'S KINGDOMS.
OUR VENERATED CHRONICLE KING... IS DEAD.
ALL WHO ARE LIFTED BY THE NARRATIVE'S POWER MUST ONE DAY BE SET DOWN. LAST NIGHT, PEACEFULLY IN HIS SLEEP, THAT TIME CAME FOR OUR BELOVED GOSOVIC.
I GRIEVE FOR MY FRIEND, BUT I DO NOT GRIEVE FOR YOU.
BECAUSE YOU, BLESSED CHILDREN OF THE NARRATIVE, WITNESS THIS, THE START OF THE NEXT CHAPTER! ONE IN WHICH THE TRUE MEN AND WOMEN OF MIRANDUS ARE CALLED FORTH TO THEIR OWN DESTINIES!
A NEW ERA OF TRANSPARENCY, UNDER THE LEADERSHIP OF ONE WHOM WE LOVE AS FIERCELY AS WE DID HER FATHER.
RAISE UP YOUR VOICES FOR THE ONE WHO WILL GUIDE US INTO A NEW NARRATIVE...
...FEOTORA, THE CHRONICLE QUEEN.
FEO TORA
FEO TORA

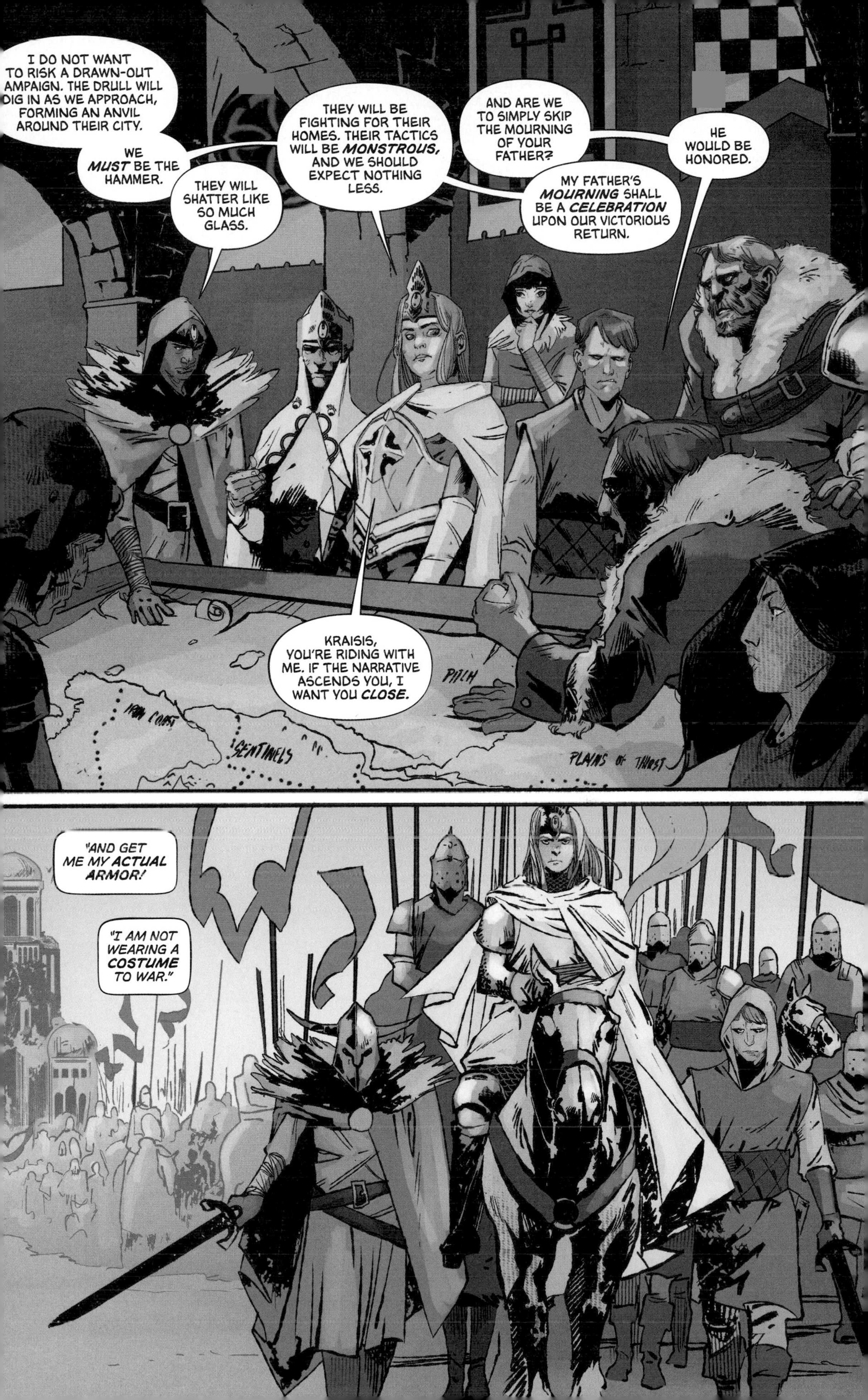
I DO NOT WANT TO RISK A DRAWN-OUT AMPAIGN. THE DRULL WILL DIG IN AS WE APPROACH, FORMING AN ANVIL AROUND THEIR CITY.
WE *MUST* BE THE HAMMER.
THEY WILL SHATTER LIKE SO MUCH GLASS.
THEY WILL BE FIGHTING FOR THEIR HOMES. THEIR TACTICS WILL BE *MONSTROUS,* AND WE SHOULD EXPECT NOTHING LESS.
AND ARE WE TO SIMPLY SKIP THE MOURNING OF YOUR FATHER?
HE WOULD BE HONORED.
MY FATHER'S *MOURNING* SHALL BE A *CELEBRATION* UPON OUR VICTORIOUS RETURN.
KRAISIS, YOU'RE RIDING WITH ME. IF THE NARRATIVE ASCENDS YOU, I WANT YOU *CLOSE.*
PITCH
IRON COAST
SENTINELS
PLAINS OF THIRST
"AND GET ME MY *ACTUAL ARMOR!*
"I AM NOT WEARING A *COSTUME* TO WAR."

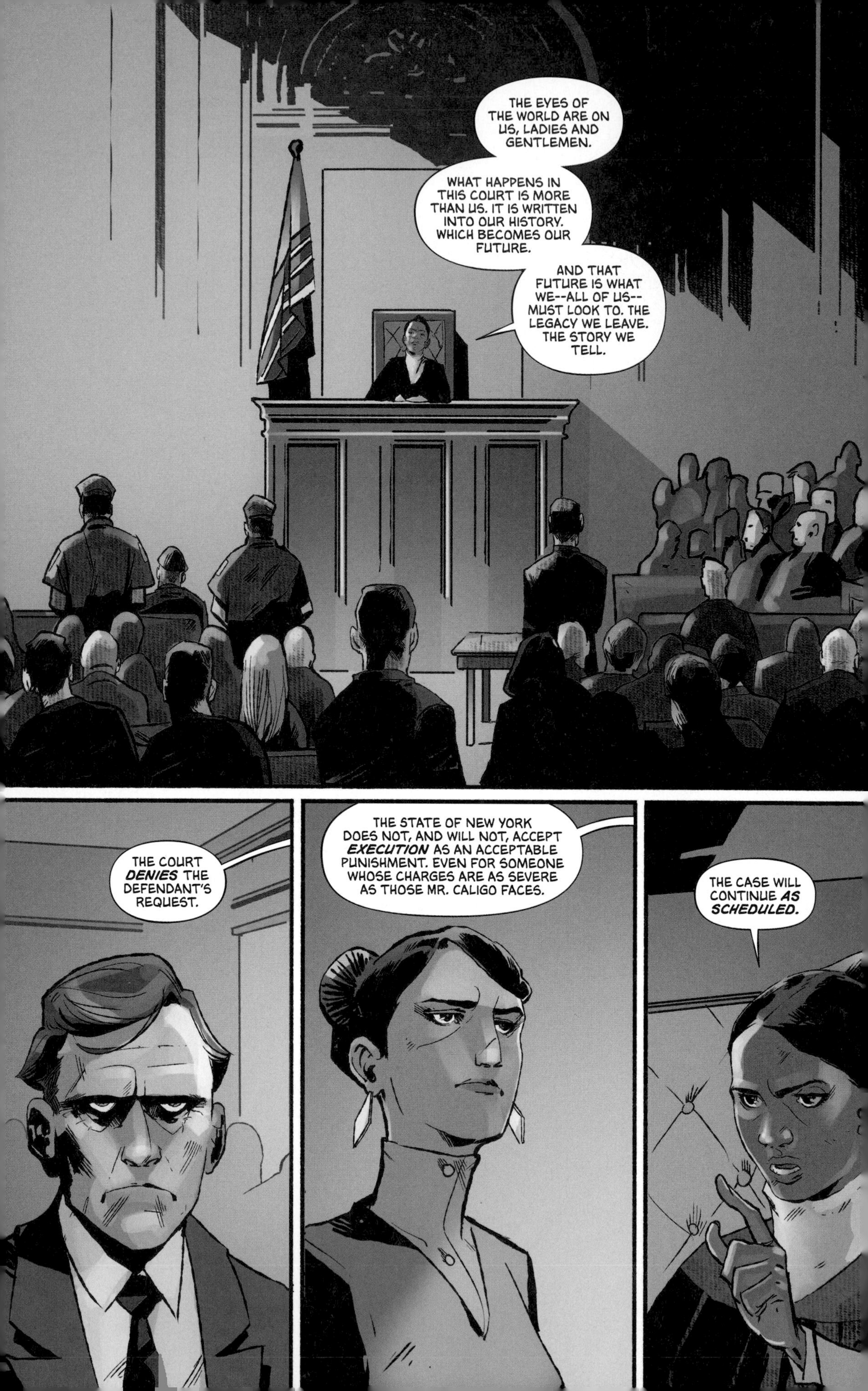
THE EYES OF THE WORLD ARE ON US, LADIES AND GENTLEMEN.
WHAT HAPPENS IN THIS COURT IS MORE THAN US. IT IS WRITTEN INTO OUR HISTORY. WHICH BECOMES OUR FUTURE.
AND THAT FUTURE IS WHAT WE--ALL OF US--MUST LOOK TO. THE LEGACY WE LEAVE. THE STORY WE TELL.
THE COURT *DENIES* THE DEFENDANT'S REQUEST.
THE STATE OF NEW YORK DOES NOT, AND WILL NOT, ACCEPT *EXECUTION* AS AN ACCEPTABLE PUNISHMENT. EVEN FOR SOMEONE WHOSE CHARGES ARE AS SEVERE AS THOSE MR. CALIGO FACES.
THE CASE WILL CONTINUE *AS SCHEDULED.*

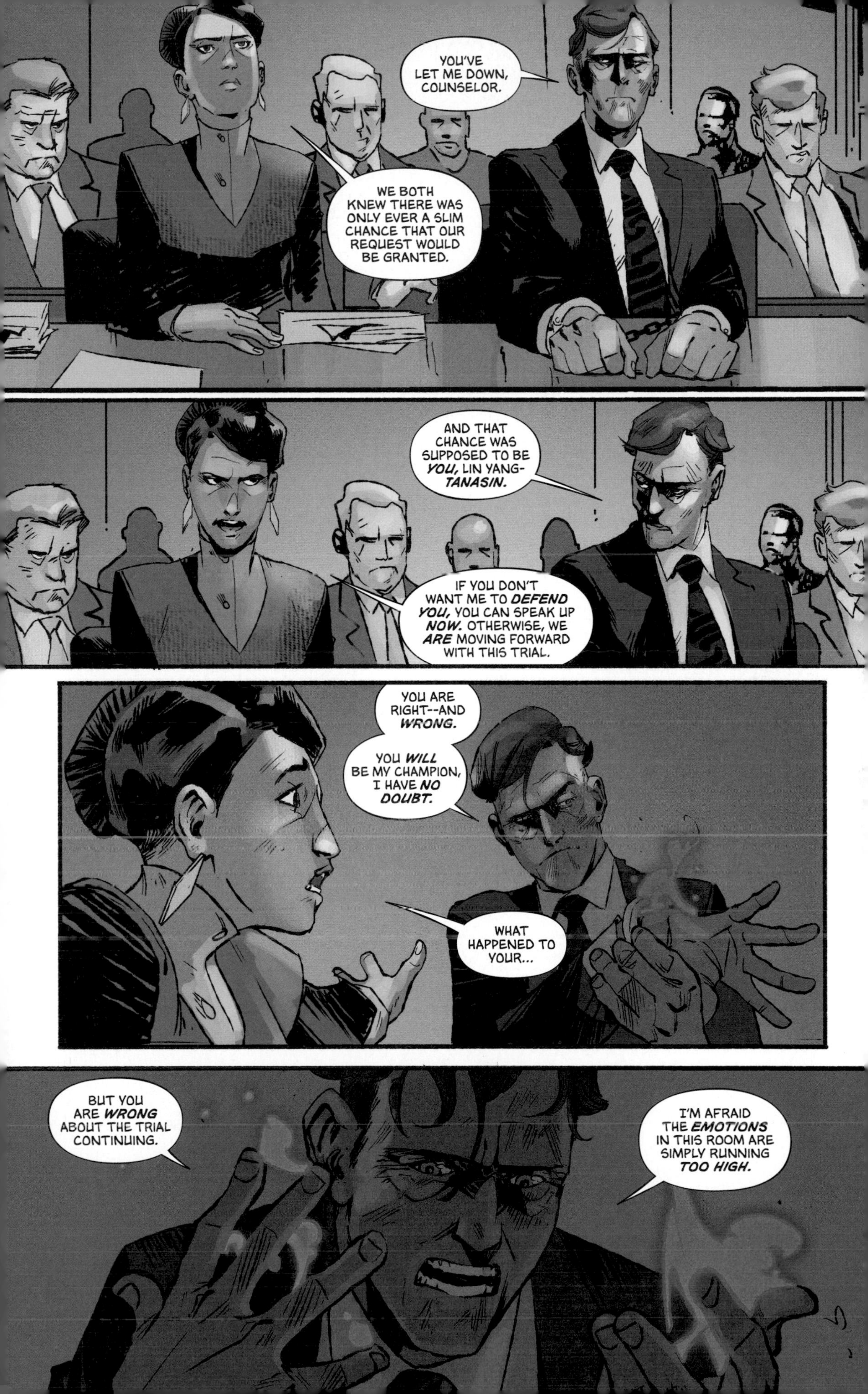
YOU'VE LET ME DOWN, COUNSELOR.
WE BOTH KNEW THERE WAS ONLY EVER A SLIM CHANCE THAT OUR REQUEST WOULD BE GRANTED.
AND THAT CHANCE WAS SUPPOSED TO BE *YOU,* LIN YANG-*TANASIN.*
IF YOU DON'T WANT ME TO *DEFEND YOU,* YOU CAN SPEAK UP *NOW.* OTHERWISE, WE *ARE* MOVING FORWARD WITH THIS TRIAL.
YOU ARE RIGHT--AND *WRONG.*
YOU *WILL* BE MY CHAMPION, I HAVE *NO DOUBT.*
WHAT HAPPENED TO YOUR...
BUT YOU ARE *WRONG* ABOUT THE TRIAL CONTINUING.
I'M AFRAID THE *EMOTIONS* IN THIS ROOM ARE SIMPLY RUNNING *TOO HIGH.*

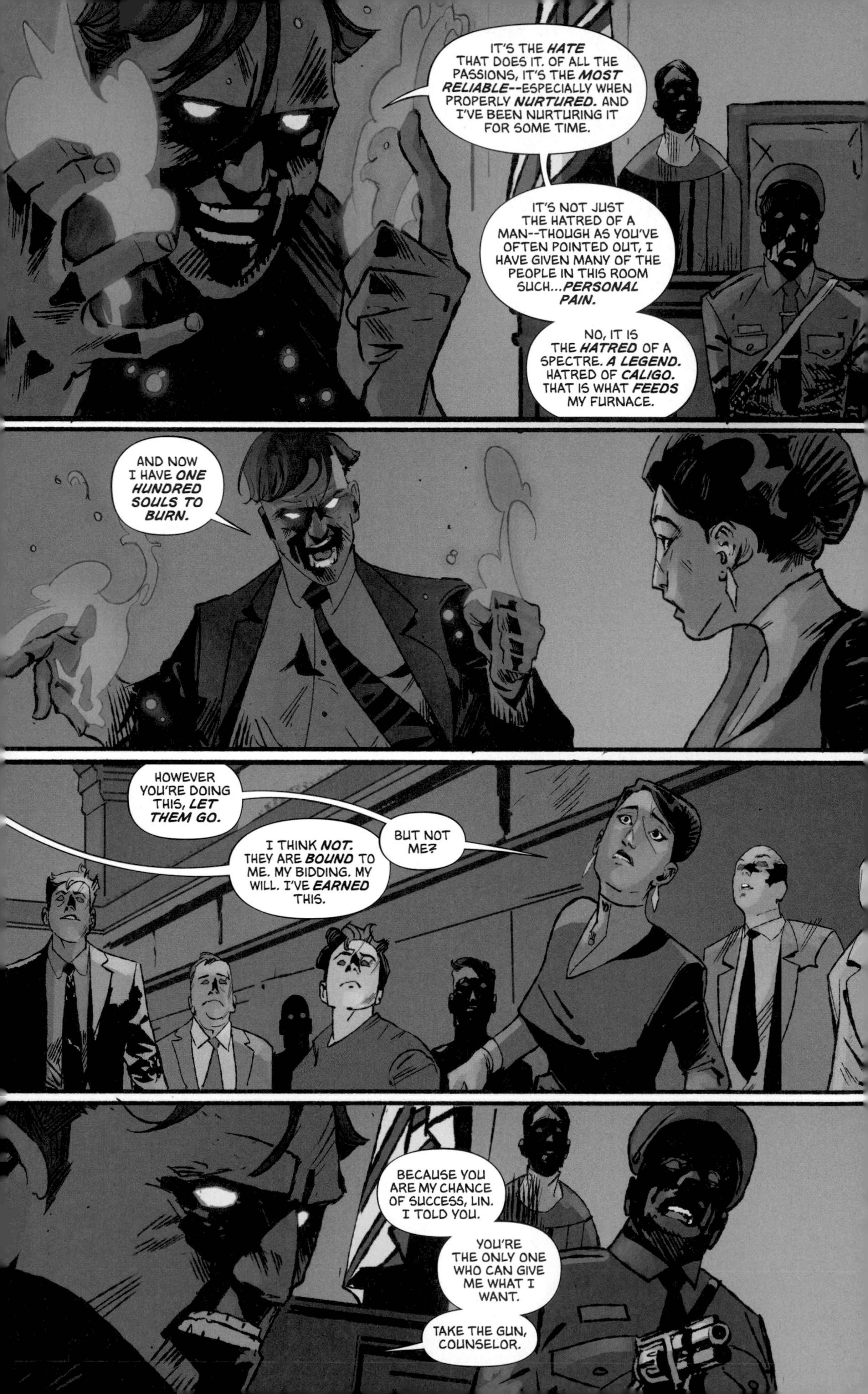
IT'S THE HATE THAT DOES IT. OF ALL THE PASSIONS, IT'S THE MOST RELIABLE--ESPECIALLY WHEN PROPERLY NURTURED. AND I'VE BEEN NURTURING IT FOR SOME TIME.
IT'S NOT JUST THE HATRED OF A MAN--THOUGH AS YOU'VE OFTEN POINTED OUT, I HAVE GIVEN MANY OF THE PEOPLE IN THIS ROOM SUCH...PERSONAL PAIN.
NO, IT IS THE HATRED OF A SPECTRE. A LEGEND. HATRED OF CALIGO. THAT IS WHAT FEEDS MY FURNACE.
AND NOW I HAVE ONE HUNDRED SOULS TO BURN.
HOWEVER YOU'RE DOING THIS, LET THEM GO.
I THINK NOT. THEY ARE BOUND TO ME. MY BIDDING. MY WILL. I'VE EARNED THIS.
BUT NOT ME?
BECAUSE YOU ARE MY CHANCE OF SUCCESS, LIN. I TOLD YOU.
YOU'RE THE ONLY ONE WHO CAN GIVE ME WHAT I WANT.
TAKE THE GUN, COUNSELOR.

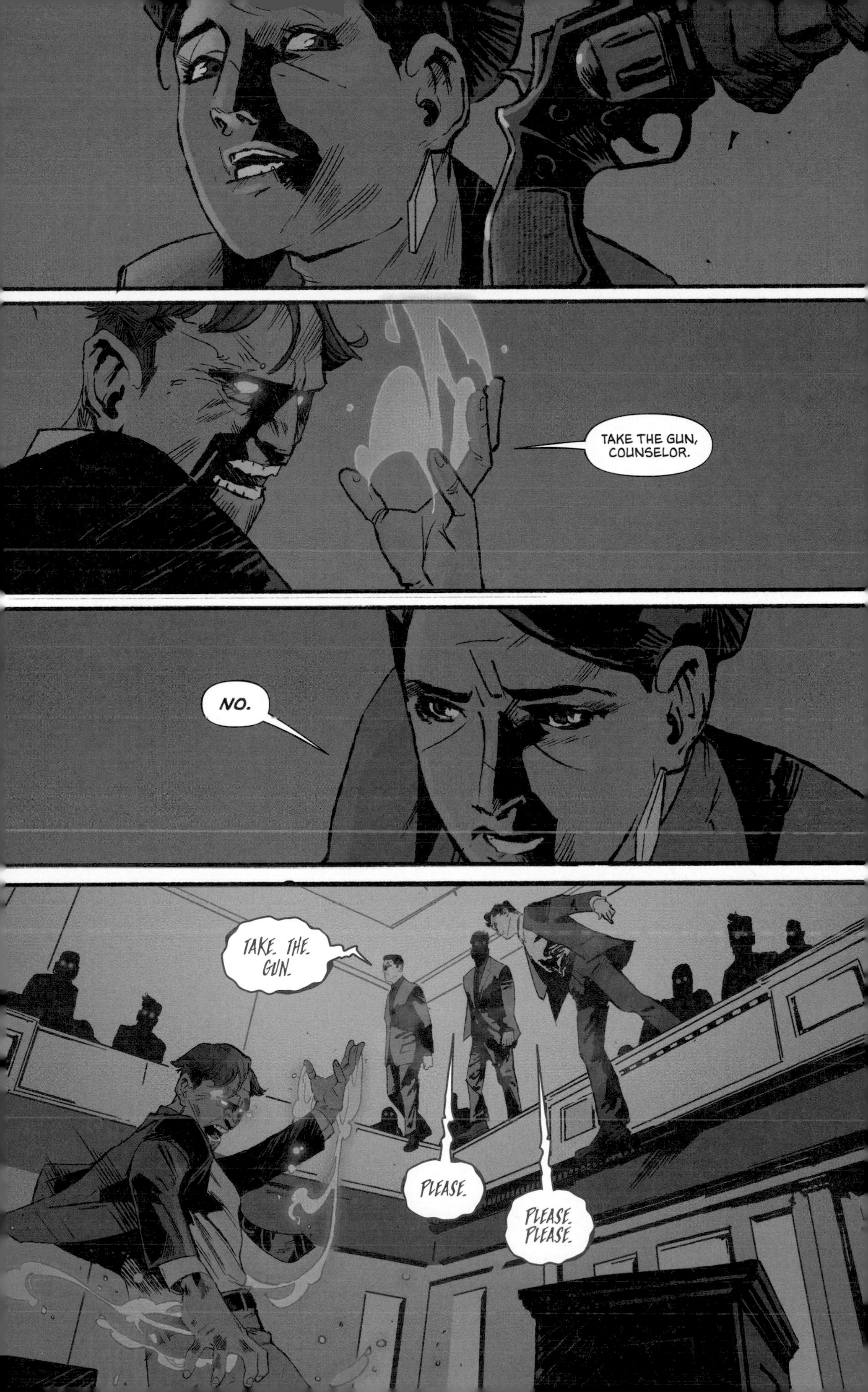
TAKE THE GUN, COUNSELOR.
NO.
TAKE. THE. GUN.
PLEASE.
PLEASE. PLEASE.

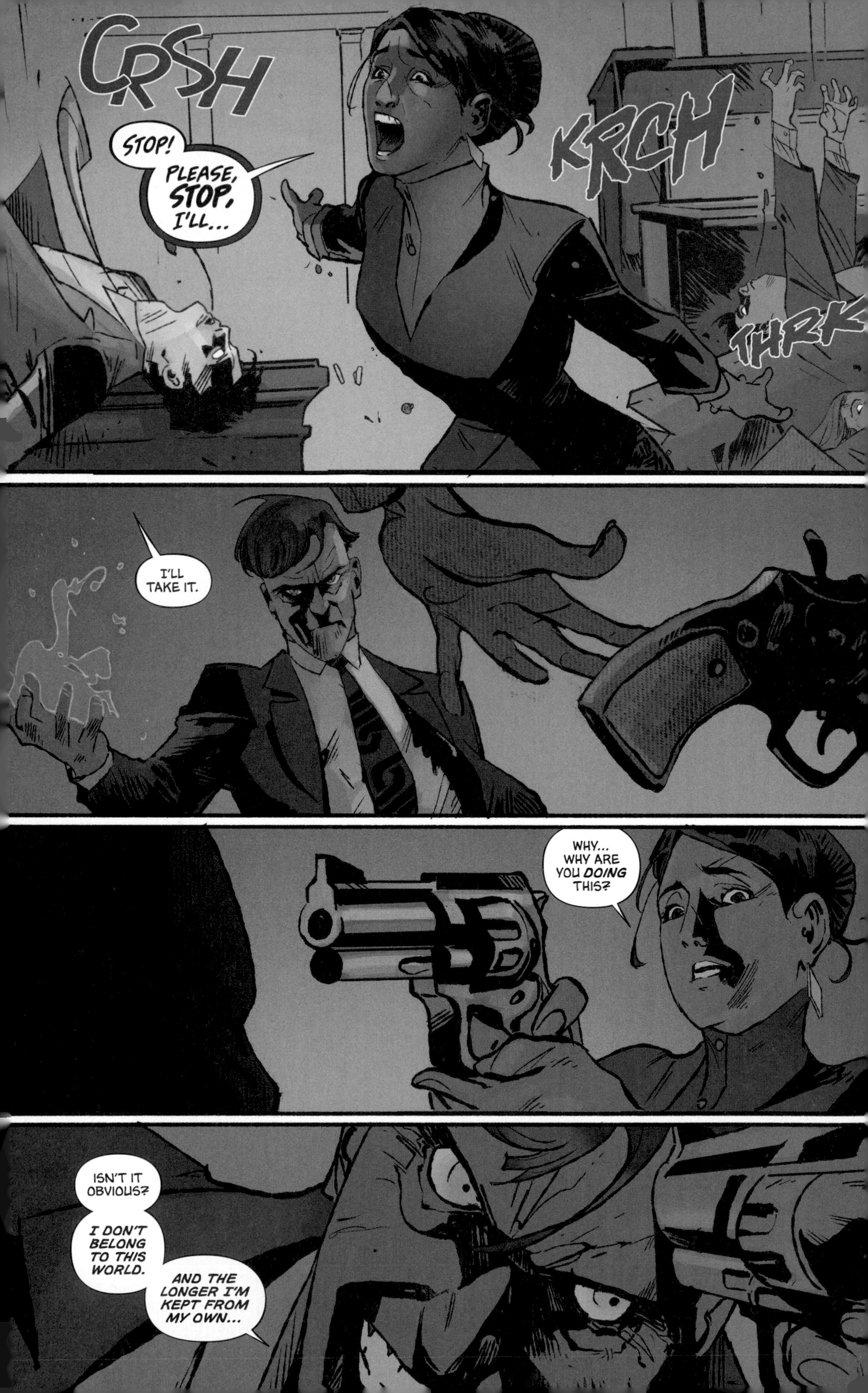
CRSH
STOP!
PLEASE, STOP, I'LL...
KRCH
THRK
I'LL TAKE IT.
WHY... WHY ARE YOU DOING THIS?
ISN'T IT OBVIOUS?
I DON'T BELONG TO THIS WORLD.
AND THE LONGER I'M KEPT FROM MY OWN...

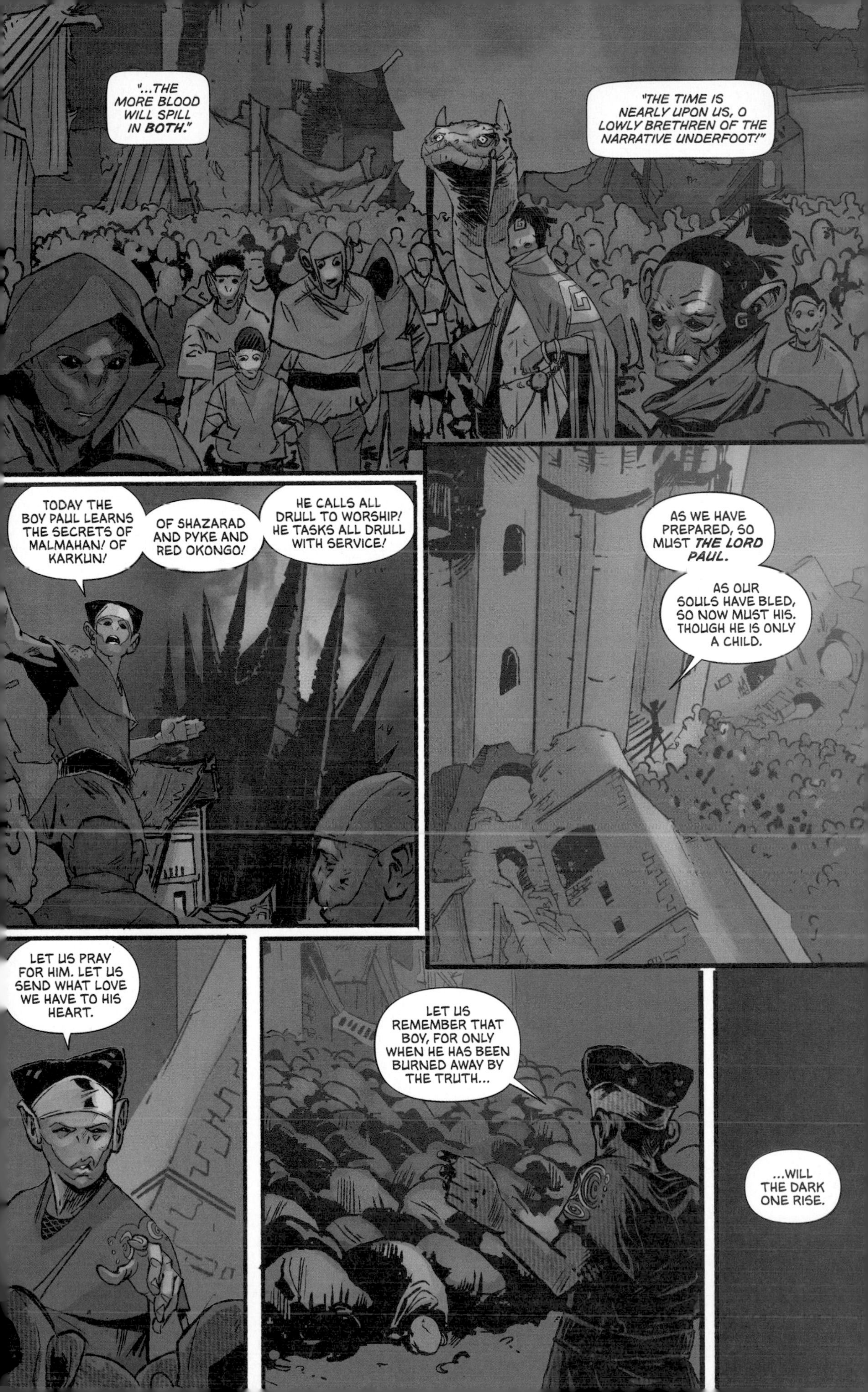
"...THE MORE BLOOD WILL SPILL IN BOTH."
"THE TIME IS NEARLY UPON US, O LOWLY BRETHREN OF THE NARRATIVE UNDERFOOT!"
TODAY THE BOY PAUL LEARNS THE SECRETS OF MALMAHAN! OF KARKUN!
OF SHAZARAD AND PYKE AND RED OKONGO!
HE CALLS ALL DRULL TO WORSHIP! HE TASKS ALL DRULL WITH SERVICE!
AS WE HAVE PREPARED, SO MUST THE LORD PAUL.
AS OUR SOULS HAVE BLED, SO NOW MUST HIS. THOUGH HE IS ONLY A CHILD.
LET US PRAY FOR HIM. LET US SEND WHAT LOVE WE HAVE TO HIS HEART.
LET US REMEMBER THAT BOY, FOR ONLY WHEN HE HAS BEEN BURNED AWAY BY THE TRUTH...
...WILL THE DARK ONE RISE.

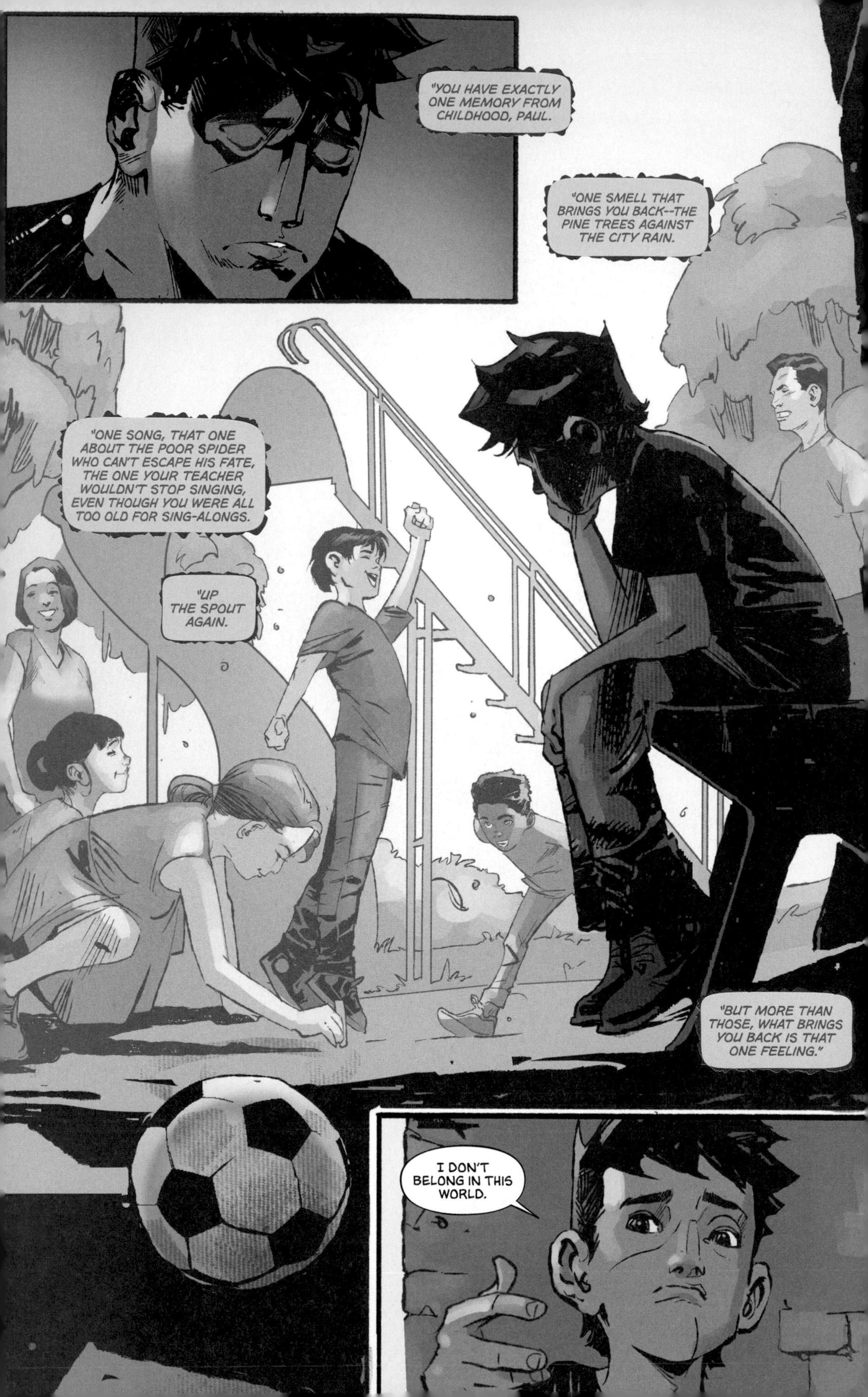
"YOU HAVE EXACTLY ONE MEMORY FROM CHILDHOOD, PAUL.
"ONE SMELL THAT BRINGS YOU BACK--THE PINE TREES AGAINST THE CITY RAIN.
"ONE SONG, THAT ONE ABOUT THE POOR SPIDER WHO CAN'T ESCAPE HIS FATE, THE ONE YOUR TEACHER WOULDN'T STOP SINGING, EVEN THOUGH YOU WERE ALL TOO OLD FOR SING-ALONGS.
"UP THE SPOUT AGAIN.
"BUT MORE THAN THOSE, WHAT BRINGS YOU BACK IS THAT ONE FEELING."
I DON'T BELONG IN THIS WORLD.

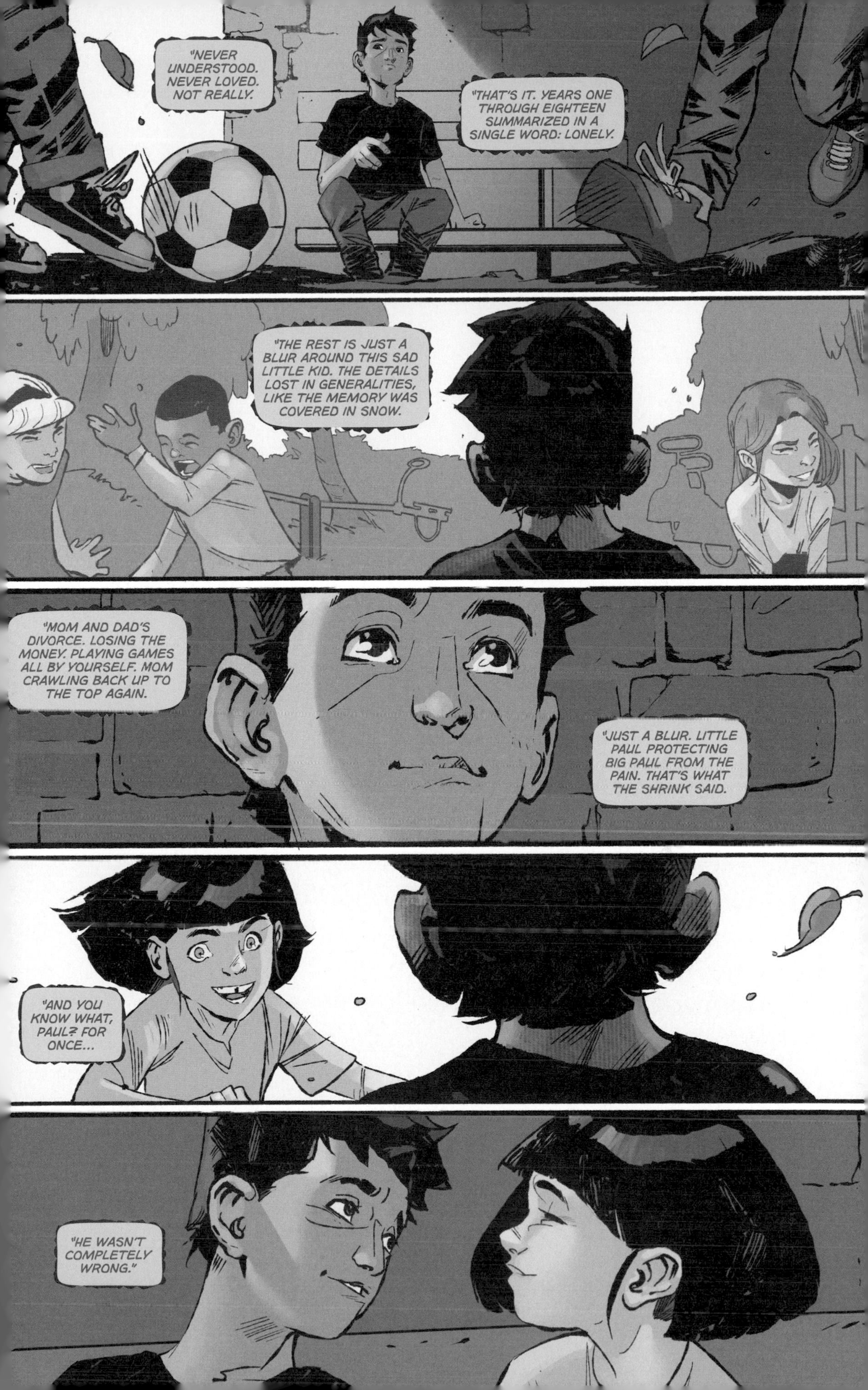
"NEVER UNDERSTOOD. NEVER LOVED. NOT REALLY.
"THAT'S IT. YEARS ONE THROUGH EIGHTEEN SUMMARIZED IN A SINGLE WORD: LONELY.
"THE REST IS JUST A BLUR AROUND THIS SAD LITTLE KID. THE DETAILS LOST IN GENERALITIES, LIKE THE MEMORY WAS COVERED IN SNOW.
"MOM AND DAD'S DIVORCE. LOSING THE MONEY. PLAYING GAMES ALL BY YOURSELF. MOM CRAWLING BACK UP TO THE TOP AGAIN.
"JUST A BLUR. LITTLE PAUL PROTECTING BIG PAUL FROM THE PAIN. THAT'S WHAT THE SHRINK SAID.
"AND YOU KNOW WHAT, PAUL? FOR ONCE...
"HE WASN'T COMPLETELY WRONG."

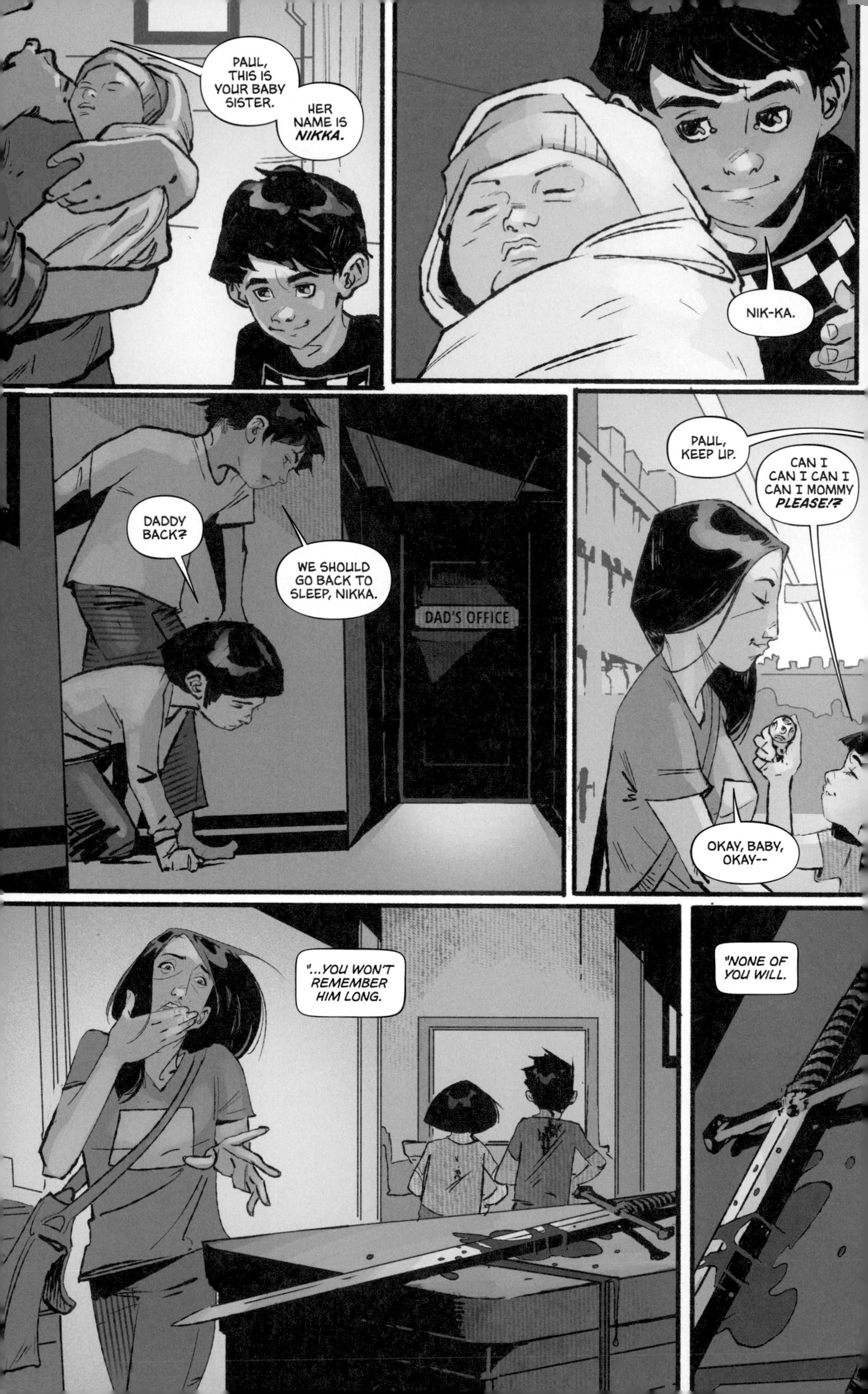
PAUL, THIS IS YOUR BABY SISTER.
HER NAME IS *NIKKA.*
NIK-KA.
DADDY BACK?
WE SHOULD GO BACK TO SLEEP, NIKKA.
DAD'S OFFICE
PAUL, KEEP UP.
CAN I CAN I CAN I CAN I MOMMY *PLEASE!?*
OKAY, BABY, OKAY--
"...YOU WON'T REMEMBER HIM LONG.
"NONE OF YOU WILL.

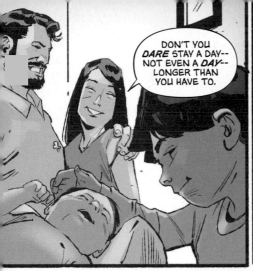

DON'T YOU *DARE* STAY A DAY-- NOT EVEN A *DAY*-- LONGER THAN YOU HAVE TO.

I KEEP TELLING YOU, LIN...

THEY DON'T HAVE *DAYS* WHERE I'M GOING.

YER DOING IT!

YER *DOING IT!*

DID YOU HEAR ME, PAUL?

KEEP UP.

"I'M SO SORRY, LIN. I TRIED. WE ALL TRIED.

"IF IT'S ANY CONSOLATION...

WE GATHER HERE TODAY TO MOURN THE LOSS OF *ZORAN TANASIN.* FATHER, HUSBAND, FRIEND. TAKEN BEFORE HIS TIME.

WOULD ANYONE LIKE TO SAY ANY WORDS?

"AFTER TWO DAYS, WE COULDN'T REMEMBER HIS FACE.

"AFTER FOUR DAYS, HIS VOICE WAS GONE FOREVER.

WITHIN A WEEK, WE WOULD BARELY EVEN REMEMBER WE HAD A FATHER.

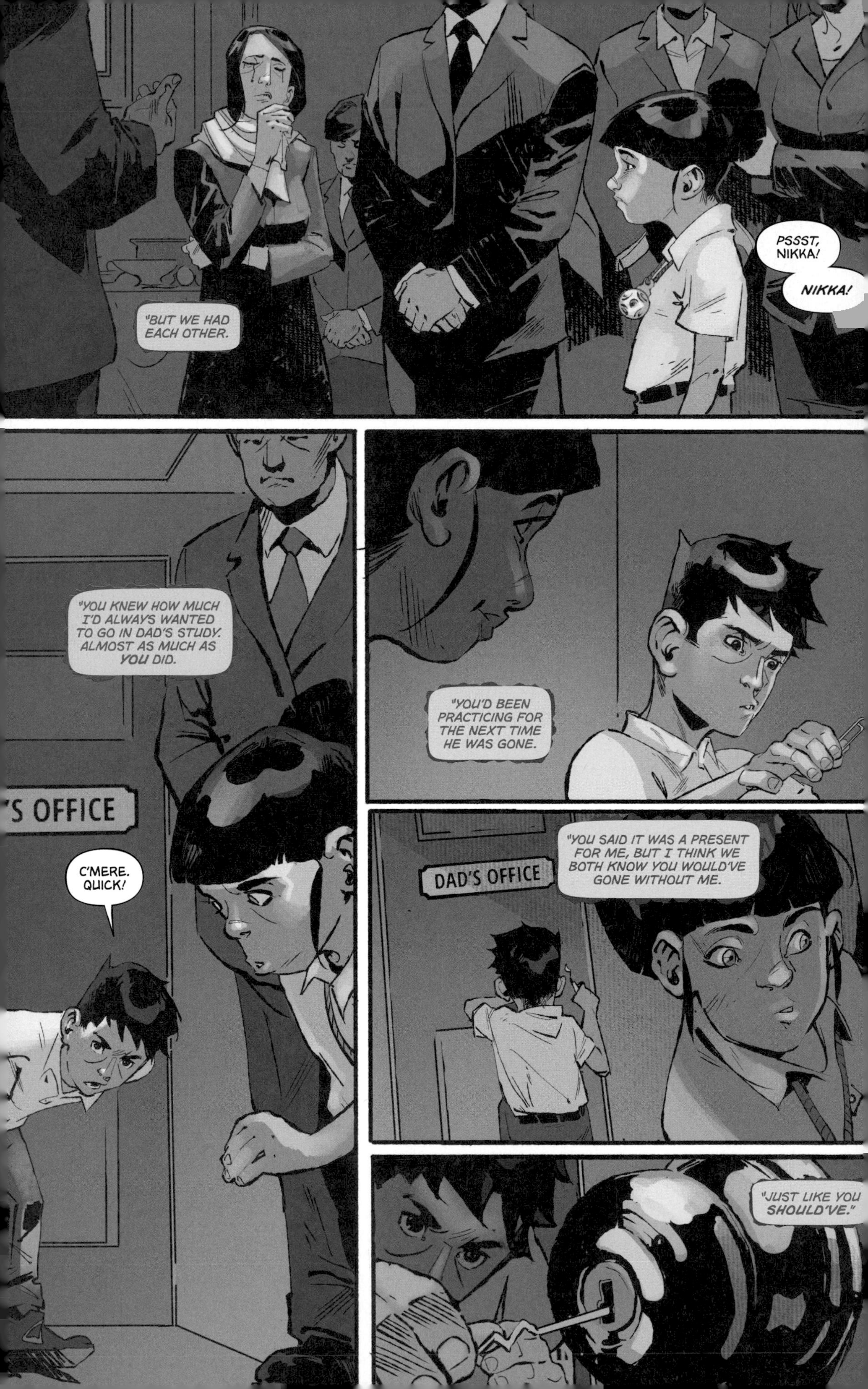
"BUT WE HAD EACH OTHER.
PSSST, NIKKA!
NIKKA!
"YOU KNEW HOW MUCH I'D ALWAYS WANTED TO GO IN DAD'S STUDY. ALMOST AS MUCH AS YOU DID.
'S OFFICE
C'MERE. QUICK!
"YOU'D BEEN PRACTICING FOR THE NEXT TIME HE WAS GONE.
DAD'S OFFICE
"YOU SAID IT WAS A PRESENT FOR ME, BUT I THINK WE BOTH KNOW YOU WOULD'VE GONE WITHOUT ME.
"JUST LIKE YOU SHOULD'VE."

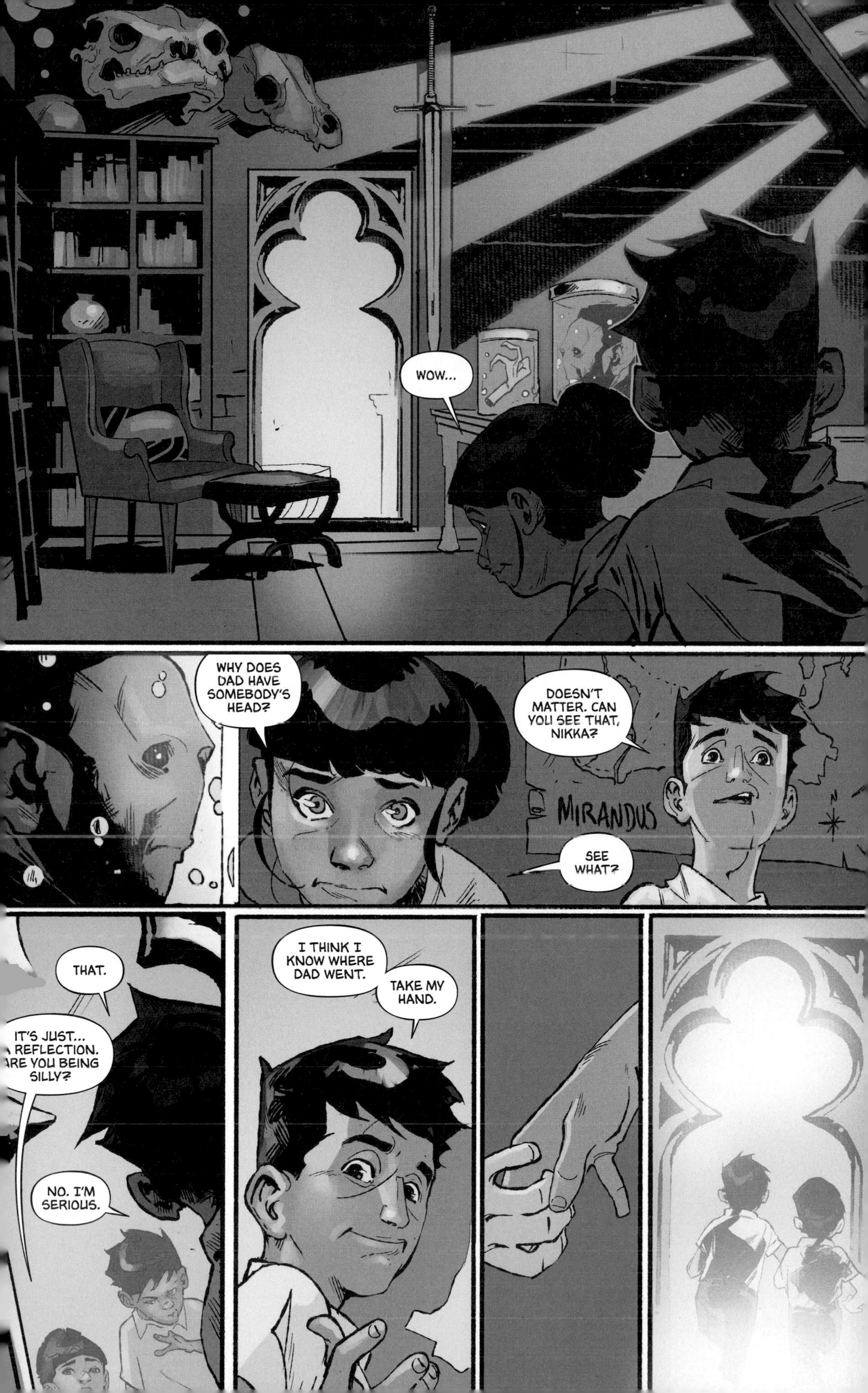
WOW...
WHY DOES DAD HAVE SOMEBODY'S HEAD?
DOESN'T MATTER. CAN YOU SEE THAT, NIKKA?
MIRANDUS
SEE WHAT?
THAT.
IT'S JUST... A REFLECTION. ARE YOU BEING SILLY?
NO. I'M SERIOUS.
I THINK I KNOW WHERE DAD WENT.
TAKE MY HAND.

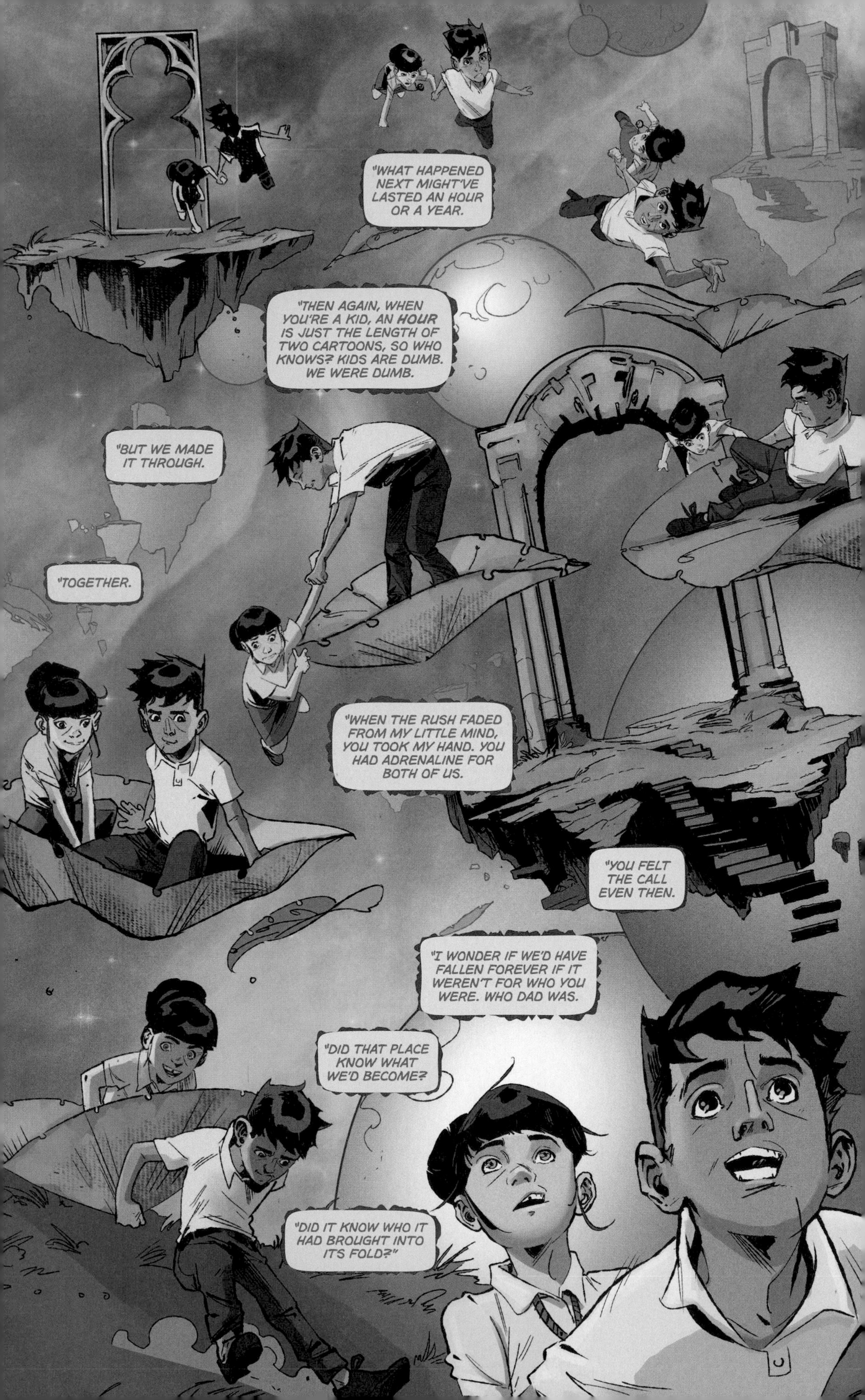
"WHAT HAPPENED NEXT MIGHT'VE LASTED AN HOUR OR A YEAR.
"THEN AGAIN, WHEN YOU'RE A KID, AN HOUR IS JUST THE LENGTH OF TWO CARTOONS, SO WHO KNOWS? KIDS ARE DUMB. WE WERE DUMB.
"BUT WE MADE IT THROUGH.
"TOGETHER.
"WHEN THE RUSH FADED FROM MY LITTLE MIND, YOU TOOK MY HAND. YOU HAD ADRENALINE FOR BOTH OF US.
"YOU FELT THE CALL EVEN THEN.
"I WONDER IF WE'D HAVE FALLEN FOREVER IF IT WEREN'T FOR WHO YOU WERE. WHO DAD WAS.
"DID THAT PLACE KNOW WHAT WE'D BECOME?
"DID IT KNOW WHO IT HAD BROUGHT INTO ITS FOLD?"

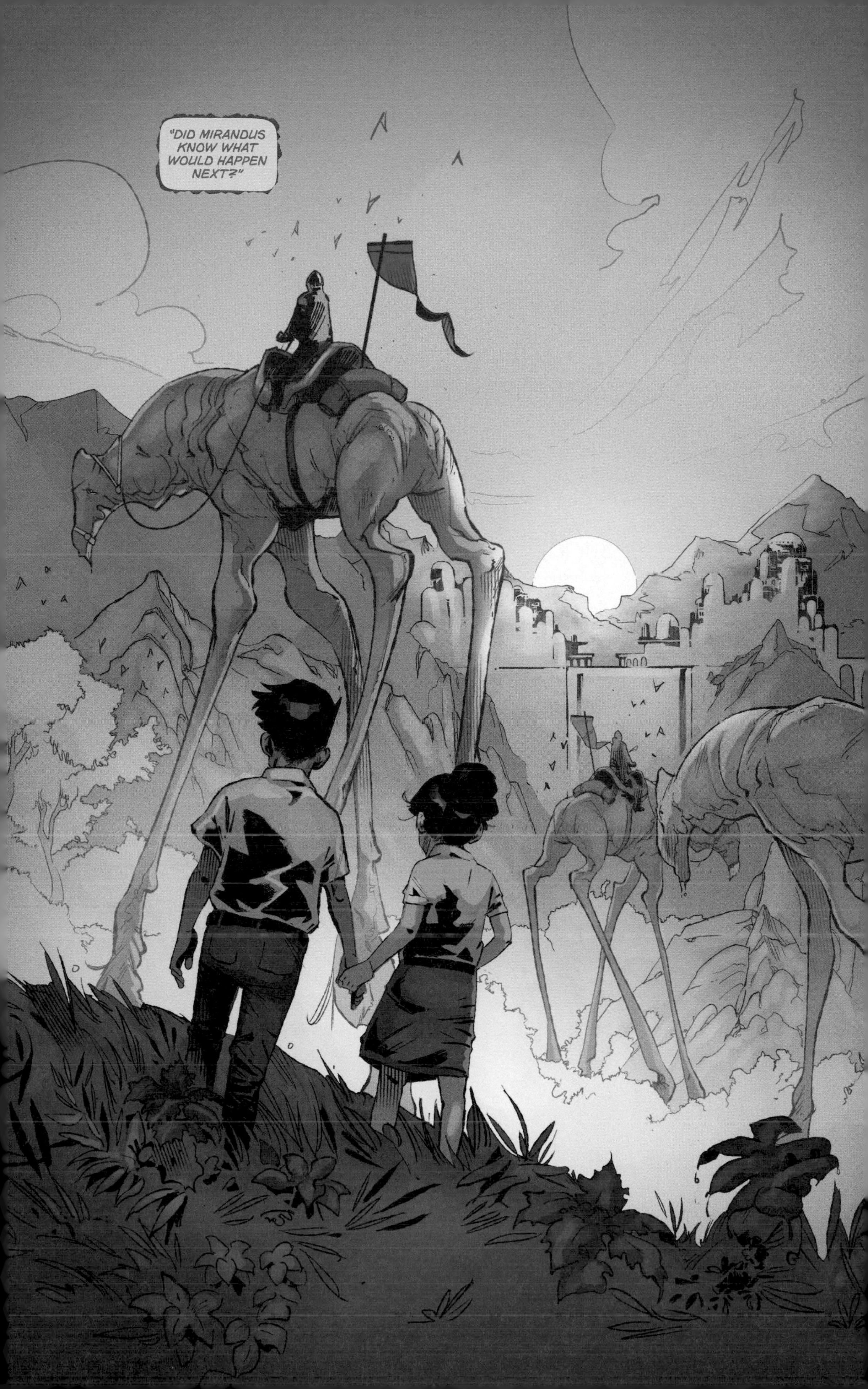
"DID MIRANDUS KNOW WHAT WOULD HAPPEN NEXT?"

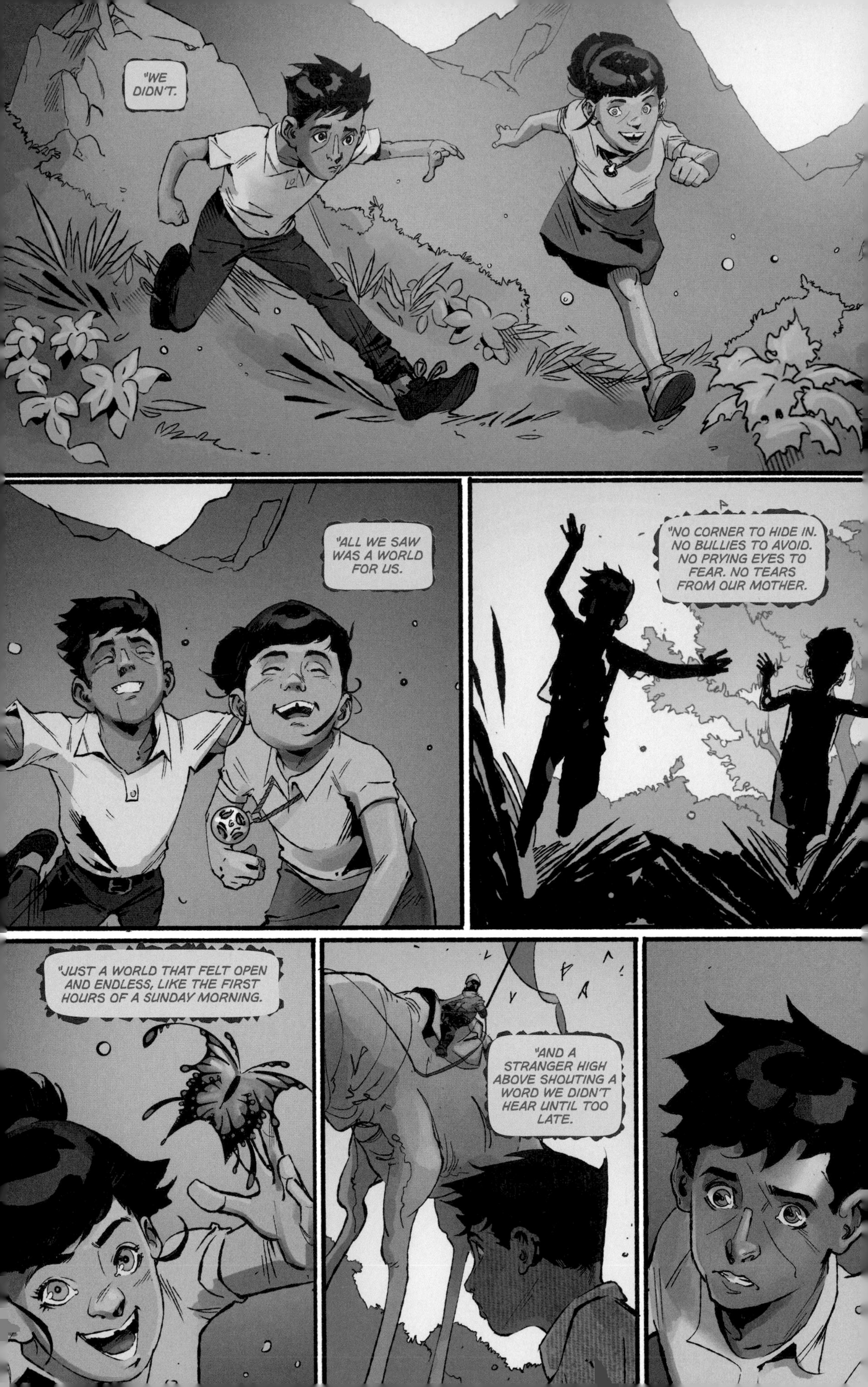

"WE DIDN'T.
"ALL WE SAW WAS A WORLD FOR US.
"NO CORNER TO HIDE IN. NO BULLIES TO AVOID. NO PRYING EYES TO FEAR. NO TEARS FROM OUR MOTHER.
"JUST A WORLD THAT FELT OPEN AND ENDLESS, LIKE THE FIRST HOURS OF A SUNDAY MORNING.
"AND A STRANGER HIGH ABOVE SHOUTING A WORD WE DIDN'T HEAR UNTIL TOO LATE.

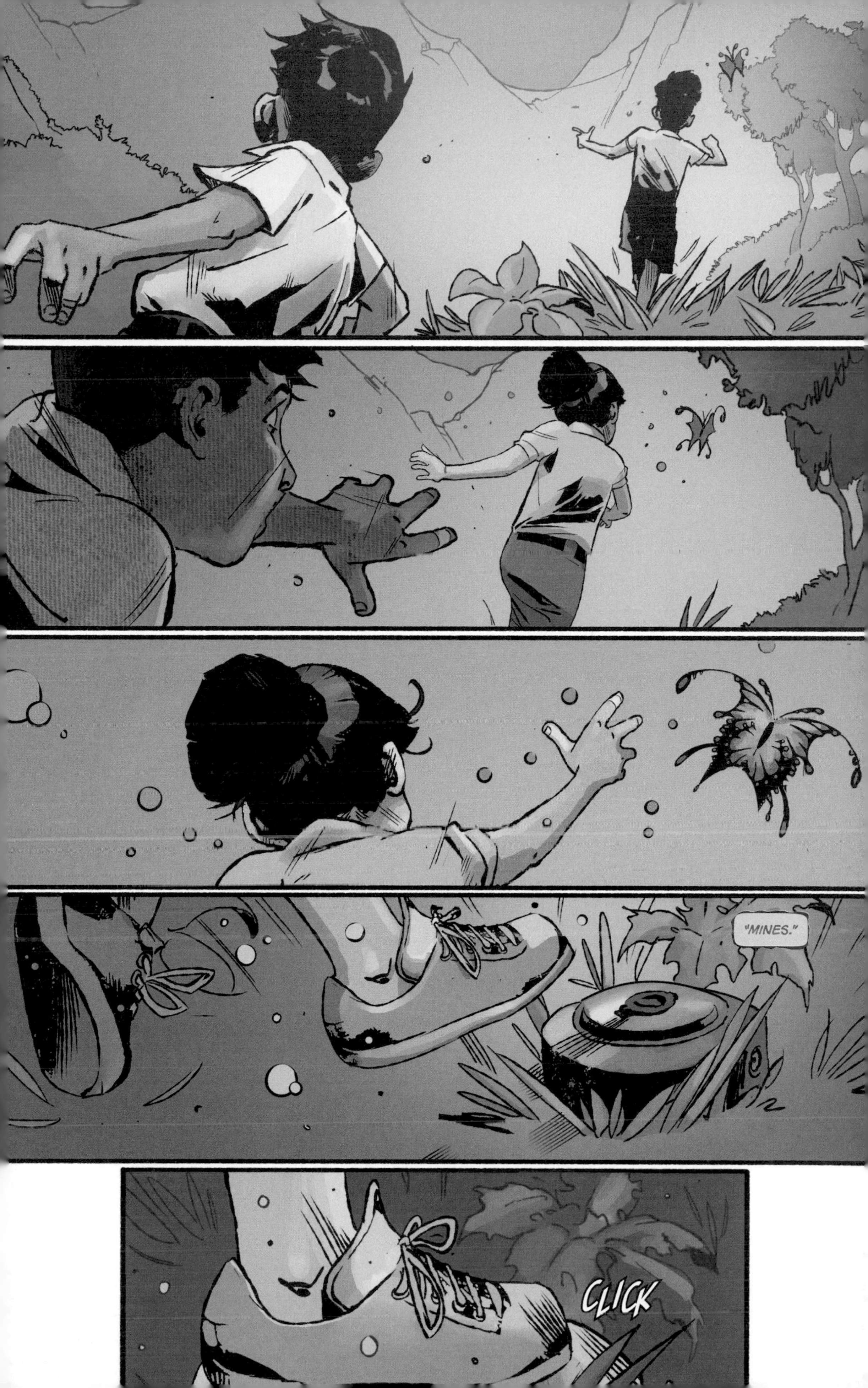
"MINES."
CLICK

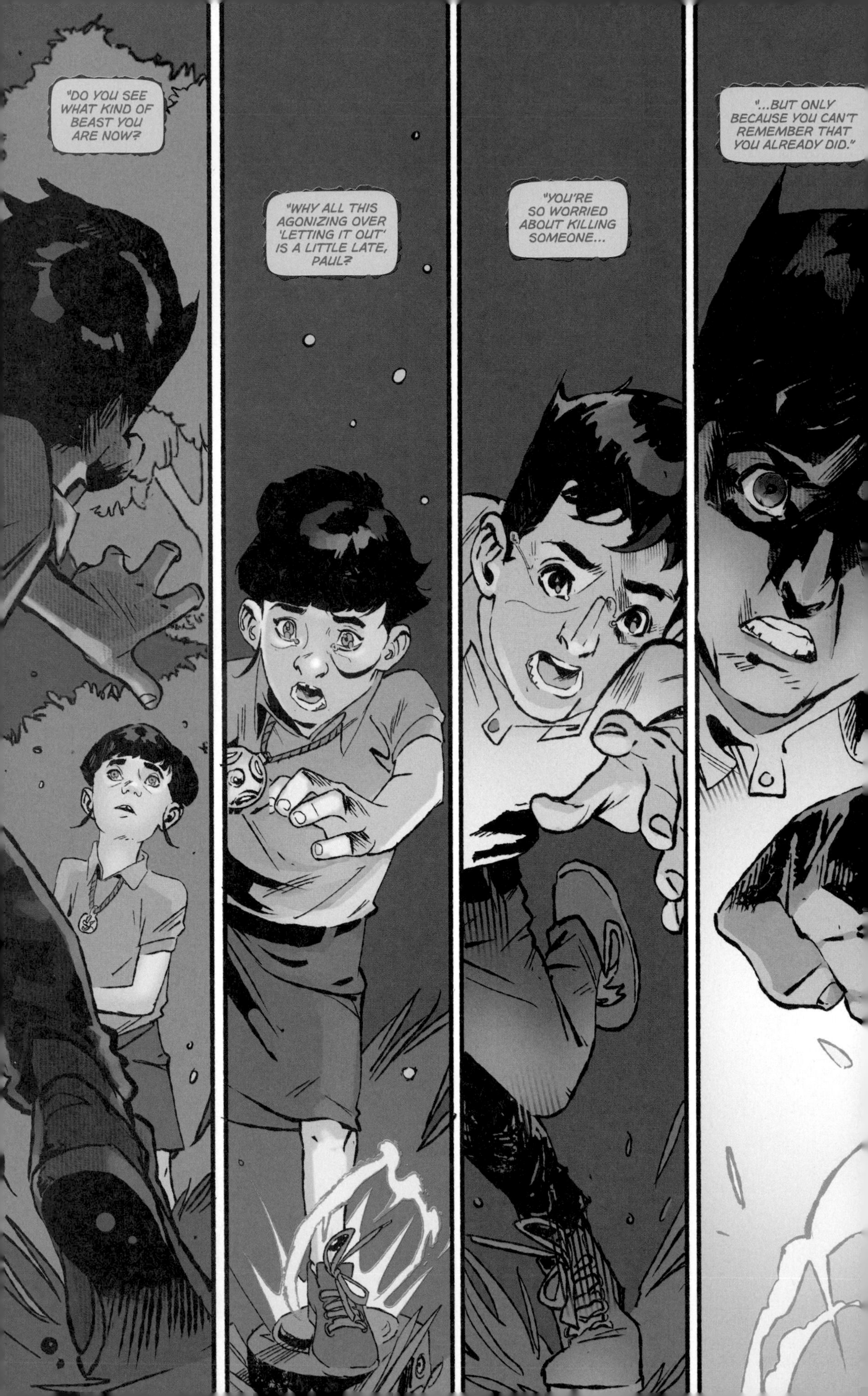
"DO YOU SEE WHAT KIND OF BEAST YOU ARE NOW?
"WHY ALL THIS AGONIZING OVER 'LETTING IT OUT' IS A LITTLE LATE, PAUL?
"YOU'RE SO WORRIED ABOUT KILLING SOMEONE...
"...BUT ONLY BECAUSE YOU CAN'T REMEMBER THAT YOU ALREADY DID."

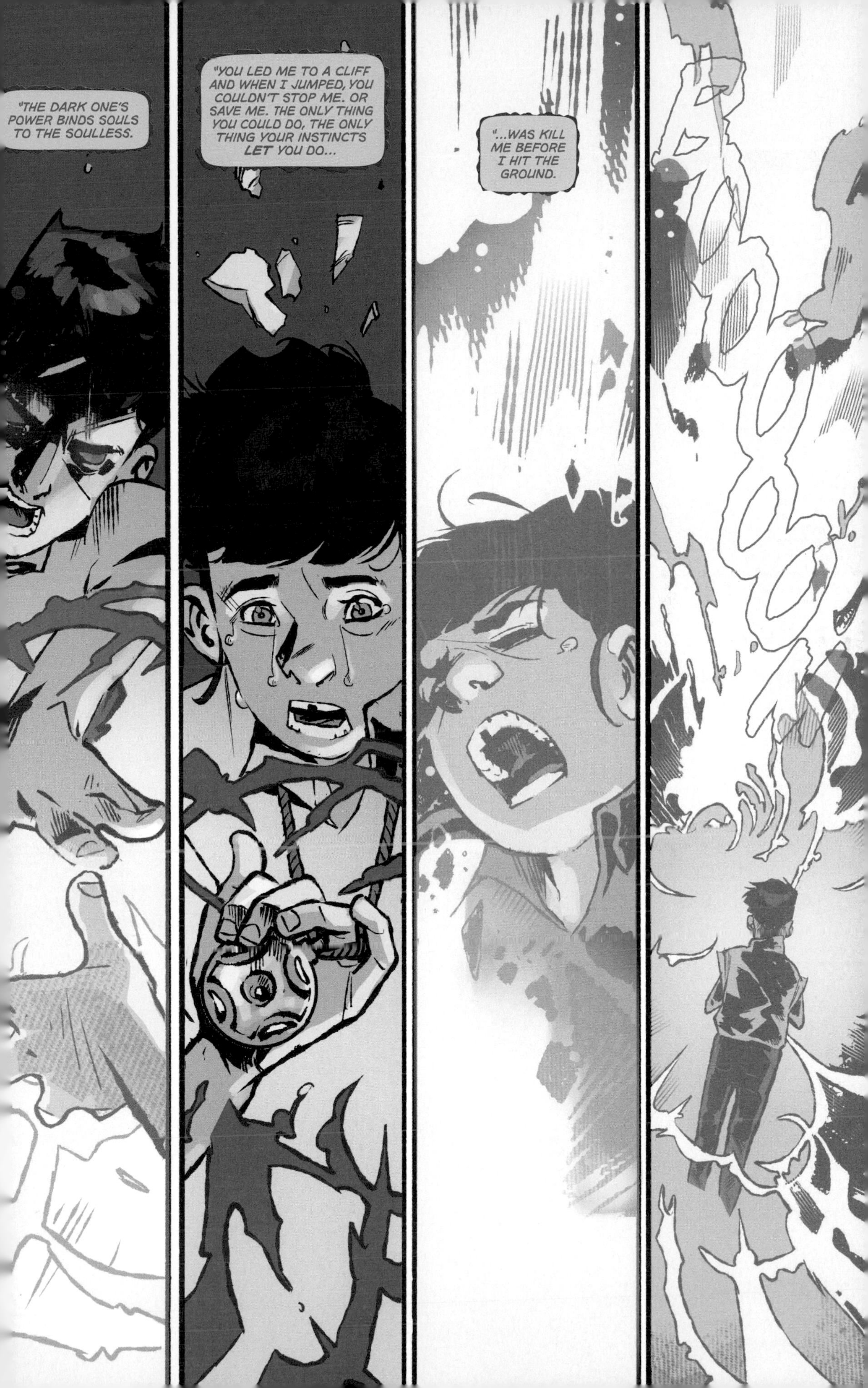
"THE DARK ONE'S POWER BINDS SOULS TO THE SOULLESS.
"YOU LED ME TO A CLIFF AND WHEN I JUMPED, YOU COULDN'T STOP ME. OR SAVE ME. THE ONLY THING YOU COULD DO, THE ONLY THING YOUR INSTINCTS LET YOU DO...
"...WAS KILL ME BEFORE I HIT THE GROUND.

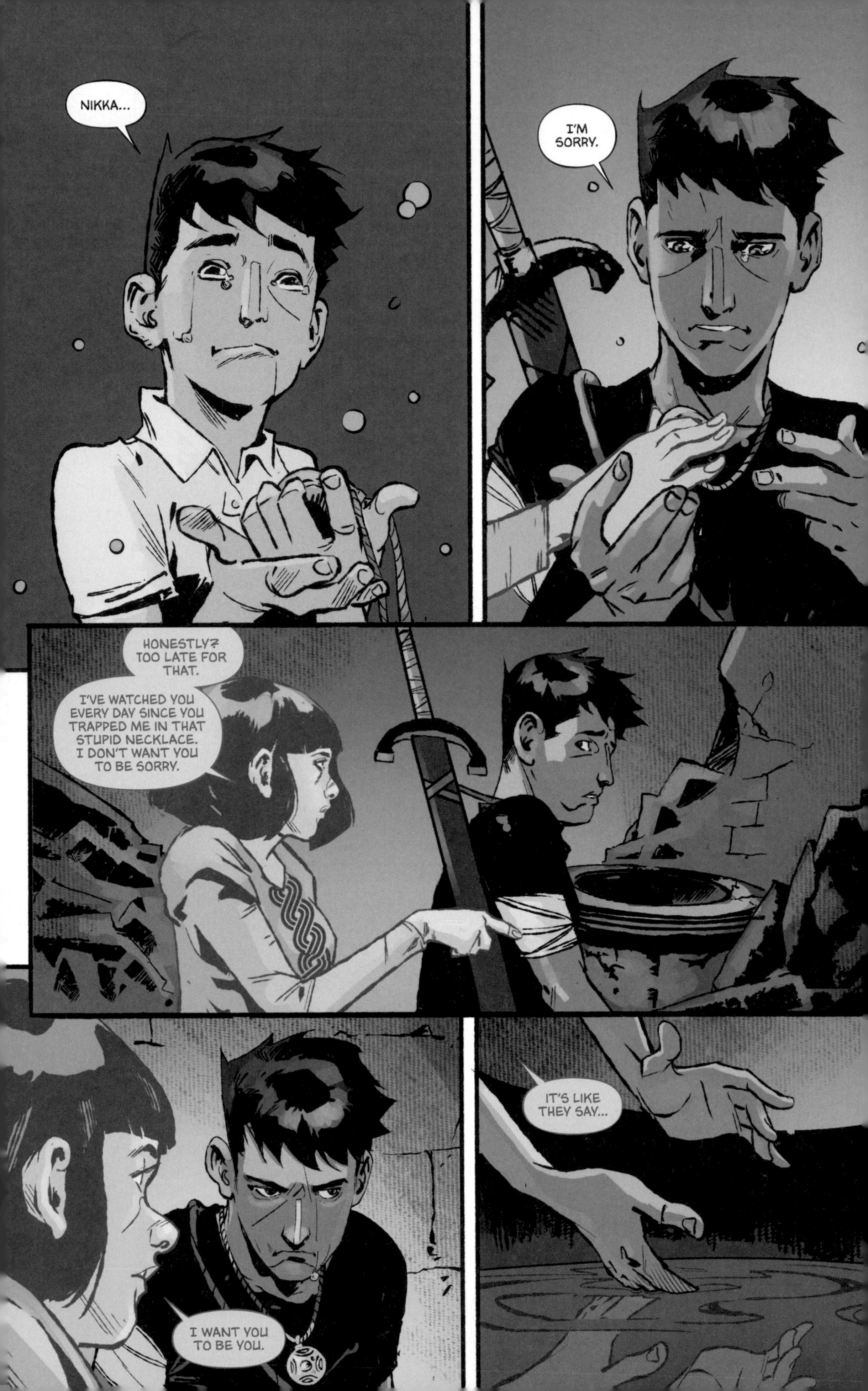
NIKKA...
I'M SORRY.
HONESTLY? TOO LATE FOR THAT.
I'VE WATCHED YOU EVERY DAY SINCE YOU TRAPPED ME IN THAT STUPID NECKLACE. I DON'T WANT YOU TO BE SORRY.
I WANT YOU TO BE YOU.
IT'S LIKE THEY SAY...

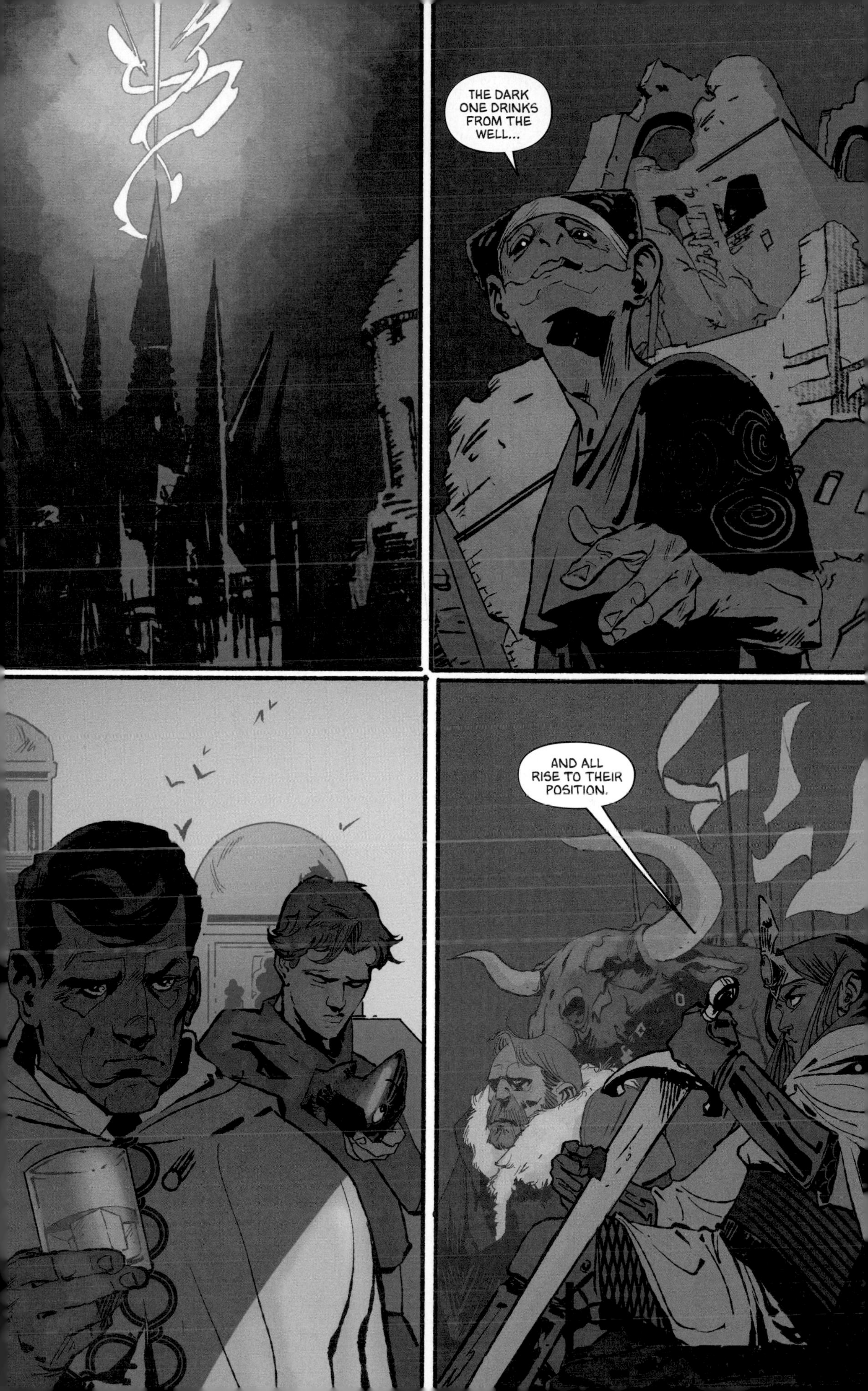
THE DARK ONE DRINKS FROM THE WELL...
AND ALL RISE TO THEIR POSITION.

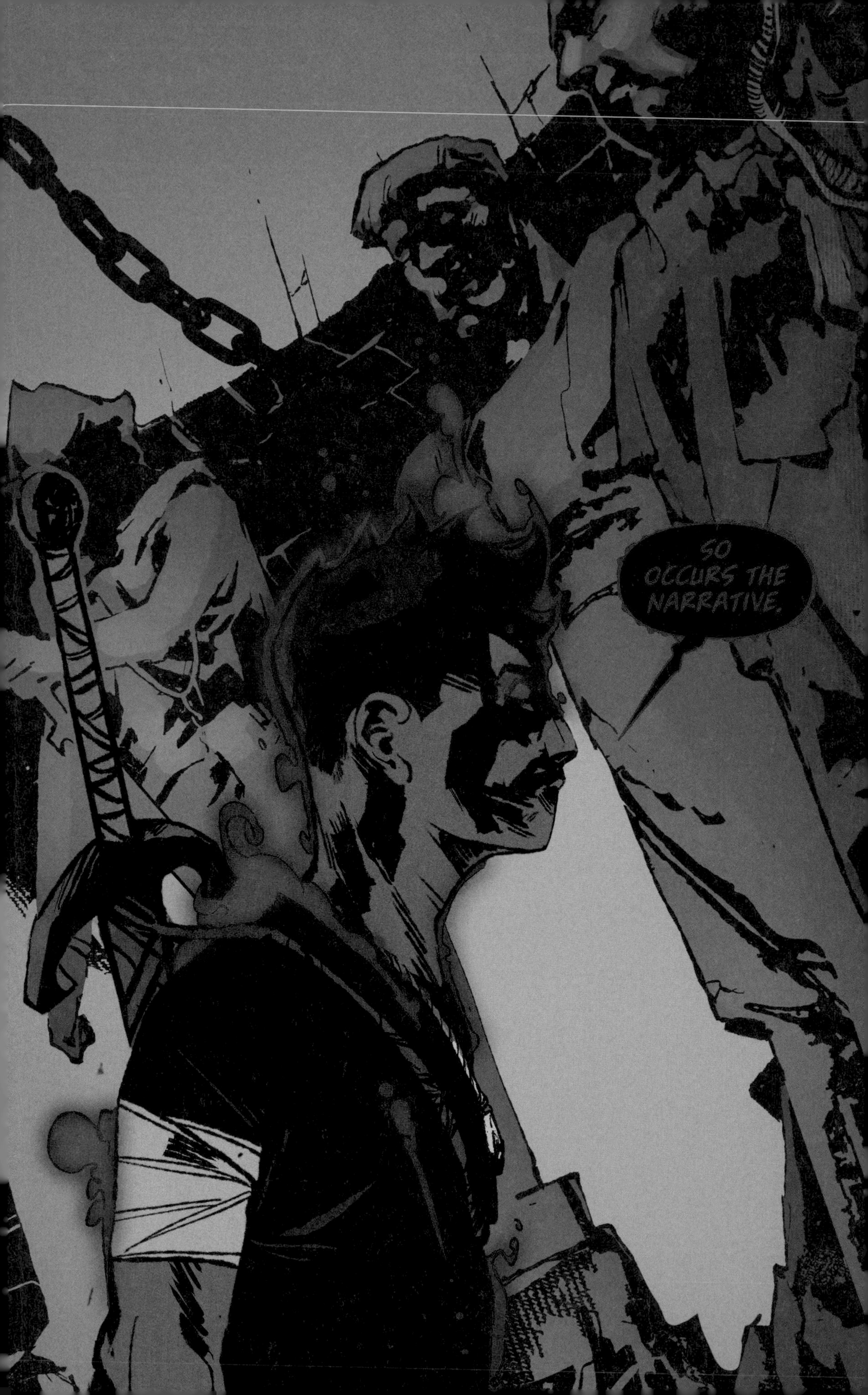
SO OCCURS THE NARRATIVE.

INTERMISSION

THE TRAGEDIE OF THE BOY KARKUN

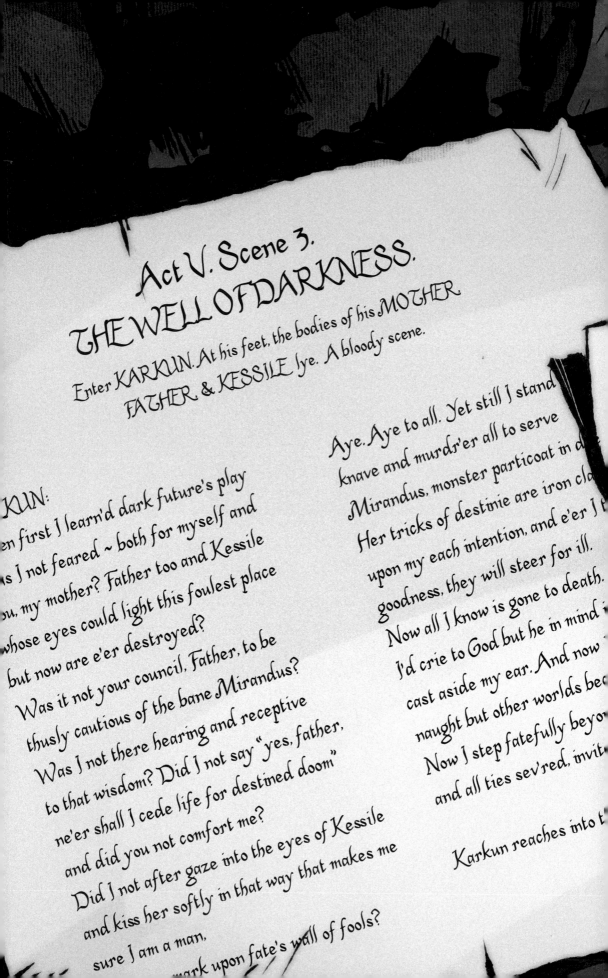

Act V. Scene 3.
THE WELL OF DARKNESS.

Enter KARKUN. At his feet, the bodies of his MOTHER
FATHER & KESSILE lye. A bloody scene.

KUN:

en first I learn'd dark future's play
s I not feared ~ both for myself and
ou, my mother? Father too and Kessile
whose eyes could light this foulest place
but now are e'er destroyed?

Was it not your council, Father, to be
thusly cautious of the bane Mirandus?
Was I not there hearing and receptive
to that wisdom? Did I not say "yes, father,
ne'er shall I cede life for destined doom"
and did you not comfort me?
Did I not after gaze into the eyes of Kessile
and kiss her softly in that way that makes me
sure I am a man,
mark upon fate's wall of fools?

Aye. Aye to all. Yet still I stand
knave and murdr'er all to serve
Mirandus, monster particoat in d
Her tricks of destinie are iron cla
upon my each intention, and e'er I t
goodness, they will steer for ill.
Now all I know is gone to death,
I'd crie to God but he in mind
cast aside my ear. And now
naught but other worlds bec
Now I step fatefully beyo
and all ties sev'red, invit

Karkun reaches into t

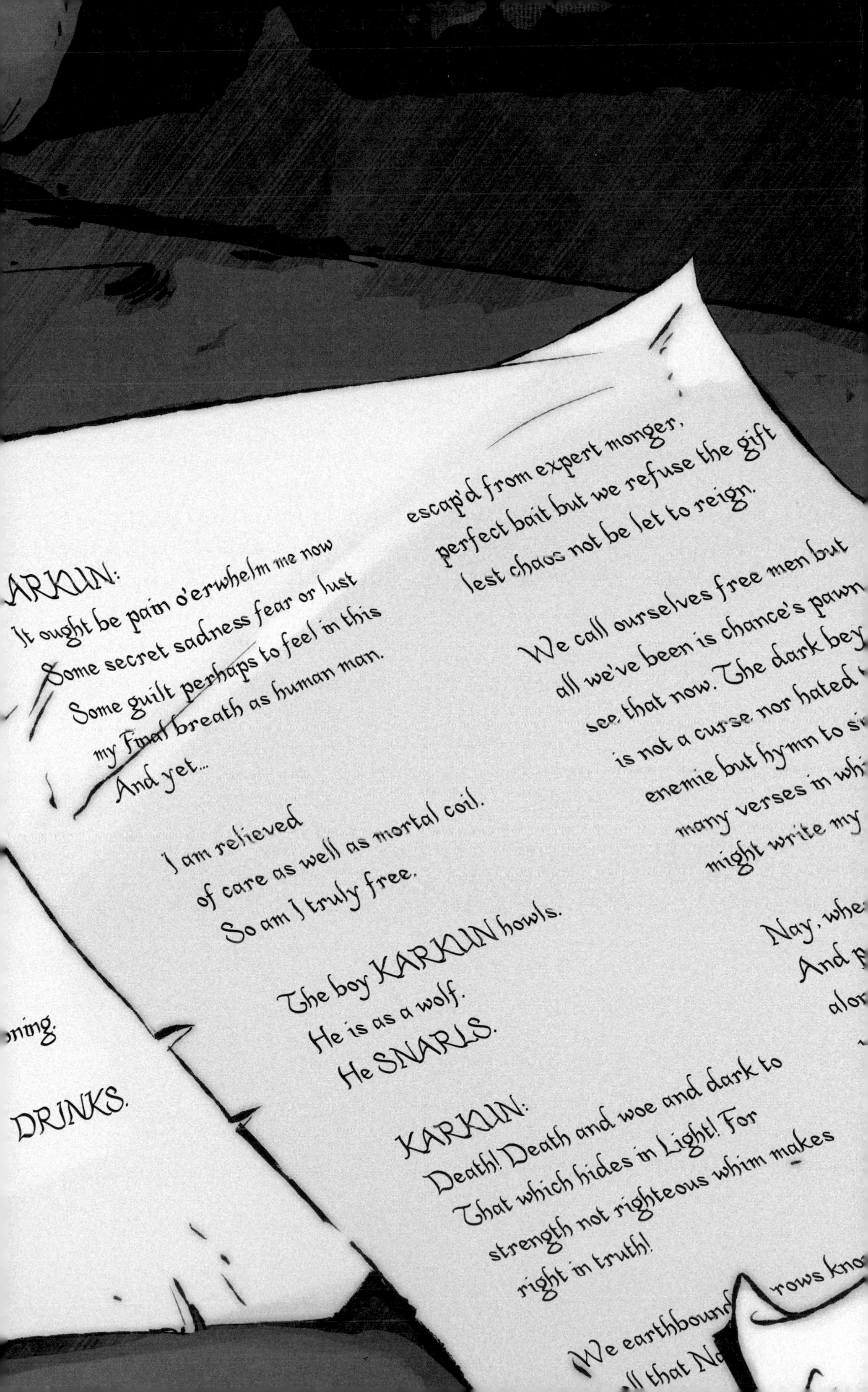
ARKUN:
It ought be pain o'erwhelm me now
Some secret sadness fear or lust
Some guilt perhaps to feel in this
my final breath as human man.
And yet...
I am relieved
of care as well as mortal coil.
So am I truly free.
The boy KARKUN howls.
He is as a wolf.
He SNARLS.
KARKUN:
Death! Death and woe and dark to
That which hides in Light! For
strength not righteous whim makes
right in truth!
We earthbound
escap'd from expert monger,
perfect bait but we refuse the gift
lest chaos not be let to reign.
We call ourselves free men but
all we've been is chance's pawn
see that now. The dark bey
is not a curse nor hated
enemie but hymn to s
many verses in wh
might write my
Nay, whe
And p
alor
rows kno
oning.
DRINKS.

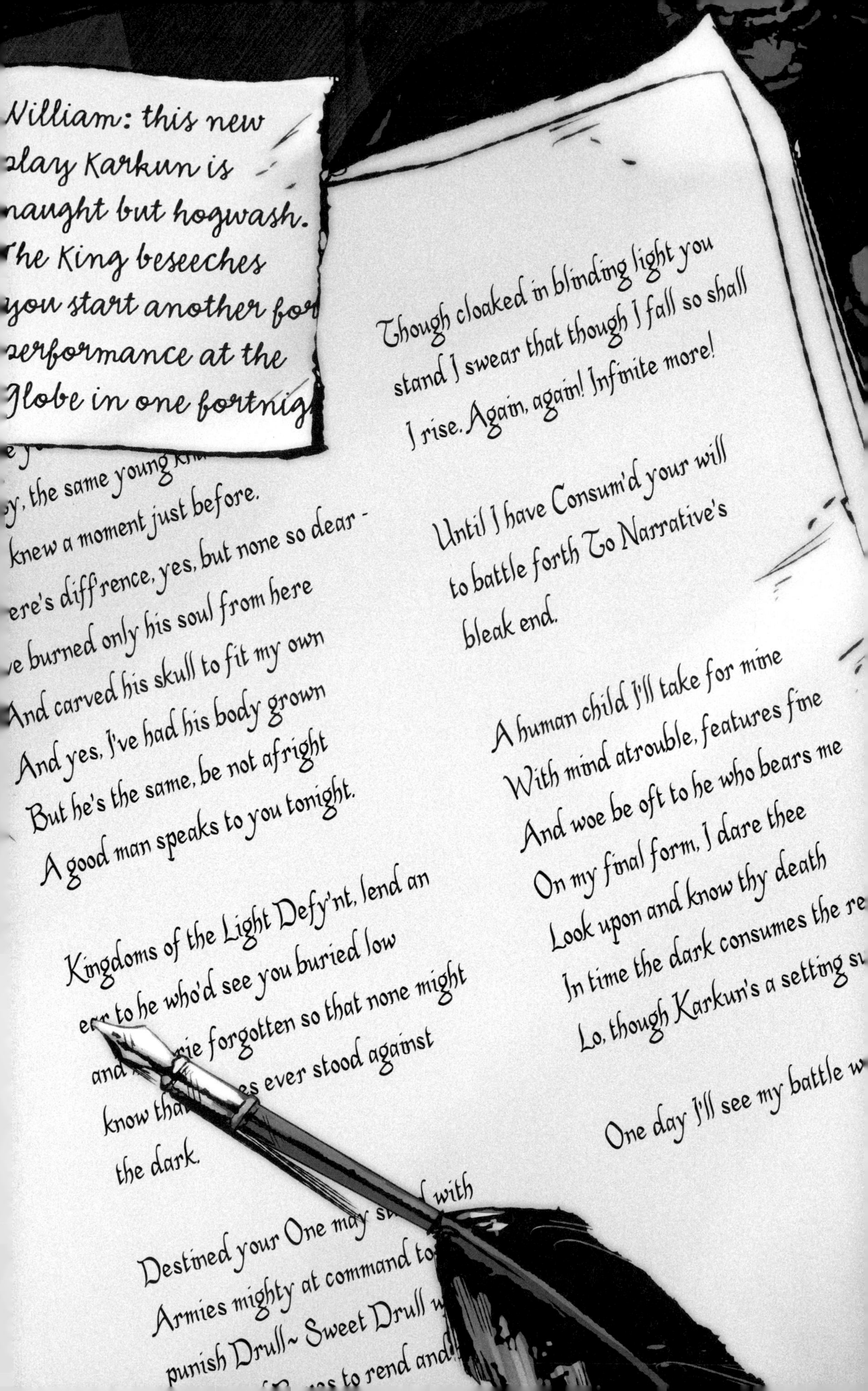

William: this new
play Karkun is
naught but hogwash.
The King beseeches
you start another for
performance at the
Globe in one fortnig
y, the same young kn
knew a moment just before.
ere's diff'rence, yes, but none so dear -
e burned only his soul from here
And carved his skull to fit my own
And yes, I've had his body grown
But he's the same, be not afright
A good man speaks to you tonight.
Kingdoms of the Light Defy'nt, lend an
ear to he who'd see you buried low
and
rie forgotten so that none might
know tha
es ever stood against
the dark.
Destined your One may s
d with
Armies mighty at command to
punish Drull~ Sweet Drull w
s to rend and
Though cloaked in blinding light you
stand I swear that though I fall so shall
I rise. Again, again! Infinite more!
Until I have Consum'd your will
to battle forth To Narrative's
bleak end.
A human child I'll take for mine
With mind atrouble, features fine
And woe be oft to he who bears me
On my final form, I dare thee
Look upon and know thy death
In time the dark consumes the re
Lo, though Karkun's a setting s
One day I'll see my battle w

A NEW NARRATIVE

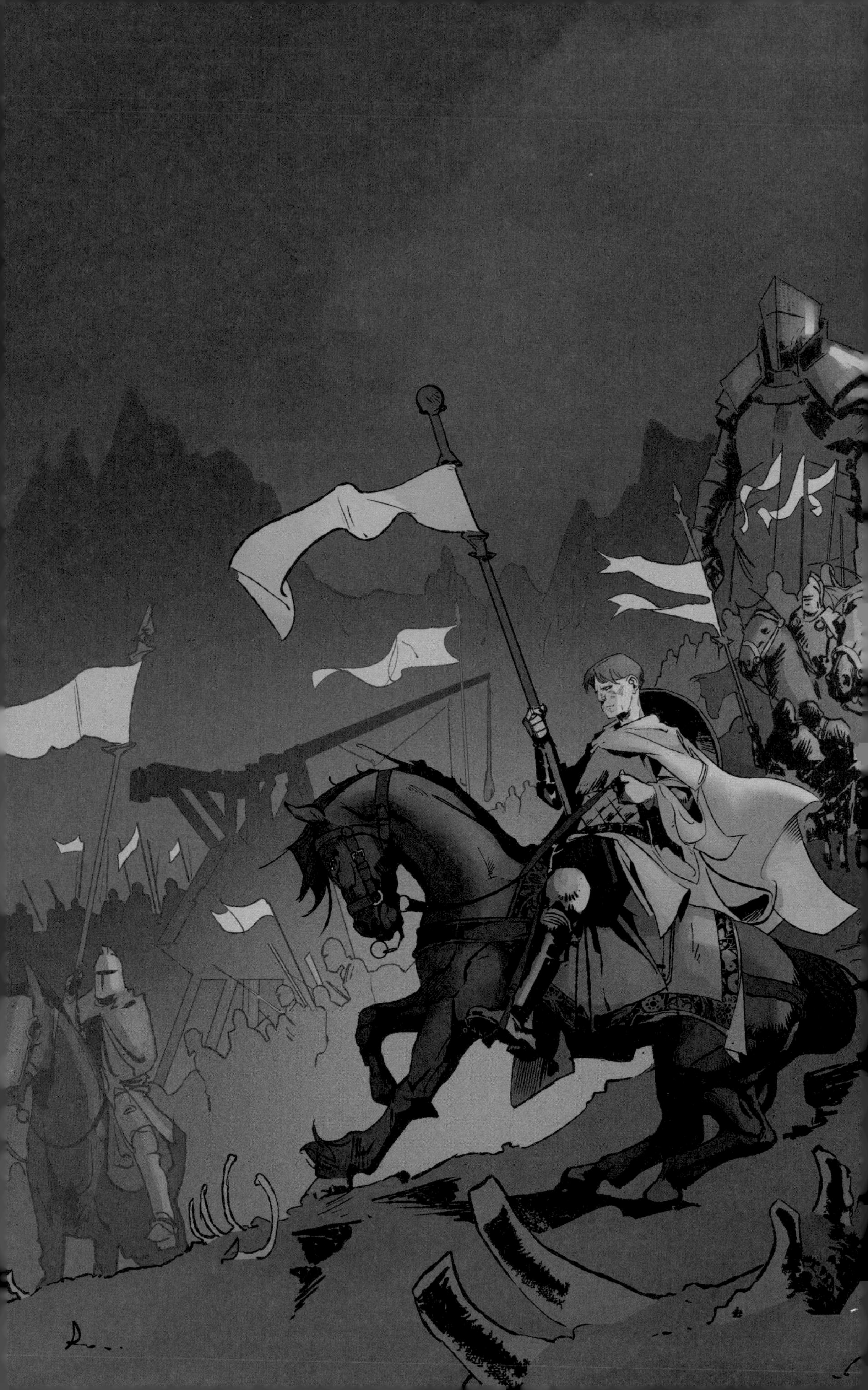

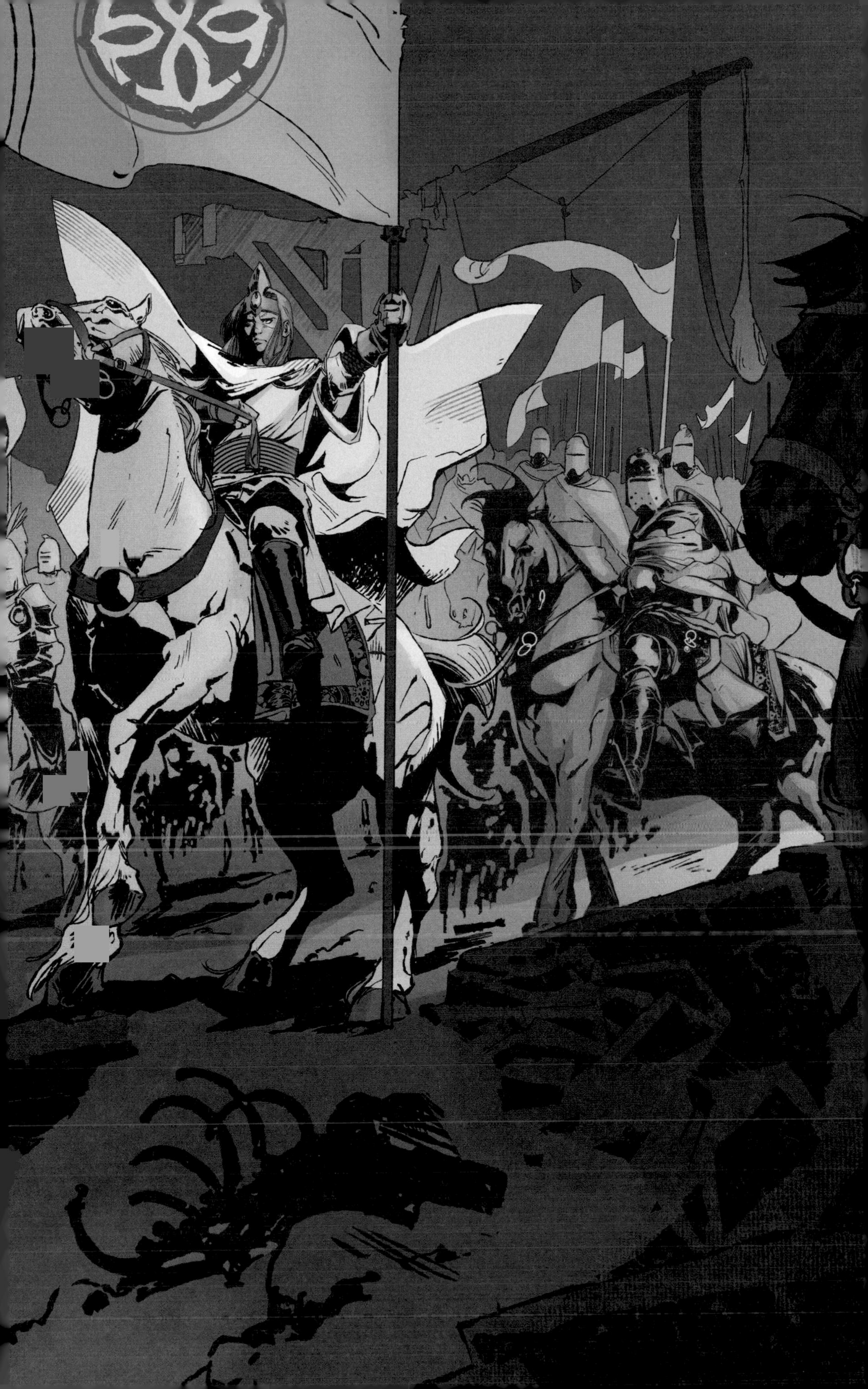

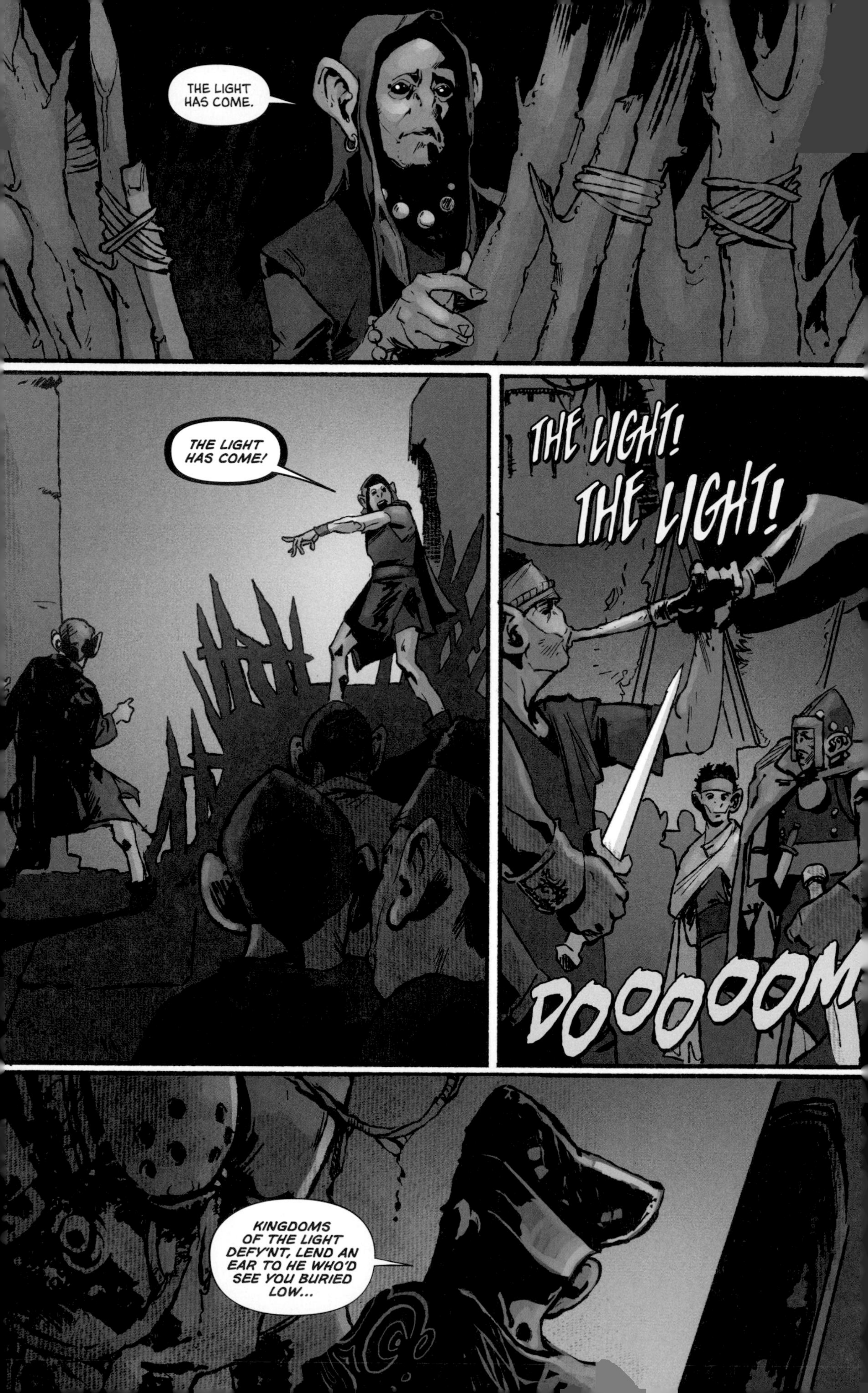
THE LIGHT HAS COME.
THE LIGHT HAS COME!
THE LIGHT! THE LIGHT!
DOOOOOM
KINGDOMS OF THE LIGHT DEFY'NT, LEND AN EAR TO HE WHO'D SEE YOU BURIED LOW...

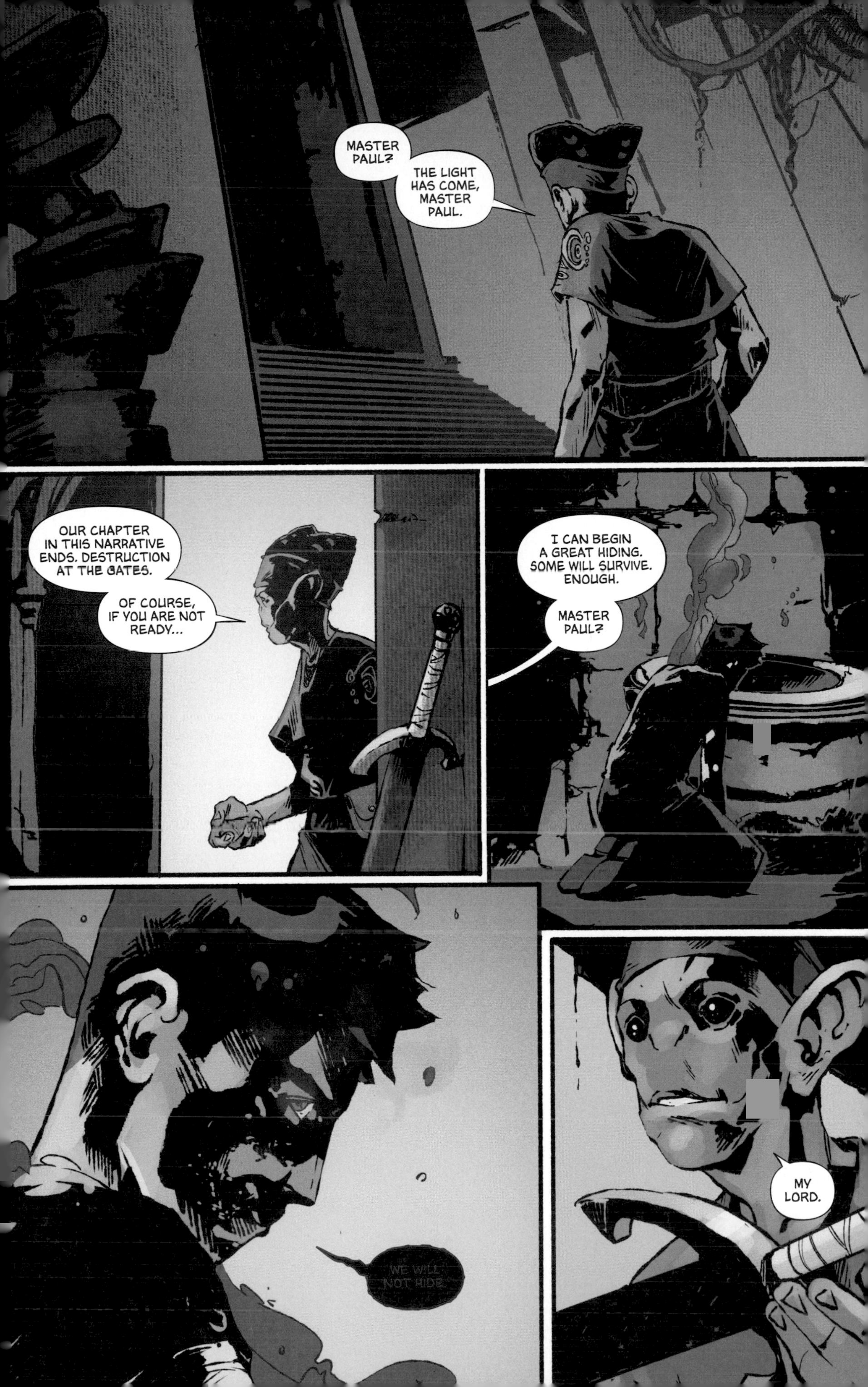
MASTER PAUL?
THE LIGHT HAS COME, MASTER PAUL.
OUR CHAPTER IN THIS NARRATIVE ENDS. DESTRUCTION AT THE GATES.
OF COURSE, IF YOU ARE NOT READY...
I CAN BEGIN A GREAT HIDING. SOME WILL SURVIVE. ENOUGH.
MASTER PAUL?
WE WILL NOT HIDE.
MY LORD.

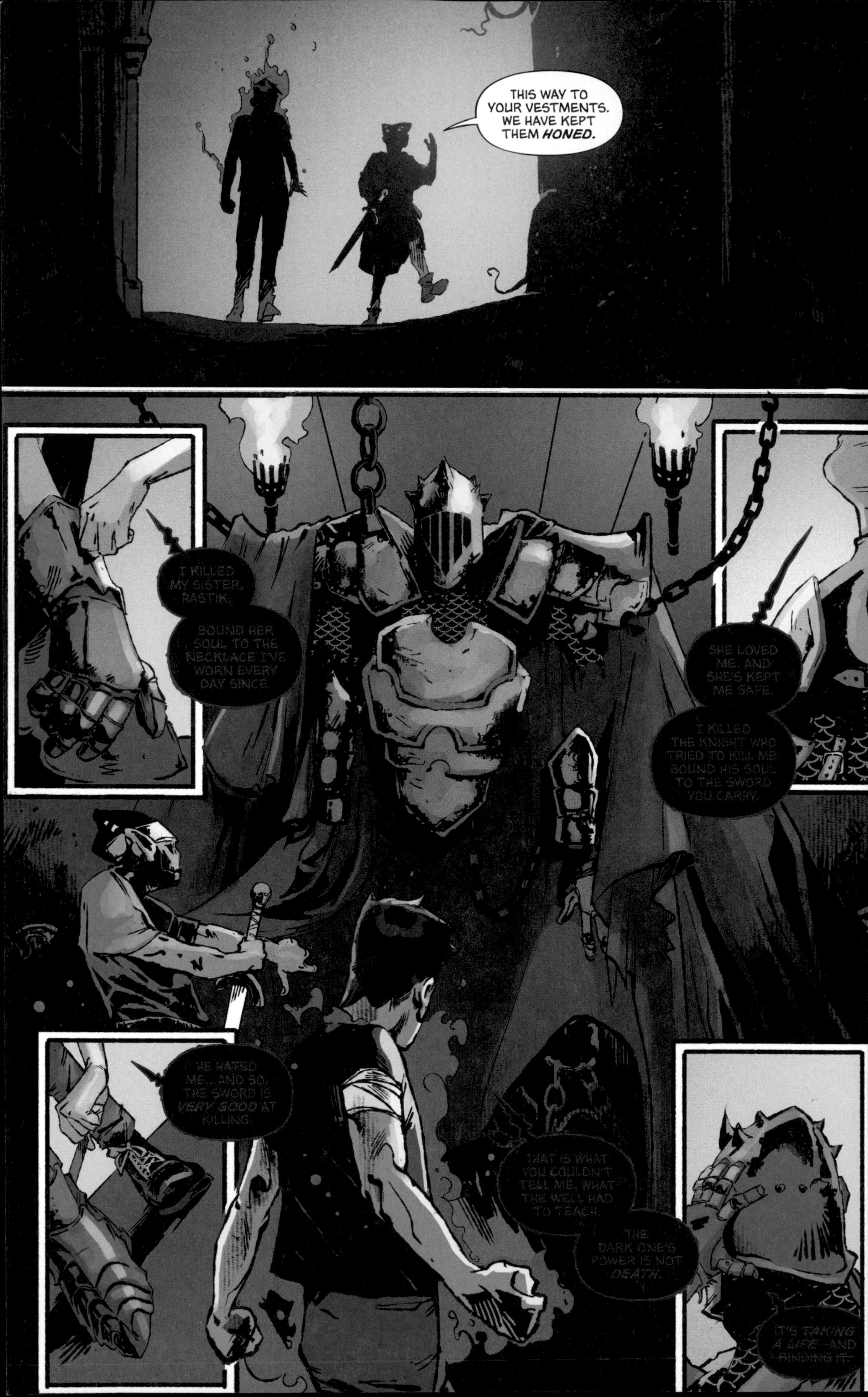
THIS WAY TO YOUR VESTMENTS. WE HAVE KEPT THEM ***HONED.***
I KILLED MY SISTER, RASTIK.
BOUND HER SOUL TO THE NECKLACE I'VE WORN EVERY DAY SINCE.
SHE LOVED ME. AND SHE'S KEPT ME SAFE.
I KILLED THE KNIGHT WHO TRIED TO KILL ME. BOUND HIS SOUL TO THE SWORD YOU CARRY.
HE HATED ME... AND SO, THE SWORD IS *VERY GOOD* AT KILLING.
THAT IS WHAT YOU COULDN'T TELL ME. WHAT THE WELL HAD TO TEACH.
THE DARK ONE'S POWER IS NOT *DEATH.*
IT'S *TAKING A LIFE*--AND BINDING IT.

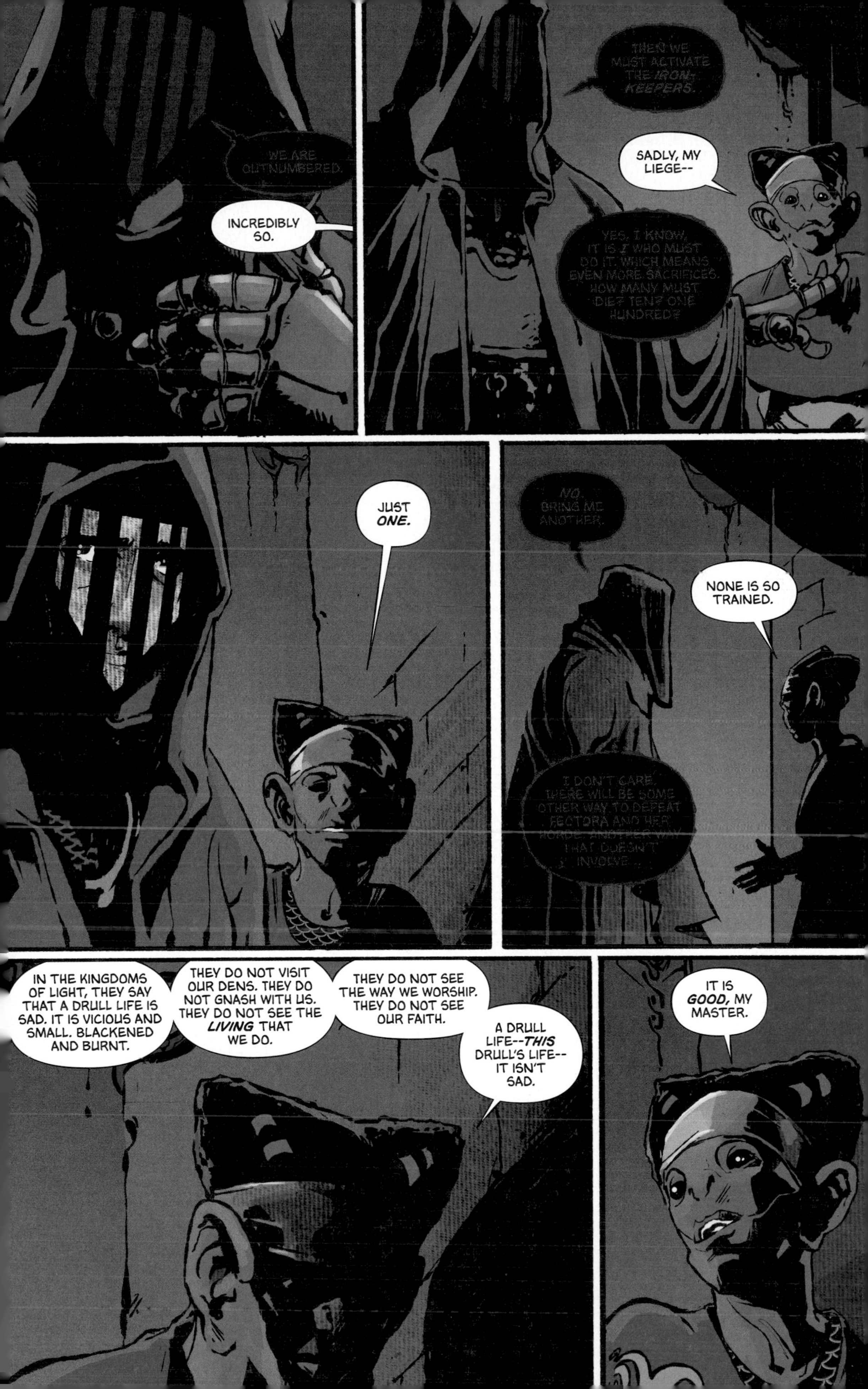

WE ARE OUTNUMBERED.
INCREDIBLY SO.
THEN WE MUST ACTIVATE THE IRON-KEEPERS.
SADLY, MY LIEGE--
YES. I KNOW, IT IS I WHO MUST DO IT. WHICH MEANS EVEN MORE SACRIFICES. HOW MANY MUST DIE? TEN? ONE HUNDRED?
JUST ONE.
NO. BRING ME ANOTHER.
NONE IS SO TRAINED.
I DON'T CARE. THERE WILL BE SOME OTHER WAY TO DEFEAT FECTORA AND HER HORDE. ANOTHER WAY THAT DOESN'T INVOLVE...
IN THE KINGDOMS OF LIGHT, THEY SAY THAT A DRULL LIFE IS SAD. IT IS VICIOUS AND SMALL. BLACKENED AND BURNT.
THEY DO NOT VISIT OUR DENS. THEY DO NOT GNASH WITH US. THEY DO NOT SEE THE LIVING THAT WE DO.
THEY DO NOT SEE THE WAY WE WORSHIP. THEY DO NOT SEE OUR FAITH.
A DRULL LIFE--THIS DRULL'S LIFE--IT ISN'T SAD.
IT IS GOOD, MY MASTER.

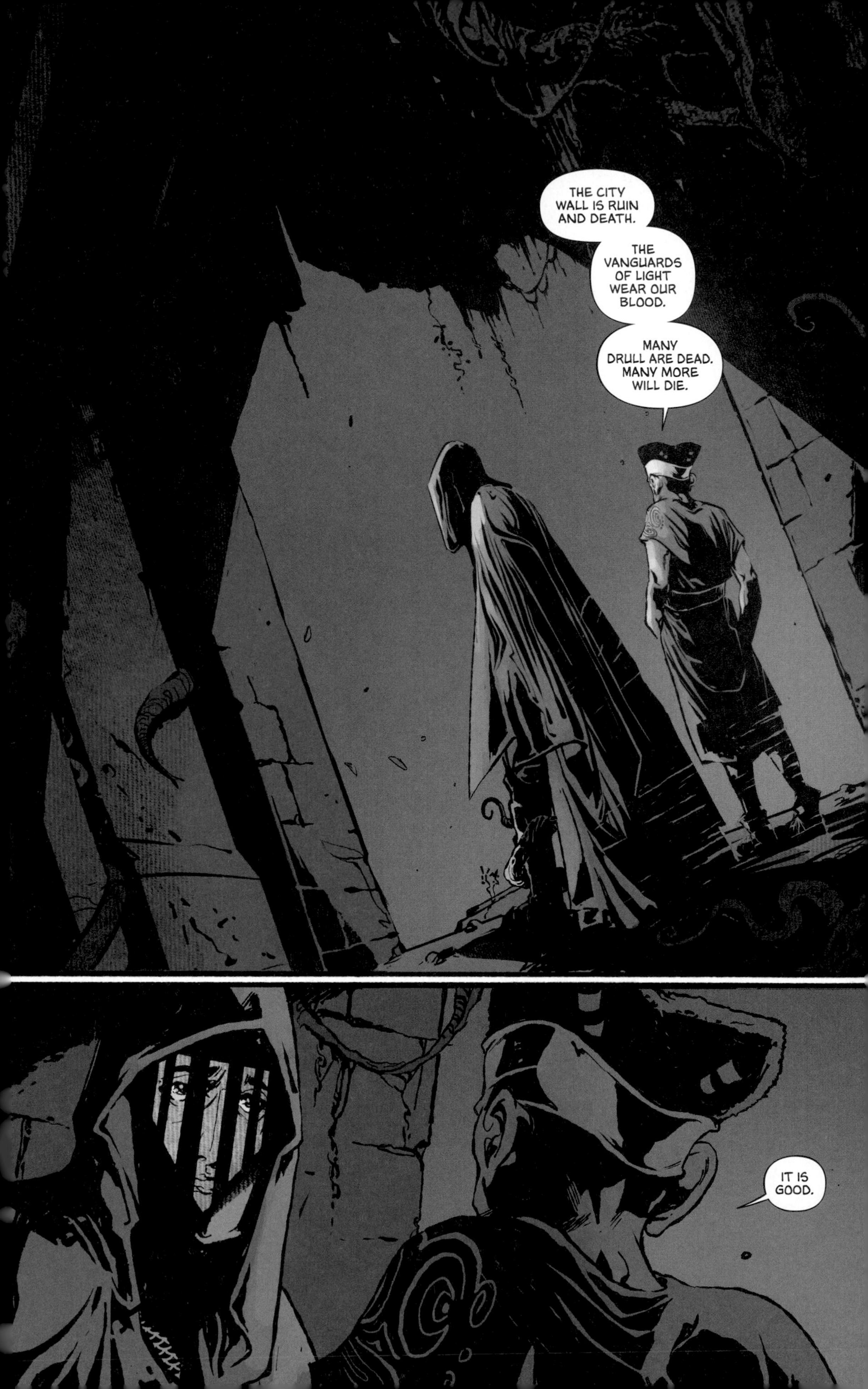
THE CITY WALL IS RUIN AND DEATH.
THE VANGUARDS OF LIGHT WEAR OUR BLOOD.
MANY DRULL ARE DEAD. MANY MORE WILL DIE.
IT IS GOOD.

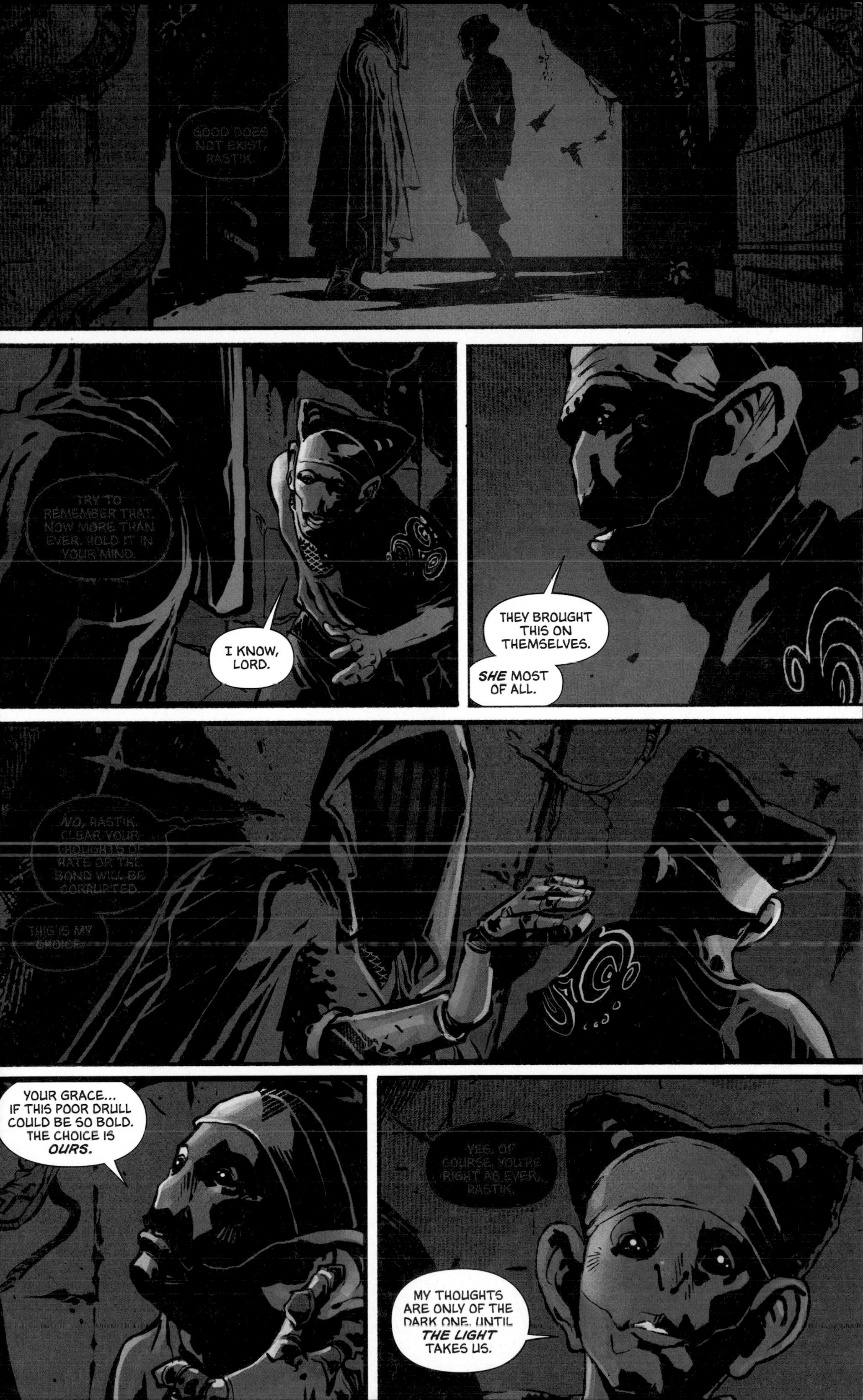
GOOD DOES NOT EXIST, RASTIK.
TRY TO REMEMBER THAT. NOW MORE THAN EVER. HOLD IT IN YOUR MIND.
I KNOW, LORD.
THEY BROUGHT THIS ON THEMSELVES.
SHE MOST OF ALL.
NO, RASTIK. CLEAR YOUR THOUGHTS OF HATE OR THE BOND WILL BE CORRUPTED.
THIS IS MY CHOICE.
YOUR GRACE... IF THIS POOR DRULL COULD BE SO BOLD. THE CHOICE IS *OURS.*
YES, OF COURSE. YOU'RE RIGHT AS EVER, RASTIK.
MY THOUGHTS ARE ONLY OF THE DARK ONE, UNTIL *THE LIGHT* TAKES US.

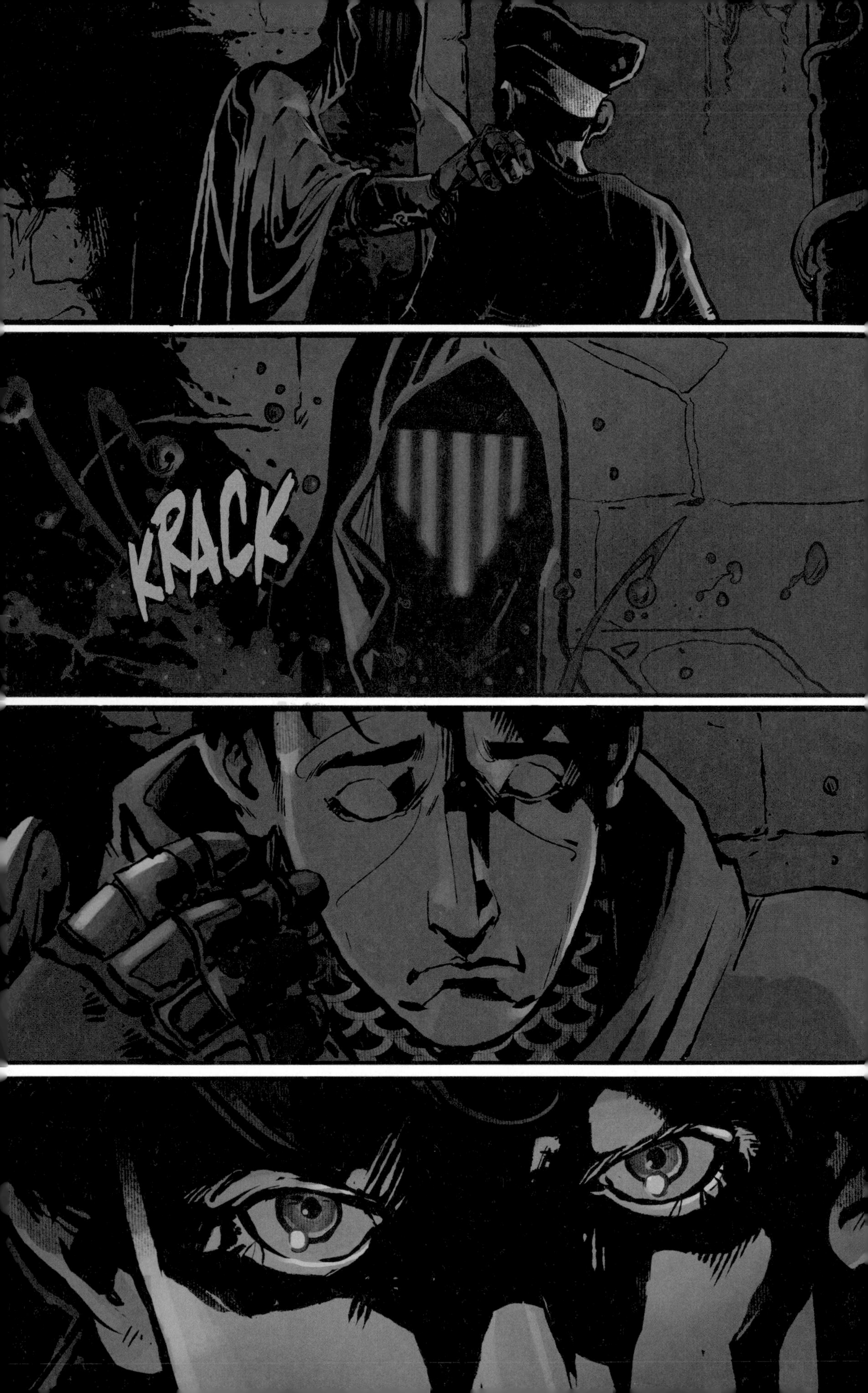
KRACK

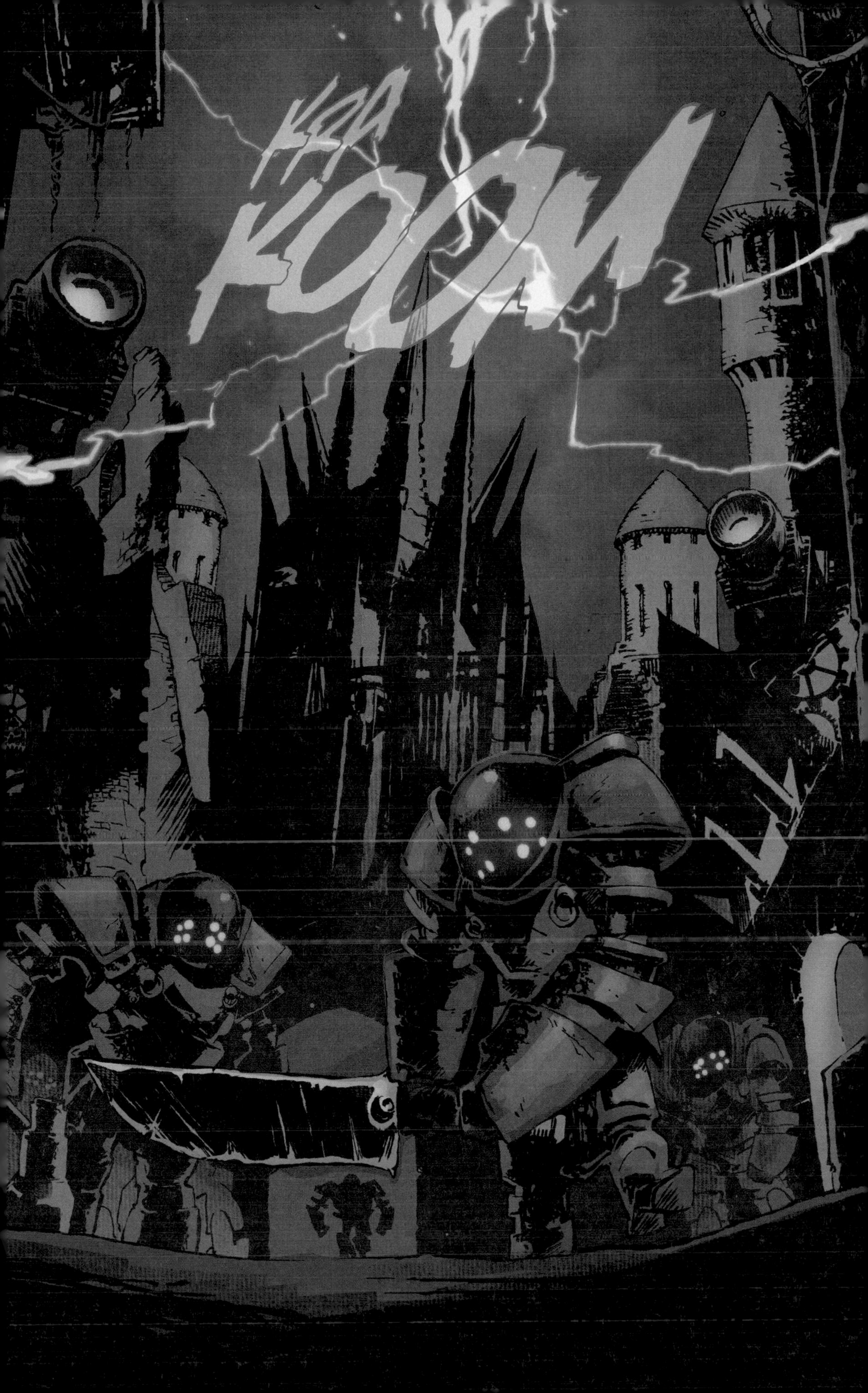
KRA
KOOM

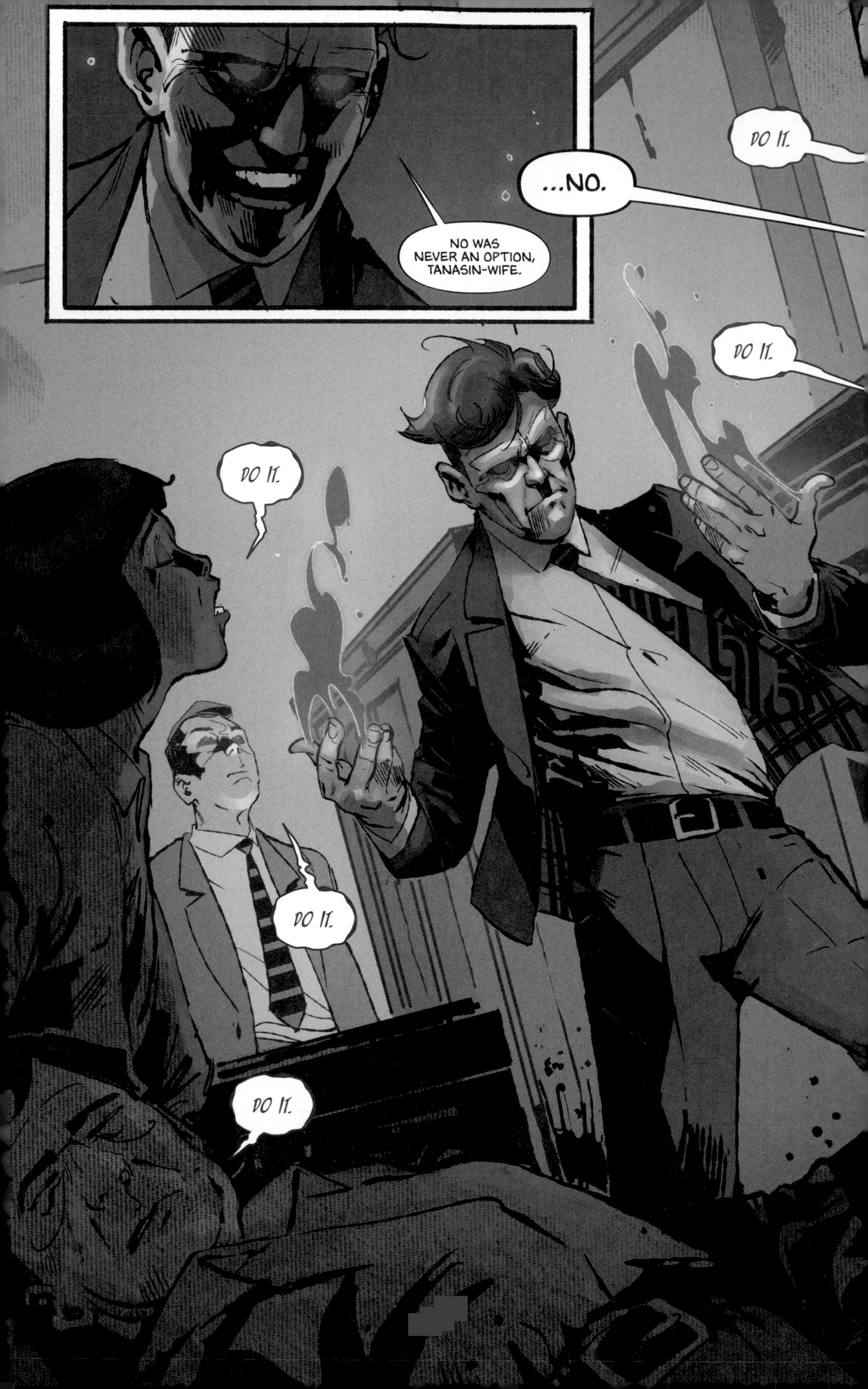
NO WAS NEVER AN OPTION, TANASIN-WIFE.
DO IT.
...NO.
DO IT.
DO IT.
DO IT.
DO IT.

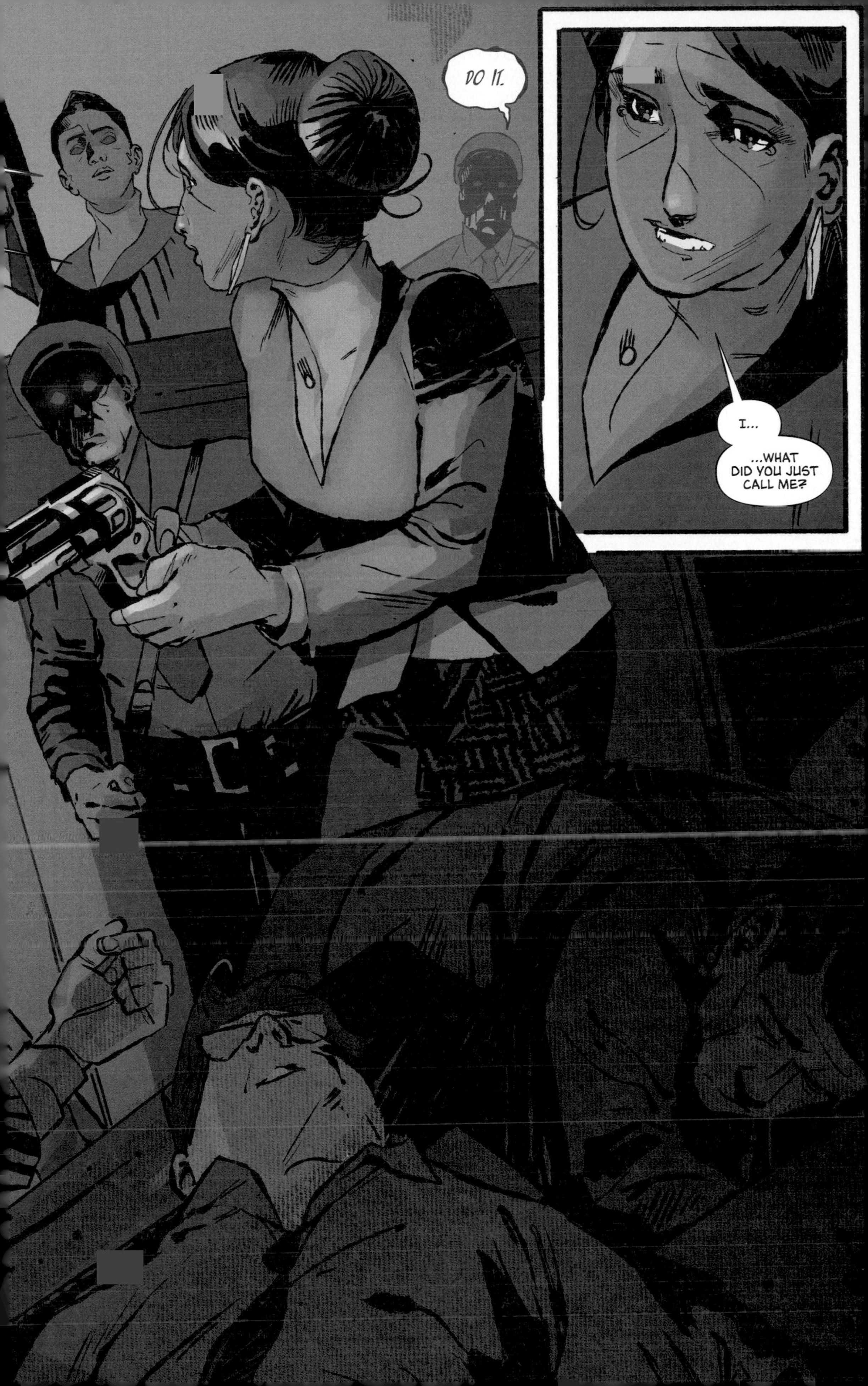
DO IT.
I...
...WHAT DID YOU JUST CALL ME?

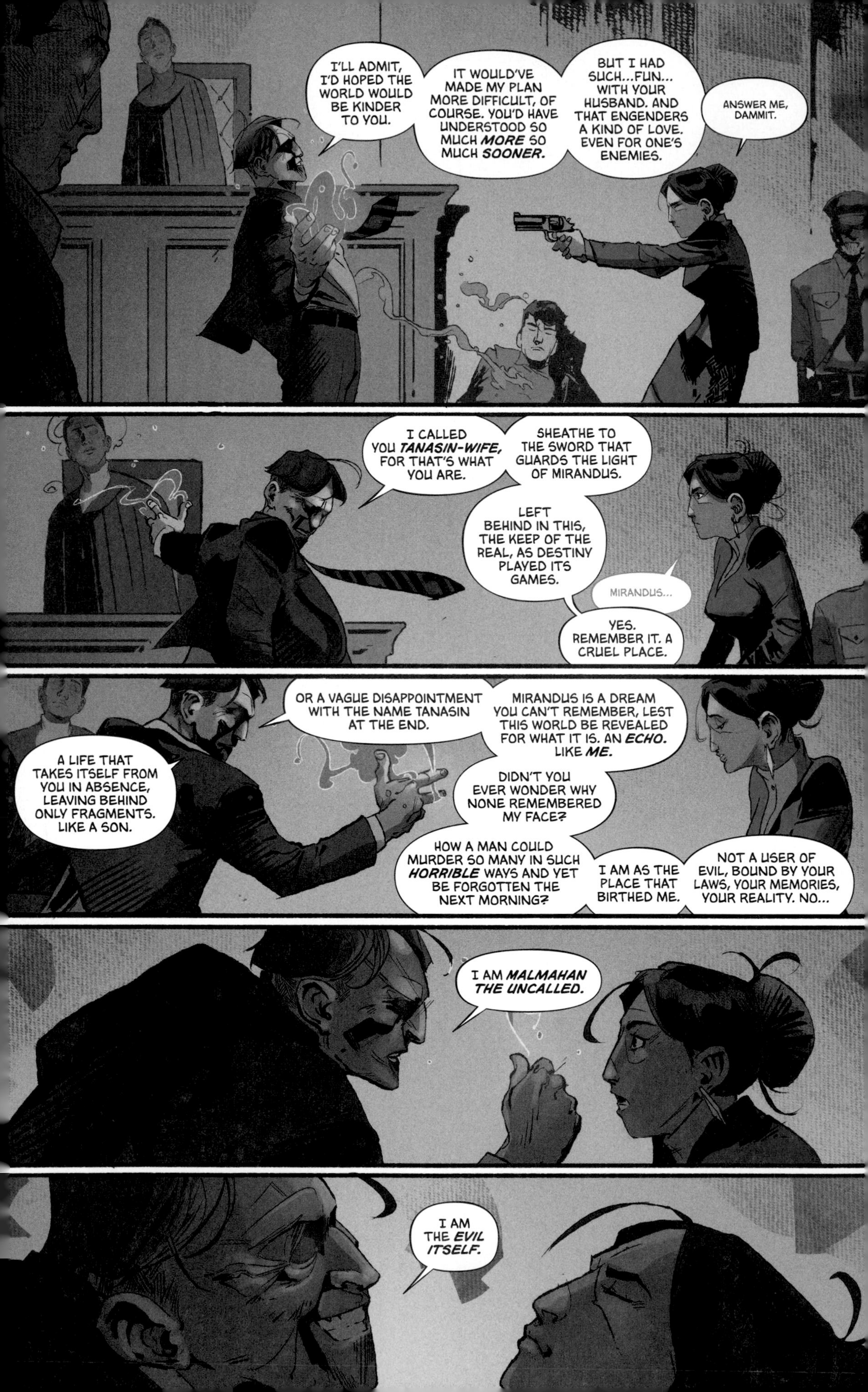
I'LL ADMIT, I'D HOPED THE WORLD WOULD BE KINDER TO YOU.
IT WOULD'VE MADE MY PLAN MORE DIFFICULT, OF COURSE. YOU'D HAVE UNDERSTOOD SO MUCH *MORE* SO MUCH *SOONER.*
BUT I HAD SUCH...FUN... WITH YOUR HUSBAND. AND THAT ENGENDERS A KIND OF LOVE. EVEN FOR ONE'S ENEMIES.
ANSWER ME, DAMMIT.
I CALLED YOU *TANASIN-WIFE,* FOR THAT'S WHAT YOU ARE.
SHEATHE TO THE SWORD THAT GUARDS THE LIGHT OF MIRANDUS.
LEFT BEHIND IN THIS, THE KEEP OF THE REAL, AS DESTINY PLAYED ITS GAMES.
MIRANDUS...
YES. REMEMBER IT. A CRUEL PLACE.
A LIFE THAT TAKES ITSELF FROM YOU IN ABSENCE, LEAVING BEHIND ONLY FRAGMENTS. LIKE A SON.
OR A VAGUE DISAPPOINTMENT WITH THE NAME TANASIN AT THE END.
MIRANDUS IS A DREAM YOU CAN'T REMEMBER, LEST THIS WORLD BE REVEALED FOR WHAT IT IS. AN *ECHO.* LIKE *ME.*
DIDN'T YOU EVER WONDER WHY NONE REMEMBERED MY FACE?
HOW A MAN COULD MURDER SO MANY IN SUCH *HORRIBLE* WAYS AND YET BE FORGOTTEN THE NEXT MORNING?
I AM AS THE PLACE THAT BIRTHED ME.
NOT A USER OF EVIL, BOUND BY YOUR LAWS, YOUR MEMORIES, YOUR REALITY. NO...
I AM *MALMAHAN THE UNCALLED.*
I AM THE *EVIL ITSELF.*

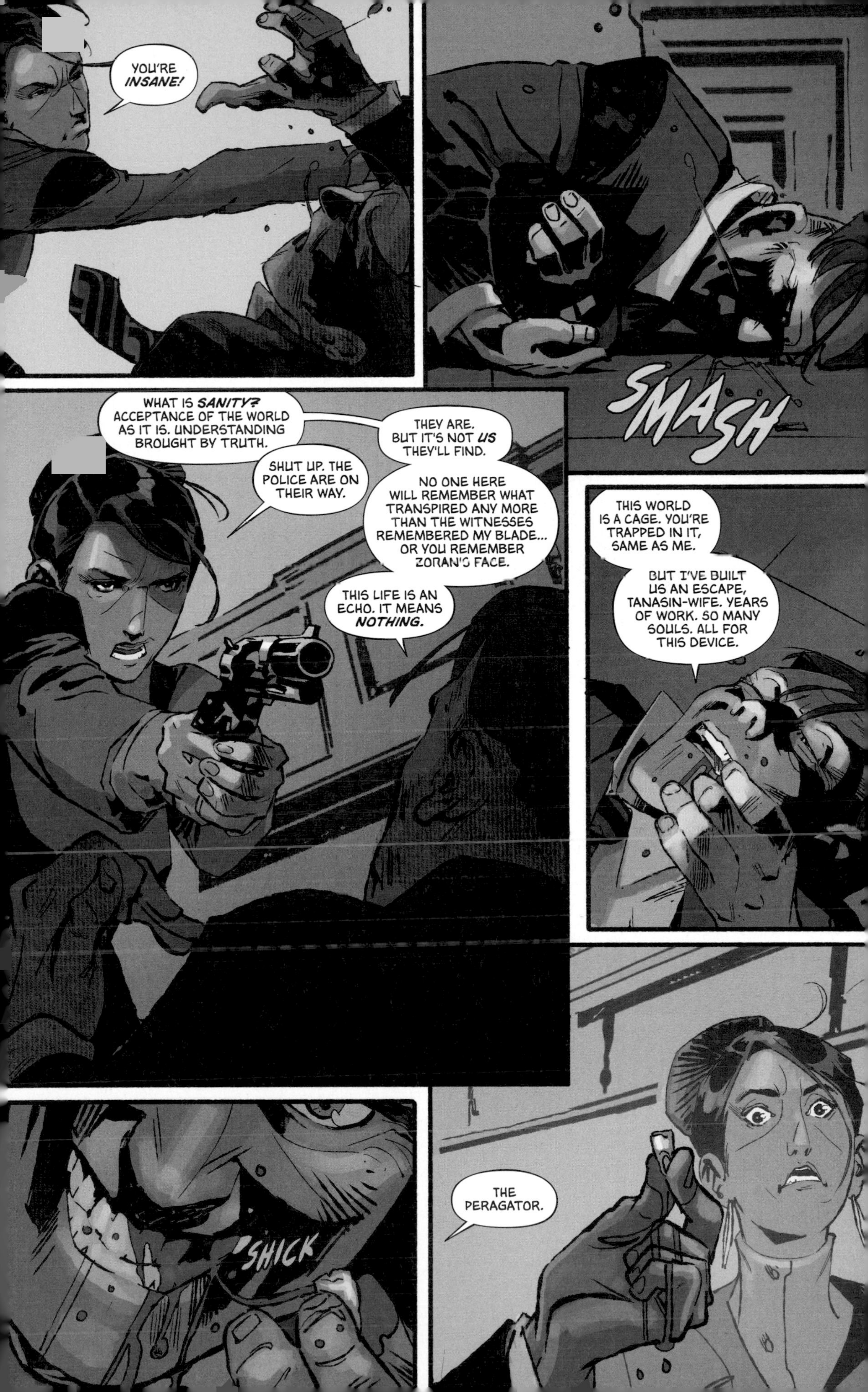
YOU'RE *INSANE!*
SMASH
WHAT IS *SANITY?* ACCEPTANCE OF THE WORLD AS IT IS. UNDERSTANDING BROUGHT BY TRUTH.
SHUT UP. THE POLICE ARE ON THEIR WAY.
THEY ARE. BUT IT'S NOT *US* THEY'LL FIND.
NO ONE HERE WILL REMEMBER WHAT TRANSPIRED ANY MORE THAN THE WITNESSES REMEMBERED MY BLADE... OR YOU REMEMBER ZORAN'S FACE.
THIS LIFE IS AN ECHO. IT MEANS *NOTHING.*
THIS WORLD IS A CAGE. YOU'RE TRAPPED IN IT, SAME AS ME.
BUT I'VE BUILT US AN ESCAPE, TANASIN-WIFE. YEARS OF WORK. SO MANY SOULS. ALL FOR THIS DEVICE.
SHICK
THE PERAGATOR.

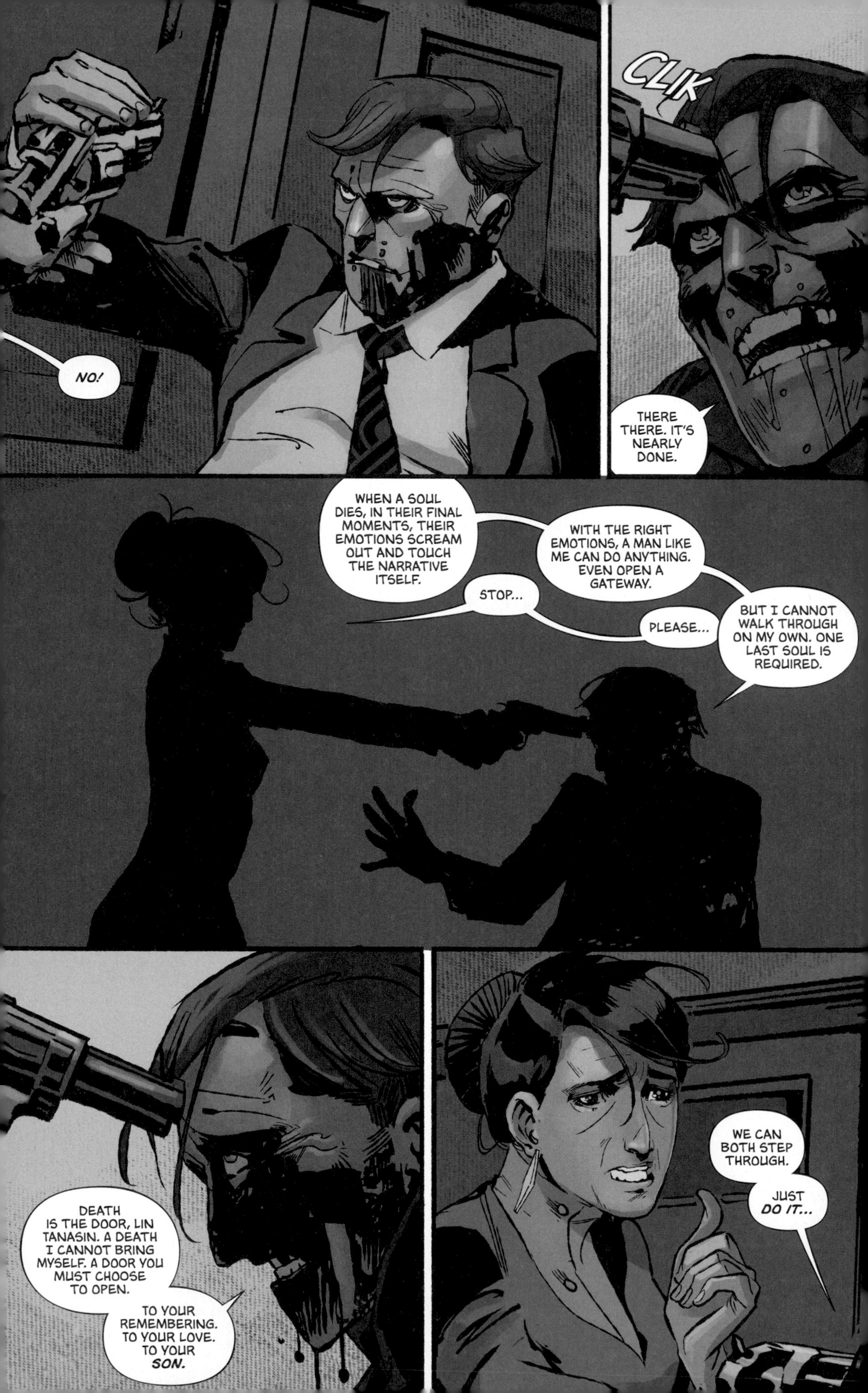
NO!
CLIK
THERE THERE. IT'S NEARLY DONE.
WHEN A SOUL DIES, IN THEIR FINAL MOMENTS, THEIR EMOTIONS SCREAM OUT AND TOUCH THE NARRATIVE ITSELF.
WITH THE RIGHT EMOTIONS, A MAN LIKE ME CAN DO ANYTHING. EVEN OPEN A GATEWAY.
STOP...
PLEASE...
BUT I CANNOT WALK THROUGH ON MY OWN. ONE LAST SOUL IS REQUIRED.
DEATH IS THE DOOR, LIN TANASIN. A DEATH I CANNOT BRING MYSELF. A DOOR YOU MUST CHOOSE TO OPEN.
TO YOUR REMEMBERING. TO YOUR LOVE. TO YOUR *SON.*
WE CAN BOTH STEP THROUGH.
JUST *DO IT...*

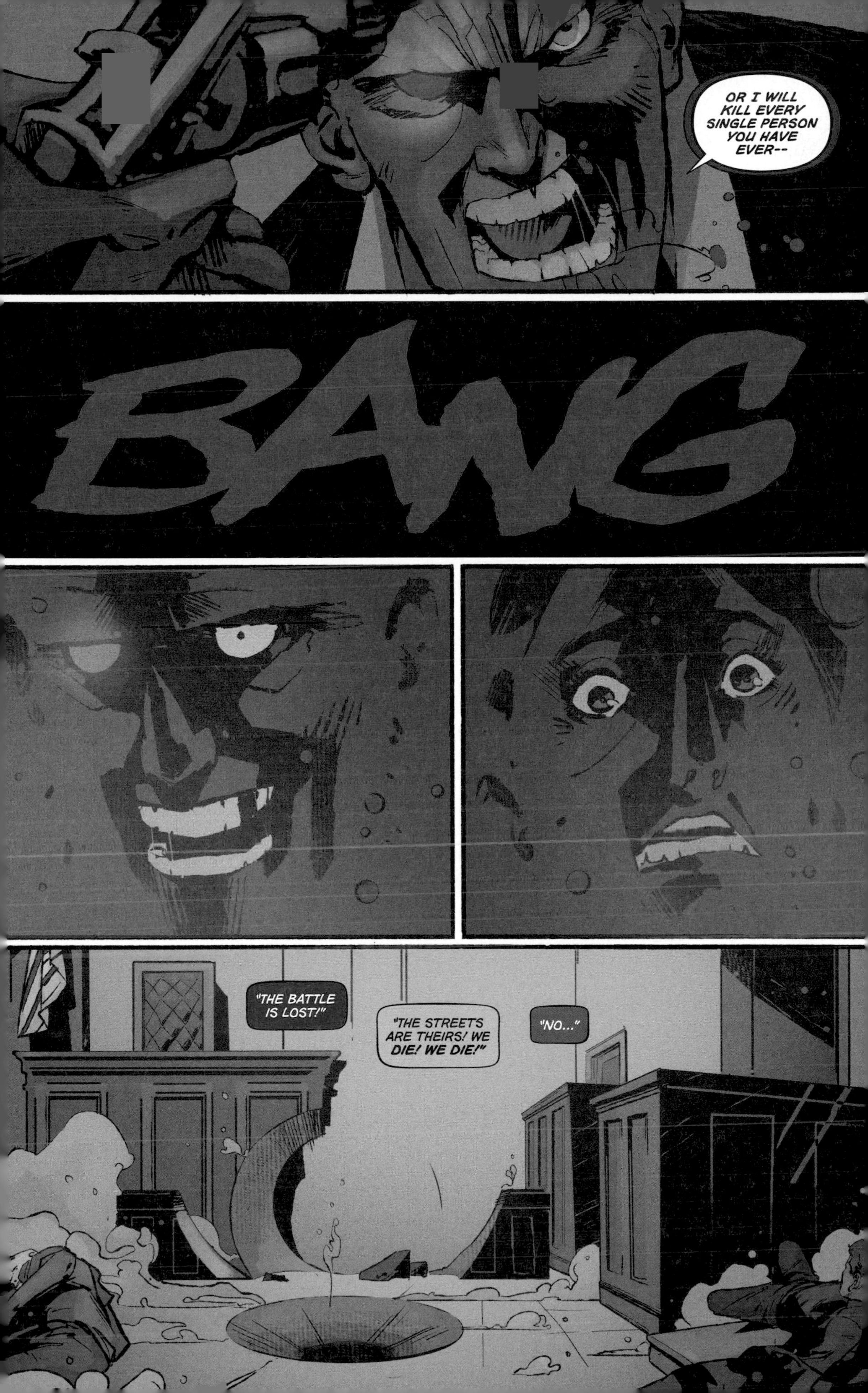
OR I WILL KILL EVERY SINGLE PERSON YOU HAVE EVER--
BANG
"THE BATTLE IS LOST!"
"THE STREETS ARE THEIRS! WE DIE! WE DIE!"
"NO..."

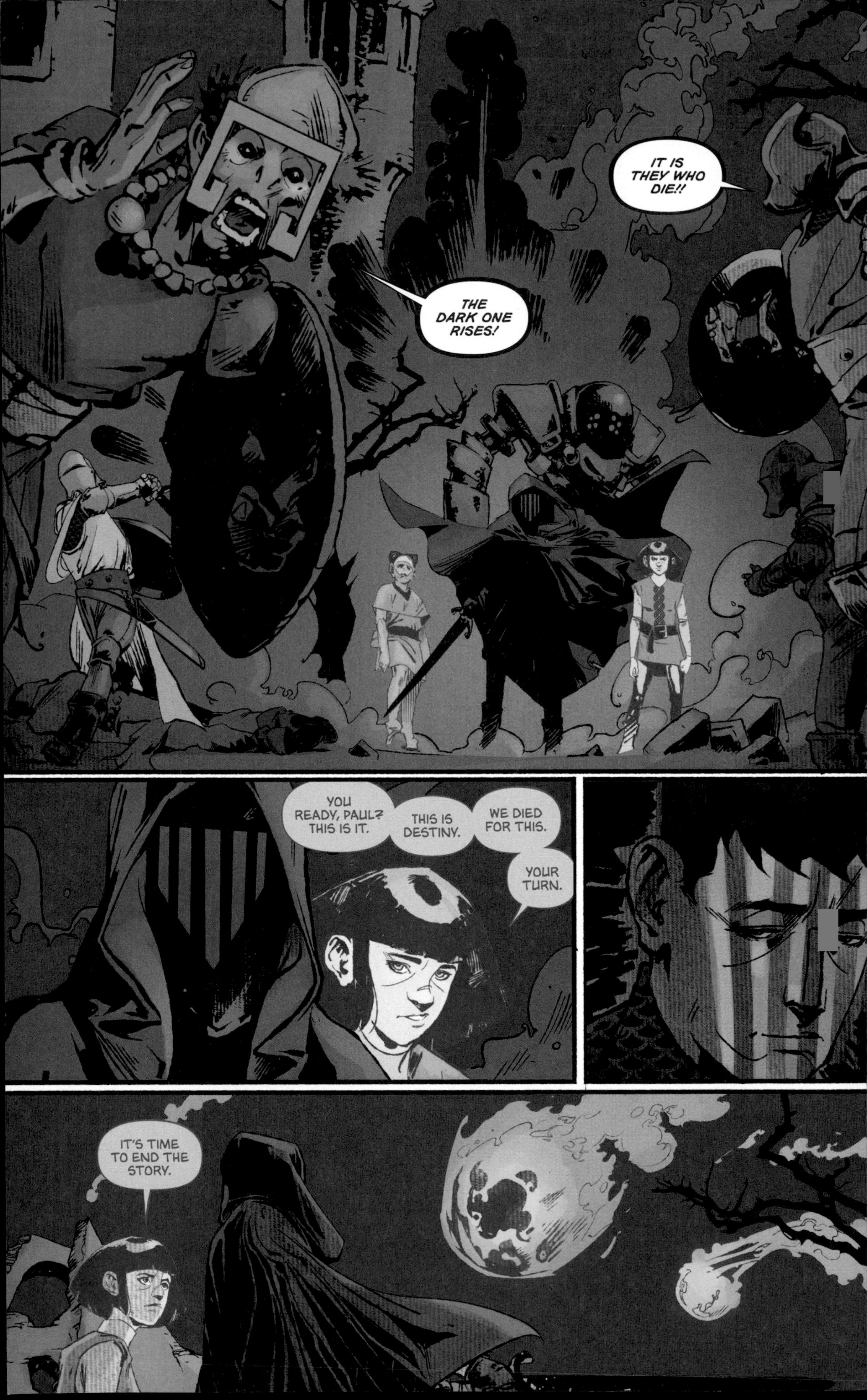
THE DARK ONE RISES!
IT IS THEY WHO DIE!!
YOU READY, PAUL? THIS IS IT.
THIS IS DESTINY.
WE DIED FOR THIS.
YOUR TURN.
IT'S TIME TO END THE STORY.

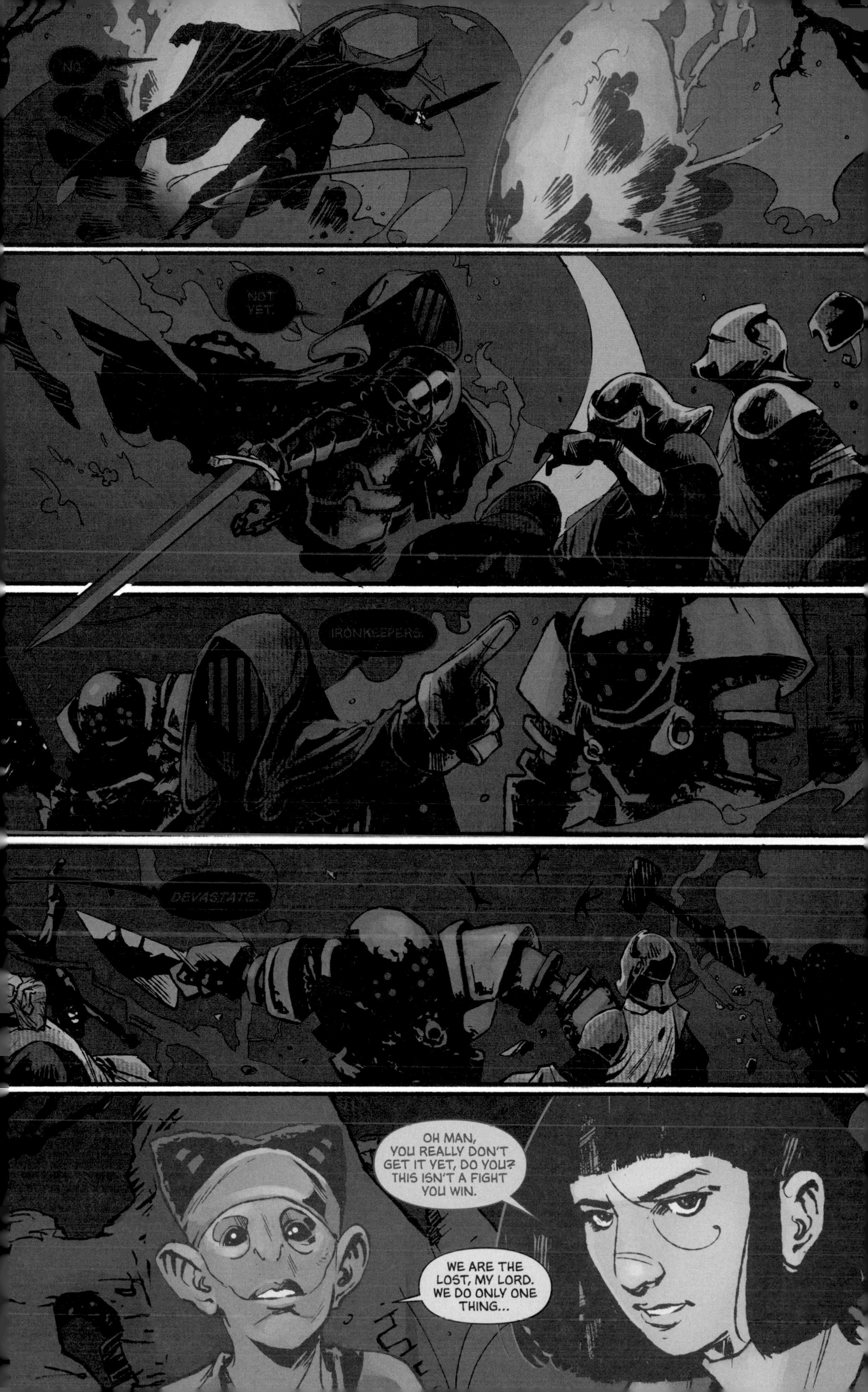
NO.
NOT YET.
IRONKEEPERS.
DEVASTATE.
OH MAN, YOU REALLY DON'T GET IT YET, DO YOU? THIS ISN'T A FIGHT YOU WIN.
WE ARE THE LOST, MY LORD. WE DO ONLY ONE THING...

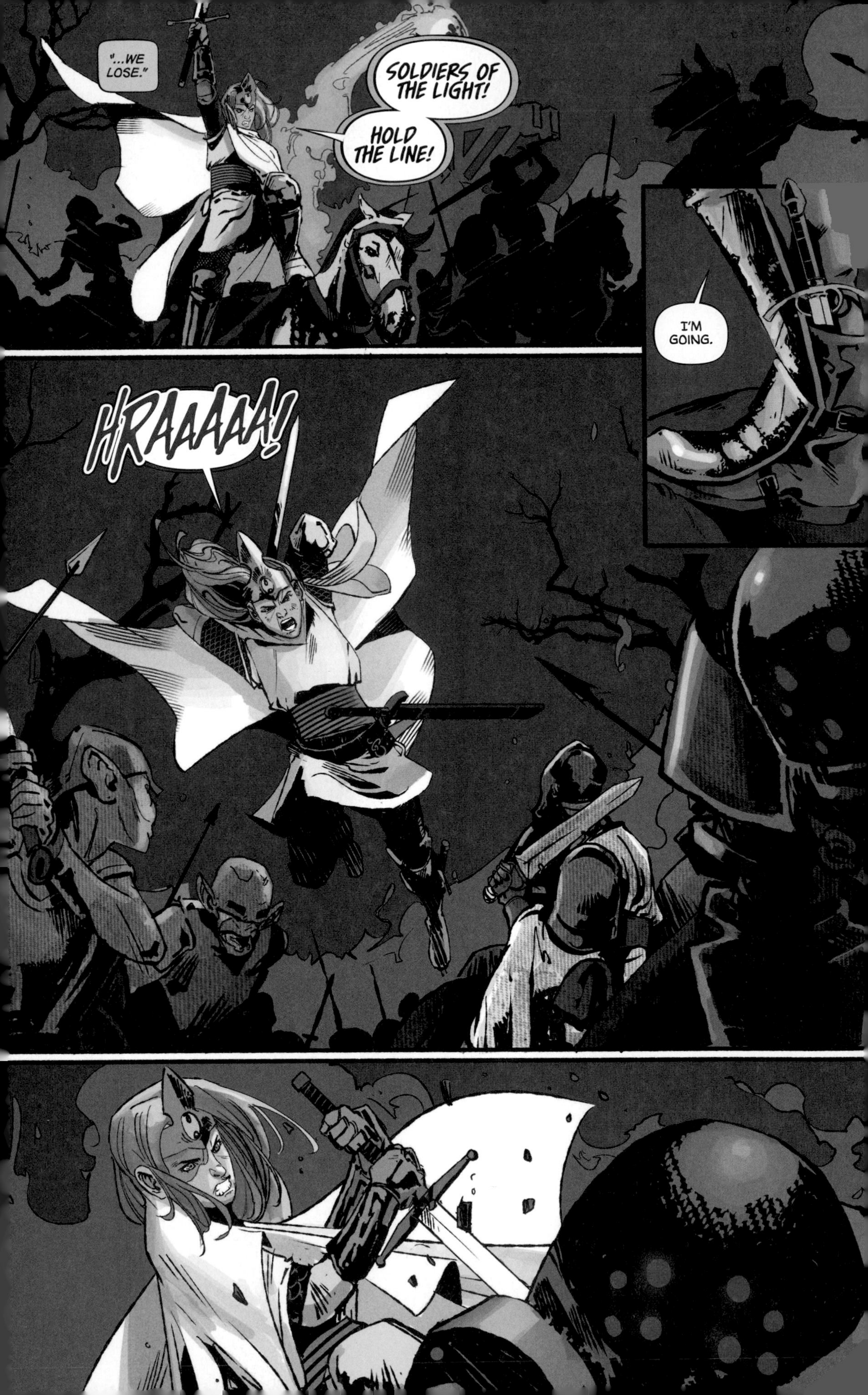
"...WE LOSE."
SOLDIERS OF THE LIGHT!
HOLD THE LINE!
I'M GOING.
HRAAAAA!

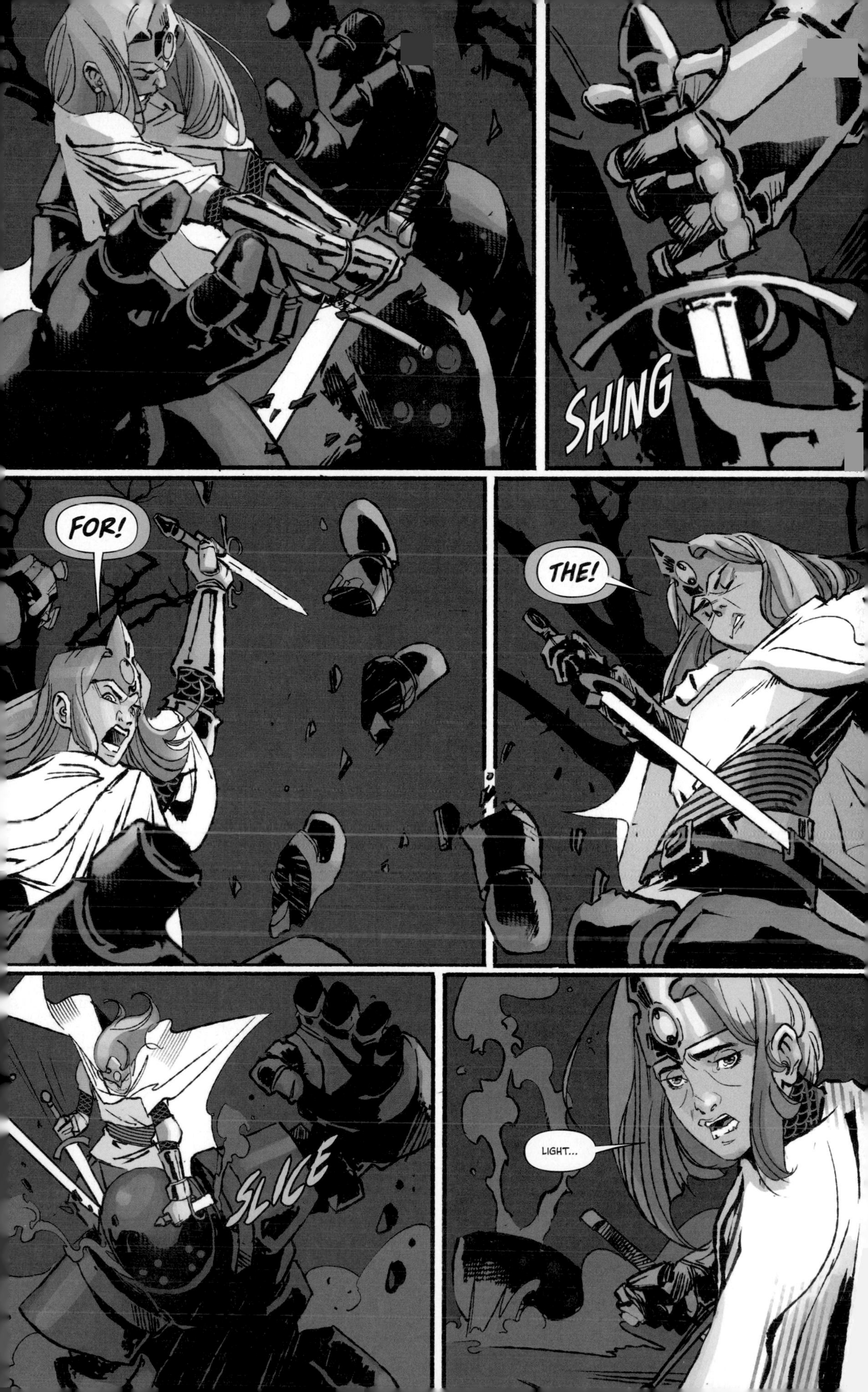
SHING
FOR!
THE!
SLICE
LIGHT...

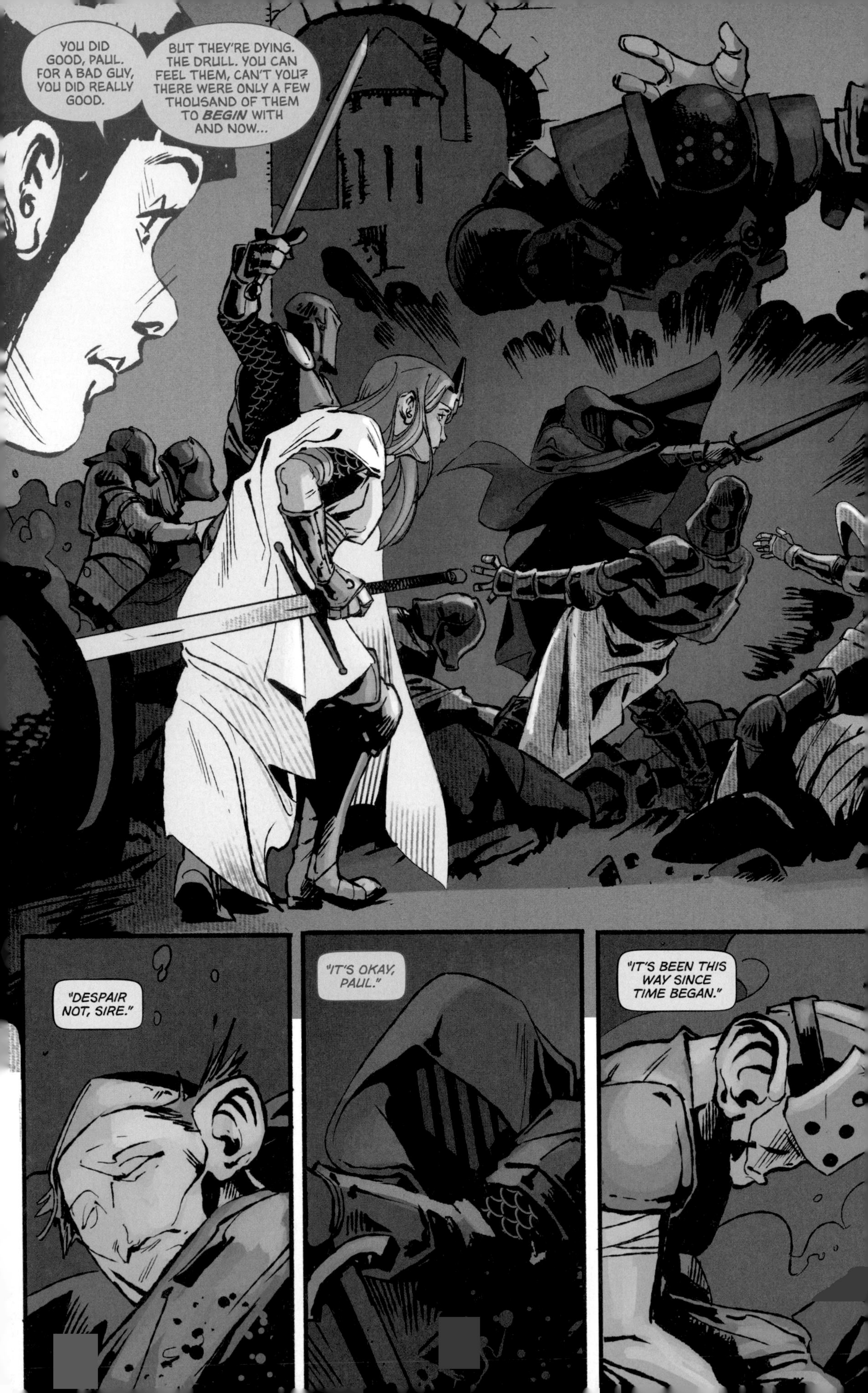
YOU DID GOOD, PAUL. FOR A BAD GUY, YOU DID REALLY GOOD.
BUT THEY'RE DYING. THE DRULL. YOU CAN FEEL THEM, CAN'T YOU? THERE WERE ONLY A FEW THOUSAND OF THEM TO *BEGIN* WITH AND NOW...
"DESPAIR NOT, SIRE."
"IT'S OKAY, PAUL."
"IT'S BEEN THIS WAY SINCE TIME BEGAN."

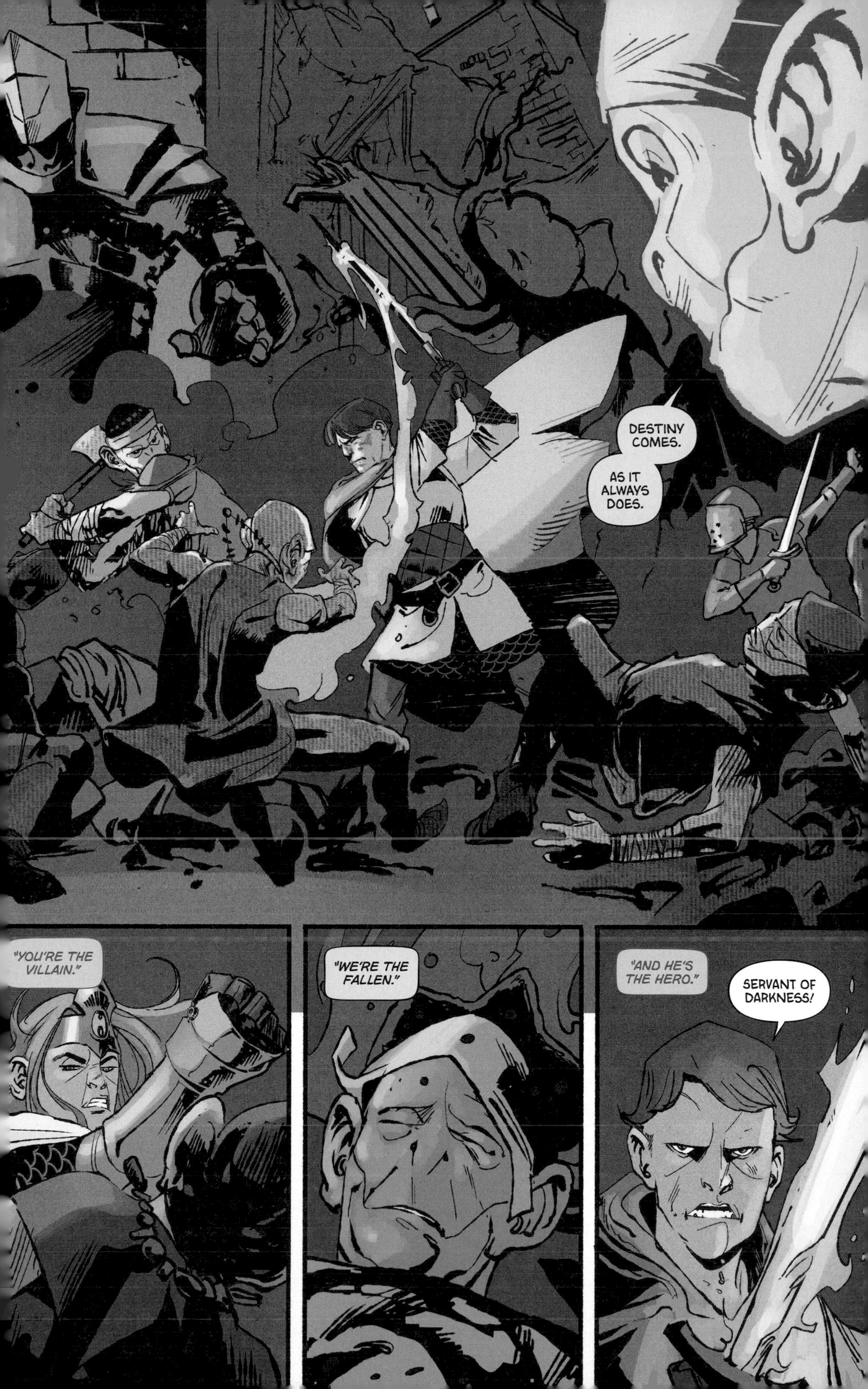
DESTINY COMES.
AS IT ALWAYS DOES.
"YOU'RE THE VILLAIN."
"WE'RE THE FALLEN."
"AND HE'S THE HERO."
SERVANT OF DARKNESS!

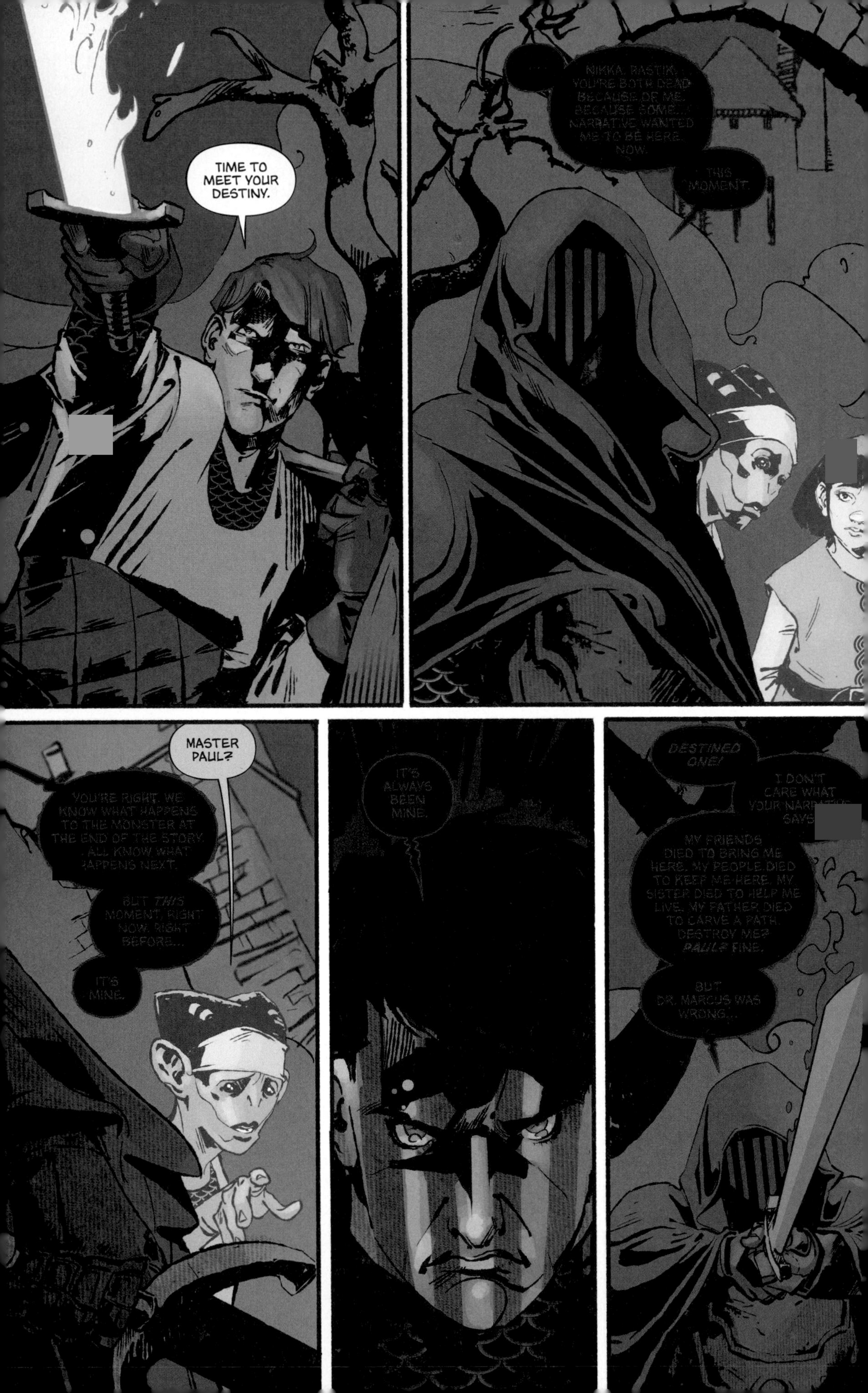
TIME TO MEET YOUR DESTINY.
NIKKA. BASTIK. YOU'RE BOTH DEAD BECAUSE OF ME. BECAUSE SOME... NARRATIVE WANTED ME TO BE HERE. NOW.
THIS MOMENT.
MASTER PAUL?
YOU'RE RIGHT. WE KNOW WHAT HAPPENS TO THE MONSTER AT THE END OF THE STORY. [redacted] ALL KNOW WHAT [redacted]APPENS NEXT.
BUT *THIS* MOMENT, RIGHT NOW, RIGHT BEFORE...
IT'S MINE.
IT'S ALWAYS BEEN MINE.
DESTINED ONE!
I DON'T CARE WHAT YOUR NARR SAYS
MY FRIENDS DIED TO BRING ME HERE. MY PEOPLE DIED TO KEEP ME HERE. MY SISTER DIED TO HELP ME LIVE. MY FATHER DIED TO CARVE A PATH. DESTROY ME? *PAUL?* FINE.
BUT DR. MARCUS WAS WRONG...

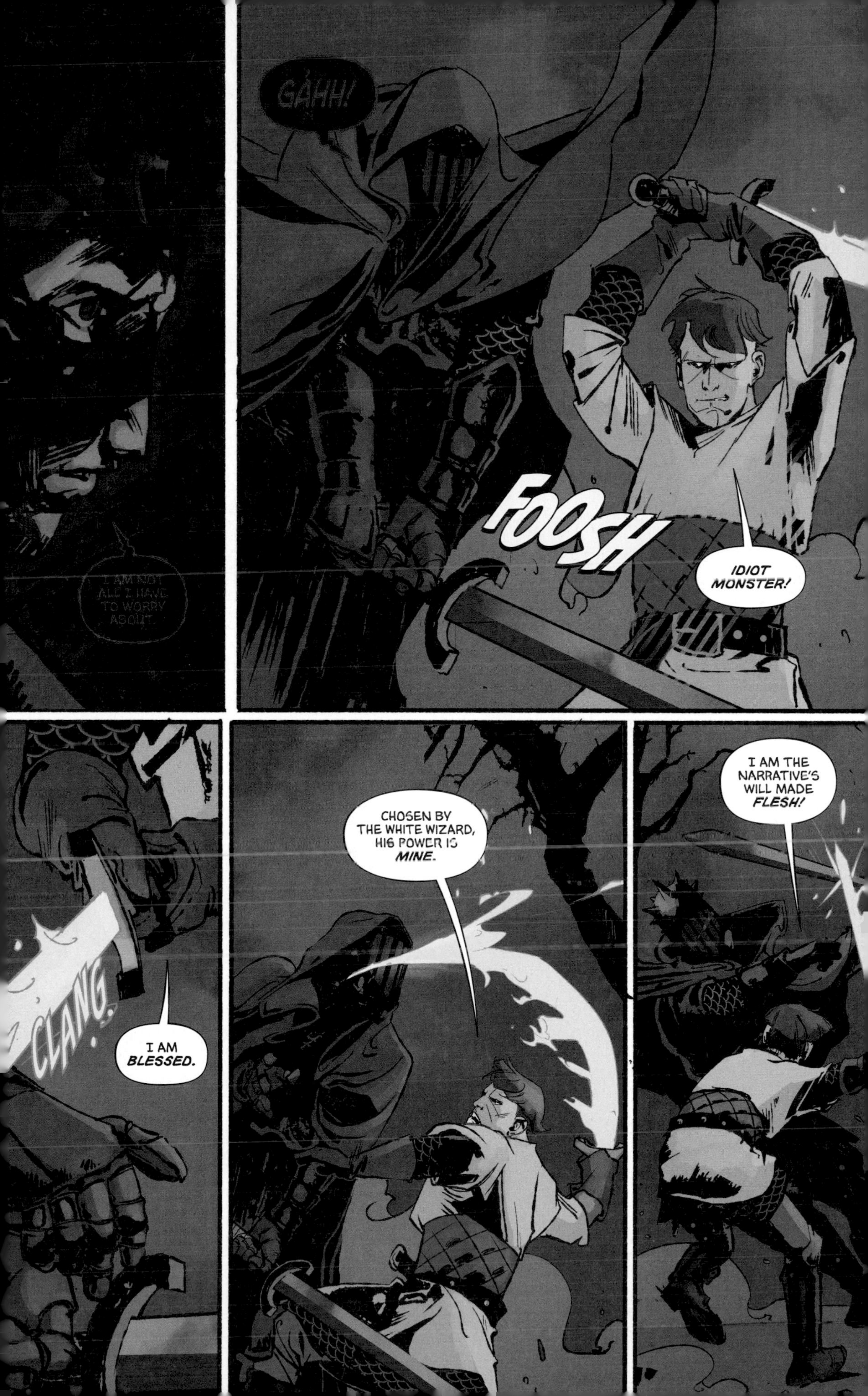
I AM NOT ALL I HAVE TO WORRY ABOUT.
GAHH!
FOOSH
IDIOT MONSTER!
CLANG
I AM BLESSED.
CHOSEN BY THE WHITE WIZARD, HIS POWER IS MINE.
I AM THE NARRATIVE'S WILL MADE FLESH!

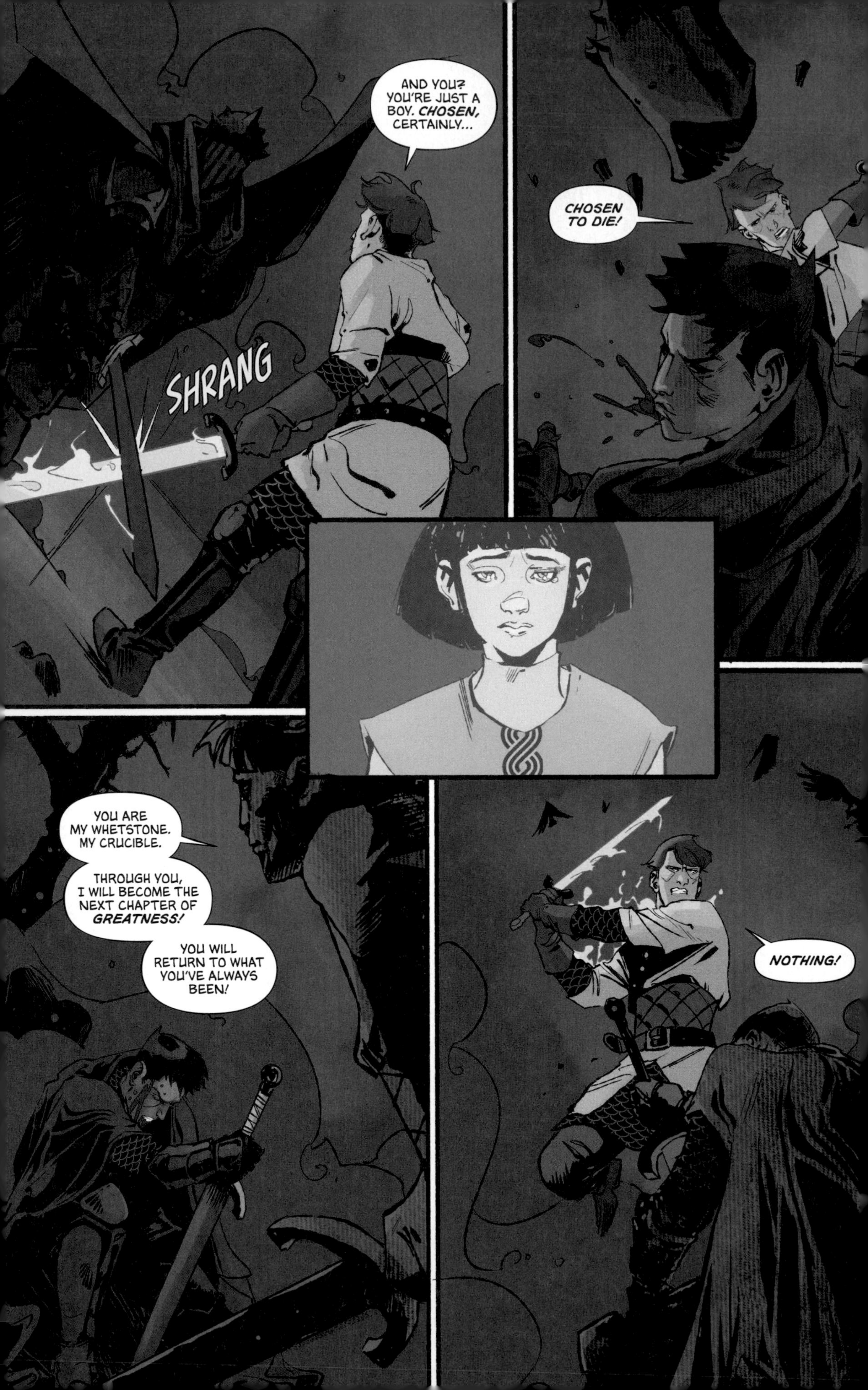
AND YOU? YOU'RE JUST A BOY. CHOSEN, CERTAINLY...
SHRANG
CHOSEN TO DIE!
YOU ARE MY WHETSTONE. MY CRUCIBLE.
THROUGH YOU, I WILL BECOME THE NEXT CHAPTER OF GREATNESS!
YOU WILL RETURN TO WHAT YOU'VE ALWAYS BEEN!
NOTHING!

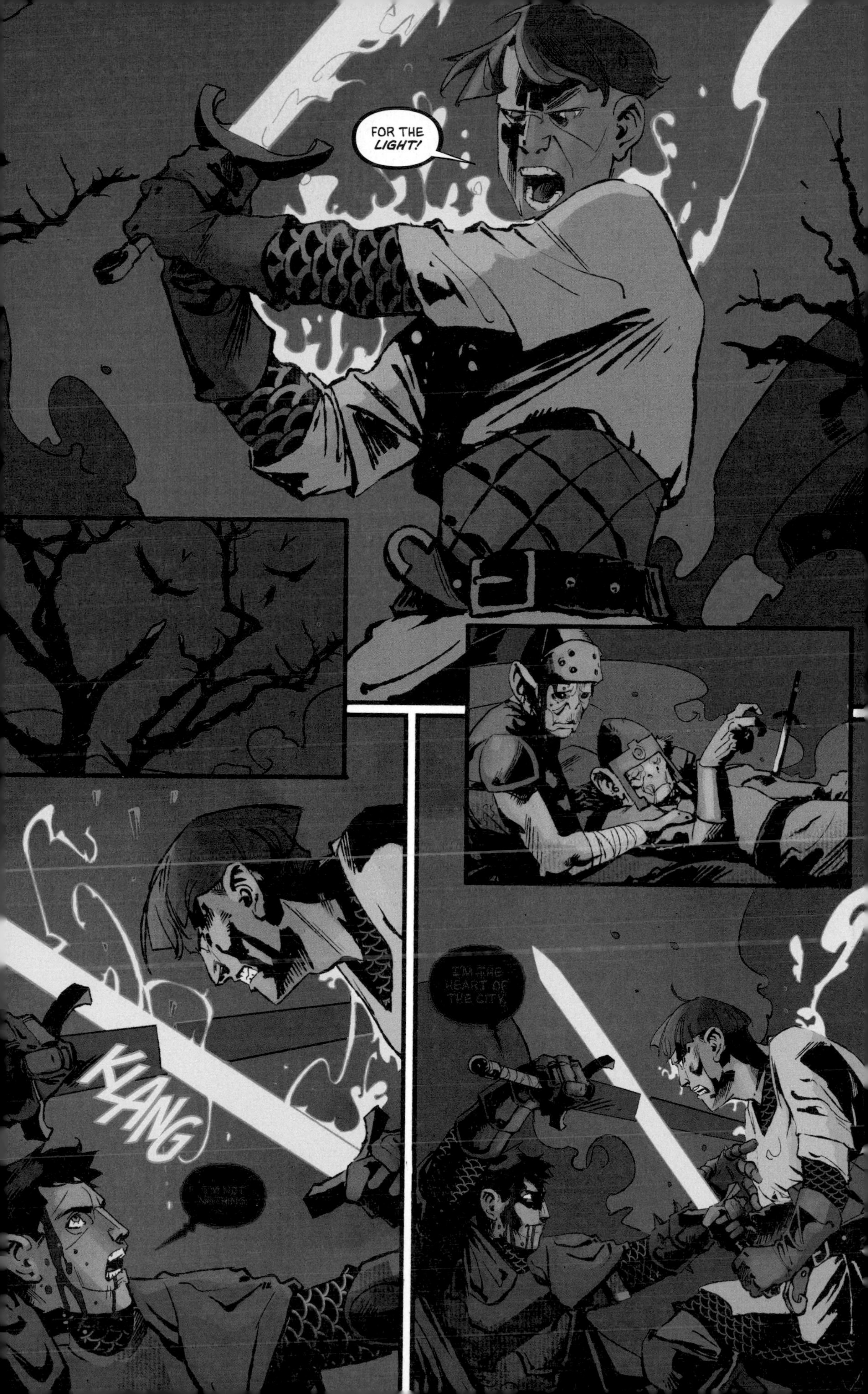
FOR THE *LIGHT!*
KLANG
I'M NOT NOTHING.
I'M THE HEART OF THE CITY.

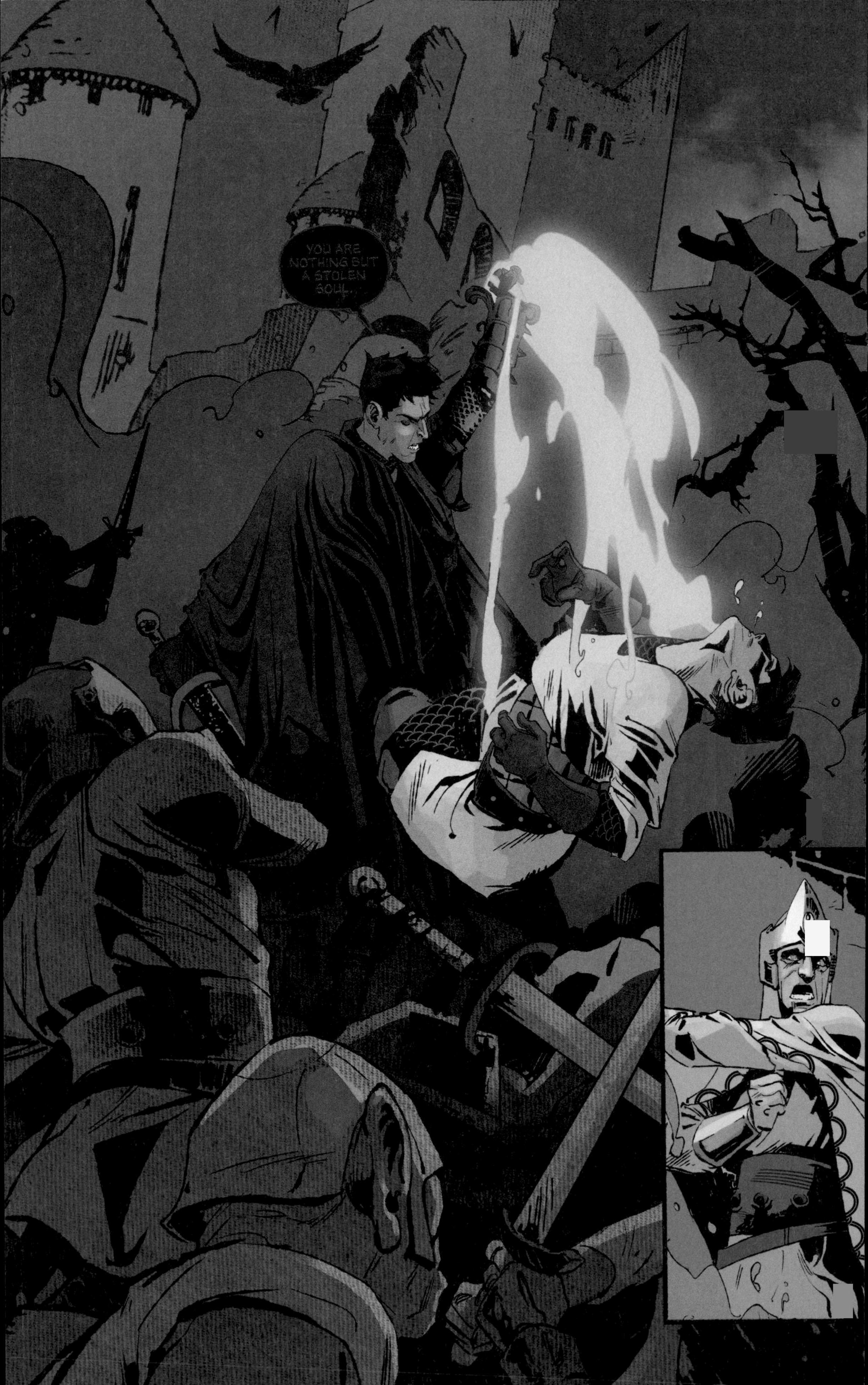
YOU ARE NOTHING BUT A STOLEN SOUL...

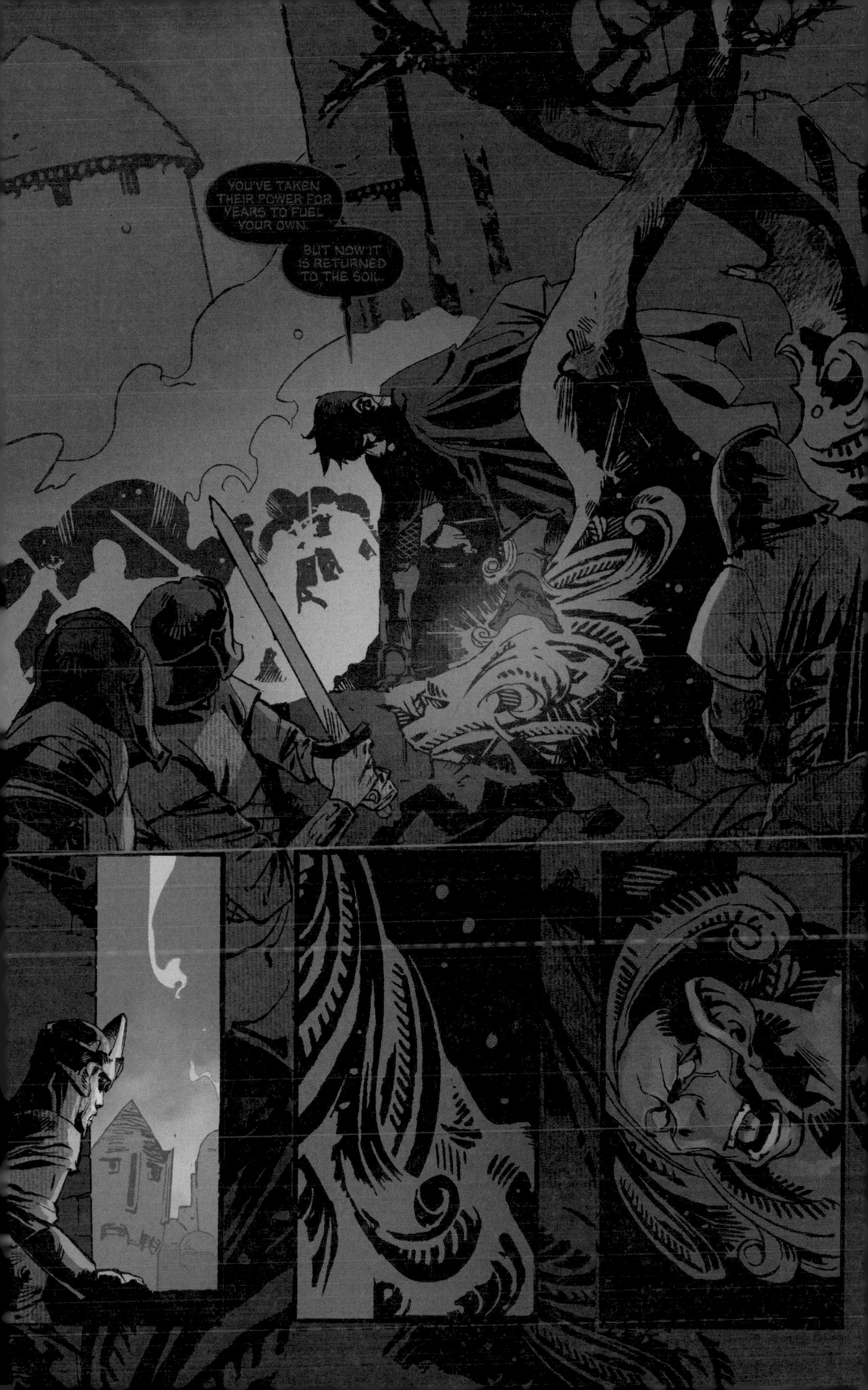
YOU'VE TAKEN THEIR POWER FOR YEARS TO FUEL YOUR OWN.
BUT NOW IT IS RETURNED TO THE SOIL.

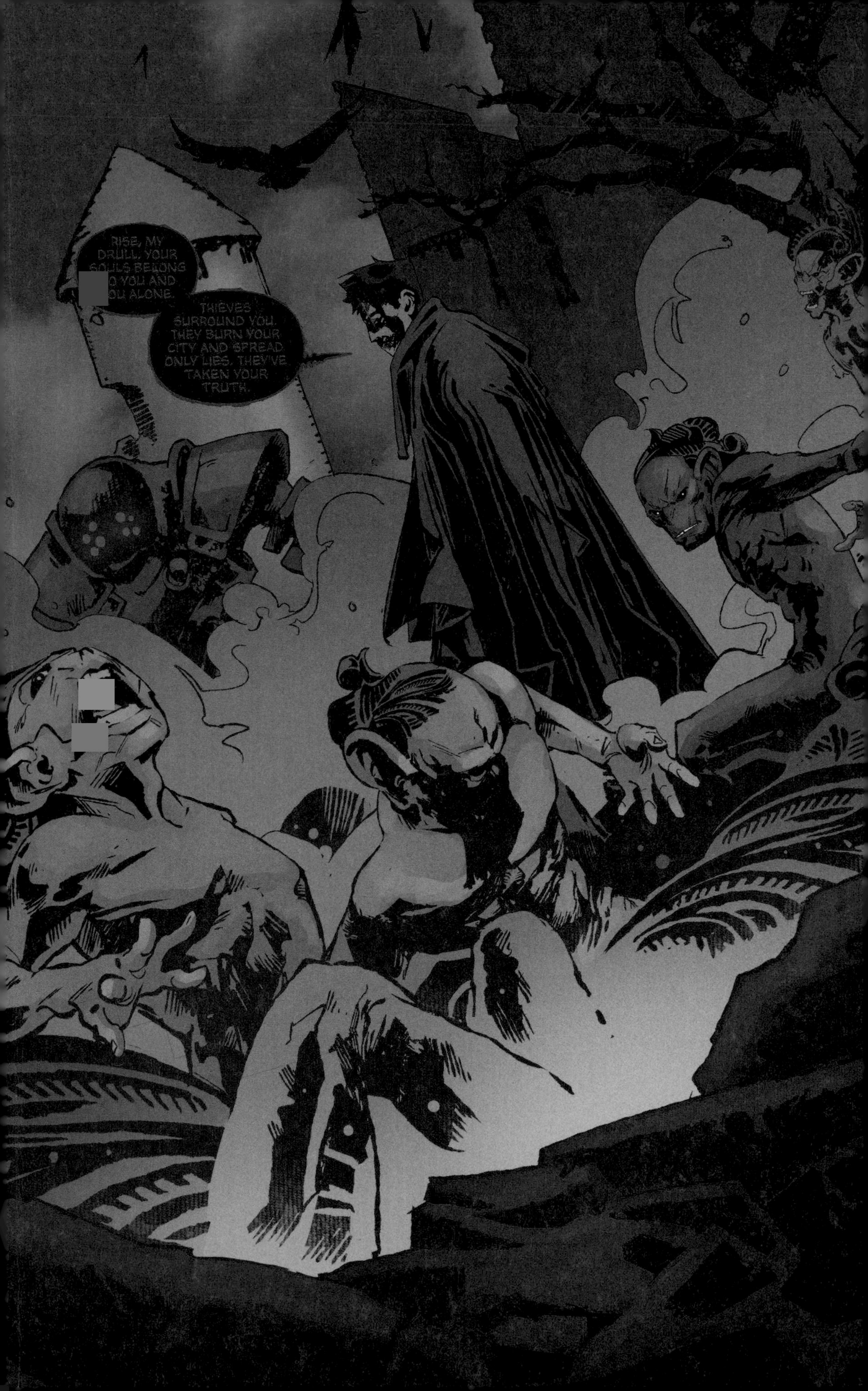
RISE, MY DRULL. YOUR SOULS BELONG
YOU AND
ALONE.
THIEVES SURROUND YOU. THEY BURN YOUR CITY AND SPREAD ONLY LIES. THEY'VE TAKEN YOUR TRUTH.

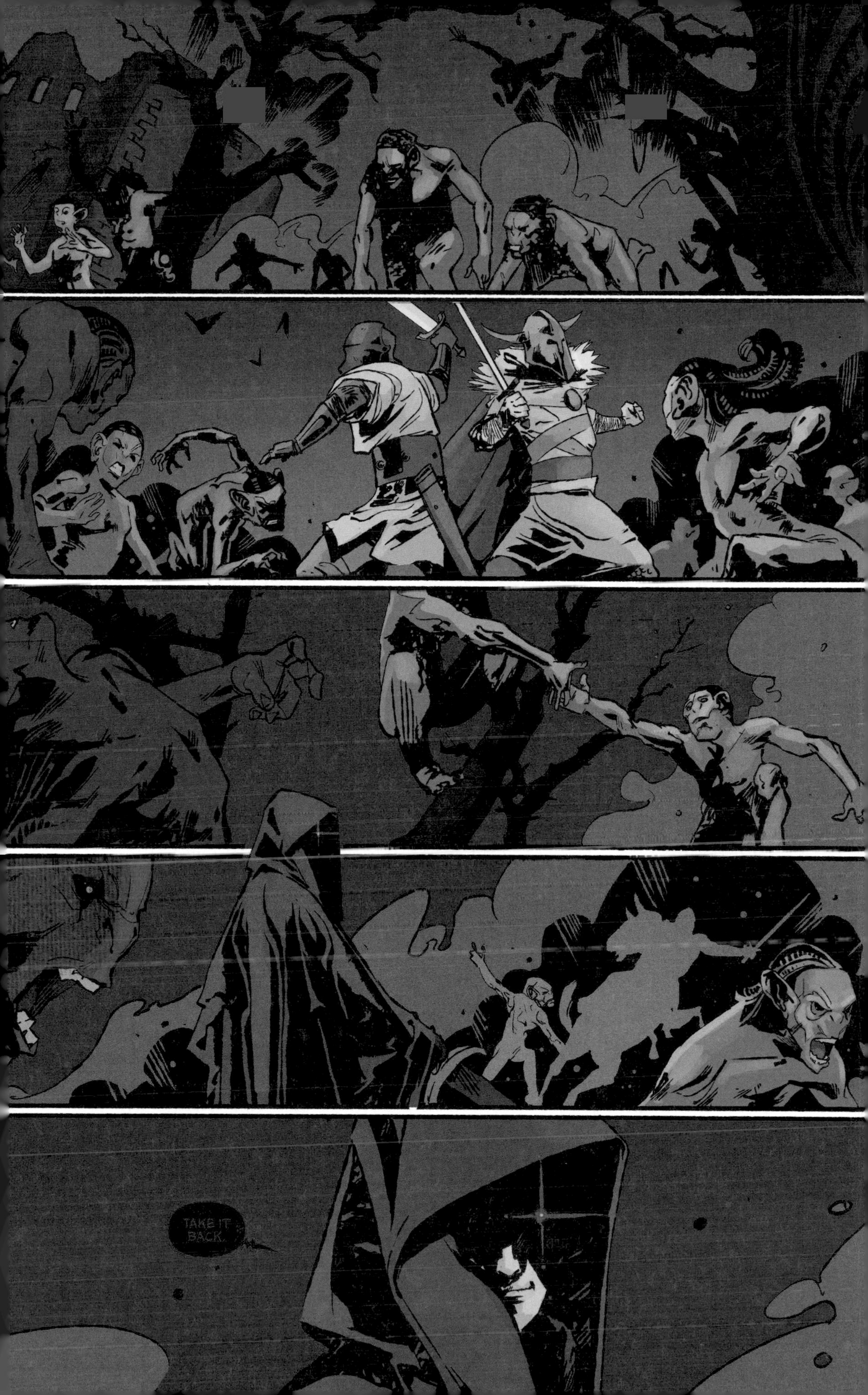
TAKE IT BACK.

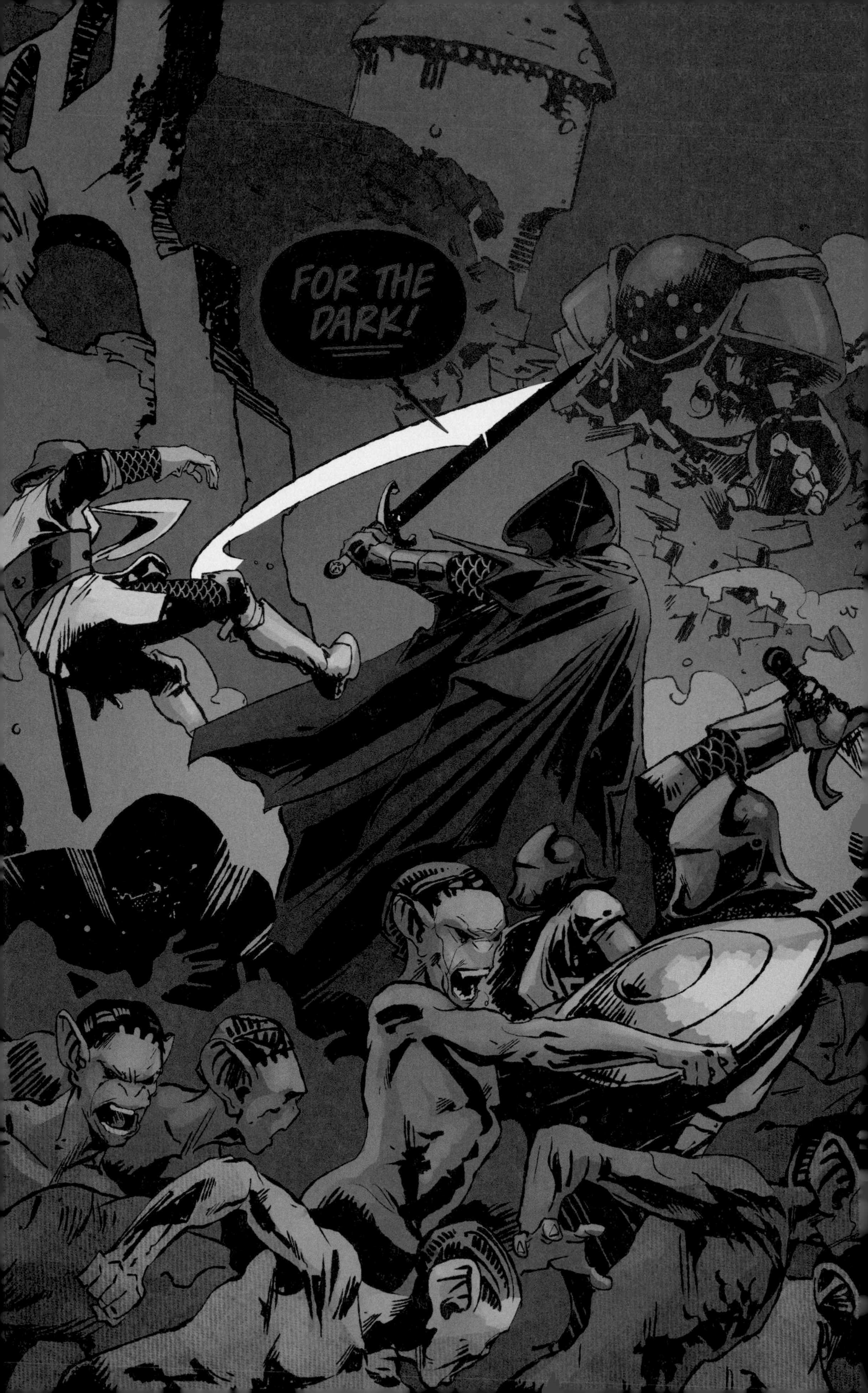
FOR THE DARK!

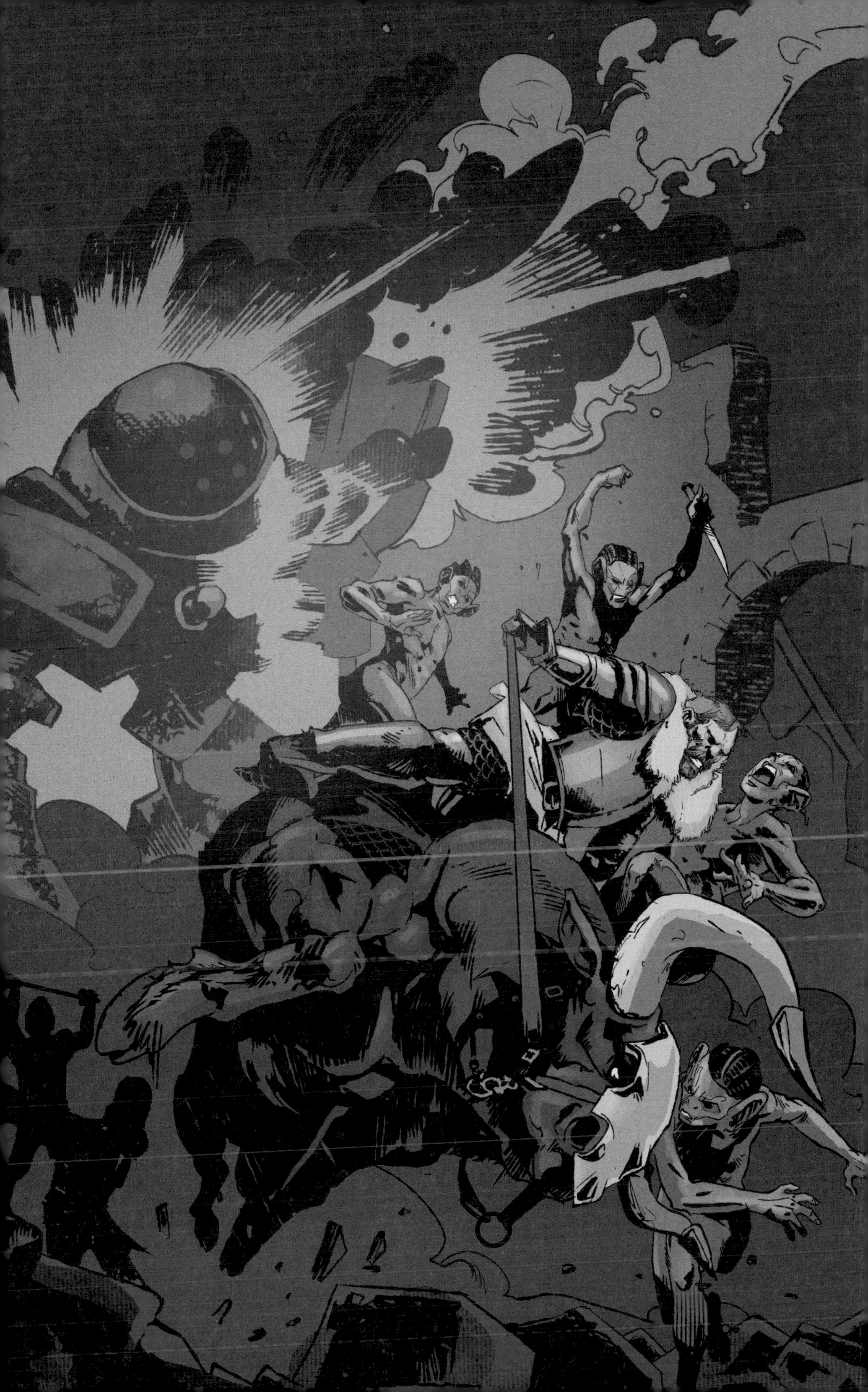

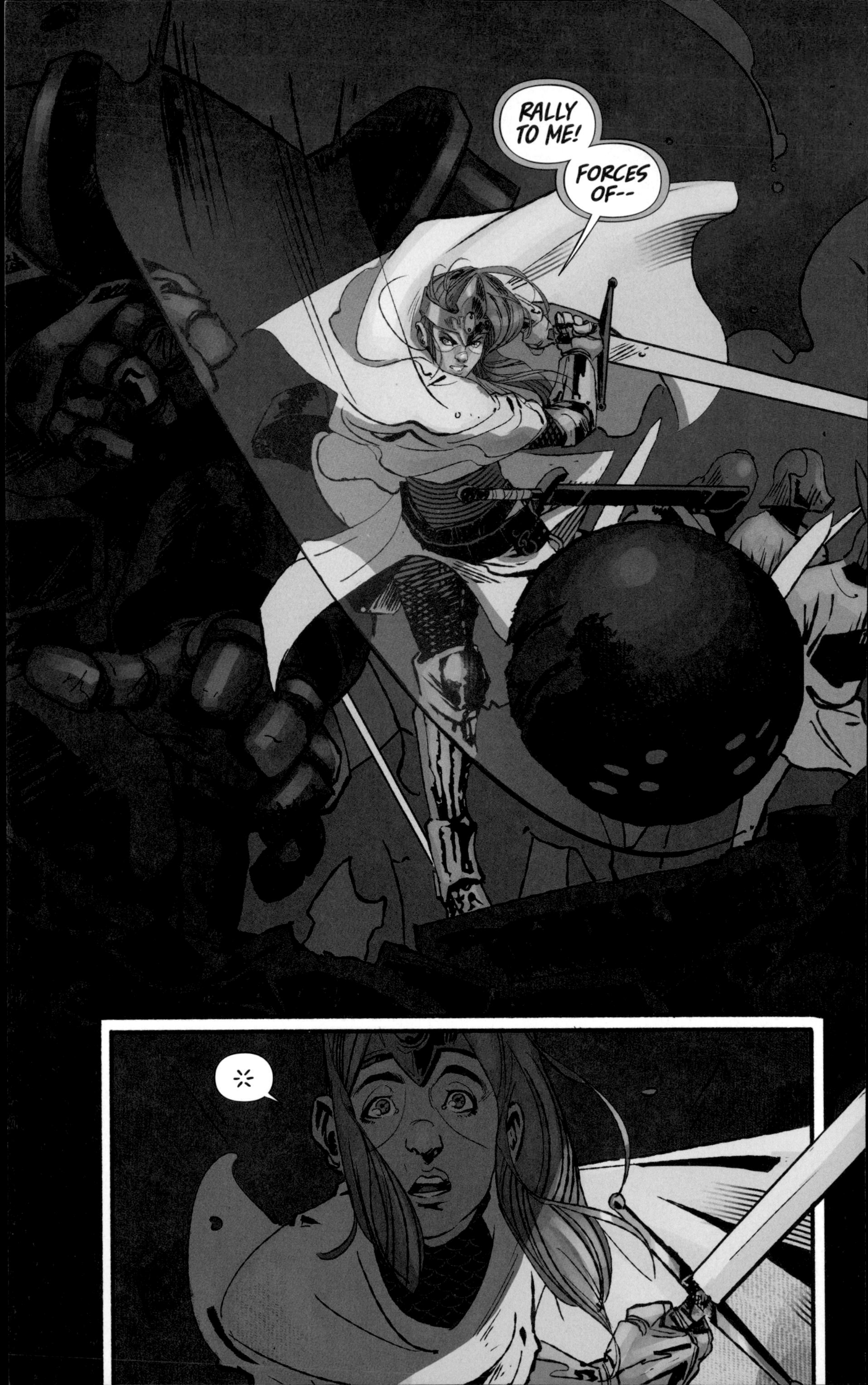
RALLY TO ME!
FORCES OF--

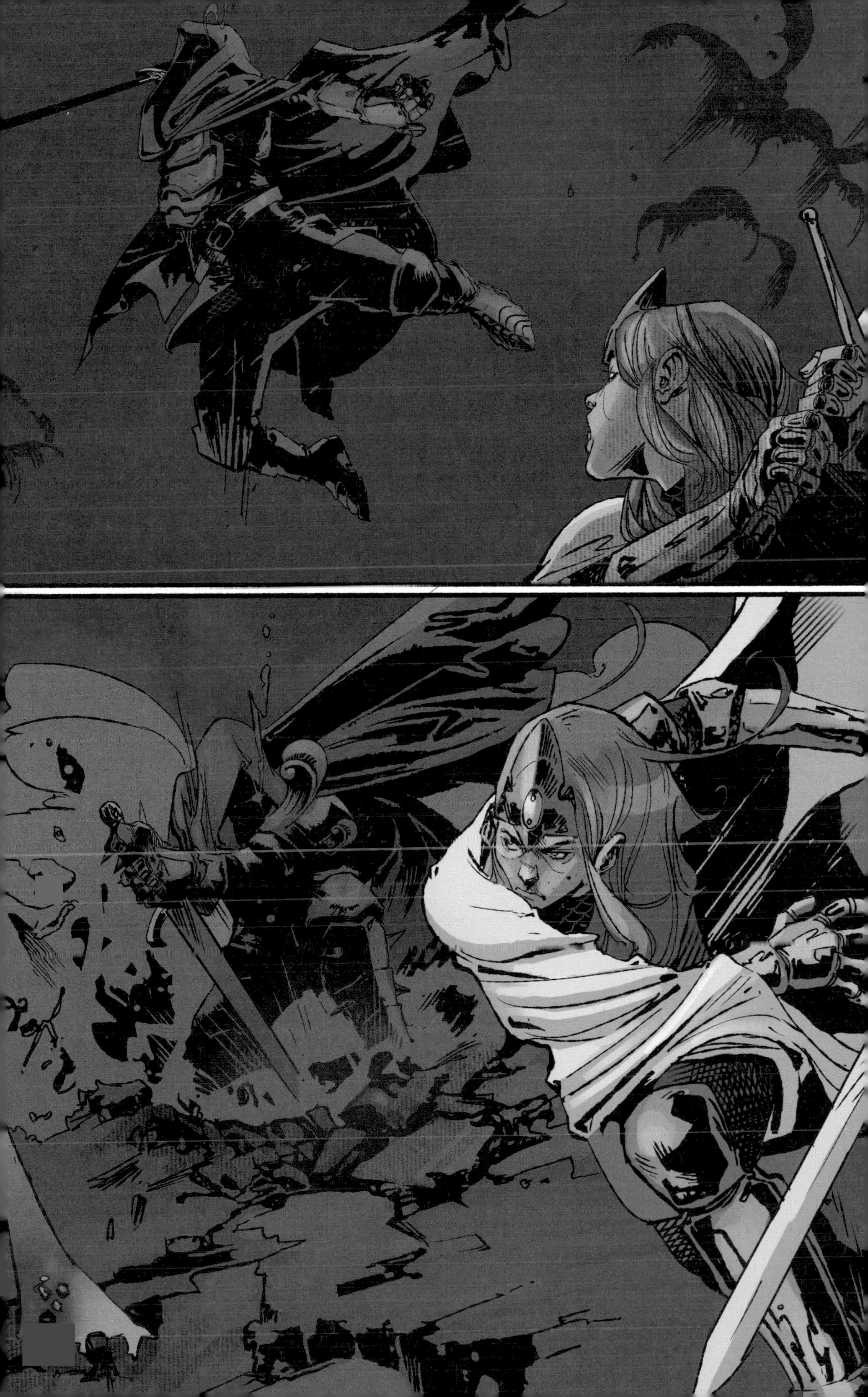

YOU'VE REVEALED YOUR *TRUE FACE!*

GIVEN *TRUTH* TO YOUR *LIE!*

I AM ONLY WHO I WAS *MEANT* TO BE!

MONSTER.

CLANG

KILLER!

CLANG

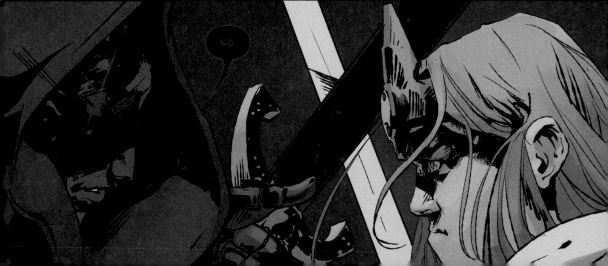

NO.

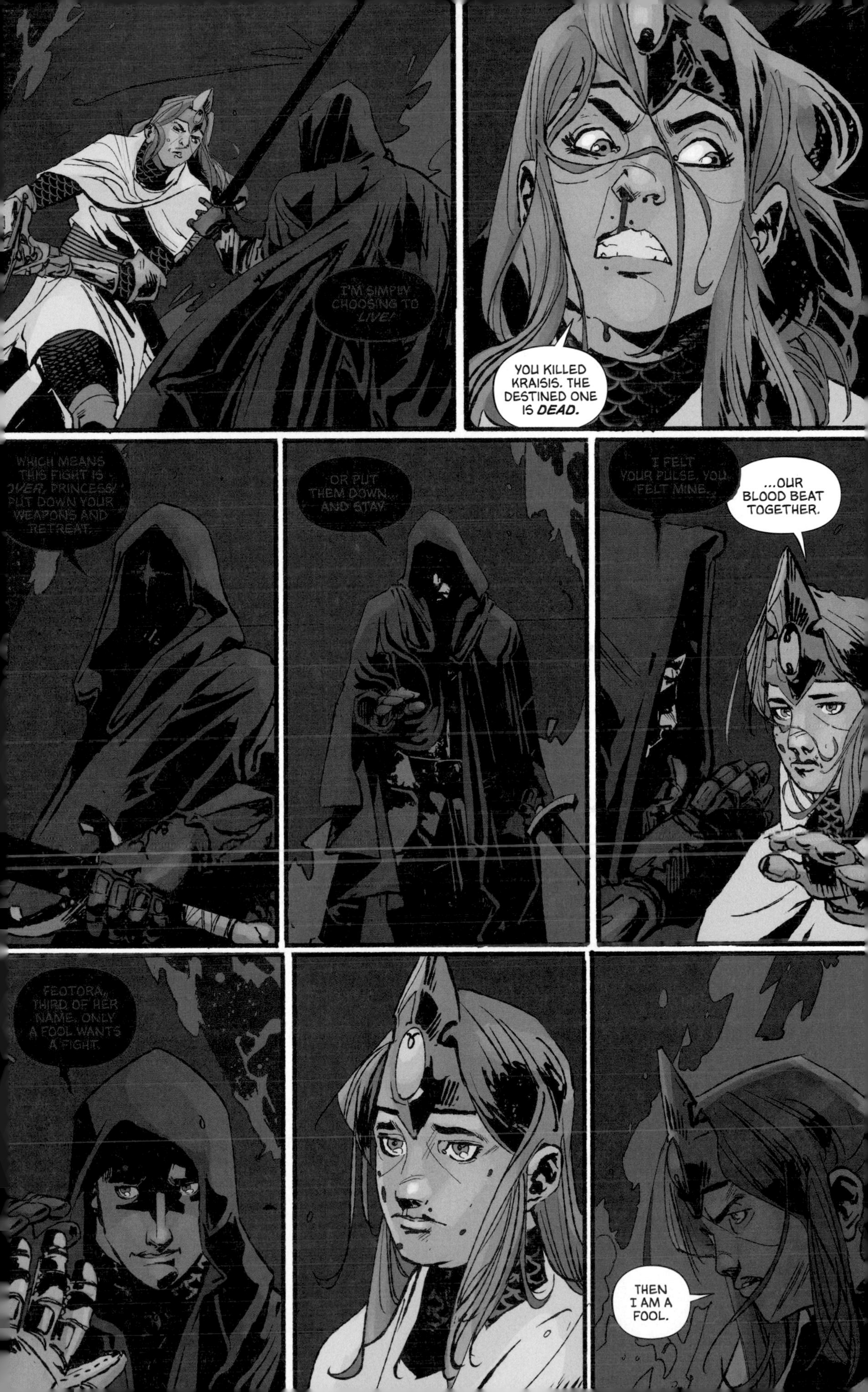
I'M SIMPLY CHOOSING TO LIVE!
YOU KILLED KRAISIS. THE DESTINED ONE IS DEAD.
WHICH MEANS THIS FIGHT IS OVER, PRINCESS! PUT DOWN YOUR WEAPONS AND RETREAT...
OR PUT THEM DOWN... AND STAY.
I FELT YOUR PULSE. YOU FELT MINE...
...OUR BLOOD BEAT TOGETHER.
FEOTORA, THIRD OF HER NAME. ONLY A FOOL WANTS A FIGHT.
THEN I AM A FOOL.

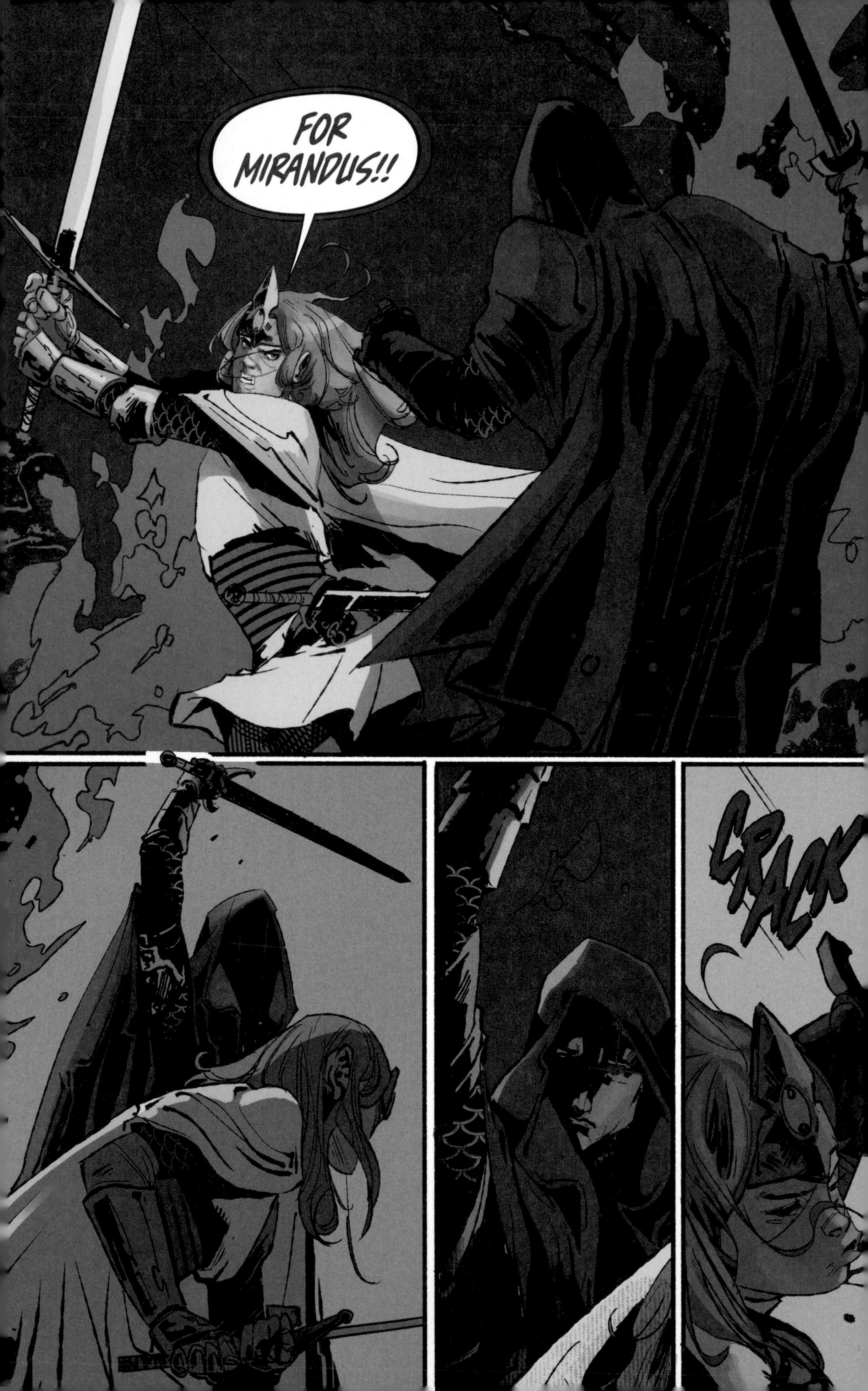
FOR MIRANDUS!!
CRACK

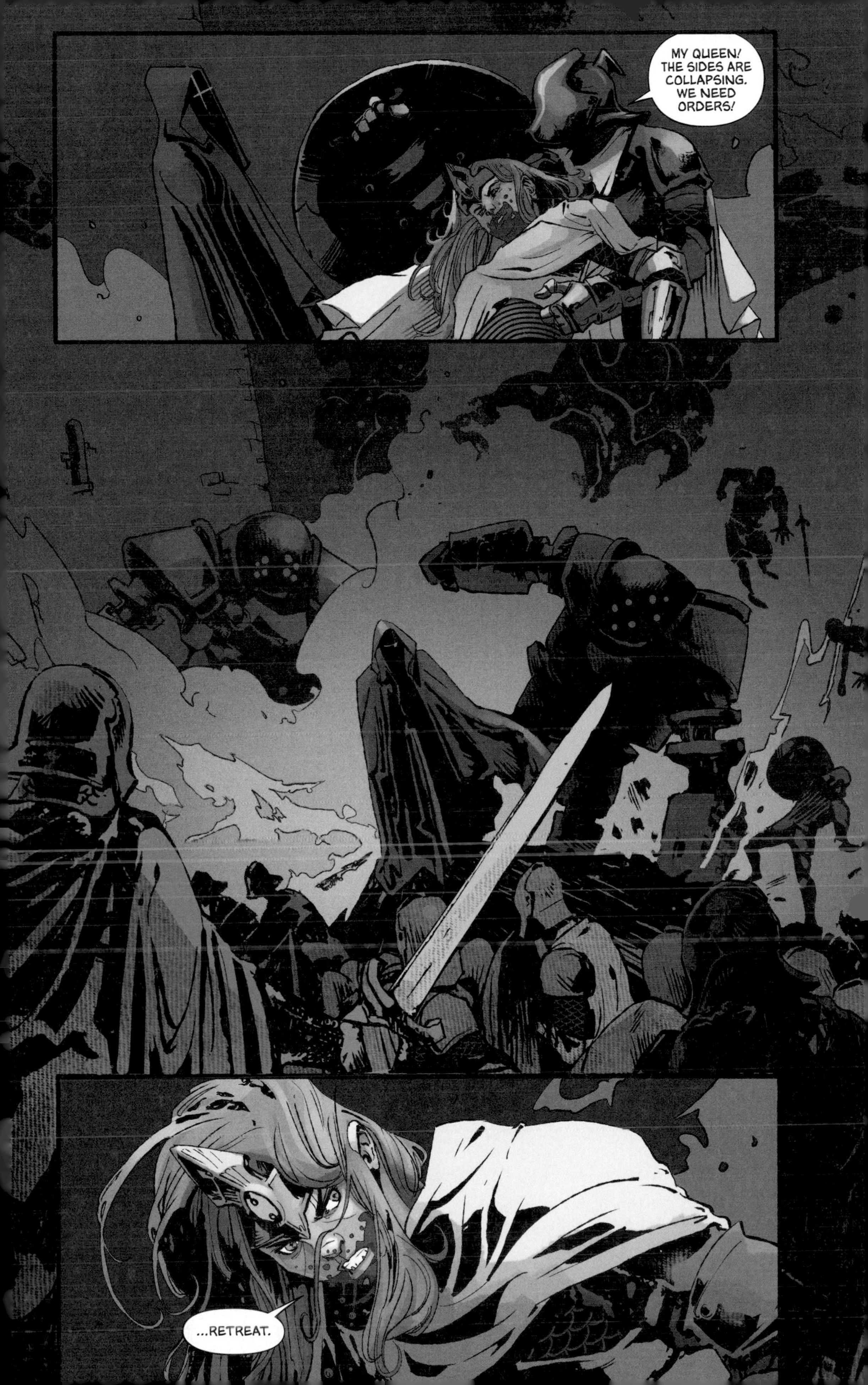
MY QUEEN! THE SIDES ARE COLLAPSING. WE NEED ORDERS!
...RETREAT.

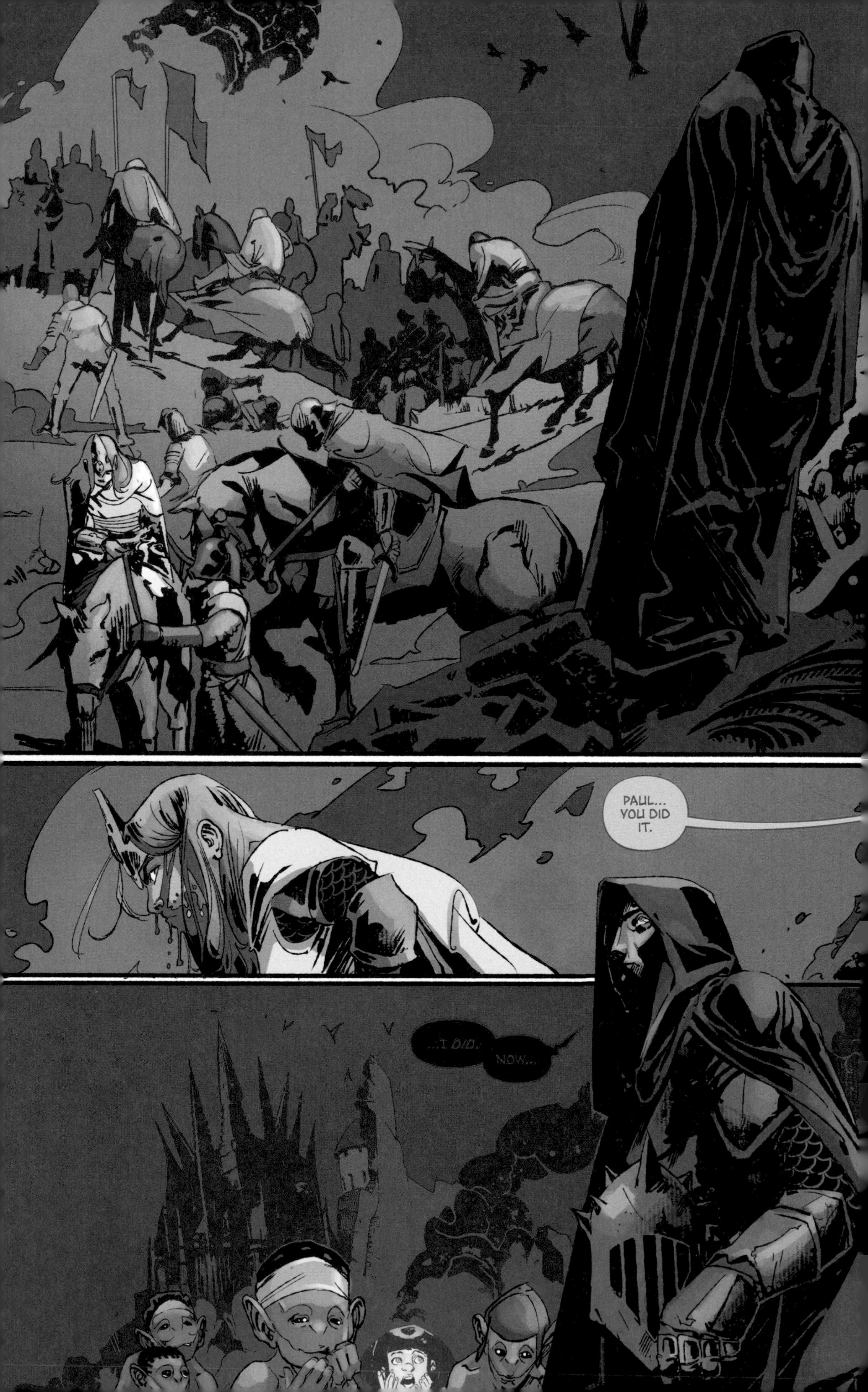
PAUL... YOU DID IT.
...I DID.
NOW...

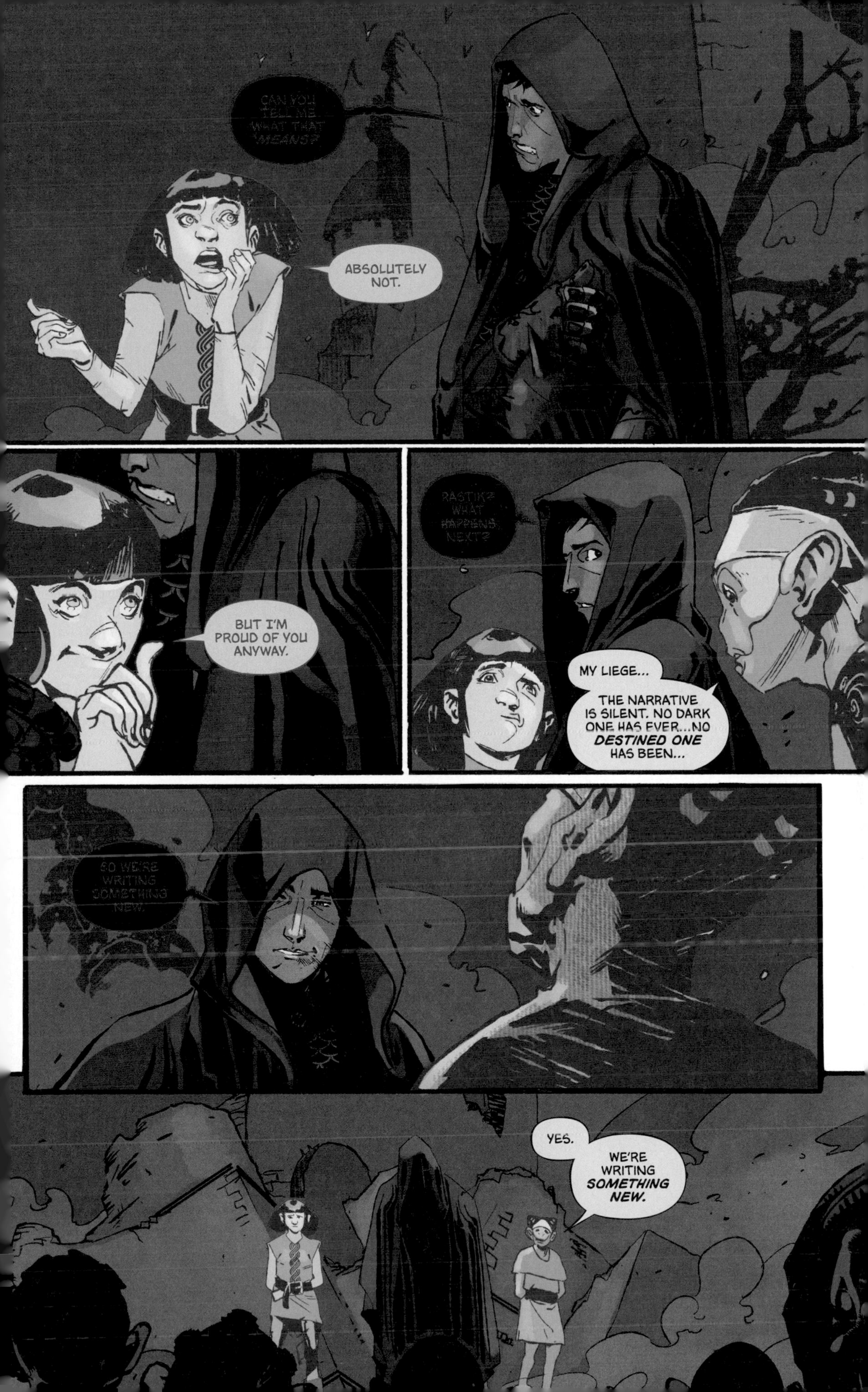
CAN YOU TELL ME WHAT THAT *MEANS?*
ABSOLUTELY NOT.
BUT I'M PROUD OF YOU ANYWAY.
RASTIK? WHAT HAPPENS NEXT?
MY LIEGE...
THE NARRATIVE IS SILENT. NO DARK ONE HAS EVER...NO ***DESTINED ONE*** HAS BEEN...
SO WE'RE WRITING SOMETHING NEW.
YES.
WE'RE WRITING ***SOMETHING NEW.***

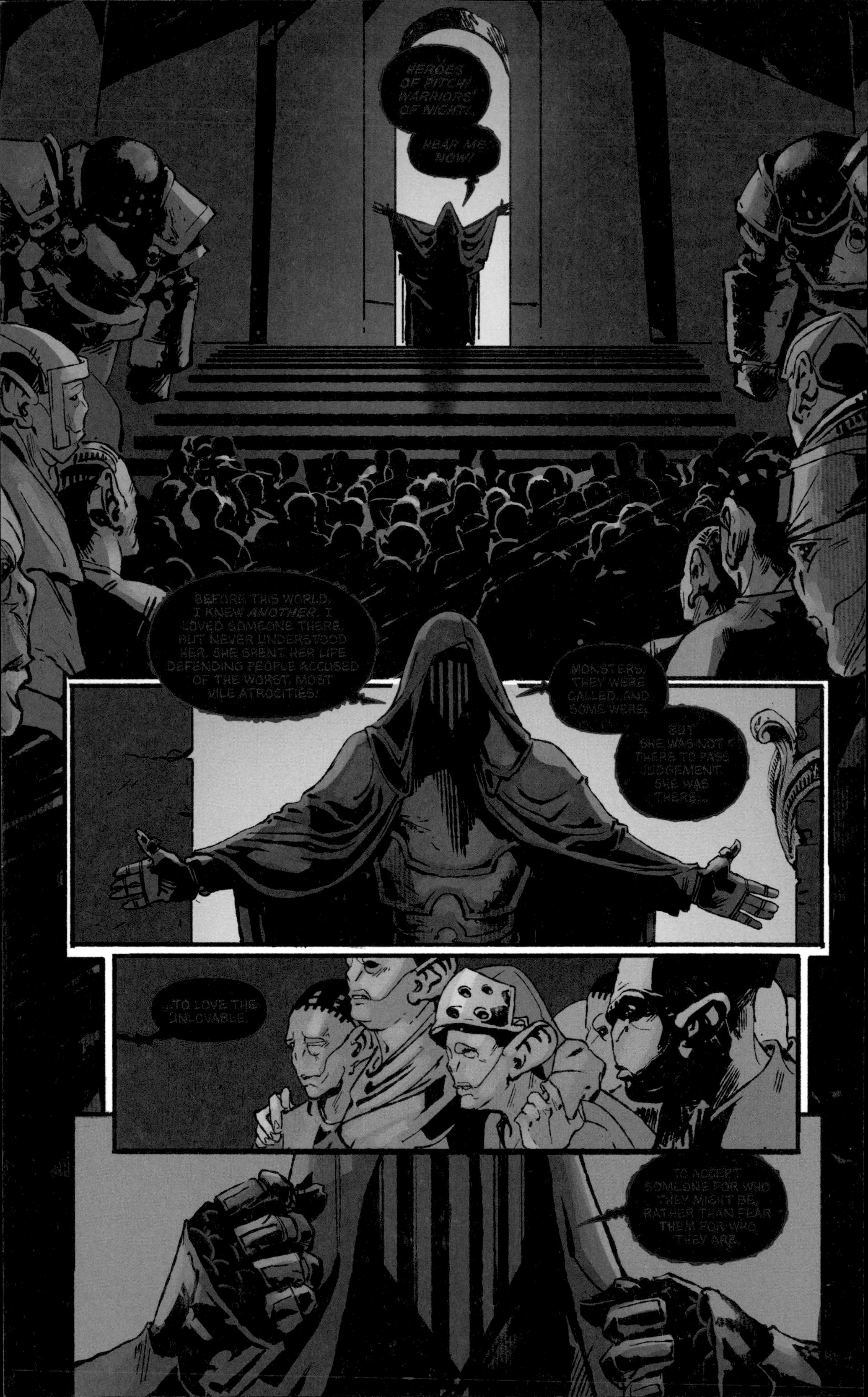
HEROES OF PITCH! WARRIORS OF NIGHT!
HEAR ME, NOW!
BEFORE THIS WORLD, I KNEW *ANOTHER*. I LOVED SOMEONE THERE, BUT NEVER UNDERSTOOD HER. SHE SPENT HER LIFE DEFENDING PEOPLE ACCUSED OF THE WORST, MOST VILE ATROCITIES.
MONSTERS, THEY WERE CALLED. AND SOME WERE.
BUT SHE WAS NOT THERE TO PASS JUDGEMENT. SHE WAS THERE...
...TO LOVE THE UNLOVABLE.
TO ACCEPT SOMEONE FOR WHO THEY MIGHT BE, RATHER THAN FEAR THEM FOR WHO THEY ARE.

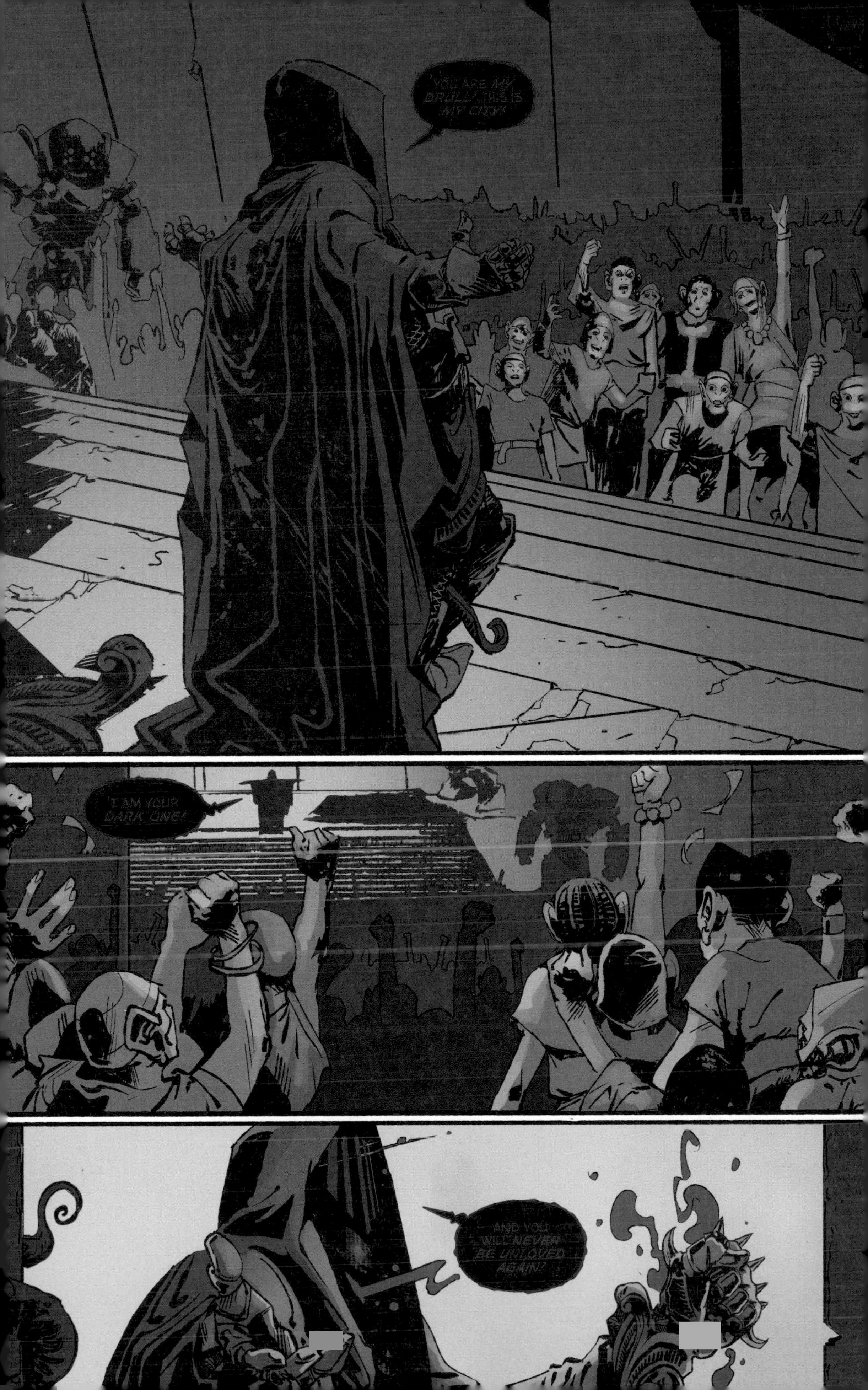
YOU ARE MY DRULL! THIS IS MY CITY!
I AM YOUR DARK ONE!
AND YOU WILL NEVER BE UNLOVED AGAIN!

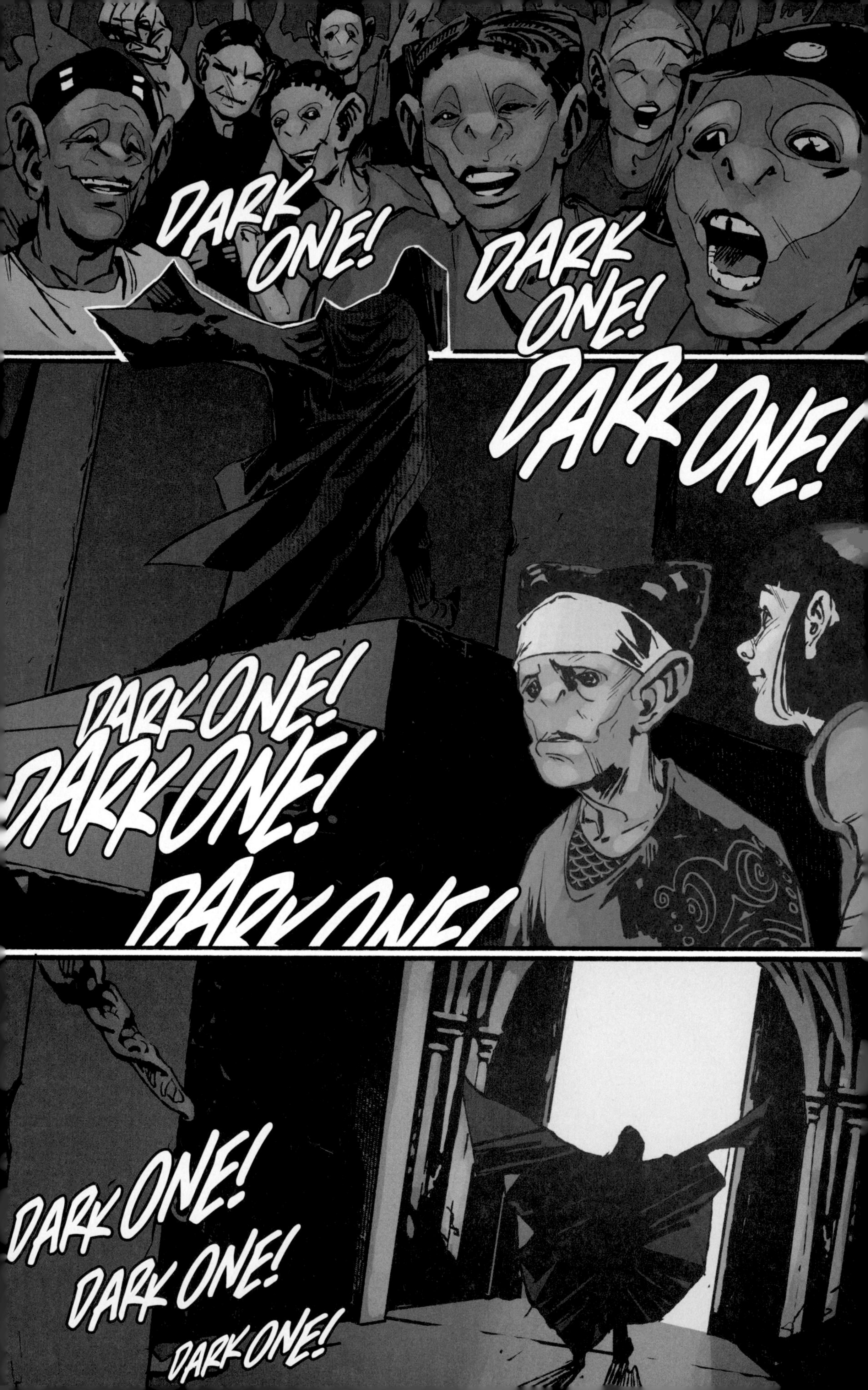
DARK ONE!
DARK ONE!
DARK ONE!
DARK ONE!
DARK ONE!
DARK ONE!
DARK ONE!
DARK ONE!
DARK ONE!

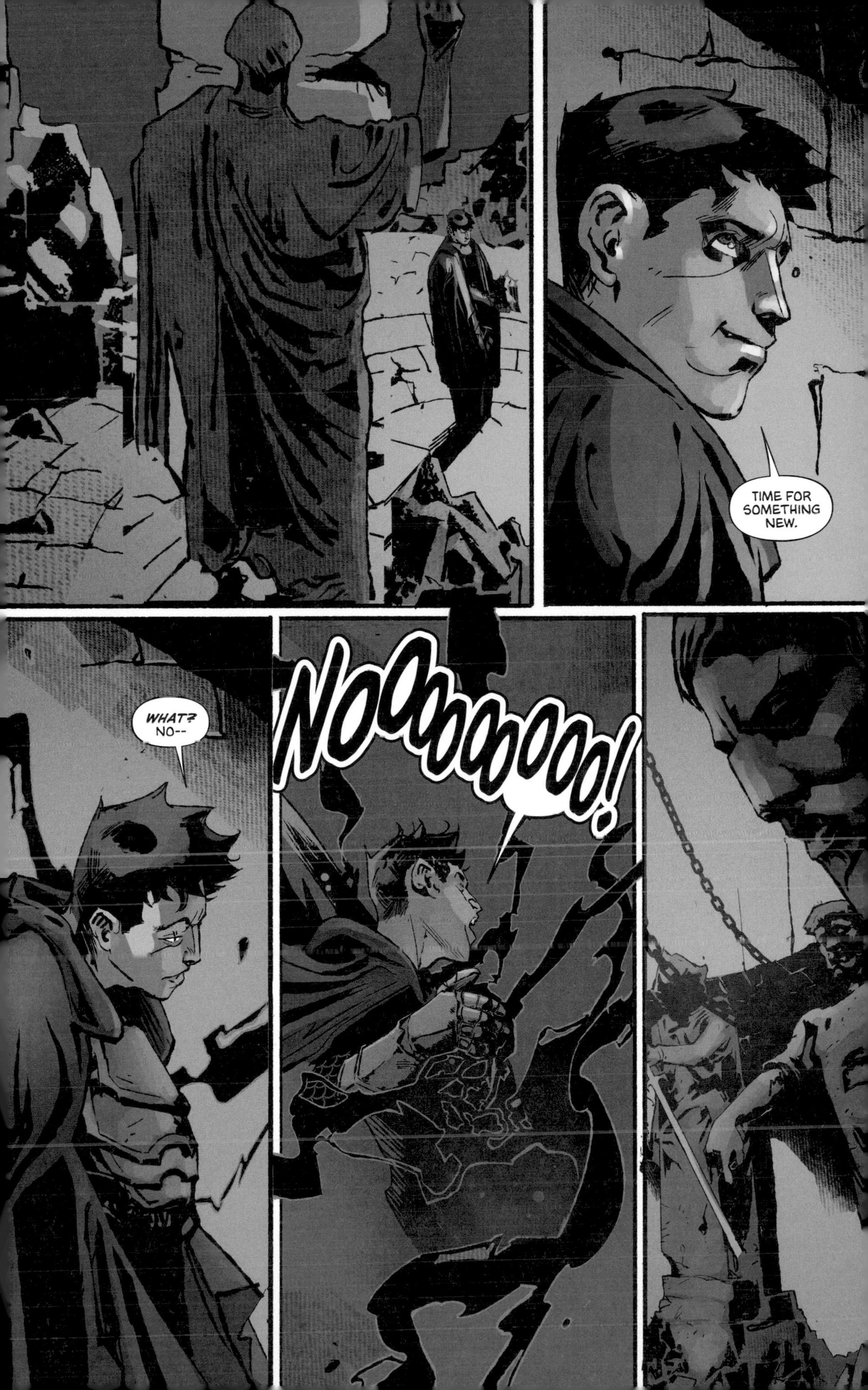
TIME FOR SOMETHING NEW.
WHAT? NO--
NOOOOOOOO!

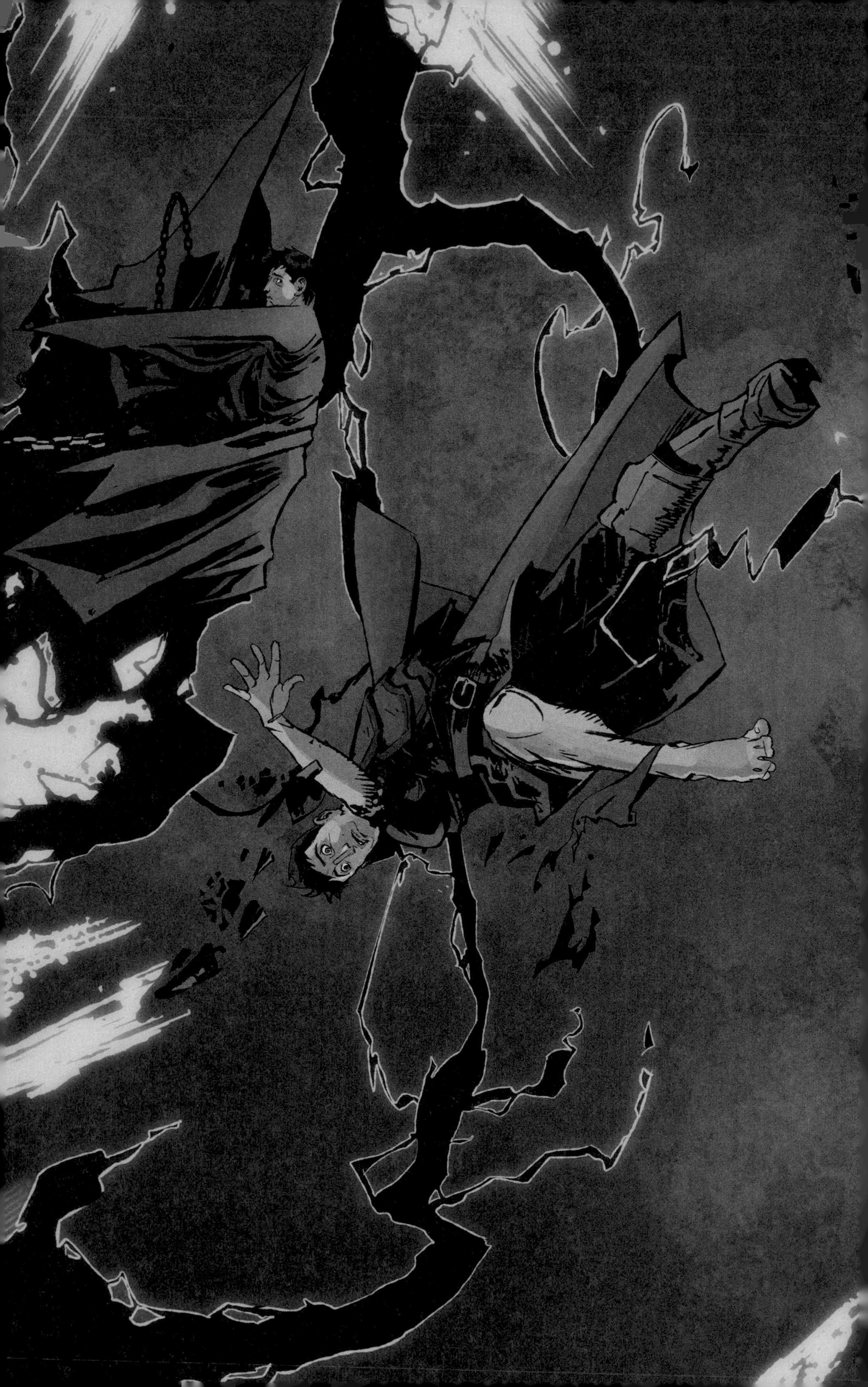

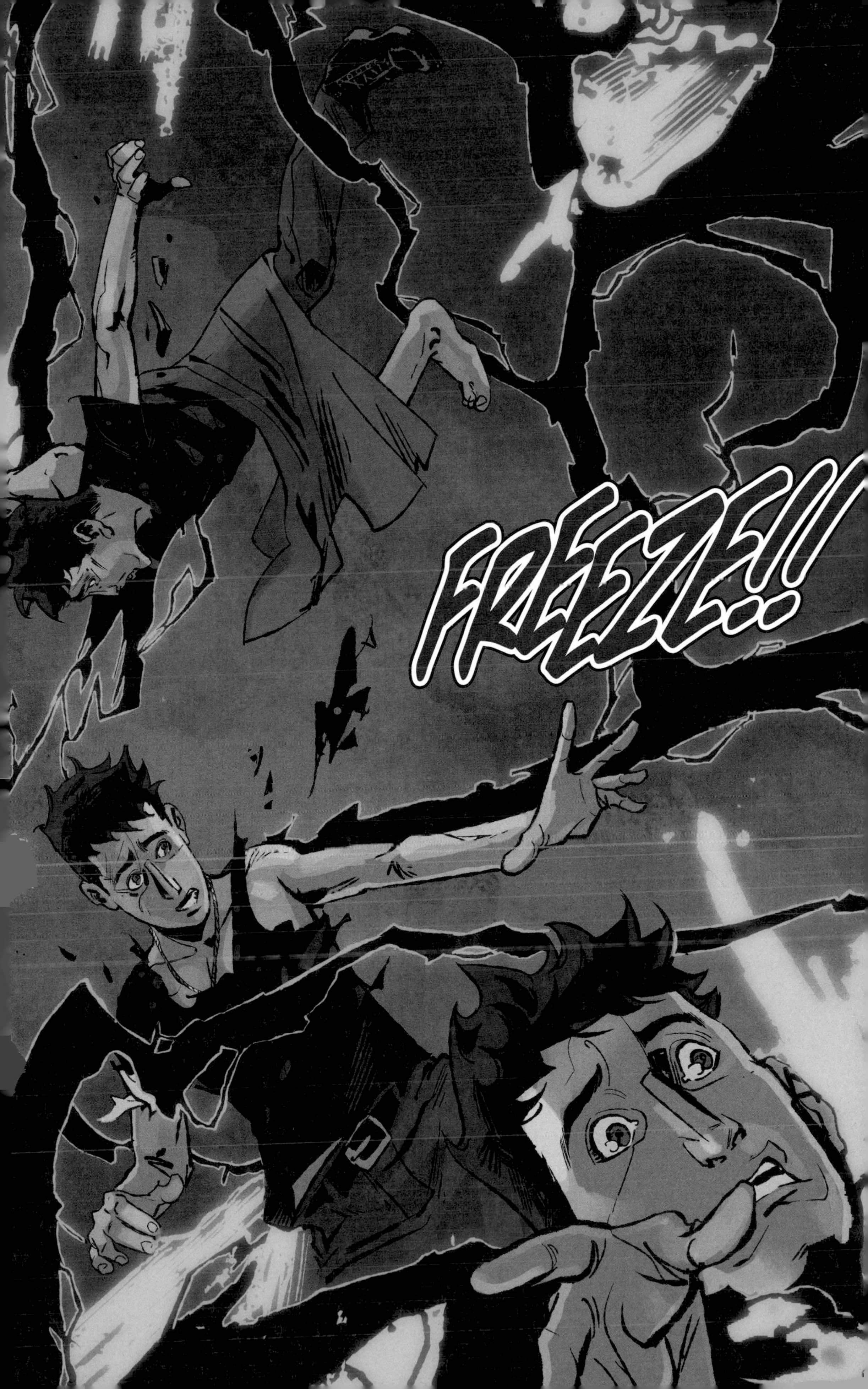
FREEZE!!

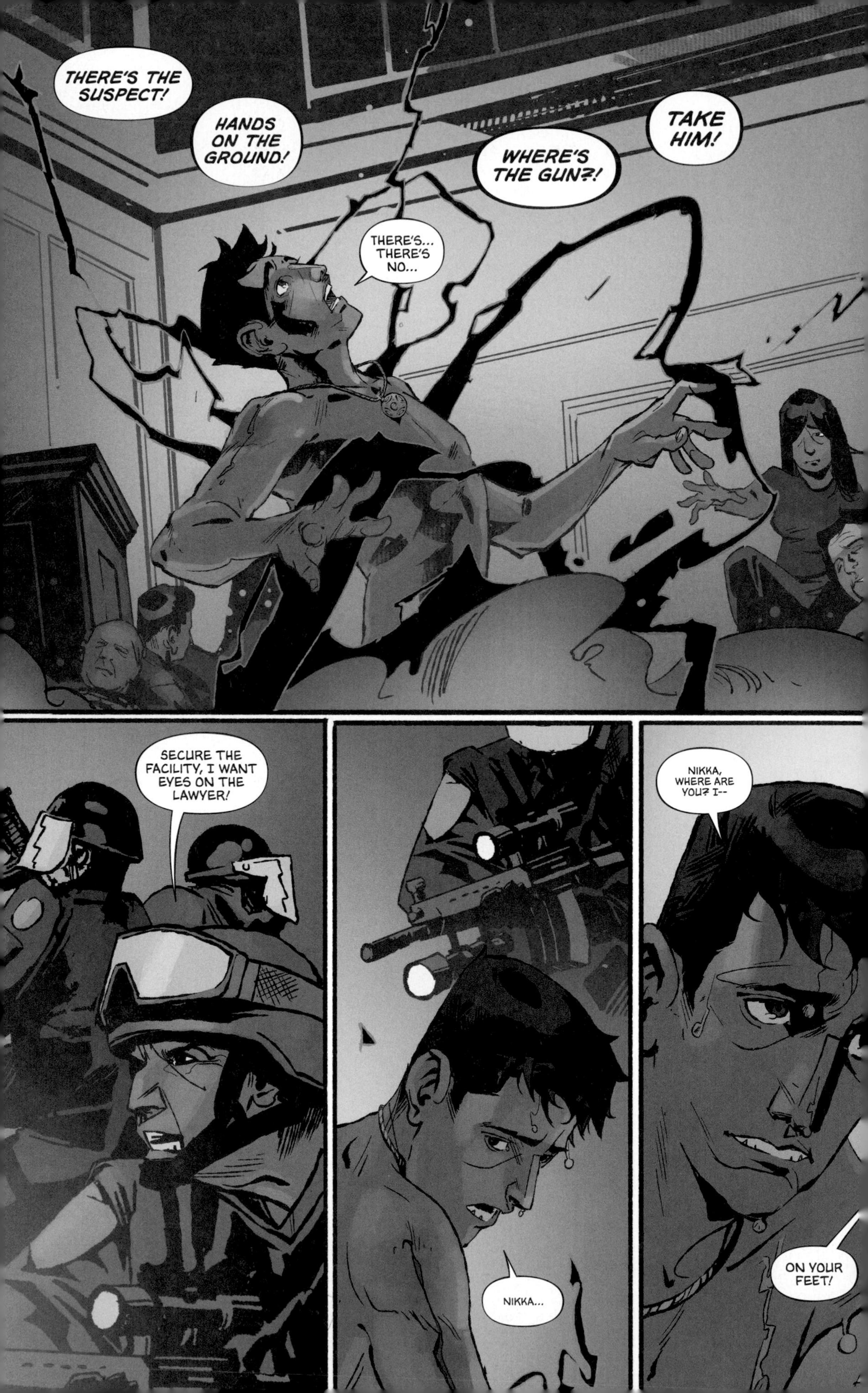
THERE'S THE SUSPECT!
HANDS ON THE GROUND!
WHERE'S THE GUN?!
TAKE HIM!
THERE'S... THERE'S NO...
SECURE THE FACILITY, I WANT EYES ON THE LAWYER!
NIKKA...
NIKKA, WHERE ARE YOU? I--
ON YOUR FEET!

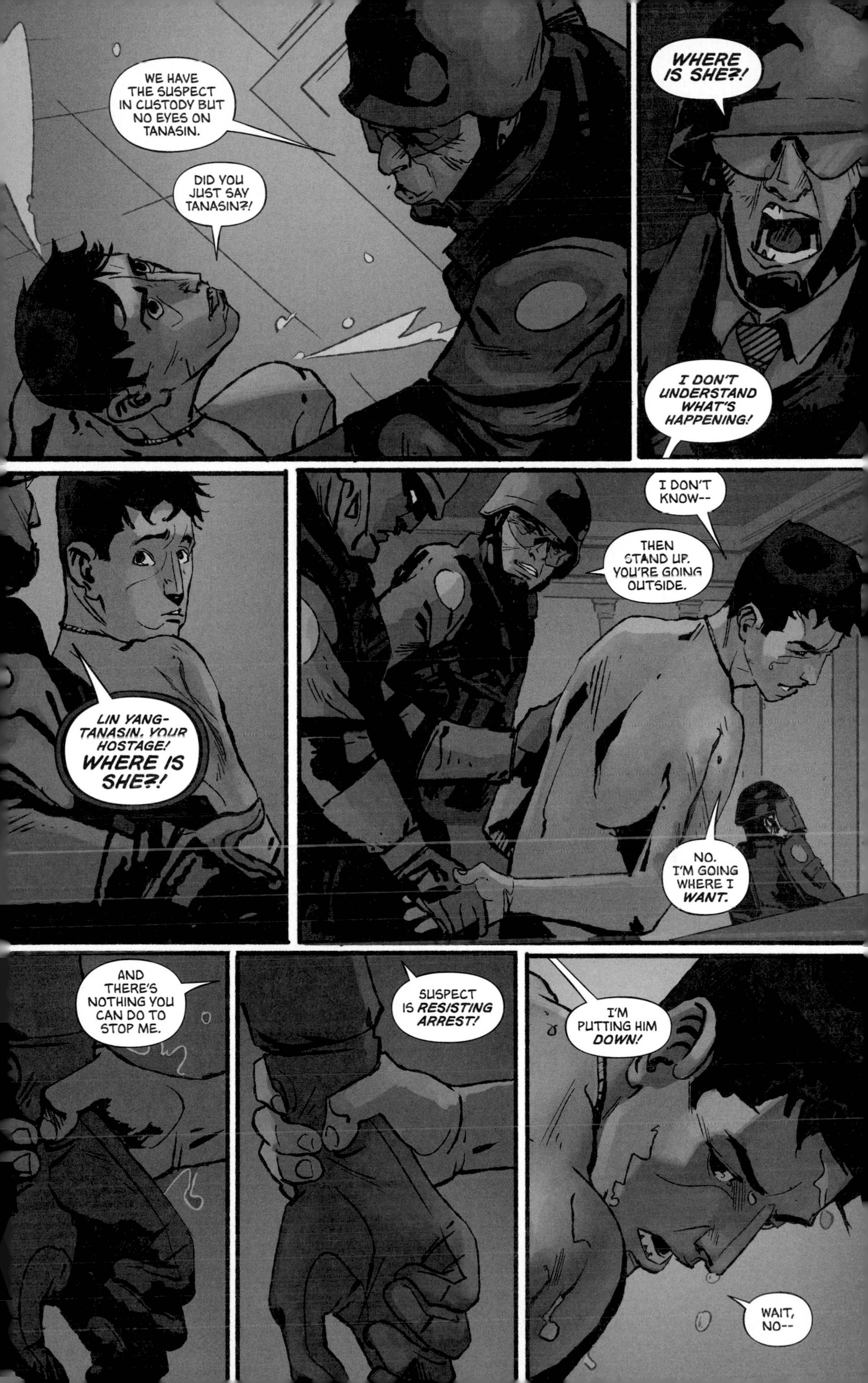
WE HAVE THE SUSPECT IN CUSTODY BUT NO EYES ON TANASIN.
DID YOU JUST SAY TANASIN?!
WHERE IS SHE?!
I DON'T UNDERSTAND WHAT'S HAPPENING!
LIN YANG-TANASIN. YOUR HOSTAGE! WHERE IS SHE?!
I DON'T KNOW--
THEN STAND UP. YOU'RE GOING OUTSIDE.
NO. I'M GOING WHERE I WANT.
AND THERE'S NOTHING YOU CAN DO TO STOP ME.
SUSPECT IS RESISTING ARREST!
I'M PUTTING HIM DOWN!
WAIT, NO--

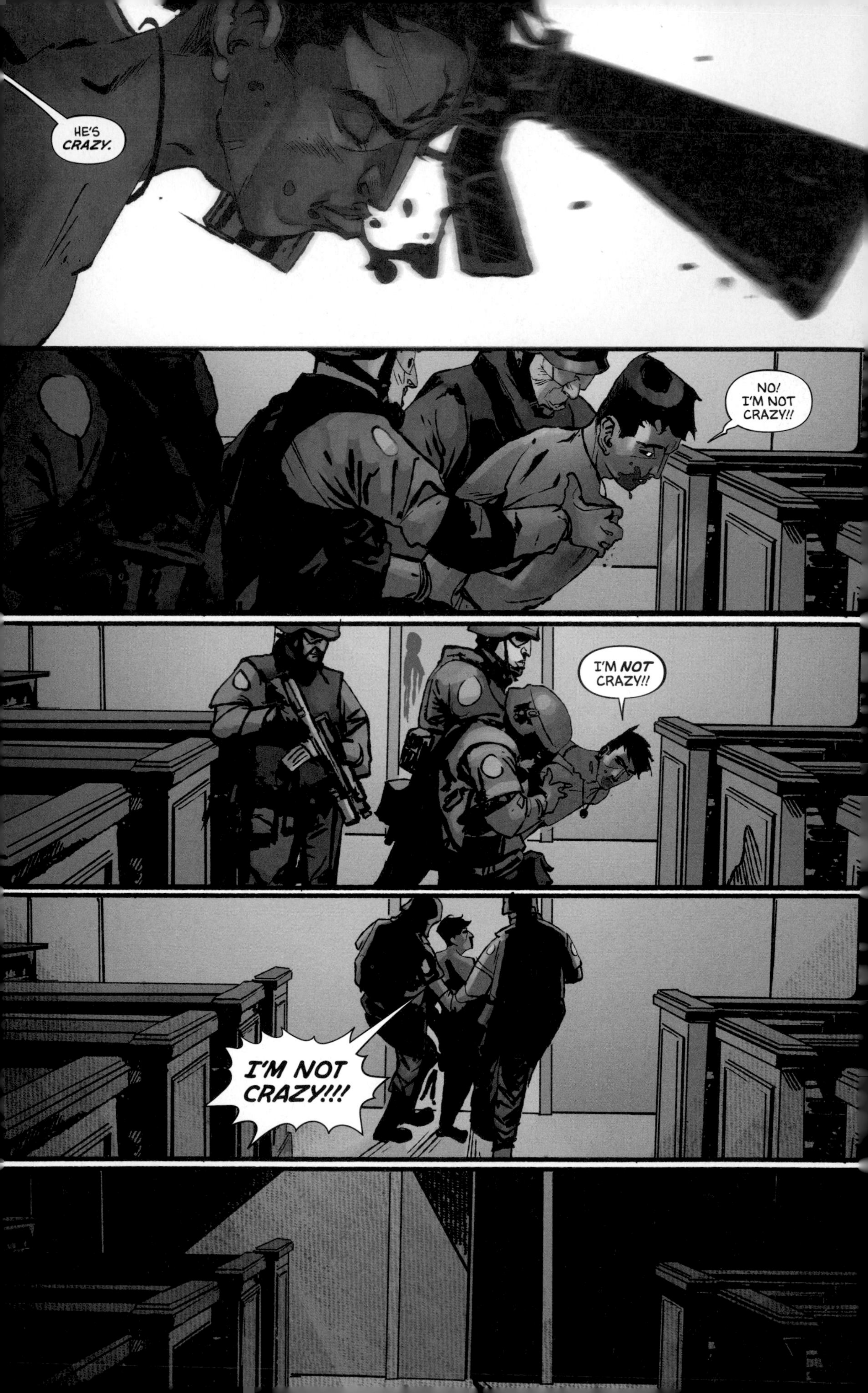
HE'S CRAZY.
NO! I'M NOT CRAZY!!
I'M NOT CRAZY!!
I'M NOT CRAZY!!!

EPILOGUE
PERAGATOR

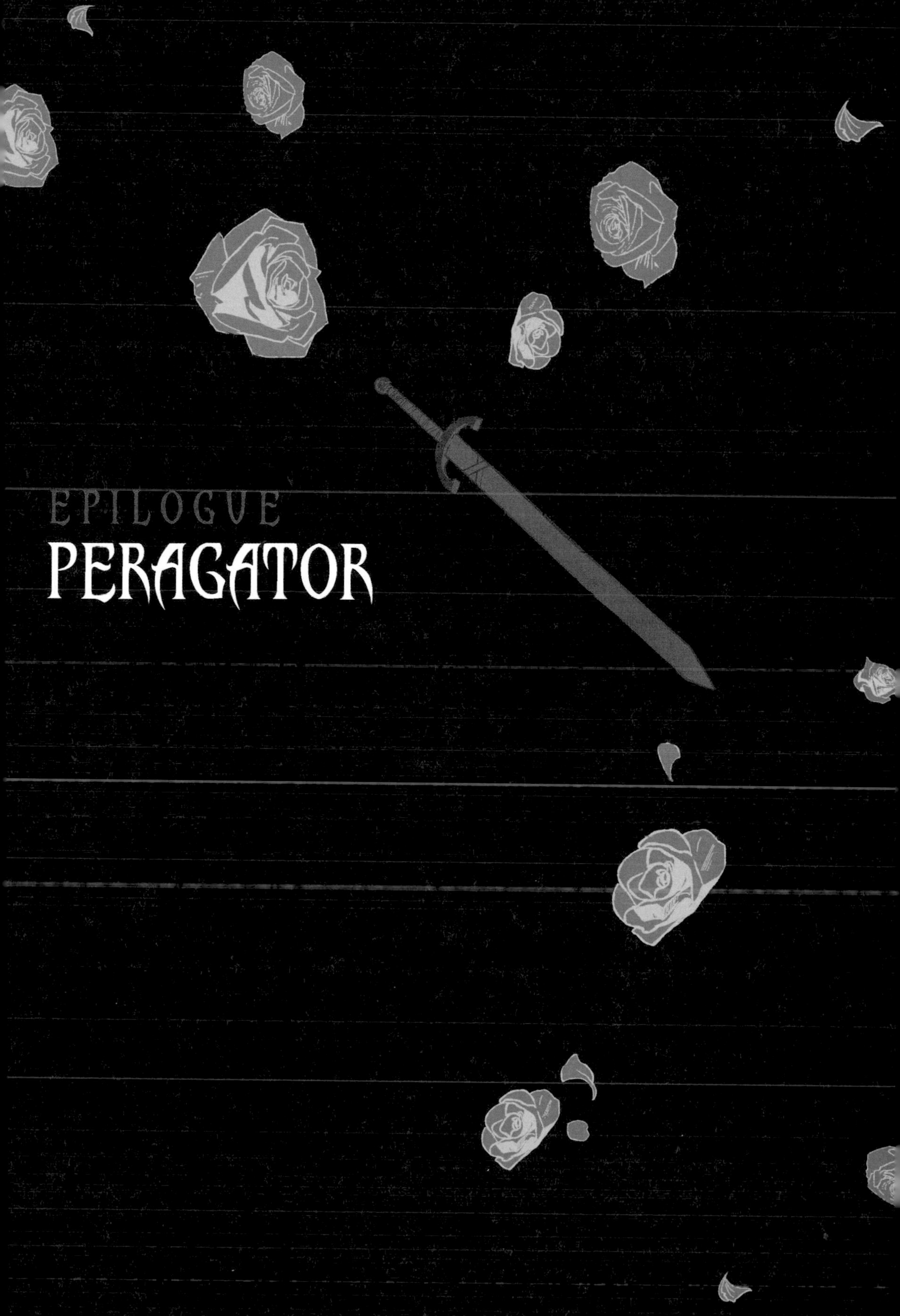

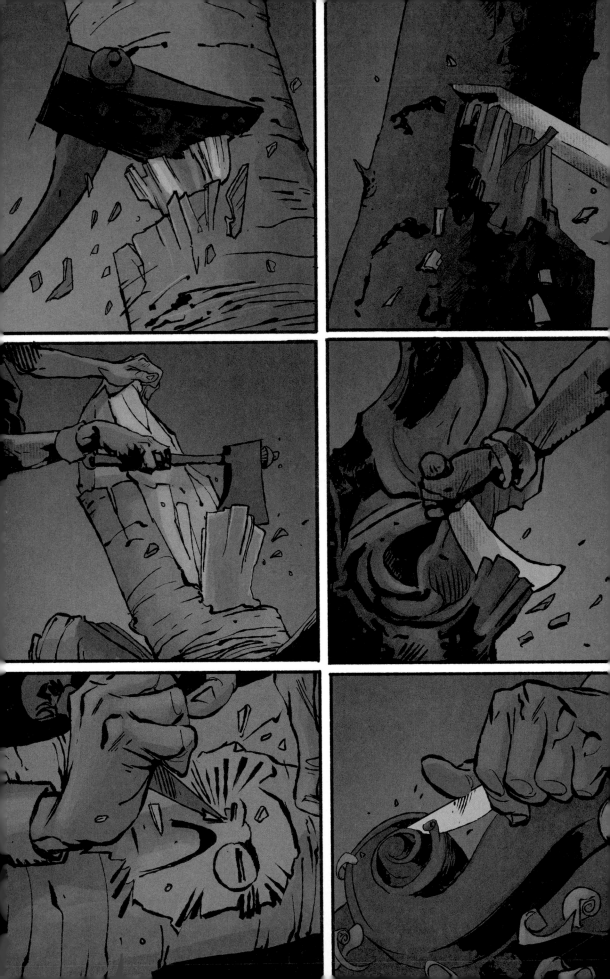

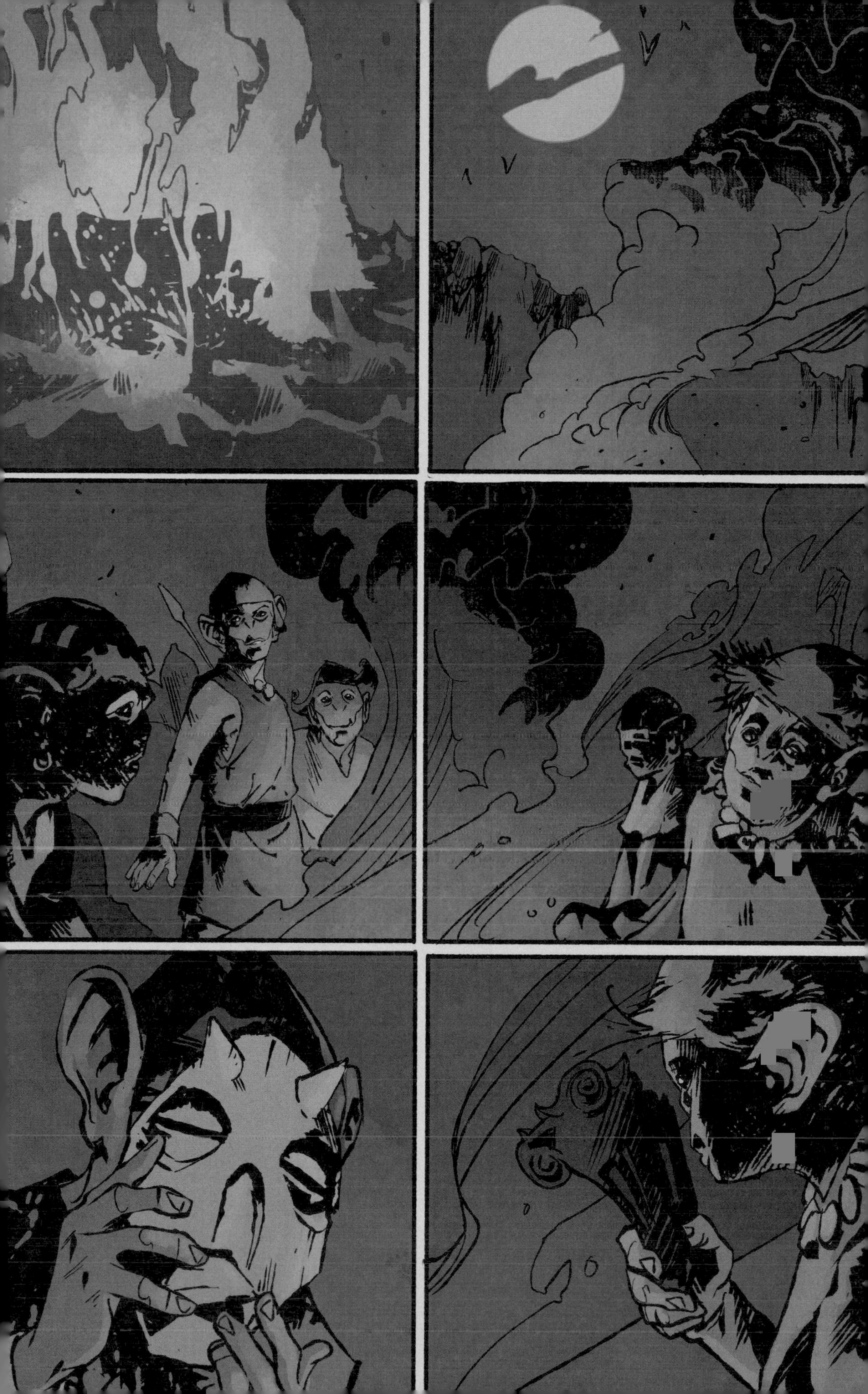

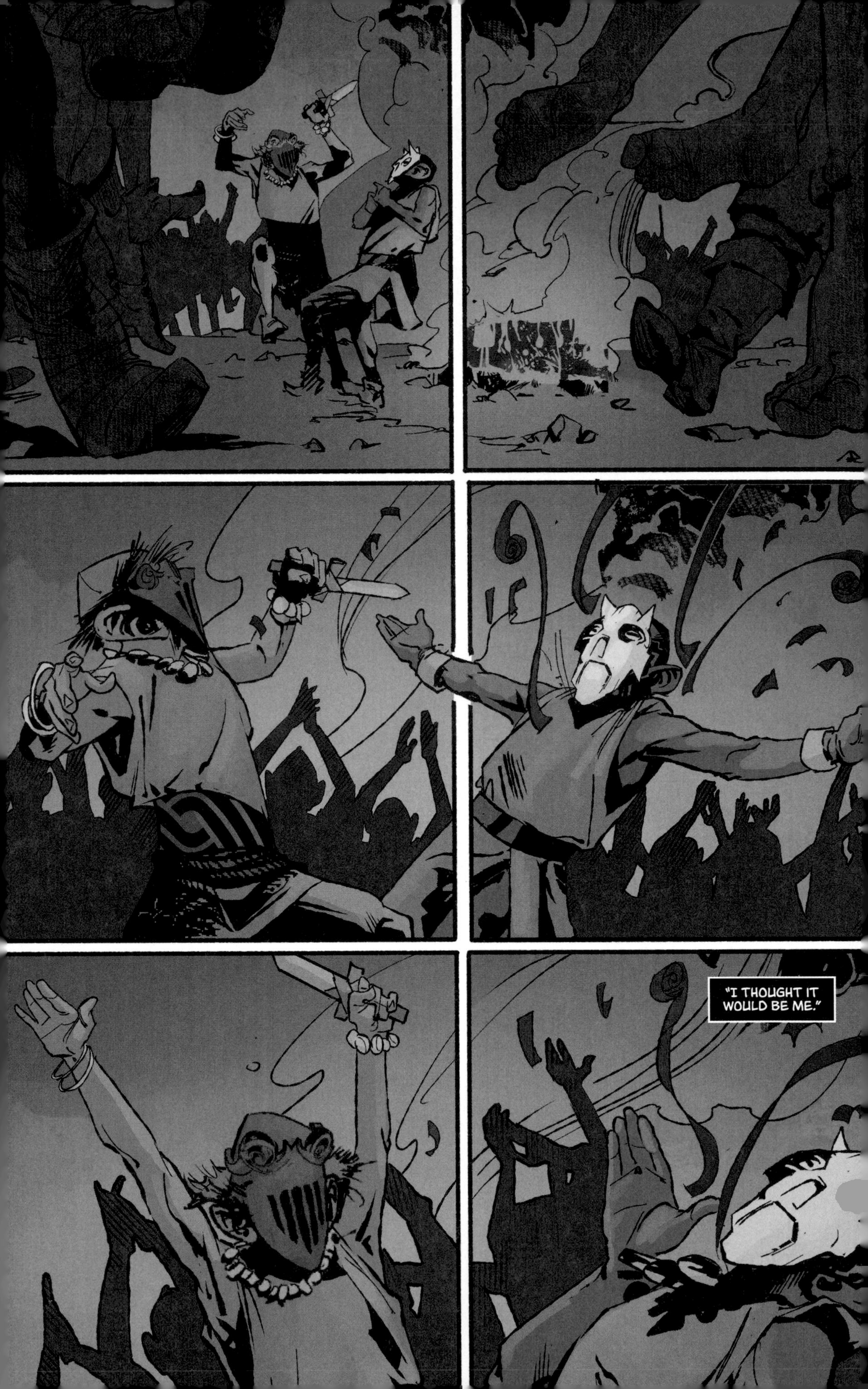
"I THOUGHT IT
WOULD BE ME."

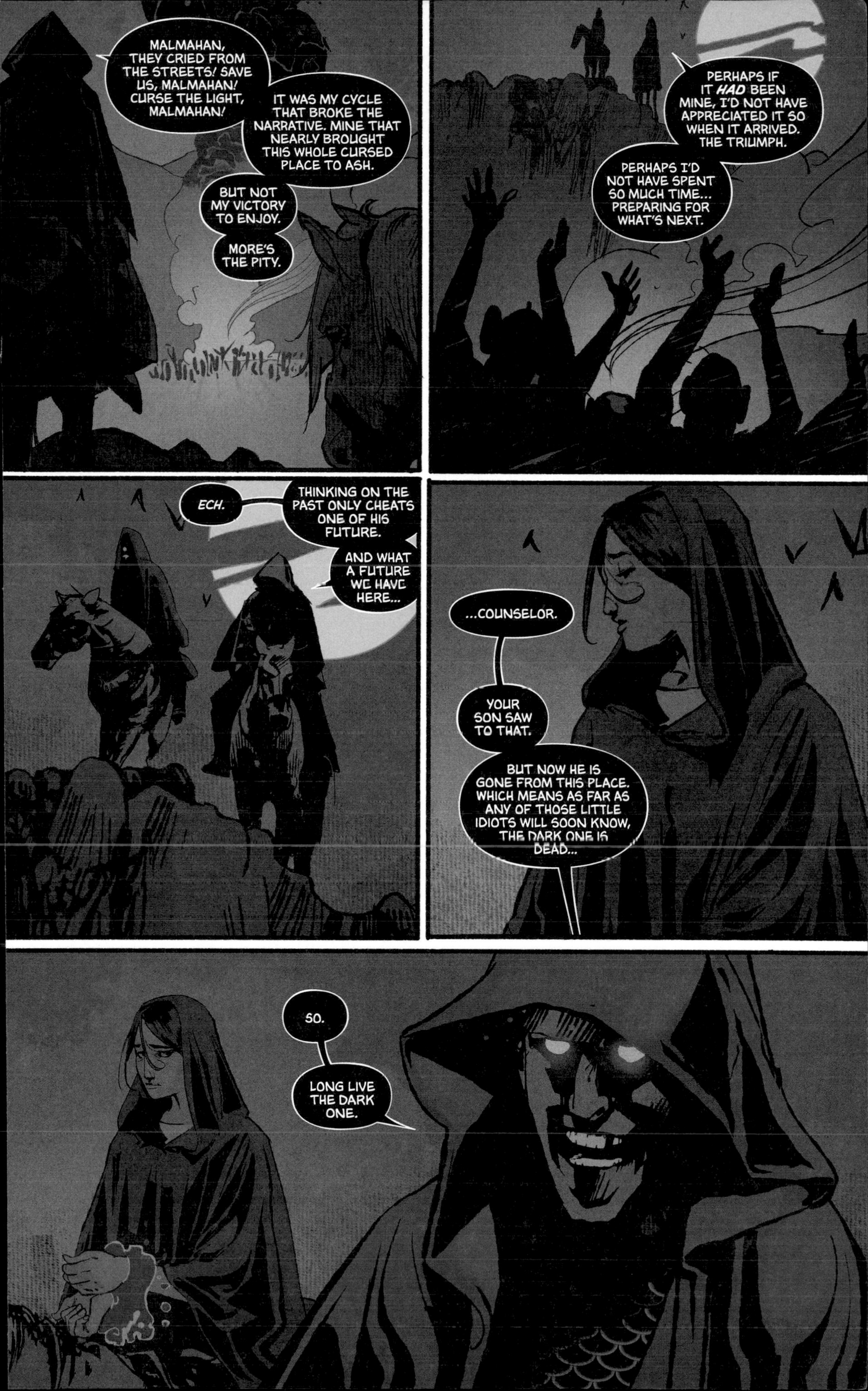
MALMAHAN, THEY CRIED FROM THE STREETS! SAVE US, MALMAHAN! CURSE THE LIGHT, MALMAHAN!
IT WAS MY CYCLE THAT BROKE THE NARRATIVE. MINE THAT NEARLY BROUGHT THIS WHOLE CURSED PLACE TO ASH.
BUT NOT MY VICTORY TO ENJOY.
MORE'S THE PITY.
PERHAPS IF IT *HAD* BEEN MINE, I'D NOT HAVE APPRECIATED IT SO WHEN IT ARRIVED. THE TRIUMPH.
PERHAPS I'D NOT HAVE SPENT SO MUCH TIME... PREPARING FOR WHAT'S NEXT.
ECH.
THINKING ON THE PAST ONLY CHEATS ONE OF HIS FUTURE.
AND WHAT A FUTURE WE HAVE HERE...
...COUNSELOR.
YOUR SON SAW TO THAT.
BUT NOW HE IS GONE FROM THIS PLACE. WHICH MEANS AS FAR AS ANY OF THOSE LITTLE IDIOTS WILL SOON KNOW, THE DARK ONE IS DEAD...
SO.
LONG LIVE THE DARK ONE.

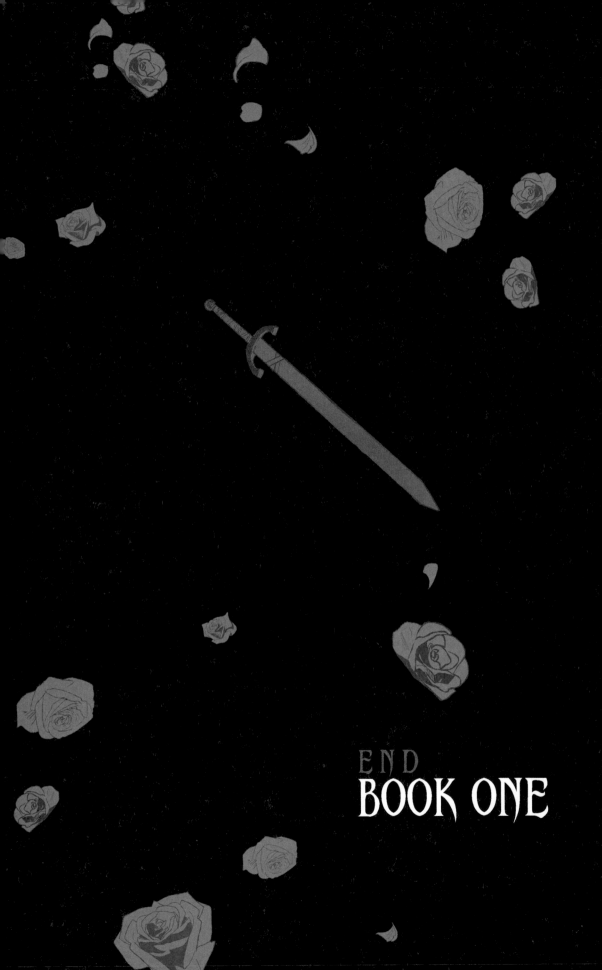

END
BOOK ONE